AMBER FISHER

SIN &
BEAR IT

SINFUL HOUSE MYSTERIES
I

one

. . .

I knew something was wrong the minute I walked into our apartment.

The bookshelves were ransacked, with books lying scattershot all over the floor around them. The couch was pushed away from the wall where it belonged, and the knick-knacks over the fireplace were missing. Clothing was strewn helter-skelter across the living room floor, and our potted plants had been moved from their proper places and were now lined up against one wall.

My throat tightened. My stomach flipped. I stood still as stone, hardly daring to breathe, my senses on high alert as adrenaline coursed through my veins.

We were being robbed.

But just as I was deciding what to do—call the cops or grab a baseball bat? Did we even have a baseball bat?—I noticed something aside from the disarray.

The astringent scent of cleaning products.

I started moving toward the bedroom. I was halfway through the living room before I noticed the suitcases lying open on the couch, half packed. I peered inside, my brow wrinkled. Shayda's blouses, t-shirts, and sweaters were neatly folded, not haphazardly thrown inside. I pawed around the garments, looking for my things, but everything in the suitcases belonged to Shayda alone.

What was happening? Why were our suitcases packed with Shayda's things in the living room? Why was our apartment in such disarray?

I smoothed the garments back into place and took another look around. On second look, it no longer appeared to be a robbery. What few valuables we had, like our PlayStation and my laptop, were still where they belonged. Plus, there was the smell. Thieves didn't usually wipe down the counters with bleach, not even if they were worried about fingerprints. So it probably wasn't burglars, but still, something was off.

I was headed toward the bedroom when I nearly collided with Shayda in the hallway. Her hair was tied away from her face with a bandana, and she wore a pair of pink rubber gloves. She stopped in her tracks, her eyes flying wide as she clutched her chest and yelped with surprise. When she realized it was me, I expected her face to flood with relief.

It didn't.

She stood still, her jaw clenched and nostrils flaring. Then, she dropped her arms to her sides and blew out a heavy breath. "I wasn't expecting you back yet," she said.

I glanced at my smartwatch. It was noon, which seemed a normal time for me to come home for lunch. "What time were you expecting me back?" I asked.

Shayda gave a lame shrug, her expression unchanged. "I don't know. I never know *anything* with you these days."

I stood still, thinking of what to say as I shuffled through the encyclopedia of Shayda's facial expressions stored in my brain. My therapist said I was getting better at recognizing emotions, especially Shayda's. We lived together, so I had a lot of practice. I still wasn't great at it, though, and I usually tried to mask my lack of emotional intelligence by talking. But that didn't work with Shayda, so as she stood there glowering at me, I kept my mouth shut.

Finally, her expression registered.

Exasperation. A lot of it.

"You're upset that I didn't come home this weekend," I said. "I know. It's just that there was a new break in the case, and you know how I get when I'm deep in my work. So I just thought—"

Shayda held up a hand to interrupt my explanation. "I don't care, Sid. Save it. All the explaining, all the excuses, none of it matters anymore. I gave this a good college try, but I think we're just…" She sighed, squeezing her eyes shut. "I think we're just done here."

I paused, letting her words sink in. "What do you mean, done here?"

Shayda sighed, shifting her weight to one leg as she crossed her arms over her chest. "What day is it today, Sid?"

I shrugged, hoping this wasn't a trick question. "Monday?"

Shayda's eyes narrowed. "Right. And what's the date?"

Again, I shrugged. Now I was pretty sure these were trick questions. "May 31st?"

Shayda tapped her fingers against her elbows, her posture rigid. "So if today is Monday, May 31st, then yesterday was what?"

"Yesterday was Sunday. May…"

I let my voice trail off. My stomach sank as I finally realized why Shayda was upset. It wasn't because I'd stayed gone all weekend without telling her. "Oh, no," I groaned, my voice low and full of remorse. "Shayda. Yesterday was your sister's wedding."

"That's right!" Shayda shouldered past me, marching into the living room and snapping off the gloves, which she tossed to the floor. "My baby sister's wedding. My *entire* family was in town, including my grandparents, aunts, uncles, and cousins who flew in from Iran—that's halfway across the world, Sid. But *you* missed it. You promised you would use this opportunity to finally meet my family. We've been together for three years, Sid, and my family's never met you, not even once. You were supposed to be there."

I raised my hands to my face and dug my knuckles into my eyes. "I know. But with everything happening at work, I just forgot."

That was apparently the wrong thing to say. Color shot into Shayda's cheeks, and the muscles in her jaw clenched. Tendons stood out like ropes along her neck. I didn't need my mental encyclopedia for this one. Shayda was furious. "You forgot. Do you know how that sounds? How do you forget something this important? You were supposed to put it on your calendar. You were supposed to set a reminder. I called you, Sid. But do you know where your phone was?"

I took a deep breath. "Here?"

"You got it," she said, her words underlined by a dry, unamused chuckle. She pulled my phone from her hip pocket and tossed it to me. "You forgot the wedding, and I couldn't even get in touch with you to find out what happened. We *talked* about this. We agreed there couldn't be any mistakes this time. And God, I just meant I didn't want you to say anything inappropriate to my family. I didn't think I had to explain that you had to actually *be* there!"

As usual, I didn't know what to say. My mouth was dry, and I tried to swallow around the lump in my throat, but I couldn't. I was desperately thirsty all of a sudden, and I wanted to go into the kitchen for a glass of water. Not only would that give me time to think, but it would get me out from under Shayda's accusing glare. Not that I didn't deserve it. I did. And if I were a normal person, I'd sweep her into my arms and apologize profusely, promising it would never happen again.

But that would be a lie. It probably *would* happen again. And worse, I couldn't apologize. The words "I'm sorry" always stuck in my throat like glue, refusing to budge. It's one of my worst flaws. I can't apologize. Ever. I'm too proud.

Or stubborn. Or idiotic. Something.

I gestured toward the luggage. "So, where are you going?"

She stared at me, mouth agape, momentarily at a loss for words. Then she blurted out, "Are you *serious* right now?"

I blinked. "Of course I am. You know I don't joke about stuff like that."

Shayda pinched the bridge of her nose and closed her eyes. When she opened them again, they were damp, and her face had gone slack. "Sid, I'm moving out."

I stared at her for a moment, too surprised to speak. I watched her fidget, knowing she was waiting for a response, but my mind was blank. So I said, "What do you mean, moving out? Hold on, Shayda. Hold on." I ran my hands through my hair, buying myself some time. I should have gone for that glass of water. "You're upset. I see that now. And I know I screwed up. I know I screwed up *bad*. But moving out? Isn't that a little… extreme?"

Shayda's shoulders slumped, and she pressed her fingers to her eyes, her cheeks ruddy. "It would be extreme if this were the first and only problem between us. But things haven't been great for a long time. I'm sick of cooking dinner for two, only to eat alone. I'm tired of you not coming home but also forgetting to call. I'm done wondering if you and I are really on the same page about this relationship. I'm so tired of you not understanding how I feel. I really wanted to make this work. I tried and tried and tried. But now I just want this to be over."

She dropped down onto the couch, trembling. Her skin had

gone pale, and her eyes were glassy. She was about to cry. I held my breath, debating what to do. I knew I should go to her, say the right words, and caress her skin. I was supposed to comfort her, but I didn't want to. Not because I wanted her to be upset, but because comforting people made me feel like a phony. On the other hand, my therapist said sometimes I have to do things for Shayda I don't want to do because that's what being in a relationship is about. But, if what Shayda said was true, then I wasn't in a relationship anymore, and I didn't have to comfort her if I didn't want to.

I stood there like an idiot, debating what to do for too long. While I argued with myself over the pros and cons of comforting my girlfriend (?), Shayda covered her face with her hands and began to sob.

Teary eyes, I could ignore. Sobbing was a whole different story. I sat beside her, awkwardly draping an arm around her shoulder and pulling her close to me. She didn't resist. I let her cry for a while until she finally pulled away and wiped her eyes dry. "I really do want the best for you," she said, her voice wet and sniffly. I wanted to get up to get her a tissue, but I didn't think that was the right thing to do, so I stayed where I was. "But I do think it's gonna be hard for you to find someone who can put up with everything. Your crazy schedule, your weird job, and all the other…stuff."

"Stuff?" I repeated. "What stuff?"

"Sid." Shayda gave me a look. "You know what I'm talking about."

Oh. She was talking about the ghosts.

I'm a ghost whisperer. I can see, hear, and interact with ghosts, and I've been doing it since I was a kid. It was a long time before I realized that not everyone could see spirits. It was an even longer time before I realized it freaked people out when I talked about them. In general, people either thought I was crazy or a creepazoid, neither of which was true, and neither of which I wanted anyone to believe. I already had enough working against me, being maladroit at interpersonal interactions and having little ability to read situations, especially emotional ones.

That's one of many reasons I loved Shayda. She didn't mind that I saw the ghosts. Well, she minded, but it didn't creep her out, and she didn't think I was nuts. Of course, I didn't tell her about all the ghosts I saw. Especially the ones I knew she wouldn't want to hear about, like the ghosts of people that jumped in front of trains or fell off bridges or especially the ones that got stabbed or shot to death. I saw those people frequently, thanks to my job. The ghosts looked exactly as they did in death: broken and bleeding and half put together. It didn't bother me, but Shayda didn't like to hear about those things. After all, she was a "normal person." Not psychic. Not weird.

"I promise I'll try harder," I said. I tried to reach for Shayda's hand, but she pulled away, climbing to her feet. "I can get better. At everything. Really, I can."

"That's the thing, though," she said, shaking her head as the corner of her mouth dipped into a little frown. "I don't think you can. Not on your own."

I held my hands out. "I'm not doing it on my own. I have a therapist."

Shayda sighed. "When was the last time you saw Dr. Xena, Sid? Like, when was the last time you *actually* kept an appointment?"

I opened my mouth to object, then snapped it shut. She was right; I technically had a therapist, but I mostly dodged her calls and avoided seeing her. The thing was, I was pretty sure Dr. Xena had already done everything she could for me. I didn't like leaning on other people. I didn't like asking for help and seeing Dr. Xena made me feel weak. I'd learned enough to make things work with Shayda, and that had been good enough for me.

Except, now I didn't have Shayda. So I didn't know where that left me.

"I know you have a hard life," Shayda was saying. Her eyes had gone soft and wet again, but I didn't think she would cry this time. "Your personality quirks aren't that big a deal. You can manage them—you just need to *ask* people what they're feeling or what they mean if you don't know. You can manage that part of it, Sid. But the stuff with the ghosts? Your job? I don't know if you can handle all that on your own. It's a *lot*. You know? And on top of your psychological stuff…"

"There's nothing wrong with my brain," I interrupted. "My brain is *fine.*"

"I never said it wasn't," Shayda shot back. "Your brain is *more* than fine. You're brilliant and funny and kind. But forgetting a wedding? Not coming home for an entire weekend and not calling me? Those aren't things…"

I knew she was going to say, *"Those aren't things normal people do,"* and I was glad she didn't because that would have pissed me off, and I didn't want to be angry on top of being hurt and scared. Instead, she said, "Those aren't things I can deal with." She was using a technique she tried to get me to use: she made her words about herself rather than about me.

But I knew they were really about me.

"Please get help, Sid. Talk to someone. Everybody needs help sometimes. It's nothing to feel bad about."

I looked down into my lap. "I don't need help," I said. "I've got everything under control."

Shayda sighed. "That pride is going to be the death of you. You know that, right?"

I said, "I don't want to talk about this, Shayda. Can we please not talk about this?"

"Fine." The woman who used to be my girlfriend zipped up

her suitcases and carried them to the door. "Either way, this is over between us. Okay? We're done. I'm sorry."

We didn't speak more after that. I didn't know what else to say, and I wasn't going to beg her to stay. Besides, I may not be good at reading people, but even I knew Shayda wasn't going to change her mind. But I didn't want to hang around and watch her pack up, either. So as she loaded up her car with plants and art and suitcases, I went for a long walk to clear my head and cry where no one would see me.

When I came back, Shayda was gone.

And then my phone rang.

two

. . .

"Is this Sidney Sheridan?"

I winced as I sat down on the sofa, now devoid of suitcases. No one called me Sidney. "This is Sid," I said.

"Hi, Sid. My name is Tricia Woodward. I'm a producer at RealTV Productions. Do you have a minute to chat with me?"

I leaned back into the cushions, closing my eyes. I got calls like these every now and then—reality TV producers who wanted me to appear on some stupid show about paranormal investigators, ghost hunters, things like that. Most of those people were actors. Phonies. I hated people like that. They made me look bad, and I didn't need any help in that department. "Now isn't really a good time," I said.

"I understand. I won't be a moment. I'd actually like to schedule an in-person meeting with you to discuss a new opportunity we think you'd be perfect for. Do you have any time this evening? I'm in town," she explained.

"Yes," I said, instantly regretting it. I naturally default to the truth, often to my detriment. "I mean, I have time this evening, but—"

"I'd be happy to meet you anywhere convenient for you. Is dinner or coffee preferable?"

I sighed. Shayda did most of the cooking, and I didn't have any idea what was in the refrigerator. "Dinner, I guess," I said. I was heartbroken, but I still had to eat.

"Wonderful! I'll text you the address. How does 8 o'clock sound?"

"That sounds fine," I agreed, my voice sounding weary even to my own ears. "Sounds great."

"Wonderful. See you then."

The line went dead.

———

The address Tricia Woodward sent me was for a fancy French restaurant on the other side of town. That was a bad sign. Bad because it meant the production company was pulling out all the stops to get me on board with whatever cockamamie project they'd cooked up in some ridiculous board room. I didn't like being pressured—I guess no one does—and even walking into the restaurant set me ill at ease. I'd almost made up my mind to turn right around and leave when I saw her.

Seated in the waiting area dressed in a simple linen dress, Tricia Woodward wasn't anything I expected. Usually, when the production companies came after me, they sent some artificial-looking person who spent too much time in front of a mirror. You know the kind. Perfectly coiffed hair, glowing white teeth, fake charisma oozing from their pores. I guess that works with some people. Not with me. Beautiful people made me self-conscious. I was nothing special: average height and build with a never-before-coiffed head of short, chocolate-brown hair. My eyes were my best feature, but they were just brown. I say they were my best feature because that's what I was told, but maybe everyone who said that was just being polite because otherwise, there was little to compliment me on.

I'm not being pitiful. That's just the truth.

But anyway, Tricia wasn't anything like that. She had dishwater blonde hair and fine lines around her eyes; not the kind that made her look old but the kind that made her look friendly. She was even wearing white Keds, which I didn't think they made anymore. She looked normal. In fact, she looked so ordinary that she reminded me of Shayda, which got me feeling all emotional again. But I swallowed it down and donned a fake smile. But not too much of a smile. I didn't want Tricia to get the wrong idea.

She rose to her feet, extending a hand which I accepted. "Thanks for agreeing to meet on such short notice," she said. "This isn't how I like to do business. But the opportunity came up, and since I was in town, I figured I would see if you were available. Looks like I had pretty good timing."

I didn't bother to tell her that her timing was actually garbage, that my girlfriend had just broken up with me, and the last thing I wanted was dinner with a shyster encouraging me to shove my ethics in a corner and do a show I didn't believe in. But I had been right about the refrigerator at the apartment: it was mostly empty. And like I said before: I had to eat.

The hostess sat us at a table in the far corner of the main dining room. After I placed my napkin in my lap, I folded my arms over my chest. "So, what's this all about?"

Tricia smiled. "You like to get right to the point, don't you? Suits me just fine. Okay. We have an idea for a new reality TV show. Now before you say anything, hear me out," she said, holding up a hand to stave off my objection. "I did my research on you. I know our network and several others have made similar offers in the past. And I understand why you were hesitant to accept those offers. Most of the shows they pitched were…" She dithered, tilting her head side to side, equivocating. "Let's just say, maybe not entirely on the level. But this new TV show is different from the others. There are no haunted locations to investigate, nor are we pitching a half-baked 'Where's Bigfoot?' adaptation. This is something entirely new." She clasped her hands on the table and leaned forward. "Have you ever seen the Japanese TV show Paris House?"

I shook my head. "No. What is it?"

"The show takes six young people and puts them in a house together. Six strangers. Most of the people coming to the show hope to find love, but others have different objectives. There's no script or interviews or anything phony like that. The participants merely live in the house together, and the crew films their lives. Simple."

It sounded simple. It also sounded like nothing I would ever watch, let alone participate in. "Okay. So, what does that have to do with me?"

Again, Tricia smiled. "I'm glad you asked. The idea for our TV show is a little different from the Japanese version. We want to take a number of strangers—seven, however, not six—and put them in a house together in sunny Odyssey, California, a beach town not too far from here. But we're not interested in just *any* strangers." Her smile deepened, and I thought I saw a twinkle in her eye. "What would happen if you took seven strangers, each guilty of one of the seven deadly sins, and put them in a house together? Would they get along? Would they learn from each other? And more importantly, would viewers learn anything from watching them?" Tricia lifted her hands, palms out, making little exploding motions with her fingers. "Seven strangers. One common theme. *Sinful House*: Which sin is your favorite?"

She was looking at me expectantly, her eyes wide and glittering, that smile growing by the second. But I had no idea what she wanted me to say. Nothing made any more sense now than when she started talking. "I don't understand what this has to do with me," I repeated.

Tricia looked only the slightest bit crestfallen as she gave a crisp nod and settled back into her chair. "All right. Let me lay it out for you like this. We're casting seven strangers to live in a house together. Each housemate has some degree of psychic ability, plus a unique personality trait that overwhelms the others. For example, one participant has anger management issues. We've cast him as Wrath. Another participant is a hoarder and doesn't like to clean up after herself. We've cast her in the role of Sloth. Envy is portrayed by a jealous young woman for whom the world is a profoundly unfair place. The other parts are still up for negotiation." She tilted her head to the side. "Including yours."

"Mine?" I leaned forward into the question, hand pressed to my chest. "You want me to live in a house with six strangers with personality defects while you film the whole thing?"

Tricia pointed a finger in my direction. "That's exactly what we want to do, yes."

"And which sin did you want me to play?"

Again, that movie-star smile. "Isn't it obvious? Pride."

It took me a minute to digest what she was saying, and I was probably staring at her like an idiot with my mouth falling open as I mulled this over. When my brain finally caught up to the conversation, I barked out a single laugh. "Is this some kind of joke?"

"I assure you, it's not. Now, our show differs from our Japanese inspiration in another important way. We are adding a competition aspect. We'll be sending you off in small groups to complete various challenges around town. Helping the elderly with household chores and errands, for example. This is all to engage the audience. And each week, the audience will vote on their favorite house members. At the end of the season, the audience favorite, determined by votes, will receive something special in return."

I leaned away from her, fidgeting in my seat. "Something special?"

Tricia cocked her head to the side, her eyes narrowing as the smile slipped from her lips. "Sid, what's the one thing you want more than anything else in the world?"

I answered without thinking. "I want my girlfriend Shayda back," I said.

"That's very noble," Tricia said. "And we can make that happen." Before I could ask how, Tricia reached across the table, pressing her palm against the white linen cloth. "You're the person for this part, Sid. I want the real deal. I want honest-to-God psychics, real witches, genuine summoners, the whole shebang. So we will reward you well. The winner will be granted their deepest true desire. There are some caveats, of course, which will be stipulated in your contract. But I assure you, this is all on the up-and-up. So what do you say, Sid? How'd you like to be famous?"

I stared at her, wondering where to start. She said she'd done her research, yet she didn't realize what little appeal celebrity held for me. Famous? I didn't want to be famous. I wanted my girlfriend back. And regardless of her promises, I couldn't see how a TV show could help me realize that goal.

"It looks like this meeting was a big waste of both our time," I said with a tight smile. "You don't want me for your show. I promise. And more importantly, I don't want to be on your show. I'm sure you'll find someone else to fill the role. This is Southern California, after all. Everyone here is a star in the making."

The woman opposite me sighed, blowing out her cheeks, her mouth twitching to one side. "I can see I chose the wrong tack. But think about it, Sid. This is a really great opportunity." When I didn't say anything, Tricia retrieved a business card from her purse and slid it across the table. "Don't answer now. Take a few days to think it over. When you decide, call me."

"I've already decided," I said, taking the card and slipping it away anyway. "I'm not interested."

But Tricia acted like she hadn't heard. "I'll pay for dinner on my way out. Please stay and enjoy the meal on the network. It's the least I could do for your time."

I was going to tell her how much I hated the phrase "It's the least I could do," because it made the person saying it sound lazy and ungracious. Why would anyone admit to doing the *least* they could do? But before I could say anything, Tricia was already on the other side of the dining room, and then she was gone.

three

. . .

The next day was Tuesday, which meant I had to go to work even though I'd worked all weekend and just wanted to sit in my near-empty apartment and sulk. When I arrived at the police station, Angela Richards, the city's head of HR, was sitting in the lobby. She was jittery, fidgeting with her hair and clothes, her leg bouncing up and down as she chewed her lips. I recognized those tells: Angela was nervous, but that wasn't any surprise. Angela always looked nervous. For someone whose job was dealing with people, she was horrible at it. Not as bad as me, but you expect more from a human resources person. Anyway, when she saw me, she stood up clumsily, her hands shaking as she reached for the necklace she wore at her throat, wrapping it around her fingers. You didn't need to be a detective to know something was up.

"Good morning, Sid." She donned a tight smile that didn't quite reach her eyes. "Have a good weekend?"

I frowned. "I worked all weekend. Angela, you know I don't like small talk. What are you doing here? I have a meeting with Detective Hidalgo in 15 minutes."

Angela bobbed her head up and down, but it wasn't exactly a nod. It was more of a tick. "Yes, right. Well, that's what I wanted to talk to you about, Sid. Can we go someplace a bit more private?"

It wasn't really a question. She grabbed me by the elbow and led me down the hallway toward an empty office she was squatting in. I gently pried myself out of her grasp; I didn't really like touching other people if I didn't have to. Part of that is my anxiety and awkwardness, but it's also because sometimes when I touch people, I see things I don't want to see. Luckily, when Angela touched me, nothing happened.

When we were safely ensconced in her makeshift office, Angela closed the door and bid me sit at the desk. Stacked on top in three piles was paperwork I immediately recognized.

I looked up as my shoulders slouched. "Are you firing me?"

Angela offered me that same tight smile, but her eyes were cloudy. "Sid, I hope you know how much we appreciate you around here. I know it was hard getting the respect you deserve at first. We're a little behind the times when it comes to using psychics in our investigations, but the people who matter? They all recognize your genius. But the mayor's up for reelection soon, and he's made it clear he's not comfortable with the scrutiny the department's been getting because we consult with you. And, besides that, there've also been budget cuts." She said this last part as if it was supposed to soften the blow, but when you've just been fired, there's really no softening that. It all sucks.

"So you see, this is out of our hands. If we could keep you on, we would. But right now…" She let her voice trail off as she dropped her gaze and shrugged. "I'm really sorry, Sid. But we have to let you go."

Officially, I'd been working for the San Diego Police Department as a contractor. I was not a full-time employee, and so, in theory, all of this was unnecessary. They could've handled the termination of my contract with a simple phone call. Doing it this way was supposed to be an olive branch. I understood that. But I didn't like it. I would have preferred a phone call and saved the trip down here.

But this wasn't Angela's fault. She was just doing her job. So I shook myself off, cleared my throat, and nodded. "Yeah, I get it. I understand. I knew this gig wouldn't last forever, so it's okay, Angela. Really." It really wasn't, but sometimes even I had to say things I didn't mean. "So, do you need me to sign something, or…?"

Angela pushed the piles of paper toward me. "Well, these are for you. This one just says we're terminating the contract. You can look it over at your leisure. This one talks about how you're going to receive the remainder of your money. And this over here is just recommendation letters from the department. You know, in case you decide you want to take your services elsewhere. We're happy to recommend you to others."

"But you don't want to use me anymore yourself."

I shouldn't have said that, and I regretted it the moment the words were out of my mouth. Angela turned an unsightly shade of pink as she tilted her head to the side, dropping her chin in her hand. "I hate this for you, Sid. I know how hard it is for you to get work. And you're really good at your job. I mean, just astoundingly good from what I hear. You realize this isn't personal, right?"

Of course I knew it wasn't personal. It was entirely professional, and that made it worse. Look, I could understand not wanting to be my friend. I knew I made people uncomfortable. But Angela was right about one thing—I was really good at my job. So I would rather hear that the department was getting rid of me because I creeped people out than because my work was deemed unnecessary or unsavory.

"I solved the Maryann Holder case," I said, almost to myself.

"I was the one that found the ghost in the parking garage. I was the one that asked the ghost what it saw. You know how unusual it is to have a ghost as the only eyewitness? No one else in the department could've gotten that information. It was me."

Angela was nodding and swiping at her nose. I couldn't tell if she was about to cry—her tells weren't the same as Shayda's. Still, she was making me anxious.

"And the Marco Gilmore murder? I found the key evidence in that case, too. Doesn't the mayor care about that? Or *all* the other crimes this department solved because of my abilities?"

Angela looked up at me, her eyes melty and downward tilting. "What do you want me to say? This wasn't my decision. Nobody really wants you out of here, but—"

I held up a hand. "Number one, that's not true. Plenty of people really want me out of here. But number two, I get what you're saying. I don't mean to make this difficult for you. I should go."

I gathered up the papers without looking at them and rose to my feet. I was already halfway to the door when I stopped and turned around. "It was nice working with you, Angela. Maybe we'll keep in touch?"

I don't know why I made it a question. I wasn't even sure I wanted her to keep in touch. What did I think might happen? We'd meet for coffee on Wednesday afternoons? Go out for drinks on Saturday nights? I couldn't see any of that happening. But that was the sort of thing people said when they separated from a job, right? That whole keep in touch thing?

I felt stupid as soon as I said it. So instead of waiting for a response, I shouldered my way out the door.

———

When I got home, I saw that Shayda had been back. More of her things were gone, including much of the furniture. I wasn't sure how she managed to move so much furniture in the short amount of time I was gone, but then I didn't think about it too hard, either.

She left a note on the refrigerator. All it said was, "Pay the rent."

That's when the reality of everything happening really hit home.

Shayda was an obstetrics nurse practitioner, and she made good money. That was how we afforded this apartment in San Diego. I never could've lived here on my own. Hell, even between the two of us, making ends meet was rough. But when you have a good attitude and a partner who loves and supports you, you can do almost anything.

(I don't know why I just said that. I must've read that on a greeting card. Or maybe I heard Dr. Xena say it. That cocka-mamie nonsense wouldn't have naturally come from my brain.)

But anyway, I had neither a good attitude nor a partner who loved and supported me. I was a loner who had just been dumped and fired, so that meant I could do pretty much nothing.

Especially pay the rent on an apartment in San Diego.

(Those thoughts were my own. That's precisely the kind of depressing thing my brain would come up with.)

I plucked the note from the refrigerator and stared at it, my mind running through the possibilities. I could call the landlord and explain my situation, but I wasn't sure that would do any good. After all, if I were the landlord, I would shrug off that sob story and start my search for a brand-new wealthy tenant.

Plus, admitting my dire straits was something I could never, ever do.

Realizing that was a dead end, I considered other options. I could get a quick temp job, though I wasn't sure what I was qualified to temp at that would pay anything close to supporting a lovely apartment a few miles from the beach. I could sell plasma, but again, while I might be able to scrape together enough money for a seafood dinner, rent was probably out of the question. I could ask Shayda for the money, but I would rather die than put myself in her debt.

That wasn't hyperbole, either. If I had a choice between begging my ex-girlfriend for money or lying in the middle of Pacific Coast Highway, I'd be face-down on the freeway before you could say "6-car pileup."

I'm not suicidal. But I do have my limits.

I thought about calling my therapist. In times like these, getting advice from a professional might not be the worst idea in the world. But just as I didn't want to ask for help from Shayda, I also didn't want to ask Dr. Xena for help. I realized that was stupid. Asking an ex-girlfriend for help is one thing; asking your therapist for help is another. Dr. Xena got paid to help me with difficult situations.

Or at least, she did.

Dr. Xena was part of my health insurance. Health insurance I got through Shayda. And now that I didn't have Shayda, I probably wouldn't have insurance much longer, either.

It's a hell of a thing to realize in one afternoon that everything you used to take for granted was gone.

I crumbled up the Post-it note and threw it in the trash. I couldn't pay the rent. That was a no-go, so it didn't make sense to waste time thinking about it anymore. I was out of options. I wouldn't ask Shayda for help. I couldn't go to Dr. Xena. The city had let me down.

And then, just as I was about to make my way down to the local bar to drown my worries in a gin and tonic, I thought of Tricia Woodward and her pretty linen dress and her sensible shoes and her mysterious smile.

No way, I thought, shaking my head even at the idea. *I'm not calling the network. Absolutely not. No, no, no—*

"Hey."

The voice startled me. I looked up to find a girl standing just a few feet away from me, arms akimbo, her dimpled face smiling out from underneath a mass of thick, chocolate-brown hair. She ambled toward me and climbed up on the couch, curling up in the corner, hugging her knees to her chest. "Whatcha doin'?"

I smiled at her, oddly comforted that she'd chosen now to appear. It was a ghost girl—but not just any ghost girl. She was the very first ghost I'd ever seen, and now I'd been seeing her my whole life. When she first appeared, we were roughly the same age. Over time, I'd grown up.

She never did.

The first time I saw her, she'd appeared in my front yard while I was spying on the neighbors with a pair of orange plastic binoculars I'd gotten for Christmas. She was wearing a pink t-shirt and khaki shorts, the same outfit she'd wear for the rest of our lives together. Anyway, that first day, she surprised me by approaching from behind, tugging on the hem of my t-shirt. When I spun around, she cocked her head to the side and asked innocently, "Whatcha doin'?"

I stammered, lowering the binoculars to my side. "Nothing. Just playing," I said.

The girl pointed to my binoculars. "Can I try?"

I wasn't sure I should insinuate anyone else in my illicit activities. Still, even as a child, I was lonely, and the idea of sharing my covert operation was appealing. Besides, the neighbors weren't naked or anything. They were just sitting around watching television. So I shrugged in agreement. She held out her hand, but when I dropped the binoculars into her open palm, they clattered to the ground.

"Hey!" I shrieked. "You gotta be careful with those! If they break, I probably won't get another pair."

I bent over to retrieve the toy, and when I stood up, the girl was gone.

I leaned back into the sofa, digging my knuckles into my eye sockets. "Now isn't a good time," I said. "What do you want?"

The ghost sucked her teeth. "You just seem sad is all. I thought maybe I could make you feel better. Did you know you can hear a blue whale's heartbeat from miles away?"

I sighed. The ghost loved to tell me random facts, especially about wildlife. She'd been doing it for as long as I'd known her. "I didn't know that."

"It's true. And did you know that crocodiles are over 200 million years old?"

"I don't think that's true," I said. "No creature can live for 200 million years."

The ghost rolled her eyes. "I mean, crocodiles have been on *Earth* for that long."

I shrugged. "That's not what you said."

"You knew what I meant. And did you know mantis shrimps have sixteen cones in their eyes, while humans only have three? They can see colors we can't even imagine."

"That one I did know," I said. "You've told me before."

The ghost pretended not to hear. "I learned all that in school."

I shook my head. "You haven't been to school in a really long time. Why do you keep hanging around here, anyway? Nobody else seems to want anything to do with me." I realized as I said the words that I sounded pathetic, which I hated, so I changed tacks. "Don't you have other people you can haunt?"

That made her laugh. "I'm not haunting you, silly. I just want to know what you're doing. I thought maybe we could play a game."

I let out a long sigh. "We've tried to play lots of games, but you can't touch things. You can't handle a video game controller, you can't move pieces around a board…Hell, you can't even skip rope. We've tried all these things, remember? I don't even understand how you're sitting on the couch right now. How come you don't just fall right through?"

She wound a stray lock of dark hair around her finger. "Yeah, I don't know. You're right about the games. But maybe we could play something like a guessing game? There's no pieces to touch in that. I could think of a number, and you could try to guess it."

I squinted at her. "A guessing game? I have a similar idea. Why don't you tell me your name?"

Now, the ghost looked sullen. "I thought we weren't gonna do this anymore," she said. "I've told you a million times. I can only tell you my name if you tell me yours."

It was true. She had told me this particular rule of hers at least a million times. Well, probably not a million, because that's a really large number, but a lot of times, anyway. What I didn't understand was:

1. Why she was so adamant about this rule, and
2. Why she thought I hadn't already told her my name. Because I had, at least a million times. Or maybe not exactly a million. But you know what I'm saying.

"My name is Sidney Sheridan," I said for the million-and-first time. "I don't have a middle name. What else do you want to know?"

The ghost sighed and dropped her face low, pressing her cheek against her knees. "That's not your real name, though. And if you won't tell me your real name, why should I tell you mine?"

I threw up my hands. "Fine. Don't tell me your name. But,

honestly, I'm not in the mood for this today. You know what rent is?"

The girl shook her head. "Sounds like some kind of boring grown-up stuff."

"Yeah, you got that right," I chuckled. "Boring grown-up stuff. Well, right now, I have to worry about my rent. And a lot of other really boring grown-up stuff."

The ghost was peering at me quizzically. "Like what?"

I sucked in a breath. "Like whether I'm going to sell my soul to the devil."

"That sounds scary," she said, making bug eyes at me.

I thought of Tricia Woodward's offer and the idea of living on camera with six strangers, each with psychic abilities and an array of personality flaws and shook my head in real horror. "Ghostie, you don't even know the half of it."

Then I picked up my phone.

four

. . .

Two weeks later, I was standing outside an ostentatious ocean-side home with my suitcase in hand. I felt like a schmuck. Not only was I carrying a mostly empty bag, pretending like I was moving into this house for the first time, but I was really about to do this. I was really about to walk into this house filled with cameras and start a "new life" with a bunch of psychologically questionable strangers. Thinking about it this way almost sent me into a panic attack, so I closed my eyes and counted backward from 10 while I thought about comforting things. The way Shayda smelled after she'd been painting. The taste of champagne. The way reading my favorite book made me feel. Pretty soon, I was feeling better, but I still didn't want to go inside. Even so, it was too late for second thoughts. Not only had I already signed a contract, but I had no other place to live, no money, no job, and no other options.

Sucking in a deep breath, I strode toward the door, threw my shoulders back, and pressed the buzzer. A moment later, a female voice answered. "Hello?"

I forced a fake friendliness into my voice. "I'm the new housemate. I'm moving in today."

I heard giggling on the other end, and then the door buzzed open.

With my weighted suitcase in hand, I entered my new home. I'd been here before to drop off my belongings, but I hadn't actually seen the place since it had been furnished.

It was sleek, minimal, and modern. Everything was white: the walls, the tile floors, the ceiling. Enormous windows overlooked the Pacific Ocean, and tall, potted plants luxuriated in the sunlight. Tasteful paintings decorated the walls, and throw rugs made the place feel inviting instead of sterile.

It was almost welcoming until I noticed the cameramen.

I wasn't supposed to look at them, of course. The whole point of the show was to appear as natural as possible. Still, each time I caught a glimpse of the lenses or the blinking "Recording" lights from the corner of an eye, I felt a chill run down my spine.

What had I gotten myself into?

As I was taking all of this in, a pair of women appeared.

They were smiling like schoolgirls. One of them reached her hand out to me, and I accepted as I set my suitcase on the floor. "So you're the new housemate," she said, a crooked smile curling over her lips. "You're the last one to arrive!"

My eyebrows shot up. "Oh, really?" I glanced around. "Where's everyone else?"

"Down at the beach, probably," one of them said with a slight frown. "I wish I had that level of carefree, wild abandon! Must be so nice to have a body you can just flaunt in front of God and country without even giving it a second thought!"

Without meaning to, I let my eyes travel the length of the woman's body. I didn't see anything wrong with it.

"You must be Pride," she said. "I'm Envy. It's nice to meet you."

The other woman waved without offering her hand. "I'm Sloth."

Although we'd all been prepped on how to address each other, hearing these women address themselves by presumably their biggest flaw was *weird*. Can you imagine some very normal-looking person walking up to you, extending their hand, and saying, "Hi, I'm Pathological Liar!" How would you respond to that? It was jarring, is what I'm saying.

But then I remembered the cameras, so I pushed the thought away and grinned. "Nice to meet you, too." I gestured toward my fake luggage. "So, where should I put this?"

"Your room's upstairs," Envy said, nodding toward the staircase. "You want me to show you around? We all have our own rooms. This place is *huge*. My room is okay, but it doesn't overlook the water like *yours* does. God, I *wish* I had your room. Let me know if you want to trade."

Sloth came forward then, holding out a hand. "Here, why don't you give me your stuff? I'll put it in your room while Envy gives you a tour."

I looked down to see Sloth's hand covered in something red and sticky. She must've caught me looking because she giggled and rushed to explain. "It's just melted popsicle," she said. "Just sugar. It'll wash right off. I promise not to get any on your stuff."

I wasn't so sure she could keep that promise, but I also knew this was part of the routine. The cameras were going to follow me and Envy around the house while Sloth took my fake suitcase to my already-prepared room. So I handed the other woman my luggage. She gave me a military salute as Envy grabbed me by the elbow.

At her touch, images flashed before my eyes. A fiery lizard, a nondescript humanoid composed of water, a short humanoid that could only be described as a gnome, and a wispy humanoid that looked to be cast in smoke. Abruptly, I yanked my arm free of Envy's grasp. The woman looked at me, her eyes betraying the slightest smile as she glanced almost imperceptibly in the camera's direction. "Is something wrong?" she asked.

"Not wrong," I drawled, rubbing the spot on my arm where she'd touched me. "But sometimes when people touch me, I see things."

Envy cocked an eyebrow. "Did you see something just now?"

I swallowed. "Yes. I saw…Well, I don't really know how to describe it. I saw four creatures surrounding you. Creatures made of air and water. A little guy, like a gnome. And a lizard made of fire."

A slow smile spread over Envy's mouth, and she popped a hand on her hip, her head listing to one side. "Interesting! I'm gonna have to keep my eye on you. Well, you'll get to know those guys soon enough, I guess. They sort of follow me around. Are you familiar with the four cardinal elements? Earth, air, water, fire?"

My eyes narrowed. "Sure, I guess." I wasn't, though. Not really. But neither she nor all of America needed to know the depths of my ignorance.

"Well, each cardinal element is represented by a different being. Elementals, some people call them. I guess you could say I have an affinity for them. They come and go as they please, of course, but sometimes, I can convince them to do some simple tasks. If they feel like it."

I wanted to ask more questions, but I saw that Envy was deliberately ending this conversation. She was trying to follow Tricia's directives. We weren't supposed to talk about our abilities. We were only supposed to *show* the audience what we could do—but only in a natural, everyday kind of way, whatever that meant.

"Okay, so this is obviously the kitchen. Get a load of these appliances. I mean, top of the line. I hope somebody here turns out to be a great cook. I can't cook at all, but I love to eat. I have to keep an eye on that, though. You know what I'm saying? It's so unfair how some people can eat anything they want, and the rest of us have to watch every single calorie, or else we'll blow up like a giant Pillsbury Doughboy. So where are you from?"

The subject change threw me for a loop, and I blinked back my surprise. "Here," I said. "Well, San Diego. You?"

"Pittsburgh. There's one other person here from California, but I can't remember who. Maybe you two know each other."

I couldn't tell if that was supposed to be a joke or not. California is one of the biggest states in the country, with a population of almost 40 million. So the odds of knowing another random Californian were slim. Only an idiot wouldn't realize that, and I wasn't sure whether Envy was an idiot, so I decided to give her the benefit of the doubt and treated her statement as a joke. I chuckled. I must have guessed right because she grinned and motioned with her head for me to follow her.

We exited the kitchen and walked through the main living room to a second open area with the dartboard, a pool table, beanbag chairs, the whole nine yards. It looked like a scene from a frat house movie. "Okay, and this is the recreation room. Haven't spent any time in here yet. But I mean, we all just got here, so. Do you play darts?"

I shook my head. "No. Do you?"

She wrinkled her nose. "No. Who the heck plays darts? I heard we might get a foosball table, but I'm not super interested in that, either."

We left the room, and Envy continued the tour. In addition to the recreation room, the house also featured a theater room, a unisex bath and sauna, beach access, a pool, and half a dozen bathrooms. "Apparently, this place used to be a beach condo," Envy explained. "But I guess it's been recently renovated to be a private house. Can you believe we really get to live here?"

Under different circumstances, I'm sure I would have been just as enthralled with the space as she was. But all I could think about was how Shayda would have hung her paintings in the kitchen, replacing the generic "Taco Tuesday" sign hanging in there now. I thought about how the house would smell faintly of floral perfume, especially after Shayda came out of the shower. But I pulled the best smile I could out of my hat and nodded. "It's amazing," I agreed.

"Well, I probably ought to let you get upstairs and get settled in," Envy said. "God only knows what Sloth is doing with your things. You better go up there and kick her out before she gets popsicle juice all over your walls or something."

I fake laughed as my stomach flipped over. Just thinking about that woman rifling through my things was enough to give me hives. "Ok, cool. Hey, thanks for the tour."

"No problem. When you get bored, come find me. Maybe we can go find a café and get a bite to eat or something? The fridge is still empty. Some of the others wanted to get the shopping out of the way earlier, but Wrath and I voted to wait until you got here."

I squinted. "Two out of six people won the vote?"

Envy chuckled. "Oh, right. You haven't met Wrath yet."

I watched in silence as Envy disappeared around a corner. I glanced surreptitiously at the cameraman, who was swallowing down a chuckle.

Heat rose in my cheeks. *What the hell have I gotten myself into?*

five

. . .

"Good morning, everyone! And welcome to your first official day at *Sinful House!*"

Tricia Woodward was dressed in a simple gray cotton shift, her hair pulled into a neat ponytail. She was too chipper for 8 o'clock in the morning. We were sitting in a semicircle around her in the main living room. Some of us were drinking coffee; others were rubbing the sleep from our eyes as we tried to hide our yawns. I was in the second group. It seemed that none of us were morning people, and for some reason, that made me feel better.

"As you all know, I'm here to give you your assignments this morning. You will be working in teams to help out various members of the local community. The teams were assigned beforehand, but each team will randomly select an assignment from the pot. You have two weeks to complete your task. After that, we'll assign new teams and challenges. There's no penalty for failing a task. But each completed challenge grants 'Good Samaritan' points. You get more points the earlier you complete your challenge. Your Good Samaritan points will be added to your Audience Favorite votes at the end of the season. We encourage every team to try their best." She flashed us a bright smile. "Any questions so far?"

No one said anything. We all knew the drill.

Tricia clapped her hands together. "Great! Then let's go ahead and get started." She retrieved a piece of paper sitting in front of her on the coffee table. "The teams are as follows: Team one is Pride and Lust. Team two is Greed and Wrath. And team three is Envy, Gluttony, and Sloth."

One of the men in the semicircle rose to his feet, hands balled into fists at his side. "What the hell? Right off the bat, the teams are unfair? Why does team three have three people and the rest of us only have two?"

Tricia's head listed to one side. "That's a great question, Wrath. But as I'm sure you can tell, seven doesn't divide neatly. Every week, one team will have three people. But don't worry. Having that extra person might not be as much of a boon as you expect. Sometimes, the more people we have to work with, the harder it can be to reach consensus and make decisions."

This didn't assuage Wrath, whose face darkened as he approached the producer. "This is rigged," he said, pointing a finger in her face. "You need to fix this, or I'll call my agent. Get an additional housemate if you have to."

"Are you stupid or something?" This comment came from another man in the group. He was tall and lean, with dark hair that brushed against his shoulders. His features were sharp, his eyes bright. "There are *seven* deadly sins, you dolt. Not eight."

"Greed's right," Envy said. "There's seven of us, and that's how it has to be. You'll just have to accept that."

Greed and Wrath shot daggers at each other before Wrath sucked in a breath and returned to his seat, face red, nostrils still flared. "I still say this is rigged," he muttered.

Now, Tricia looked to me, her hands folded in her lap as she leaned forward. "Pride, as the last person to arrive, you get to choose the first mission." She pointed to a wicker basket sitting on the table between us. "Go ahead and make your selection. But do me a favor and don't look until everyone has chosen their assignment."

I did as I was told, retrieving a paper from the basket. My skin prickled over at the feeling of everyone's eyes on me. I didn't like being the center of attention, which was pretty stupid considering I was now on a reality TV show where my every move would be broadcast to homes all across America. I ignored the cameras with the "Recording" lights that blinked in the background and sat back down.

The other teams chose their assignments, and when the basket was empty, Tricia leaned back and crossed her legs. "All right! Everyone, please find your teammate and see what you got. You're free to begin your task immediately. If you get stuck, you can ask other teams for help. But of course, no one is obligated to help you. I wish you all the best of luck, and may the best Sins win!"

Everyone got to their feet. I glanced around the room, unsure which of the remaining people I didn't know was Lust. I'd already met the short, round-cheeked girl with hay-colored pigtails and peaches and cream skin: that was Sloth. I also ruled out the pasty, wiry dude with sharp eyes: that was Greed. Wrath was the handsome but volatile Asian fellow with bleached blond hair, and Envy was the girl-next-door woman who'd given me a tour of the house.

So that left two people I hadn't met: Lust and Gluttony.

It didn't take long to figure out who was who. A tall woman approached me, raven hair undone and tumbling in loose curls. She wore an off-the-shoulder t-shirt that revealed smooth, cinnamon-brown skin and cut-offs so short they left nothing to the imagination. Even at this hour, her face was painted to perfection, and she sauntered over to me with the grace of a cat on the prowl. She placed a hand on my forearm. Strangely, I didn't want to pull away. "We didn't get a chance to meet yesterday," she said. Her voice was both husky and melodious. "I'm Lust."

I cleared my throat. "Pride," I said, extending a hand. "Nice to meet you."

"Likewise. So." She glanced at the paper in my hand. "Should we go ahead and see what the network has in store for us?"

Obediently, I unfolded the paper. Lust peered over my shoulder, and I read the contents aloud for the cameras. "Help Linda and Eric Wong discover who's been tampering with their fortune cookies."

I looked up, my brow creased in confusion. "That's it? There's no address or phone number or anything."

Lust took the paper from my fingers, flipped it over to confirm, then folded it and slipped it in my pocket. "Well, my guess is they own a Chinese restaurant, so maybe we start there."

Lust whipped a phone from a pocket. She tapped in a Google search and, after a quick browse, snapped her fingers in victory. "Aha. Here we go. There's a story from the Odyssey News website about a Chinese restaurant having trouble with pranksters altering the fortune cookies. Apparently, the locals are pretty mad about it."

"Okay. What's the name of the restaurant?"

Lust shoved the phone in my face before announcing aloud, "Wights and Wongs." She chuckled, a throaty sound that made my spine tingle. "Oh man, that's good. That's *funny.*"

"Why's it funny?"

Lust peered at me a moment before answering. "Well, it's a pun, sweetie. Like Rights and Wrongs, but Wights and Wongs? Get it?"

I didn't get it, but I wasn't going to admit that. So instead, I said, "I wonder why they named it that."

Lust looked back down at her phone before answering. "Probably because it's owned by the Wong family and—get this—they don't have human servers. All their food is served by ghosts—wights, to be exact."

"Oh." That was a twist I hadn't expected. "Technically, wights aren't ghosts," I mused aloud. "Ghosts are spirits of dead people. Wights are cursed, immortal spirits forced to wander the Earth in never-ending servitude."

"*Okay*, Professor Freak Show! Hey, don't me wrong, knowledge is sexy. Keep those random factoids coming. Just not right now, though," she said, interrupting the speech I was about to give about various kinds of earthbound spirits. "We should get going. I don't know about you, but I'm not about to lose to any of these other clowns. What do you say? Are you in the mood for some moo goo gai pan?"

I gestured over my shoulder with my thumb. "I thought we were going to help the Wongs figure out—"

Lust barked a laugh, her eyes wide. "Wow, you're super literal, aren't you? Come on, Freak Show. Let's go solve the fortune cookie caper."

six

· · ·

Wights and Wongs was on the other side of town but still only a ten-minute drive from the house. Unlike other Chinese restaurants tucked away in strip malls, Wights and Wongs was an ornate standalone building designed to look like a Chinese palace. The exterior was red and black, with an ornate tiled roof adorned with stone dragon guardians. A lighted path led up to double front doors that swung open easily despite their size.

Stepping through the doorway was like entering another world. The eerie sounds of wind whistling through trees and somber organ music drifted from unseen speakers. The inside was dark, lit by strategically placed red candles. The walls were adorned with paintings featuring dark, moody scenes from a forest where specters peeked out from behind gnarled trees. The combined effect of lighting, art, and music was fantastic and unlike anything I expected. Whoever designed this place was a genius. A bit twisted, maybe, but a genius.

Standing behind a podium, a bored hostess, no older than eighteen, hardly looked up from her seating chart. She wore a vintage graphic t-shirt with the words "Save the whales!" splashed across the front. "Welcome to Wights and Wongs. How many?"

I cleared my throat. "Actually, we're looking for Linda or Eric Wong? Are they here by any chance?"

The girl looked up, and when she saw the cameramen behind us, her eyes went wide, and her hands flew to her mouth. "Oh my gosh! You must be those people from that show! I heard you were coming today, but I totally forgot! Oh my gosh, am I going to be on television?" Her cheeks turned an alarming shade of red as she tittered, shifting her weight from foot to foot and combing her fingers through her long, dark hair. "No, don't tell me. I know I'm doing this all wrong. I'm supposed to pretend like the cameras aren't here and stuff, right? Well, I guess they can edit this part out. I'm such a moron! Okay. Let me start over."

The girl shook herself, arranged her hair around her shoulders without obscuring the lettering on her shirt. Then she looked up, a bright smile on her face. "Hi! Welcome to Wights and Wongs! How many will be dining with us today?"

I choked down a chuckle at her acting job. She certainly had a future in the spotlight if she wanted it. "We're here to see Linda or Eric Wong. Are they available?"

The girl brought an index finger to her chin, tapping lightly as she pretended to think. "Yes, I think they're both in the back. Would you like to be seated, and I can have them join you when they're ready?"

Lust nodded. "Sure. Sounds great."

The girl stepped out from behind the podium with menus in hand and motioned for us to follow her. "Excellent. Right this way."

As we wended our way through the restaurant, I noticed how empty the place was. It was lunchtime, and I expected the place to be bustling. But as we walked through the main dining hall, I noticed at least 80 percent of the tables were vacant. I elbowed Lust in the side. "Place is pretty empty. No way they can cover their overhead with a crowd like this. You think they do most of their business at dinner?"

Lust leaned in to answer. "Could be. But I have a feeling the lack of customers has something to do with the fortune cookie shenanigans."

Upon hearing the words 'fortune cookie,' the hostess turned around. "It's really awful what's been happening here," she said. "Mom and Dad are really torn up about it. I hope you guys can get to the bottom of it. Okay, here we go." She'd led us to a private room large enough to seat eight people. The cameramen ensconced themselves in the corners where they could shoot the whole room from different angles. I chose a seat facing the door, and to my surprise, Lust chose to sit beside me rather than across. She was so close, I felt her thigh pressing against mine.

The hostess handed us our menus and said, "A wight will be with you shortly." Then she excused herself and disappeared down the dim corridor.

Lust whistled as she looked around the room. "This place is wild," she said. "Have you ever seen anything like this? I feel like I'm at some haunted amusement park ride."

She was right. Our private room boasted a chandelier that was professionally designed to look like it hadn't been dusted in about 20 years. Artificial cobwebs glittered on the ceiling. The art on the walls featured graveyards with shrines in the background. But the chairs were comfortable, the table didn't wobble when you leaned on it, and there were real linen napkins for place settings.

I barely had a chance to peruse the menu—which was extensive—before two people entered our room.

They were both Asian. The woman was tall and severe, with thin lips and long, dark hair. The man with her was shorter and more relaxed, with wire-rimmed glasses and hair styled away from a broad, handsome face. They were both dressed simply in slacks and button-down shirts.

"Hello," the woman said, tucking a stray lock of hair behind her ear. "Thank you for coming. I'm Linda Wong." The woman shook hands with Lust first, then me. "It's nice to meet you."

"I'm Lust," my companion said, one hand placed on her chest. "And this is my friend, Pride."

Linda gestured toward the man with her. "This is my husband, Eric. You already met our daughter, Ruby." The Wongs slid into their seats beside us, their hands folded on the table. "How would you like to begin?" Linda asked.

I shrugged. "We don't know anything about what's been going on here. So how about starting from the beginning?"

Eric nodded, clearing his throat as he adjusted in his seat. "It all began a few weeks ago. I'd gotten a new shipment of fortune cookies. We get them from a company up in San Francisco. We've been ordering from the same place for years. Never had a problem. Anyway, our sous chef, Ping Lau, sent the fortune cookies to Table 31 just as she normally would. Later that night, our daughter, Ruby, who was hosting, received a complaint from one of our guests. The guest's name was Charmaine Young. She said her fortune was inappropriate."

My brow wrinkled. "Inappropriate how?"

"Well, you know how fortune cookies are. They usually say dumb, innocuous things like, *'You are the life of the party.'* Or sometimes they give actual fortunes like, *'Expect a windfall of money coming your way soon.'* But Charmaine claimed her fortune said, *'A dark horse rides at midnight, bringing an untimely death to the family.'*"

Lust and I exchanged looks. "That is grim," Lust said, propping her cheek against a fist. "Then what happened?"

"Well, she showed the fortune to Ruby, but when Ruby looked at it, the fortune read, *'The best gift you can give is your smile.'*

Charmaine was furious, claiming Ruby was lying, and she demanded to speak to us." Eric gestured between himself and his wife. "When we read the fortune, we saw what Ruby saw."

"I assumed she was nuts or just trying to get a comped meal," Linda admitted. "The fortune obviously didn't say what that woman claimed it said. But then…"

The Wongs glanced at each other before looking down at the table, their cheeks coloring red. "Less than a week later, that woman's uncle passed away. He was the mayor of the next town over."

A chill ran down my spine. "So the fortune came true," I said. "Probably just a fluke, though, right?"

Linda sucked in a breath. "Well, that's what we thought, too. But unfortunately, the awful fortunes continued. One woman got a fortune predicting layoffs at her company, and days later, she was let go. Another patron was told to expect heartbreak. His wife filed for divorce. So as you can see, it's not just that the fortunes are dark and only appear to the person they're destined for. It's that they're also accurate."

Lust murmured a thinking sound as she absently stroked a lock of hair. "Very strange, indeed."

"After that, we checked the cookie shipment," Eric said. "Ruby and I opened about thirty fortune cookies, and none of them said anything bad. Just the same old stuff. Still, we threw the rest of the batch away, and my wife called our vendor to complain. They sent us a replacement batch for free. When they arrived, we went through those the same way, opening a couple dozen at random, and they seemed untainted. But…" Eric sighed, shaking his head miserably. "That night, one of Ruby's friends, Lee Jordan, got a fortune that said, 'Troublesome times await you. Expect family to be detained against their will.' And sure enough—"

"Lee's dad was arrested for money laundering and other

fraud," Linda finished. "After that, journalists got a hold of the story. Charmaine Young was on every news station crying about how we cursed her uncle. She was in the papers. And she grew a following, too. Thanks to her, people stayed away."

I folded my arms over my chest. "I guess I can see how this might be a problem."

"This is our family business," Eric said, his voice strained. "It's our income. Our livelihood. Ruby is about to graduate high school. Soon, we'll have to pay for college. But people don't want to eat here anymore. The idea of inviting a curse freaks them out. And I can't say I blame them."

I was opening my mouth to suggest that diners who didn't want to know their future shouldn't eat fortune cookies when the air in the room suddenly chilled. I looked over to find that an apparition had materialized at the side of our table. At first glance, it looked like a pillar of swirling smoke. But soon, I realized the shifting image was that of a skeletal figure wrapped in a gauzy, hooded cloak, its eyes glowing with a green, lambent glow.

My breath caught. It was a wight. An actual, honest to God wight.

And it seemed to be waiting to take our orders.

"Combination lo mein for the table, please," Eric said to the wight. Then, reconsidering, he glanced around the table, eyebrows raised. "That's our house specialty, but if someone wants something else…"

Both Lust and I shook our heads. "Combination lo mein sounds great," I said.

"Egg rolls, too," Eric amended. He waved his hand, and the wight vanished.

"That's a hell of a trick," I said. "Never visited a haunted Chinese restaurant before. How did that happen, anyway?"

Linda sighed, running a hand through her hair. "It was my grandmother's fault," she said, a bit of ice in her voice. "When

Eric and I first opened our restaurant, we didn't anticipate how expensive it would be to run. We were in danger of going under when I complained to my grandmother. She's a busybody, and in retrospect, I should've known better than to open my mouth. But I guess I'm glad I did. We certainly would have gone out of business if I hadn't."

At this, Eric's expression darkened. "Still, it was something we should've discussed together."

This was obviously an old argument, and Linda only rolled her eyes in response. "A few days later, my grandmother offered me a gift. She said it was a blessing she'd bought off a shaman recommended by one of her friends. She told me if I read the blessing in the middle of the restaurant, we'd receive an influx of money." Linda gave a dry, bitter chuckle. "That's how desperate I was, you see. I'm not superstitious. I don't really believe in those old Chinese blessings. Some people obviously have inexplicable abilities, but that's directed. Purposeful. I don't see how the universe just randomly bestows blessings on someone because they read words off a piece of paper."

"The universe is stranger than you imagine," Lust said.

"Hmm. Maybe." Linda frowned and smoothed her hair away from her face. "In any case, like an idiot, I read the blessing. Except it wasn't a blessing, and Grandmother didn't buy it from a shaman. It was a curse, which she bought from a disreputable curse vendor."

At my side, Lust chuckled. "Are there reputable curse vendors?"

Linda shrugged. "I don't know. Anyway, I was cursed from that moment to be haunted by twelve hungry wights. I don't know if you know this, but wights are bound spirits forced to spend eternity as servants." I did know that, but I let her keep talking. "They don't have free will, and they're immortal. So my grandmother cursed me with a lifetime of free labor, which was her way of solving our overhead problem. I'm still not sure how I feel about it," she admitted. "Anyway, when word got out that our food was served by ghosts, we became a curiosity. People came from all over to see our spirits. We had our fair share of people who tried to debunk us, of course. Some reporter from the next town even accused us of piping hallucinogens through the air vents to make people *think* they saw ghosts." Again, she rolled her eyes. "But over time, the *food* kept people coming back. Our sous chef, Ping, is a *miracle*. I don't think we could have done it without her. It wasn't long before we almost couldn't keep up with the demand. Our little restaurant was full to bursting every day."

"That's right," Eric said, nodding. "Within a year, we had enough money to upgrade. We left that little store in the strip mall, upgraded our appliances, and bought this place. Business has been booming ever since." His shoulders drooped, and he sighed, deflated. "Well, until recently."

An idea struck me, and I leaned forward onto my elbows. "I'm guessing some of the other local restaurants weren't too happy about your success," I said. "They might have reason to sabotage your business. Anybody in particular you think might be up to no good?"

Linda pursed her lips together, her eyes downcast. "Helen Park," she said. "She's been giving us trouble for years. She isn't even Chinese. She's Korean. She has a Chinese restaurant a couple of blocks away. Until recently, she hadn't been able to compete with us. But now, with everything going on here, she's doing better. Her business is picking up. I wouldn't be surprised if she had something to do with it."

Eric, however, didn't look convinced. "Helen Park has indeed been troublesome in the past, but I don't think she would do something like this. She has nothing against us personally. In fact, she's been teaching our daughter piano since she was a kindergartener. I can't imagine she would try to put us out of business, knowing the effect that would have on our daughter."

"And that right there is your problem," Linda said, turning to face her husband. "You always see the best in people. Just because Helen is nice to Ruby doesn't mean she wouldn't turn on her in a moment to save herself. I wouldn't put anything past that woman." Linda faced me, her eyes ablaze. "You should start there. She has to know something."

The room's temperature shifted again, and this time, a half dozen wights appeared at the table with our order. Four of the wights carried platters of noodles while the other two had plates of egg rolls. They set our food before us and then drifted from the table, lingering shoulder to shoulder (if wights had shoulders) in a straight line. Eric offered the wights a tight flick of his fingers. "Thank you, that's all."

One by one, the wights silently disappeared.

Lust pressed her fingertips to her lips. "This really is spectacular," she breathed. "Even if people are getting fortune cookies they don't like, wouldn't they still want to come see this in person? I know I would."

Linda shrugged. "Newcomers and tourists, sure. But most of our business is the locals. They've seen this before. For them, the novelty wore off a while ago. They come for the food. Or did, anyway. So you see the problem."

"We'll look into Helen Park," I said, taking a tentative bite of steaming hot noodles. They were fantastic. I could see why this place had become locally famous. "Anyone else who might want to see you suffer?"

"There are plenty of people who would like to see this place disappear," Linda said with a frown. "The conservation groups have picketed here several times, claiming our property sits too close to the coastal lagoon, which is the habitat for the endangered…What is it? The freshwater gimlet?"

"Tidewater goby," her husband supplied.

"Right. Tidewater goby." She rolled her eyes, shaking her head. "And then there's the entire city council, which is full of racists. But if you ask me, the person doing this wants our *business*. There are other Chinese restaurants in town besides Helen's, but most of their business is delivery. Helen Park is the only person directly profiting from this fiasco."

Now, Lust leaned forward, drumming her nails on the table. "What about your grandmother?"

Linda's brow creased. "What about her?"

"Could she have anything to do with this? If she had access to a curse vendor to purchase a dozen eldritch servants, maybe she has the power to conjure up cursed fortune cookies, too."

"No." Linda folded her arms and shook her head. "Grandmother wouldn't do anything like that. Why would she? She spent a lot of money to help us become successful. Curses aren't cheap," she pointed out.

"Besides." Eric sighed heavily. "She's dead."

Just then, a wight appeared at our table bearing a tray of fortune cookies. It placed the tray in the center of the table and then vanished into thin air.

Discomfort washed over me as I stared at the tray. I looked up to meet Linda's gaze. "You're still offering the cookies?" I held up my hands, imploring. "Why?"

"People expect them," she answered. "You can't have a Chinese restaurant without the cookies."

I reached out to pluck one from the tray. My fingers closed around the cellophane, and across the table, Linda said, her voice catching, "I wouldn't."

I ripped the paper off, my heartrate speeding up. It's not every day that opening a cookie makes you nervous. My better judgment agreed with Linda—don't open the cookie. Some futures aren't meant to be known.

But I had to know. I had to see for myself what the cookies held in store for me.

I broke the cookie into two pieces, revealing a slip of familiar white paper. I pulled the fortune free and, my breath held, read my destiny.

"A friend is a present you give yourself."

"In bed," Lust added, reading over my shoulder. "You have to add 'in bed' to any fortune."

Small relief flooded through me, and I placed the fortune on the table. "Just to cover all our bases, we should probably talk to your staff," I said to the Wongs. They might have heard or seen something. Unless that's a problem."

Linda shooed this away. "Of course not. I'll make sure you get the contact information for anyone you need. Is there anything else?"

I glanced at Lust, but she was already going to town on her noodles. I turned to Linda. "If we think of something else, we'll be in touch."

seven

. . .

Afbefore we finished lunch, I headed out to the street where I called Helen Park. It was a quick conversation. The woman cursed me out, called me a spineless mongrel, spit when she said Linda Wong's name, and then agreed to meet with us the next day. Afterward, I made a half dozen other phone calls to the staff, but no one answered, so I left voicemails.

"I'm not sure what else we should do today." I shoved my phone into my pocket and mopped beads of sweat from my brow. The day was warm, and I was overdressed. "Should we head back to the house? Or should we, I don't know, go get ice cream or something?"

I didn't want any ice cream, but Tricia made it clear we were supposed to entertain our viewers. That included going on fun, cute outings. Going for ice cream was about the cutest, funnest thing my brain could conjure up.

Lust didn't answer, and for a minute, I thought she hadn't heard me. But when I peered into her face, I saw something was wrong. Lust looked the way Shayda sometimes looked when she watched Hallmark movies or talked to her family in Iran. "Hey. Are you okay?"

Lust swept her fingertips across her cheek, and only then did I realize she was crying. Her face wasn't red or splotchy, which is why I hadn't noticed. Shayda's face always turned colors when she wept. She was what some people might call an ugly crier, though I wouldn't say that. To me, everything Shayda did was beautiful.

"It's fine. I'm fine," Lust lied. "I'm just being silly."

"Emotions are silly," I agreed, "but you're supposed to acknowledge them. At least, that's what my therapist says."

Lust chuckled. "Oh yeah? My therapist says something similar. No, really, it's nothing. It's just…sometimes seeing happy families makes me weepy."

I glanced over my shoulder toward the restaurant. I didn't get the impression that the Wongs were a particularly happy family, but what did I know? "I see. Any reason? Do you not get along with your family?"

Lust looked like she would answer but then shut her mouth, a curious expression taking over her face that I couldn't read. "Actually, let's change the subject. Why don't you tell me about you? Where's your family from?"

This was a line of conversation I really didn't want to have, but if it prevented an episode of crying, I'd embrace it enthusiastically. "I don't know," I said, wavering. "It's kind of a weird story."

Lust rubbed her palms together as if to warm them, her previous melancholy quickly evaporating. "Ooh, now *that* sounds interesting. Do tell."

We started walking, though we weren't heading toward the car. We were just sort of ambling along, soaking up the sunshine, the wind blowing through our hair. "Well, I'm an orphan. I don't know who my family was because they all disappeared."

Lust's eyes went wide. "Disappeared?"

I nodded. "Yeah. It's…kind of a famous story. You ever heard of the Lovelace Commune out in Santa Barbara?"

Lust shook her head. "I'm from Ohio."

I was pretty sure they had Netflix and libraries even in Ohio, but I let it go. "Oh. Well, the commune was kind of infamous, even before it disappeared. It was an artist's colony started by this guy Sam Lovelace. He was a religious fanatic who believed Jesus was an alien and that the lost books of the Bible taught psychic powers like telekinesis and co-location. He believed deep artistic expression could unlock psychic powers in the mind, so he started this commune."

"I believe that, too," Lust said. "I mean, I don't know about the aliens and stuff. But I do believe deep artistic expression can unlock your inner power."

"Anyway," I continued, "this journalist went out there to do some interviews for a story she was writing. But when she arrived, the entire place was empty. People's cars were still there. The houses were furnished, and closets were filled with clothes. But all the people were gone. The journalist, Anne Lovett, said it was the strangest thing she'd ever seen. Most of the houses were unlocked, so she'd gone inside a few, trying to find someone. Anyone. It was lunchtime when she arrived, and many of the dining rooms were set with plates and untouched food and everything. She said it was like people were there one second, and in the next second, they vanished. She was dialing the sheriff's department for help when she heard a baby crying."

Without warning, Lust reached over and linked her arm in mine. At her touch, an image flashed through my mind—a woman wearing an elaborate, cream-colored saree with jewels in her hair, a man in an officer's uniform. But just as quickly as they'd come on, the images subsided. "Was that baby you?"

I nodded. "Anne Lovett ran into my house and found me in

my cradle. I was the only person she found in the commune, alive or otherwise. The sheriff's department investigated, but none of the other commune members were ever found. Not even their bodies. There was no evidence of foul play or anything like that. One minute, it was a bustling community filled with people, and the next, it was a ghost town. Empty except for me."

Lust whistled and squeezed my upper arm. "My God. It's your very own Lost Colony of Roanoke story, isn't it?"

I had no idea what she was talking about, but I wasn't about to tell her that. Instead, I shrugged. "Yeah, I guess so. There's been lots of books written about it. There was even a popular documentary a few years ago. They wanted to interview me, but I wasn't interested. Never really wanted that kind of notoriety."

Lust glanced surreptitiously at the cameras following us. "Kind of a weird situation for you to be in, then, isn't it, Freak Show?"

I looked down at the sidewalk, trying to hide my face. Something about the way she said *Freak Show* felt intimate, which freaked me out, but not in a bad way, and the fact that I kind of liked it *also* freaked me out. "I didn't have a lot of choice," I said.

Lust purred knowingly. "Yeah. When Tricia gave me that line about fulfilling my deepest desire, I was hooked, too. I'd do *anything* to win this thing. I mean it." There was a fierceness about her when she said this, a tension in how she held her shoulders. "But I guess most people would do just about anything to get what their heart really wants, huh?"

I couldn't answer that, though, so again, I shrugged. "I guess, but that's not me. I mean, I'm not here to win some stupid wish."

Lust cocked her head to the side. "You're lying."

I opened my mouth to say I wasn't, but then I reconsidered. Maybe there *was* a part of me that was here to win my heart's deepest desire. But I wasn't going to be contradicted on camera, so I said, "I'm not lying."

"So then why are you here?"

"I had nowhere else to go after my girlfriend dumped me. I needed a place to stay. Tricia was offering, and no one else was. So that's why I'm here. It's as simple as that."

Lust squeezed my arm again and pressed her body closer to mine. "So what you're saying is, you're single?"

I couldn't help it. I blushed.

———

When we arrived back at the house, someone was screaming.

I pushed Lust aside and flew up the stairs, taking them two at a time, following the screams. Without thinking, I threw open the door to one of the bedrooms and immediately wished I hadn't.

The room was a disaster. Pigsty hardly began to describe it. In addition to the clothes piled in heaps across the room, the trashcan overflowed with tissues and junk food wrappers. The bed was unmade, with a tangle of stained sheets lodged at the base of the footboard. A bare mattress was covered in books, makeup brushes, and decks of tarot cards. Empty beer bottles, discarded jewelry, and wire hangers added a bit of sparkle to the rest of the detritus.

Amid all of it was Sloth, standing in the center of the room, her hands buried in her hair, fully clothed and dripping wet. She was wailing at the top of her lungs.

"Sloth?" I stepped over a pair of muddy shoes as I approached her. "Are you okay? What's wrong?"

Instead of answering, however, Sloth squeezed her eyes shut, shaking her head wildly from side to side. *"I need everybody to stop thinking about me!"* she screeched. Her whole body was trembling, and I couldn't tell if it was because she was cold and wet or because she was having an episode. I took another step toward her, but before I reached her, I stopped in my tracks.

Something—some kind of translucent, undulating creature—was hovering at the side of the room. Water dripped from slender, human-like limbs, and long hair floated around its head like the being was underwater. As I watched in disbelief, the being evaporated, only to reappear on the other side of the room where it began to nonchalantly shower Sloth's belongings with water.

"Stop that!" Sloth squealed, angry tears streaming down her cheeks. "You're *ruining* my things! Why are you even doing this? Why is this happening?"

I didn't have an answer to that. I was still staring at the impossible existence of this miraculous water creature when someone else burst into the room.

It was Envy. Her skin was blanched, her eyes wide and red-rimmed. She, too, looked as though she'd been crying. A cameraman stood behind her, a blinking camera perched on his shoulder.

"I don't know what to do!" Envy was trembling as she looked around the room. The creature had floated to a new area, dousing everything it found in water. "The undine was supposed to help, but it's making everything *worse!*"

Well, that was an understatement. The books were ruined. The clothes were fine—in fact, they looked like they needed a good wash—but the papers, tarot cards, electronics, and other things that didn't interact well with water, well, they were long past saving.

Envy stomped a foot and thrust out her arm, pointing in the water creature's direction. "Undine! Stop that! Stop *that right now!* Dissolve! Get out of here!" She turned to me, eyes pleading. "I don't know how to command these things. Sometimes they just get out of control."

My jaw dropped as I waved about, indicating the soggy mess all around us. "You did this? You summoned this creature?"

Envy tilted her head back, wrapping her hands around the

back of her neck. "*Summoned* is a strong word. I just thought that if we had some help around here, you know, to keep Sloth in line? You know, to balance out her mess? I just thought it would be nice for everybody. It's fine to live in a house with somebody with cleanliness issues, but that means someone else has to take up the slack. I figured I could do that. So I just sort of thought that an undine might be able to fix the situation. But now I can't get her to stop!"

As if on cue, the undine disappeared and reappeared again, soaking a stack of laundry that lined the far wall. I sighed, taking a careful step toward Sloth, who had stopped screaming but was still crying and shaking. "Let's get you out of here," I said, gently placing an arm around her shoulder. But as soon as I touched her, intense images flashed behind my eyes, their accompanying emotions shuddering through my body. Greed scowling at her from across the living room. Wrath sneering, shouldering past her in the hallway. Lust seeing her approaching and going the other way. I saw people I didn't recognize ridiculing and mocking her, their disgust etched all over their faces. I felt their name-calling like so many daggers in my gut: Pig. Deadbeat. Repulsive. Worthless.

My instinct was to pull away, to break the connection that allowed me to see her memories and feel her pain. But if I withdrew, she would think it was her. She would think I was just like all the other people who treated her like she was less than human. But I wasn't like that, and I didn't want her to think I was. So I held on.

As my grip tightened around her, Sloth's crying ceased, her face upturned to mine. Her eyes were wide and round, her lips parting as she exhaled, "Really? You care what I think about you?"

I balked, blinking in surprise. "I—huh? Wait. How did you know…?"

She offered me a tentative smile. "I read minds. I try not to," she explained hurriedly. "But sometimes I can't tune it out. Especially when I'm upset. And right now, I'm *very* upset!" She shot an accusing glance at the undine that was still floating around the room, drenching her things in water. "I'll try very hard not to read your mind, Pride. But do you think you could stay with me awhile? Until I calm down?"

"Sure," I said, guiding her around a growing puddle in the middle of her room. "Let's go downstairs. Envy?"

Envy startled, looking up. "Yeah?"

I sighed and lifted my chin toward the undine. "Please have that fixed by the time we get back."

She nodded vigorously, chewing on her lips. "I will. I promise. I mean, I'll try."

I ushered Sloth downstairs where she settled into the couch, feet tucked beneath her as I hurried to the kitchen to pour her a glass of water. "You need anything else?" I called.

"No," she called back. Her voice sounded calmer. "Thank you."

I returned with the water, which she accepted gratefully. "I'm sorry to be such a nuisance. It's just…that *thing* burst into my room and started spraying water all over my stuff." She sniffled and wiped away the snot that leaked from her nose. "The *nerve* of Envy to sic one of her elementals on me! Who does she think she is? She didn't even *ask*. She just *assumed* I'd want that thing in my room."

I grunted as I settled into the couch beside Sloth. "To be fair, I don't think Envy really thought it through at all. I think she really believed she was doing the house a favor."

But Sloth wasn't listening. "People think because I'm messy, I don't care about my things. But I actually care very much. It's just that so much goes on in my head all the time. I don't have the energy to worry about my physical space. I'm constantly trying to arrange things in my *head*. Especially other people's things." She looked down at her hands, her head shaking as her chin wobbled. "Being a mind reader isn't all it's cracked up to be, you know? People think such awful things all the time. Not just about me. But about each other. And especially about themselves."

I didn't know what to say to that, so I changed the subject. "How did your task go today? You're with Envy and Gluttony, right?"

Sloth nodded as she took another sip of water. "Yeah. It was fine, I guess. Our task is to help this old lady find her son." She rolled her eyes and set the glass on the table. "She swears he's missing because she hasn't heard from him in a week or so, but the police say she does this all the time. She reports him missing, but then he shows up like nothing happened. Apparently, the old woman is kinda…" She whirled her index finger around her temple and made a cuckoo sound. "It seems like a dumb task to me."

I settled into the cushions, crossed my legs, and folded my arms over my chest. "Why does it sound dumb? Even if he's not really missing, imagine the peace of mind you're giving her. Sounds like she needs the help. Anyway, it has to be better than helping a Chinese restaurant figure out who's been meddling with their fortune cookies."

Sloth's cheeks turned pink as she choked down a laugh. "You have to help a Chinese restaurant with a cookie problem? Yeah, that's…Okay, I feel less bad about mine. Hold that thought, though. We'll get back to that. Anyway, I see what you're saying about old Mrs. Romanowsky, but it's *impossible*. She wants us to walk around town and ask people. 'Have you seen this man?'" She dug her phone out of a pocket, tapped something in, and showed me a photo. I leaned in, squinting to get a better look. The photo showed a middle-aged man dressed in a camouflage hunting outfit. A vest was strapped over his chest, sporting various tools and accoutrements attached with velcro. I could barely make out his face.

"*This* is the picture she gave you?" I asked. "Does she think he walks around dressed like this all the time?"

Sloth snorted. "I told you. She's not all there. Luckily, we got a better photo from the police, though they also told us we were wasting our time." Sloth sighed and rubbed her forehead with the heel of her hand as she slipped her phone back into her pocket. "You see what I mean? It's just a lot."

It did sound like a lot. "Do Gluttony and Envy have any ideas?"

Sloth sucked her teeth, her expression melting into something like annoyance. "We didn't get a lot done, to be honest. Envy just walked around the house admiring everything and complaining that this woman's house was so much more pleasant than her own. Gluttony made a beeline for the kitchen to make snacks for everyone. To be fair, he whipped up a *great* pasta dish. But with Gluttony in the kitchen and Envy giving herself a private tour, that left me to deal with the old lady alone. She showed me stuff she collects—stamps and plates and stuff." Sloth wrinkled her nose and threw a glance up to the ceiling, where we heard shuffling and the occasional curse in Envy's voice. She cringed. "I hate to say this only one day in, but as a trio, I'm not sure we're working out."

"The good news is, you'll have a new team eventually," I said.

Sloth waved this away. "I guess. Okay, your turn. Tell me about this fortune cookie situation."

I gave her the short version of the story, and when I was done, she was utterly enthralled. She had stopped crying, which was good, and she even seemed to have forgotten about the undine destroying her bedroom. "So what does your gut say? Do you think it's the Korean lady?"

I scratched my chin, dithering. "Not sure. It's too early to say. We have to investigate all leads, of course. But the Korean lady angle just seems too obvious, you know?"

"Maybe," Sloth drawled, her voice heavy with uncertainty, "but this isn't a detective movie, Pride. It's real life. Sometimes the obvious answer is the answer."

I opened my mouth to object but then quickly snapped it shut. She was right. This wasn't a scripted assignment from the network. This was a real problem affecting a real family. The Wongs were genuinely and rightfully upset, losing much-needed money, and needed Lust and me to help them. I groaned with chagrin as the realization dawned. "Wow. I'm an idiot. I've been approaching this all wrong."

Sloth leaned forward. "What do you mean?"

"In my regular life, I'm a paranormal investigator," I said. "It's not as glamorous as it sounds. I consult with the police department on special cases. Murders and missing persons, mostly. I see things when I touch people, and I run into more than my fair share of ghosts. I solved a recent case by interviewing a ghost that was the only eyewitness to a murder. So if this were a case, I'd be working from a list of suspects the cops gave me, but I'd also be thinking about who can do something like this."

Sloth nodded. "Right. You mean like the people who had access to the fortune cookies or whatever?"

"No. See, the weird thing about this case is that the fortunes only appeared to the person the fortune was about. Anyone else who read the fortune just saw some innocuous message. That's why the Wongs had a hard time believing the accusations at first. But when their daughter's boyfriend confided that he'd also gotten a dark message and then it came true, that's when they believed. So that makes me wonder."

"Wonder what?"

I drew in a sharp breath. "Who can make people see things that aren't there? A random cook or server or somebody couldn't do this because the *cookies* aren't the problem. There's something else at work here. Something more ominous."

"Like magic?" Sloth breathed.

"*Mind* magic," I agreed. "Thanks, Sloth. You just gave me my first solid lead."

eight

. . .

My personal cameraman followed me as I went upstairs to find Lust. Her door was open, and she was lying in bed reading a book. When she saw me, she set the book aside. "Didn't think I'd see you again so soon. You come to keep me company?" She patted the space beside her on the bed.

I ignored that and jammed my thumb over my shoulder. "Get up. I need you to come with me. I have an idea."

Lust frowned but pulled herself out of bed and slipped her feet into a pair of shoes. "Where are we going? An idea about what? I thought we were done for the day."

I nodded, rubbing my palms together. I was getting excited. They say the best way to get over someone is to get under someone else. But the next best way was to get busy with work. "Yeah, we were, but then I was talking to Sloth, and she gave me a great idea."

Lust's eyebrows shot high on her face. "*Sloth* gave you an idea? That's interesting. I wouldn't have thought that girl had an original thought to call her own."

I felt my expression darken as my eyes narrowed. "Why would you think something like that? Because she's sloppy? That doesn't make her stupid. And second, I don't know if you know this, but she's a mind reader. So she probably heard you think that."

Strictly speaking, I didn't know if that was true. I had no idea how far Sloth's abilities extended, but I made my point. Lust's cheeks blushed crimson, and she glanced down, avoiding my eyes. "You're right. That was mean. Don't tell her I said anything, would you?"

I grunted. "Assuming she didn't hear you herself, maybe the network will edit it out before they air this episode."

Once outside, Lust and I climbed into the front seats of our car. Our camera crew crowded into the back while I fiddled with the Go-Pro on the dashboard. We were supposed to have it on any time we used the car. "So you never told me where we're headed," Lust said.

"I worked a case a few years ago where people were receiving threatening emails requesting big sums of money. Lots of victims from all over the county. But when our forensic computer guys looked into it, nobody could find these emails. They weren't in the inboxes of the victims, and they hadn't been trashed or archived. They simply didn't exist, even though the victims swore up and down they'd received these emails demanding payment."

"Did the people pay?"

I whistled. "They sure did. Some of them forked over thousands of dollars out of fear of retribution or a secret getting leaked."

Lust clucked her tongue. "Lots of husbands afraid of their wives finding out about their mistresses, I bet."

"You got it," I agreed. "Well, at the same time I was working that case, I was…seeing someone."

Lust hrmmed. "That girlfriend you're trying to win back?"

I grunted, shaking my head. "No, that's not what I mean. I was actually seeing someone. She was showing up a lot at that time. This…girl. A ghost girl." I cleared my throat and waited for a snide jab, but surprisingly, it never came. I plundered on. "Anyway, sometimes I forgot other people couldn't see her. One day, I was talking to her at the park, and this homeless guy shouts at me, '*You people say I'm crazy, but you're the one seeing things ain't there!*' And that got me thinking—what if nobody could find the emails because they were never there to begin with? What if the victims just *thought* they saw them?"

"And were you right?"

I nodded. "Turned out, all the victims had gone to see this magic show over in La Jolla. This guy, Jack Dempsey, was a mentalist. You know, an entertainment psychic. But he was also a con man. His show included subliminal suggestions that tricked susceptible people into thinking they were being blackmailed. Which they were. Just not in the way they claimed."

Lust pulled her feet up into the seat, wrapping her arms around her knees. "That's crazy. So they caught the guy? We aren't going to a *prison*, are we?"

"Nah, he got out a while ago."

"Well, that's something." Lust wound a lock of hair around a finger. "Forgive me if this is a dumb question, but what's that got to do with our task?"

"I don't think anybody's been messing with the fortune cookies. I think somebody's been messing with people's minds."

Lust made a thinking sound as she looked out the window. "Oh, I get it. I guess that makes sense. So let me ask you for the third time. Where are we going?"

I grinned. "Andre's Spooktacular Bowling."

———

Andre's Spooktacular was on the opposite side of the county in a run-down strip mall featuring a pawn shop, a Payday loan, two lingerie shops, and a laundromat. As we climbed out of the car, Lust looked around, hands dug into her hip pockets. "Reminds me of home," she said, nose wrinkled. "I didn't come all the way to California to spend time in a place like this."

"Even California has poor parts of town," I chided her. "But I take your point. This place looks like where Hollywood dreams go to die."

It was the middle of the day, and Andre's was mostly empty. The smell of decades-old cigarette smoke and stale beer hung in the air, and the soles of our shoes stuck to the moldy carpet as we walked. Lust made a disgusted sound in her throat, and though I didn't acknowledge it, I agreed with her sentiment. Andre's had seen better days.

"I guess I can see why they call this place Andre's Spooktacular." She glanced around at the stained walls, the grimy tables and chairs, the paint peeling off the ceiling. "It's absolutely terrifying."

"You think so?" I indicated the dollar store Halloween decor someone had halfheartedly displayed. Ancient plastic skeletons yellowed with age hung from the ceiling, covered in dust and cobwebs. Cheesecloth ghosts haunted the corners, lopsided and decayed. The muffled sounds of a moaning ghost and rattling chains fluttered in from overhead speakers that crackled due to faulty wiring. It somewhat marred the effect. "Seems cheesy to me."

Lust stared at me with an unreadable expression. "Right. Super literal. I forgot." She patted me on the arm. "I like you, Freak Show. You're not like anyone else."

I didn't know how I was supposed to take that, so I let the conversation drop and headed to the check-in counter. The girl working the desk didn't look up from her phone. "You guys here to bowl a game?"

I shook my head. "Here to see Jack Dempsey. He in?"

The girl looked up then, her face slack. She wasn't really a girl, though. Now that I could see her face, she was older than her cotton candy pigtails and blue eyeshadow led me to believe. She looked like a middle-aged woman who called in some heavy favors to get cast as a teenaged girl in a terrible horror film. "Who's asking?"

I hesitated, thinking of the cameras and Tricia Woodward's adamant direction not to use our real names during filming. But I couldn't exactly go around to old acquaintances calling myself Pride. I'd never hear the end of it. "Sid Sheridan," I said finally. The network could edit out my real name if they wanted. "And tell him I'm in a hurry."

The 40-year-old teenager snapped her gum and threw me one last skeptical glance before picking up the phone—an actual landline—and pressing a button. "Jack? Someone's here to see you. Sid Sheridan? Says it's urgent." A pause, then a nod. "You got it."

She hung up the phone and tilted her head in a vague direction. "He's in the back."

I thanked her, and we made our way in the general direction she'd jerked her head. I had no idea what 'in the back' meant— he could have been in the parking lot or the john for all I knew. But it didn't take long to find him. He was sitting alone in a dusty room behind a desk covered in papers and empty soft drink cans. He looked just like I remembered. Tall and balding with a potbelly and a nose too large for his face, Jack Dempsey didn't so much as give me a second glance when we walked in. He only had eyes for Lust. He leaped to his feet, a smarmy smile on oily lips as he admired the view. "Well, now, it's not every day a beautiful woman comes asking for me. I should play the lotto or something, eh? Gotta be my lucky day."

Lust walked up to him, all confidence and steel, and with a voice that could have frozen the devil's spit, said, "Hey buddy. My eyes are up here."

Dempsey recoiled, his lecherous grin morphing into a sneer. "Feminazi type, eh? Shoulda known. Equal rights this, I'm not a piece of meat that. Bet you change your tune when the bill for dinner comes, though, right?"

Lust didn't miss a beat. "I promise you will *never* find out."

As gently as I could, I nudged Lust aside, interrupting before things got nasty. Dempsey was a pig, but we needed his help. "Hey, knock it off, okay? We're not here to pick a fight. We're working on a case."

Dempsey tumbled into his chair, brushing aside a mound of papers as he kicked his feet up to the desk. "Bully for you, Sheridan. You don't actually think I'm gonna *talk* to you, do ya? I served time on account of you. Penitentiary time."

"You served time for committing a *crime*," I reminded him. "I had nothing to do with it. Come on, Dempsey. Be the bigger man. Think of it this way—I'll owe you."

"You already owe me," he growled. "That's the point, Sheridan. That's what I'm saying. You're in a hole so deep, you couldn't dig your way out."

That was a ridiculous thing to say because the depth of the hole had nothing to do with whether further digging would get you out. It really depended on the nature of the hole and the tools at hand, but that wasn't the point, so I let it slide. "Dempsey—"

But before I could make my pitch, Lust sauntered around to the other side of the desk and planted her butt on the edge. For all that he'd dismissed her as a feminazi a few moments ago, Dempsey couldn't take his eyes off her now. She leaned in, lowered her voice, and said, "You're gonna help us with this case, Jack Dempsey. And you don't want anything in return. You just want to help."

Dempsey's jaw went slack as his eyes glazed over, a blank expression replacing his earlier sneer. His whole body relaxed, and he blinked lazily until whatever cloud had settled over him dissipated. He sat up, loudly clearing the phlegm from his throat. "I'm feeling generous today, Sheridan. Must be your lucky day. How can I help?"

Lust looked over her shoulder and dropped me a wink before walking back around the desk, coming to stand at my side. I gave her a questioning look, but when all she did was shrug in response, I dove in. "Let's say you wanted to make people read something ominous in their fortune cookie messages. How would you go about doing that?"

Dempsey narrowed his eyes at me. "I heard you got canned at the county. What's this about?"

I shot a quick glance toward the cameras. "Private customer," I said. "Pay's not great, but." I shrugged and offered an awkward smile. Guys like Dempsey liked it when you admitted things weren't going so hot. Made them feel big.

Dempsey grunted. "Private customer. Right. And this is the case? Fortune cookies?"

My face grew hot at the scorn I noted in his voice, and before I could reel in my ego, I said, "You're assistant managing a run-down bowling alley, Dempsey. Your mother's not exactly boasting about you to the ladies at Bridge club."

Lust elbowed me in the side, throwing me a reproving glance. She was right; insulting him wasn't going to get me any information. The first rule of interrogation was to butter up the other party. Wheedling and flattery weren't exactly my forte, but at least I didn't have to tick him off. I tried again. "Look, I didn't come here to bust your balls. Just answer the question."

Dempsey glowered at me, lips pinched as he stroked his chin and clucked his tongue. I waited, but with each second that passed, the more confident I became that I'd overstepped. Dempsey wasn't gonna talk. I was thinking of something to say to put him back in the driver's seat when he sighed and threw his hands up. "Whatever. Look, there are two ways to go about this: blanket the whole venue in suggestion, or go after individual people. For the venue approach, you have to get the crowd susceptible first—get them in a hypnotic state. Several ways to do that: music, smell, even certain lighting. But like I said, it doesn't always work. People are talking, flirting, drinking—they're not necessarily tuned in to their environment. Anyway, you still gotta plant the suggestion in the ones you managed to influence. Best and easiest way to do that is to encode it into music. It isn't hard. Anyway, the suggestion always has a trigger—in your case, reading a fortune cookie. They read the cookie and BAM! They think they read a message that wasn't there."

I nodded. "Okay. How popular is this tactic?"

"Very. It's what most good con artists—including yours truly —go for. Less chance of getting caught. Plus, the bigger the area of effect, the more marks available. But it's hit-or-miss. You can't guide it, can't tailor it to any specific person, you see what I'm saying? It's generic."

I said, "Right. Okay. Let's say that's my guy—Joe Schmoe Con Man using suggestion. Gimme a profile. What kind of person am I looking for?"

Dempsey folded his arms across his chest and blew out a puff of air. "Pretty much anybody with basic brainwave training and a decent audio editing program could do it."

"And where do you get brainwave training?"

Dempsey snorted. "These days? YouTube."

That wasn't the answer I'd hoped for, and my increasing optimism took a hard left. But then Lust said, "Well, but the person responsible would need access to the restaurant, right? To cause the hypnotic state in the first place? And then to play the track with the suggestion?"

Dempsey nodded. "Oh, sure. Once the marks leave the venue, they're not susceptible anymore. They wake up."

Lust looked at me with wide eyes. "In that case, it has to be one of the staff," she said. "Or at least someone with access to the sound system."

"Not necessarily." Dempsey held up two fingers. "Your suspect could have used method number two—up close and personal. It's way more difficult but more effective. You can even plant a suggestion in advance and set it to go off at a certain time and place—like, say, when the mark reads a cookie at a certain restaurant." He couldn't keep the ridicule from his voice as he said this. Honestly, I couldn't really blame him.

"And for the up close and personal kind, anybody could do that, too, right? Anybody with access to the marks?"

"Anybody with the right talent," Dempsey corrected. "And there's not a lot of those folks running around."

Now we were getting somewhere. "What do you mean?"

Dempsey twitched his over-large nose and rearranged his feet on the desk. "People always think the large-scale tricks are the hardest, but it's actually the up close and personal stuff that's the doozy. Think about it this way. When you've got a whole audience in front of you, there's a million ways to distract their attention from what you're trying to pull. You got sparkly lights, amazing sounds, a hot woman on stage." He glanced at Lust and winked when he said this. "But when it's up close and personal, that person's attention is a hundred percent on you. You got to be at the top of your game to get what you want from them. I always admired the guys who could pickpocket. Distract you while they touched your body, removing jewelry and watches and stuff? Man, what a gift."

I ignored the wrongness of referring to swindlers and cheats as having a gift. "So what kind of person can do the up close and personal attack? Can you learn that from YouTube?"

Dempsey waved that away. "Nah. Those folks aren't manipulating music tracks. They do it with their voice. Or a look. Maybe the way they smell—hell, I don't know. It's not something you can learn—you're born with it. Kinda like you and your ghosts."

For some reason, that made my skin crawl. Goosebumps broke out over my skin, and I grimaced, unreasonably insulted. "I'm not a con artist," I said.

"Never said you were. Just meant maybe she's born with it, maybe it's Maybelline." Dempsey removed his feet from the desk and stood, stretching his arms over his head and arching his back. The buttons at the belly of his shirt strained. "Are we done here?"

I glanced at Lust. "You have any more questions?"

She shook her head. "No, I'm good."

I returned my attention to the con man. "Thanks, Dempsey. You were a big help, whether you wanted to be or not."

He scratched his nose with one hand and made a rude gesture with the other.

We took that as our cue to leave.

———

"Okay, so we know the mechanism for how this is happening. Or at least we have some leads. But I'm still not sure how to figure out the bigger question."

Lust cocked an eyebrow at me as we climbed into the car. "And what's that?"

"The victims in this case didn't just read an ominous message. They read an ominous message that also came true. That's the part I'm struggling with. Even con men like Dempsey can't predict the future. So whoever implanted those suggestions is not only an accomplished mentalist, they're also some kind of fortuneteller. And that's the part I just can't wrap my brain around."

I started up the car, and we drove in silence for a while, my mind combing over the facts of the case. As I was replaying the meeting with Dempsey in my mind, however, an unnerving feeling crawled up my spine.

"Hey, Lust? Can I ask you something?"

She shrugged. "Sure."

"How did you do that thing with Dempsey back there?"

She hesitated, winding a lock of hair around a finger. "What do you mean?"

My grip tightened on the wheel. "He wasn't going to talk. Dempsey doesn't exactly hate me, but we're not buddies, either. I was prepared to butter him up good, but I didn't have to. You just walked over there and turned on your charm, and suddenly, it was like he was a zombie. Or hypnotized." I paused to let the effect of my words sink in. "So, what did you do back there?"

Silence engulfed the car. The only things I heard were the noise from the highway and the cameramen in the backseat squirming, trying to get comfortable. But finally, Lust answered, her voice softer than usual. "I'm a siren."

I snapped my head around. "A what?"

"It's my psychic ability. It's why the network cast me on the show. That and these personality flaws." She grabbed her breasts as she said this, and from the corner of my eye, I saw the color crawl up her cheeks. "I can get people to do things. Not any person, of course. But certain people. I use my voice to…*seduce* them into giving me what I want. I don't even really know how I do it. Not really. I just decide to convince someone to do something, and they do it."

"I see." I wanted to leave it at that because part of me really didn't want to hear more. But the rest of me was too curious for my own good, so I asked, "So, what're the criteria for someone being susceptible to your charms?"

Again, she paused. "Well." She looked down, fidgeting with the strings that hung from her cut-off shorts. "They have to be into women."

I felt my cheeks flush red as beads of sweat popped out on my brow. "So it would work on me, then?"

Lust shrugged. "I guess so, yeah. If you like women."

The energy in the car shifted as the full meaning of Lust's words registered. Even the cameramen made subtle disapproving sounds at her revelation. I was suddenly anxious, my mouth going dry while my palms began to sweat. I felt like a rabbit who just smelled a nearby wolf, and I swallowed down the instinct to get as far away from Lust as possible. She must have felt my growing discomfort, too, because she sighed and shrank away from me, drawing herself closer to the car door. "Now you think I'm a manipulative sociopath," she said.

I shot her a sideways glance. She didn't look like a wolf. Maybe that made it worse. "I don't know exactly what I think. I *am* worried that you're dangerous."

My words hung in the air, stark and naked and true. I *did* think someone like that was dangerous. But I also didn't want to hurt Lust's feelings because I needed her to help out with our case. So I said, "I guess I don't like the idea of someone planting ideas in my head. I'm garbage at understanding other people's motivations and emotions, but at least I can control my own, you know?"

"You don't, though." She said this without looking at me. "Nobody does. You've already been conditioned to think a certain way just by being alive in Western society. Advertisers, social media, even your family and friends—everybody puts ideas in your head all the time. Lose weight. Buy name brands. Make more money. Vote Democrat." She ticked these off on her fingers without missing a beat. "Everyone around you has an agenda, even if they don't know it. Even *you* have an agenda."

That last part was definitely true, but my agenda was simple: get Shayda back. It had nothing to do with influencing other people. "That's different," I said. "That's not personal."

"Oh, really?" She angled her body so she was fully facing me. I couldn't look directly at her, but I saw how taut her body was and how her eyes flashed in the sunlight. "Tell me something, Pride. And be honest. When you see a fat person wearing a bikini, what's the *first* thing you think?"

"That maybe they should have worn a one-piece instead." As soon as I said that, however, I felt terrible. A hot flush crept up my neck. "Wait, no. That's an awful thing to say, and I'm not even sure I believe that. Yeah, on second thought, people should wear whatever they want."

"Bingo." Lust pointed a triumphant finger at me. "But that was the *second* thing you thought. Your first thought was conditioned by society. Let that sink in, Freak Show. Your *second thought* was your own. Your *first thought* belonged to someone else."

I wanted to argue, mainly because she'd just proven me wrong, and I hated that, but I *couldn't* argue because she was right, and no amount of arguing would make me less wrong. So instead, I said, "Well, I see your point, but I still don't like the idea of someone else putting ideas in my head."

She turned away from me then, pressing her forehead against the window. "Of course you don't. No one does. You don't have to worry about me, though. I won't try to charm you. I like you. But I can't help that this is the way I am. Not any more than you can help seeing ghosts."

Everything she was saying made sense, but the more sense she made, the more I didn't like it. And sometimes, when I was upset and flustered, I said things I later regretted, which is why I said, "Well, at least this conversation helped me learn more about the person we're looking for."

"It did?"

I nodded. "Yeah. Turns out, we might be looking for a sociopath like you."

nine

. . .

Things were tense between Lust and me after that. We drove the rest of the way in silence, and when we arrived back at the house, she went straight up to her room without greeting the other housemates. She brushed past Envy on the stairs, who gave me a questioning look as she jabbed a thumb over her shoulder.

"What's wrong with Lust?"

I plopped down on the couch, kicking off my shoes as Envy took a seat next to me, still looking puzzled. "Do you know what her ability is?"

"Sure." Envy's puzzlement deepened. "She's a siren. So what?"

I chuckled dryly and made a face. "Let me guess. You're straight."

Envy peered at me for a moment, then folded her arms over her chest. "Oh, I get it," she said. "You're worried she's gonna mind-trick you into doing something you don't want to do." I noted a trace of disapproval in her voice. "That's not how it works, you know."

"Isn't it?"

Envy made a disgusted sound and looked away. "Did you even *ask* her about her talent? Or did you just assume the worst?"

"I assumed the worst," I admitted.

"Well, according to what she told me, she can only override your social conditioning. She can only give you an impulse. If you're a thoughtful person—someone who really considers their actions—your own convictions will kick in, and her suggestion gets thrown out."

"I guess that makes me feel better," I said.

Envy smiled. "Good."

The thing was, though, hearing these words *didn't* make me feel better. I only said that because it seemed like the right thing to say. But the truth was, it made me feel worse. I considered the reasons:

1. I didn't bother to ask Lust more questions about her ability. It was selfish and short-sighted, two things I was supposed to be working on if I wanted to get Shayda back.
2. I wasn't a thoughtful person. I ran on instinct almost all the time. So if Lust wanted to brainwash me, she probably could, and she wouldn't even break a sweat.

"Do you want me to go talk to her?"

I hesitated. "You can go talk to her if you want. I don't mind. Or you can stay here. I don't mind that, either."

Envy chuckled. "I meant, do you want me to go talk to her on your behalf?"

"Oh." I shook my head. "No, that's okay. Thanks, though."

Envy lingered a moment before rising and reaching out to muss my hair. "Cheer up, okay? I'll see you at dinner."

I wasn't hungry, but according to my contract with the network, I was supposed to attend house meals any time I was home. Apparently, it would be good for ratings. So I went to my room, got cleaned up, and came back down to dinner, which turned out to be a feast.

Gluttony was bustling to and from the kitchen carrying dishes that smelled so good, my mouth watered despite my lack of hunger. The table was already heaped with roast chicken, buttery green beans, fresh-baked dinner rolls, and baked sweet potatoes. I followed Gluttony into the kitchen and gestured around. "Anything I can do?"

"Ancestors help me," he muttered, eyes turned to the ceiling. The utterance was half prayer, half curse. "These fools think I actually want their help." He elbowed me aside with a meaty arm. "No, get on outta here. People always think offering to help in the kitchen is friendly, but you just in my way. Step on out."

Gluttony shooed me out into the dining room, and while he grumbled and complained and carried out more plates, I sat down at the table next to Sloth. She looked happy to see me. "You guys make any progress on your task?" she asked, chewing on the end of a pigtail.

"Some," I said. "You?"

"Not really." She sighed and helped herself to a serving of sweet potatoes. She spilled most of them onto the table. "And tomorrow already doesn't look good, either."

One by one, the rest of the housemates gathered at the table. Everyone had come down except Lust. The table had been set for seven, so the empty seat was conspicuous. Wrath pointed at it with his fork.

"Is anybody gonna go get the nympho?"

A few snickers went around the table, but they died out when Envy snapped, "Stop it." She gave Wrath a withering stare. "She has a name."

Wrath snorted. "Calling her Lust is better than Nympho?"

Envy opened her mouth to retort but shut it again, looking down into her lap.

"She'll come down when she's ready," Gluttony said. "I'm not about to let this food get cold, not after I been in the kitchen all afternoon. Let's eat."

Greed dug into the green beans with a vengeance. "This is phenomenal," he said. "I mean, really great. If anybody's not going to eat theirs, let me know. I mean, just fantastic."

"Better be after all the work I put in," Gluttony said with a grin. "I wanted this dinner together to be special, so I added a little something extra."

I glanced up from my still-empty plate. "What kind of something extra?"

Gluttony winked. "Eat it and find out."

After the earlier debacle with Lust, I wasn't so sure I wanted to deal with any more surprises. Still, I also didn't want to appear ungrateful, so I took small samplings of everything. I took one bite of the roasted chicken, and then another, and then another. And as I ate, my muscles relaxed, my mood lifted, and my appetite ignited in a blaze of glory. I was just about to go in for seconds when I realized what was going on.

"You're a kitchen witch!" I exclaimed, delighted by the discovery. I'd never met a kitchen witch before. They aren't as plentiful as social media might have you believe. Just because you can follow a recipe for chocolate chip cookies and you're handy with a camera and lighting doesn't make you a wizard. "This is incredible. Like, wow, Gluttony. You're really talented."

The big man huffed. "I know it." He gestured toward the green beans. "Those are my specialty. They make you gabby. I don't like silence. Secrets live in silence. Green beans'll make you the life of the party."

Everyone went for the green beans at once.

As we ate, tensions melted away, and laughter flowed. We

shared the highlights of our days and traded questions back and forth. After a while, it was like we'd known each other for years, which was precisely the point. Gluttony's magic was the most fun I'd had in a long while.

But as good as dinner made me feel, I couldn't stop thinking about Lust.

Later that night, as I was climbing into bed and preparing a mental checklist of tomorrow's activities, I heard a familiar voice in the dark.

"Boy, did you ever mess up today."

I squeezed my eyes shut and rolled onto my side, giving the specter my back. "Now's not a good time," I said.

The ghost girl snorted, and I sensed her rolling her eyes at the back of my head. "You always say that. It's never a good time with you. But you messed up this time. So you need to fix it."

"I can't," I said into the darkness. "I know I messed up. But it's not something I can fix."

I heard the shuffling of spectral feet coming around to my side of the bed. I didn't open my eyes, but I sensed the ghost hovering near my face. "Apologize," she said.

I pretended to be asleep, but the ghost didn't move. "I know you're awake," she said. "Nobody falls asleep that fast. Even goldfish need 30 seconds to fall asleep."

Exasperated, I opened my eyes. The ghost's face was mere inches from mine. Her eyes were wide and round in the dark, the corners of her mouth turning down into a frown. I never would've thought a child could look so disappointed in someone. I rolled over onto my other side. "I can't apologize, so don't ask."

The ghost sucked her teeth. "You're such a jerk."

I pulled the blankets up over my head, hoping to muffle the sound of her voice. But I heard her perfectly when she said, "You can't just go around hurting other people because *you* feel uncomfortable or because *you* don't understand what the big deal is.

Maybe Shayda's sister's wedding wasn't a big deal to you, but it was a big deal to her. You made a promise."

"That was an accident!" I cried. "I know it was a big deal! I screwed up!"

"You *let* yourself mess up. If it really mattered, you would have set reminders. You would have told the detective you couldn't work that day. You would have done *something!* But you didn't because the only person you think about is yourself because you're too *scared* to think about other people. You're supposed to be a grown-up. Grown-ups are supposed to know better."

"Children are supposed to do what they're told," I retorted. "Go away."

"No."

The ghost didn't so much as twitch. I rolled over again to find her still standing there, hands on her hips, head tilted to one side, toes tapping. I kicked off my blankets and sat up. "If I apologize in the morning, will you give me a break? I need to get some sleep. I have a lot to do tomorrow."

The ghost lifted her shoulders, a halfhearted attempt at a shrug. "Depends."

"Depends on what?"

"Depends on how good of an apology you give her. You really hurt her, you know. She didn't deserve that. She didn't do anything except tell you the truth."

Shame lit me up and set my skin on fire. I hated getting admonished by ghosts, especially pint-sized ghosts with boundary issues. I threw myself back into the pillows, flinging my forearm over my eyes, trying to blot the day from my memory and the ghost's words from my ears. But she was right. I messed up, and I had to fix it.

"I promise I'll make this right," I told her. "I promise. Now get out of here. Go."

I didn't see her leave, but after a few moments, I felt alone. And not just alone, but lonely.

I pulled the blankets up under my chin and tucked my knees to my chest. I closed my eyes and tried to breathe low and slow, but I didn't fall asleep for a long, long time.

The next day, Lust and I arrived at our appointment with Helen Park fifteen minutes early. She had agreed to meet us at her house. We parked the car, and as we crossed the street, I reached out, grabbing Lust's wrist. She halted and turned, gently freeing herself from my grasp. Her expression was neutral when she asked, "Can I help you with something?"

It's now or never, I told myself. I sucked in a steadying breath. "About what I said yesterday. I shouldn't have called you a sociopath."

"If that's what you think about me, then I'm glad you said it." She crossed her arms over her chest, shrugging like none of this mattered. But her face didn't match her carefree body language, and that's how I knew she was acting. "I'd rather know where I stand. I would hate to have someone be nice to my face only to slag me behind my back."

I shook my head. "I wouldn't talk bad about you behind your back. I'm not much of a gossip. It's one of my few good qualities."

Lust's eyes flickered toward me, and I saw some of the tension ease from her shoulders. She still didn't say anything, though.

"Look, Lust, we have to work together. I genuinely want to help the Wongs get the restaurant back on its feet. I know you want that, too. Right? You want to win. This will go better if the two of us are on good terms."

Lust stared me down, nostrils flared. "Is that supposed to be an apology? Because I never heard the words 'I'm sorry.'"

I rubbed the nape of my neck, avoiding Lust's gaze. "Come

on, Lust. I'm trying here." *Good job*, I thought sullenly. *You're making it all about* you *now. That's the opposite of what you're supposed to do.* If I ever went back to therapy, Dr. Xena would have a field day with this one.

If Lust noticed my inner turmoil, however, she didn't let on. She was winding a lock of hair around her finger as she looked up, eyes blinking quickly. It was a moment before I realized she was trying not to cry. "You really hurt my feelings, Pride. I opened up to you, and you made me feel like a jerk."

I shoved my hands in my pockets and looked down at the ground. "I know."

"I want to help the Wongs, too. And that's the only reason I'm accepting your non-apology. I rarely give people second chances." She took a step toward me and placed two fingers under my chin, lifting my face to meet her gaze. "I promise I'll never use my powers on you," she said. "And I always keep my word."

Before I could say anything else, Lust was already turning away, heading for Helen's house. It wasn't exactly the reconciliation I'd imagined. But it was better than nothing.

ten

. . .

I rang the doorbell, and after a moment, I heard shuffling on the other side of the door followed by a shout of, "Keep playing! And don't rush!"

The door opened to reveal a small, scowling Asian woman with perfectly coiffed hair and not a speck of makeup out of place. She had an ageless face—she could have been anywhere between 30 and 100, but the silver in her hair told me she was older. When she saw us, her scowl deepened, but she opened the door wider, stepping to one side. "Well, don't just stand there. You might as well come in. I'm almost done with my lesson."

Piano music drifted in from another room. Lust and I followed Helen into a living area, where our host gestured impatiently toward the couch. The piano playing continued as Lust and I took our seats. I didn't know anything about the piano, but whoever was playing seemed very talented. I recognized the tune, but I couldn't have named it if you'd paid me. Helen held up a finger as she disappeared into the adjoining room. The music halted. "No, you're rushing again. Go back to the coda. And this time, play with your emotions. This isn't an act, Ruby. The audience can tell if you're faking it. You have to love each measure, or you might as well get out of here right now."

After a brief silence, the music picked up again, but this time was subtly different. The tempo was slower, more languid. I closed my eyes, imagining the pianist curled over the keys, eyes darting over her score, caressing the ivories as she breathed in time with the music. After a while, the playing stopped, and the house filled with silence. I heard the smile in her voice when Helen Park said, "Much better."

The squeak of the piano bench was accompanied by the thump of a piano lid closing, and a moment later, Helen Park entered the living room, followed by Ruby Wong. Ruby smiled and waved, arranging her hair around her shoulders just like she did the first time we'd met. Today, she was wearing a faded t-shirt that read, "I brake for dolphins." That didn't even make sense, but I guess that was par for the course with teenagers. Their prefrontal cortex wasn't fully developed, and that's why they made such terrible decisions, like spending money on illogical t-shirts. At least, that's what I'd heard.

"Hello again!" Ruby said, coming to stand before Lust and me. She was holding sheet music in both hands. "What are you guys doing here?"

Lust glanced from the girl to the older woman, who was now standing with her arms crossed, her scowl still etched into her brow. "Your parents said we should talk to Mrs. Park. You know. About the disturbances at the restaurant."

Ruby cringed, her mouth falling open. Her nostrils flared, and her cheeks grew hot pink as she cursed under her breath, shaking her head. "They just don't listen," she hissed. "What did they tell you? Did they say Mrs. Park had something to do with our fortune cookie incident? Is that what they said? Did they say she's the only one who would benefit from their misfortune?"

Lust and I exchanged looks. "Something like that," I agreed reluctantly.

Ruby dropped into an armchair, setting her sheet music aside as she leaned forward onto her knees, pointing a finger at us. "I'll tell you what's causing the problem at the restaurant," she said. "It's not Mrs. Park or anybody else in this town. It's the wights."

Now, I sat up taller, wrinkling my brow in confusion. "The wights? You mean the supernatural waiters?"

"Servers," Lust corrected me.

I nodded. "Servers. Right. Them?"

"Yes," Ruby said. "*Wights*. I've been reading a lot about them, and it turns out it's not uncommon for earthbound spirits to drive people crazy. They can get in your psyche and make you believe things. See things. It happens a lot more often than people think. Sometimes, especially in older people, it can look like mental deterioration or senility."

This was new information to me, but then again, I was an expert on ghosts, not non-corporeal, non-human entities. And even calling me a ghost expert was a stretch. "So you're saying the wights are making the customers see things? But your parents have had the wights at the restaurant for years. Why is it just happening now?"

Ruby nodded like she'd been expecting this response. "According to the experts I've been reading, wights grow increasingly vicious over time. The longer they're connected to a place, the more likely they are to do mental damage to those around them. So the wights may be just now becoming powerful enough to harm my parents' patrons." Ruby sighed, settling back into the armchair. "I've tried to explain this to my parents, you know. But they don't listen. They think someone is behind this." She gestured toward her piano instructor. "But Mrs. Park wouldn't do anything to hurt them. I know she wouldn't."

"And I don't have to, anyway," Helen said. She'd been

standing this whole time, but now she came to sit next to Lust and me. "My restaurant is doing fine. I do enough business to stay busy, but not so much that I don't have a moment to myself. I enjoy teaching piano. I couldn't do that if I was working all the time at the restaurant. My husband helps, but you know how men are." She tittered as she said this, and Lust and I both smiled even though I was pretty sure only Lust knew what she meant. "So you see, I have no motive. But the Wongs are stubborn people. They want to believe it's me, so they've convinced themselves it's true. And now here you are, asking questions and trying to make me look bad."

Lust waved her hands in front of her face, her mouth falling into a frown. "No, we're not here to make you look bad. We just want answers. We want to help the Wongs get the restaurant back on its feet. I do have a question, though." Lust reached up toward her hair, stroking it absently. "Eric said they've had trouble with you in the past. Do you know what he was referring to?"

Helen huffed and rolled her eyes, pinching her lips together. "Oh, sure, I know what he's talking about. Old news. It was back when they first opened. They were subletting the place from another tenant. That was illegal in Odyssey at the time. I explained to the building owner what was happening because he was my cousin. I was looking out for his interests. That's all it was. I wasn't trying to stop the Wongs from renting the space. I just wanted to make sure that they had a contract with my cousin and not with the previous tenant." She held up her hands questioningly. "Is that so wrong?"

"That seems reasonable," I agreed. "Have you and the Wongs had other beef over the years? Any other reason Linda Wong would be so convinced you're behind all of this?"

Helen glanced toward Ruby, and the girl tilted her head forward, a subtle but unmistakable nod. She was giving Helen permission to say something. The older woman sucked in a breath and twisted her hands in her lap. "I hate to say this because I don't like to start rumors. But I think Linda might be jealous of the relationship I have with Ruby. She's here almost every day, and I spend more one-on-one time with her than her own mother does. That's not a criticism," Helen said, holding up a hand to preempt an objection that wasn't coming. At least, not from me. "It's just a fact. Linda and Eric work hard to keep that restaurant running. That doesn't always leave a lot of time for family. That's a choice that Linda made, but now I think she's regretting it. Ruby is all grown up now and moving out, and her mom realizes what little time they have left. I think she wants to turn her daughter against me so they can have more time together." The older woman lifted her shoulders in a defeated shrug. "I know how women get when their nest goes empty. It happened to me, too. I keep trying to tell Linda it will pass. Over time, she'll find her happiness again. But she doesn't listen. To her, I'm still the enemy."

I'd only been half-listening to this, partly because family dynamics didn't interest me and partly because I'd been distracted by Ruby's t-shirt. I must've been mulling it over subconsciously because the meaning finally struck me, and I snapped my fingers. "Oh, I get it. Like a Sea-Doo."

Ruby blinked. "Huh?"

"Your shirt," I said, smiling. "I've been wondering how you could brake for dolphins since dolphins aren't in the streets. But Sea-Doos have brakes, don't they?"

Ruby glanced down at her shirt, brows knit together, and then looked back up, offering a shrug. "Oh, I don't know. I guess? I've never actually been on a Sea-Doo. That's more of a rich people thing," she explained.

That made sense. "So then what's the deal with the t-shirt?"

Ruby puffed out her chest and grinned. "Oh! Well, I'm super into the animal rights community here in Odyssey. It's important to look out for creatures who can't look out for themselves. After all, fish are friends. Not food." She gave a smug smile as she said this. "I'm also a vegan. Imagine how difficult it is to be working at a Chinese restaurant," she said, her nose scrunched.

Lust murmured her agreement. "I can only imagine. You're such a good daughter for going against your ethics to work for your parents."

Ruby cast a sidelong glance at Helen Park. "Well...I mean, it's not like I have much choice. In my culture, kids are expected to obey their parents. But my parents are really cool," she added hurriedly. "They are. I mean, they let me join ORCA, and they really, *really* didn't want to."

I was ready to let this line of conversation drop because my interest in Ruby's relationship with her parents was low. But Lust leaned forward, her curiosity piqued. "What's ORCA?"

"Odyssey Repertory and Community Artists," Ruby said. "It's the local acting company. They offer classes, workshops, all kinds of stuff. Agents and casting directors from Hollywood come down every so often to scout talent. I don't have enough of a portfolio yet to attract attention," Ruby said, a self-pitying frown marring her expression. "But I'm playing Hermia in our production of *A Midsummer Night's Dream.* Opening night is coming up. You should come!"

I couldn't think of anything less appealing than watching amateur actors butcher Shakespeare, but I smiled anyway. "Thanks, but I'm not really into theater."

"I wasn't either at first," she said. "Stage acting isn't the same as being in the movies, which is what I really want. But it's helping me become a better actor, and as a result, my YouTube channel has really taken off. It's hard letting it all hang out, though, you know? Hiding emotions is way easier." (I almost snorted. Out of the mouths of babes.) "Especially around here. There's a pretty big difference between the haves and the have-nots, and it pays to look like it doesn't really bother you, even when it does. At my school, especially."

Despite my best intentions to stay aloof, this line of conversation piqued my curiosity. "What do you mean, especially at school?"

"Well, I know it's been a long time since you were in high school, but don't you remember how it was?" I cringed, and Lust nudged me in the side, covering her face to hide her laughter. Ruby didn't seem to notice. She continued, "Cliques and stuff, you know? In our school, it's money that divides us. The rich kids run the school. They run the student council, the athletic teams…everything. Most of them are jerks. They act like because they have money, they can do whatever they want. Unfortunately, here in Odyssey, they're not entirely wrong."

Helen nodded at this. "It's true. From the outside, Odyssey looks like a perfect beach resort town. A nice place to vacation, relax, get some sun. But underneath all that?" She shuddered. "It's just rich people doing what they do best. Lying, cheating, being corrupt. That's why it's ridiculous that Linda and Eric Wong think I'm behind sabotaging their business. People much more influential than me would love to see their restaurant shuttered for good."

Finally, we were getting back on track, uncovering the kind of information we came here for in the first place. "Oh yeah? Like who?"

Helen Park pinched her lips together, huffing noisily. "The city council has been trying to shut down that place for the past six months. It's an eyesore. That building? The haunted house facade? It's contrary to how they want to portray the city. The city has been trying for years to lure Hollywood magnates and other big-name, new-money people down here. And they've been successful. Our real estate prices have shot through the roof, and they weren't reasonable to begin with. Beach town, you know," she said. "Last month, the city council introduced a proposition to prohibit buildings that didn't fit into a beach aesthetic from operating within the city limits. But the voters shot it down, though narrowly."

Lust turned to me, sucking her bottom lip thoughtfully. "The Wongs *did* say the city council was full of racists that wished them harm." She turned back to Helen. "Have *you* had trouble with any of them?"

Helen shook her head. "Not like the Wongs. I don't think the city council is racist. I think they're just capitalists looking for the most profit."

"Mom thinks everyone is racist," Ruby said, rolling her eyes. "Anyway, I need to get going." She climbed to her feet, retrieving her sheet music as she headed toward the front door. "I'll be back tomorrow, Mrs. Park. Thanks for today's lesson." She raised her hand in farewell and was halfway out the door when she doubled back. "Oh! If you want to look into the thing about the wights causing psychological trauma, check out the work of Gary and Melissa Kimball. They're on YouTube and stuff. Okay, bye!" Then she disappeared out the door.

"We should probably go, too," I said. "You've been really helpful, Helen. We appreciate your time."

Lust and I got to our feet, and Helen walked us to the front door. As she was ushering us outside, she said, "Forget about the wights. Look into the city council. I'd start with Portia Cameron. She owns Cameron Realty California. The council members are supposedly all equal, but you know what they say. Some are more equal than others." She hesitated, her lips quirking into a tentative frown. "Also? Be careful. When you start looking under rocks in this town, you're gonna find a few snakes. Good luck."

She shut the door and was gone.

eleven

. . .

"Okay, so what's the plan?"

We were piling into the car, or at least trying to. The cameramen were having trouble loading their equipment into the backseat. I tapped my fingers impatiently on the steering wheel as I waited for them. The network really should have gotten us a larger vehicle. "I was thinking we should go back to the restaurant. Now that we have that lead about the city council, I'd like to ask Eric and Linda about it."

"Good idea. While we're there, we should pick up that spooky soundtrack they play in the dining room. If someone embedded subliminal suggestions in it, at least we can prevent further hallucinations from happening."

The cameramen were finally locked and loaded, and I pulled out into the street. "I have no idea how to tell if an audio file's been tampered with. Any ideas?"

Lust perked up. "Oh, sure. When we get back to the house, I'll ask Wrath to analyze it for us."

I groaned, mouth twisting like I'd tasted something bad.

"Wrath? I don't know if I want his help. He called you a nympho at dinner last night."

"I am a nympho," Lust said, not missing a beat. "Plus, I'm sure I can get Wrath to do anything. Of all the housemates, I bet he's the most susceptible to my feminine wiles."

I didn't like Wrath, but I also didn't like the idea of Lust using her powers against our housemates. It felt wrong. "I don't know if that's a good idea. Envy explained your power to me, so I know it's not foolproof, but—"

"Good grief, Pride." Lust's laugh was deep and throaty. It was the type of laugh that turns heads, the type of laugh that makes other women uncomfortable, the type of laugh that gets husbands in trouble with their wives. "I don't have to use my powers on Wrath. All I have to do is this." She tugged down the front of her t-shirt, revealing an impressive amount of cleavage. "They're called boobs, honey."

My eyes lingered on her exposed bosom a second too long, and by the time I caught myself, Lust was already chuckling and tugging her top back into place. I cleared my throat and refocused on the road. "Anyway, why would we get Wrath's help? Is he a sound engineer or something?"

My partner cocked an eyebrow. "Oh, you don't know? Then I won't tell you. It'll be more fun when you discover it for yourself."

While I drove to Wights and Wongs, Lust pulled out her phone and tapped something in. After a minute, she angled her body toward me, gathering her hair over one shoulder, stroking the strands absently. "Hey, Pride, listen to this. This is what the Kimballs have to say about the wights. 'While often considered a nuisance, wights are some of the most biologically evolved noncorporeal supernatural creatures.' " Lust snickered. "Can you call a non-corporeal being biologically evolved? Is that even a thing?"

She had a point. "Bad choice of words, maybe. Keep reading."

She cleared her throat. " 'They first appeared in ancient Egypt as guardians of the pharaoh's tomb. They protected the dead from being pillaged by the living. Archaeologists believe wights contracted their services to the royal family. Today, wights are sometimes coerced or tricked into serving similar contracts. However, the nature of their services ranges from protection to simple housework. Due to these circumstances, wights have developed the ability to psychologically manipulate their human cohabitators to drive them to madness. In some cases, wights have been known to *curse their human cohabitators* to earn their freedom.' "

"Interesting," I said. "Does it explain how the curse works?"

Lust shook her head. "No, but there's more. 'While wights can and do manipulate their human cohabitators, psychological influence works the other way as well. Some people have reported that soothing music and daily affirmations can calm an agitated wight, while heavy metal music and shouting can incite anger and rebellion in these naturally non-violent creatures.' "

Lust looked up from her phone, chewing on her lips in thought. "Have you ever heard of this before?"

I shook my head. "No, but I've never researched wights before, either."

We arrived at Wights and Wongs where Linda was working at the reception desk. When she saw us, a blush crept up her cheeks. She stammered, glancing around at the empty room. "I had to send our day hostess home. There's not enough work to justify… well. Are you here to eat?"

"We were just at Helen Park's place," I said. "She said you've been having trouble with the city council."

Anger flashed behind Linda's eyes, but it quickly gave way to annoyance. "Portia Cameron is a pain in the rear," Linda grunted. "But she has bigger fish to fry than running me out of business."

"Like what?"

She ticked off the fish that needed frying on her fingers. "There's the growing homelessness problem that needs to be addressed. Our crime rate has been steadily climbing as our population increases. We don't have enough room at the high school for the number of new students we get each year. The city council seems to forget that along with growing our population and tax base—the only thing they really care about—they're also inviting more problems. Rumor is, Portia Cameron is thinking about running for mayor next year. If she wants to do that, she has to address the problems our city faces. They won't go away on their own. The last thing she needs to worry about is my little Chinese restaurant."

I was about to ask another question about the city council when the doorbell tinkled, and a delivery man walked in carrying a large box. "Excuse me a moment," she said. To the delivery guy, she asked, "Is that my order from Peteman's?"

The delivery guy nodded. "Want me to put it in the freezer for you?"

Linda shook her head. "Nah, I've got some other stuff I need to organize back there. Just set it down, and I'll deal with it in a minute. Thanks, Randy."

Randy set the box on the floor, and when he stood up, he looked Lust up and down with an expression like a dog eyeing a prime rib. He rubbed his palm on his pant leg and then extended his hand to Lust, ignoring me altogether. "Hi, there. Never seen you before. You must be new in town. I'm Randy."

Lust purred her response as she shook his hand. "Yes, you sure are."

The delivery man flushed and looked back at Linda. "Have a good day, Ms. Wong." He tucked his chin to his chest as he strode out the front door with Lust and Linda giggling in his wake.

"That wasn't nice," I said.

"But it *was* funny," Linda giggled. "And he deserved it. Randy's married with three kids. Look, Portia Cameron is a dead end," she said. "I've considered that possibility already. What else did you find out at Helen's?"

"Ruby was there," Lust said. "She seems to think the problem isn't a person in town. She thinks it's the wights themselves."

Linda sniggered, shaking her head. "My daughter spends too much time on Reddit," she said. "She needs to stop listening to charlatans trying to make names for themselves. It's not the wights," Linda repeated. "It's Helen Park."

I still wasn't convinced that Helen Park had anything to do with this, but I didn't have enough evidence to rule her out, either. I was working from my gut, and while my intuition was good, it was no substitute for hard evidence. Then I remembered my encounter with Jack Dempsey. "Another lead we're following is your audio," I said, pointing to the ceiling. A haunted organ was playing something chilling over the speakers. "It's possible someone embedded subliminal messages in the music. It's a thing con men do, and apparently, it isn't very difficult."

Linda looked up, her brows furrowed. "We've been using the same audio track for, I don't know, as long as we've been at this location. I can't imagine anybody would bother to tamper with it, but if you think it will help, I'm happy to hand it over."

I nodded. "Yeah, great. We'll look at it and see what we find."

Linda leaned over to pick up the box and jerked her head toward the back, indicating we should follow. "The audio's in the office. Come on back with me, and I'll get it for you."

We wended through the dining room, cutting through the kitchen. Wights appeared at odd intervals, their green eyes glowing in the dim light. Although I was used to seeing the human dead wandering the streets, I was unnerved to see spectral beings floating around a restaurant as servants. As I passed them, the chill of their presence sent shivers down my spine. I couldn't help but wonder if they were messing with my mind.

Would they make me see things that weren't there?

Between them and Lust, I needed to keep on my toes.

Once in the office, Linda dropped the box on her desk and then moved to the corner of the room where an ancient stereo was hooked up to what I assumed was the restaurant audio system. She ejected a disc, and my jaw dropped open. "You're still using CDs?" I said, incredulous. "I haven't seen one of these since I was a kid."

Linda chuckled as she handed me the disc. I handled it carefully, treating it like the prehistoric relic it was. "That's the only copy I have, so be careful with it. If you find anything, let me know. Hey, do me a favor? Help me with this box. My shoulders have been giving me trouble, and I need to get it in the freezer. It's fish," she said, wrinkling her nose, undoubtedly imagining the stink it would make if the fish started to defrost.

I handed the CD to Lust and hefted the box up onto my hip. I followed Linda back into the kitchen, which was occupied only by the sous chef, Ping, and an assistant cook. Linda guided me over to the large walk-in freezer and pulled on the handle to open it. She had hardly stepped inside when she let loose a bloodcurdling scream.

Adrenaline pulsed through my body, and I snapped into action, dropping the box and elbowing my way past Linda. I stepped into the freezer and blinked, letting my eyes adjust to the dim light. I followed Linda's gaze to the floor and froze. When I was sure I was seeing what I thought I was seeing, I fished my phone out of my pocket and dialed.

"Hello?"

"Hey, Sloth? Is this you?"

"Yeah, it's me. Who's this?"

"It's Pride. Listen. Are you still looking for that guy? The old lady's missing son or whatever?"

Sloth sighed heavily into the receiver. "We're still looking, but no dice so far. We're *totally* gonna lose this challenge. I don't think Envy or Gluttony cares, either. I don't even know why they're *on* the show if they're not gonna try to win." She paused long enough to sigh again, more dramatically this time. "Why do you ask?"

I glanced over my shoulder at the shadowy area Linda was still staring at, hands pressed to her mouth in horror. "I think I found him."

Sloth gasped. "You did? Where?"

"At Wights and Wongs. The Chinese place."

On the other end, Sloth cursed under her breath. "You gotta be kidding me! Really? He just waltzed in there to have lunch? God, what rotten luck. Do you think we'll get credit even though our team didn't find him? Should I call Tricia? I should've known we'd—"

"He's not having lunch," I said. "He's in the freezer." I paused and toed the corpse with my shoe. It was frozen solid. "This probably goes without saying, but I'm pretty sure he's dead."

twelve

. . .

The sound of sirens briefly proceeded a bevy of cops pouring through the front doors. The film crew did their best to stay out of the way while also trying to get the best shots they could. Lust and I retreated to the corner of the main dining room, away from the commotion. Eric, Linda, Ping, and the assistant cook whose name I still didn't know huddled together in a booth opposite ours, swearing, crying, and barking orders. Police were taping things off, snapping photos, and strutting around like peacocks. I wondered idly when they'd last seen anything as major as an actual murder in Odyssey. They all had that "kid in a candy store" look about them.

Which was an entirely different look than the one the Wongs were sporting. Linda's face was pale, her cheeks tear-stained. Every so often, she crumpled against her husband, who cooed soothing words to her and stroked her hair, trying his best to be the rock she needed him to be. But he, too, had a haunted look in his eyes.

I guess it wasn't every day you found a corpse in your freezer.

Eventually, a lanky cop approached us, retrieving a pencil

tucked behind his ear and flipping open a notebook. I didn't know cops still did that. I figured even the Odyssey PD had gone digital. He pointed the pencil at Lust and me. "You the two that found Walter?"

"Walter?"

The cop raised a brow at me. "You're not from Odyssey."

"I know that," I said, frowning.

The cop's mouth twitched in a half-grin. "The dead fella is Walter Romanowsky. Local weirdo. Thinks he's a hunter. You the two that found him?"

I shot a glance over toward the Wongs. "Linda and I found him," I said.

The cop narrowed his eyes at Lust, his gaze traveling inevitably to her bosom before he reluctantly turned his eyes to me. "What were you doing when you found the corpse?"

"Putting fish in the freezer."

The cop clucked his tongue. "Right. You notice anything strange?"

I paused. "Just the dead body in the freezer," I said.

The cop glowered at me, and I returned his stare, unblinking. I didn't know why cops asked stupid questions if they didn't want stupid answers. He cleared his throat, continuing. "We found a cat carrier in the kitchen. The staff say it's not theirs. The Wongs also don't recognize it. Does it belong to you? Did you or she—" he gestured at Lust without looking directly at her—"bring that here?"

I shook my head. "A cat carrier? No. I don't have a cat. I don't even like cats." I paused, thinking. "Did you know cats are the only mammals that can't taste sweetness? I don't trust anything that doesn't like sugar."

I must've gotten that information from the ghost girl at some point, though I don't know why I brought it up just then. Nerves, maybe. Or maybe the wights were getting to me.

My stomach roiled at the idea.

But anyway, if the cop noticed my mental deterioration, he didn't let on. "You're not going anywhere, are you? No sudden travel coming up? You'll stay in town to answer any questions, won't you?"

I donned my best pie-eating grin. "I'll be here if you need me, Officer. Happy to serve."

"Don't be a smartass," the cop said. "I'll be in touch."

Lust and I hung around long enough to ensure neither Linda nor Eric needed anything more from us before we left. When we arrived back at the house, news of the corpse in the freezer had preceded us. As soon as we stepped through the front door, the questions started.

"Was there really a freaking body at the restaurant? Holy smokes! How can anyone be so incompetent they overlooked *that?*"

"Did you see his face? Who was it?"

"Was it gross? Oh my God, I bet it was so gross. I can't *believe* you got to see a frozen corpse and I didn't. Some people have all the luck!"

Lust and I took turns fielding questions as Gluttony hustled to and from the kitchen, bringing snacks and beverages to everyone. For himself, he'd brought out an entire gallon of ice cream, which he proceeded to eat with a giant spoon as he plopped down beside Wrath on the couch. "How did you know the dead guy was our missing person?"

"Sloth showed me his photo. He was wearing the same camouflage hunting suit. So unless there's a lot of guys in town running around like that, I was pretty sure it was him."

"I expect the police will tell the public before long." Envy was studying her phone, scrolling endlessly. "Social media's already hashtagging the department asking who it was. God, poor Mrs. Romanowsky." She curled forward, sinking her chin into her hand. "She's been trying to get the police to look for her son since before we got here. And now he shows up dead? I hope she sues them into oblivion."

Silence settled over the room, punctuated only by the sounds of chewing and slurping. Gluttony had graced us with another amazing meal, though I wasn't sure what magic he'd put in this one. Sometimes good food is just good food.

"Do you think our two cases are related?" Sloth peeled off her socks as she asked this, dropping them to the floor. "Like, if you're trying to put a restaurant out of business, no better way than to stuff a dead body in the freezer. I can't imagine people will want to eat somewhere a murder occurred." She threw a sideways glance at Wrath. "Stop thinking about me," she hissed.

"I can't help it!" Wrath gestured wildly to the dirty socks on the floor. "You just drop your nasty, sweaty, *disgusting* socks in the middle of our living room, and you act like it's no big deal! It's gross, Sloth! Everybody else is thinking it, too; they're just too polite to say anything!"

"They *weren't* thinking it before," Sloth said, her own anger rising. "But they are thinking it now!"

"Nobody would be thinking anything if you weren't such a pig!"

Lust tapped me on the knee, and I peeled my eyes away from the growing pile of laundry Sloth was accumulating on the floor. She'd just unclasped her bra, pulled it out through an armhole, and dropped it on top of her socks. "Do you think the wights had anything to do with this?"

I snickered. "Wights? Come on. No."

Lust looked surprised. "Why are you so sure? You don't think wights can drag a person into a freezer?"

I thought about the ghost girl I'd tried to entertain over the years. For the most part, she was incapable of interacting with the physical world. "Seems unlikely. They don't have bodies. How would they drag a fully grown man into a freezer?"

"They serve food, though," Lust pointed out. "So they can carry things. Who's to say how strong they are?"

I frowned. I hadn't thought about that. "Still. I don't think—"

"And maybe they didn't drag him in there at all. Maybe they lured him in there. Or," Lust said, her face going serious, "maybe they used mental manipulation to get him in there. Either way, once he was inside, all they'd have to do is close the door."

I dismissed these ideas with a wave of my hand. "If that was the case, the victim could just *open* the door. Industrial freezers can be opened from inside," I reminded her.

Lust hesitated, then whispered, "Mental manipulation, Pride. Hypnosis. Plain old fear."

I was uncomfortable with these speculations, but Lust was right—I had no reason to think the wights couldn't have murdered this person. My skepticism had little to do with facts and more to do with my feelings. I didn't want to believe anyone could be manipulated into walking into a death trap. The idea that wights could do that was terrifying to me.

But it was more than that. The idea that *Lust* might be able to do that was terrifying to me.

Sloth chewed on the end of her pigtail as she dug her bare feet into the crevice between the couch cushions. "What mental manipulation?"

Lust explained what she'd read about manipulation and curses on the Kimball's website. When she finished, she shrugged. "It seems plausible is all I'm saying."

Sloth frowned. "Could just be propaganda. Or, you know. Total BS."

I laughed, wagging a finger in Lust's face. "Never get too excited about a theory," I said. "Your pet theories will almost always turn out to be BS."

Lust ignored me and turned to Wrath. "Hey. I need a favor."

Wrath's scowl immediately slid into a grin, eyebrows arching on his face. "Oh yeah? What's up?"

Lust smiled playfully, her finger trailing lightly over her lips. "You're pretty handy with technology stuff, right? If I gave you a CD, do you think you could analyze it and see if anybody tampered with it?"

"Tampered with it how?"

Lust shrugged seductively. "Like, could you find an embedded message if it was there?"

Wrath nodded, his eyes glued to Lust's chest. "Yeah, sure, man. I can do that. Easy. I thought you had a challenge for me."

Boobs, I thought as Lust dropped me an I-told-you-so wink. *They really do work.* I shook off my dismay. "So, is that your day job? Are you a sound engineer or something?"

Instead of answering, Wrath pointed to the television. The power was off. "Channel 4," he said. At his command, the television flickered to life. An anchorwoman was standing before a camera at Wights and Wongs, reporting on what we had just seen with our own eyes. The ticker across the bottom read, "Man found dead in Chinese restaurant freezer."

"How did you—"

Wrath pointed to the smartwatch I wore at my wrist. "Text a message from Pride's girlfriend," he said.

Now, my smartwatch buzzed and lit up with a new message. Stunned, I looked down to see a message from Shayda lighting up the watch face. It read, "I'm not coming back. Get your life together, Sid."

I dropped my hand into my lap, my mouth agape as I stared at Wrath. "How did you do that? What the hell was that?"

Wrath looked very pleased with himself as he linked his hands behind his head and leaned back into the cushions. "I'm a technopath, man. I can get technology to do anything I want."

"This is quite serious, you know." Greed ambled into the room, hands tucked casually into his pockets. "The situation with the Wongs. You should let the police handle it. They're trained for this kind of thing. You're not. You'll just get in the way."

"I know how to stay out of the way during an ongoing investigation," I said. "I assist the police on cases like this all the time."

"Excellent!" Greed clapped his palms and rubbed them together. "Then you don't need us. You should already have the resources you require, right?"

"I don't need *you*," I agreed warily. "I need *Wrath*. What do you care anyway? Why—"

I stopped short as understanding dawned. Greed was Wrath's partner. They hadn't completed their task yet, whatever it was, and Greed didn't want Wrath's attention divided. Greed wanted to win—or at least, to beat us.

Lust figured it out the same time I did. "You're a schmuck," she said, lip curling.

"Might be, but I'm a schmuck that isn't gonna let you horn in on my victory. Nobody on our task is dead, so it stands to reason we should win this round. As long as Bottle Blond over there doesn't blow his cool or waste time solving other people's cases, we've got this in the bag."

Envy wriggled to the edge of the sofa, showing her palms as she gaped. "Do you know how heartless you look right now? A person is frozen as solid as a grocery store turkey, and you're talking about winning a stupid competition?"

"Hey, if it's so stupid, feel free to drop out any time," Greed crooned, that slimy smile growing wider. "You all knew what you were getting into when you signed the contract. The rest of you might be in this to play Good Samaritan, but I'm in it to win. I intend to be America's favorite sin, and I won't let any of you jackholes get in my way."

And with that, Greed backed away, flashed double peace signs, and left.

With Greed gone, Lust returned her attention to Wrath. "So, about the audio—"

"Yeah, yeah," he cut in with a sigh. "I'll get to it when I can."

Lust batted her lashes. "Thank you."

Wrath scowled. "Don't mention it. Especially to Greed."

"I hate that guy," Sloth said to no one in particular. Then, turning to me, she asked, "So what's your plan? Are you guys gonna keep trying to solve the fortune cookie thing or what?"

"The way I see it, the Wongs are in an even worse position than before," I said. "If people weren't saying the place was cursed before, they'll start now. So, I'd like to keep working on it." I turned to Lust. "I mean, if you do. I'll understand if you don't want to touch this with a ten-foot pole."

But Lust waved that away. "Like hell am I dropping out now. I'm with you, Pride. Whether these cases are connected or not, *something* bizarre is going on here. I want to find out what it is."

That was a relief. I *could* continue investigating on my own, but having Lust around would likely make it easier. She had skills I could use, as much as I hated to admit it.

Plus, I enjoyed her company, which I hated to admit even worse.

"All right, then. I guess you know what we need to do first." When Lust just stared at me blankly, I said, "We have to interview Walter."

Lust continued staring. A long moment passed before she stated, "He's dead, Pride."

I grinned. Not because it was a funny situation—it wasn't, and I knew that. I'm awkward, not a moron—but because she looked so concerned, like maybe she was wondering if I actually *was* a moron. "That's okay. I'm a ghost whisperer. If the dead have secrets, I'm the one to find them."

thirteen

. . .

I'd been to the city morgue plenty of times, but never without the police department's blessing. I was relatively sure I didn't stand a snowball's chance in hell of getting to the corpses on my own, so I took some precautions and dressed for the occasion. I traded in my old jeans and t-shirt for proper slacks, a sensible shirt with actual buttons, and ditched my Chucks for the only nice shoes I owned. I felt like a tool, but when Lust saw me, she whistled, her eyebrows leaping toward her hairline. "Well, hello, Pride! You clean up good! Why do you look so spiffy?"

"I don't know if this will actually work," I said, tucking my shirt into my pants. "But you know how people are. Easily tricked by appearances. I figure this whole thing might go smoother if I look professional."

"Not a bad idea," she said. "What about me? How do I look?"

You know that expression "like a deer in headlights"? I imagine that's how I looked at that moment as I searched for the right response to this question. The truth was a no-go: Lust looked like she was auditioning to be the first person killed in a horror movie. Her shorts were so short, the pocket lining peeked out from beneath the hem. Her blouse—if you could call it that—exposed most of her midriff and an amount of cleavage that would have made the devil blush.

On the other hand, she had a part to play, and if she did need to seduce someone, well, at least she'd have an advantage.

"Charming," I said finally. Which was true, depending on your definition of "charm." "Let's go."

On the other side of the room, one of the film crew started moving toward me, but I held up my hand, palm out. "Not this time," I said.

The cameraman clucked his teeth. "You know the deal. Where you go, I go."

"Today, where I go could get you arrested," I said. I noticed how Lust stiffened at that. "You're way too conspicuous with that camera. You're not coming with me, and that's final. Take it up with Tricia later if you want."

"Do us both a favor, then," he said. He gestured toward my pocket. "Video it for me. On your phone. The network might be able to use that footage at least."

I felt my pocket to make sure I had my phone, gave a crisp salute in agreement, and then we were off.

Seaside County didn't have its own morgue, so homicide victims were taken to the morgue at the local hospital. I didn't know precisely where the Odyssey morgue was, but most hospital morgues were in the basement, so that's where we headed. Inside the elevator, I dug out my phone. I scanned the Odyssey General website, hoping to find the morgue attendant's name. I flipped through three pages before I found it. Dennis Parker. Bingo.

As the elevator made its slow descent, I prepped Lust for how this would all go down. "What we're hoping for today is run-of-the-mill incompetence," I explained. "Homicide victims are supposed to go straight into the tank, where they're locked up until it's time to autopsy them. That way, unscrupulous people like you or me can't waltz in and start messing with them. To get into the crypt, you need the right credentials, which we don't have. So, the first thing we'll try is the 'act like you own the place' method."

"Okay." She swallowed hard before asking, "What's that?"

"It's where you just walk in and act like you own the place," I said. Really, that seemed self-evident. "People are tricked by confidence. It works in some cases, but I doubt it's gonna work for us here. Still, it's worth a try."

Lust blew out a puff of hot air and fidgeted with her hair. By now, I was getting familiar with her tells: she was nervous. Nervous was no good. Nervous people didn't look like they owned the place. I clasped her by the shoulder and gave a little squeeze. "You can do this," I said. "But you have to act natural."

Lust bobbed her head up and down, but it wasn't exactly in agreement. "And if it doesn't work? What's Plan B?"

I wasn't so sure I really had a Plan A, so calling our failure option Plan B was maybe giving ourselves too much credit, but I let it slide. "Then we wing it. If you can charm the attendant into letting us in, you do that. If not?" I shrugged. "We'll cross that bridge when we come to it." When the elevator doors opened and we stepped out, I added. "Also, when we get to the stiffs, please try not to throw up."

I followed the signs that directed us to the morgue. I pushed through the heavy double doors that separated the respectable part of the hospital wing from the place nobody wanted to visit. I walked past a reception desk on my right, repeating silently to myself, *I own the place. I own the place. I own—*

"Ah, excuse me? You there?" The woman behind the desk was on her feet, waving a hand at me, her expression pinched. "Where do you think you're going? You can't go in there."

I looked around, pretending to be confused as I donned my

best award-winning grin. "Eh? What's the problem? I was just going to see Dennis." I jammed my thumb over my shoulder in the general direction I hoped Dennis was. For that matter, I hoped Dennis still worked here. Hospital websites were notoriously unreliable.

The attendant shook her head, all business. "Authorized personnel only, no exceptions." She looked me up and down before doing the same to Lust. Neither outfit seemed to impress her, and I felt our chances of slipping into the crypt evaporating by the second. "Look, I don't know what you're playing at. But you're not getting in there. Don't make me call security."

Calling security would be bad, so I eased up on the fake charm and headed back in the same direction we'd come from. "No problem. I'll just give Dennis a ring. I'm okay to stay out in the hallway, aren't I?"

The woman shrugged. "Suit yourself."

I took a quick inventory of her desk before Lust and I pushed back through the double doors, regrouping in the hallway.

Lust leaned against a wall as a fluorescent light flickered overhead. "Okay, so now what do we do? I can try to charm her, but I don't think it'll work. She didn't seem to like my outfit."

I rejected the suggestion with a flick of my fingers. "Too risky. If it doesn't work, she'll definitely call security, and then we're toast. But I think we might be in luck. I noticed a keycard on her desk. She wasn't wearing it around her neck like she's supposed to. Remember what I said when we got here? We're hoping for basic, run-of-the-mill incompetence."

Lust chewed her lip and peered over my shoulder, looking through the windows on the double doors we had just passed through. "I don't know, Pride. She seemed pretty serious about doing her job."

I, too, turned to look over my shoulder, peering through the glass. From my vantage point, I could just barely see the woman sitting behind her desk, rifling through papers. I cracked my knuckles and heaved a sigh. "You don't have anywhere else to be, do you?"

Lust frowned. "No, why?"

"Because I have a feeling we might be here a while. We're just gonna have to wait."

Lust held her hands out, imploring. "Wait for what?"

"For nature to call. We're gonna stake out the place until she has to go to the bathroom."

Lust exhaled, running a hand through her hair. "Well, poop."

"Yes," I agreed. "Hopefully sooner than later."

I had to admit, staking out a hospital morgue was incredibly boring. There were no people to watch, and Lust and I ran out of conversation pretty quickly. Even social media wasn't holding my interest. After 45 minutes, I started to seriously question whether the morgue attendant was getting enough water in her diet when, blessedly, she finally got up from her seat. My heart skipped a beat when I saw her reach for the keycard on her desk. If she took the keycard with her, we had just wasted a bunch of time. But she reached past it and grabbed her purse, tucking it under her arm and heading for what I presumed was the ladies' room.

When the attendant was out of sight, I grabbed Lust by the wrist, and we pushed through the doors. I lifted the keycard from the desk and hurried through the halls, looking for the crypt.

We'd turned down several hallways and tried several locked doors when I found it. "This is it," I said, stopping at an unmarked door decorated only with a keycard reader. Lust sidled up behind me so close, I could feel her breath at my back. She squeezed my elbow, her nails digging into my skin.

I swiped the card, breath held. To be honest, I wasn't 100% sure this was the right door. For all I knew, I could have just swiped into the admin break room. We could be about to walk in on a clandestine game of strip poker. You wouldn't believe some of the stories I've heard about what goes on behind the scenes in the morgue.

The door beeped.

I turned the handle and pushed open the door. We stepped into a refrigerated room, and I shivered both with cold and relief. No strip poker. Just dead bodies.

Lots of them.

We were surrounded by corpses. Some were wrapped in heavy plastic and tied up with rope. Those were the bodies that had already been autopsied and were awaiting transport somewhere else. But many of the bodies were merely draped in a shroud. That's what we were looking for. Unless, of course, the city's administrators had actually done their jobs and took our victim to the tank. I crossed my fingers and hoped again for run-of-the-mill incompetence.

I looked over at Lust, whose skin had blanched to near color-lessness. "You okay?" I asked.

She swallowed and swayed on her feet. "I will be. Let's just get on with this and get out of here as soon as we can."

I paused, remembering what the camera guy had requested. "Maybe you should film this," I said. "If we don't bring back any footage, the network goons might insist on tagging along next time. Assuming there's a next time."

Lust looked a little green around the gills, but she dug out her phone anyway and held it up, framing the shot. She brushed the hair from her eyes and said, "Ready when you are."

We moved quickly from body to body, flipping tags and reading names. How did a town as small as Odyssey have so many bodies waiting to be autopsied? I thought of Helen Park and her admonishment to be careful lest we overturn the wrong rock and uncover some nasty snakes. A shiver ran down my spine. I was beginning to think there was more to Odyssey, California, than they advertised on the billboards plastered along Pacific Coast Highway.

As I was contemplating all this, Lust's voice cut through the silence. "Found him."

I strode over to where she was standing. Sure enough, the tag around his toe read, "Walter Romanowsky." Gingerly, I moved Lust aside as I drew nearer the corpse. As I reached out to remove the shroud, Lust grabbed my hand. "Wait." She licked her lips, unsure. "Aren't you worried about fingerprints or something?"

I hesitated, curling my fingers into my palm. I hadn't worried about that in the past because I'd been working with the police. But this time, I could be putting myself in jeopardy. And the last thing I needed was legal trouble on top of everything else.

Still, I had a job to do. And not just for the Wongs, either. The wrongful dead had stories to tell. They deserved to be heard.

I flexed my fingers and blew out a sigh. "It can't be helped, Lust. I have to touch him for my ability to kick in. Let's just hope for the best." I closed my eyes and brought my hands to the corpse's cheeks, pressing my palms against the cold, gray skin.

Slowly, the Wong's kitchen glimmered into view. I was inside Walt's memory, seeing things from his perspective. He sauntered into the kitchen to find Ping coming out of the Wongs' office, something clutched in her hand. When she saw Walt, she drew up short, her free hand pressed against her heart. Her muscles were stiff, her face drawn into an expression I couldn't read. Her lips moved—she was talking, but I couldn't hear the conversation. The longer the discussion wore on, the more Ping fidgeted, shifting her weight from foot to foot. She chewed on her lips, eyes darting around the room.

And then, without warning, Ping stepped over to the stove and lifted a frying pan. Walter closed the distance between them in a few long strides. Ping swiveled, bringing the pan down on Walter's head.

Everything went black.

I pulled my hands away from the cadaver and folded them against my chest. Lust stepped closer, closing her fingers around my upper arm. "Pride? Did it work? What did you see?"

I groaned, scrubbing over my eyes before I remembered I'd just been touching a corpse, and dropped my hands quickly to my sides. "Damn, Lust. Maybe it's not our lucky day after all."

fourteen

. . .

"Ping? No, that's impossible. There has to be some kind of mistake."

A few days had passed since we'd sneaked into the hospital morgue, and Lust and I were sitting across from Mr. and Mrs. Wong at the restaurant. We had Sloth along with us, too, because it was mostly her case. Plus, I suspected that her ability to peek inside other people's minds might come in handy.

I folded my hands on the table and leaned forward, giving my head a slow but certain shake. "I'm sorry, Linda. But I saw with my own two eyes. My own two mind's eyes?" I glanced at Lust to see if the joke landed, but she just stared at me with a "What are you doing?" look on her face, so I guess it didn't. "Anyway, the point is, I'm not wrong about these things. I touched Walt's face, and I saw Ping. Clear as day. She hit him over the head with a cast-iron frying pan."

I knew this was a lot of information for the Wongs to take in. I couldn't blame them for not wanting to face the facts, especially if Ping was the superstar asset they believed she was. Linda was looking at her husband, eyes wide and unblinking. Her mouth was working, but words weren't coming out.

"It's just that we've known Ping for years, and she doesn't have it in her," Eric said. "She doesn't have a violent bone in her body! Besides, what would be her motive?"

"Well, that's what I'm here to find out," I said. "I'd like to talk to her if you don't mind. I know I should probably leave this to the police, but between you and me, I'm not so sure the officials in this town are all that capable."

Snickers of agreement went around the table. "You don't have to convince us that the people running this city leave much to be desired," Eric chortled under his breath. "Still, I agree with my wife. There has to be some mistake about Ping. I trust her utterly. She can't have done this. She just can't."

"We just want to talk to her," Lust said, her voice melodious and even. "And we promise, we won't say anything to the police if you don't want us to. We're doing this for *you*. You deserve answers, and we want to find them."

Linda Wong squared her shoulders and tossed her hair away from her face. "Okay. Fine. If nothing else, maybe talking to Ping will prove that you must've misunderstood what you saw. You'll see. She's not the person you say she is."

We found Ping in the kitchen stir-frying something at the stove, expression grim and focused as she worked the wok. She wore a neat, floral print dress with a long, white apron. Her hair, an eye-catching auburn shot through with silver, was tucked into a hairnet. When she saw us, she turned off the stove and stepped away, frowning. She glanced from Eric to Linda and back again. "Is something the matter?"

Linda gestured in my direction. "Ping, these people would like to have a word with you. They have some questions about what happened the other night." She swallowed and tried on a smile, but it didn't stick, sliding off her lips almost as quickly as it had appeared. "Why don't you all step into my office? I'll handle the kitchen the best I can."

At first, Ping didn't move except to brush her hands along her apron, fidgeting. Finally, she nodded, lips twitching. "Sure. Okay." She patted her hairnet, checking that everything was still in place.

Lust, Sloth, and I followed Ping into a small office at the back of the kitchen. My housemates took their seats, but Ping and I remained standing. I closed the door behind us, giving us a bit of privacy. "Ping," I said. "I have some questions about the murder."

Ping's troubled expression deepened. "Murder?" Her voice was high and squeaky. "The police said it might have been an accident."

I linked my hands in front of me and dropped my gaze. "I haven't spoken to the police," I admitted. "That's not why I'm here. I'm a psychic. When I touch people, I see things. When I touch dead people, I often see the last thing they saw before they died." I paused, hoping to see a flicker of something in Ping's eyes—guilt or confusion, maybe. But she remained stoic, so I pressed on. "I went to see Walt in the morgue. I laid my hands on his face. And what I saw…"

I had everyone's rapt attention. Lust and Sloth were both staring at me, eyes wide, perched on the edge of their seats. Before now, I had only given Lust the barest details. Now, I was about to detail exactly what I'd seen. Ping had to know. More importantly, I wanted to see how she reacted. And I wanted Sloth to have good context for when she rooted around in Ping's gray matter.

"I saw you, Ping. I saw you clear as day. I could tell that you were talking, but I can't hear in my visions. I only see. So I don't know what you or Walt said, but I know you were the last person he saw before he died. You hit him in the head with a frying pan. I saw the whole thing. Walt never woke up after that."

Everyone was still. I heard nothing but the whirring of the air conditioner and the pounding of my heart against my eardrums. And then, as if breaking free of a spell, Ping erupted into tears.

"I don't know what you're talking about!" she wailed. "I don't know why you're doing this. I don't know what you're trying to prove here. I had nothing to do with Walter's death. Nothing! It wasn't me!"

Lust dug into her purse and pulled out a tissue, which she handed to Ping. The older woman accepted gratefully, blowing her nose while she trembled. "I don't have any reason to hurt Walter," she said. "There has to be another explanation. I don't know anything about psychics or visions, but *surely* you make mistakes. I could never kill anyone."

I nodded slowly. "Well, you're right about one thing. There is another explanation. After you hit Walt in the head with a frying pan—that part's not up for debate, Ping, I *saw* it—he could have just fallen unconscious. Someone else could have dragged him into the freezer."

This concession seemed to reinvigorate Ping, who was nodding frantically. "Okay, yes! It had to be someone else, right? Someone else who stuffed the body into the freezer?"

"It *could* be," I stipulated, "but besides you and the Wongs, who else has after-hours access to the restaurant?"

"The wights do," Lust said, her voice soft.

I swiveled, throwing her my best "What are *you* doing?" look, but she ignored me. She was gazing at Ping. "Ping, have you ever noticed the wights acting strangely? Agitated or violent? Anything like that?"

Ping's mouth worked, lips twitching as the cords in her neck strained. She swallowed several times before shaking her head, her shoulders slumped. "No. I wish I could say yes. That would be much better for me." Her voice broke as she choked down a fresh sob. "But I don't like to lie. I've never seen the wights do anything but serve food."

Silence grew thick between us, and after a while, Lust stood from her chair and walked over to the crying woman, enveloping her in a hug. She stroked her back and squeezed her arm until Ping's crying subsided. I had to give her credit. Lust was a lot better at dealing with people than I was. Which I guess wasn't saying much.

"Let's start at the beginning," Lust said. "Did you know Walter?"

Ping bobbed her head side to side, dithering. "Not personally. I knew *of* him. Everyone does. He's a bit of a legend in this town."

That piqued my curiosity. "A legend? How so?"

Now, Ping rolled her eyes and sniffled, swiping at a drop of liquid falling from a nostril. "Well, you've seen him. He wore that weird camo outfit pretty much all the time. He lived with his mom. He claimed to be a hunter, but there's nowhere to hunt in Odyssey, and he wasn't the outdoorsy kind, anyway. You know what I mean? He was pretty much a loner. A very eccentric, creepy loner." She gave a dry laugh, but there was no mirth in it. "Everyone in town knows he's crazy, but they give him a wide berth because his mother has money. And anyway, he's harmless. Or, was," she amended.

"Do you remember seeing him the night of the murder?"

Ping hesitated before taking the last empty seat in the executive chair behind the desk. "I...yes. I do remember seeing him," Ping admitted. "I'd come back to the restaurant late in the night after we closed. I'd left my keys behind, and I needed to come collect them. When I came in, I didn't lock the front door, so I guess he just walked in. He found me back here and started asking me weird questions."

Lust narrowed her eyes. "What kind of weird questions?"

Ping shrugged miserably, sinking down in the chair. "I don't know. Nonsense stuff. Asking me how old I really was, where I was from, stuff like that. *Creepy* stuff like that."

Lust nodded. "That *is* creepy. No one should ask a lady how old she is. And then what happened?"

Ping hesitated, her lips parting as her eyes drifted upward as she thought. Then she shrugged, wringing her hands in her lap. "That's all I remember," she said.

"That's it?" Sloth had been quiet this whole time, but now she leaned forward, eyes glowing as she caught Ping's gaze. "You're *sure* you don't remember anything else? Maybe he attacked you? Something like that?"

But Ping was adamant, shaking her head vehemently. "No, nothing like that. He asked me a bunch of weird questions, I told him to leave me alone, and then I left. That was the end of it."

Frustrated, I blew out my cheeks. "This is a waste of time," I said, folding my arms across my chest. "I *saw* you hit Walt with a frying pan. I *saw* it."

"I don't know what you saw," the woman said, her words still thick from crying. "But I didn't hit anyone. It wasn't me."

"Okay, Ping," Lust said. "Thanks for being so cooperative. I don't know what's going to happen next," she admitted. "The police will probably want to talk to you if they haven't already. You shouldn't—"

Now, the sous chef grew frantic, a wildness growing behind her eyes that made my throat tighten. She bared her teeth in a snarl, and for a split second, she reminded me of a trapped animal. But then her fierceness melted away, and she was herself again, a small, scared slip of a woman caught in an impossible circumstance. "God, you're not going to tell them what you *think* you saw, are you? You can't do that. You might as well kill me yourself if you do that."

"Why?" It was Sloth who asked, her head titled to one side, her face open. "No, really. Why would you say that?"

"You don't know what this town's really like," Ping replied, a sharp undercurrent cutting through her words. "It's full of vipers. If you tell the police you imagined me killing Walter—"

"I didn't imagine it," I interjected.

"—they'll arrest me for sure. It'll be a witch hunt, even without evidence. I'm *Chinese*," she said. "An *immigrant*. They'd love to blame this on me. You think they'll hesitate to throw me in jail? And even if I can prove my innocence, my reputation will be destroyed. Whatever you think I did, at least don't tell the *cops*. Please."

I sighed. "Don't worry. We're not gonna tell the cops anything. But if I were you, I'd stick around and keep a low profile. Don't do anything to arouse their suspicion, like skipping town. You got it?"

Ping nodded miserably. "I got it."

I dug my hands in my pockets. "Okay. Well, best of luck to you." I jerked my head toward the door, and both housemates followed me out of the office. I spoke briefly with the Wongs in the kitchen, collecting a few more bits of information and sharing what we'd learned, which wasn't much. They thanked us, shoved the stir-fry Ping had been making into our hands, and walked us to the parking lot. We piled into the car, and only when the doors were closed did I say, "So, Sloth. What do we think of that?"

In the backseat, Sloth chewed thoughtfully on the end of her pigtail. Finally, she said, "She was telling the truth."

I turned quickly in my seat, craning my neck to get a better view of Sloth's face. "I'm sorry, *what?*"

Sloth shrugged, her face pink and splotchy. "I don't know what to tell you. I was reading her mind the whole time she was talking, and she wasn't lying. Or at least, she believed everything she was saying." She paused. "There *was* something strange, though."

I rolled my hand in a "Get on with it" motion. "Strange how? What was it?"

"When she talked about Walt asking her the creepy questions, her mind got dark and hazy. It reminded me of TV static. Or like I was watching a videotape, and someone had erased part of the film."

That *was* interesting. "Have you ever seen anything like that before?"

Sloth shook her head. "No. And that wasn't the only weird thing. Most people's thoughts are jumbled and nonlinear. People think of lots of different things at a time. They'll be talking about how much they hate their jobs, for example, but they're also thinking about what they need from the grocery store, the rent that's due, the time they lied to their spouse about why they'd come home so late, and what to get Mom for her birthday. It's all in there, jumbled together like the clearance section at Walmart."

"Okay. And her mind wasn't like that?"

"No. Ping's thoughts were very organized. *Too* organized. Like she was trying very hard to only focus on the present."

"And what do you make of that?"

Sloth shook her head again. "I don't know. I'm not a psychic detective. I can only tell you what I saw."

I turned around and started up the car, lost in my own thoughts. Ping *couldn't* be telling the truth. I'd seen her strike the victim with my own eyes. There had to be another explanation.

But then I remembered Sloth's caveat: that Ping *believed* she was telling the truth. And according to Sloth, some of her memories were missing. That might explain the contradicting facts.

I still didn't know what to make of the weirdly organized thoughts, though.

All of this wanted further investigation, but I was tired. It was all starting to feel overwhelming, the evidence spinning out of control. And though there was no hidden camera footage to corroborate my hunch—yes, I asked, I'm not *that* bad at my job —I didn't believe the wights were involved. No one else had dragged the victim into the freezer.

Ping had done that.

The question that would keep me awake that night and every night until I solved this case was—why?

fifteen

. . .

The following day, I was surprised to find Sloth already awake and dressed when I came downstairs for breakfast. She was usually the last one up, coming to the dining room in her ratty slippers and housecoat crusted with various spilled foods. But today, she was wearing a clean sundress, sandals, and even her hair was properly brushed.

"Good morning," she chirped, handing me a mug of coffee. "How did you sleep?"

"Fine," I said, taking a careful sip. "You?"

Sloth tutted. "I've always been a poor sleeper. Being in this house doesn't make it easier. I hear people's thoughts more clearly at night. Drifting through the walls. It's disconcerting. I've asked my doc for something to help me sleep or at least block out all the constant inputs. But so far, nothing seems to work."

I gestured toward her outfit. "Is that why you're up so early? Do you have an appointment to see your doctor?"

Sloth laughed and shook her head, going to the fridge for orange juice, which she immediately sloshed onto the floor. It didn't faze her at all. She merely swatted at it with the toe of one sandal. "No, nothing like that. I was actually going over to see Walter's mom, Eleanor Romanowsky."

I retrieved a paper towel from the counter and bent down to wipe up Sloth's mess. Wrath would lose his mind if he came down later to a sticky kitchen. "Really? But your case is already solved. We found her son. Just not alive."

Sloth nodded and gulped her juice. "I know. But I guess I feel bad. When I first got assigned to her case, I made assumptions about her. I called her crazy and stuff." Sloth frowned at the memory. "I don't think she's crazy now. She suspected something was wrong, and she was right, but not a single person believed her. So, anyway, I thought it might be nice if she had some company. Someone to distract her."

I wasn't so sure that a grieving mother wanted to be distracted. Still, I couldn't deny it was a kind sentiment. "Would you mind if I tagged along? I'd like to get more information on Walt. Something personal."

Now, Sloth gave me a dubious look over the rim of her juice glass. "I don't know, Pride. You're not gonna ask her a bunch of insensitive questions and start her crying and everything, are you? I don't mean to be rude, but you're not super great with people, you know?"

She was right about that, but I was pretty sure I could be on my best behavior. "I just want to ask her some questions about her son. Find out what he was like. What were his hobbies? What was he like as a kid? Things like that. I'm not gonna ask anything pointed like what he was doing on the night of the murder."

She still looked doubtful. "You promise?"

I drew a cross over my heart and held up two fingers. "Scout's honor," I said. Which meant exactly nothing at all since I wasn't and had never been a Scout, but Sloth didn't need to know that.

My promise seemed to do the trick. Sloth's face brightened, and she nodded, slurping down the last of the juice. It dribbled down her chin, but, miraculously, she wiped it away before it ended up on her chest. "Okay then! I was going to leave now. Are you ready?"

Today was the film crew's day off. They didn't film every second of every day, and I was looking forward to a day without them. Still, I wanted to get *some* footage of the day's adventure. Just to be safe. "Let me get my phone."

A few minutes later, we were out the door and in the car, making the short drive over to Eleanor Romanowsky's house. Like Sinful House, the Romanowsky place was a few blocks from the ocean. As we emerged from our vehicle, I saw a flock of seagulls circling overhead. Not far away, ocean waves crashed on the shore. The sound of the surf was comforting. It was hard to believe we were here investigating a murder. Everything looked so peaceful.

On the other side of the street, something caught my eye. A couple was walking up the sidewalk, hand in hand, oblivious to everything except each other. I paused, watching them, a familiar shiver running down my spine. The woman looked up and saw me. When she saw that I saw her, too, she stopped in her tracks, tugging her partner back. She pointed at me. I swallowed.

"Wait a minute, Sloth," I said.

She stopped in the middle of the street, turning with her hand pressed to her forehead, making a visor above her eyes. "What is it?"

"Over there," I said, gesturing with my chin. I don't know why I did that, because Sloth couldn't see what I saw.

She looked around. "Over where?"

The couple was walking toward me now, their smiles growing wider even as my stomach rolled. I glanced from the woman to Sloth and back again. "Ghosts," I said.

Now, Sloth hurried to my side, catching me around the arm. "What? Where? What are you talking about?"

"I see them sometimes," I explained. "There's two coming toward us now. I almost missed them. They almost look alive except…"

Sloth waited, her mouth agape. When I didn't continue, she squeezed my arm tighter. "Except *what*?"

I swallowed again. "They're wearing swimsuits, and they're dripping wet. But it's their skin. Their lips. Too blue."

The color drained from Sloth's face. "Did Envy's undine get them?"

I almost laughed at the absurdity, but Sloth was very serious, and I didn't want to hurt her feelings. "No. They died by drowning."

The couple approached, and I stood still, unsure what they might want from me. Usually, ghosts ignored me completely. Other times, they were frightened and demanded help. That happened most often with the newly dead. But these two appeared neither newly dead nor distressed. Their pace was steady, and they were smiling. But the closer they came, the stranger they looked. The woman's hair was knotted with snarls of seaweed. The man's bare torso was severely abraded.

The man raised a hand in greeting. I raised mine back. "Hello there," he called. "Can you see us?"

I nodded. "I see you," I said. Even though I'd been engaging with ghosts my whole life, starting conversations with them was always awkward. You couldn't exactly ask, "How's it going?" or anything like that. It's obviously not going well, because they're dead.

"I wonder if you could help us, then," the woman said. "We…well, we're obviously dead, right?"

I nodded again. "You are. My condolences," I added.

"Oh, it's fine. We figured it out a while ago." The man put his arm around the woman and squeezed her close. "But we haven't managed to go…well, this is gonna sound stupid, but…aren't we supposed to go somewhere? Heaven or the other side or something? I mean, as nice as Odyssey is, this can't be everything, right?"

"Probably not," I agreed.

"Well, then, since you can see us, maybe you can help? Do you have…I don't know, directions? On how to find the others? The other dead, I mean?"

I sighed. I knew what they were asking. I'd been asked this at least a thousand times before. Maybe not a thousand, but many times, anyway. And even after all this time, it was a question I couldn't answer. I wasn't sure anyone could. "No, I don't. I have no idea how to get…*there.*"

Sloth squeezed my arm again. "Get where? What are they saying?"

I shushed her, keeping focused on the ghosts. Their smiles faded, and their cheeks sagged, eyes drooping at the corners. Even I recognize that disappointment, and it stabbed me right in the heart. "Okay. Well, thanks anyway. Hey, have a good rest of your day. And take it from me—steer clear of the riptides."

The ghosts retreated, turning their backs to me and continuing their walk up the street. They left the barest trace of watery footprints in their wake. A moment later, they were gone.

I turned to Sloth. "They're stranded here," I explained. "They were asking for directions to the other side. Or the afterlife. Or wherever."

Sloth's mouth dropped into an *o* as she craned her neck to look around as though maybe with this new info, she'd be able to see them. Of course, it didn't work. "Those poor things," she said, peeling herself away from me. "Why does it happen? Why do some people get stuck here after they die?"

I snorted, shaking my head. "If you find out, write a book about it. You'll be rich. It's one of the greatest paranormal questions of our lifetime."

She blinked. "Really? No one knows?"

"No one. But hey, don't let it get to you." I saw the way her lips trembled, how she reached for that pigtail to chew on. "Those two, at least, didn't seem too upset about it. They have each other."

For a moment, Sloth looked doubtful. But then she shrugged it off and nodded, confirming something to herself. "You're right. We have other things to worry about. Let's see Mrs. Romanowsky."

———

Sloth rang the doorbell. A few moments later, the door creaked open, and a small, gray-haired woman appeared. Her eyes were red and swollen, and she was sniffling, a handkerchief clutched in one gnarled hand. She looked to be in her seventies or eighties. She smiled when she saw Sloth, but when she glanced in my direction, that smile faltered. "Sloth," she breathed. "It's nice to see you, honey. I wasn't expecting any visitors." She glanced at me again. "Who's your friend?"

Sloth put her hand on the small of my back and encouraged me forward. "Mrs. Romanowsky, this is Pride. Pride, this is Mrs. Romanowsky. We live at Sinful House together on the same TV show. I thought it would be nice to bring one of my housemates along. Is it all right?"

The woman looked me over from head to foot, evaluating me. I was glad I'd worn my good jeans and not the ones with the holes in the knees. After a moment, she gave in and stepped aside so we could enter.

The inside of her home was modest, especially for a woman who was supposed to have money. I saw nothing ostentatious or conspicuous. Nothing stood out as extravagant. In fact, the place was downright cozy. Everything was decorated traditionally, with plush upholstery and floral paper on the walls. Still life paintings added homey accents to the living room and hallway. Upstairs, I heard the twittering of birds.

"Sun conures," she said, gesturing toward her second floor. "A gift from my son. I've never been much of a pet person myself, but strangely, I find those birds comforting. Although they do make a bit of a racket. I apologize for that."

Eleanor led us into the living room, where Sloth and I sat on a couch covered in afghans. The accompanying coffee table was dotted with doilies. Eleanor ambled toward the kitchen. "Can I get you two anything to drink? I have a kettle on for tea," she said. "I know most young people don't drink tea, though."

My enthusiasm for tea was very low. "I'm fine. I'd really just like to ask you—"

Sloth elbowed me sharply in the side and shot me a dark look. I took the none-too-subtle hint and called out, "Tea sounds lovely," just as Sloth said, "I'd love some!"

While Eleanor busied herself in a kitchen, I leaned toward Sloth and whispered, "I hate tea."

Sloth held a finger to her lips. "You don't have to drink it. But it's nice to accept hospitality when it's offered. Plus, you can't just launch into an interrogation. You *promised.*"

A moment later, Eleanor returned with a tea tray set for three. She poured our cups and dropped sugar cubes in each. I accepted mine but didn't drink, placing it on my lap. Sloth gave me an almost imperceptible smile.

"I'm sorry to hear about your son," I said. I hoped that wasn't too direct, but I really wanted to get to Walt sooner than later. "Were the two of you very close?"

Eleanor sighed and dabbed at her eyes. The teacup rattled in her hands. "Yes. Very. For most of his life, it was Walt and me against the world. Walt was an oops baby; I was 45 when he was born. His father left early on, but Walt and I were like peas and carrots. We did everything together. I was a very involved mother. It wasn't until recently that we started to drift apart. And by recently, I mean, oh, the last five or so years. That's when things started getting strange."

I tried not to look too eager when I asked, "Strange how?"

Eleanor sighed, her eyes traveling the room as though the knickknacks and tchotchkes would give her the answers I was seeking. "Walt was involved with an organization he discovered online. I don't know much about them, but…" She sighed and looked down into her tea. "Well, Walt was always a strange boy. I don't deny that. Today, they'd say he was somewhere on the spectrum, but we just called him peculiar back then and didn't overthink it. He was a loner most of his life, and as an adult, he wasn't much different. So when he met that group on the internet, I was glad for him. It gave him something to do. A social life, you know. But after a while, I admit I grew a bit jealous. He spent so much more time with them than with me."

I nodded and tried a sip of the tea. It tasted like hot water and leaves, like all other teas. I didn't know how people drank this stuff. "He was spending time with them online?"

Eleanor's eyes grew wide as she shook her head. "Oh, no. He met up with them in real life. Days at a time, sometimes. At first, it was just a day or two. But as time went on, his trips got longer and longer. His check-ins grew more infrequent. And to make things worse, when I *did* see him, he seemed troubled. Secretive. I didn't like the change I saw in him, not at all. I tried to ask him about it. But you know how men are. They don't like women to get involved in their private lives. Especially their mothers."

I didn't know anything about men and their mothers, but I was willing to take her word for it. "So he met this group about five years ago?"

Eleanor nodded. "That's right."

I set my tea on the table, hoping that my attempt at drinking it would be noted and appreciated, at least by Sloth. I sank back into the couch and crossed my legs, folding my hands in my lap. "Do you know *anything* about the group?"

For the first time, Eleanor looked nervous. She, too, set her teacup on the tray and began fussing with her hair, brushing stray locks behind her ears. She cleared her throat a few times and fiddled with her necklace, twining the chain around wrinkled fingers. Finally, she met my eyes. "They called themselves hunters," she said. "I found that hard to believe because my Walt had a soft spot for animals. I couldn't imagine him killing for sport. But I did find strange things in his room. A spiked collar much too big for a dog. A muzzle. And when the police found him…" She choked up, dabbing at her eyes with a handkerchief. "They said he had handcuffs in his pocket."

I glanced at Sloth to see if she was thinking what I was thinking, but Sloth was just gazing at Mrs. Romanowsky with a sorrowful expression, which wasn't helpful. So I took a chance and said, "Isn't it possible Walt was just into bondage?"

Sloth shot me a horrified look. "Pride!"

Mrs. Romanowsky looked like I'd just casually suggested she try cannibalism. "Excuse me?"

I gulped, knowing that once again, I'd stepped in it, but I couldn't turn back now, could I? "I'm just saying—"

"No, Pride, we all know what you're saying," Sloth interrupted. She gave me a look that I clearly read to mean, "Shut up right now." She turned back to our hostess. "Please, Mrs. Romanowsky. Continue."

The old woman gathered herself, angling her body toward Sloth—and away from me. "I tried to ask him questions about all this, but he wasn't saying much. He wouldn't even tell me the name of the organization. And he had a password on his computer, so I couldn't look it up myself. Believe me, I tried. I know that might make me a terrible person. But when your son is getting involved in strange activities and staying out for days without contacting you, well, you go a little crazy. You just want to keep your children safe."

Sloth reached over and took the old woman by the hand, squeezing softly. "Nobody thinks poorly of you for trying to protect your son," she said.

I wasn't so sure about the nobody part. I would be pretty pissed if I discovered someone was snooping through my stuff for information I clearly didn't want to share, but that was beside the point, so I let it go. "Sloth mentioned you reported him missing a few times, but nobody took you seriously. Is that true?"

Eleanor's cheeks flushed hot and pink. "The Odyssey Police Department is an absolute disgrace," she spat. "When I first filed a report, they looked into it. My family comes from money, you see. And here in Odyssey, money talks. You know how it is."

I didn't, but that seemed to be the common theme over the past couple of days. "So the police helped you out because you're rich. That's what you're saying?"

She offered a matter-of-fact nod. "Yes, exactly. But after a while, all the money in the world couldn't get them to do their jobs properly. I would call and report that Walt had gone missing again, and they told me to just settle down and he'd show up eventually. Which, of course, he did. Until he didn't."

I saw the way her eyes grew liquid, and for a moment, I worried she would start crying. But it seemed she was more angry than sad. "I was fit to be tied when I heard the police referred my case to a TV network. Imagine my mortification when RealTV contacted me and asked if they could send *actors* to help me find my son." She glanced at Sloth and offered a lopsided, apologetic smile. "I didn't understand until later that you're not an actor. Which is a good thing, if you ask me. Actors are horrible people. Terrible. The only one I can remotely stand is that Charmaine Young woman, and even that is a grudging acceptance."

I frowned, pulled suddenly into my own thoughts. Why did the name Charmaine Young pique my attention? But then I remembered. She was the first victim of the fortune cookie scandal. "You know Charmaine Young?"

Eleanor shrugged one shoulder. "She was a friend of my son's—a member of a very exclusive club, if you catch my meaning. They were as different as night and day, yet thick as thieves. Charmaine has wanted to be an actress since she was a girl. Not an ounce of talent in her entire body, mind you, but that didn't stop her any. I never liked her, but I was grateful that she befriended my son. Even after all these years, they maintained their friendship. She was the first person to offer her condolences after the police announced Walt's death."

Sloth tilted her head to one side. "Is there a particular reason you don't like her, Mrs. Romanowsky?"

Eleanor heaved a sigh, her lips pressed into a thin, hard line. "My son was special, as I've said. He had a delicate mind—prone to flights of fancy. Charmaine encouraged his eccentricities. They talked frequently about the habits and habitats of supernatural beings. Leprechauns, mermaids, fairies." The older woman couldn't keep the disdain from her voice. "They took trips together—Area 51 to look for aliens. The Blue Mountains to search for Bigfoot. What kind of person does that? Who takes advantage of a delicate mind like that?"

To be honest, it didn't sound like a big deal to me. Lots of people were interested in things like aliens and pseudo-monsters; I didn't see the harm in it. I'd seen much more toxic friendships in every teen movie that came pouring out of Hollywood. But maybe there was something Eleanor wasn't telling us.

I reached for my tea, pretended to take a sip, and then placed the teacup back on the saucer. "Eleanor, would it be all right if I saw his room?"

The old woman wrinkled her chin, hands wringing at her chest. "His room? Whatever for?"

Sloth took the old woman's hand, squeezing her fingers softly. "Pride is a psychic who sometimes sees things. It might help us understand what happened to Walter."

Eleanor glanced up the stairs, still looking unsure. "Well, in that case, I suppose it won't hurt anything. It's the first room on the left. But please don't touch anything."

I left Sloth with Eleanor and headed upstairs. The door to Walt's room was slightly ajar and squeaked as I pushed it open. The room was small and neat and looked nothing like the bedroom of an adult man. It was more like a time capsule, a room forever preserved in Walt's youth.

I stepped inside, breath held in my throat. A double bed was pushed against the far wall. The bed was neatly made, and atop the pillows were a collection of stuffed animals. A roll-top desk sat in the corner, stacked with papers, books, a tablet, and a laptop. In the other corner was a bookshelf, but instead of books, it held a variety of curious items: spiked dog collars, a heavy chain, a thick leash, a metal muzzle. These must be the items Eleanor had mentioned finding.

The walls were covered in unframed paintings done in the same style as the still life paintings downstairs. These, however, were not paintings of fruits and flowers. They were of fantastic monsters: griffins, manticores, phoenixes, and others I couldn't name. I leaned in closer to examine the artwork and saw that each had been simply signed, "Walt."

On the next wall, the paintings changed. These featured cryptids: Bigfoot, the Chupacabra, the Loch Ness monster. Underneath the Bigfoot and Chupacabra paintings were plane ticket stubs—undoubtedly from the trips he'd taken with Charmaine.

On the last wall, the paintings were of regular animals—

foxes, raccoons, and crows, mainly. But the last picture was the most elaborate. It depicted a seal on a beach with a cityscape in the background. I thought I made out the telltale, red-tile hip roof of Wights and Wongs. It must have been a still life of something Walt had seen here in Odyssey.

Underneath the seal was a single word scrawled in the same hand as Walt's signature. It read, "Charmaine."

I know I promised not to touch anything, but I guess I was a liar because I plucked the painting from the wall and slipped it into the back of my pants, hidden by the tail of my shirt.

————

I was heading back downstairs when a blood-curdling scream ripped through my eardrums, squeezing my heart up from my chest and into my throat. I shot down the stairs, but neither Sloth nor Eleanor were in the living room. I was about to look for them outside when I heard the scream again.

It was coming from upstairs.

I ran back up the stairs, throwing open doors and shouting for Sloth and Eleanor. The rooms were all empty. When I came to the last room, I threw the door open, beads of sweat popping out on my skin, my clothes sticking to my body. I was prepared for the worst—an intruder with a gun, a lunatic with a knife, an escaped wight with a wok of stir fry.

But I didn't find any of that.

This was Eleanor Romanowsky's bedroom. The room was larger than Walt's, with huge bay windows that faced the beach. A canopy bed took up the center of the room. At the foot of the bed stood a tall, black cage the same width as the bed.

Inside that enormous cage were two beautiful birds, both sporting red and orange plumage that mimicked the colors of the sky as the sun set over the Pacific.

And one of those birds was screaming its head off.

I crumbled with relief, leaning my weight into hands rested on bent knees. "Sun conures," I breathed, repeating what Eleanor had said when we'd arrived. When I finally caught my breath, I straightened up and stepped nearer to the cage for a better look.

I didn't know a sun conure from a pit bull, but I could see the appeal. They looked like miniature parrots with the same hooked, black bill and the same shining, black eyes. I'd never seen birds like this, not in real life. I tapped the cage with a finger, and both birds turned, heads cocked comically to one side.

"Polly wanna cracker?" I said, my voice pitched up an octave. "Polly wanna cracker?"

The birds continued to stare at me, blinking as though perhaps I'd lost my mind.

"Well, I guess you don't talk," I said, standing up straight and shoving my hands in my pockets. "But you sure can scream. You almost gave me a heart attack."

I turned to head back downstairs when a voice behind me said, "Did you know sun conures can live 30 years in captivity?"

I spun around and should not have been surprised to see the ghost girl peering into the cage, her nose pressed right up against the wires. Why she didn't go through, I don't know. The physics that ruled her world continued to mystify me. "What are you doing here?" I asked.

"What are *you* doing here?" she retorted. "This is that old woman's bedroom. I don't think you're supposed to be in here."

"I heard screaming," I said.

The ghost girl turned away from the cage, a knowing look in her eye. "Oh, yeah. They do that. That's why some people don't think they make great pets."

"Well, these were a gift," I said. "Eleanor got them from her son. And now he's dead."

The ghost's eyes grew wide. "He gave her the birds, and then he died?"

I shook my head. "I don't think the two events were related."

The ghost blew out a breath, wiping the back of her hand across her brow. "Phew. That's a relief."

I watched her from the corner of my eye, wondering not for the first time what she was doing in my life. How did she choose when to show up? *Did* she choose, or did something else precipitate her appearances? What was she still doing here on Earth? Why hadn't she gone on to…wherever the dead were supposed to go?

It was useless to ask her these questions, though. I'd already asked her a million times over the years. Well, maybe not a million. But enough to know she had no more answers than I did.

"I better get back downstairs," I said. I turned away from the birds, still watching the ghost from the corner of my eye when something strange snagged my attention.

The cage was pulsating with a faint golden glow.

I stopped, turning to face the cage again, but when I did, the glow disappeared. I stepped toward it, eyes narrow as I examined it more closely. It was a standard, if large, birdcage—or at least, it seemed that way to me, someone who knows absolutely nothing about birdcages. It stood about five feet tall with a domed top and four wheels on the bottom. It was not ornately decorated. A small plaque in the lower corner read simply, "Chenoweth." I turned my face away from the cage until it nearly disappeared from my peripheral vision. And just as it slipped almost beyond my view, the glow reappeared.

"Strange," I said, turning back around. "Does the cage glow for you?"

The ghost shook her head. "No. Does it glow for you?"

"Only sometimes." I pulled my phone from my pocket and set it to record. "I wonder—"

"Pride! Pride? Hello?"

I ducked out of the bedroom and headed down the stairs to find Eleanor and Sloth standing in the living room. "There you are," I said, acting like I'd been looking for them. "Where'd you go?"

"Mrs. Romanowsky was showing me her garden," Sloth said. "We should get going. We're expected back at the house soon." Turning to our host, she asked, "Would it be okay if I visited you again sometime?"

Eleanor's face cracked into a smile, the sadness easing out from the creases of her skin. "I would like that very much, darling. And you're welcome to bring your friend here, too," she said, flicking kindly eyes in my direction. "It's good to have the energy of young people in the house."

I helped Eleanor gather the tea and other accouterments and carry them into the kitchen. Even Sloth helped, wiping down the counters as best she could, which wasn't very good at all. Sloth and Eleanor exchanged hugs while I offered only a handshake. Still, the older woman accepted gratefully. "You two be careful," she said. "And come see me again soon."

sixteen

. . .

We weren't actually expected at the house for another few hours. So once we were on the road, I said, "I want to talk to Charmaine Young."

Sloth raised an eyebrow. "Oh yeah? What for?"

I slipped the painting out of my pants and handed it to Sloth. When she saw it, her face blanched. "Are you kidding me? Did you steal this?"

"Yes," I said. There was no point in lying. "I had a feeling about it, Sloth. I'll return it. But I also want to ask Charmaine about it."

"Charmaine," she repeated. "Walter's friend? Why?"

"Don't you think it's weird? A painting of a seal with his friend's name on it?"

Sloth examined the painting, lip curled beneath her teeth. "Is it weird? His mom said she was his only friend. Maybe he painted this for her."

"Then why didn't he give it to her? Why was it hanging on his bedroom wall?"

Sloth raised an eyebrow. "I guess those are good questions.

But is that all you came up with? I thought you investigated crimes for a living."

I frowned, ignoring the reproach in her voice. "I need to know more about Walt to understand what he was doing at the restaurant that night. I like getting to the bottom of things. In my line of work, it's important."

Sloth was chewing her hair again as she gazed out the passenger window. "I can see that. If someone I loved was murdered, I'd want answers. I'd want to know why."

"Knowing why isn't always satisfying," I told her. "In fact, it rarely is. It doesn't help the families when I tell them the murderer killed their loved one because they wanted her wallet, and slitting her throat was the best way to get it. It doesn't help when I tell them their loved one died because they were in the wrong place at the wrong time. When I investigate murders, I'm trying to get justice, yes, but mostly I want to help the person lying cold in the ground. I want to help them share their final chapter. Sometimes when I touch the cadavers, I don't see their final moments at all. Sometimes I see their favorite memories. You know how they say your life flashes before your eyes when you die? It's true, at least for some people. And when I touch them, I get to see those, too. Their most private home movies."

Sloth shuddered, her skin pimpling over with goosebumps. "I wouldn't want anyone to see what's in my head," she said. "I see what's in other people's heads all the time, and believe me, it's better not to know."

I glanced over at her. "Can you read my mind right now?"

She whipped her head around and peered at me before breaking into a grin. "I don't need to read your mind to know you wanna call Charmaine Young." She fished her phone from her pocket. "I'll find her number."

I nodded. "Call her and put it on speaker."

Sloth dialed and, a moment later, placed the phone in the dashboard phone holder. "It's ringing," she said.

"Hello?" The voice on the other end was breathy and hurried.

"Is this Charmaine Young?"

A pause. "This is she. Who's calling?"

"Um, hi. This might sound weird, but my name is…Pride." I didn't know when I would stop feeling ridiculous introducing myself this way, but it wasn't today. "I'm with a reality TV show called *Sinful House* filming here in town. I'm helping Eleanor Romanowsky find out what happened to her son, Walter Romanowsky. I understand you were a good friend of his. Do you have time this evening for an interview? I'd love to ask you some questions."

I heard a scuffle and rattling on the other end like someone was rifling through a junk drawer. Charmaine sighed heavily into the receiver. "I'm sorry, but that's *absolutely* impossible. Tonight's opening night at ORCA. We're performing *A Midsummer Night's Dream*, and I'm playing Titania." I heard the wet smacking of lips and deduced she was applying lipstick. "So, as you can see, I couldn't possibly spare a moment."

"I understand," I cooed. "Perhaps later this afternoon, then? I can even meet you after the play if that works better for you."

"I'm in the middle of getting dressed even as we speak," she said. "My hair needs time for the curls to set. I need to pick up my costume from the dry cleaner, and I like to enjoy a cocktail on my own to calm my nerves before curtain. So I'm very sorry. I would love to help you, but the timing is impossible. You know how it goes for actresses," she tittered. "The show runs until next week, so I won't have a free moment until then." She paused. "Just a moment. Did you say *reality* TV show? Are you bringing a film crew?"

I balked, unsure what she meant. "What?"

"To the interview. Will I be on television?"

I blinked hard. "Well, I don't know for sure. The producers—"

But Sloth reached over and punched me in the arm. "Just say yes," she mouthed to me.

"Yes," I stammered into the phone. "Yes, you'll be on TV. Of course. Does that mean you can meet with me after all?"

"There's a party starting at 10. VIP only," she said. "I'll leave word with my manager that I've invited you as my guest. *Do* make sure to bring the film crew."

"I won't forget," I said. "Thank you for your time. You won't regret it. I'll see you then. And good luck tonight!"

Charmaine paused on the other end. "In showbiz, we say *break a leg*."

"Okay then. Break a leg!"

The line went dead.

"You almost bit the big one!" Sloth said with a laugh. "What would you have done if I hadn't been here?"

I shrugged, a grin of my own spreading over my face. "Scuffed it, I guess. Like I said, I don't like to lie, and I'm not good at it. It's a good thing you were here to keep me straight."

"You mean to remind you to fib," Sloth said.

"Toh-may-to, toh-mah-to," I said. That was another phrase I didn't like. I don't actually know a single person who says Toh-mah-to. Maybe they say that in England. I've never left the continent, though, so I have no frame of reference. "The point is, we made a good team today."

Sloth's cheeks blushed a soft pink, and she grabbed a pigtail, stuffing the end in her mouth as usual. "Yeah, it was fun. I'm glad you came with me to see Mrs. Romanowsky."

"Speaking of that," I said, "you should come with me to the party. The camera crew is off tonight, and I'll need someone to play the part. You in?"

Sloth's smile faltered, the confidence fading from her face. "Wish I could. But I try to avoid crowds. In that situation, I'd have to work so hard to keep everyone else's thoughts out of my head that I couldn't appreciate what was happening around me. It's been forever since I've gone to see a movie, even. Netflix and me? We're like this." She held up two crossed fingers.

I nodded as I maneuvered the car back toward the house. "I guess that makes sense. I should probably invite Lust to come along, anyway. This is her case, too. Besides, I know how much she wants to win this thing."

Sloth was quiet for a moment, chewing thoughtfully on her hair. Then she said, "Am I a complete jerk for thinking she doesn't have a chance to win?"

Confused, I glanced over to my companion. Her cheeks were splotchy, and she looked like she'd just tasted something unpleasant. "Why do you say that?"

"Because this is America," Sloth said with a roll of her eyes, more than an ounce of disgust cutting through her words. "The show's about finding America's favorite sin, right? But Americans are so phony. We love sex, and we revile it at the same time. We *especially* hate women who enjoy it. And even though Lust is a perfectly sweet human being, women won't vote for her because they're jealous of her, and men won't vote for her because they can't have her. Of all the housemates, Lust is the only one I feel sorry for. When the show airs, she's gonna be the one that catches the most heat."

I frowned, though not because I disagreed with Sloth's assessment. I didn't like the idea of Lust being demonized on TV. "What about Wrath? Or Greed? Those guys are awful."

"They are," Sloth agreed. "But they're also guys. People overlook that kind of behavior from men. They'll get plenty of votes."

When we arrived back at the house, Sloth went up to her

room, but I was starving. I made a beeline for the kitchen but stopped when I got to the dining room. Gluttony had both a giant plate of Chinese food and a look of rapture on his face. He was so absorbed in his meal that he didn't even sense me standing there. When I spoke, he jumped. "Gluttony? Did you get that from the fridge?"

The big man stuffed a forkful of stir fry into his mouth. "Mary and Joseph, don't sneak up on a brother like that!" he exclaimed, clutching his chest in a faux heart attack. "My cholesterol's so high, it won't take much to send me to my grave."

I pointed to the food. "Was that in the fridge?" I repeated.

"Sure was," he said, shoving in another forkful. "It's not yours, is it?"

"Not anymore," I agreed. "I never would have pegged you for the jerk who steals other people's food. I thought you *liked* cooking."

Gluttony held up a fork to punctuate his words. "I like *eating*," he said. "If I have to cook to get good food in my belly, I will. But when there's leftover Chinese and nobody around to enjoy it? I'ma go in." He took another bite, his eyes rolling to the back of his head. "Plus, this food *magically* delicious, you know what I'm sayin'? This stir fry *slaps*."

"That's what I hear," I said. "Wights and Wongs is supposed to be the best Chinese in Odyssey." My stomach growled, reminding me of my mission of finding my own lunch. "Hey, you seen Lust around today?"

Gluttony gestured toward the ceiling with a fork. "She's upstairs. She ain't in a good mood, though. Fair warning."

I glanced upward, my brow furrowed. "Why, what's wrong?"

"Beats me," Gluttony said, returning his attention to his plate. "I'm just sayin', if you gonna go up there, you best be on your guard."

I stopped into the kitchen long enough to make myself a

sandwich. I went ahead and made two. History told me that even upset people could be consoled by food. I wrapped Lust's sandwich in a paper towel and headed to the second floor.

Lust's door was open. I peeked my head inside and saw her lying face down on top of her covers, still as a corpse. I knocked gently on the door frame. "Lust?"

Her voice was muffled. "Go away," she called.

I stepped into the room and padded over to the bed. "I brought you a sandwich," I said. "It's not much. Just salami and swiss." I waited for a reply. When it didn't come, I said, "Want me to leave it on your nightstand?"

"I'm not hungry," she said, turning her head away from me. I heard her sniffling. "Just go away, Pride. I want to be alone."

"Sure, I get it," I said. I set the sandwich on the nightstand. "But I need your help. I need to interview Charmaine Young tonight. And I need you to pretend to be a videographer."

Lust rolled over then, turning her face toward me. Her brow was creased in either anger or frustration—I couldn't tell which. Her mouth was twisted in a frown, her liquid eyes staring daggers in my direction. "What's your problem, Pride? I said I want to be alone."

"I know what you said," I countered. "But I also know how bad you want to win this contest. Talking to Charmaine Young will boost our popularity. I'm sure of it."

Lust groaned. "We already lost the challenge. Sloth, Envy, and Gluttony solved their case."

"We only lost some Good Samaritan points," I said. "We can still win over the viewers. You still want that, right?" When Lust didn't answer, I took a chance and sat on the edge of the bed. I rested a hand on her arm, and images flashed before my eyes: a white man in a military uniform. A South East Asian woman in a saree. They were slow dancing, gazing into each other's eyes. Then the image changed: the same man and woman, but much older, and no longer dressed in their finery. They were sitting on a couch, crying.

I withdrew my hand and pressed it against my chest. My fingers tingled. "Who are they, Lust? The woman in the white saree and the man in the military uniform?"

She was silent for a long stretch before she opened her eyes and folded her hands atop her stomach. "You saw them when you touched me?"

"I did."

She bit down on her lip, a single tear falling from the corner of her eye. "My parents," she whispered.

I swallowed. "Are they dead?"

A short, bitter laugh croaked from Lust's throat. "No," she said. "No, Pride, they're not dead. I'm just dead to them."

I fell quiet, half wishing I'd never asked and half wondering what I should say next. Finally, I slumped forward, dropping my chin into my hand. "Do you want to talk about it?"

"Does it matter what I want? I asked you to leave, but you're still here." She uttered that same mirthless laugh, and when I didn't move, she sniffled, a slow hiss of air escaping her lips. "We had a falling out, I guess you'd call it. It happened a long time ago. I've mostly made peace with it, as much as a person can come to terms with their parents disowning them. But today's my dad's birthday. I tried to call and wish him well—"

She choked on the last of these words, fresh tears seeping from the corners of her eyes. "He pretended he didn't know who I was," she said. "Said he didn't have a daughter and hung up the phone."

It's times like these when I felt most like an orphan. I had parents growing up, of course. I was adopted as a baby by a very charming, All-American couple who loved me very much and gave me everything I wanted. But my whole life, I never felt close to them. It was nothing they did. It was me. I felt like an impostor, like a…like a changeling. And while I never had the urge to seek out my biological family—after all, they'd famously disappeared with the rest of Sam Lovelace's cursed compound—a part of me felt I would never be complete without them. So I could only imagine what it felt like to be rebuked by someone who was supposed to love you unconditionally. Parents were the only people who could love you that way, really. Everyone else's love came with terms.

"I can't help who I am," she said, her voice raspy with grief. "And I wouldn't change even if I could. I just wish…I just wish it hadn't cost me my family."

We sat together in silence for as long as I could stand, which wasn't long. After a while, I got to my feet. "Party's at 10," I said. "We'll leave here around 9:30. I'm counting on you, Lust."

I didn't wait for a reply. I slipped out of the room and closed the door softly behind me.

seventeen

. . .

Since I had hours to kill before the party, I decided to pick up the reins to the cookie investigation once again. I found my dedicated camera guy in the kitchen, drinking straight from the milk carton while standing in front of an open fridge. When he saw me, he grimaced and wiped his mouth with his sleeve. "Sorry," he said. "Old habit."

This kind of stuff is why you can't eat over at just anyone's house.

"Get your camera," I said. "We have work to do."

The cameraman, whose name I still didn't know, set the milk back in the fridge and slammed the door. He gestured vaguely in my direction. "Where's the hot girl?"

"She's not coming," I said. "She needs some alone time."

The cameraman made a sour face. "You should bring the hot girl."

"Cameramen should be seen and not heard," I said. He seemed to get the message because he just gave a lame shrug as he retrieved his equipment and followed me out to the car.

Cameron Realty California was on some of the nicest beachfront property Odyssey had to offer. The building looked like it was made entirely of glass. Portia Cameron's office was on the top floor overlooking the beach. Her receptionist was a red-haired, perky thing who flashed a smile bearing too-white teeth when I came through the door. She glanced curiously at the camera guy, who made a "Don't look at me" motion, redirecting the woman's attention. Without a hitch, she looked at me, her smile growing even wider. "Good afternoon! How can I help you today?"

I gestured with my chin. "I'm here to see Portia Cameron."

The receptionist nodded. "And is she expecting you?"

I tilted my head to the side, bemused. "How should I know?"

The woman stared at me for a moment, her mouth agape. Then she smiled awkwardly and tried again. "Do you have an appointment?"

Ah. At least that was a question I could answer. "No. I'm not here to look at houses. I'm here on city council business."

The receptionist's shoulders sagged, and she offered me a tight smile. "I'm sorry. But Miss Cameron doesn't see constituents when she's in the office. If you have a city matter, there's a website where you can add items to the next meeting agenda. Would you like me to give you that URL?"

I shook my head and peered down the hall. I could just barely make out a glass door with the name "Portia Cameron" etched in frosted letters across the front. "Is she in? I'll just be a minute."

Without waiting for an answer, I headed toward the office door. The receptionist jumped to her feet, hurrying toward me. "I'm sorry, but you can't just go back there. It's not—"

But I had already opened the door to Portia's office. Crisp, conditioned air that smelled faintly of fresh paint blasted me in the face. As I stepped inside, a woman sitting behind a desk looked up in surprise. The receptionist ran up behind me, flustered, and blurted out, "I'm sorry, Miss Cameron. They wouldn't wait. They barged right past me."

Portia held my gaze a moment before flicking her eyes to my cameraman. Then she pulled her shoulders back and sat up straighter, glancing to her assistant. A stiff smile formed on her mouth. "It's fine, Lindsey. Thank you."

Lindsey muttered a final apology before slinking out of the office, the door clicking shut behind her. Portia was sitting forward in a leather executive chair, legs crossed at the knee, hands folded atop the desk. She was the picture of icy cold professionalism. She wore a black suit precisely tailored to her diminutive frame, and a cornflower blue silk blouse. White-blonde hair was pulled into a low ponytail. Her face was framed with blunt, perfectly straight bangs. Her lashes were long and black, her eyes ice blue, her lips painted deep red. When she smiled, there was no warmth in it. "You must be from that television show *Sinful House*," she said.

I jerked my head toward my sidekick. "Camera give it away?"

For all that her smile was frigid and unwelcoming, her voice was velvety. "Which one are you, exactly? Greed? Wrath? I know you're not Lust," she said, eying my outfit with a scornful chuckle.

"Pride," I said.

When she was done sizing me up, she relaxed. "Pride. I see. Well, it's nice to finally meet you. I worked with the network for weeks. I'm glad to see my labor finally paying off."

"You worked with the network?"

Portia smirked, her eyes glittering. "Who do you think found the property for the show? I don't just find properties for people. I find people for properties."

I sighed. "I don't know what that's supposed to mean."

"Every property is special in its way. Each house, apartment, condo—even office buildings attract a certain kind of soul. Put the wrong person in the wrong abode, and it's a disaster for everyone. But when the network contacted me about this project, I knew exactly where to put you. It was paramount that I not dump you just anywhere. We had to construct exactly the right look for America's 7 Deadly Sins. I didn't want you coming to my town and living out of some hovel. How would that make us all look? I sit on the city council." She tossed her bangs from her eyes. "I have Odyssey's reputation to uphold."

"Speaking of that," I said, taking a seat across from Portia. I was only mildly annoyed that she hadn't offered. "I've been asked to look into the fortune cookie fiasco at Wights and Wongs. I'm trying to figure out who might want to sabotage their business." I offered my own icy smile. "Some sources tell me you're a good person to talk to about that."

"What exactly do you want me to say about it?"

I shrugged. "I'd take a confession."

Now, Portia's eyes came to life as she laughed, a good-natured sound only slightly edged with something bleaker. "Do you *really* think I have time to mess around with a Chinese restaurant's fortune cookies? Really, if you're the best the network has to offer, I'm worried the poor people of Odyssey stand no chance of solving their petty crimes and mysteries."

I crossed my legs, shrugging off the insult. "I understand you proposed legislation that would put the Wongs out of business. Or at least force them to remodel or move. Something about their restaurant being an eyesore? Do you have anything to say about that?"

Portia placed her elbows on the desk. She leaned forward, resting her chin in her hands. Her nails were short and square and painted red to match her lipstick. "Do you have any idea how many Odyssey residents would love to see the Wongs go out of business? Not just because their building is hideous, which it is. Not just because their gimmick is tacky, which it is. No. That horrific building is sitting on prime real estate. That lot is worth at least twice what the Wongs paid for it. This town is booming, and our moneyed families want their piece of that pie. Leland Jordan, a long-time friend and client, tried to buy the property last year. He offered the Wongs $100,000 more than the property is worth. The Wongs wouldn't sell. And if you think Leland Jordan is the only person trying to get his hands on that property, you're wrong."

I chewed on that for a minute. From my years working with the police, I knew people were almost always motivated by two things: love (or whatever they mistook for love) and greed. If someone stood to make a wad of cash from the Wongs losing their business, that put them squarely in my crosshairs. "So, who else was interested in buying the property?"

But instead of answering my question, Portia pulled out a compact mirror and flipped it open. She raised her chin, examining her lipstick. "Help me understand. You're looking for the person behind the fortune cookie situation, right?"

I nodded. "That's right."

"And let me guess. You think someone might have financial reasons to shut down the Wongs. Is that right?"

I sensed she was going somewhere with this line of questioning. I'd seen the cops do it plenty of times. She was setting me up to knock me down, and I didn't like it. "It's a good theory," I said.

"It isn't." Portia's smile slid off her lips as she snapped her compact closed. "Look, I'll be frank with you. I don't like the restaurant. I would love to tear down that building and put up a chic swimwear boutique or a lovely tea shop. But the Wongs are small potatoes. I'm in the real estate business to make *money*. I have much bigger concerns, and frankly, if I *did* want to spend my energy on ruining that restaurant, I wouldn't do it with fortune cookies. I'd do it the old-fashioned way. With blackmail and bribes." Her smile returned, but now it had a wicked bite to it. "And that's how my clients would do it, too. What's the point of having money and power if you can't use it to get what you want?"

As much as I hated to admit it, my gut said Portia was telling the truth. A quick glance around her office made it clear what her priorities were. Framed photographs of expensive properties adorned her walls with their price tags etched into the frames in gold. All the properties were in the high millions. She also had framed photographs of herself with a senator, a business mogul, and even a previous first lady. Portia Cameron loved money and clout, and I couldn't imagine her wasting her time or reputation on fortune cookies.

And if this Leland Jordan and others of his ilk were like Portia—and experience told me they were—fortune cookies were way outside their wheelhouse.

"However." Portia leaned forward aggressively, an arrogant smirk curling over her lips. "There are *others* in this town who'd love to put the Wongs out of business for reasons that have nothing to do with money. And not that you asked for my opinion, and you certainly don't deserve it, but if I were you, I'd rule out the sharks with teeth. You're looking for the soft-hearted and tender. The predator that guiles you with its vulnerability right before it tears out your jugular." When my expression betrayed no understanding—I really had no idea what this woman was talking about—Portia huffed out a disgruntled sigh. "*Liberals.*"

I stared mutely at the woman in front of me, debating whether I'd heard her correctly. *Liberals?* I searched her expression for some amusement, some telltale sign she was pulling my leg. I didn't see anything. Finally, I blurted, "What are you *talking* about?"

"Liberals!" She threw up her hands in exasperation. "Progressives! Left-wing socialists! This town is bursting with them.

Ethical politics is the name of the game in Odyssey. Black lives matter. Trans rights are human rights. Animals are people, too."

I gaped at her, my brain unwilling and unable to process this train of thought. "Wait, are you saying that's a *bad* thing?"

Portia looked at me like I was a moron—and to be fair, I was starting to feel that way. This whole conversation had just taken a hard left. "I'm saying it's a *motive*. The only people in Odyssey who have it in for the Wongs *and* would turn to such a ridiculous *modus operandi* are those godforsaken animal rights groups. If anyone has the time and inclination to tamper with fortune cookies, it's those people."

I didn't like how she said "those people," but I couldn't deny my curiosity was piqued. "What do the animal rights people have against the restaurant?" I asked. But then I remembered something Linda had told me at the beginning. "The tidewater goby thing? They're endangered, right?"

Portia fluttered a hand cavalierly, her expression bordering on bored. "Oh, the conservation idiots. No, I'm not talking about them. The animal rights people. Different group. Much more robust."

"Okay. Well, what about them? What do they have against the Wongs?"

Portia chuckled. "The wights, of course."

I blinked. "The wights? I don't understand."

Portia pushed away from her desk, standing. She strode over to the window, turning her back to me and gazing out over the city. "I can see that. Outsiders don't understand Odyssey at all. The town is so much more than it looks, even from this vantage point. Take the Star of the Sea, for example. That statue is supposed to guard City Hall. But for the past several months, she's been traveling all over town, appearing in the most unexpected places. Last week she showed up in front of Tigh's Dry

Cleaning. The statue even had the audacity to wear a sneer instead of the beatific smile the artist gave her."

I blinked. "You have a traveling statue in this town?"

"Well, she isn't *supposed* to travel," Portia said. "And I'm sure there's a logical explanation behind her disappearances. Kids pulling a prank is my guess. But you never can tell with Odyssey. Tell me, Pride. Do you know much about supernatural creatures?"

I stammered, scratching a temple as my brows squished together. Another sharp left in this conversation. I was going to need a map to find my way back to the reason I'd come here in the first place. "Supernatural creatures? Uh, no. I can't say that I do."

Portia shrugged, unbothered. "That's okay. Most people don't. Which is why the Odyssey animal rights group has adopted their more inclusive stance. They're not just pro animal rights. They advocate for *all* sentient nonhuman entities. Animals and supernaturals alike. Since no one else is speaking up for the wights, they've added them to their platform. They want to end the indentured servitude of wights."

On its face, the idea seemed ridiculous. But the more I mulled it over, the more reasonable it seemed. If Walt Romanowsky had some kind of pro-wight liberation agenda, it might explain what he was doing at the restaurant after closing *and* why Ping attacked him. "Was Walter Romanowsky a member of these groups?"

Portia turned to face me, her brows knit together. "Who?"

"The man who was recently *murdered*?" I couldn't keep the incredulity from my words. "Surely you remember him."

Portia tsked, pressing her red lips into a hard line. "Oh, the hunter weirdo. I couldn't say. We ran in different circles."

I grunted. I bet they did. "Did the restaurant have run-ins with the activists in the past?"

"As far as I know, just demonstrations," Portia said. "Liberals with too much time on their hands virtue signaling with picket signs. You know the drill. Of the animal rights people gunning for the Wongs, Amanda Rutherford is the most vocal. She frequently solicits signatures for petitions—and she's not particular. She's an equal opportunity thorn in our flesh. Save the whales. Free the greyhounds. Reanimate the woolly mammoths, I don't know," Portia said with a roll of her eyes.

As much as I hated to admit it, a pro-wight agenda fit the crime. With a sigh, I climbed to my feet and ran a hand through my hair. "I appreciate your time, Portia. Thanks for the tip about Amanda Rutherford. Any idea where I can find her?"

"She runs a vegan bakery right by the beach called Bake Some Waves. Now, if you'll excuse me, I really need to get back to work." She gestured toward her laptop with a flick of her hand.

I smirked at the dismissal. I was already headed for the door, but maybe people like Portia always need to feel in charge. "Sure. And if I have more questions?"

She turned her attention to her computer screen and said, "Then you can make an appointment with my assistant. Good day, Pride."

———

Just as Portia promised, I found the Bake Some Waves bakery just a block from the beach. It was a cute building with a pink-and-white striped awning and hand-painted illustrations of ocean waves on the front door. A bell tinkled overhead as I entered, alerting the proprietor to my presence. A dark-skinned woman with her hair pulled into two apple-sized afro puffs greeted me. She was dressed casually in a t-shirt and jeans with a half apron tied at her waist. Her t-shirt read, "Vegans do it batter." I was sure that was a brilliant pun, but I didn't get it.

As I stepped up to the counter, the woman wiped her hands on her apron and pointed with her elbow to a display of frosted cookies. "The almond ones are half-off today," she said. "I added too much food coloring to the royal icing. Still good. But not perfect. So can I get you something?"

I folded my arms over my chest, fingers hooked under my armpits. I leaned toward the glass case, my stomach flipping with desire. My sandwich hadn't quite quelled my appetite, and the pastries looked phenomenal. Aside from frosted cookies, she had lemon bars, chocolate brownies, jelly rolls, hand-dipped macaroons, and an assortment of other things I couldn't even name. Everything looked scrumptious. "You've got quite a selection," I said. "I think I'll try a lemon bar."

The woman grinned. "You wanna try it, or you wanna buy it? I don't do samples."

"I'll take three," I said, thinking both Lust and Sloth would happily accept an offering of sugar. The woman selected the three largest from the case and put them in a bag, which she handed to me. "Anything else?"

"Yes," I said. "I'm looking for Amanda Rutherford."

The woman pressed a hand to her chest, her smile flickering almost imperceptibly. "I'm Amanda. And you are…?"

I gestured to my cameraman as I pulled a lemon bar from the bag. "I'm from a TV show that's filming in town. *Sinful House.* Have you heard of it?"

Amanda nodded carefully, her expression growing wary. "Sure. Everybody knows about the show." She paused, wariness sliding toward suspicion. "What do you want?"

I took a bite of the lemon bar. Tart, sugared goo melted on my tongue. My toes curled. "This is delicious," I said, hand in front of my mouth as I talked and chewed. "Wow."

"Thanks," she said. "Family recipe modified to be vegan. You don't know how hard it was to get the texture right." She paused. "So, how can I help you?"

I popped the rest of the dessert into the bag. "Sorry. Well, I'm looking into the fortune cookie debacle over at Wights and Wongs. Have you heard about it?"

Amanda nodded, misgiving easing from her face. "Of course. Everybody knows about that. I feel awful for poor Eric and Linda. They've worked hard for their success. The Wongs don't come from money or anything, you know? They're just regular people. I know how hard that is," she said, glancing around her own establishment. "I had to fight tooth and nail to get this property. But I had luck on my side. My store at least matches the aesthetic the city council wants to portray. Wights and Wongs doesn't."

I nodded. "Yeah, so I've heard. In fact, I was just talking with Portia Cameron about that very thing. She said the council has nothing to do with the Wong's troubles, though." I paused, wiping my mouth free of lemon crumbs with the back of my hand. "She also mentioned you're an animal rights activist. She said you've been pretty active in your campaign against the Wongs."

Amanda sighed, and the friendliness she'd exhibited just a moment ago seeped right out of her body. "Look," she said. "It's not a secret how I feel about the use of wights at that restaurant. Those creatures are sentient beings. They should be allowed to come and go as they please, not bound to serve shrimp fried rice to every Tom, Dick, and Harry that wanders in off the street. Besides, those wights are taking jobs that should belong to real people. Odyssey already has a growing inequality problem. Imagine if instead of using slave labor to serve their noodles, the Wongs hired local workers. A good job like that could feed a family, pay the rent. You know? It's not right what they're doing.

But." She held up a hand and shook her head. "That fortune cookie business? That's got nothing to do with me."

"Do you have any thoughts on who might be involved in it?"

Amanda pressed her lips together and made a motion like she was locking her mouth with a key. "My name's Paul, and this is between y'all."

I scowled. "Your name's Amanda."

Amanda snickered, hiding her smile behind her hand. "Right. I'm just saying."

I hated it when people were obtuse. Guessing games were my least favorite. "*What* are you saying?"

"I'm saying I don't know anything, and this interview needs to be over."

What little ground I had gained earlier in our conversation was quickly giving way and I hadn't learned a thing, so I decided to change tacks before Amanda threw me out on my ear. "Did you know Walter Romanowsky?"

Amanda was still a minute before her face softened and she breathed a little sigh. "I know the name. Terrible what happened to him. They found him in a freezer," she said with a shudder.

I nodded. "It is terrible. But I have a hunch the reason he was at the restaurant that night had something to do with the wights. Was he a member of any animal-rights groups you know of?"

Amanda's shudder deepened. "That guy? No. I don't mean to speak ill of the dead, but he wasn't exactly...he wasn't someone you'd *want* in your group, you know?"

"Because he was weird?"

Amanda grunted. "Weird is putting it mildly. That's not nice, but it's true."

"Can you think of any reason he would have been at the restaurant that night?"

The baker placed a hand on her hip and shifted her weight. "Look, I barely knew the guy. I don't think he was friends with the Wongs if that's what you're asking. And as far as I know, he didn't have business with the restaurant. But beyond that, who knows?"

Amanda seemed to be holding something back, but my intuition wasn't giving me any new ideas. It seemed everyone had the same thing to say about Walt. He was a weirdo and a loner who had no particular reason to be at the restaurant after hours. And yet, he'd been there. He'd *died* there. There had to be a reason for that.

Then an idea struck me. "What about the sous chef? Ping Lau?"

Amanda's brow darkened. "What about her?"

"Is she an animal rights activist?"

"I don't know," Amanda said. "I've never seen her at any of our demonstrations. Even if she were, why would she sabotage her own company? Wights and Wongs pays her bills, and a girl has to eat. Listen." Amanda's eyes softened as she gave her head a slow shake. "Don't tell anyone I said this, but in Odyssey? Activism is more like Slacktivism. We're not like PETA. We don't throw paint on people or destroy personal property. We write petitions. Sometimes we get published in the newspaper. And sometimes, *rarely*, we demonstrate. But actually *doing* anything isn't part of our MO."

I mulled all this over, trying to find my way through this information. I wasn't sure any of it helped. "What about the conservation people?"

Amanda's eyes narrowed. "What about them?"

"What can you tell me about them?"

Amanda turned her back to me, opening the faucet and wetting a cloth. When she turned back around, her expression was murky. "I wouldn't touch those people with a ten-foot pole. Around here, you get in bed with conservationists and you make some powerful enemies. Conservationism and real estate development do not go hand in hand. And real estate is the biggest cash cow in Odyssey. You feel me?"

"I do," I said. "I appreciate your candor. Thanks for talking with me. If you think of anything, though…" I reached for a napkin and scribbled my phone number on the back. I pushed it forward, and Amanda accepted it, folding it before putting it in a pocket. "Give me a call."

"If I hear anything, I will," she said. "But don't hold your breath."

eighteen

. . .

"Is that what you're wearing?"

It was 9 p.m., and I was sitting in the living room listening to Spotify while I waited for Lust to come down. Envy appeared in front of me, plucking the earbuds from my ears.

"What are you doing?"

She gestured to my outfit. "Is that what you're wearing?" she repeated.

I looked down. I didn't know the dress code for the party, but I thought I'd chosen well. I was wearing a pair of pressed khakis, a pinstriped shirt, and my favorite suspenders. I thought I looked great, but Envy's expression said I was wrong. My cheeks burn hot with embarrassment. "What's wrong with what I'm wearing?"

Envy frowned. "Well, nothing if you're going for that Old Navy clearance rack look."

I stammered, blinking back my surprise. "I'm not," I said.

"No, I didn't think so. Look, you can't accompany Lust to a party looking like that. She'll outshine you. I mean, she'll do that anyway, but you don't want to be *completely* mortified, do you?"

"I suppose not," I muttered.

Envy smiled, grabbing me by the wrist and pulling me to my feet. "Great. Then let's get you changed. I'm *positive* we can find something that won't make you look like Tilda Swinton's reject body double."

I didn't think I looked *that* bad, but nonetheless, I let Envy drag me up the stairs. But I drew up short when she tried to tug me into Greed's bedroom.

"Why are we going in there?" I asked.

Envy continued inside, throwing open the door to Greed's closet and rummaging around, pushing aside garments, checking out the inventory piece by piece. "You and Greed are about the same size," she said, chewing on her lips as she examined a pair of plaid trousers. "I'm pretty sure we can find you some pants in here."

I held up my hands and backed away. "Nuh uh. No way. I'm not gonna borrow Greed's pants without permission."

Envy chuckled as she rejected the plaid pants and moved on to the next pair. "What's the problem? We all live together. What's yours is mine."

I was pretty sure that wasn't how the saying went, never mind the fact that we were talking about *Greed's* things, not hers. "Come on, Envy. This is a step too far. Don't you think—"

"Aha!" Envy snatched a pair of trousers from the closet and held them up to better examine them. They were black with white pinstripes with a slight sheen in the light. She walked over and held them up to my body. "Your hips are a bit wider than Greed's, so these should hit you just above the ankle, which is *perfect!* You have very shapely ankles."

"Thanks," I said, "but I'm not wearing Greed's pants."

Envy floated out of the bedroom, stolen trousers in hand. "I think I have a blouse that will look great with these."

Still objecting to the pilfered pants, I followed Envy into her bedroom. She stalked over to the closet and began picking through her own clothes. "I *know* I brought it. It's one of my favorite blouses, and with your frame, it will just look so avant-garde."

"I don't wear *blouses*," I said, unable to keep the disdain from my voice. "Seriously, Envy, I appreciate the gesture, but—"

"Here it is." She removed the hanger from the closet and showed me the garment she'd selected. It was a bright blue oversized silk shirt—almost a tunic—patterned with white geometric line art. It clashed ridiculously with Greed's pinstripe chinos. "This is perfect."

"That is *not* perfect," I said. "I'd look like a clown. Thanks for trying, though. Honestly. I appreciate it. But no."

But Envy wasn't listening. "Let's go to your room. Can I style your hair? I love your haircut. I've toyed with cutting mine that way, too, but I don't think I have the face for it." She sighed wistfully as she reached out and ran her fingers through my hair, which I'd already styled. "Come on, Pride. Let me have some fun."

I tried objecting again, but Envy looped her arm in mine and tugged me into the hallway. However, she wasn't watching where she was going, and as soon as we tumbled into the hall, we crashed into Sloth coming up from the stairs.

I felt something cold and wet spilling down my shirt and pants. I looked down to see a dark red stain blooming through my clothes.

"Oh my God!" Sloth gasped as she bounced away from me, surveying the damage. "Oh, Pride, I'm so sorry! I wasn't watching where I was going!" She looked at the empty wine glass in her hand. "Oh, wow, I can't believe I did that."

"It's Envy's fault," I said, arms raised at my sides as the red stain continued to spread. "You couldn't have expected us."

"Your outfit's ruined," she said, staring mournfully at my midsection. "That'll never come out."

At my side, Envy smiled widely as she held up the mismatched outfit in her hands. "Thank goodness we have a spare!"

By the time I was changed into Greed's pants and Envy's blouse (we'd added leather boots and suspenders to the mix), Lust was already waiting for me in the living room.

She glanced up the stairs as I came down, her expression unreadable as she looked me up and down, taking in my outfit. "What have you done with my friend Pride?" she asked. "This is not the Pride I know."

"We had a wine accident," I said, blushing profusely. "I don't look too ridiculous, do I?"

"Not a bit," Lust said, and the look in her eyes said she wasn't kidding. In fact, her expression had gone from unreadable to *wolfish.* When she smiled at me, I felt precisely like a piece of meat.

Which, for some reason, I didn't mind at all.

"You look beautiful," I stammered.

And she did. Lust was dressed in a pair of skin-tight black and red striped pants, stilettos with razor-thin heels, and a black lace corset top. Her long, dark hair curled around her shoulders, and she'd chosen tasteful gold earrings to complement the look. Really, beautiful wasn't the right word. She looked exquisite. Breathtaking.

I was going to burst into flames if I blushed any harder. I looked away.

"We should get going," she said, glancing at the time on her phone. "We want to be fashionably late without missing all the fun."

I held up a finger. "One minute. You need a prop for tonight's ruse." I scurried off to find one of the cameramen who was done filming for the night. When I came back, I had a small video camera.

"Do you think this'll work?" I asked, showing the camera to Lust.

She smiled. "This lady's an aspiring actor, right? Yeah. I think that should work just fine." She stood up and took the camera, linking her arm in mine. With her body pressed to my side, she looked up, bright eyes twinkling. The funk she'd been in earlier was clearly gone. "Shall we?"

A frog was lodged in my throat. All I could manage was a nod.

———

The party was held at the Odyssey Regal Hotel, one of the fanciest hotels in the area. As we wended our way through the ballroom, I kept my eyes peeled for Charmaine Young. Not that I had any idea what the woman looked like. But Lust had set the video camera on her shoulder, and I was walking around smiling at everyone like a lovesick puppy. If luck was on our side at all, Charmaine Young would find us.

We had barely completed one lap around the ballroom when high, shrill laughter from the center of the floor snagged my attention. I spun on my heel to find a woman surrounded by young men, drinking prettily from a champagne flute. Unlike the other cast members who had shed their costumes for more comfortable attire, this woman was still dressed in her Titania, Queen of the Faeries costume. An elaborately curled wig strewn with glitter and flowers was topped off with a sparkling tiara. Her cheeks were painted an obscene red, and her fake lashes were so long, they hit her eyebrows. Her gown was made of sheer pink gossamer and fake leaves dotted with rhinestones to appear damp with dew.

Charmaine lifted her gaze from her admirers just long enough to catch my eyes across the room. When she saw me with Lust, and more importantly, Lust with her camera, the woman turned on a smile so bright, it burned my retinas to look directly at her. She pushed through the crowd of young men, dropping her empty glass at a nearby table as she sauntered over to us. She extended a hand to me first. "You must be Pride," she said, her words lightly accented in a manner I suspected was entirely affected. "I'm so glad to see you could make it! You didn't have any trouble getting in, did you?"

I accepted her handshake. "None at all. We were on the guest list, just like you promised. Allow me to introduce my videographer…" I turned to Lust, blind panic on my face. I had forgotten to arrange a fake name for her, and I couldn't very well introduce her as Lust or the jig would be up for sure. Luckily, Lust was quicker on her feet than I was. She stepped forward and extended her free hand. "Sita Varaprasathan," she said.

Charmaine slowly accepted Lust's handshake as she mouthed the syllables to the surname. I glanced away, choking down a chuckle at her consternation. "Should we get started, then?" I took Charmaine by the elbow and guided her to a quieter corner. "I don't want to keep you from your fans any longer than necessary."

The woman tossed a lock of curled, glittering hair behind one shoulder and nodded. "Excellent. So, how should we begin?"

"I understand you and Walt Romanowsky were friends. Is that right? How long did you know each other?"

Charmaine's eyes took on a faraway look. She licked her lips and sighed gloriously, her gaze neatly avoiding Lust, who was pretending to record the conversation. However, I couldn't help but notice that she had turned her body to a slight diagonal, undoubtedly to appear slimmer on camera. A pro move if I'd ever seen one. "We grew up together. We were in the same class at school. Both of us are from Odyssey, which is unusual now. We're so overrun with transplants. Back then, Odyssey was a tiny, nothing beach town, and everyone knew each other. Walt was a bit of an outsider. He didn't have a lot of friends. He was strange, but I found him charming in his own way."

I made encouraging sounds as I nodded, trying not to appear impatient. I'd heard enough about Walt's strangeness. "Charming how?"

The woman dithered and twirled a hand in the air as though trying to summon an explanation from the ether. "Oh, I don't really know how to say it. Walt was fanciful. The daydreaming type. He was the kid that doodled all over his math tests, you know? Unicorns and mermaids and things like that. Even in high school, he was the kid you found alone in the art studio painting during lunch."

I nodded. "That's right. He was an artist."

Charmaine pressed her lips together. "Yes. Watercolor paintings, mostly. It was an easy escape for him. A place for him to explore his imagination."

"I see. Mrs. Romanowsky says the two of you went on cryptid hunting trips together."

"Guilty as charged," she said. "My uncle was into cryptids. He passed away recently, God bless his soul. No one knew he was ill except—" She stopped short, then shook herself as though pushing away the sad memory. "Growing up, that was something my uncle and I did together. We were very close, right until the end. I was the only person in the family that shared his cryptid fascination. So when Walt suggested we go find a Chupacabra or the Jersey devil, I was game. It was fun. And it reminded me of my uncle."

"Did you ever find anything?"

Charmaine gave me a withering look. "Well, no. They're not real, you see."

I chuckled, chagrined. "No, of course not. Right. Well, can I ask you about this?" Lust retrieved the painting of the seal from her bag and handed it to Charmaine. "Have you seen it before?"

Charmaine took the painting, her fingers tracing over the seal at its center. "It's a portrait of me," she said, her voice soft.

My brows shot high in surprise. "A portrait?"

Suddenly, the cheerful facade that Charmaine had worn for us slipped from her features. She rolled her eyes, her cheeks puffing out in irritation. "All that supernatural business got *way* out of hand," she said. "It started off as a joke, but…"

"Hang on," I interrupted. "How is this a portrait? That's a painting of a *seal*."

"I know what it is." Charmaine groaned, pressing her fingertips to her forehead. "Do you know what a selkie is?"

I blinked and shook my head. "No. What is it?"

"It's a Scottish sea creature capable of shifting into a human," the woman said matter-of-factly. "I'm told they live as seals in the ocean, and when they come ashore, they shed their seal skin and live as humans." She looked around, fingers grasping nervously at strands of hair. "What does a woman have to do to get a glass of champagne around here?"

"I'll find you something in a minute," I said. "You were saying? About the portrait?"

Charmaine huffed, dragging her teeth over her bottom lip. "I asked Walt to paint me one day. This is what he came up with. I thought he was joking, but he said he saw the real me. That he knew what I *really* was—a selkie living as a human. He assured me he wouldn't tell anyone. It would be our little secret. I went along with it for a while, because why not? What could it hurt? But I should have set him straight. I should have made it clear everything we did together was all in fun. It wasn't *real*. But I never said anything. And I'll take that to my grave because that's how he got involved with those online idiots that pushed him away from me. And from his mom."

Now we were getting somewhere. "His mother said something about an organization he was involved with. Are those the idiots you're talking about?"

"You can't air that I called them idiots," Charmaine said quickly. I thought I detected a jolt of fear underlying her words. "Promise me you won't air that."

"I won't," I said, drawing an X over my heart. That wasn't a lie. None of this conversation was getting aired anyway.

Momentarily appeased, she turned to look over her shoulder, checking for eavesdroppers. When she found none, she heaved a sigh and continued. "A couple years ago, Walt got involved with this group. I don't know a lot about them except that they called themselves bounty hunters." Even beneath the electric red of her rouge, I saw a blush rise in Charmaine's face. "And not just any bounty hunters. They supposedly hunted supernatural creatures."

"Supernatural creatures?" I paused. "Like wights?"

Charmaine hesitated, then dropped her chin to her chest. "Sure. Wights, selkies, you name it."

With that simple revelation, things finally started to make sense. If Walt were a supernatural bounty hunter, it explained the secrecy, the camo outfit, and what he'd been doing at Wights and Wongs that night.

Walt hadn't been trying to *free* the wights. He'd been trying to *capture* them.

Aloud, I said, "How on Earth do you capture a wight?"

Charmaine blinked at me. "What's that?"

"A wight," I repeated, still thinking it all through. "If Walt went down to the restaurant to try and capture a wight for a bounty, wouldn't he have equipment with him?"

Still confused, Charmaine held out her hands, imploring. "Capture…? Well, I'm not sure, I…What kind of equipment?"

"I don't know," I admitted. "Ectoplasm detectors? EMF recorders? Night vision goggles? Assuming catching a wight is something you can actually do, you wouldn't just walk up and grab it, would you? They're non-corporeal. Your hand would go right through." I thought of the ghost girl and the many times I'd tried to touch or interact with her. My hands always slipped through as though she was nothing more than mist. "You'd need some kind of equipment, right?" I looked to Charmaine. "Did Walt have things like that?"

At my side, Lust sucked in a breath. "Yes, Pride. He *did* have equipment with him. The cat carrier they found at the scene. That had to be his—the Wongs said they'd never seen any of that stuff before."

I frowned, chewing on a lip. "That's true. And his mother said the police found handcuffs on his body. But can you handcuff a non-corporeal being, even with magic handcuffs? And what's the point of the cat carrier?"

For a moment, the three of us were quiet. Then Charmaine uttered a dry grumble, something between a mirthless chuckle and a groan. "You're not really filming this, are you?"

Lust and I exchanged looks. If I looked anything like she did, we looked like a couple of cats with canary feathers hanging from our mouths. "I guess the jig is up," I admitted as Lust dropped the video camera to her side. "The real camera crew is off tonight."

Charmaine waved her hand, the cloud that had settled over her evaporating as quickly as it had landed. "Oh, don't worry about it. I understand why you'd lie. You really had me going there for a minute," she said with a sly grin. "Devious bastards. You know, I've heard about the show. Seven sinful psychics living together? I auditioned with the casting director," she said with an important sniff. "But obviously, I wasn't a good fit, what with not being a psychic and all. Anyway, did you have any more questions about Walt? I really would like to get back to the party otherwise."

We were already moving back toward the center of the room, where Charmaine obviously felt most comfortable. I extended a hand, which the Queen of the Faeries graciously shook. "Thanks for your time. And don't worry—your secret's safe with me."

"What secret?"

I flashed my best impish grin. "Shapeshifting selkies must be hard to come by."

Charmaine gave me a puckish smile as she turned to drift away. But for a fleeting moment, I saw the twitch of a seal's long whiskers beneath her nose and caught the scent of seaweed floating on the air.

I blinked, and they were gone.

I watched Charmaine melt into the crowd, my eyes playing no other tricks on me. She was merely Titania, Queen of the Faeries, a dashing middle-aged woman pinning her hopes on a dream.

The whiskers and seaweed were just my imagination.

Right?

nineteen

. . .

"Come on, Pride." Lust had dropped the camera off in the coat room and was now tugging me by my shirt tails across the ballroom. "This is one of my favorite songs. Dance with me."

The deejay was playing something fast and fun from the 80s that I only vaguely recognized. But when we found ourselves in the middle of the dance floor, I folded my arms over my chest.

"I don't dance."

Lust rolled her eyes and put her hands on my arms, her fingers digging into my skin. "Of course you can dance," she said. "Just wiggle your hips to the beat. Come on."

I shook my head, refusing to budge. "I never said I *couldn't* dance."

Lust cocked her head to the side, still holding onto my arms. "So you just don't like to dance?"

"I like to dance," I said slowly. "Alone. In my room. Where no one else can see me."

She threw her head back, shoulders shaking at my expense. "You're so funny, Freak Show! Come on, I'm not taking no for an answer. I haven't had anyone to dance with in ages. No one's even looking at us."

Before I could object further, Lust wrapped her arms around my waist and pulled me close. Her hip bones jutted against mine as she rocked and shimmied to the music. She pressed her lips against my ear. "We're the best-looking couple here, you know," she teased. "Everybody wants to be us right now."

I wasn't going to look around to verify this, so I had to take her word for it. It was impossible to remain still as Lust wriggled her body this way and that. I hadn't had anything to drink, but being so close to Lust made me feel giddy, like bubbles were floating around in my stomach, but not in a bad way. Lust had a way of getting to me that was both thrilling and embarrassing. But at that moment, I didn't care. In a minute, I was laughing, and before I knew it, I was swaying in time with her, a stupid smile plastered over my face.

Next thing you know, we were dancing.

One dance turned into seven, and just as I was about to beg relief, a familiar voice rang out behind me. "Pride! Lust! You made it! I didn't know you were coming!"

I turned around to see Ruby Wong beaming at us, her eyes glittering with the joy of the evening. Unlike Charmaine, she'd changed out of her Hermia costume—at least, I didn't think Hermia wore zebra leggings and a t-shirt that said, 'How to Shoot Animals' with a camera icon beneath—and was carrying a plate of something bite-sized and delicious. I realized I was starving.

"Did you like the play?"

I disentangled from Lust's arms and scrunched up my nose. "*A Midsummer Night's Dream?* We didn't watch it. I can't stand Shakespeare."

Ruby's face crumpled, and her shoulders drooped, but she

recovered quickly. "Oh. I thought—well, never mind, at least you're here now."

"I'd never watch a Shakespeare play on purpose," I continued. "Especially the comedies. They're not even funny, and *A Midsummer Night's Dream* is the worst of all. Othello at least tackles real issues—racism, ageism, you know. But the comedies—"

I was about to launch into an anti-Shakespeare diatribe when Lust elbowed me in the side, effectively shutting me up. She cut her eyes at me with a "What are you doing?" glare before turning to Ruby. "Sorry we missed it. But tonight's just opening night, right? The other nights aren't sold out, are they?"

Ruby's face brightened again. "I don't think so! You should come. Maybe just don't bring Pride." She said this last bit with more than a hint of disdain.

A moment later, a young man sidled up to Ruby, slipping an arm around her waist. He looked to be Ruby's age, handsome in a non-threatening way, and wore a v-neck t-shirt beneath a purple leather jacket. Black jeans and white Chucks with no socks completed the outfit. He looked ridiculous. He kissed the girl on the cheek before turning toward us. "Friends of yours?"

She nodded, her cheeks glowing pink from his attention. Oh, young love. I knew absolutely nothing about it. "They're helping my parents with the restaurant." Turning to Lust and me, she added, "This is my boyfriend, Lee Jordan. He's studying forensic accounting at university. He played Lysander tonight."

We all shook hands, and Lust gestured to Lee's jacket. "Nice duds," she said. She probably meant it, too. My housemates had much more adventuresome taste in clothing than I did.

Lee did a little flourish that was so mortifying, it gave me dizzying secondhand embarrassment. He didn't seem at all fazed. "It's faux. I'm vegan."

That's when I recognized his name. I snapped my fingers, jabbing the air for emphasis. "Aha! Lee Jordan. I know you. You were the last guy to get one of those creepy fortunes," I said. "You got that prediction about family being detained, and then the FBI raided your house. How did that all work out? Everything okay?"

Lee shrugged and ran a hand through his hair. "Yeah, it all worked out. That whole thing was wild, though, you know? Crazy. Right, Rubes?"

Ruby nodded. "Yeah, a total nightmare."

Something about him was tickling the back of my mind, however, and it wasn't his taste in clothes. It wasn't even the fortune cookie notoriety. It was something else. "Is your dad still in prison?"

Lee shifted his weight from foot to foot, gaze darting around our little group as he obsessively cleared his throat. "Uh, yeah, I guess? He's awaiting trial."

I nodded. "What did the FBI get him on, again?"

Lust laid a hand on my arm, squeezing gently. "Hey, maybe this isn't the time," she said.

Lee licked his lips, jamming his hands in his pockets. "Embezzlement," he said. "Some shady real estate stuff."

That's when it struck me. "Your dad's Leland Jordan, right?" I turned to Ruby. "His dad tried to buy your parents' restaurant, right?"

Ruby gaped as her eyes shot wide, and she turned abruptly to Lee. "I have no idea," she said, crossing her arms over her chest. "Did he?"

But instead of answering, the snappy dresser chuckled nervously and said, "Look, I don't know what my dad's up to. His business is his business." His smile faltered as Ruby's face remained impassive. He jammed a thumb over his shoulder and stepped back. "Hey, I'm gonna go hit the head. Catch you later." He flashed us all a peace sign before making his way to the john.

"I think I'm ready to head home," I said, feigning a yawn. I really was exhausted, but mostly I was just done being around people. "Lust, let's go fetch the camera."

As I dragged Lust through the crowd toward the coat check, my housemate looked over her shoulder, blowing a kiss at Ruby. "I'll make it to your play. Promise!"

If Ruby responded to that, I didn't hear it.

Ten minutes later, we were outside, an ocean breeze riffling our hair and raising goose pimples across my skin. I was fumbling with the keys, trying to get the car unlocked. Lust was standing next to me—too close, as usual—yawning hugely and stretching like a cat. "I had a great time tonight," she said. "You were a great date."

I finally got the door unlocked. "It wasn't a date," I said. "But I enjoyed it, too."

And then, before I knew what was happening, Lust grabbed me by the chin and crushed her mouth against mine. I was so surprised, I don't even know if I kissed her back. When she pulled away, she was smiling. "Now, it's a date."

I stared at her, my face burning hot, my mouth dry. Before I even gathered my wits, Lust was climbing into the back seat, eying me with that wolfish grin she'd worn earlier. "You coming?"

I stood on the street, keys in hand, staring at my housemate. Her hair was mussed from the dancing, her lipstick smudged from the impromptu kiss. She looked amazing. Ravishing, even. The network didn't cast her as Lust for nothing. But even as my libido begged me to throw caution to the wind and have some fun for once, my heart denied me, breaking into a thousand pieces. I stood there like a mute fool, conjuring up memories of Shayda. Her smell. Her laugh. Her eyes. Her everything. Even one romp with Lust could cost me a future with the woman I loved.

On the other hand, there were no cameramen around to

capture this moment. If I jumped into the backseat with Lust, no one would ever have to know.

But I'd know.

I must have stood there too long because Lust's expression changed, cloudiness rising behind her eyes that disclosed something worse than disappointment. However, at that moment, I didn't know what it was. "I thought you liked me," she said.

I swallowed hard, shaking my head, fingers clenched hard around the keys. My heart was beating a mile a minute, and not just from desire. "You promised," I whispered, my voice thready.

"Promised?" She stared a moment, her lips moving, eyes blinking quickly as her brows knit together. But then her expression changed. Her forehead went smooth, and color rose in her cheeks. She swallowed hard, a vein in her temple pulsing. "I'm not *charming* you, you ass. I'm seducing you the old-fashioned way. But you know what? Never mind." She threw me a dark look as she buckled in, angling her body away from me. "Your loss. You don't know what you're missing."

The awful part was, I was pretty sure I did. "Lust—"

"Forget it, Pride. Moment's passed. Just take me home."

I stood there a moment longer, questioning whether I was the biggest moron in the world and even deciding that I probably was. But it was too late now. I said nothing more as I climbed into the driver's seat and started the engine.

We were pulling into the driveway of Sinful House when I finally recognized the look I'd seen in Lust's eyes.

It was betrayal.

———

I got a late start the next day. I slept in longer than usual, then went for a jog on the beach before the rest of the house was awake. Although I was getting used to the constant cameras and the need to feel "on," I still jealously guarded my alone time.

Plus, I was avoiding Lust.

I wasn't sure what had prompted her advance, but I wasn't ready to deal with it. I was even less prepared to deal with my rejection of her, which I still wasn't sure was the right move. Weren't you supposed to take a rebound lover to get over a relationship? But I didn't want to get over Shayda. I wanted to get her back, even though a little voice in the back of my head was saying on repeat, *She's never coming back.*

What can I say? There were reasons I was supposed to be in therapy.

Freshly showered, I was sitting on the couch reading a murder mystery when Wrath walked into the living room. He was dressed in Hawaiian board shorts with a set of enormous headphones hung around his neck. When he saw me, he snapped his fingers multiple times in quick succession.

"I was just looking for you," he said.

I set my book aside. "Yeah? What for?"

"Man, you ask a guy for a favor, and then can't even be bothered to remember it!" He looked mildly disgusted, but then Wrath always looked mildly disgusted. "I analyzed that file you asked me about," he said. "Took me longer to get around to it than I thought, but hey, it's free, right?" He snorted at his own joke. "You wanna come see what I found? Or should we wait for the nympho?"

My face flushed at the mention of Lust. "Wait for her? What, is she not here?"

Wrath motioned for me to follow him upstairs. "She left with Sloth about an hour ago. You guys weren't supposed to be working together today, were you? Have you solved your case?"

I shook my head. "No, still haven't solved it. But maybe whatever you found on the audio will help."

Wrath rubbed his hands together in wicked glee. "I was pretty pumped when I found it, man. Not that it was hard, though. Beginner stuff. We're not dealing with pros here."

I'd never been in Wrath's room before, so I was utterly unprepared for what awaited me. Stepping inside was like walking into one of those 90s-era hacker movies. Aside from the tiny twin bed shoved into a corner, Wrath's room consisted entirely of monitors, computers, gaming consoles, speakers, sound mixing boards, even a turntable. The room was dark, illuminated primarily with purple and blue neon lights that glowed behind his multiple monitors. It was also hot due to the heat output from all the electronics, and the ever-present whir of computer fans provided a semi-private background for our conversation.

Wrath pulled out his gaming chair and slid into it. "Computer, turn on." The monitor came to life, and an interface for audio software glimmered onto the screen. Wrath pointed to it.

"Okay, so this is the file you gave me. By the way—where did you even get that? Who uses CDs anymore? I had to order a drive from eBay to even read the file. That's why it took so long." He didn't wait for me to reply. "Anyway, you see this waveform here?" He pointed to a dense, wavy line. "That's the original audio track—chains rattling, ghosts moaning, organ music, stuff like that. Really amateur stuff, seriously. All the testosterone tried to leave my body each time I listened to this trash."

I thought Wrath had plenty of testosterone to spare, but I kept my mouth shut.

He pointed to the second waveform beneath the first. "This was embedded within your original audio. Separating audio tracks like this isn't easy, especially since the second track was designed to not be heard by the naked ear. But I was able to differentiate between the two tracks based on background noise spikes and overall frequency."

"I'm sure this is all very impressive," I said, "but aren't you a technopath? Couldn't you just, I don't know, snap your fingers and separate the two tracks?"

Wrath gave me a sullen look. "You need to appreciate my skill, man. Computers can only do what I *tell* them, okay?" He made an exasperated sound in his throat, then continued on. "Anyway, once I separated the two tracks, I listened to the new track. It sounded like whales humping, man."

I frowned. "What does that mean?"

"It was real slow. All the words were drawn out. That's how they hid the track without anyone noticing it. Pretty cool, actually. So I had to speed up the track. And once I did…" He grinned. "Well, I'll let you hear it for yourself."

Wrath hit the space bar, and the file started to play. The beginning of the track was blank. Then a thin, reedy voice spoke. "Freedom is the only truth. Freedom is your basic right. Win your freedom at all costs. Forget the danger. Escape."

The voice faded away, and Wrath hit the space bar again, and the audio stopped. He looked up at me expectantly. "What do you think? Cool, right?"

I worried my tongue against my teeth, brow furrowed in confusion as I thought. "What's that supposed to be? Performance art? Spoken word poetry or something?"

Wrath rolled his eyes and leaned forward, tapping fervently on the monitor. "No, man, you gotta listen with better ears than that. This is liberation philosophy, man. This is abolitionist stuff. Hardcore. Close your eyes this time and listen to it again."

I shut my eyes and let my head fall slightly forward. I took a few steadying breaths, hearing only the whir of the computers. Wrath hit the space bar again, and the audio played a second time. The ghostly voice repeated the same words. "Freedom is the only truth. Freedom is your basic right. Win your freedom at all costs. Forget the danger. Escape."

A shiver ran down my spine. I hadn't recognized the voice the first time because it was distorted and artificial, probably from either the embed or the extraction. But with my eyes closed, the voice sparked a recent memory, and an image rendered in my mind's eye, plain as day.

I knew that voice.

My mouth dropped open as realization struck. I opened my eyes. "Oh my God. That's—" I scrubbed my hands over my face, chuckling darkly to myself. "Wow, Wrath, you did it. You solved our case."

"Hell yeah, I did!" Wrath slapped his thigh with gusto. "This is for all the teachers and step-parents who said I wouldn't amount to anything." He flipped the bird at no one—or maybe everyone—in particular.

"Yeah, you saved our hide. Or at least you saved the Wongs' restaurant. I know exactly what happened with those fortune cookies. You know, Greed's not gonna like this at all. Looks like you guys are coming in last."

But Wrath barked out a laugh, shaking his head as he spun around in his chair. "We solved ours yesterday, man. You and Lust are the big losers this week. Eat my dust." He made a rude gesture and grinned maniacally. "Now, get out of my room."

I didn't need to be asked twice.

twenty

. . .

Since we'd already lost the challenge, I didn't feel any big need to rush over to the Wongs' place to tell them what I had discovered. It could wait a few hours more. It was more important that I cleared the air between Lust and me.

I wrote a note for her that said, "I'm waiting for you in my room. Please come at your earliest convenience. –Pride." I left it on her pillow.

The door to my room squeaked open a few hours later. I'd fallen asleep while waiting for her, and when she saw me bleary-eyed and only semi-conscious, she tried to ease out of the room as quietly as she'd come in. But I sat upright and beckoned for her to come back. "I'm awake," I said. "Don't go. I was hoping we could talk."

Lust shuffled into the room and perched daintily on the edge of the bed. She twiddled her thumbs in her lap, refusing to meet my gaze. "What did you want to talk about?"

I rubbed my palms over my face and pulled myself into a fully seated position. "I want to talk about the party," I said. "I hope you understand why I rejected you."

Lust looked up sharply then, her eyes narrowed. "I'm not upset that you rejected me," she said. "I'm upset that you thought I went back on my word. I promised I wouldn't charm you, and I didn't. I was just trying to get in your pants the way any regular person would. You made me feel like a jerk. *Again.* I told you I'd only give you one chance. I won't allow anyone to make me feel that way. Not anymore."

I tried to swallow but found that my throat was dry. This whole 'confessing your feelings' thing was so much harder than it looked when other people did it. "I didn't mean to make you feel bad," I said. "I just misread the situation. I didn't think that someone like you… I mean, you know…would be interested in someone like me."

"Why would I charm you if I weren't interested in you? That doesn't even make sense." Her words were sharp but edged with something else. Hurt.

"I don't know. To get something from me?"

"Of course," Lust said, her voice cool. "That's what you really think of me, even now. It couldn't be that I was just *into you,* right?"

Silence hung thick in the air between us. Lust still wasn't looking at me, and I wasn't sure that my half-assed attempt at fixing things was working. Why was it so hard for me to just say the words "I'm sorry"? That's all I needed to do. Apologize. But instead, I was making everything worse. I knew that, and yet I couldn't make myself say the thing that would get me out of it.

That, after all, was my biggest sin. Stupid, stupid pride.

Finally, Lust looked up, and her cheeks were damp with tears. "I was 22 when my parents stopped talking to me," she said. "And the worst part is, the whole thing was a giant misunderstanding. At least, that's the gracious way to look at it. It's the way I prefer to look at it. I would rather think my family misunderstood the situation so I don't have to believe they purposefully ignored the truth staring them in the face."

I said nothing, but I hoped she could read the interest in my face. I hoped she understood I cared about her story.

"My dad had this best friend. Growing up, I called him Uncle Rick. He was a friend of the family, and we did everything with him. We went camping, went to concerts, festivals, things like that. He was closer to me than some of my actual relatives. I loved him. We all did." She sighed, flipping her hair over a shoulder. "As I got older, though, I noticed Uncle Rick looking at me differently. You know what I mean when I say differently, right?"

I felt a flush creep up my neck. "I think I get the gist of it," I said. "He was noticing you the way people who like women notice you."

Lust nodded. "Exactly. Anyway, around the time I started college, Rick started coming around a lot more often. Sometimes even when Dad wasn't home. I realized pretty quickly he was coming around to see me. I thought it was flattering. A successful, older man, showing interest in me, you know? He flirted with me. Bought me gifts. We even kissed a few times. I was eighteen and insecure…but also curious. Not just about him, but also about what I could do with my abilities. So…I'm not proud of this, but when I got a little older, I charmed him. And the little gifts turned into bigger gifts. He bought me a car. I didn't think that much of it—after all, I had just graduated from college, and that's not an outrageous gift for a college grad. Not for someone like Rick, who could afford it. But my parents saw it for what it was. An older man trying to buy his way into a young woman's life. A young woman who happened to be their daughter. A daughter who, they realized to their eternal embarrassment, was a siren."

She swallowed as a fresh tear slid down her cheek. "My

parents confronted me about it. Asked if I had used my charms on Rick. At first, I said I didn't. Rick's attention began long before I charmed him. But they kept insisting. *'Rick's been a friend of the family for years! He never would have behaved this way on his own! You must have done something!'* And then I started doubting myself. Like, maybe I *had* charmed him from the beginning. My parents were mortified. Embarrassed beyond belief. I kept trying to explain how it all started, but soon, even I didn't believe it. I figured I must have done it."

She was crying openly now, shoulders shaking, her voice growing thick as her throat closed up. "I thought that was the end. But my parents went on vacation, and Rick showed up at the house again. I knew I hadn't charmed him that time. But he showed up at my house and told me he was in love with me, and he wanted to run away with me." She groaned at the memory. "I was so angry, Pride. So I did the only thing I could think of."

I gulped. "What did you do?"

She shrugged. "I called his wife and told her everything." She smirked at the memory, but there was no warmth in her face, and the grin slipped quickly from her mouth. "You should've heard the names she called me. I bet you can imagine. Instead of getting upset at her husband, the man she shared a life with, the man who vowed his life to her, she took out her anger on me. And my parents? They went ballistic. They were so furious that I tried to bust up a 'perfectly good marriage' that they stopped speaking to me. My father said he didn't have a daughter, and that was the end. I've tried for years to mend the fences between us. But they don't believe me. They won't listen. And before you ask, yes, I've talked about this in therapy. But some wounds just won't heal."

We were quiet for a long time, with only Lust's sniffles punctuating the silence. After a time, I said, "Is that why you want to win, Lust? Is your wish to earn your parents' love again? Because I hate to say this, but I don't think that's a prize the network can give you."

Without saying anything further, Lust crawled into my lap and wrapped her arms around me, face buried in the crook of my neck as she sobbed in my arms. I held her tight, not saying anything. I still hated comforting people. But Dr. Xena used to say sometimes silence is golden. I hoped this was one of those times.

When the tears finally subsided, she pulled away, wiping her nose with the back of her hand. She turned her eyes to me, and there was no longing or passion in that gaze. Just the simple desire of someone who wanted to be loved and accepted. Part of me wanted to be that person for her. Mostly, I just didn't know how.

"I'm sorry to put all that on you," she said. "I just feel like I can open up to you."

"Don't apologize," I said. "It's nice to be trusted with something intimate like that. It's awful what happened to you." I paused. "Can I ask you a very personal question?"

Her jaw clenched, and she pinched her lips, but then she relaxed and breathed, "Okay."

"That name you gave Charmaine. Sita something? Is that your real name?"

She grinned, wiping the last of the tears from her eyes. "That's my mother's maiden name," she said. "Sita Varaprasathan. I'm half Sri Lankan. I've always thought it was a beautiful name."

I waited to see if she would offer her real name, but she didn't, so I didn't press. That was part of the mystique of the show, anyway. Some mysteries weren't meant to be solved.

Lust brushed a stray lock of hair from her eyes. "Anyway, my point is this: I never use my charms on people I care about. I don't want my ability to push people away. But, I do want to find someone to love. Someone to be in a relationship with. But it's hard because once I tell people my secret, they always think I'm using it against them. Always. I don't know why. And believe me, it causes no small amount of shame and embarrassment. It's like —what, people can't just be attracted to me? It's easier to believe I manipulated their emotions than to think they just *like* me? I mean, I know I'm a lot to handle. But am I not worthy of love?"

I absolutely didn't know what to say to that, and as usual, I was quiet for too long. Finally, Lust reached up and placed a hand on my cheek, turning my face to hers. She was so close, I felt her breath on my skin. "You don't have to say anything, Pride. I appreciate your being here and listening to me."

Again, I felt the desire to say the right thing, to be the person Lust wanted me to be. Something about her made me feel warm and fuzzy, like a kid in pajamas on Christmas morning. But I wasn't sure what that meant.

Well, that wasn't entirely true. The more I thought about it, the more I knew one thing.

I wanted Lust to win this competition. Even if losing meant I didn't get Shayda back. I wanted Lust to have the chance at happiness she deserved. And I was going to do my best to help her get it.

"You know," she said, cutting into my thoughts, "when we get our new partners for the new assignments? That'll be weird. I don't think anybody else in this house can hold a candle to you. You really are a great partner, you know?"

"Speaking of that." Gently, I eased Lust out of my lap and took her by the shoulders. "I solved the case."

Lust blinked in surprise, sitting up straighter, her shoulders squaring. "You did? When? Who—"

I released her and held up a hand. "I'll tell all of you everything at the same time," I said. "What do you say we go down and pay the Wongs a visit?"

Lust hopped to her feet, all traces of sorrow gone from her face. "Let's get this show on the road," she said. "I'll go find the camera dude."

twenty-one

. . .

It was dinnertime, but as usual, we were nearly the only people in the restaurant. We were sitting at a large table where the wights had just brought us several platters of dumplings and a heap of noodles. The food smelled delicious, but I wasn't in the mood to eat. There was a lot to say, and I wanted to get it all out in the open as quickly as possible.

Lust and I sat next to each other, across from Linda and Eric. On the third side of the table, Ruby and Lee were making goo-goo eyes at each other. My stomach flipped over when I looked at them.

When the last of the food arrived, Linda Wong ripped the wrapper off her chopsticks and viciously snapped them into two pieces. "So, on the phone, you said you had something important to tell us. It's good news, I hope?" She popped a large helping of noodles into her mouth.

I sucked in a breath. "We've solved the case," I said. "We know who's behind the issue with the fortune cookies."

The Wongs exchanged a surprised look and then turned wide, incredulous eyes back to me. Their gaze darted between

Lust and me as though they didn't know who to look to for answers. Finally, Eric blurted out, "Well? Don't keep us waiting! Who did it? Who's responsible?"

My heart was beating loudly in my ears, but I kept my calm, turning my attention to Ruby. I kept my voice low and even when I said, "Before I reveal what I found out, Ruby, is there anything you want to say to your parents?"

The girl's brow wrinkled as she looked at me and stuffed a massive helping of dumplings into her mouth. "What are you talking about?"

I sighed. "Okay. Have it your way. But don't forget, I tried to give you an out." Reluctantly, I turned my gaze back to Linda and Eric. "It was Ruby. She was behind the whole thing from the beginning."

Ruby's eyes flew wide. "Me? That's ridiculous! This is my family's business! Why would I do something like that?"

"I wondered the same thing," I said. "But then I realized people don't always act in their own best interest. Sometimes, they act in the best interest of others." I looked to my left at the wights that floated past our table. "You were trying to free the wights. You brake for dolphins. You're a vegan. And since you admire the Kimballs so much, I guess you also believe the wights are sentient. So you wanted them free."

Linda frowned, dropping her chopsticks and dabbing her mouth with a napkin. "I'm sorry," she drawled. "But I have a hard time believing our daughter would sabotage our business."

Ruby looked at her parents, her eyes wide and round with her innocence. Her body trembled. "I *wouldn't*," she insisted. "You know I object to the wights being here, but this…this is…" She turned her gaze back to Lust and me. "How can you sit there and *lie* about me like that?"

"I took the audio from the restaurant's soundtrack to a friend who analyzed it for subliminal suggestions," I said, unfazed. I turned to face Linda Wong. "There *was* a message encoded in your soundtrack after all. At first, I was confused about what the message said. Because I *thought* the culprit was using the subliminal suggestions against your patrons. But the track said something about freedom at all costs. Escape. Strange message if it's intended for the patrons, right? But then I remembered what Portia said about the animal-rights people and how they adopted the wights into their cause. The message on the CD was never intended for the patrons. Ruby meant to implant that subliminal suggestion in the wights. She wanted them to fight for their freedom. She wanted them to escape."

"This is crazy," Ruby said. But I noted a tremble in her voice. Her facade was crumbling bit by bit.

I gave her a reproachful look. "It was *your* voice on the audio, Ruby. Do you want me to play it for everyone?"

She looked down into her plate, her shoulders sagging. I was glad she didn't call my bluff. I had no recording to play, but she didn't know that.

Eric and Linda were staring at their daughter, their faces unreadable. Ruby continued to stare away from us, muttering to herself, but Lee was silent. *Mysteriously* silent. His gaze was in his lap, and he hadn't looked up the entire conversation.

"I'm not sure I understand," Linda admitted. "Even if Ruby tampered with our audio, what does that have to do with the fortune cookies? That's what we need to understand. Who messed with them?"

I looked at Ruby, hoping she'd take over and explain herself, but she sat still and quiet, avoiding my gaze. I sighed. "No one," I said. "The whole thing was a ruse. No one received mysterious fortunes. No one saw the future. They were all in on it with Ruby."

Eric scrubbed his chin with the back of his hand, clearly agitated. "I don't understand."

"Everyone who claimed to get a strange fortune was friends with Ruby, had a motive, and knew a secret," I said. "They used the fortune cookie fiasco to reveal those secrets. It had nothing to do with predicting the future." The Wongs continued to stare at me, so I sucked in a breath and pressed on. "The first victim was Charmaine Young, a local actress. An actress who, by all accounts, would do or say anything for her 15 minutes of fame. Turns out, she knows Ruby. They each had leading roles in *A Midsummer Night's Dream*. If I recall correctly, her fortune said something about a family member getting sick and dying, right?"

Linda nodded. "That's right. Her uncle passed away not long afterward. It was a shock to the community. No one knew he was sick."

"Charmaine did," I said. "She and her uncle were close. I spoke with her at the ORCA party, and she admitted she knew things about him no one else did." I recalled Charmaine's face when she'd confided in me: *"My uncle was into cryptids. He passed away recently, God bless his soul. No one knew he was ill except—"*

She hadn't completed that thought, but I had enough evidence now to finish it myself. "No one knew he was ill except *me*."

I glanced over at Ruby, who was now white as a sheet, her eyes staring holes into her lap, just like Lee. "Then there was Lee Jordan." At the mention of his name, Lee momentarily looked up, bit his lip, and looked back down. "Lee's father is Leland Jordan. I heard from Portia Cameron that he tried to buy your property, didn't he?"

Linda Wong nodded. "He made several offers, in fact. Wouldn't take no for an answer."

I nodded. "Not too long after that, Lee Jordan claimed to get a fortune cookie about a family member being detained, and then the FBI raided his house." I looked over at Lee. "Lee, do you want to tell your side of the story? Or should I keep going?"

Lee looked up, his eyes twitching as he gulped and stammered. "Freeing the wights was important to me, but this was about more than just their liberation. It wasn't even about you, Ruby," he said, casting a quick look at his girlfriend, cheeks pink with emotion. "You don't know my father. He's a bastard. He'll take advantage of anyone to make a buck. When I found out he targeted the restaurant, I was pissed. I didn't want him to get his hands on this place, so I started snooping around."

Lee gulped and ran a hand through his hair. "I had suspected my father was doing illegal business for a long time, but I couldn't prove it. I don't know how to spot fraud or whatever. But I snuck into his office and downloaded some of his files. I shared them with my accounting professor, and he tipped off the FBI. After that, I had a feeling they were going to raid our house. So when Ruby asked for my help with the fake predictions, I agreed. I knew I had something I could offer. And I knew the wights needed all the help they could get."

I turned to Ruby. "That's the gist of it, right? You got your friends—actors and animal rights people—to share secrets. Things they knew were going to happen that no one else knew about. I never talked to any of the other 'victims,' but I'm guessing they all follow the same script. Do I have that right?"

Ruby was silent for a long while, and when she finally looked up, she had tears in her eyes. "I tried to talk to you and Dad about freeing the wights," Ruby said to her mother. "I told you I believed they were sentient. I told you I didn't feel good about keeping them prisoner. They're *slaves*, Mom! But nothing I said made any difference to you. So I thought maybe if you believed the wights were harming our patrons—cursing them with unlucky fortunes—" Ruby closed her eyes, squeezing out more tears. "I had to turn to the one thing I knew you really cared about. The customers." She was crying freely now, wiping her face and sniffling as she shrank back into her chair. "I tried to talk to you. I really did. But I'm not sorry. I did what I had to do."

Linda stared at her daughter, mouth agape, methodically popping her knuckles as she mulled over the admission. "You convinced all those people to *lie* about the fortune cookies? The whole thing was fake?"

Ruby nodded dolefully. "Like Pride said, I convinced Charmaine to do it because she knew she'd be on TV. She loves the attention. Convincing Lee to do it was easy, obviously. Plus, he had a great secret to share. The others agreed for various reasons. Some of them are animal-rights advocates, just like me. Others were actors I knew from ORCA, like Charmaine. And some of them just wanted to see our business go away."

Eric, who had been mostly silent this whole time, cleared his throat and leaned forward, elbows on the table, as threatening as anyone could look seated behind a bowl of noodles. "You did serious harm to our family business, Ruby. Do you understand that? How do you expect we'll pay for college now? Where do you think the money comes from to send you to ORCA? Did you think any of that through before you conspired with our enemies to destroy us?"

I cringed at the harshness of those words, but Ruby sat up taller, thrusting out her chest and lifting her chin in defiance. "I did think about it," she said. "And I decided our financial comfort isn't as important as their basic rights. Free them. Our restaurant doesn't need a gimmick. People will support us for our food alone. Find someone who can release the wights from this contract. I *know* it can be done. If you can find someone who sells curses, you can find someone to break them. You just have to *want* to do it. You can find *anything* online," Ruby rushed to add.

Linda and Eric fell silent, staring down into their plates. After a while, Lust broke the silence with a gentle sigh. "Your daughter didn't mean to hurt you," she said, a quiver in her voice. I looked over at her and saw the emotion in her face. I knew she was thinking about her relationship with her own parents. "She was following her heart. She's learning to be her own person who cares passionately about animals—and that includes the wights. Maybe she went about it in the wrong way," Lust said, turning an admonishing glance to the teenager, "but you should be proud of her. She's coming into her own. She's figuring out her power and how to use it in the world. She's a change agent, that one. Heck, if she doesn't have a career in acting, she definitely has one in politics!"

After another drawn-out silence, Linda turned to face her daughter, her expression softer than before. "What you did was wrong, but Lust is right about one thing. You are blossoming like a flower, and we should have taken your concerns seriously. I'm sorry about that. And if it means so much to you, your father and I will find a way to release the wights." Eric opened his mouth to object, but Linda stared him down hard until he looked away, shoulders slumped in defeat. "In the future, however, I recommend you find other ways to reach people who don't listen. Wrecking their livelihood is a bit extreme." She raised an eyebrow and stared pointedly at her daughter as she said this last part. "And Lee?" Lee looked up, a hangdog look around his eyes, his Adam's apple bobbing up and down. "I don't know if your father deserved what he got, but I'm sorry your family is going through hard times. And I forgive you for your participation in all this."

Eric leaned back, folding his arms across his chest. "I still have one last question, though," he said, his brow furrowed. "Why was Walt Romanowsky in my freezer?"

Lust and I exchanged looks, unsure where to begin. "We don't have definitive answers there," I said. "But from what we can tell, it looks like Walt was a bounty hunter."

Eric stammered. "A bounty hunter?"

"Yes," I nodded. "A *supernatural* bounty hunter. Apparently, he was here to collect the wights. We don't know how and we don't know for whom. But we suspect Ping tried to protect the restaurant. So when she saw what he was up to, she hit him over the head with a frying pan and, in her panic, dragged him into the freezer."

Linda pinched the bridge of her nose, closing her eyes, her shoulders falling low. "If you figured that out on your own, it's only a matter of time before the police reach a similar conclusion."

I bit down on my lip, glancing around to make sure no one could overhear our conversation, but the restaurant was still mostly empty. "I don't think they've figured it out yet," I said. "But you're right. Unless they're profoundly inept, they'll get there eventually. You all should be prepared for that. I know how much she means to you. And this restaurant."

The Wongs' faces blanched as they digested that information. Not only were they going to lose the wights as an attraction, but they were also likely to lose Ping as their sous chef. And they still had the city council and real estate magnates after them like hawks.

It wasn't looking good for the Wongs, and I felt terrible for my part in that. But no one ever promised justice would feel good.

What can I say? Even in Odyssey, California, life's not always a beach.

twenty-two

. . .

While the Wongs, Lust, and Lee Jordan finished their food and discussed the implications of getting rid of the wights, I went outside to stretch my legs and get some fresh air. It was a pleasant afternoon. The sky was cloudless, and a gentle breeze was blowing off the Pacific Ocean. I had half a mind to take a stroll down to the beach, but I wasn't dressed for it. I hated getting sand in my tennis shoes.

Enjoying the sunlight on my skin, I ambled around to the side of the building, admiring the property for what it was. I could see why so many real estate magnates wanted to get their hands on it. It was just a short walk to the ocean, and it was conveniently located close enough to Pacific Coast Highway for easy access, but not so close that highway noise was a nuisance. As I was making my way toward the back of the property, however, something stopped me in my tracks.

I blinked, narrowing my eyes as I pondered whether sunlight was playing tricks on me. Up ahead, a shadow danced along the wall of the restaurant. I knew that shape, but my mind wouldn't grasp it. I'd lived in California beach communities most of my life, and I'd never seen the creature capable of throwing that shadow.

It was a fox. The pointy ears, sharp little snout, and elegant legs gave it away, but there was something strange about the shadow. It didn't have just one tail. I counted approximately nine, each moving independently from the others, the shadow slithering on the wall almost like a gaggle of serpents.

I was still staring at the shadow when a voice behind me said, "You see it too, don't you?"

I didn't need to turn around to know who the voice belonged to. The ghost girl sidled up beside me, her hands in her pockets, her head tilted to one side as she watched the shadow undulating with the afternoon sunlight. "Do you know what that is?"

I shook my head. "I'm guessing it's not my imagination," I said.

The ghost laughed. "Of course not, silly. If it were your imagination, I couldn't see it, too. But I can see it, all right. That's a nine-tailed fox."

I couldn't take my eyes off the shadow. "Nine-tailed fox? I've never heard of such a thing."

The ghost girl sucked her teeth and folded her arms over her chest, glowering incredulously at me. "That's because they're not animals you can find at the zoo," she said. "They're supernatural creatures. Pretty rare here in America. You mostly only find them in Japan."

I was so used to the ghost telling me random facts about wildlife that I often tuned her out. But in light of all my recent discoveries, this information was noteworthy. "A supernatural Japanese fox? What would one be doing in Odyssey, California?"

The ghost scratched her chin, thinking. "Hard to say. They like adventure and playing tricks. Most often, they shapeshift to look like humans. They especially like to be female humans. Sometimes, they try to trick rich men into marrying them. The problem is, even in their human form, they can't get rid of all of their tails. They always have at least one they can't transform." She grinned and looked up at me, her eyes wide and sparkling. "Did you know that if you put magical handcuffs on a supernatural creature, they shift back to their natural form?"

I stared at her, my mouth softly agape as my brain processed that. "Is that right?"

I was about to ask another question when the creature casting the shadow stepped into view, interrupting my thoughts.

It wasn't a nine-tailed fox, though.

It was Ping.

I glanced at the shadow and back at Ping and then to the shadow one more time. When Ping saw what I was doing, the color drained from her face, and she backed away from me, holding her hands palm out as if warding me away. "It's not what you think," she said. "It's not—I mean, I'm not—"

"I'm not going to hurt you," I said. At my words, Ping stopped moving, hands still up in the air. "I have no interest in supernatural creatures. Not even nine-tailed foxes."

She hesitated, mouth opening as she undoubtedly prepared a retort. But then she dropped her chin to her chest, her hands falling to her sides. She knew she'd been caught, and I knew I was right. Or, more accurately, the ghost was right.

Ping was a nine-tailed fox masquerading as a Chinese woman.

"Walt wasn't here for the wights," I said. I hadn't even realized I would say these words until they were already out of my mouth. All the pieces were finally falling together, and I felt stupid for not having realized it before. Of course, I didn't have all the information before. Who knew nine-tailed foxes could be running around in Odyssey, California? "Walt was looking for *you*. That's why he had the handcuffs and the cat carrier."

I glanced at the ghost, who was smiling and nodding,

confirming my thoughts. "They weren't just any handcuffs," I continued. "They were *magic* handcuffs. He intended to cuff you, forcing you to shift into your true form. And then he was going to put you in the cat carrier and take you away."

Ping's hands were folded beneath her chin as her lips quivered and tears gathered in her eyes. "People like him are dangerous," she breathed, her voice strangled. "He's not good. Those people aren't good! I've heard stories. Things they do to supernaturals. Experiments. Torture. I couldn't let him take me. I'd do anything to fight for my freedom. To escape."

With these last words, her face transformed into a snarl. And for a fleeting moment, I saw Ping as she truly was—a ferocious creature terrified for her life.

A ferocious creature who'd been bombarded with subliminal messages about escaping. About protecting her freedom at all costs. And about forgetting the danger.

I tilted my head back as I laughed toward the sky. Now, finally, everything made sense. "Ruby's subliminal message got to you. She meant to force the wights to fight for their freedom and escape. But she infected *you* with that message, too. That's why you forgot the encounter. You forgot the danger." I leaned my head to the side. "But you seem to remember now. I guess the subliminal effect wore off since the CD hasn't played since I took it."

Ping was still shaking like a leaf. Hands up to show her I meant no harm, I took a cautious step toward her. When she didn't move away, I reached down to lift the hem of her dress. Sure enough, I saw a flash of gold and red fur, the one tail she couldn't hide.

Indignant, she swatted my hand away and stepped back, cheeks glowing red with embarrassment. "That's not for you to see," she said. "Please."

I sighed and stuffed my hands into my pockets. "Listen. The

police will come for you soon. They'll eventually put two and two together and determine you were responsible for Walt's death. I don't know what those supernatural bounty hunters want with you, but I *can* tell you what the police department will do with you as a human. They'll put you in jail for a long time. And just take it from me, that's not a place you want to be." I tried to smile, but it felt false, so I let it fall away with another sigh. "It's time for you to get on out of here, Ping. Change back into a fox. Get as far away from here as you can. I can't tell you what to do after that. The future is up to you. But I think your time in Odyssey is over."

Ping was still for a moment, no doubt mulling over everything I'd said. But after a while, she looked up, sad eyes down-turned, lips trembling. "Tell them goodbye for me?" she asked.

I nodded. "I will."

Without another word, the trembling woman lowered her head, and her body began to shrink, dwindling down to the size of a large house cat. Red-gold fur shot with silver sprouted from her skin. Her body was compact and strong, with liquid amber eyes that glittered with intelligence. Best of all, nine glorious tails fanned around her like a halo, catching the light from the sun.

She was miraculous.

When her transformation was complete, she posed for me, showing off her otherworldly beauty. Her mouth opened, and her tongue lolled in what I think was laughter. In the next moment, she skipped away, disappearing into the shadows where I was unlikely to ever see her again.

"Well, I guess that's that," I said to the ghost. "Your dumb facts paid off for once. Thanks for—"

But when I turned to finish my thanks, she was already gone.

twenty-three

. . .

Two weeks later, all the housemates were sitting in the living room, laughing and talking, sharing a tray of appetizers Gluttony had kindly whipped up for us. The TV was on, but nobody was watching anymore. Tensions were too high.

Today was the day. The first episode of *Sinful House* had finished airing just two hours ago. Viewers all over the country had seen us for the first time, and we were on pins and needles waiting to hear how the show was received.

"I'm so nervous, I could croak," Lust said as she dropped beside me on the couch, a fresh glass of pink champagne in her hand. "I haven't been this nervous since I took my first pregnancy test in high school."

I couldn't tell if she was joking, so I let that comment slide. "I have no doubt the public will love you," I said. "They showed all your best moments this episode. And you look amazing on camera."

Lust blushed and took a deep sip of her drink. "You're just being nice."

"No, I'm not," I countered. "I don't do that."

"That's true," Sloth said from across the room. "Pride is a no-nonsense kind of person. And I don't just know that because I can read minds."

"Get out of my head!" I snapped playfully. "You're leaving a trail of crumbs in there."

Sloth poked out her tongue. "No promises."

The front door opened, and everyone looked over to see Tricia Woodward floating through the entrance, a dazzling smile plastered on her face. As usual, she was immaculately dressed in a simple linen dress, white Keds, and hair pulled into a neat ponytail. She had a laptop tucked under her arm, and a purse slung over her shoulder.

"Hi everyone!" She pitched her voice into her trademark singsong, drifting into the living room and taking her place on an overstuffed love seat. "So, did you all watch? What did you think?"

"The editing was way unfair, man," Wrath submitted, his face twisted in a scowl. "I hardly got any screen time, man. So wrong. Plus, every scene I was in made me look like a total skeeze!"

Tricia chuckled as she crossed her legs and bounced her foot. "Maybe that's because, generally speaking, you act like a total skeeze." Her smile widened. "What about the rest of you? How do you feel about how the first assignment went?"

"I agree with Wrath," Greed said. "I definitely think our team deserved more screen time than we got. Also, the editors played up the animosity between us and the other housemates. Like that scene where Wrath called Lust a nympho? That could have been left out completely. It just made him look bad. And *me* by association."

Lust snorted, winding a lock of hair around a finger. "But he *did* call me a nympho," Lust said. "Why should that have been edited out?"

"Because it made me look bad!" Wrath shouted.

Lust sucked her teeth and smirked. "If you wanted to be portrayed in a better light, maybe you should have acted less like a twit."

Tricia held up her hands to interrupt the argument. "All right, all right. I'll take that feedback back to the editing room. Can't promise anything, though. I don't think the network will want to mess with a good thing. Preliminary numbers show our ratings were *sky high*." Tricia's eyes were large and round, glittering with the good news. "In fact, I have a feeling this may be the network's best premiere so far."

Whistles of appreciation fluttered around the room, and even I couldn't help but feel a bit chuffed by this information.

"How long do we have to wait for the official numbers?" Sloth asked. Her face was damp with nerves or excitement, and she reached for her ponytail, inching its tip toward the corner of her mouth. "I mean, I know one successful episode doesn't mean much, but I still can't stand the suspense. Am I the only one who wants to know?"

"Of course not," Envy said. "I'm so nervous I can't even keep food down. I'm so jealous of all of you who can just snack on Gluttony's food like it's no big deal. I wish I could enjoy it."

Gluttony gestured toward the tray of finger rolls sitting on the coffee table. "Try one," he said. "I put magic in them to keep the anxiety down. Really, Envy. You ought to know better. After all this time we worked together, you still don't know how I operate?" He shook his head. "Some people just don't learn."

Envy reached for a roll and popped it in her mouth. She was still chewing when she said, "I don't feel anything."

Gluttony glowered at her. "Give it a minute, dang."

Suddenly, Tricia's phone rang. The room fell silent. Wrath snapped his fingers, and the television shut off. Tricia pressed a finger to her lips as she put the phone on speaker, setting it on her lap. "Hi, it's Tricia. You're on speaker."

The caller's voice was barely audible over the background noise on their end. It took me a minute to realize the caller was in a room full of people shouting. *Celebrating.* "Have you seen the numbers, Tricia? We did it! *Sinful House* is officially the most successful premiere the network has produced to date!"

Around the room, the housemates pressed their hands to their mouths, eyes wide. We were so quiet, you could have heard a pin drop.

"That's *amazing* news," Tricia exclaimed, making victory fists she pumped into the air. "I wish I could be there to celebrate with you guys. But I'm here at the house now. Everybody's waiting with bated breath for audience responses to start rolling in."

"I'm sending you some initial numbers and sentiment scores now," the man on the other end said. "Do you want to read them for yourself, or should I share the news with everyone at once?"

Tricia blinked in surprise, sitting up straighter. "We have comments already?"

"We do. Shall I go through the highlights?"

Tricia nodded, her hands clasped at her chest as she bit down on her lower lip. "Sure, do us the honors. We're dying here!"

The voice on the other end cleared his throat elaborately, clearly enjoying every minute of this fresh torture. "Overall, viewers identify the least with Wrath. Only 10% of audience sentiment was positive about him. Viewers liked Gluttony but say they didn't get to see enough of him to know for sure. Lust and Greed were both perceived neutrally, with very few viewers loving or hating either. Surprisingly, Sloth was well liked among all age groups, though she performed better among female viewers. Envy was also well liked, and viewers are speculating whether summoning is the extent of her abilities. And topping the charts as the most-liked housemate is Pride with a positive sentiment score of over 80%! Well done, all of you!"

Tricia hit the disconnect button on her phone. When the line went silent, the room erupted into shouting.

"Oh my God, Pride! Congratulations!"

"This is a sham, man. Last place? This is obviously Asian oppression, man. I'm being stereotyped!"

"Wow, what a ride. I wonder what'll happen next week."

"This whole thing was rigged. I want a recount."

I was sitting there like an idiot, unable to process what had just happened. It didn't mean anything. Audience sentiment mere hours after the first episode didn't mean a thing in the grand scheme of things.

And yet? It meant something to me.

Lust pulled me into a hug, lips pressed against my ear in a half whisper, half kiss. "You deserve it, Pride. Congratulations."

I disentangled myself, swallowing hard around the lump in my throat. My tongue felt huge in my mouth. "Thanks," I said. "I got lucky, I guess. They edited me well. As the show wears on, you'll pick up fans. I'm sure of it."

"Don't worry about me." She was grinning now, a twinkle in her eye. "I'm pulling out all the stops on the next assignment. We've still got a *long* way to go before any of us is crowned America's Favorite Sin!"

She slapped me on the back before standing and raising her glass in a toast. "To Pride! Freak Show outdid us all. But for the next challenge, let's show America how super sinful the rest of us can be!"

The room broke into shouts of hearty agreement. Someone shoved a glass of champagne in my face. I took a small sip and then a bigger one. Moments later, I'd downed the whole thing and was going for a second. The celebration was infectious, and before I knew it, I was laughing and taking bets on who would win the next challenge.

My money was on Lust, but who could say? Americans enjoyed all kinds of sinful pastimes.

As I downed my third glass of champagne, I was feeling good. Positive, even. Maybe coming on this stupid show wasn't the worst thing that ever happened to me, after all.

———

"Pride? Can I talk to you a moment?"

Tricia pulled me upstairs, away from the other housemates. Once in my room, she closed the door behind her. "I'd like to read you some of the viewers' comments about you. These were taken from Twitter and our Facebook page." She looked down at her phone screen and began to read. "*Pride is my favorite housemate by far. Awkward and weird, just like me. I hope the show investigates that stuff with the commune that vanished. I'd never heard of that before.*"

She looked at me like she wanted me to say something, but I had nothing to say to that, so I kept quiet.

Tricia continued reading.

"*I thought I recognized Pride from that documentary about the missing artist commune! I would love to know more about that. It would be so rad if Pride looked into it. Maybe a personal challenge for the future?*"

Tricia looked up at me, her face carefully blank. "There are dozens more like this," she said. "Viewers want to know more about what Anne Lovett found when she went up to that commune. Where those people went. What happened to them."

"There are plenty of books and documentaries about it," I said. "They can find out anything they want. All that information is available."

"It's available," Tricia agreed, "but it leads nowhere. There's no closure. No one has ever found that lost commune."

I shrugged. "Some mysteries aren't meant to be solved."

"And some are." Tricia dropped the phone to her side and took me by the elbow, leading me to the bed, where she sat on the edge. "Of all the documentaries that exist, *none* of them include you. At most, they show still photographs of your face. But none include your story. No interviews with you on the matter exist. But people want to know. What became of the baby? What does the lone survivor think happened? What's that story?"

I had a bad feeling about what Tricia wanted. I stared her right in the face. "Tell me what you're getting at, Tricia."

Her face tightened. "While you live here, the network wants you to investigate—on camera—what became of the lost commune. Where did those people go? What was really going on there? There's no one better to unearth that story than the innocent soul left behind—the baby found alone and crying who happened to grow up to become a psychic who sees ghosts."

"No."

Tricia sighed. "Don't you think they're related? Don't you wonder if whatever happened to those people is the reason you have the talents you do?"

I folded my hands in my lap, shaking my head. "I've never thought about it."

"Don't you wonder," she pressed on, "if the child ghost that's visited you your whole life has something to do with your mysterious past?"

I stared at her, questions running through my head like wildfire. How did Tricia know about the ghost girl? None of the footage of me talking to her—or even about her—aired. "How do you—"

"I did my research before I cast you," she reminded me, her voice gentle. "I'm not an idiot. And neither are our executives or producers. They know the money shot when they see it." She licked her lips, twisting her body to face me more fully. "Let me say it this way, Pride. The network *invites* you to look into your past. It'll make for great TV. But if you don't choose to do it on your own terms, they'll find other ways to get what they want. Am I being clear?"

I chuckled, a bitter sound in the back of my throat. "Sure, Tricia. I understand. You're blackmailing me."

"It's not blackmail," she corrected. "It's *encouragement*. Look into your past, Pride. Investigate what happened to those poor people. Even if you don't find out, you'll be better off for having tried."

I knew perfectly well this conversation had nothing to do with my wellbeing, but I also knew better than to press the matter. "I'll think about it," I grunted.

"You do that," she said, standing up. "And who knows, Pride?" She flashed me a thousand-watt smile. "Maybe you'll even thank me later."

———

As I was returning to the party, I ran into Sloth in the hallway.

"There you are," she said. "I was just looking for you." She examined my face, her head cocked to the side. "Are you okay? For someone who just won this week's vote, you sure don't look great."

"I'm fine," I lied, still thinking about Tricia's marginally veiled threat. "What's going on?"

Sloth sucked in a breath, twisting the end of her pigtail around a finger. "It's Mrs. Romanowsky. She's asked for my help —and I think I'd like *your* help."

I blinked. "Help with what?"

"After everything came out about Walter being a bounty hunter, Mrs. Romanowsky did some snooping. She hired someone to break into his laptop, and she found his emails.

Apparently, Walt was in pretty deep with this group, and Mrs. Romanowsky is worried that they…well, that they're not good people."

I raised an eyebrow. They were bounty hunters capturing supernatural creatures. It was a safe bet that they weren't people you wanted to have brunch with. "Ok. And what does she want you to do?"

"She wants me to help her find out who they are and what they're doing. Why are they hunting supernaturals? And more importantly, what happens to the supes once they're caught?"

I recalled the afternoon outside Wights and Wongs when I'd confronted Ping about being a nine-tailed fox. I remembered her words clearly. She'd said, "Those people aren't good! I've heard stories. Things they do to supernaturals. Experiments. Torture."

Experiments.

Torture.

I shuddered.

"Okay," I said slowly. "Okay, yeah. I'll help you look into it. Do we have any leads at all? What did she find out?"

"Not much," Sloth said. "Just their name, really. Chenoweth International."

Something about that name tugged at a memory, but I couldn't quite place it. I was chewing on it when a voice from downstairs shouted, "Pride! Sloth! Get your butts downstairs. Tricia has an announcement!"

———

The party was well underway, and the other housemates were all inebriated when Sloth and I bounded down the steps to join the fray. "I just got the new assignments from the network," she said. "We're changing up how we do these from now on. Instead of the housemates selecting assignments randomly, producers will assign teams specific tasks. And before anyone complains," Tricia said, holding up her hand, her gaze directed pointedly at Wrath, "I'm sure they're doing it to maximize ratings, which is what we all want. After all, wish fulfillment is expensive." She said this last part with an extra gleam in her eye.

Swaying on our feet (some of us more than others—Sloth looked like she might pass out any second), we gathered around Tricia, awaiting our assignments. She looked down into her cell phone, scrolling through messages before finding the information she was looking for. "Okay, here we are. For the next challenge, the teams are as follows: Wrath, you'll be happy to know the network paired you with Pride, our audience favorite."

I felt the blood drain from my face at the thought of being stuck with Wrath for days on end. Even though I knew I'd partner with everyone eventually, I had hoped I'd get lucky and find myself with Envy or even Sloth. But though my heart was sinking with the news, Wrath was blissful—as blissful as he ever was, anyway. He was punching the air, bottom lip folded beneath his teeth. "Oh, yeah! That's what I'm talking about! We're gonna be an unstoppable team, man." Wrath pointed to me, a wicked smile spreading ear to ear. "The fan favorite with the house's smartest member? We got this in the bag."

"Continuing on," Tricia said, her voice rising only slightly, "Gluttony, you will be paired with Sloth. Envy, Lust, and Greed, you'll make up the final team."

Sloth turned to Gluttony, high-fiving him. "Working together again! We got it this time," she said.

"Your assignments have been sent to your email addresses," Tricia said. "Filming for the new challenge begins in the morn-ing, but you're free to read your assignments now. And with that, I'm off. Good luck, everyone! And may the best Sin win!"

Wrath sidled up next to me, his phone already in hand. "Show me my next assignment," he said. His phone's screen flashed, and an email with the subject, "Wrath and Pride: Challenge #2" appeared.

Wrath might've been a pain in the neck, but his technopathy was pretty cool, I had to admit.

He clicked the email and read the assignment aloud. "Heiress Bailey Preston is concerned that her sister, Tamora, is being hoodwinked. For the past six months, Tamora has been talking to a man online who claims he loves her and wants to marry her. However, the two have never met or even video chatted. Help Bailey find out if Tamora's lover is who he says he is or if he's got other ulterior motives."

Wrath and I looked up, twin expressions of puzzlement on our faces. "Is this some kind of joke?" he said. "They want us to find a potential catfish?"

"There's already an entire reality show dedicated to this premise," I agreed. "Is this the best the network could come up with?"

Wrath's phone flashed again, this time with a second message, the subject of which read, "The catch."

Wrath clicked it.

"The challenge isn't as simple as it seems," he read. "The catch? Tamora's online lover claims to be the spirit of her dead husband trapped in a medium's body. Good luck!"

Again, Wrath and I locked eyes, our mouths hanging ajar. "A dead guy trapped in a medium's body? How are we supposed to prove or disprove something like that? We're psychics, but come on! Even we have our limits!"

I chuckled darkly, clapping my new partner drunkenly on the shoulder. "Welcome to Challenge #2, Wrath. Don't overthink it. We'll get started in the morning. And hey." I grinned like a fool as I stumbled toward the kitchen, looking for one more glass of champagne. "Good luck. With a challenge like this, we're probably gonna need it."

ONLY SIN DEEP

AMBER FISHER

SINFUL HOUSE MYSTERIES

2

intro reel (recap)

Welcome to *Sinful House*, a reality TV show where the 7 Deadly Sins live together in the sunny beach town of Odyssey, California, and compete to become America's Favorite Sin!

Previously on *Sinful House:*

1. Pride and Lust were assigned the task of figuring out who was behind the cursed fortune cookies at the Chinese restaurant Wights and Wongs.
2. Sloth, Gluttony, and Envy won Good Samaritan points for completing their task first. They were tasked with finding Mrs. Romanowsky's missing son…
3. ….Who turned up dead in an industrial freezer at Wights and Wongs.
4. Upon investigating, Pride discovered that the dead man, Walt Romanowsky, was a member of a supernatural bounty hunting organization called Chenoweth International. His mother asked Sloth and Pride to investigate the organization.

5. After breaking into the morgue, Pride laid hands on Walt's corpse and had a vision of the person who killed him. It turned out to be the sous chef from Wights and Wongs, Ping…

6. ….Who was later revealed to be a nine-tailed fox disguised as a human.

7. The network's producer, Tricia Woodward, asked Pride to investigate the missing Sam Lovelace art commune and discover the truth about Sid Sheridan's (aka Pride's) past.

You're all caught up! Stay tuned for more rollicking adventures. And don't forget to vote for your favorite sin at the end of each challenge.

Happy watching!

one

. . .

"I don't think that should go there."

Gluttony placed his hands on the brand new foosball table and leaned into his palms. Envy stood akimbo, scowling at the game. Her brows were furrowed, and her mouth twisted as though the table had done something naughty and she was deciding its punishment.

"Then where exactly do you think it should go, Envy?"

Envy hrmmed, thinking as she looked around the space, analyzing potential placements. "I'm not sure, but my intuition says it can't go there."

Currently, the foosball table sat in the center of the room, which made sense since foosball required a lot of space. It couldn't go flush against any of the walls. "If you have a better idea about where to put it," Gluttony said with exaggerated patience, "I'm all ears. But I'm not about to let you tell me that this ain't a good place without you telling me where *is* a good place."

Envy circled the offending foosball table, rubbing her chin with her fingertips as she considered her options. "No, I get it,

Gluttony. And I'm not trying to be difficult. But if we're gonna do this, we should do it right. Putting the table there blocks the energy flow between the entry and the doors leading to the patio. That's just bad feng shui. It'll screw up the house energy. Is that what you want? Do you want to live with bad energy?"

Gluttony threw up his hands. "*What* bad energy? Besides the obvious, I mean." He stood tall then, shoulders square, and I realized for the first time how imposing Gluttony could be. I'd always thought of him as a giant teddy bear—which he was—but given his heft and height, he could pull out the intimidation with the best of them.

Envy blinked. "What obvious? Do you feel bad energy? Is there something I should know?"

Gluttony sighed, shaking his head. "I meant we are seven psychopaths living in a house together competing to win a reality show. I'd say any good juju we had coming into this mess has long since fled the coop."

I cleared my throat as I walked into the room, letting the other two know I was there. "We're not psychopaths," I corrected. "Well, I can't speak for Wrath or Greed. But the rest of us are not psychopaths. Psychologically damaged, sure. Mentally—"

"Were you even invited to this conversation?" Gluttony asked.

I hesitated, eyes darting between my housemates. "Not that I'm aware of," I stammered.

"Then you best see your way out of it. Unless you know where this table should go."

"I'm just saying you shouldn't say glib things like calling the other housemates psychopaths." I gestured discreetly toward the room's always-on camera. "We don't want to give people the wrong impression."

"Either way," Gluttony continued, returning his attention to Envy, "there isn't a better place to put the foosball table. I don't know anything about feng shui, but this is the only place big enough. So unless we put it on the patio—"

"It can't go on the patio," I interjected. "If it rains, it'll get destroyed. Plus, the heat will probably warp it, and the humidity will definitely rust it." I had no idea if that was true, but it sounded plausible.

"I know it can't go outside," Gluttony grumbled, running his hands over his afro. "I was being facetious. Do you know what that means? Facetious?"

I glowered at him. "I'm not an idiot."

"Then quit acting like it!" Gluttony cursed under his breath, then pointed a finger at Envy. "You know what? You don't like where I put the table, put it wherever you want. I'm gonna go make breakfast."

We watched as Gluttony stalked out of the room. After a moment, Envy's shoulders slumped, and she let out her breath in a whoosh. "Well, if there wasn't negative energy in here before, there is now." She hugged her torso and made puppy dog eyes at me. "I was just trying to be helpful. In a house this size with this many people, protecting our energy is really important. You'd think Gluttony would understand that."

I cocked an eyebrow. "Why would Gluttony understand that?"

"He's a kitchen witch," she said, as though this were the most obvious thing in the world. "Witches work with energy, don't they? I think I read that somewhere."

I shrugged. "Maybe, but I don't get the feeling Gluttony is that kind of witch. Outside of food, magic doesn't seem to be his bag."

Envy didn't respond to that, but I saw the way her nose wrinkled and her ears perked up, like she sensed something was amiss. "Yeah, I can feel it. Negative energy all over the place. It's too bad our housekeepers can't do spiritual cleanses. Maybe I'll just…"

Before Envy finished her thought, a breeze fluttered through my hair, raising goosebumps on my skin. The faint smell of incense filled my nose. Across the room, a diaphanous creature composed of smoke materialized before the large glass doors overlooking the beach. She shimmered into view like a mirage. She had long, slender limbs like a human's, except she had no hands or feet. Her limbs merely faded into nothingness. The creature moved gracefully, wafting around the room and moving her arms in choreographed patterns. She looked like she was dancing. Or perhaps casting a spell.

I watched the elemental for a moment before I turned to Envy. "Did you do that?" I lifted my chin in the creature's direction.

Envy, too, was watching the creature with rapt attention. "I guess so," she said. "Not consciously. But sometimes, the sylph appears when the energy around me needs cleansing. Look at her! She's trying to purify this space." A soft smile played over her lips as she whispered, "Good girl! You clear out mean old Gluttony's bad juju."

I watched the sylph float around the room, its graceful movements mesmerizing. The air elemental appeared to change colors like a chameleon, the hues of its smoke shifting to match its surroundings. I'd never seen a creature composed of smoke before, so part of me was enthralled. But the rest of me was apprehensive.

"Don't take this the wrong way," I said, "but do you actually have control of this thing? We're not gonna end up in a situation like last time, are we?"

Envy's cheeks glowed pink as she recalled the previous summoning. In a kind-hearted attempt to keep the house clean, Envy accidentally summoned a water elemental and immediately lost control of it. Left to its own devices, the undine had sequestered itself in Sloth's room, where it drenched everything she owned in water. It was a disaster. Half of Sloth's belongings were ruined.

Envy leaned her head to the side, her eyes trailing the sylph's movements around the room. "Control of the sylph? I wonder if such a thing is even possible. They do what they like. But don't worry!" She must have sensed my growing unease because she laughed and patted me on the shoulder. It was supposed to be reassuring. "Unlike the water elemental, the sylph is harmless! What could possibly go wrong?"

I groaned, clasping my hands on top of my head. "Envy, why did you *say* that? Everyone knows you're never supposed to say that. The minute someone says nothing can go wrong, *something goes catastrophically wrong*. Geez, they made a whole movie about that!"

Envy looked surprised. "They did?"

"Yes!"

"Which movie?"

I held out my hands, exasperated. "*The Titanic!*"

Envy snorted, running a hand through her hair. "Good grief, Pride, that's not what that movie's about. But okay, I take your point. Sylph," she called out, "don't mess anything up, okay? I don't need to be in hot water with America's Favorite Sin."

I made a disapproving sound in my throat and waved away the hyperbole. "Don't call me that," I said. "I haven't earned it. I had one good episode, that's it. I would hardly call that a victory."

We had been living at Sinful House for almost a month, our everyday lives filmed as we adjusted to living with six strangers in the cozy beach town of Odyssey, California. We were the stars of a new reality TV show, competing to become America's Favorite

Sin. So far, I was a fan favorite. But the show was still in its infancy. I had plenty of time left to lose.

"The camera loves you," Envy crooned as the two of us walked over to the couch, settling in. "You never can tell who's gonna look good on camera. I thought Lust would be the one to beat. Who would've known it would be you?"

I didn't think Envy intended that to be a slight, so I tried not to take it that way. However, she was right about one thing: I, too, expected Lust to have a better showing than she did. In any case, although the show premiered to record-breaking numbers, there was still a lot of road to travel before any of us would be crowned America's Favorite Sin. The lucky winner would take home an epic prize: their heart's ultimate desire.

"Speaking of being America's Favorite Sin," Envy said, "you're paired up with Wrath for this challenge, right? What's your task?"

"Some rich lady is worried that her sister is being catfished," I said. "Wrath and I are supposed to find out the truth behind her online love interest. Real deal or a shark in sheep's clothing?"

Envy chuckled. "Not a bad challenge, really. Better than the fortune cookie thing, at least. I'm surprised they didn't give you a case with a more supernatural element, though. You know, since you can see ghosts and everything? Especially since you worked the wight case, it seemed like magic and mayhem would be right up your alley. But maybe there's not much paranormal activity in this town aside from us."

"Well, you'll be glad to hear our case does have a paranormal aspect to it. You ready for this?" I stretched the moment out, enjoying torturing my housemate more than a little. From the corner of my eye, I saw the sylph continuing its journey around the room, the smell of incense thickening in my nose. I hoped she was almost done with her cleansing. My allergies were getting to me. "The online boyfriend claims to be the spirit of this woman's dead husband trapped in a medium's body."

For a moment, Envy didn't move. She didn't even blink. Then, as her shock wore off, she burst into laughter. She covered her mouth with her hands, her eyes wide above her fingertips. "You've got to be kidding me! The ghost of her dead husband trapped in a medium's body? And this woman fell for it?"

I shrugged. "I can't say for sure if she fell for it. Wrath and I haven't started investigating, so we haven't even spoken to her. But that's the challenge. So if that is the gist of it…" I shook my head, running a hand through my hair. "They say there's a sucker born every minute. In my experience, the more money a person has, the more likely they are to be a mark."

"Well, I guess that's true," Envy said. "Still, even if it meant everyone would target me, I sure wouldn't mind having all that money. *Or* fame. Can you imagine what it must be like to see yourself in every magazine or be invited to every talk show? To be adored by fans all over the world? Oh, I wouldn't mind that at all. I feel *destined* for stardom. I just *know* it." Her eyes fluttered closed as she smiled dreamily, no doubt imagining herself surrounded by sycophants snapping her photo.

I frowned. "Fame and celebrity aren't what they're cracked up to be. Believe me. I know."

Envy's eyes grew wider. "Oh, you mean because of the missing Sam Lovelace colony thing?"

I nodded. "An entire colony vanished off the face of the Earth, except for me, the baby left behind. People always want to hear my story. I can't tell you how many pitches I've heard for documentaries, books, movies…Even our network told me I need to be investigating my past for this show. They say the viewers are wild for it or something. It's annoying."

Envy nodded, absently tapping a finger to her lips. "Well, what *do* you think happened to them?"

I rolled my eyes. "Not you, too. Look, I don't know. Whether they stepped into another dimension or were abducted by aliens is anyone's guess."

And plenty of people *had* guessed. But I never saw the point in navel-gazing about the past. Besides, it seemed disrespectful. I was raised by two kind people who loved me very much. And despite never feeling very connected to them, they had done their best to make me into a respectable human being.

It wasn't their fault I was nowhere near respectable. Heck, some days, I wasn't even sure I was human.

"Anyway, you wanna help me find a new spot for the foosball table? I think if we move some of the furniture around, we can make it work."

My desire to do physical labor in the interest of improved feng shui was very low, so I checked my watch and made a disappointed face. "Can't. Wrath and I are meeting our client soon." I stood up and gave the sylph a quick parting glance. Turning to Envy, I said, "Keep an eye on that thing, will you?"

My housemate rolled her eyes as she climbed to her feet. "You're overreacting. She's not causing any trouble. By the time dinner rolls around, the energy in this place is gonna be spic and span. You just wait."

I had time for a quick shower before pounding on Wrath's door. He flung it open and flashed me the brightest smile I'd ever seen him wear. "You ready to rock and roll, man?" he asked.

"We're meeting Bailey Preston in fifteen minutes," I said. "Whether I'm ready or not, it's time to go."

We tumbled out the door with a cameraman on our heels. As we pulled out the driveway, I noticed faint tendrils of smoke seeping from the rec room windows.

two

. . .

"You gotta be kidding me! Is this really it? This is the place?"

As we pulled up to Bailey Preston's mansion, I understood why Wrath was about to have a conniption fit. Don't get me wrong, beautiful homes were in no short supply in Odyssey. But even by Odyssey standards, the Preston mansion was incredible.

We'd already driven down a long private road to get to the house. Now that we were here, it seemed we were in a secret oasis. Palm trees surrounded us, providing welcome shade from an unrelenting sun. The lawn was emerald green and immaculately tended. Precisely sculpted topiaries featuring an array of tropical birds lined the walkway leading to the home's front entry, marked by an enormous stone fountain.

"Pretty impressive," I said to Wrath as the cameraman followed us up to the door. "I've never seen anything like this."

Wrath spun on his heel, his brow creased, eyes cut in narrow slits. "Impressive? Really? That's what you see? Something beautiful and luxurious?"

I shrugged, digging my hands into my pockets. "Sure. Isn't that what you see?"

Wrath was quiet a moment, his lips pressed into a thin line. Then he said, "How much do you think this house is worth?"

I scratched my chin, dredging up memories of the beautiful buildings I'd seen in Portia Cameron's real estate office. It was the only thing I had for comparison. "I don't know, $10 million? $20 million?"

"$20 million is probably undervaluing it," Wrath said. "I'd put this place closer to $30 million. You see where I'm going with this?"

I considered the question carefully before answering. "Not really," I admitted.

"Where you see beauty and luxury, all I see is excess, selfishness, and the blood, sweat, and tears of the people who paid dearly so that one woman could own a home like this."

"I guess I never thought of it that way," I said, reaching for the doorbell. While I understood Wrath's point, we weren't here to discuss the ethics of extreme wealth. We had a job to do, and the sooner we got started, the sooner we could go back to Sinful House and enjoy some of Gluttony's amazing food. Plus, it was just easier to agree with Wrath. It kept his diatribes to a minimum.

"I see the oppression of the working class," Wrath continued, hands balled into fists at his sides. My finger paused just before hitting the doorbell. "I see people exploited for their labor. I see hungry families, sick children, and parents working two, three jobs just to make ends meet. This isn't beautiful," Wrath said, throwing the house a grievous look. "This is disgusting."

I said nothing as my finger punched the doorbell.

The door opened. Standing in the doorway was a petite woman with sun-streaked blonde hair. She wore a pair of loose-fitting white linen slacks, bejeweled sandals, and an off-the-shoulder yellow peasant blouse. She held a tiny dog in her arms. It was one of those purse dogs, those awful things that yip and yap and snarl, having no idea they were as threatening as the Easter Bunny. I hated those stupid dogs. But this woman's dog didn't bark. It merely looked up at us with wide, shining eyes, its tongue lolling from the side of its mouth.

I hated this particular dog a little less.

"You must be Pride and Wrath," the woman said, a smile spreading over her face. "I'm so glad you could make it! Please, come in."

We stepped inside and were greeted with piano music drifting in from another room. I couldn't tell if it was live music or a recording. In this house, both seemed equally likely. "I'm sorry, where are my manners?" The woman pressed the dog into the crook of her arm and extended a hand. "I'm Bailey Preston. Welcome to my home."

Wrath took her hand first. "Nice to meet you, Bailey. I'm Wrath." He clapped me on the shoulder. "And this is my buddy, Pride." He glanced around him, taking in the ostentation of our surroundings. As I watched his face, my heart skipped a beat, my breath lodged in my throat. The last thing we needed was for Wrath to utter even a fraction of his anti-capitalism screed in front of Bailey. But before I could say anything, his expression changed, a lightning-bright smile breaking out over his face as he gave an appreciative whistle. "Man, this place is off the charts. I've never seen anything like it."

Bailey looked around the entrance hall as though seeing her home for the first time. "Thanks. I can't take credit for any of it, though. My interior designer is an angel. Anyway, I poured drinks for us in the sitting room. Please, follow me."

As Bailey moved down the hallway with her dog tucked under her arm, I got a better look at the place. Disgusting display of obscene wealth aside, the house was terrific. The hallway we were moving down was lined with life-size black-and-white portraits of a man whose style reminded me of Elvis Costello. Alongside these portraits were framed platinum albums. At least two dozen accompanied our trek down the hallway.

"The albums," I said. "Are they yours? Are you a singer?"

Bailey Preston turned around, her eyes wide as saucers. My heart lurched into my throat, and I worried that I'd stepped in it once again. I'm not exactly what you might call a pop culture connoisseur. So if Bailey Preston expected me to recognize her face from a magazine or even a commercial, I wasn't the right person for that. Still, I didn't like to look like a fool, either. I stopped in my tracks, chewing the insides of my cheeks.

But Bailey's bewilderment quickly faded to laughter. "Me? A singer? Oh my goodness, no. Unfortunately, I don't have a musical bone in my body. No, these records belonged to my father. Perhaps you recognize his name? Adam Preston?"

I opened my mouth to say I knew the name—I didn't, but neither she nor the rest of America needed to know that—but Wrath beat me to the punch. "Of *course* we know Adam Preston. He was only the biggest music producer of our time. A mogul. A phenomenon."

"Daddy was unique, that's for sure," Bailey agreed. "When he died, I inherited most of his paraphernalia. Tammy didn't want any of it. I don't know why. But then again, I guess no one really understands Tammy."

We had arrived in the sitting room, which was much more comfortable than I expected based on the furnishings in the other rooms we'd passed by. Instead of chandeliers and Queen Victoria-style fainting couches, the sitting room was decidedly normal. A jumbo-size TV hung over a gas fireplace. An oversized leather couch took up the center of the room, and completing the U shape of the seating area were two smaller love seats. I could see an expanse of beachfront from the enormous windows that composed most of the wall opposite where I stood. The coffee table was set with liquor bottles, club soda, and a silver tray with finger sandwiches.

Wrath and I sat on the couch, and Bailey sat on the loveseat beside us. Her dog curled up in her lap. She pointed to the drinks on the table. "I hope you don't mind what I selected for us. Gin and tonic is my go-to," she said with a grin. "If there's something else you prefer, just let me know. I'll have Baxter bring it in."

Wrath raised an eyebrow. "Baxter?"

Bailey smiled. "One of my personal assistants. When you run a house this size," she gestured around her vaguely, "it's more than a full-time job. And with everything else I have going on, I need all the help I can get. So!" She clapped her hands at her chest, an obvious change in subject. "The two of you are here to talk about the case, right?"

I nodded. "We got the assignments yesterday," I explained. "The email from the network was pretty light on details. Want us to read what they sent?"

Bailey nodded and settled back into the pillows. "Sure, that would be great."

Wrath pulled out his phone. "Show me the Bailey Preston assignment," he said to the device.

His phone flickered to life, taking him immediately to an email from the network presenting the details of our case. Wrath was a technopath—he could get technology to do just about anything he wanted. It was a pretty helpful skill if you asked me. Too bad the guy wielding it was, well, Wrath.

Wrath read aloud. "Heiress Bailey Preston is concerned that her sister, Tamora, is being hoodwinked. For the past six months, Tamora has been talking to a man online who claims he loves her and wants to marry her. However, the two have never met, or even video chatted. Help Bailey find out if Tamora's lover is who he says he is or if he's got other ulterior motives."

Bailey looked down into her lap, but I saw color climbing up her cheeks. "They included something else, right?"

Wrath cleared his throat and read, "The challenge isn't as simple as it seems. The catch? Tamora's online lover claims to be the spirit of her dead husband trapped in a medium's body."

Bailey looked up, and her face aged before my eyes. For a moment, she was no longer a vibrant socialite with a dumb purse dog. She had a haunted look in her eyes, a darkness that pulled her lips into a frown. "That's the gist of it," she said. "I guess I better start at the beginning."

Bailey leaned forward and selected a tumbler from the coffee table. She filled it with ice before adding the gin and tonic. "Tammy is my older sister. Don't let that fool you. We're about as different as night and day. And although we've always gotten along, we've never been close, if you know what I mean. Still, she's my sister. I look out for her. Because to be honest, she's not very good at looking out for herself."

"What do you mean by that?" Wrath asked.

Bailey took a sip. "She's gullible. She doesn't trust her brain. She relies on gut instinct and 'spiritual advisement,'" Bailey made finger quotes around the phrase, "to make even the most basic life decisions. She's kind of the perfect mark for a scam like this." She stroked the dog in her lap absently, her head listing to one side as she conjured up a memory. "Tammy's husband was Jeff Bishop. Really nice guy. Everybody liked him. And he adored Tammy. I mean, just head over heels in love with her. His family was like ours—big in the music industry. His father was Kerry Bishop, the big-time producer, and his grandfather was Berry Bishop—founder of Bishop Knight Records. Anyway, he and Tammy were married for over five years. And then he had the accident."

Again, she sipped from her drink. Wrath, too, reached for his glass. I left mine untouched. I'm not a teetotaler or anything. But I hadn't even had breakfast yet.

"He trained for years to climb Mount Everest. It was his driving passion—his *raison d'être*. But I guess no matter how hard you prepare or how badly you want something, some people just aren't meant to climb Mount Everest. You know what I mean? So he died up there, just like so many others. Tammy was devastated. She was in mourning so deep, I thought she might never come out. She wouldn't even get out of bed most days."

Bailey heaved a heavy sigh, her shoulders pressed low as she shook her head at the memory. "I was the one who recommended she try online dating. I should've known better. But she was so adamant that she didn't want to date anyone from our circle. She wanted someone normal, someone who knew what it meant to struggle. Jeff was a philanthropist. She wanted someone Jeff would have approved of. A project."

Wrath leaned forward expectantly. "And did she find someone like that?"

Bailey pinched her lips together, her nostrils flaring. "Well, she found *someone*. Leave it to my sister to find the biggest charlatan the Internet has to offer." Bailey lifted the dog from her lap and put him on the ground. She got to her feet and began pacing, arms wrapped around her torso as her fingertips tapped her elbows nervously. "She met this guy online. And at first, it seemed good for her. She was getting back to her old self. But over time, she started acting strange. Tammy's always been strange," she amended, "but… I don't know how to describe it. She got worse. I finally got her drunk one night, and she told me she was seeing this online guy she'd never met, and he wanted to marry her. And the crazier part was, she was considering it. Strongly considering it. Like, she wanted to go wedding dress shopping and everything."

I found all of this fascinating, but maybe not for the reasons other people might be drawn into the story. The part I didn't understand was the *dating* part, let alone online dating. I never dated. Not really. The idea of auditioning to be someone's lover made me want to shrivel up and die. I'm not kidding. I would rather walk into the surf and let my body turn to sea foam like in *The Little Mermaid* before I'd consider *dating*.

(I'm talking about the Hans Christian Andersen original. Not whatever cockamamie nonsense I watched as a kid. In real life, little mermaids rarely get their happy endings. Not that fairytales are real life, but life is hard is what I'm saying.)

"When did your sister reveal, you know. The catch."

Bailey was staring out the window, her back to Wrath and me. I couldn't see her face or read her expression—not that I was very good at that anyway—but I heard the weariness in her voice when she said, "Three or four weeks ago. She said she was determined to make the relationship work because the online mystery man was Jeff. Just… Jeff trapped in someone else's body."

"And how does *that* work?" I asked.

Bailey turned around slowly, refusing to meet my eyes. "You'll have to ask my sister. I didn't ask for the details because I don't care. There's no such thing as an afterlife. There's certainly no such thing as ghosts. When Jeff died, he just died. No piece of him lingered around. No energy got left behind. Jeff's just gone. Like my dad and my mom. Like everyone else who has ever died and will ever die. So this idea about him being trapped anywhere, let alone in someone else's body? It's hocus-pocus nonsense. And I need my sister to understand that. I need her to get her act together and gather the pieces of her life before it's too late."

I cleared my throat and cracked my fingers. "Well, sure, but you're wrong about the ghosts, though. They're absolutely real."

When Bailey turned a dubious look in my direction, Wrath scooted forward, placing a hand on my knee. "What Pride means is people believe in that stuff. So we have to take it seriously."

I stared at Wrath. "That's not what I meant. I meant exactly—"

"Anyway," Wrath interrupted, shooting me a dark glare, "it doesn't matter about the ghosts. Even if Jeff was trapped in some other dude's body, that wouldn't make him a ghost, right? Ghosts are a dead end." He said this last part more to me than Bailey. "No pun intended."

I returned Wrath's glare but said nothing. Pun or no, Wrath was dead wrong. Ghosts were real. I saw them all the time and had been seeing them since I was a kid. Mostly, they left me alone. Once in a while, they asked for help. Sometimes they wanted to contact a loved one. Occasionally, they wanted revenge. Most of the time, they just wanted to talk to someone about why they hadn't crossed over. But like Bailey, I didn't know anything about the afterlife. I had no idea if spirits could travel back and forth. The paranormal left many mysteries unsolved, but I knew one thing for sure. Life—and death—were both stranger than most people gave them credit for.

Which isn't to say that the deceased Jeff Bishop was trapped in someone else's body. Even a ghost whisperer like me could be skeptical of a claim like that.

"Anyway, that's why I contacted the network. I knew the police couldn't help. He hasn't asked my sister for money or anything like that. So I can't even press charges— not that I would know what charges to press. But I need someone to help with this. I'm so afraid that this person is taking advantage of my sister. She's already emotionally fragile. The last thing I need is for her to be financially fleeced as well. So can you help? Do you think you can discover who's been pretending to be my sister's dead husband?"

"We're for sure gonna try," Wrath said, once again turning on a charm I had never seen him display before. "Don't you worry, Bailey. Pride and I are on the case. We're gonna win this thing."

He blinked and started, shaking himself. "Uh, I mean, we're gonna solve this thing. It's all gonna work out. You'll see."

It was in that fleeting moment that I finally understood. All Wrath's fake charm? It wasn't about helping Bailey. It was about the viewers. Of course it was. How could I have missed it earlier? The real Wrath was a short-tempered, foul-mouthed pain in the neck, just like I thought. This new person was a caricature. A figment of the audience's imagination.

To be honest, I wasn't sure if I was revolted or impressed. It was probably a useful talent to have. The ability to adopt an entirely new personality, I mean. If I could do that, I might try it. The personality I was born with wasn't working out so hot, after all.

three

. . .

When we arrived back at Sinful House, it was on fire.

Wrath stared at the house, eyes wide with shock. "What the…?"

I swore, fumbling to unbuckle my seatbelt. "You've got to be kidding me." When I got it unlatched, I threw my door open.

Wrath and I jumped from the car, running pell-mell toward the house. I threw open the front door and immediately began coughing. Enormous clouds of billowing smoke poured out of the entryway, stinging my eyes and the back of my throat.

It wasn't just any regular smoke, however. It smelled alarmingly like patchouli.

I darted into the house. "Envy! Sloth! Is anybody here?"

Outside, I heard the scream of sirens as fire trucks pulled up to the property. The smoke was so dense, I could scarcely see, but I wasn't about to let my housemates be asphyxiated. I buried my nose in the crook of my arm as I searched the house for anyone passed out on the floor. I made it all the way upstairs before I heard someone shouting my name.

"Pride? Outside! We're all outside!"

I dashed back down the stairs and was almost at the front door when I saw her—that stupid sylph Envy summoned to cleanse the house. She was still drifting from room to room, tendrils of herbal smoke trailing in her wake.

I growled. When things settled down, Envy and I were gonna need to have a serious talk.

I raced out the door to find firefighters lugging hoses from the truck. I waved my arms overhead, trying to get their attention, but to no avail. They were doing firemen things, shouting to each other and going into the house looking for the fire.

Little did they know, there was no fire to locate. Just a nuisance of a sylph wreaking billowing, herbal havoc.

When I could finally breathe again, I found Envy sitting on the curb, her head cradled in her arms, shoulders shaking. I sat down next to her, but not too close. She, too, reeked of patchouli. "The sylph?" I asked.

Envy didn't raise her head. "I don't understand why this is happening," she said. "I've had problems with the elementals before, sure, but never anything like this. It's like the more I try to help out, the more determined they are to destroy everything!" She sat up now, her face turned toward me. She wasn't exactly crying, but she didn't exactly look thrilled, either. If I had to guess, I'd say she looked scared.

Well, if I were in her position, I'd be scared, too. Scared of Wrath screaming at me. Scared of Gluttony giving me the cold shoulder. Scared of the other housemates being furious all their belongings would smell like hippies for a long, long time.

"I think one of the neighbors called the fire department."

I looked up to find Lust ambling toward us, her hands dug in her back hip pockets. "We were on the other side of town, and even we heard the sirens. I don't think anybody was home once the smoke started getting bad. Everybody wants to win so much, we all got an early start on the day. Even Sloth was actually out of the house before the morning was over."

I stood and dusted myself off, turning my attention back to the house. I noticed now that all the windows were open, smoke billowing out like from a dragon's nostrils. If I had to guess—I was doing a lot of guessing today, apparently—Envy had done that. She was trying to air the place out. It might've worked if she'd been able to reel in the sylph. But that thing was still inside, making more smoke.

I would have liked to see the firemen's faces when they saw what they were up against.

"I guess we're going out to lunch," I said, trying to change the subject. "It's not like we can cook with the house like this. Anybody have any suggestions? I'm starving."

Behind me, I heard Envy sniffle. "I'm not hungry."

"I could go for some seafood," Lust said. "Should I get the group together?"

As contestants on the show, our contracts required us to spend time together as a household. Of course, investigating our cases and solving mysteries for the locals was our top priority. But the second priority was camaraderie. And by camaraderie, I actually mean drama. You just can't have a good reality TV show without a healthy dose of drama. Forcing us to get together for meals was one way the network hoped to stir up theatrics.

"Sure, get a group together," I said. "Looks like we're all gonna need the distraction. So." I cleared my throat and rubbed my hands together, feeling the heat rising in my cheeks. Talking to Lust always turned me into a stammering idiot. "How did your morning go?"

Lust flipped her hair over her shoulder and shrugged. "Fine, I guess. It's weird not to be working with you, though. Your instincts are so much better than everyone else's."

I felt the color in my cheeks deepen at this small compliment.

Of course I was better than the other housemates at investigation. After all, that's what I used to do for a living. Before I got fired, I worked with the San Diego Police Department on cases with a paranormal bent. My most recent claim to fame was finding the key witness in a high-profile murder case. There'd been a ghost in the parking garage who had seen everything. I found the spirit, interviewed him, and found the key evidence against the prime suspect. That guy was going away for a long time, thanks to me.

Of course, my skills being second-to-none didn't matter in the end. Budget cuts, you see. The almighty dollar always wins out.

"Everybody will get better at their jobs as time goes on," I said. I wasn't sure I believe that, but it was likely. Possible. At least plausible. "What is your case, anyway?"

Lust sighed, her nose wrinkled. "Helping some old guy locate his missing antique guns."

"The police weren't interested in the case?"

Lust shrugged. "Apparently, the Odyssey Police are too busy investigating suspicious deaths. I guess this town has a super high death rate?"

I nodded, looking down at my hands. "That would explain why you and I saw so many corpses in the morgue. Well, holler if you need me." I cringed as soon as the words were out of my mouth. I wasn't a "holler if you need me" sort of person, but sometimes Lust made me say and do things out of character.

"Of course I need you," she said, her voice so low, I almost missed it.

I turned, blinking in surprise. But she was already going the other way, heading over to gather the others.

My face caught fire, and my heart skipped. As much as I hated to admit it, I was grinning like a moron.

Lust said she needed me.

Sinful House might be coughing out ungodly amounts of patchouli smoke, but my day was looking up.

———

Later that night, long after the fire department left and the house had aired out enough for human habitation, it was time to visit Tamora Preston—our possible catfishee.

Tamora lived only a few blocks away from Bailey, but her home was much less ostentatious than her sister's. That was a relief because I wasn't sure I could take another of Wrath's rants about the capitalist agenda. We rang the doorbell, and a moment later, the door creaked open.

The woman standing in the doorway looked nothing like I expected. Unlike Bailey, who was petite and tan and blonde, this woman was tall and milk pale with hair as black as a raven's wing. Her hair was cut in a severe bob that ended just beneath her ears. Her bangs were cut into a sharp triangle, the point of which sat directly between two perfectly arched black brows. She was wearing something black and flimsy and silky that looked more like lingerie than a dress. She'd paired the slip with a pair of clunky black combat boots with a 2-inch platform. A silver pentagram hung around her neck. Her lips were painted black, and heavily lined eyes squinted at us in the darkness.

I was so stricken by her appearance that I just stood there, staring. Thankfully, Wrath found his voice easily. "Uh, hey. Are you Tammy Preston?"

The woman in the doorway gave Wrath a long, slow blink. Her face was a mask of ice and venom when she said, "Call me Tammy again, and those will be the last words you ever speak."

I didn't mean to smile, but I did. I understood that sentiment. I didn't respond well to people calling me Sidney, either. I preferred Sid. Names are important.

"Sorry. Tamora," Wrath supplied. "My name's Wrath. We're here with —"

Tamora held up a hand, interrupting the introduction. "I know who you are," she said, eyes flickering toward the cameras behind us. "You're the idiots from that show. My sister sent you. She said you were coming."

Wrath nodded. "Yeah, that's right. Is it cool if we come in?"

Tamora looked us up and down, sizing us up. I wasn't sure how we rated. I was dressed in a casual t-shirt and jeans, but Wrath looked like something out of a cyberpunk movie. He had taken extra time with his bleached-blond hair today, spiking it out all over his head. He wore a pair of skinny black pants with entirely too many pockets pushed up to his calves. A spiked leather belt at his waist dripped with silver chains, and his wrists sported matching black sweatbands. He also wore combat boots, but he'd left them unlaced, their tongues hanging out. A cropped black hoodie completed the outfit, even though it was almost 80 degrees out.

The door creaked as Tamora swung it open and led us through the living room. The overall effect of the place was something like a baroque nightmare. Every flat surface was covered with black candles, taxidermy ravens, and statues of nude goddesses. The walls were adorned with paintings derived from Tarot cards, each depicting the darker scenes: Death, the Tower, the Devil.

Along one wall, Tamora had created a shrine to her late husband. Photographs of Jeff Bishop interspersed with candles and various gemstones cluttered an altar. There were photos from their wedding, photos of Jeff as a child, even hand-drawn portraits of him. He'd been a good-looking man. In the photos of them together, they looked very much in love. Not that you can't fake that sort of thing, but.

Wrath nudged me in the side. "Do you have holy water on you?" he whispered. "I think we might need it."

Tamora called over her shoulder, "I heard that."

We continued through the dark, overly air-conditioned house to climb a set of winding stairs. When we reached the landing, Wrath sidled up to our host, pushing up the sleeves on his hoodie. "Thanks for having us. Do you think we could get some water or something? I'm parched. We had a fire at our house, and the smoke did a number on my throat," he explained.

She answered without turning around. "I heard it wasn't a fire. I heard one of the other idiots who lives with you summoned an air elemental she couldn't control and filled the whole place with incense."

Wrath looked at me, and I shrugged. News travels fast in small towns.

"Yeah. Envy's not an idiot, though. I mean, she's okay. So anyway, about that water…"

The woman turned to Wrath and brought a finger to her lips. "I'll get you anything you want, but it'll have to wait. Right now, we have other business to attend to."

"Other business?"

Saying nothing more, the woman pushed open a door and led us into an enormous library. In the center of the room was a rectangular table covered with flickering black candles. That explained the air conditioner, then. Candles put out more heat than you think.

The candles were nestled among pink and red rose petals strewn across the table. A cone of incense burned on a censer shaped like a pentacle to match the star Tamora wore at her throat. Framed photographs were lined up in the center, and seated around the table were six other people who all looked up as we entered the room.

There were three empty chairs.

Tamora swept her arm in front of her. "Take your seats," she said to us. "It doesn't matter where. Any empty seat is fine."

I hesitated, hands clenched at my sides. I don't do well in new situations, and I definitely had no idea what was happening here. Who were these people? What was going on? We were supposed to be interviewing Tamora, not participating in…whatever this was.

Oh God, was this an intervention?

I was deciding whether to turn around and get out of there when Wrath pulled out the nearest chair and slid into place.

Tamora lifted her eyes to me. I was still standing, rooted to the spot. A smile cracked over her lips, but it wasn't exactly friendly. She looked more like a snake about to strike. "We can't get started until you sit down," she said.

What choice did I have? I sat down.

Tamora chose the last seat and folded her hands on the table, smiling for real now. "Thank you all for coming," she said. "And special thanks to you, Madam Andromeda. We are so honored that you broke your vow of seclusion to be with us today."

Now I snapped to attention. Before that moment, I hadn't looked at the faces of the other guests. I don't exactly suffer from face blindness. It's just that my interest in other people is pretty low. But now, I looked. I recognized one of these people. Seated at the head of the table was someone whose persona I knew well.

Andromeda Clark was the premier psychic medium in the country, if not the world. She had appeared on countless talk shows, and for a while, even had a show of her own. I was addicted to her show—I watched every episode, and not just because we shared a professional interest in spirits.

It was because she was captivating.

A few years ago, she canceled her show and went into seclusion, withdrawing from the world to pursue what she called "communion with her holy guardian angel," whatever that meant.

And yet, here she was.

Which meant this wasn't just some weird gathering of friends.

This was a séance.

"Please, just call me Andromeda." The woman grinned, a cupid's smile if I ever saw one. Long, curly pink hair fell over her shoulders. She was wearing something transparent and silvery that could have been the dressing gown to the lingerie Tamora wore. Still, it worked for her. Andromeda had always had an otherworldly style.

"I assume this is everyone, then?" Andromeda asked, turning her attention to our host.

Tamora nodded. "We're ready to begin."

Andromeda cleared her throat and sat forward, placing both palms flat on the table. She looked around the room and slowed her breathing, her eyelids growing heavy. "As most of you know, this world is not conclusion. Beyond what the average person can see, hear, smell, touch, or taste is another realm just as rich and abundant as this one. It is separated from us not by fact but by fiction. We have been conditioned not to believe, but our belief is not required. The other world stands between and among us, and sometimes within us." She dipped her chin toward her chest, her voice growing deeper and more mysterious. "At your invitation, tonight I will endeavor to channel your friends and family from the other side. Do I have any requests?"

I looked around the table and saw that everyone else was doing the same thing. Most everyone looked sheepish, hesitant to speak up. Finally, an older man sitting directly across from me raised a hand. "I have a request," he said. "I'd like to speak to my mother."

Andromeda smiled, tossing a stray curl from her face. "It's

always the mothers," she teased. The man blushed, but Andromeda tutted, her smile growing. "I'm only kidding. And your mother's name?"

"Caitlin Pratchett," he said.

"And is Ms. Pratchett's photograph among those on the table?"

The man nodded and selected the photo nearest him, passing it down the table. "That's her," he said.

Andromeda took the photograph and gazed at it before replacing it on the table with a crisp nod. "She was a beautiful woman. I usually like to have an item from the deceased," she said. "Did you bring anything personal of your mother's? Perhaps a piece of jewelry or a special item of clothing?"

The man reached into his smoking jacket's breast pocket and pulled out a glittering tennis bracelet. This, too, he passed down the table. "My father gave this to her on their 50th anniversary," he said. "She should have been buried in it. But my sister…" The man's lips pulled into a frown. "Well. You know how catty some people can be when money is involved."

Andromeda said nothing as she fingered the diamonds, clenching the bracelet in her palm and closing her eyes. A moment later, she breathed out a low, controlled breath and placed the jewelry on the table. Her eyes fluttered open. "Let us begin. Please, everyone. Join hands and close your eyes."

The people on either side of me reached for my hands, and I panicked. I don't like to touch people. Sometimes, I see things. To be fair, it was usually innocuous things. But sometimes… Let's just say some people have darkness about them.

I don't like darkness. I guess most people don't.

Still, I wasn't exactly in a position to get up and leave, so, against my better judgment, I slipped both my hands in theirs.

Instantly, a barrage of images shot through my mind. A kitchen table with a stack of chairs forming an impossible tower.

A metal bedframe rattling violently, the finials spinning illogically. Dishes flying off the shelves. Doors banging open.

I gasped.

Poltergeists?

I snapped my head from side to side, looking at the people to my left and right. I couldn't tell whom the images came from. Both people were frowning at me, brows furrowed. I didn't want to cause a scene, but one of these people had experienced poltergeist activity, and that just wasn't normal.

Suddenly, I had a bad feeling about this.

"Gathered here tonight are friends and loved ones, mortals seeking the immortal, the faithful seeking that upon which we place our faith." Andromeda was speaking again, swaying to a tune only she could hear. "Tonight, we call out into the void to seek one Miss Caitlin Pratchett, beloved mother of…?"

Andromeda looked to the man in question, her eyebrow cocked. He nodded. "Chase Pratchett," he said.

"Beloved mother of Chase Pratchett. We come in perfect love and trust and open our hearts to you. Ms. Caitlin Pratchett, if you have a message for your son, please share it now. Begin by letting us know you hear and accept our invitation."

The room was deathly still as we collectively held our breath. I'd never been to a séance before, so I didn't know what to expect. Still, I expected *something*—a voice or a crack of lightning at least.

But nothing happened.

With my eyes closed, I could only gauge the others' reactions by listening to their breathing and the squeak of the chairs as they shifted in their seats. Someone let out the smallest of sighs. Was it disappointment? Or maybe fear?

"Caitlin Pratchett," Andromeda said, louder. "If there is such a being as Caitlin Pratchett, I bid you appear before us with an indication that you hear and accept our invitation!"

The woman at my right closed her hand more firmly in mine. The man to my left breathed in sharply through his nose.

Otherwise, the room was silent.

Too silent.

I chanced opening my eyes just a slit. Andromeda sat in the flickering darkness, eyes still closed, a perplexed frown on her face. "Perhaps you should try speaking, Chase." Andromeda said. "Is there a question you'd like to ask your mother?"

With a sharp inhale, Chase Pratchett spoke. "Mother, are you there? Sometimes I feel your presence. Are you watching over me? Are you watching over Rachel?" He stopped speaking abruptly, and I thought I heard his voice catch as emotion caught him off guard.

But Chase's plea was met only with an eerie silence.

"Everyone, please open your eyes. Perhaps we'll come back to you," Andromeda said softly. "Is there anyone else who wishes to speak with a loved one?"

"I know." At the other end of the table, Tamora leaned forward onto her elbows, placing her chin atop clasped hands. "Why don't we see if we can talk to Pride's family? I think everyone here would love to know what happened to Sam Lovelace's vanished commune."

I gazed at Andromeda, my heart in my throat. "I don't have any personal effects of theirs," I stammered. "I don't even know their names."

Andromeda leaned her head to the side and offered me a lopsided smile. "That's certainly a challenge. I prefer to address the dead by name, while in possession of a personal item. But in this case, we'll have to make an exception."

I didn't want to make an exception. I wanted to turn this

séance around and go home, but then Andromeda's back stiffened, and her shoulders squared. "All right, everyone. Let's try again. Please close your eyes. Think about that lost commune, the poor souls who disappeared into thin air and were never seen again. Please hold in your mind the image of the sole survivor of that mysterious incident— Pride, discovered as a wee babe. Let us hold these thoughts in our minds as we try to access the dearly departed."

The man and woman at my sides squeezed my hands tighter, and I swallowed down my objections, an icy chill running down my spine. I didn't know what else to do, so I closed my eyes and let my chin drift to my chest. Andromeda's words filled my ears.

"Spirits of the great beyond, we call out with a most unusual request. We have no name and no personal effects. But as we sit with Pride today, we beseech the very people who brought this lovely person into the world. If you're there, please let us know."

Silence stretched for several agonizing moments. Then, just as I thought maybe I would be spared, a cold draft whistled through the room, fluttering through my hair. My skin pimpled over, and I opened my eyes, searching the room. The other guests' eyes were open, too, their bodies held taut, their faces frozen.

The candles on the table stuttered and then went out.

A collective gasp went around the room. No sooner had smoke begun to rise from the extinguished flames that the table started to shake. The temperature dropped, and the table jerked violently to the right, screeching loudly as it scraped across the floor and then lifted into the air.

I sat in stunned silence as the table levitated, climbing higher and higher before my eyes.

Throughout the library, something else was happening. Books tumbled from their shelves, spines cracking as they landed haphazardly on the hardwood floor. A sound like thunder cracked through the room as the darkness above our heads split open to reveal a pool of eerie blue light dotted with white. It shimmered and danced, undulating.

At the head of the table, a voice spoke into the darkness.

"Find some of all profits," the voice said.

I turned my head, blinking in surprise and—I admit it—absolute terror. Andromeda's head was tilted back, and her mouth hung open, her eyes rolled to the back of her head. Her cloud of pink hair floated from her shoulders, fanning around her like a cotton candy halo. The voice was coming from her body, but it wasn't her voice.

I couldn't place it. And yet, somewhere in the pit of my soul, I recognized it. It was as familiar to me as my own name, something I heard long, long ago, and it plucked my heart strings. Another chill ran down my spine.

"Find some of all profits on vinyl," the voice repeated. "Start there. That's where you began. Some of all profits on vinyl."

Then Andromeda's head snapped forward, and her eyes opened wide, her gaze trained on me. Whoever or whatever had taken over the medium's body was staring holes into my skull, and my skin crawled under the scrutiny. I'm garbage at reading people's faces, especially possessed people channeling spirits of the dead.

But I think the expression Andromeda's hijacked face wore was astonishment.

She lurched to her feet and grabbed me by the shoulders. Then, in a hushed voice, she said, "Sam warned us this might happen."

Then Andromeda's face fell slack, and she collapsed at my side.

The table crashed to the floor, knocking the candles on their sides. They rolled to the edge, spilling wax across the table's surface before clattering to our feet. The overhead pool of light vanished. The aftermath of the chaos was frightening in its stillness.

Finally, Tamora released the hands of the guests at her sides. I snatched my own away as well, dropping them in my lap. Tamora stretched her fingers and adjusted the thin straps of her slip. "I think that's all for tonight," she said, her Cheshire Cat grin growing ever wider, her eyes never once leaving my face.

four

. . .

"You set me up."

The four of us were alone in the library. Tamora had sent everyone else home and was now sitting at the table, smiling at me. Wrath and Andromeda were still seated as well, wearing twin looks of confusion. I was on my feet, trembling with fury, an accusing finger pointed in Tamora's face.

"You set me up," I repeated. "Did the network put you up to this?" I whirled on my heel to face Wrath. "Were you in on this?"

Scowling, Wrath held up his hands, palms out. "Man, I had nothing to do with this. From my perspective, this whole thing was a giant waste of time."

Andromeda sat silently at the head of the table. She'd woken up, but she looked drowsy, like she wasn't fully back in her body yet. "Please stop shouting," she said, her fingers pressed against her temples. "Could I please get some water?"

"Good luck with that," Wrath said. "I've been asking for water since we got here."

I studied Andromeda, my blood still boiling. She wore a grimace, eyes squeezed shut. She didn't *look* guilty, not like someone who had just exploited a stranger's past for her own amusement.

Though, to be fair, Tamora didn't look remorseful, either.

She looked delighted.

At least one of us was amused.

"I did set you up," Tamora said finally. "When Bailey said you were coming out to the house to investigate my—how did she put it? My catfishing case?—I knew I had to do something. I wasn't going to let you come into my house and try to make me look like a fool. Plus, how many opportunities does a person have to investigate one of the most famous disappearances of our time? When you look at it like that, it would be a sin *not* to set you up."

"It was cruel and unnecessary," I said. I was too amped up to sit down, so I paced around the room, stepping over candles and heaps of books. "You could have just *asked* me. You could have—"

"You would have said no, and anyway, that wasn't the point. You wanted to humiliate me. I wanted to humiliate you first."

"I *never* wanted to humiliate you!" I shouted. "I don't even know you! I just wanted to do the job I was hired to do. Your sister thinks you need to be protected from a charlatan after your fortune. But you know what? Now that I've met you, maybe it's the rest of *us* who need to be protected from *you!*"

"Oh, *do* keep shouting," she cooed, fluttering her lashes. "You're *very* pretty when you're angry."

If the cameras weren't filming, I think I might have slapped that smile right off her face. I'm not usually a violent person, but Tamora Preston was pushing all my buttons.

I turned to Andromeda. "I suppose you were in on it as well?"

The medium blinked, slowly coming out of her haze. She crossed her arms over her chest, her eyes cut into narrow slits. "I came out of retirement for this," she said. She shot a dark glance at Tamora as well. "Tamora told me you'd be here. And I admit, I wanted to see if I could channel your family. On my own, it would have been impossible, not to mention unethical. With you here, we at least had a chance. But I had no idea you didn't volunteer for this. I'm sorry about that."

"You have nothing to apologize for," Tamora said. She climbed to her feet and walked to the other end of the table. She slid into an empty seat next to Andromeda and placed her hand on top of the medium's. "Something happened here tonight. You channeled something. Some*one*. For decades, no one has made any progress toward finding that missing commune. Tonight, we received a clue. A precious clue!"

I stared at her. "What clue? What are you *talking* about? The table flew around, the books and candles fell to the ground, and the bloody ceiling turned into a lake of light but how is any of that a clue?"

"Are you dumb?" Tamora was looking at me as though she truly questioned my mental state. "Didn't you hear what Andromeda said when she was under?"

My jaw clenched. "Find some of all profits on vinyl? How is that a clue? It doesn't even make sense!"

"Not that," Tamora whined, growing impatient. "'Sam said this might happen.' She meant Sam Lovelace! It was his commune!"

Wrath looked just as confused as I felt. "How is that a clue? Sam said *what* might happen? Hang on, why are we even talking about this? We're supposed to be talking about *your* dead husband!"

"Please, everyone, stop." Andromeda shrank back into her chair, withdrawing her hand into her lap. "I don't know what happened here tonight," she said. "I didn't see it, and I won't understand it until I watch the footage." She jutted her chin in the cameraman's direction. "You'll turn over the footage to me before you edit or release any of it," she instructed. "I haven't signed any release form, and I'm not afraid to sue your network into the ground if any of this gets leaked. You understand?" She returned her attention to Tamora. "But you shouldn't have tried to channel a loved one without consent. Regardless of what may or may not have happened. That was wrong."

My anger was already fading—it was never an emotion I liked the cling to. But as my fury dwindled, something else began gnawing at me. "This doesn't make sense," I said. "Your sister said you've been talking to someone online who claims to be your dead husband trapped in another person's body. Right?"

Tamora stiffened, obviously taken aback by the change in subject. Good. Let her be uncomfortable. "That's right," she said.

"So if you have access to the world's greatest psychic medium," I gestured toward Andromeda, "why use her to play a trick on *me?* Why not take advantage of her talents to find out the truth? All you have to do is channel your husband's spirit. If he's not trapped in someone else's body, he should make an appearance, right?"

Tamora sat back in her chair, crossing her legs at the knee and shaking her head. "You don't understand," she said. "I don't need proof. I've been talking to this person online for six months. I know what I felt. I know what I experienced. I'm not talking to a fake. I'm talking to Jeff."

"How on earth can you possibly know that?" I exclaimed.

"He knows things only Jeff would know," she said, her voice suddenly breaking with emotion. "Moments we shared. Things I said to him. There's no way those things could be faked. It's Jeff. I know it is."

"He could have told *anyone* those things before he died," I said.

"He would never," she said. "Jeff was very private. Especially where I was concerned."

"Why not just test it?" Wrath was also on his feet now, pacing around the room like I was. "Have Andromeda channel him and see what happens. If he shows up, he's not stuck in anyone's body and you can get on with your life. If he doesn't show up…" He shrugged. "At least you'll have data. So why don't you do that? You have nothing to lose, right?"

"That's where you're wrong." Tamora wasn't looking at either Wrath or me. She was peering at Andromeda. "Let's say Andromeda successfully channeled Jeff. What if he gets stuck again? I can't very well marry Andromeda, can I?"

I stopped pacing, gaping at Tamora, incredulous. "What? He might get stuck *again?* Tamora, what if he never got stuck in the first place? Isn't it more likely your husband is on the other side, enjoying his afterlife, and whoever you've been talking to is just *lying to you?*"

"It's *not* more likely," Tamora insisted. "He's *trapped in someone else's body!* I've heard his voice. How do you explain that? It's Jeff's voice on the phone!"

"This is getting us nowhere," Wrath said. He jammed his knuckles into his eyes, rubbing them wearily. "Andromeda, maybe you can talk some sense into her."

"I've never heard of a spirit getting trapped in a medium's body," the psychic said slowly, "but that doesn't mean it can't happen. If I tried to channel a spirit residing in an earthly host, probably nothing would happen. But it's *possible* it could be disastrous, both for the spirit and the host. We just don't know. And frankly, I'm not interested in proving anything to anyone. I only work with people who want my help. Live and let live is what I say."

Tamora's black-painted lips broke into a smile, but there was no warmth in it. "You and my sister are the ones who need proof," she said to me. "I have something better than proof. I have faith." She placed the flat of her palm against her chest as she said this. "It doesn't matter what you think. It certainly doesn't matter what Bailey thinks. And although all of you would love to discredit me and my experience, I know what I have with Cecil is the real thing."

Wrath and I replied in unison. "*Cecil?*"

Tamora's grin widened. "Yes. That's his name. The host, I mean. Jeff is trapped in Cecil's body. And although on paper I'll be marrying Cecil, I'll really be marrying Jeff."

In the years I'd worked with the San Diego Police Department as a paranormal investigator, I'd come across many unhinged people. But I'd met nobody who believed their dead husband was hanging out in someone else's body and was willing to marry a stranger to reunite with their spouse.

I mean, you just can't make this stuff up. RealTV Productions was definitely getting their money's worth.

"So that's it then? You just don't want to know the truth." Wrath plopped down in a chair, slouching, legs spread wider than necessary. I think they call it manspreading. "Look, man, that's fine and everything. That's your right. But you know we're gonna look into this with or without you, right? This is our challenge, man. And you may not want our help, but *I* want to win. So for me, this isn't about you at all."

Tamora sniffed disdainfully. "Believe me, Wrath, I was never under the misconception that it was." She rose to her feet, making shooing motions with her hands. "Do whatever you like," she said. "Reverse search Cecil's phone number. Message his friends on Facebook. I draw the line at trying to channel him, though. Do you understand? I *do not consent* to that. Am I clear?"

Given what she had just done to me, I thought it pretty rich that she was refusing consent, but I just shrugged. "Whatever."

"And do me one favor," she continued. "When your investigation leads you to the same conclusion that I've already reached? That Jeff and Cecil are one and the same? Have the backbone to come back here and tell me to my face. Admit you were wrong."

I almost laughed at that. I didn't get cast as Pride for nothing. Admitting I was wrong on national television? Fat chance of that.

But I didn't have to say anything because Wrath answered for both of us. "You got a deal," he said, rising to his feet. "I guess we might as well get out of here."

We were halfway to the door when I stopped and turned. "I have one question before we leave. Who were those people who sat next to me tonight?"

Tamora squinted, thinking. "The man was Balthazar Andros. The woman was Victoria Webster. Why?"

I hesitated. The ethics around psychic revelations aren't exactly clear-cut. "I saw something when I held their hands. I'm not sure who the visions came from, but I saw evidence of poltergeists. Stacked chairs, dishes flying around the kitchen." I shrugged. "Might have been nothing."

Slowly, Tamora walked to where I stood, her eyes locked on mine. "Who put you up to this?" she asked.

I blinked, confused. "Excuse me?"

"The poltergeists," she said. "You said you saw *poltergeists*. The chairs and the dishes. What else did you see?"

I floundered, racking my memory for the exact images that had come. "A brass bedframe rattling. Doors being thrown open, things like that." I narrowed my eyes at her. "Why?"

Tamora sucked in a long breath. "Those were Jeff's memories," she whispered. "He was tormented by poltergeists growing up. How did you know that? Nobody knew that. How could you have seen that?"

"Somebody knew it," I said. "Either Victoria or Balthazar. Maybe one of them is the one catfishing you."

"Or one of them is Cecil," Wrath suggested, "and Jeff really is trapped inside that body."

I shot Wrath a dubious look. "You don't really believe that."

Wrath snorted and thumbed his nose. "Man, I'll believe anything if it gets me the votes. Now come on. It's late, and I'm still thirsty. Let's get a good night's rest, and in the morning, we'll go hunt down a dead guy."

five

. . .

The next day, I found Sloth in the living room, lying on the couch. She was dressed in an old, ratty bathrobe and a pair of slippers that had long since needed to be retired. Her hair was in a messy bun, and a laptop was propped on her stomach. When she saw me, she waved lazily and scrubbed her face with her free hand. "Hey, Pride."

"Hey, Sloth," I answered. "What're you up to?"

Sloth frowned and gestured at the computer. "Me? Nothing. I mean, I was doing something, but I'm not getting anywhere. I'm too stupid to do detective work."

"Most people are," I said. "What are you investigating?"

Sloth heaved a sigh and sat up, shifting the computer into her lap. "Remember I told Mrs. Romanowsky I would help her find that organization her son was working with?"

I nodded. "Yeah, sure. I remember." As part of the last challenge, I'd stumbled upon a dead body. The victim was a loner named Walt Romanowsky. He was involved with an enigmatic organization that appeared to hunt down supernatural creatures.

His mother had asked Sloth to find out what she could about them. "I told you I would help."

"Well, I got Walt's laptop from Mrs. Romanowsky," she said, gesturing to the machine in her lap, "and I've been looking through these emails. But none of it sounds suspicious at all. I found his exchange with somebody at Chenoweth," she said. Chenoweth International was supposedly the name of the organization we were investigating. "But it's just dumb *guy* stuff."

"Dumb guy stuff? What do you mean?"

Sloth patted the cushion next to her, and I plopped down at her side. She handed me the computer. "Here. Look. This is what I found so far. Like I said, maybe I'm just too stupid to understand what I'm looking at. But none of this has anything to do with hunting bounties."

I clicked on Walt's inbox, and the first thing I noticed was that it was surprisingly empty. He had a few confirmation emails from local retailers, some general newsletter spam, and quotes on car insurance. (That lizard wanted to save him 15%.) But I didn't see a single inbound message from Chenoweth.

Walt kept a meticulous inbox. Good for him; bad for us.

"Did you look in the sent folder?" I asked.

Sloth nodded. "Yeah, that's where I found the dumb guy stuff. I mean I'm stupid, but I'm not *that* stupid."

"You're not any kind of stupid," I answered absently. I clicked open the sent folder and began browsing. Unlike the inbox, which was squeaky clean, it looked like he'd never scrubbed his this one. Most of his outgoing messages were sent to Ghost@ChenowethITL.com.

I clicked the most recent one.

It read:

"Hey Ghost,

Haven't heard back from you. I still have your SuperHawks.

If you can't pick them up, I can bring them to you. Otherwise, I'll have to transfer them to another garage. You know how it is; gotta make space for new customizations. Get back to me,

-Walt"

I glanced at Sloth. "What's a SuperHawk?"

"According to the internet, it's a motorcycle," she said.

"Oh, so that's what you meant by dumb guy stuff."

She nodded. "Uh huh."

I opened the next email in the list, which chronologically was actually a previous email. It read:

"What's up, Ghost!

So, I've got your Honda SuperHawks ready. I gotta say, they look sweet! I gave them new wheels and repainted them, so they look brand new—you won't even recognize them. I've got them locked up in my garage, so everything is secure. When do you want to come pick them up?

-Walt"

I clicked through about half a dozen other messages. It was more of the same. The recipient of his emails changed—Ghost, Jackal, Wolverine, etc.—but the gist was always the same. Your bike is ready, please come get it.

"Did his mom or anyone say anything about him doing motorcycle customization?" I asked.

Sloth shook her head. "No. But then again, we didn't ask, did we?"

"I guess not," I agreed. "Well, you're not stupid. I don't know what to make of these emails either. Unless…"

I switched tabs and ran a Google search for Chenoweth International. Their website was the first search result, and I clicked it.

It was a website for motorcycle customization enthusiasts. The site was a mixture of upcoming shows and events, with articles about motorcycle repair, maintenance, and customization. Apparently, they held conferences and workshops all over the world. There was even a store section. I clicked SHOP, and a pop-up informed me the store was members only. I could either log in or request an account.

"Let's see if we can log in as Walt," I suggested. His email address was already populated on the login screen. I clicked "Reset password" and received a notification that someone would get back to me within 10 business days with a new password.

"It's not automated?" Sloth asked with a frown. "An actual *person* has to reset our password?"

"Looks like it," I said. "Well, I guess that's all we can do with this for now. Though it is *weird*."

"The password thing *is* weird," Sloth agreed.

"Not that. I was in Walt's bedroom. He had tons of paintings of animals but nothing about motorcycles."

"To be fair," Sloth said, "he's a grown man. What grown man puts up pictures of motorcycles in his bedroom?"

"The kind of grown man who lives at home with his mother?"

Sloth hrmmed, nodding. "Okay, fair point. Still, we don't know *anything* about him. Not really. Maybe his mom was wrong. Maybe there's nothing nefarious about Chenoweth after all."

"Maaaybe," I drawled. But even though I saw where Sloth was coming from, things weren't adding up in my mind. The cops found handcuffs on Walt's body. In addition, they'd found a cat carrier at the scene of his death which was presumed to belong to him. Of course, neither of these things meant he was a supernatural bounty hunter. But his mom claimed he was a member of a secret organization, and Walt's good friend Charmaine

confirmed it, saying the organization hunted supernatural bounties.

These two women were the closest people to Walt in the world. Could they both be wrong?

Maybe, maybe not. Either way, I wouldn't know more until Walt's password on the Chenoweth website was reset.

I handed the laptop back to Sloth. "I wish I could be more help," I said. "but I need to get going. Wrath and I have an appointment. Will you be around later? Maybe we can grab a bite to eat."

"We'll see," Sloth said, returning to her previously prone position on the couch. I noticed her bathrobe had at least three new fresh stains. "I'm pretty tired."

"Suit yourself," I said. "I'll look for you when I'm back. If you look halfway presentable, I'll treat you to ice cream."

Sloth smiled sleepily. "Thanks, Pride. I can see what Lust sees in you. You treat everyone like they matter."

I paused, frowning. "Everyone does matter," I said.

Her smile faltered, and she looked away. "You're pretty much the only person I've ever met who really believes that."

———

"Is this the place?"

I checked the address on the building against the address pulled up on my phone and nodded. "Looks like it," I said. "Not exactly what I expected."

Our appointment today was with Balthazar Andros, the guy who'd been sitting next to me at Tamora's séance. He was apparently some kind of shamanic healer. He must be doing pretty well for himself. The office was in a posh, upscale building.

Wrath shook his head, killing the engine. "I expected something more, you know, down to earth? Homey? Isn't this guy supposed to be a New Age consultant or something?"

"Whatever that means," I agreed. "To be honest, I didn't read that much about him on his website."

Wrath and I got out of the car and headed towards the building looming before us. We checked the directory in the lobby, confirming our destination. I pointed to Balthazar's name. "Third floor."

Three floors up, we walked into Balthazar's office, and a chill ran down my spine. There was nothing wrong with the place, strictly speaking. A plump receptionist sat behind the desk where we signed in. The waiting area was mostly empty except for a few anxious-looking people thumbing through magazines, checking their phones, and perusing the various pamphlets available.

That's when I realized what was bothering me. Balthazar's office reminded me of Dr. Xena's office. My therapist. The therapist I hadn't seen in months. So that wasn't a chill running down my spine.

That was guilt.

I was too nervous to sit, but Wrath took a seat next to a middle-aged woman holding a pamphlet. The title was, "Losing Weight After Menopause: A Guide to Mid-Life Beauty." He gestured at her reading material and said, "You know, diet culture is a tool of the patriarchy."

The woman looked up and blinked. "Excuse me?"

"These people are only trying to make you think you have a problem so they can sell you a solution," he said. "Who made them an authority on what you should look like? Do you think it's just rotten luck that men supposedly get better looking as they age while women don't? That's nonsense, man! It's based on the idea that women have to be young to be valuable. It's breeder propaganda. You look great. Don't let anybody tell you different."

The woman blushed bright crimson and set the pamphlet aside. "Thanks, but I'm not trying to lose weight for my looks. I'm doing it for my health."

Wrath rolled his eyes and leaned forward, dangerously close to invading the poor woman's personal space. "Losing weight for your *health?* Do you know what a load of hogwash that is? Look, man. You can be totally healthy and fat. I'm not saying you're fat. I'm just saying."

I cleared my throat. "Wrath—"

"You gotta look at your *numbers,* man," he continued, ignoring me. "What does your cholesterol look like? What's your resting heart rate? How about your glucose? Those are the numbers to watch. Not the numbers on a scale. And don't get me started on BMI charts," he said, holding up his hand to stave off an objection that wasn't coming. The woman looked far too stunned to speak. "BMI charts were created by insurance companies, not health experts. BMI has nothing to do with your health! It's about maximizing profits."

"Wrath," I said, raising my voice a little. He was causing a scene, which was mortifying. "I don't know if now is the time for this."

But Wrath continued to ignore me. He was really on a roll. "Listen to me, man. If you want to lose weight because you have an idea in your head about what you want to look like – I guess that's fine. After all, if you told me you wanted to dye your hair pink or something, I wouldn't try to talk you out of it, even though your natural hair looks great. Aesthetics are okay, man. It's cool to want to look a certain way. But *you* should decide what you look like! Come on, man. Doesn't this stuff tick you off?" He gestured to the now-abandoned pamphlet. "I know it ticks me off."

The woman looked at me, cheeks still flaming red. She

gestured towards Wrath and adjusted in her seat. "Is he your friend?"

"Friend is maybe putting it too strongly," I said. "But he's with me."

Wrath sucked his teeth and rolled his eyes. "I'm not with anybody, man. I do my own thing. I'm just saying. If you're here to see that shamanic healer about losing weight? Rethink it is all I'm saying. Make up your own mind."

The woman hesitated a moment, fidgeting with her wedding band. Then, as though confirming something to herself, she gave a crisp nod, gathered up her things, and stood. "You know what? You're right. I'm not even sure I want to lose weight. It seems like such a hassle, but I thought…well, it doesn't matter what I thought. I guess I needed to hear that today."

Wrath jabbed a finger in the air. "Yeah, you did! Everybody needs to hear it sometimes. Truth to power, man. That's what I'm here for."

As the woman left, closing the door behind her, I slid into her spot, leaning in close to Wrath and lowering my voice. "Don't be too proud of yourself. I don't think you changed her mind. I think you freaked her out. Why do you do that? Why do you go on these crazy rants?"

"Somebody has to, man. I don't want to live in a society ruled by self-hatred and capitalism. Do you?"

I gestured around me. "Who is ruled by self-hatred and capitalism? We are literally sitting in a shaman's office. As things go, that seems pretty counterculture to me, don't you think?"

But Wrath folded his arms across his chest and leaned back, shaking his head in disgust. "A shamanic healer with weight loss pamphlets in his lobby, man. That dude needs to do some serious self-reflection."

I was about to open my mouth to suggest that maybe Wrath should take his own advice when the receptionist cleared her throat and waved us over. "Wrath? Pride? Balthazar will see you now."

I followed Wrath down the hall. At the end of the hall was a room cordoned off with a curtain. We pushed through it into a dimly lit space furnished with two low tables and a half dozen floor cushions. Balthazar sat on one of the two cushions flanking a small brazier. Flames licked the bottom of a stone bowl that rested on coals.

"Welcome in," he said. "Please, make yourselves comfortable."

Since there were no chairs, we were forced to choose floor cushions, and though we took our seats, I don't know that I'd go so far as to say I was comfortable. Here's why:

1. I wasn't sure anyone should be lighting fires in an office building. That seemed like it would be against the lease, at least.
2. Balthazar looked so different than he had at Tamora's. Instead of a suit and tie, he wore a pair of sweatpants pushed up to his knees and his broad, deep brown chest glistened with sweat. His dreadlocks were pulled into a neat ponytail, and he wore a purple paisley bandanna on his head.
3. Sitting on the floor just isn't what it's cracked up to be.

I felt like I was at some kind of culturally appropriated sweat lodge, and I was way, way outside my comfort zone.

Balthazar hunched over the brazier, reaching into the flame and coaxing it with a pair of iron tongs. As he did, the coals shifted, and a strange odor filled the room.

"Please, not more incense," Wrath complained. He turned to me. "What is it with this town and incense?"

Balthazar grinned and put the tongs aside. "It's not incense, strictly speaking," he said. "This is chamomile, St. John's Wort, and Holy Basil. These are herbs I use for their ability to uplift the spirit. It has a balancing effect on the mental body. I'll be using this cleansing rite to purify the pathways of your being so I can better understand the nature of your concerns."

"The pathways of our being are already pure, thanks," Wrath said, inching away from the coals. "Can you put that out? Seriously, we just want to talk. We've had enough voodoo for a lifetime."

Balthazar chuckled, his grin widening. "This isn't voodoo, but sure, I understand. My patients usually appreciate the more spiritual approach." He put a lid on the bowl.

"Well, we're not patients," Wrath said. "We want to talk to you about poltergeists."

Balthazar leaned back on his wrists and studied us, his smile faltering. "Poltergeists," he repeated. When neither of us said anything, he sighed, the smile slipping away completely. "You're gonna need to explain that."

I told Balthazar everything I knew, which wasn't much. I explained Bailey's suspicions, Tamora's attitude, and the experience I had when I touched him and Victoria at the séance. When I finished, the shaman rubbed his hands together, eyes narrowed in thought.

"Wow, that's a lot. Can I ask you something stupid?" he asked.

"You seem capable," I said.

The slightest smile cracked over Balthazar's face. "I've been practicing the metaphysical arts for a long time. I've helped people overcome addictions and heal childhood scars. I've mended broken people and helped them tackle new life adventures. But in all my time, I've never seen any proof of life after death. I think that's why I help people achieve their potential here and now. We're not promised tomorrow."

He stopped talking long enough for me to think he was done, but he hadn't actually asked a question. I kept waiting, but he kept on not saying anything. Finally, I said, "Is there a question in here somewhere?"

Balthazar laughed, a full sound that rumbled in my belly. "Sorry, yeah. I guess I just want to know what you know. What happens after we die?"

"I have no idea," I said simply.

The shaman blinked. "Really? But you said you were a ghost whisperer."

"I am," I agreed. "I see ghosts. That doesn't mean I have the answers to life, the universe, and everything. I mean, what about you? You were at the séance. If you don't believe in life after death, what were you doing there?"

Balthazar hrmmed and placed his hands lightly on his knees. He straightened his back, tipping his chin up to the ceiling. "You want to know the truth? I'm not sure. I told myself it was research. But that's only half the truth. I was also curious about Andromeda Clark. I wanted to see her do her thing in person."

"And what did you think?" Wrath asked.

"I don't know," the shaman admitted. "It didn't go the way I expected."

"That makes two of us," I growled under my breath.

"It was scary," Balthazar continued. "The way the table levitated and the books fell and everything. It makes me wonder, though. Why would that happen? Why would a spirit's appearance cause such a disruption? It never happened that way on Andromeda's show," he pointed out. "In fact, she never used rituals. She just invited a spirit into her body, and it showed up. So why the theatrics? Why a séance at all?"

These were valid questions. But like everything else Balthazar had asked today, I had no answers.

Balthazar breathed in sharply and shook himself as though

casting the memory aside. "Anyway, you didn't come here to hash all that out. Back to the matter at hand, then. Can you tell me more about poltergeists in general? Are they evil ghosts? Angry beings in life that became angry beings in death?"

"Well, no. Poltergeists aren't ghosts," I explained. "Ghosts are spirits of dead people. Poltergeists are something else. There's an entire world beyond what you or I can see or experience. It's out there. I didn't even know wights existed until I moved to Odyssey and encountered them at Wights and Wongs. But sure, poltergeists exist. Whether they're angry, I don't know. They throw things. They make a lot of noise. They scare the bejesus out of people who live with them, but they're not ghosts. They're their own thing."

"I see. Is there a reason a person would attract a poltergeist? I'm sorry I have so many questions. But you don't run into this every day."

"That's true," I agreed, "but to be honest, I don't know. I'm not an expert in paranormal activity. Just ghosts."

The shaman looked disappointed, but he was good-natured about it, shrugging and smiling. "Ah. Well, sorry, then. I just thought I'd ask. So, tell me. What does any of this have to do with Jeff?" Balthazar asked.

"I was hoping you could tell me," I said. "Tamora said those were his memories. I don't know what to make of that. Usually, when I touch people, I see their most emotional moments. The death of a pet, getting their first big job, a wedding, things like that. But I've never touched a person and seen someone else's memories."

The shaman was quiet for a while, staring down at the burning embers. He lifted the lid from the bowl, and a thick pillar of smoke billowed out. Wrath coughed loudly, burying his nose in the crook of his arm. But Balthazar leaned forward and breathed the smoke in deeply. I bet his lungs were just garbage by now.

"I started working with Jeff about 18 months before the climb," he said finally, replacing the lid. "I was quite surprised when he came to me for help. I knew about him, of course. Big-time philanthropist, often in the news, you know. Plus, when he moved down here, the city council made a big deal about it. They used his name in their advertising for the various real estate properties for sale. So when he came to my office, it caught me off guard. I didn't figure him for the spiritual sort."

I quirked an eyebrow at that. "Any reason?"

Balthazar waved a hand, dismissing my question. "Oh, you know how it is. People with money often come off as soulless, you know?"

"They come off that way because they *are* that way," Wrath interjected. "Money makes people into monsters. Life becomes all about winning, and the winner is the one with the biggest cash pile. It's the worst blight we suffer from as humans. Left unchecked, capitalism will destroy—"

"Maybe we can talk about this later," I interrupted, throwing Wrath a remonstrative look. He scowled but clamped his mouth shut, looking away.

I returned my attention to Balthazar. "You were saying?"

"Jeff's reasons for coming to me were twofold. The first part was physical training. He wanted to learn how to breathe properly to maximize his oxygen efficiency. There's a spot up there called the death zone where people really suffer physically. Their brains and lungs are starved for oxygen, and the body begins to die. The mind plays tricks, and they become psychotic. They hallucinate people who aren't there. Things like that. Jeff wanted to be prepared. His physical training included the basics like calisthenics, but it also included body and mind purification. I taught him how to breathe and what to eat for optimum performance. We based his regimen around his astrological sign and blood type."

Wrath and I exchanged looks. Look, just because someone has money doesn't mean they can't buy into bunk science, okay? Money makes you rich. It doesn't make you a genius.

"But aside from the physical, there was a spiritual aspect to his visits, too. I don't really know how to explain it, and if I'm honest, part of me feels like discussing this with you might be an ethical breach. Doctor-patient confidentiality and all," he said with a weary smile.

I stared at the shaman through the smoke. "Good thing you're not a doctor," I said.

Balthazar stiffened. "I have a Ph.D. in holistic healing."

"My baby cousin has a driver's license from a Cracker Jack box, too, man, but it wouldn't hold up in court," Wrath interjected sharply.

I turned to Wrath and pressed a finger to my lips, giving him the best *Can you please shut up and let the guy talk?* look I could muster. Again, Wrath turned away in a huff.

Balthazar was silent for a long stretch, and I worried Wrath had cost us the rest of the interview. But finally, he took a deep breath and let it out in a loud exhale. "Jeff had his fair share of demons. I guess we all do. He spoke little of his childhood. He was very private that way. But he credits his parents with instilling philanthropic ideals in him from a young age. He had several foster siblings over the years. Still, his life was missing something. That's why he climbed Mount Everest. He needed to push his limits and see what it did for his soul. He came to me to learn what was possible up there."

"Possible in what way?"

The shaman groped for the right words, searching for a way to explain. "It's kind of like when you go to the symphony," he said finally. "Beautiful music is beautiful music, and you don't need to know a thing to appreciate the notes. But when you understand more—world events that inspired the music, the composer's love life or living situation, things like that—it adds another dimension to your appreciation. For instance, knowing Beethoven was deaf makes the marvel of his music even more profound. That's what Jeff wanted from me. Context. He wanted to understand the spirit better, so he'd know what to look for when he reached the top of that mountain."

"Which he never reached," I said.

Balthazar nodded, the corners of his mouth falling into a frown. "Which he never reached," he agreed. "It was a blow to the community, losing Jeff. He was such a wonderful man. Admittedly, we were all baffled by his relationship with Tamora. They were very different, those two. But the more distance I get from his death, the more I believe he wanted to save her."

Now, I cocked my head to the side, blinking in the dim light. My eyes still burned from the smoke. "Save Tamora? How? From what?"

Balthazar sucked his teeth. "You've been to her house," he said. "She has an unhealthy relationship with darkness and death. An unhealthy relationship with the metaphysical—and that's coming from me. What kind of woman relies on séances and mediums to make even the most basic decisions in life? She's broken. I don't know why or how—that's between her and her maker. But I think Jeff saw that and wanted to fix her, so he had to fix himself first."

This was a lot of information, but I wasn't sure any of it was getting us closer to the answers we sought. "Okay. Well, back to the poltergeists," I said. "Did he ever talk to you about them? Do you know anything you can tell me?"

Balthazar just shook his head, his shoulders falling low. "I would tell you if I knew something," he said. "But Jeff never mentioned any poltergeists. If it happened when he was a kid, I'm not surprised he said nothing. Like I mentioned, he kept mum about growing up. Childhood and family were something he didn't like to discuss. I wish I could be more helpful. I really do. But that's all I know."

With some discomfort, Wrath and I climbed to our feet. My legs were tingling from sitting cross-legged for so long. I really needed to start doing yoga or something. "Thanks for your time," I said. "Maybe we'll see you around."

Balthazar led us out of the curtained area and back into the hallway, where we welcomed the smoke-free blaze of the fluorescent lighting. As we were leaving, the shaman placed a hand on Wrath's shoulder, stopping him. "You seem like someone who could benefit from spiritual advisement," he said. "I can help you release that anger. Teach you calming exercises. Think about it. The first session's on me if you'd like to come in."

Wrath offered a tight smile and thrust his hands into his pockets. "My anger keeps me alive," he said.

When we were outside and loaded into the car, I turned to Wrath. "Do you think you'll take Balthazar up on his offer?" I asked. "Maybe you can do a shamanic journey or something."

My housemate laughed, maybe the first real laugh I'd ever heard him utter. "Seriously, I think I'd rather set myself on fire, man."

I couldn't help but smile. Finally, something Wrath and I agreed on.

six

. . .

"So, what should we do first?"

We were in Wrath's room back at the house, surrounded by his electronics. The cameraman was having trouble settling in and getting a good shot because of all Wrath's equipment. But every time the guy tried to arrange Wrath's things, Wrath slapped his hand and shouted at him in a language I didn't speak.

"By the way," I said as Wrath muttered something I didn't understand under his breath. "What language is that? Am I allowed to ask, or is that racist?"

"Vietnamese," he said. "Why would that be racist?"

"I don't know," I admitted, "but lots of things I don't recognize as racist actually are, and I don't want to be offensive."

"First of all, ignorance doesn't offend me, so don't worry about it. Ask me whatever, man. But secondly, you worry too much. It would be racist if you assumed I was speaking Chinese or if you asked me if I'm good at math. But it's not racist to be curious. You know what really ticks me off?"

"Everything," I answered earnestly.

"Well, right. But no. It ticks me off when people think ignoring differences is somehow progressive. It's nonsense, man. We're different. People, I mean, not you and me. Although you and me are pretty different. Where did you grow up, anyway?"

"Around here," I said. "San Diego."

"That's what I thought," Wrath muttered. "You seem comfortable here with these rich people and idiot charlatans like that shaman. You can't help how you grew up, man, so don't get defensive. But I grew up outside Salt Lake City. You know? Where the Mormons are."

I had no idea where he was going with any of this. "Are you Mormon?"

Wrath's eyes grew wide. "Do I look Mormon?"

I had no idea what Mormons were supposed to look like, but I wasn't so dense I didn't recognize his incredulity. "I guess not?"

"Of course not. Look, man, the point is, we're all different. We should celebrate those differences and learn from them. But anyway, I'm comfortable with charlatans, too. I grew up with them. Mine are just different from yours."

That seemed like an avenue of conversation rife with blind alleys I didn't want to turn down, so I changed the subject. "So, what should we do first?" I repeated.

"I guess we need to learn what we can about the guy pretending to be Jeff," Wrath said. "Here's all the info we have from Bailey Preston." He pointed to the computer screen, and an email from Bailey popped up listing everything she knew about the person Tamora was dating.

"He claims his name is Cecil Bradshaw from San Francisco. Let's look up his social media profiles."

Without anyone touching the keyboard, several new windows popped up in the browser. The first took us to a Facebook profile for Cecil Bradshaw in San Francisco. I pointed at it. "Is that him?"

"Looks like it," Wrath confirmed. "See, he's friends with Tamora Preston. Ok, this is a red flag."

I squinted at the profile, trying to see what Wrath had noticed, but everything looked normal to me. Not that I was an expert. I didn't have a Facebook page. It was too mortifying to post daily updates about banal minutiae, and I was absolutely not posting pictures of my meals, no matter how photogenic. "What is?"

Wrath gestured at the screen. "He's only got, like, 45 friends. A real profile would have in the hundreds."

I nodded like this made sense, but really, I was surprised. I didn't know forty-five people I cared enough about to follow on Facebook, so maybe Cecil didn't, either. But then I remembered I was the socially awkward weirdo on this cockamamie TV show, so maybe I wasn't the best judge of things like that. "So you think this profile is fake?"

Instead of answering, Wrath navigated away from the page, and a new browser window popped up. "Search the internet for photos of Cecil found on his Facebook page," he told the computer. "Show me anything that matches." He folded his arms across his chest. "If he took his profile photos from another website, we'll find them."

A moment later, a new window opened, and Wrath snapped his fingers in victory. "Man, that was too easy. Look at this, Pride." He clicked the first search result, and an image gallery popped up. "This guy didn't even *try*. This is an Instagram profile for—get this—a model from Israel named Amit Nagad." He tapped the screen to emphasize his point. As he scrolled down, my jaw dropped. Every picture he'd sent Tamora and every photo from his Facebook page were stolen from this Israeli model's page.

"But Amit Nagad has, like, *millions* of followers," I said, bewildered. "Who would be so stupid to steal photos from a popular profile like this?"

"Liars and charlatans are liars and charlatans," Wrath grumbled. "No one said they were mental prodigies."

"Okay, so it's obvious the person Tamora has been talking to isn't the person in the photos," I said, musing aloud. "So, what should we do next?"

Wrath scratched his head, thinking. "Well, I guess we have a couple options. Let's message some of his female Facebook friends and see if he's having a romantic relationship with any of them. If he's pulling a scam on Tamora, he may be pulling a scam on other people, too."

"That's a great idea," I said, rubbing my palms in excitement. "And if it turns out he's scamming other people, that should be enough to convince Tamora that he's a liar, right?"

Wrath scrubbed his face with his fingers and then swiveled in his chair to face me. "That's something I've been thinking about," he said. "You know, we actually have two different objectives. Bailey and the network want us to find out who's behind the profile. That's our challenge. But it's only half the battle. We still have another obligation, at least from my point of view."

I cocked an eyebrow. "What do you mean obligation?"

"I'm talking about justice, man. Doing the right thing. Tamora says she doesn't care who Cecil is, but if we can prove he's lying about having her husband's spirit stuck inside him, she'll cut him loose. Right? And I know that's not our challenge," he conceded, "but I couldn't live with myself if I let her continue a relationship with a charlatan. Even though she's a capitalist princess and I hate everything she stands for, I don't want anyone to take advantage of her, either. So, our challenge is to find out who Cecil is, but we *also* have to rescue Tamora."

As much as I hated to admit it, Wrath was right. "Okay, I see your point. But how do you propose we prove that this Cecil person is lying? I mean, not just about his profile picture and stuff. But about the things Tamora actually cares about."

"The only thing I can think of," Wrath said slowly, "is we have to get information out of him that only Jeff would know."

"And how are we supposed to find out something only Jeff would know?"

Wrath pointed a finger at me. "Exactamundo, man," he said. "I have no idea."

Wrath swiveled around again to face his computer. He folded his arms across his chest and leaned his head back. "Computer, I want to compose a message. Find all of Cecil Bradshaw's female friends and send them this note."

Wrath leaned forward and placed his fingers on the keys. "Easier if I just type this out myself," he said. "I feel like a jerk dictating an email message aloud."

The email message Wrath composed went like this:

"Hi there, <insert name here>,

I'm from a reality TV show called *Sinful House*. We investigate minor crimes for the locals in Odyssey, California, and solve mysteries the police are too busy to help with. Right now, I'm looking into this Cecil Bradshaw person—it looks like you're friends with him on Facebook. What can you tell me about him? Have you ever met him? Have you ever talked to him? And most importantly—are you in a romantic relationship with him? We think someone on our case might be getting catfished. I appreciate any help you can offer."

I read the email a couple times before nodding my approval. "I think that works," I said. "I can't believe we're actually doing this. This feels so… I don't know. Like high school? Like when someone would slip an anonymous note in your locker confessing their love and you had to figure out who it was."

Wrath shot me a sideways glance. "I definitely have no idea what you're talking about," he said.

I felt a flush creep up my neck. To be honest, I had no idea what I was talking about, either. Nothing like that had ever happened to me. But I'd seen it on television, so it must have happened to someone somewhere, right?

Don't answer that.

"Okay, let's move on. Bailey gave us all of Cecil's contact information, right? Should we look up his phone number?" I asked.

Wrath grunted. "Yeah, good idea."

A few moments later, Wrath pulled up the relevant information on the computer. According to the Internet, the phone number Cecil Bradshaw was using to talk to Tamora was registered to Cecil Bradshaw in San Francisco, California.

"Bollocks," Wrath swore. "It's his own phone number."

I picked up my phone. "Should we call him?"

Wrath grabbed my phone and laid it face down on the desk. "Not yet. We'll only get one chance to call him—then he'll be onto us. We should wait until we have more information."

"Okay…? What kind of information?"

Wrath ran his hands through his hair, mussing it from the roots. "Like where he really lives, if he's catfishing other girls, stuff like that. Cecil says he lives in San Francisco, which is where this phone is registered. So that's a match. We need to find info that *doesn't* add up."

"True," I agreed, "but a phone number's not hard to fake. You could use one of those internet phone numbers."

"I guess. But right now, we have no reason to doubt this person lives in San Francisco, do we?"

"No," I drawled, "it's just that… Have you ever seen the movie *Silence of the Lambs?*"

Wrath made bug eyes at me and held out his hands. "Yes? Hasn't everybody seen that movie?"

"Right. Well, in it, Hannibal Lecter says something that stuck with me my whole life. He says something like, *We covet what we see every day.* I mean, let's say you're a conman looking to marry rich. You could catfish any number of women. If it were me, I'd target women with self-esteem issues. You know, someone desperate to be loved. Why go after someone like Tamora—who, let's face it, doesn't suffer self-esteem issues. And the even bigger question is —why pretend to be someone's deceased spouse? Doesn't that feel intensely personal? Like, really targeted?"

Wrath tipped his head back, nodding in thought. "Yeah. Yeah, maybe you're right. So you think this is someone she knows."

"Not necessarily," I said. "But someone who knows *her.*"

Wrath paused. "You think it's someone in Odyssey?"

I shrugged. "I don't know. Her dad was a big-time producer. Her husband was a famous philanthropist. People all over know who she is. But still…this feels personal. I can't shake it."

"Well, trust your gut, I always say," Wrath said. He glanced down at his watch. "Hey, man, I gotta take a break. I'm starving."

"Sure. I've got some stuff I need to do, anyway."

Wrath wriggled his eyebrows and gave me a lascivious look. "Stuff? Or Lust?"

I snatched up my phone and kicked his chair before leaving his room.

Then I went to go look for Lust.

What can I say? I'm only human.

———

I searched the house for Lust, but she wasn't anywhere to be found. I didn't have anything I wanted to talk to her about or anything. I just missed her company.

Since I had some free time on my hands, I went down to the beach to soak up some sun and dip my feet in the water. In all the time I'd been at Sinful House, my trips to the beach had been few. First of all, the stupid cameraman followed me everywhere I went, and it's absolutely mortifying to be out in public with a camera following you around. I felt like a self-involved schmuck, and people stared at me. I don't know how vloggers do it. I really don't.

But aside from all that cameraman business, I grew up in San Diego. The beach wasn't exactly a novelty to me. It was, however, a place I liked to go to think. And right now, I had some thinking to do.

Initially, I'd agreed to come on the show because I didn't have much choice. I'd lost my job and my girlfriend and had nowhere to stay and no money. I let myself get invested in the show because whoever won America's Favorite Sin would win their heart's true desire. And so, for weeks, I grinned like a horse's ass for the cameras because I wanted my girlfriend back.

I wasn't so sure I wanted that anymore.

Don't get me wrong. It wasn't that I didn't love Shayda anymore. I did. I do. I'll probably feel that way about her forever. But I was beginning to think there was more to life than the love of one person. I hated to admit that something as corny as a *Sinful House* assignment got me thinking about it, but working on Tamora's case really did a number on me. Here was a woman who was obviously being swindled, and she couldn't even see it because she was so blinded by love for one person.

Look, I don't know much about anything. But even I know that's no way to go through life.

When I reached the shore, I rolled up the bottom of my

pants and waded into the water, letting the sand squish through my toes. The water was cold and felt good on my hot skin. Overhead, seagulls circled, looking for fish. The beach was sparsely populated today, which made it easier to pick out the ghosts. There were only a handful out today, but still more than I expected. None of them were looking at me. They were lying in the sand, fully dressed in the clothes they'd died in, sunbathing.

I don't know if there's a ghost-specific term for lying in the sun. Sunbathing doesn't sound right, but I don't know how else to describe it.

I was contemplating why ghosts would come to the beach at all when my phone rang.

"Hello?"

"Is this Sid Sheridan?"

I rubbed the back of my neck and looked around. I wasn't supposed to use my real name on the show, but then again, I guess the camera wasn't picking up the voice on the other end. "Yeah. Who's this?"

"Hello, Sid. This is Andromeda Clark."

I was so surprised, I just stood there like an idiot, mouth agape, saying nothing. After a moment, the voice on the other end said, "Hello? Are you still there?"

"I'm here," I said. "I'm just surprised, that's all."

"I guess that means you aren't the kind of psychic that sees the future."

"I'm definitely not," I admitted.

"So much the better, I say. Every movie would be ruined for you. And what would be the point of getting into a relationship? You'd already know how it was going to end. And the anticipation is the *entire* point!"

I hesitated. "The anticipation of a relationship ending is the point?"

"Well yes, depending on your point of view. Will it end after only seven weeks because you found out you can't stand the way he slurps his soup, or will he die at your side eighty years into the future? If you already know ahead of time which scenario you're walking into, it rather defeats the point of entering in at all, don't you think?'

I wasn't sure I agreed with any of that, but it was something to think about. Just not now. "Did you want something?"

"Of course. I didn't call you for my health. I wondered if you could make some time to speak with me."

I hesitated. "I am speaking with you now," I said matter-of-factly.

Andromeda laughed. "Yes. That's not what I meant. It's hard for me to hear you over the sound of the waves in the background. I hoped we might meet somewhere more intimate. Quieter. Would you be able to come to my hotel room? Sooner would be better than later," she amended.

I kicked at the sand and scratched my jaw. "Sure, I guess. I don't have any plans right now. Is now a good time?"

"Right now would be wonderful. I'm texting you my address. And please," Andromeda said. "I would appreciate it if you came alone. That means no cameramen and no sidekick. Understand?"

I glanced at the cameraman who was circling around me, no doubt trying to get the perfect shot of me against the sunlit ocean, wind in my hair, a slight burn on my nose. I did my best to keep my back to him. "I don't know if I can promise no cameras," I said. "But I'll do my best."

I didn't wait for a response before I disconnected.

seven

. . .

Andromeda Clark's hotel room looked like a unicorn vomited all over it.

Not that it wasn't extremely classy. It was. It was just that it was absolutely overflowing with pink femininity. Dozens of bouquets of pink roses and peonies were scattered throughout the suite. The couches were stuffed with pink satin pillows, and pink candles covered nearly every flat surface. Pink throws and area rugs were layered over top of the hotel's banal décor.

Andromeda was wearing a fluffy pink bathrobe, her pink hair pulled away from her face in a high, messy bun. She was ensconced in the corner of one of her couches, her feet tucked into the crevices between the cushions. She was holding a champagne flute filled with pink champagne.

Like I said. Unicorn vomit. Everywhere.

"Do you drink champagne?"

I laid a hand on my chest and looked around. "Me?"

Andromeda giggled, her head cocked to one side. "I wasn't speaking to the shadows. Why are you so jittery? Pour yourself a glass of bubbly and sit down with me."

I poured myself a glass of the pink champagne, and Andromeda scooted over, making room for me on the couch. I sat on the other end of the sofa, keeping a cushion's distance between us. I didn't want to invite too much intimacy. I couldn't imagine what might happen if I touched her skin. I might see anything.

And after what had happened the last time I met with her, I wasn't taking any chances.

"So," she said, smiling around the rim of her champagne glass. "We finally meet in private. The famous Sid Sheridan."

I felt my cheeks grow warm, and I took a sip of the champagne to hide my discomfort. "I wouldn't go so far as to call myself famous," I said. "I'm not exactly a household name."

"Well, but that's not true, is it? At least, you are very well known among people who study the occult and the metaphysical. People like myself. And people like Tamora."

I shifted uncomfortably, taking another sip from my glass. "Is that what you want to talk about? The commune? Because I have to tell you, I don't have much to say about that."

Andromeda peered at me, her lips pressed together as she considered my response. "We'll get to that. First, I want to talk about the séance. I watched the footage, you know. Helluva thing that happened."

I snorted. "You can say that again," I said. I looked up sharply, grinding my back molars. I hoped she wouldn't say it again. I really hated when people did that. It wasn't nearly as funny as they thought.

But Andromeda didn't say it again. Instead, she clucked her tongue against the roof of her mouth. "I've been doing this work for a long time," she said. "Are you familiar with my work? Did you ever watch the show?"

I nodded. "I've seen a few episodes." I don't know why I lied. I'd seen every episode at least once.

Andromeda hrmmed. "Then you know that isn't how I usually conduct business. I usually like to meet with people one on one and channel their loved ones into my body. No pomp, no circumstance."

"So why were things different at Tamora's? Why the séance?"

"That was for you," she said. "Well, not *for* you. It was *because* of you. Tamora told me you were coming, and she said you wanted to contact your family. I know she lied about that," Andromeda said, interrupting my prepared objection. "But I didn't know it at the time. Anyway, I knew my traditional methods wouldn't work under those circumstances. No one knows who your parents are, including you. And I knew you didn't have any of their personal effects. Lacking those very critical pieces of information, I thought it would be best to hold the séance. It creates more energy, helping the universe home in on our request. So that's why the séance. But even so."

She scooted towards me, so close I could smell her perfume. It was something fruity and overly feminine, like an upscale version of something you might find at Victoria's Secret. "All the theatrics with the books and the table? All of that is par for the course with any séance. So you have to look past all that. What struck me was that it *worked*."

My brow creased in confusion. "What do you mean, it worked? All I heard was nonsense."

Andromeda smiled, a soft stretch of her lips. "Nonsense words? Is that what you heard? Because I agree with Tamora about one thing: you got a clue to your past, Sid. 'Find some of all profits on vinyl'?" Unexpectedly, she took my free hand in both of hers, squeezing her fingertips against my knuckles. A thousand faces flashed before my eyes, each of them wanting something. Even the sight of it was exhausting.

"*On vinyl*, Sid. I think that means we're looking for a *record album*. A record album titled, *Some of All Profits*."

I blinked. "That's plausible," I admitted. "Thanks for the tip."

Andromeda sat quietly for a moment. Then she said, "You don't seem…enthusiastic."

I hesitated, not wanting to hurt her feelings. She was obviously feeling chuffed that she'd figured this out on her own. But I wasn't nearly as excited as she was. "I am," I lied.

Andromeda pursed her lips and leaned in closer to me. "Sid, sweetheart, is this something you want to pursue?" she asked.

I shook my head, exhaling heavily. "No. It really isn't. I know everyone is cuckoo for Cocoa Puffs over the missing commune, but it doesn't interest me. Not in a personal way, anyway. My parents are dead. I'm on my own in this world. That's the only thing that matters."

Andromeda nodded, her expression growing soft and serious. "You're not really alone in the world, though, Sid. You have a tremendous light inside you. Others are drawn to it, and they'll accompany you on your journey if only you'll let them. Like the ghosts."

I stared at her. "The ghosts are drawn to me because I have a tremendous light inside me?"

Now, the psychic smiled, laughing. "Yes! Didn't you know that?"

"I didn't," I confessed.

"I see. I suppose there are a great many things you don't know. Not you in particular. But most of us are blind to our positive traits. Well, if you change your mind about pursuing your past, or if you need anything—"

"I do need something," I interrupted. I stood up to retrieve the champagne bottle and refreshed both glasses. "Did you know Jeff Bishop?"

Andromeda reached her hands into her hair and unwound her bun, letting her hair fall in billowing pink clouds around her shoulders. She massaged her scalp with her fingertips, eyes closed. "I've known the Prestons for decades," Andromeda began. "I met Adam Preston when I was just a young woman, new to the Hollywood scene. I'd just started gaining some notoriety, and Adam offered to help with my career. Not that I was a singer," she added with a laugh. "But powerful, famous people know other powerful, famous people, and he wanted to open doors for me. So I let him."

Andromeda reached for her champagne glass and took a deep sip. "I'm a few years older than Tamora, and in some ways, she treated me like an older sister. I wasn't as close with Bailey. See, Tamora has always been keen on the metaphysical, and I, obviously, have some insight in that arena. She relied on me for spiritual and psychic advice about everything—where to go to college, who to date, where to purchase a home. When Jeff proposed, she asked me if she should marry him. But I told her I didn't know."

The psychic sighed and set her glass on the table. "Jeff was a nice enough guy, don't get me wrong. But there was something about him I never could unlock. If I say he was secretive, it gives you the wrong idea. I don't think he was hiding things. It's just that he kept everything very close to his chest. He never talked much about himself. He never volunteered his thoughts and opinions. For a philanthropist, he didn't have many friends. Some people called him eccentric. I don't think that's accurate. It was more like Jeff was an anthropologist objectively observing the rest of the world without participating in it. Does that make sense?"

"I'm getting the picture," I drawled. "So you told Tamora you weren't sure about the marriage because you couldn't get a bead on him?"

Andromeda nodded. "Yes. That's exactly it. Of course, she married him anyway, and he made her very happy. Maybe he opened up to her over time. I don't know. But he certainly never opened up to me. I wish I could tell you who to talk to. Who might know him better. But I'm not sure anyone knew Jeff Bishop. Not really."

I cleared my throat and popped my knuckles. "Andromeda, do you know anything about poltergeists?"

Andromeda blinked. "Poltergeists?"

"Yes. Did Jeff ever mention them to you?"

The psychic sighed, shaking her head. "I don't know anything about that," she said.

I couldn't think of anything else to ask, so I finished the last of my champagne and got to my feet. "Thanks for all your help," I said. "I really appreciate it. And if I need anything else, I'll be in touch," I added.

"You do that," the psychic said, only a bare hint of a smile playing on her lips. "You do that."

———

Later that night, I was in bed reading a sci-fi novel when the temperature dropped, and a familiar sensation riffled over my skin. A small ghost climbed into bed with me, waving a hand in front of my face. I knew this ghost. I'd been seeing her ever since I was young. I grew up, but she never did. And she had a habit of showing up when I was least in the mood to deal with her.

I set the novel down with a sigh. "Can I help you with something?" I asked.

"Did you know cows sleep standing up?" she said.

I nodded. "Everybody knows that."

"Oh. Well, did you know some people are too stupid for their own good?"

I leaned my head back, tilting my face toward the ceiling. "If you have something to say, just say it."

"Andromeda wants to help you find your family." The ghost said tersely. "You should let her."

"You know what's funny about you?" I asked. "You think you know things, but you actually don't know anything at all."

The ghost looked at me with wide eyes, her mouth falling open in disbelief. "Why would you say that? What are you talking about?"

I tucked my hands into my armpits and gave the ghost a stern look. "You don't know anything about how the world works. No, don't look at me like that. I'm not being mean. It's the truth. It's not your fault, but you don't know how much you don't know. It's called the hubris of youth," I explained.

In the darkness, the ghost glowered at me, her eyelids heavy and the corners of her mouth reaching for a frown. "I'm not *young*," she said. "Don't you remember the first time we met? You were little, and so was I. I've been on this earth every bit as long as you have."

I opened my mouth to object, but she had me there. After all, she didn't say she'd been *alive* as long as I had. "Fine, but as a ghost, you don't understand how people operate. Especially adults. You don't know why Andromeda says she wants to help. Maybe she really does. Maybe there's goodness in her heart, and she just wants to reconnect me with my past. It's possible."

"It's *more* than possible," the ghost said. "Andromeda has pink hair. Ladies with pink hair can't be bad."

"It's also possible she has a book deal in the works, and she's using me for a story no one else can tell," I said, ignoring her comment about pink hair. That didn't even warrant discussion. "Maybe it's something bigger than a book deal. Maybe it's a movie. Maybe it's a new television series. The point is, I can't read minds. I don't know what Andromeda wants. Maybe she wants to help me. Maybe she wants to help herself."

The ghost threw up her hands in exasperation. "Who cares?

Don't you want to know what happened to those people? Don't you want to know where you came from?"

It took me a long time to answer. But finally, I shook my head. "Not really. I know you don't understand that. No one does. I just don't see the point in digging up the past. What good will it do?"

The ghost blinked. "What *harm* can it do?"

"I don't know, and that's the problem. I'm happy with my life. Why would I want to look for trouble?"

The ghost was quiet for a long time. Then she said, "Are you?"

"Am I what?"

"Happy," she said with a roll of her eyes, as if this were the most obvious thing in the world. "Are you happy?"

I sighed. "I don't know. Maybe. I think so. Or at least, I'm getting there."

The ghost smiled and leaned her head to the side. "I'm glad. You deserve to be happy."

"Do I?" I asked. "Sometimes, I wonder."

The ghost nodded. "I know. And that's the real reason you won't let Andromeda or anyone help you. Because you're not sure you deserve it."

"All right," I groaned. "Let's just do this, okay?"

The ghost frowned. "Do what?"

I retrieved my phone and began a Google search. I typed in the phrase, "Some of all profits +album". Google returned a bunch of links for fundraisers saying things like, "A portion of all profits will be donated…" or "Some of all profits will go toward funding…" so I nixed that search and tried another, this time adding "-fundraiser" to my search string. That didn't yield anything, either. I varied my search terms, looking for anything to point me in the right direction. But nothing turned up.

"There, I did my due diligence," I said, putting the phone

away. "I searched for an album called *Some of All Profits*, and I didn't find anything. Are you happy?"

The ghost rolled her eyes. "This isn't about making *me* happy. Geez."

I yawned and glanced at the clock. It was getting late. I reached to my bedside table to turn off the lamp. "Well, I did it to shut you up, anyway. The truth is —"

But when I looked back over to where the ghost had been sitting, she was gone.

————

I woke up to the smell of muffins.

I wasn't especially hungry, but the smell coming from downstairs made my mouth water. I dressed quickly, ran a brush through my hair, and headed downstairs. I found Gluttony in the kitchen, pulling a tray of fresh blueberry muffins from the oven. A second batch was already cooling on the counter.

I slid onto a stool at the island and plopped my chin in my hands. "You're up early," I said. "Couldn't sleep?"

Gluttony huffed and slid the muffins onto the counter. "That pan's hot." He untied the apron at his waist and hung it on a peg by the pantry. He ran a hand over his afro and huffed out a sigh. "I slept fine. Had to get up early to get a jump start on the day, though. Sloth and I have a lot to do, and she hasn't been herself lately. I thought these muffins might help."

"Not herself how?"

Gluttony grimaced and pulled a cooling rack from underneath the sink. "She's depressed," he said, using his fingertips to lift the hot muffins from the tray and drop them onto the rack. "And depressed people can't solve mysteries."

The muffins smelled terrific, and I reached for one, but Gluttony smacked my hand away. "Those are for Sloth."

I scowled but withdrew my hand into my lap. "I hate to break this to you, but she's always depressed. That's kind of why she's here. As a sin, I mean. Sloth doesn't just mean laziness like most people think. It has more to do with a general ennui of the soul."

Gluttony tilted his head back and barked out a laugh, placing a hand on each hip and standing akimbo. "I know you're not about to school me about the Bible," he said. "I been going to Sunday school since I was knee high to a grasshopper, and two of my uncles are ministers. I know what sloth means."

He picked up the now-empty tray with a pair of mitts and dropped it into the sink. "It's gotta be tough being a mind reader," he said. "I think she been hearing things lately she rather not hear. Things ain't goin' good for her, and I worry. And that ain't selfish. I mean, yes, I want to win this challenge, but I also care about the girl. Don't you tell nobody I said that." He jabbed an index finger at my face. "I'll just deny it."

Just then, Wrath bounded into the kitchen, a pair of headphones around his neck. As usual, he was dressed like something out of a cyberpunk comic, with an oversized black T-shirt reaching almost down to his knees and a pair of polyester cargo pants with way too many zippers. "Hey," he said, slapping me on the arm. "You busy today?"

"Not especially," I said. "Why, you got a lead or something?"

Wrath smiled and lifted his hands, jabbing his thumbs toward his chest. "Who's got two thumbs and an appointment to talk to Victoria Webster?"

I spread my hands, supplicant. "Is this a riddle?"

"This guy," he said, breaking into a smile.

I sat up straight, blinking back my surprise. "Really? You got us an appointment with Victoria Webster? Why did you do that?"

"Well, you didn't *ask* for my help," Wrath said, his voice taking on an accusing tone. "But since that shaman didn't know squat about poltergeists, I figured maybe Victoria Webster would."

I spun around on the stool, still eyeing the muffins. "Yeah, definitely, but I thought it was more important to stay focused on the case. I'm afraid the poltergeists might be a dead end," I said.

Wrath pointed to the muffins. "Can I have one of these?"

Gluttony glanced at Wrath. "No."

"Anyway," my partner said, sliding his headset up onto his ears, "if talking to Victoria helps us understand Jeff better, I'm all for it. Only problem is, she doesn't have time to see us in private. She agreed to meet us while she's getting her hair done."

I shrugged. If she was willing to talk, I was ready to listen. I didn't need privacy for an interview. "That's awesome, Wrath, thanks. What time's the appointment?"

He looked down at his smartwatch. "10 minutes ago," he said. "Let's bounce."

Incredulous, I stared after Wrath as he slipped from the kitchen. I turned to Gluttony, brow raised. "Can you believe that guy?"

Without waiting for an answer, I plucked a muffin from the island. The pastry was halfway to my mouth when Gluttony shouted, "Yo! Those are for Sloth!"

I bit into the muffin, and hot blueberry juice squirted over my tongue. "She won't mind. Tell her I said thanks," I said through a mouthful of blueberry juice and sugar.

Gluttony said nothing as he watched me devour the rest of the muffin. Then he smiled and tossed a rag onto his shoulder. "Have a great day, Pride."

Something about the way he said it stopped me in my tracks. "Gluttony? Wait! Did you—what did you put in the muffins? Gluttony?"

Gluttony tsked as he walked away. "I told you they were for Sloth. Next time, mind your manners."

eight

. . .

The Beachin' Blondes hair salon was a quick 5-minute drive from the house. The entire time, I scolded Wrath for our lateness. "It's just so rude and unprofessional," I said, shaking my fists in the air for emphasis. "You of all people should understand that! You're so invested in social justice and everything."

Wrath gripped the wheel so hard, his knuckles went bloodless. "You think punctuality is on the side of the little guy? Oh man, you've got some serious deprogramming to do," he said, not waiting for my answer. "Let me tell you about *time* discipline, man. It cheats laborers out of optimizing their labor based on their natural rhythms, for one."

I pressed a hand to my forehead, closing my eyes as I leaned back into the seat. "You've got to be kidding me," I moaned.

"Think about it, Pride. Clock-time is what allowed the industrial revolution to be successful, man. Forcing people to work on the company's schedule instead of their own natural rhythms? That's what breaks people down. You think everyone in the working world wants to wake up at 6 a.m., work 8 or 9 hours, and then get in bed by 10? Our society shows no respect for different circadian rhythms, man. It's unjust."

"Why did I say anything?" I muttered to myself.

"And that's not all," he continued. "Time discipline and punctuality are tools of white supremacy."

I held up a hand. "I'll take your word for it," I said.

"Showing up late is an act of anarchy," Wrath said, ignoring me. "When we show up late to places? Especially appointments with rich ladies with more dollars than sense? We're sticking it to the man, you know? We're taking back our value."

As usual, Wrath's view of the world was too ridiculous to respond to. And anyway, the longer we drove, the less I felt inclined to change his mind. In fact, I was in a good mood. I felt lighter. My mind was clear, and negativity seemed to melt off me.

That was new to me. I kinda liked it.

The salon was exactly what you'd expect of a salon called Beachin' Blondes. It was decorated in the local beachy style, which I'm sure the city council appreciated. Most of the guests sported a head full of artificially blonde hair. The shades of blonde ranged from dark and sultry to silver so rich, it was almost purple. Bubblegum pop played from the speakers overhead, and as soon as we walked in, a woman draped in a black cape with her head full of foil lifted a hand.

"Wrath? Pride? Over here," she said.

The cameramen followed us over to Victoria's chair. We'd brought two cameramen today. I say we brought them like we had a choice, which we didn't. But judging by the look on Victoria's face, two cameras were better than one.

One thing I've learned in my time in Odyssey? Everybody in this town has their sights set on stardom. Which, I won't lie, makes getting them to talk to us on camera easier.

"Nice to see you again, Victoria," Wrath said, turning on the charm.

Victoria smiled, flashing artificially white and even teeth. "I'd offer my hand, but this cape just gets in the way," she tittered. "Good to see you, too, Pride."

"Great to see you, too, Victoria. I have to say, you look just as lovely underneath that cape as you did the other night at the séance."

As soon as the words were out of my mouth, I blinked in shock. Why on earth had I said that? That wasn't anything I'd usually say. It wasn't even anything I'd typically think. Even Wrath was looking at me like I'd lost my mind. But I just shook myself and smiled, covering my bemusement. "So did Wrath tell you what we wanted to talk about today?"

Instead of answering, however, Victoria looked to her stylist and gestured toward a couple of empty chairs in the waiting area. "Shelley, would you mind bringing those chairs over here for our guests? We have so much to talk about, and I think they'd be more comfortable if they weren't on their feet the whole time."

Shelley hurried away to carry out the request, and Victoria rolled her eyes, making a disgusted sound behind the other woman's back. "Seriously, you'd think she would've known to do that on her own. Sometimes, it's just impossible to get good help."

When Shelley returned with the chairs, I clapped her on the arm, giving her shoulder a gentle squeeze. "I really appreciate this," I said, surprising even myself. "You really didn't have to do that."

Shelley's cheeks turned from pink to bright red as she fluttered her lashes, chewing her lips with what I think was embarrassment. "It's not a problem," she breathed, returning her attention to Victoria's head full of foiled hair.

"Anyway," Wrath said, settling into his chair, "we want to talk about Jeff."

Victoria nodded sagely. "Jeff Bishop," she cooed. She said his name like she was uttering a prayer. "It was such a travesty, the way he died. But at least he went out the same way he lived his life, right? With gusto. Doing the thing he loved."

I quirked an eyebrow. "Did Jeff love climbing?"

"It wasn't about the climbing," Victoria assured me. "It was all about conquering. Doing things the average person couldn't do. Jeff was not content with ordinary. How do you think he ended up with a woman like Tamora? Anyway, not everybody gets to die on top of Mount Everest. That's my point. Jeff was different. Right from the start."

I cleared my throat and leaned forward, lowering my voice. "Did you know him well? Did he confide in you?"

Now, the woman's eyes narrowed ever so slightly, and I caught a glance from the stylist in the mirror. "I don't know if I would call myself a confidante," she said. "We were close, though. I've known Jeff for a long time."

"How long?" Wrath asked.

"That's too close to asking a lady how old she is," Victoria said, dropping us a coy wink. "But I've known him since college. No, not like that." Victoria was glaring in the mirror at her stylist, pointing to a section of foils around her face. "I want these highlights to be thinner. You can't use such chunky sections."

"Sorry," Shelley apologized, removing the foils from her client's hair. "I wasn't thinking."

As she rearranged the foils, my eyes trailed up the stylist's bare arms. She had an array of artwork on her skin done in bright colors and bold lines. "Your tattoos are beautiful," I said. "Did you get that work done here?"

"Not in Odyssey," she said. "I had to go all the way to Toronto for these."

"It was worth it," I purred, still admiring her art. "Do they have special meaning for you?"

Even as I asked the questions, I had no idea why these words were coming out of my mouth. Not because her tattoos weren't lovely—they were—but because giving out compliments like Halloween candy was so far outside my comfort zone that I'd need a GPS to find my way back. And yet, I couldn't stop. "You have a real sense of style," I continued. "Do you do your own hair? The color is outstanding."

The stylist flushed red and touched her hair absently. "I do the color myself," she said, eyes glowing. "I change it too often to let anyone else do it. The expense would be outrageous." She chuckled, the color creeping higher into her face. "Someone else cuts it, though. It's really hard to cut your own hair."

"Well, whoever does it does a great job. The way it frames your face is just perfect."

Shelley sucked in a breath and dropped her eyes, but that smile lingered on her lips.

Suddenly, I felt Wrath's hand close around my upper arm, and he stepped away, dragging me along with him. "We'll be back in just a second," he said to Victoria.

Wrath's grip tightened as he pulled me across the salon and into a quiet corner. When we were out of earshot, Wrath practically threw my arm down. "What are you *doing*?" he demanded. "Why are you blathering on with the stylist? Are you trying to get her digits or something? I thought you had a thing for Lust!"

I wrapped both my hands around my throat and shook my head, my eyes wide. "First of all, nothing is going on between me and Lust. But second, I don't know what's happening! I can't help it! My brain is absolutely overflowing with positive thoughts! Like right now, I'm trying really hard not to tell you what nice hands you have. Your fingers are elegantly shaped, and your skin is so soft."

Wrath grabbed me by the shoulders, digging his fingertips into my skin as he gave me a good, hard shake. "Get it together, man! That rich lady's not gonna talk to us if she thinks we're lunatics."

"I'm trying," I whined. "But I feel like I've been drugged or something."

Wrath released me, arms falling limply to his sides. His mouth formed a soft *o*, and he let his eyes flutter closed as his head tipped backward. "You ate Gluttony's muffins," he said.

"He put something in them," I said, realizing it was true. "Some kind of magic to make people have nice thoughts. Probably so Sloth wouldn't have to hear everyone's internal garbage for just one day."

Wrath slapped me on the shoulder. "You gotta be careful what you stuff into your piehole, man! We're trying to win this thing. What if he'd put in magic to sabotage us?"

I frowned, shaking my head. "Gluttony wouldn't do that."

"That's not the point. You need to be more careful." He jerked his head back toward Shelley's station. "Okay, so, we're gonna go back over there, and I need you to *stay on target*. Focus on your questions, okay? Leave the stylist alone."

I tried to respond, but Wrath was already tugging me back across the salon. Victoria's face was pinched, and even I could tell she was growing irritated.

"Sorry about that," Wrath said. "We don't want to take up too much more of your time. But Pride had one question." He held out his hand, gesturing for me to speak.

"Right. One question," I said, trying hard to focus. It was harder than you think. All I could think about was how Victoria had nicely shaped eyes and a perfect nose and how Shelley's neck was the perfect length for her body. "Victoria, did Jeff ever mention poltergeists to you?"

Victoria's head snapped up, and her eyes met mine in the mirror. Her gaze was icy cold, her face frozen. But the expression was fleeting; as quickly as it had appeared, the ice melted, and her carefree aloofness returned with a cavalier smirk. "Poltergeists? You mean invisible ghosts that throw things around and scream in the middle of the night?"

I sucked in a sharp breath. This town seriously needed re-education about the supernatural. "Well, technically, poltergeists are not—"

"Yes," Wrath interrupted. "Exactly. Did he ever mention anything like that to you?"

Victoria shook her head. "No. Like I said, Jeff was very down to earth. Something like that would never come up in conversation."

But as she said it, her eye twitched.

I watched her in the mirror, waiting for her to change her tune, but she just stared back at me, not even blinking. "Okay," I said finally. It didn't look like she was gonna talk. But I couldn't ignore that twitching eye. She was definitely holding something back. "Listen. We're going to catch this person who's pretending to be Jeff," I said. "But to do that, we need to ask him questions —things only Jeff would know. Do you have anything? Something we could ask that maybe only you and Jeff shared?"

Victoria's mouth twisted, and her eyes listed toward the ceiling as she considered my question. But finally, she let her breath out in a controlled exhale. "I can't think of anything off the bat," she said. "If you're asking me for secrets—I'm sure I told him secrets over the years. But I couldn't tell you what they were about. And as for him sharing secrets with me? That wasn't really how Jeff operated."

I turned my attention back to Wrath. "I can't think of anything else," I said. "You?"

Wrath shook his head. "Nothing from me. But listen, Victoria. If you think of anything, would you call us?"

Victoria flashed us another of her bright smiles. "Of course! I'd do anything to help Tamora."

We were halfway to the car when a voice called out behind us.

"Wait."

We turned around to find Shelley hurrying over to us, her eyes darting around wildly, checking over her shoulder as though she was worried about being followed. She sidled up next to us, holding her hands at her chest. She twisted her fingers together and chewed on her bottom lip. "Can I talk to you for a second? In private?"

I shrugged, looking around. "You're talking to us in private right now."

Shelley swallowed hard a couple times, nodding. But she wasn't really agreeing. It was more like she was building up courage or convincing herself of something. After a little while, she said, "I don't have a lot of time, but Victoria's lying to you."

"Lying?" Wrath repeated.

Shelley smoothed her hair behind her ears (even though she already looked perfect) and continued to scan the parking lot for eavesdroppers. "I've been her stylist for a long time. She doesn't trust anybody else to make her blonde but me. And you know what they say about stylists and their customers? When people sit in that chair for a long enough time, they talk. They talk about all *kinds* of things."

I nodded, rolling my hand in a get-on-with-it motion. "Okay. What did she tell you?"

"I wouldn't feel right telling you everything," she began, "so I'll just tell you this. The Topanga Canyon Music Awards. They were only hosted for one year before they were canceled. Jeff was there, and he had a guest."

"A guest?"

But Shelley was already backing away, holding her hands out to ward off more questions. "Just look into it," she said. "I think it'll be worth your time."

Before we could ask her any more questions, she turned on her heel and ran back into the salon.

Wrath whistled as he watched her hurry back inside. "That was weird, right? Why didn't she just tell us what she knew?"

"No telling," I said, studying Wrath's profile. "You have a really nice jawline."

Wrath's cheeks burned pink, and he rolled his eyes, jamming a thumb toward the car. "Stop flirting with me and get in. Man, I hope that stupid muffin wears off sooner than later."

But he wasn't exactly frowning as he said it.

nine

. . .

I slept until noon the next day. I could easily have slept longer, but sometimes, my housemates were the most inconsiderate people on earth. Someone was banging on a wall, and someone else—or maybe the same person, who knew?—was shrieking with laughter. Music was playing somewhere in the house, just loud enough to hear but not loud enough to make out what it was.

Grumbling, I pulled the covers over my head, foolishly hoping for a little more shut-eye. I was desperate to remain asleep, to ward off getting out of my cozy bed and dealing with cameramen just a little while longer. But then I smelled coffee and my body betrayed me, choosing the warm, steaming seduction of caffeine over another sixty minutes of dreamland.

Cursing under my breath, I climbed out of bed and pulled on a pair of sweatpants, an oversized t-shirt with glittery cupcakes on the front, and stuck my feet into a pair of slippers I'd inherited from Envy—fuzzy hedgehogs with pointy noses and whiskers and everything. How could you not want them?

I pulled a comb through my hair and went downstairs.

I found Lust in the kitchen. As usual, she looked great. Her long, dark hair was pulled away from her face in a high ponytail, which made her cheekbones look like they could cut glass. She wasn't wearing any makeup, and still she looked like America's Next Top Model. She was wearing a black Metallica t-shirt and cut-off shorts with the pockets peeking out of the bottom. I immediately regretted not putting on real clothes. But at least my loungewear was clean.

Lust took one look at me and turned to the coffeemaker, pouring me a fresh mug she shoved into my hands. "You look awful," she said, nose wrinkled. "Rough night?"

I wrapped my hands around the mug and took a deep breath of the steaming brew. I didn't know why Lust had a fresh pot of coffee on at 12 o'clock in the afternoon, but I sure was grateful for it. "Just couldn't sleep is all," I said, blowing across the top of my drink. "I keep thinking about poltergeists and dead guys and missing communes. It's just a lot."

Lust nodded and wound her ponytail into a bun. "I bet it is. If I had a vision of poltergeists like you did, I don't think I'd sleep for a week."

"Well, I've seen worse," I said. I tried to sip the coffee, but it was too hot. Luckily, just holding it made me feel better. "When I was still consulting for the police department, I once touched a guy and saw him murdering his own wife. And I saw it from his perspective, too, since that's how my gift—if you can call it that—works. I didn't want to touch anyone for months, and sleep was pretty much out of the question."

Lust's face paled, and I immediately realized my mistake. This was too heavy for morning conversation. Even though it wasn't technically morning. "Anyway, I don't want to talk about this right now."

Lust recovered quickly, pushing herself away from the counter and flashing me a bright smile. "Great! I don't want to talk about it, either. Anyway, listen. I'm glad you're awake. I was wondering if you wanted to accompany me into town."

"We are in town," I ventured cautiously. "This is town. Or did you mean another town?"

Lust shimmied up to me and wrapped her arms around my waist. I was so caught off-guard, I sloshed my coffee over the rim of the mug as I tried to maneuver the cup out from between us. With her hands clasped at the small of my back, she pulled herself right against me, giggling as I squirmed. I tried to wiggle free, but she was having none of it, pulling me closer the more I wriggled.

Not that I was wriggling *too* hard.

"I mean this town," she said with a laugh. She pressed her lips to my cheek in a quick peck and then let me go. She stepped away from me just as quickly as she'd moved in. "So what do you say? You up for it?"

The coffee was just cool enough to drink, so I closed my eyes and took a sip. Warmth flooded through my body, and the knots in my back and shoulders slowly gave up the ghost. "Getting out of the house would be good for me," I said at last. "Give me 20 minutes to get ready."

"You have 10," she said, bouncing away. "Don't be late!"

And before I could object, she disappeared around the corner.

———

"City-wide garage sale?"

We were walking toward the Cameron Events Center, merging with the throngs of bargain hunters who had come from miles around to rummage through castoff junk other people didn't want. Children in flip-flops with grubby faces squealed as they ran past me. Teenagers too cool for school meandered away from their parents, bumping shoulders playfully as they snickered and gossiped behind their hands. I turned to Lust, giving her my best "Are-you-serious?" look.

"What's this all about?"

Lust laughed as she linked her arm in mine and dragged me toward the entrance. She fished two 5-dollar bills from her pocket and turned them over to an attendant who stamped our hands and welcomed us inside. A frigid blast of conditioned air ruffled my hair as I stepped through the door.

"Shopping!" she exclaimed, spinning in a circle with her arms flung out at her sides. "I haven't been to a real, live flea market in something like fifteen years. I used to go all the time when I was a kid. When I heard this was happening, I couldn't get here fast enough."

I looked around, taking it all in. I'd heard of flea markets before, of course, but I'd never actually been to one for several reasons:

1. I hated shopping.
2. While I'd heard the aphorism "One man's trash is another man's treasure," I had not found this to be true.
3. Flea markets seemed like something old people did.
4. I hated shopping.

"Where should we start?" Lust asked, already tugging me toward a display of taxidermy alligator heads. Why any person would have an entire collection of stuffed alligator heads was beyond me. She picked up the smallest one and thrust it in my face. It had pointy teeth and marbles for eyes. "What do you think of this?"

"What are we doing here?" I asked, shoving the alligator

aside. "I know you didn't bring me all the way out here to help you select Halloween décor."

Frowning, Lust set the alligator head aside and moved on to a display of insects cast in resin. "I want to get a gift for Gluttony. He's been taking *very* good care of Sloth, and I want him to know someone noticed."

"That's nice of you," I said, wondering if buying gifts for people showing minimal displays of courteousness was common. Nobody had ever given me a gift for having basic human decency. But maybe baking Happy Thoughts muffins for depressed mind readers was above and beyond. I had no idea. What passed for normal social behavior continued to mystify me. To hide my confusion, I picked up a giant African beetle and looked for the price tag. When I found it, I put it back down.

People wanted way too much money for their worthless junk.

"Do you think he'd want an alligator head or some insects?" I asked, eyeing the rest of the wares at the booth with skepticism. "He doesn't strike me as the type."

"Well, he's from Louisiana," Lust explained. "So."

"Just because he's from Louisiana—look. I have a better idea." I grabbed her by the hand and led her away from the taxidermy animals, past some vintage photographs of other people's families, and past a huge collection of eyelet pillowcases. When I found what I was looking for, I stopped.

"He'll like this much more," I said.

Lust's eyes grew wide as she took in the vintage copper bakeware. Rooster-shaped cake pans, bread pans shaped like squash, and various Jell-O molds shaped like fish covered two folding tables. "You know you're an absolute genius?" She selected a muffin tin, examined it, and set it aside. "I don't know why I didn't think of this. Well, yes I do," she said, heaving out a sigh. "We're stumped on our case, and it's really getting to me. When you and I worked together, I felt like everything just gelled, you know? But this feels like work."

I nodded, rifling through the bakeware just to give my hands something to do. I had no interest in used cooking utensils. Frankly, the idea gave me the willies. Which doesn't make sense if you think about it. Eating at a restaurant is no different from eating from a stranger's kitchen. But at least restaurants have health inspectors. I'd seen too many pictures online of cats sitting in mixing bowls to believe most people's kitchens were anyplace I'd ever want to dine.

Lust chose a bundt pan shaped like a sandcastle. "What do you think of this one?" She held it with both hands against her chest.

"Looks impractical," I said.

She turned to the old man manning the booth. "I'll take it."

With Gluttony's present secured, I assumed we were done. But as Lust looped her arm through mine and began slowly meandering through the crowds, I realized I was wrong. We had ambled maybe fifty feet when she squealed in my ear and dashed toward a booth.

"Won't you *look* at these," Lust cooed. We were standing at a booth selling antique dolls of all shapes and sizes. "How *cute* are these?"

"Not cute at all," I said, my brow scrunched in a frown. "Old dolls are creepy. That you like them is weird."

Lust chuckled, tilting her face to meet my gaze. "Why is it weird that I like them?"

I swept my hand vaguely along the vertical lines of her body. "Because in some ways, you're so normal. Like, profoundly normal. Like Miss America poster girl normal. And then you go and say stuff like how you're into creepy dolls."

Lust selected a doll wearing a red velvet dress with white fur on the collar and cuffs. If you'd told me the doll was supposed to be Mrs. Claus as a weird baby, I would have believed you. "And in other ways, I'm as abnormal as they come," she reminded me, running the velvet between her fingers. "That's how I ended up on the show. Well, that and a completely broken sense of self-esteem."

It was hard to tell whether this was a topic Lust wanted to talk about or not, so I said nothing, letting her lead the way. She replaced the doll she was holding and chose another. This one was African and draped in traditional Kente cloth. "When Tricia first presented the idea of living with a bunch of strangers, I was completely put off. To be honest, I thought it was the most ridiculous thing I'd ever heard. I had a good job, and I was happy. I wasn't in a committed relationship, so that wasn't ideal, but everything else in my life was going fine. So why would I want to move to California into a beach house and live with a bunch of strangers?"

"The grand prize," I answered. "You wanted to win your heart's desire like everyone else."

"That's true," she drawled, the corner of her mouth dripping into a frown. "But there was more to it than that."

She hesitated, her bottom lip folded beneath her teeth. Her eyes darted aimlessly, like she was debating whether to tell me something. Finally, she looked away and said, almost offhandedly, "It also felt like fate. Do you know what I mean?"

I was quiet a beat too long, and Lust laughed nervously, shaking her head. "No, look. I mean, I get it. They wanted psychics in the house. And there's probably not a ton of real psychics out there. Certainly not a ton of psychics with my particular personality flaws." She reached for her hair. Lust usually wound a lock of hair around her finger when she was nervous, but with her hair in a bun, she had little to play with. Instead, she stroked absently at the baby hair at her temple. "But in a way, that confirms my point. I felt like I was made for this role. And I know it's not a role. I mean, I know it's real life. Sort of." She blew out her frustration in a noisy raspberry. "Gah. I don't know what I'm trying to say."

We were walking again. I didn't know what Lust was trying to say, either, but I got the feeling she just needed to talk. So I made encouraging noises and slowed my pace to match hers. "I guess what I'm saying is, it wasn't a rational thought that led me to the show. It was more like a guiding hand. Something I needed that I didn't even know about."

I was about to respond that I didn't believe in fate when Lust shrieked.

We had just wandered to a booth selling a large variety of tiaras—silver ones, gold ones, metal ones, plastic ones. She thrust the bag with Gluttony's present into my chest. Then she darted to the table, immediately choosing a silver tiara with several tiers of glittering rhinestones. Gingerly, she placed it on top of her head, examining herself in the provided mirror.

I cringed. Not because Lust looked bad—that was impossible—but because knowing countless other people may have tried on that accessory gave me the willies. What if somebody had lice? Could you get lice from trying on a tiara?

Luckily, I schooled my face into a more neutral position before Lust turned to me, expectant. "Does this work?" She placed both hands on her hips and turned in a slow circle so I could admire her from every angle. The fake jewels atop her head sparkled in the overhead fluorescent lights. She looked ridiculous, but not in a bad way. But you can't tell someone they look ridiculous without them taking it the wrong way. So instead, I said, "Excellent. You look excellent."

Gently, she removed the tiara and placed it on the table, pawing through the other options. "I've always wanted one of these," she confessed. "I feel like this is a sign. The universe wants me to have a tiara."

I wasn't sure why a table full of tiaras was a sign from the universe while a table full of taxidermy beetles wasn't. Still, I wasn't in any position to argue. Instead, I tucked Gluttony's gift under my arm and helped Lust sort through the tangle of headwear. I found one tiara that reminded me of Lust. It was more ornate than the others, but also elegant. "What do you think of this one?"

Lust lifted the tiara from my hands and placed it daintily atop her head. She peered down into the mirror, her face lighting up like candles on a birthday cake. "It's gorgeous," she breathed. She straightened up, her lips twisting into a smile as color rose into her cheeks. "Can I tell you something? Promise not to tell anyone ever."

I drew an X over my chest. "Cross my heart," I said.

Lust raised an eyebrow. "And hope to die?"

I hesitated. "No?"

My housemate stepped closer to me and lowered her voice. "Years ago, there was this website called Like It or Leave It. It was basically a vanity site for dumb girls like me who were insecure about their looks. You posted pictures of yourself, and complete strangers voted on how much they'd like to date you. You had to register, so it wasn't like any troll could randomly drive by and drop you a 1 out of 10. Well, I was so insecure that I posted my very best picture, and after a week or so, my average was something like a five."

I didn't say anything, but if she was only getting a five, the site was definitely full of trolls, required registration or not. But I kept that to myself.

"Anyway, to make myself feel better, I made a fake account. Actually, I made multiple fake accounts. Then I logged into my main account and added my fake accounts as my friends. You know, to give them the look of legitimacy. I know it's stupid," she said. "That's how desperate I was. I voted for myself with my various fake accounts. I left messages to myself and everything." She rolled her eyes, removing the tiara from her head and gazing down at it lovingly. "I figured if it looked like I was desirable to others, I would *become* desirable to others. I know that's pathetic, but in some ways, I'm still that girl," she said. "Still looking for validation. Still…" She looked up at me and made a face. "What is it? What are you thinking?"

I hadn't even realized I wasn't fully listening to Lust until she called me on it. But what she just said about making fake accounts and friending them sent bolts of lightning down my spine. I pressed a hand to my forehead as realization dawned. "*That's* how I'll find him," I said aloud, but primarily to myself. "Why didn't I think of this sooner?"

Lust narrowed her eyes and tilted her head to the side. "Find who?"

"The real identity of Cecil Bradshaw," I said. "I just realized—"

"Are you thinking about your case?" Lust gave me a long blink and a slight shake of her head. "I'm pouring my heart out to you—revealing my deepest vulnerabilities—and you're thinking about your *case?*"

I took the tiara from Lust's hands and gave it to the woman behind the booth. "I'll take this one," I said. Then I turned back to Lust. "Do you remember why my girlfriend left me?"

Lust's face softened, but only a little. "Yes. You missed her sister's wedding."

"That was the final straw," I agreed, "but it wasn't the real problem. The real problem was that I have attention deficit. I get hyper-focused on work, and I lose track of everything else. Lots of times, I didn't even come home. I slept in my car or at the office. It never occurred to me that Shayda was expecting me. I wasn't thinking about her at all."

Lust's nostrils flared. "I suppose you're telling me this so I'll feel sorry for you?"

"I'm telling you this because you can't take it personally," I said. The salesclerk returned the tiara wrapped in a bag, and I handed it to Lust. "This is who I am. You're a siren who flirts too much. I'm a forgetful, attention-challenged moron with no feel for relationships."

She looked down at the package in her hands. "Is that why you bought me the tiara? To make up for your shortcomings?"

I shook my head. "No. I bought it because you liked it, so I wanted you to have it. That's all."

Without warning, Lust pulled me into an embrace and whispered, "Thanks, Pride. That really means a lot to me."

"You're welcome," I said, wriggling free of her arms.

The truth was, it meant a lot to me, too. But unfortunately for both of us, I could never, ever admit it.

———

When I got back to Sinful House, I barged into Wrath's room without knocking. He was sitting at his computer, headphones on, lights out. He didn't turn around at my entry, so he must not have heard. I glanced at his monitor—he was playing a classic first-person shooter game. I snatched the headphones off his head and tossed them onto the desk.

Wrath spun around, fury and disbelief scrambling his features. "What the crap do you think you're doing, Pride? That was a championship PvP match! Do you know how bad that's gonna tank my rating?" He noticed the cameraman over my shoulder and regulated his tone. "This better be important."

"I have an idea how to figure out who Cecil Bradshaw is," I said.

A loud, annoyed sigh rattling in his throat, Wrath ran his

hands through his hair, making it stand up in pale yellow spikes. "Man, this better be good. You're so gonna owe me otherwise."

"Go to Cecil's Facebook page," I instructed.

Wrath frowned as he swiveled around to face the monitor. He typed the URL into the browser. "We already *did* this, remember?"

"We did," I agreed, "but we didn't know what we were looking for. Now I do."

Cecil's page loaded up, replete with that ridiculous photograph of the Israeli model. I pointed to his friends list. "Click that," I said. "I want to go through all his friends. He doesn't have many, so it shouldn't take long."

Wrath clicked the link, still scowling. "And what are we looking for?"

"The real Cecil Bradshaw."

I quickly explained what Lust had told me about making fake accounts for herself and then friending them to give herself more legitimacy. "...So that got me thinking Cecil might have done the same thing. One of his 'friends' may actually be him."

"Not a terrible idea," Wrath said with grudging admiration. At least, I think it was admiration. It was hard to tell with Wrath. "You know, this'll go quicker if we both use our own computers."

I leaned down to whisper into his ear. "It'll look better for the cameras if we do it together."

He grunted but didn't argue. He clicked the first link.

"What *exactly* are we looking for?"

"I have no idea," I said, scanning the first friend's profile. "Something that stands out."

"What kind of something?"

I grimaced, hands dug deep in my pockets. "I don't know. Let's just see what we see."

The first profile was for a man named Linton Bonner. Linton was older, maybe mid-sixties, with salt and pepper hair and a lined, tanned face. His profile featured his wife and grown kids, even a grandchild. I shook my head. "This isn't him."

Wrath backtracked and clicked the next link. "Andy Garcia," Wrath read aloud. "Looks like he's the right age. Not that there's an age limit on scammers, but." We scrolled through his pictures. No sign that he was married. Most of his photos featured him wearing Civil War reenactment garb.

"Guys who play dress-up might fake being a medium," Wrath said after clicking through a dozen photos. "We like him for Cecil?"

"Maybe," I said, jotting his name down on a stray piece of paper. We couldn't rule him out, but it wasn't pinging my psychic senses, either. Not that I was an expert in this sort of thing.

The next profile was for Britni Newsome, who was dressed in scanty bikinis in every photo. Wrath clicked more of her photos than was necessary. After the fifth or sixth, I cleared my throat loudly. "This is definitely a fake account," I said. "Next."

We clicked through profiles, jotting down the names of anyone we couldn't rule out. More than half the profiles were private, but Wrath bypassed those limitations by sweet-talking the computer, a feat that I was learning to envy more each day.

We'd been at it for about forty-five minutes when Wrath froze, his mouse wheel stopping mid-spin.

"Whoa, Pride. Look."

We were looking at the profile of a man named Jace Thornburgh. According to his profile, he studied at Carnegie Mellon University, was from Little Rock, Arkansas, and now lived in San Francisco. He was the CEO of Triplex Virtual. He had no relationship status listed.

He was a good-looking man: late thirties, olive skin, tousled, dark hair, and bushy eyebrows. His profile picture showed him laughing, his face pressed alongside the slobbering muzzle of a Golden Retriever. He looked like your typical all-American guy.

And then I saw what Pride saw. "Click the thumbnail," I said. I was so excited, my voice had risen an octave.

The photograph loaded, and both Wrath and I stared in mute awe. Jace Thornburgh was dressed in a red Gore-Tex shell coat with a hood over a wool hat with built-in earmuffs. His face was red with cold, but he was smiling brightly.

Standing next to him, arms around his shoulders and face pressed close was a very familiar face.

"You've got to be kidding me," I breathed, leaning in for a closer look. "Is that…?"

"Jeff Bishop," Wrath confirmed. "The guy with Jace Thornburgh is Jeff Bishop. And look where they are."

Quickly, I read the caption. "Can't believe my luck. Met my idol Jeff Bishop on this expedition. He was cool enough to take a selfie with me. I knew Mt. Everest would change my life. Little did I know it would save my career."

"Mount Everest," I said. "That's where Jeff died."

"Yeah." Wrath nodded, pointing to the date. "This photo was posted before his death."

I scanned the rest of the page, my heart thumping loudly in my ears. "But these comments weren't," I said. "At least, not all of them."

Here's what the original comments from Jace Thornburgh's friends said:

Becca Caldwell:

OMG! That's crazy! You are so lucky!

Kyle Harabedian:

My brother met him once. Said he was a super nice guy even in real life.

Jace Thornburgh:

He totally is. Very down to earth. We even talked about him

potentially investing in DuGood (and saving it!!), and he told me to ping him once we were both back in the States!

Albert Qian:

Only you could use your last dollar to climb Everest to "find yourself," and then meet a crazy rich donor. Somebody upstairs must really like you.

Jace Thornburgh:

I know! When I told my business partner I was doing this, he said I was out of my mind. He said no investor would touch us with a 10-foot pole if word got out I went bankrupt to climb a mountain. Rofl. Looks like I won't need them after all!

Brandon Ward:

Wow, cool!

Jackie O'Neil:

Awesome! You look great, by the way—very happy for you!

But then time elapsed, and the comments changed.

Kyle Harabedian:

Wondered if this photo was still here. So sad about his death. So glad you made it back down safe.

Anne Preacher:

I hope you got his autograph! You might be able to sell it and get the money he was gonna give you for your startup! LOL!

Brandon Ward:

WOW. That's the tackiest thing I've ever seen anyone post in public.

Anne Preacher:

Lighten up. It's not like he's gonna read this.

Joey Barber:

RIP Jeff Bishop.

Anne Preacher

RIP DuGood Virtual. 😭

"Wow, that Anne Preacher chick is a real jerk," Wrath said.

"Yeah, but thanks to her, I might have an idea." I tapped a finger against my lips, thinking. "Can you look up DuGood Virtual?"

Wrath navigated away from the page and googled the company. The first result was the website for the startup; we ignored that. The second result was a news story from Righteous Startup News. It was dated three weeks ago.

Wrath clicked it.

Here's what it said:

"Founded just two short years ago, DuGood Virtual was destined to change the world with its cutting-edge app. Early funding put the company on the map as a darling of Silicon Valley. In a sea of tech companies crowing that they would 'change the world,' DuGood Virtual was notable for actually attempting to do what others only gave lip service to.

"The technology connected underprivileged, third-world teenagers with venture capitalists who would mentor them and fund projects intended to eradicate poverty and education disparity in developing countries. However, the company today announced its dissolution. According to founder and CEO Jace Thornburgh, the company's finances were mismanaged, forcing them to shutter their endeavor when no other investors were willing to bet on Thornburgh's vision.

"But the world hasn't seen the last of Jace Thornburgh. While he wouldn't give details, the serial entrepreneur says he has another ace up his sleeve and a new company in the works. 'I'm just waiting for my funding to pan out,' Thornburgh says with a smile. 'Private donor. I can't really talk about it. But give me time. You haven't seen the last of Jace Harris Thornburgh.'"

Wrath swiveled around in his seat, facing me. His hair was still sticking up all over his head, which, paired with the maniacal grin, made him look like a villain from a children's cartoon. "So let me get this straight. Jace Thornburgh founds a tech company. But it's not going well, so he climbs a mountain to clear his head. While he's up there, he meets Jeff Bishop and hits him up for money. But Bishop dies before Thornburgh can get the money, and his company goes belly-up. So, then, what, he hatches a plan to marry Bishop's widow hoping to get the money he was promised?"

I rocked back onto my heels, my head swimming. I knew people were inherently selfish. But this seemed like a lot for someone wanting to change the world. "I hate to jump to conclusions, but yeah. Assuming Jace Thornburgh is the real Cecil Bradshaw, that's what this sounds like to me."

Wrath whooped, pumping his fists in the air as he leaped to his feet. "Did we just do it, Pride? Did we just *actually* solve this thing?"

I looked back to the monitor, the slightest smile breaking across my face. "It's too early to say for sure," I said. "Let's follow the trail wherever it leads."

Wrath clapped me on the shoulder, his smile so big, it threatened to crack his face in two. "Should we go tell Bailey? Should we go break the good news?"

"Yes," I said, my own smile broadening to match my housemate's. "Let's do it."

ten

. . .

At Bailey's house the next day, we shared everything we had learned about the case. We nestled in the couches in her sitting room and told her about the photos of the Israeli model and the strange visions about the poltergeists. We also told her about the women we'd messaged on Facebook, none of whom we'd heard back from yet. "We also looked up his phone number. It is registered to a guy named Cecil Bradshaw in San Francisco, so that's something. But we haven't called him yet."

Bailey's eyebrows shot high. "Why not? Seems like that would be the most logical thing to do."

"If we call him too early, we'll just spook him," Wrath said. "We were waiting until we had something on him. We wanted to ask him about something only Jeff would know. But so far, everyone we talked to says the same thing: Jeff was crazy private. They couldn't really think of anything notable Jeff shared with only them."

Bailey nodded, looking thoughtful. "Well, that's true. He was private. Still, you'd think *somebody* shared a moment with him, right? Maybe a funny inside joke between just the two of them? I mean, you can just make something up, can't you? Like, say, remember the time at Jenny's party when you got so drunk, blah blah blah, and if he says he remembers, you know it's a lie."

Wrath shook his head. "Only an idiot would fall for that. If I were pretending to be a dead guy, I'd pretend like I remembered almost nothing. It seems logical that a lot of your memories would go by the wayside after you kicked the bucket. We have to ask about something significant. Something you wouldn't forget, even in death."

"I see," Bailey said. "Well…I know you've been hard at work, and I don't mean to be rude, but it seems you haven't made that much progress at all."

Wrath and I exchanged looks. "Well," I drawled, "we haven't told you the best part yet."

Bailey's brows shot up. "Well, don't keep me waiting! What else did you find?"

Instead of telling her, I pulled up Jace Thornburgh's profile on Facebook and showed her the picture of him with Jeff. She read through the comments, her eyes wide, her hand pressed to her mouth. When she was done, she shook her head in amazement. "This is the guy, right? This has to be the guy."

"We think so, too," Wrath said. "But when we call and confront him, we want to really shatter his world. Hit him with all the evidence at once. So we're still following up on every lead. Which is where you come in."

Bailey leaned forward, intrigued. "Okay?"

"Victoria Webster's hairstylist said something weird," Wrath said. "She told us to look into the Topanga Canyon Music Awards. Do you know anything about that?"

Bailey tapped her fingers against her chin as she thought. "Vaguely. It was a cross between a music awards show and a fashion show. It was over 20 years ago, though. I was just a child. If I recall correctly, that show only happened once."

"That's right," I said. "Shelley—that's the stylist—said the same thing. She also said Jeff was there with a guest. You wouldn't know anything about that, would you?"

Bailey's mouth curved into a frown, and her shoulders sagged. "No, I'm sorry. I wasn't there. Dad went with Mom, and Tammy and I stayed home. But you know…" She pressed a hand to her cheek and looked up toward the ceiling. "I think there was a write-up in PopCharts Magazine about the awards show. Maybe there's something in there you can use."

"It's worth a look. Does the Odyssey library have archives? Micro-whatever?" Wrath asked.

Bailey grinned enthusiastically. "Microfiche. But anyway, you don't need the library! I still have most of Daddy's music stuff, including all the magazines he was in. It's all upstairs. Come with me. I'll show you."

We followed Bailey up the winding staircase and through the hallways until we came to an office. Or, more accurately, what used to be an office but had recently been ravaged by a tornado. The room was packed with junk—photographs, awards, papers, CDs, and more.

"Sorry about the mess," Bailey said, "but nobody uses this room. It's just where I keep Dad's stuff until I can figure out what to do with it." She pointed to a wall piled high with banker's boxes. "All of Dad's paper memorabilia is in there. If he still has a copy of PopCharts from the Topanga Canyon year, it'll be in there."

I gestured to the wall of boxes. "Any particular place the magazine is most likely to be?" I gulped as I took in the task before us. "This is a lot."

Bailey shook her head. "No, sorry. None of it's organized. At least, not that I'm aware of." She blew out a breath and stood up straight, squaring her shoulders. "Well, I guess I'll leave you to it. I hope you find what you're looking for. If you need anything, I'll just be downstairs."

As soon as Bailey was out of the room, Wrath took charge. He pointed to one end of the wall. "I'll start on this end," he said. "You start at that end, and we'll meet in the middle." Wrath whistled as he surveyed the mountain of boxes in front of us. "We've really got our work cut out for us." He turned to the camera crew. "Why don't one of you idiots put the stupid camera down and help us search?"

The camera guy shifted and snapped his gum. "We don't get paid to do nothing but work the camera. It's not in our International Cinematographers Guild contract."

Wrath blinked. "There's a guild for camera guys?" He turned to me, eyes wide. "Did you know there's a guild for camera guys?"

"Yes," I said, which was a lie, but I didn't need to admit my ignorance in front of the cameramen. Or the rest of America. "Wrath, forget about them. We have work to do."

"I'm just saying, man. I want a guild! There's no guild for reality show contestants. I asked my agent about it. She said we're not even covered by SAG because technically, we're not actors! We're supposed to *be ourselves*, whatever that means!" He kicked at a pile of books. "This is oppression, man! I feel exploited!"

I sighed. It was going to be a long day.

"Wrath, please just get to work."

He muttered one more thing about sticking it to the man before opening his first box.

It's surprising how much stuff a person can accumulate throughout their lives. And I'm talking about regular people, not even pack rats and stuff. As I sorted through the boxes looking for magazines with any reference to the Topanga Canyon Music Awards, I came across all kinds of things: letters from fans, signed photographs, sheet music, scratch paper with lyrics jotted down. I also found notebooks filled with random stuff: ideas, poems, shopping lists. It was like rifling through Adam Preston's mind.

It was unnerving.

"After I die, I hope all my stuff gets thrown away," I said, flipping through what felt like my millionth magazine. "I don't want anybody pawing around my personal stuff. This is mortifying."

Wrath was holding a Playboy magazine at arm's length, rotating it so the centerfold fell out vertically. He looked at it for a minute, brows wriggling. Then he tossed it aside. "You won't care," he said, picking up another Playboy. "You'll be dead."

"Wrath." I pointed to the magazine. "Really?"

He made a disgusted face and tossed the magazine into a pile with the others. "What? A guy can't look?"

"No," I said. "Not when we're trying to stop a woman from marrying a shyster trying to take half her fortune."

"We don't know that for sure," Wrath said, digging through a fresh box. "He could be trying to take *all* her money."

Wrath was almost to the bottom of his box when he clapped his hands together and shouted in victory. "I think I found it!"

I dropped the magazine I'd been holding and walked over to where Wrath was flipping through an old, tattered copy of PopCharts. "I think this is it, man," he said. "There's a photo on the front page of the Topanga Canyon event. This has to be it. Please, *please* be something in here we can use."

He paged through the magazine until he came to the cover story. I leaned over his shoulder, trying to read the text, but Wrath was only looking at the pictures. He flipped through almost to the end of the article, which was long. With each page turn, I felt my heart sink a little more. If there was nothing in the article about Jeff Bishop's guest, we would have to track Shelley down and get her to talk. I wasn't sure that would be so successful.

But just when I was losing hope, Wrath stabbed the magazine with a finger. "That's it," he said. "Read this."

I leaned in to get a better look. Sure enough, the picture was a black-and-white image of Jeff Bishop's father, music producer Kerry Bishop. On Kerry's right was a younger version of Jeff. Even though he was a young teenager in the photo, he looked much the same. On Kerry's left was a young woman. She was gazing up at Kerry adoringly. Kerry's arms wrapped around both young people, and both he and Jeff were smiling brightly at the camera.

The caption underneath read, Kerry Bishop with son, Jeff, 15, and foster daughter, Tori Webb, age 13."

I pondered this for a minute. "This must've been what Shelley was talking about. Doesn't really seem like she's Jeff's guest, though. She's more—"

"His foster sister," Wrath said, snapping his fingers as a light bulb went off in his head. "Holy Godzilla, Pride. Take a closer look at that picture. Does that girl remind you of anyone?"

I studied the photo. Not only was it in black and white, which didn't help, but the young people in the picture were adults by now. And while Jeff looked recognizably the same, the woman could have been anyone.

"She doesn't look familiar," I said.

Wrath thumped the photo and made a popping sound with his lips. "Man, you need to get your eyes checked. Imagine this girl with blonde hair instead of brown and a smaller, straighter nose. Who does it look like?"

I examined the picture a moment longer, and then it hit me. "Victoria Webster?" I asked, incredulous.

Wrath was beaming. "That's her, man. That's Victoria Webster. Look. The girl in the photo is named Tori Webb. Tori Webb/Victoria Webster? It's the same girl."

I stared at Wrath, hardly even daring to blink. "Victoria Webster was Jeff Bishop's *foster sister?*"

Wrath grinned like a madman. "Looks like we gotta go talk to Vicki again. Somebody's got some 'splainin' to do."

———

"I don't owe you any explanation. Please, just leave me alone."

Thanks to Wrath's charm (?) and a very chatty assistant, we tracked Victoria down to the beach. She was walking her dog, an enormous and playful Labrador, as she kicked her way through the sand, arms folded petulantly across her chest.

I put a hand on her shoulder, but she yanked away, her stride quickening. "Victoria, please. I just want to understand. You said you met Jeff in college, but that's not true. You grew up with him. You two lived together in the same house."

She whirled on me, a finger pointed in my face. "Just because you saw an old photo in some stupid magazine doesn't mean—"

"When I touched you, I *saw* the poltergeists," I pressed on. "I told Tamora about the visions, and she said those were Jeff's memories. I didn't understand how I was seeing someone else's memories through a third party. But if you grew up with Jeff, it all makes sense. I didn't see Jeff's memories at all, did I? I saw yours."

Victoria shook her freshly blonde bangs away from her face. I couldn't see her eyes behind her massive black sunglasses, but I saw the taut pull of her lips as her mouth arced into a frown. "You had no right digging into my past," she said. "I didn't ask for that, and I don't want it. I want to help Tamora, too. But not if it costs me my privacy. Nothing is worth that."

"I understand," I said. "That night at the séance? I didn't know Tamora was going to ask Andromeda about the disappeared commune. I was angry about it. I don't want anyone digging into my past, either." I softened my voice, trying to make myself sound vulnerable. That was especially hard for me since *vulnerable* is the thing I try hardest not to be. "We're calling Cecil in the next few days. I need to prove he's not who he says he is. The only anecdote I have to use against him is the poltergeists. Please, Victoria. Help us out here."

Victoria stopped walking and turned her head towards the cameramen. "I won't say a word on camera," she said. "Not a single word. But get rid of them… and I'll talk."

Turning away, Wrath strode over to the camera crew. "Go on, get outta here," he said, shooing them off with grand, swooping arm gestures. "She's not gonna sign any release forms, so there's no point filming this. I'm serious. Get outta here!"

The cameramen walked backward, still filming. "Just let us get some B roll, man. We'll turn off the audio."

Wrath bent down and picked up a sand bucket and hurled it at the cameramen. He launched a second and a third, too. They each hit their targets squarely in the chest. "I'm not asking! Get outta here! You don't want to tick me off, man. I have no problem grabbing that camera and throwing it in the ocean. Just watch me."

That seemed to do the trick because the crew grumbled something and lowered the cameras to their sides. The red blinking lights went out. We watched them head back towards town, and only when we were sure they were out of earshot did Victoria relax a little.

"I moved in with the Bishops when I was nine," she began. "My mother was an alcoholic, and I was taken away from my family. My mother was supposed to regain custody once she got sober, but that never happened. I ended up living with the

Bishops until I was 15." She sat down in the sand, and Wrath and I followed suit. Her dog was still running around, splashing and barking, tail wagging a mile a minute. Victoria watched him, a ghost of a smile playing across her face, but it quickly evaporated when she returned to the story. "You can't imagine what it's like to go from living in poverty to living with wealthy people. I can hardly tell you what my life was like. On the one hand, I felt blessed. The Bishops treated me well, and I had everything I wanted. On the other hand, I had terrible survivor's guilt. All the kids I grew up with, kids I knew from other homes? I knew they weren't doing half as well as I was. And I struggled with that. But before long, that survivor guilt stuff went away. And in a lot of ways, the guilt was better."

Victoria looked down at her hands, worrying the diamond rings on her fingers. "The first time I experienced the disturbances, I was alone. Jeff was in his room, and the Bishops were out. A book fell off a shelf in the middle of the night. I got up and replaced it. When I got back into bed, a second book fell. Then a third. That's when I got freaked out. My heart was pounding in my ears, but I couldn't let the books just lay on the floor. It felt disrespectful. So I climbed out of my blankets and put the books back on their shelves. When I got back into bed, I looked, and all the shelves were empty. Everything was on the floor."

She looked up and removed her sunglasses, revealing liquid eyes. "I was terrified. I pulled the blankets over my head and prayed for it all to end. Luckily, nothing else happened that night. Nothing else happened for several weeks. But then one night, Jeff and I were watching movies in his room. His closet door started banging open, shut. Open, shut."

Victoria wiped a tear with her fingers and cleared her throat. "They happened frequently after that. Dishes flying. Door slamming. Items falling off shelves. The disturbances only happened when Jeff's parents were out. We told them about it, but of course, they didn't believe us. And this was long ago, before everyone had a video camera in their pocket."

"How long did this go on?" Wrath asked.

Victoria shrugged. "Years. Until Jeff moved out for college. After he left, the disturbances stopped altogether. I never saw another dish fly off a shelf or another door slam in my face. But soon afterward, Mrs. Bishop died. Kerry either couldn't or didn't want to care for me after that. I got moved to a different foster home."

"That must've been hard for you," I said.

The freshly-blonde woman chortled. "You don't know the half of it."

"Did you keep in touch with the Bishops afterward?"

Victoria shook her head. "No. I never saw Kerry Bishop again. But one day, a lawyer called and asked me to come into his office. Jeff was there. We took one look at each other and burst into tears. His father had recently died, and Jeff inherited everything. He called me there because he said he owed me. I said he didn't owe me anything, but he insisted. And that day, Jeff signed over half his wealth to me. I became an instant millionaire. I used the opportunity to reinvent myself. I changed my name, my hair, my nose…I didn't need to be the trailer trash girl that grew up in foster homes anymore. I could be Victoria Webster. I could be someone."

"And you never told anyone about the poltergeists?" Wrath asked.

Victoria sneered. "Definitely not. Even Jeff and I never talked about it. We suffered through the disturbances, but after a certain age, we *never* spoke of them. Only Tamora knows. Well, and now the two of you."

We were quiet a while, nothing but the sound of the surf

rolling in to fill the air between us. Finally, Victoria said, "I think we should call him. Together."

Wrath looked dubious. "Call Cecil-Jace-Jeff? Just like that?"

A sly, unfriendly grin replaced Victoria's sneer. "No one knows more than I do about pretending to be someone you're not. Fake it till you make it, right? But even actors need something to go on. A little truth to sell the lie." She nodded as if confirming something to herself. "I'm the only person who can prove this Cecil character isn't who he says he is. I should have done it from the beginning, but I didn't want anyone to know who *I* really am. I like letting the debutantes of Odyssey think I'm one of them. But now you know my secret, so." She squared her shoulders and took a breath. "So are we doing this?"

Wrath turned the decision over to me with a lift of his shoulders and a glance. I sighed. "All right. Let's go someplace quiet."

Victoria beckoned for us to follow as she turned to head back toward town. "I have just the place."

<hr>

The three of us plus Victoria's Labrador piled into her SUV and drove a few miles to our destination. We climbed out of the car and found ourselves in front of a café and bakery called Déjà Brew. Like many of Odyssey's shops, the exterior was pale turquoise with a pink-and-white striped awning and a glass door with a hand-painted image of a witch stirring a cauldron full of coffee.

Inside, a middle-aged man behind the counter dusted his hands on his apron. When he saw Victoria, he reached for a paper cup and headed toward the espresso machine. "Hey, Vic. What are you doing here? Today's not your day."

Victoria gestured toward the coffee cup in the man's hands and then drew her fingers across her throat in a cut-it-out motion. "No americano for me today, Felix. I'm not here for treats, unfortunately. I have some business to take care of." Felix placed the cup back on the stack and leaned against the counter as Victoria kept talking. "Do you mind hanging out with Charlie for a bit? You know how he gets when he goes downstairs."

Felix snapped his fingers and whistled. Charlie—the Labrador—trotted around the counter and lay obediently on the cool tile. As the dog got situated, Felix glanced at Wrath and me. "Who are your friends?"

Victoria straightened, sniffing importantly. "They're from that TV show filming in town. You know the one. Portia scoped out the property for the network." She turned to Wrath and me. "That was all Portia talked about for *weeks*, like finding a venue was the most important problem anyone could have. Really, it was *very* annoying." She redirected her attention to the barista. "*Sinful House?*"

The barista snapped his fingers, nodding with understanding. "Oh, that's right. I remember. Has it aired yet?"

I nodded. "Every weeknight at 8," I said.

"Anyway," Victoria interrupted, "I was hoping for some quiet time. I thought I'd take these two down to the Crypt. There's nobody else down there, is there?"

Felix shook her head. "Nope, empty. The whole basement's yours."

I blinked. "Basement?"

Wrath rolled his eyes. "Big, dark rooms underneath the house used for man-caves and storing garbage from the past most people should just get rid of," he explained.

"I know what a basement is," I sighed. "I've just never seen one in California."

Wrath shrugged. "Guess you're about to."

If you know much about Southern California, you already know it's not exactly the land of basements. (Contrary to popular belief, the lack of basements has nothing to do with earthquakes. It has more to do with the housing boom post World War II. It was just more expedient to build homes without them.) I had never seen a basement until I was in my late 20s and the police department sent me to Ohio on an investigation. So you can imagine my surprise when Victoria led us down a set of winding steps and through a wooden door that took us into the cool dark of my very first California basement.

And the surprises didn't stop there.

As my eyes adjusted to the chowdery darkness, shapes swam into view, coming together like puzzle pieces to form an incredible picture.

We were in some kind of underground lair.

That was the only word I could think to describe it. The large, hexagonal room looked like something from a rich superhero's dungeon—if the superhero was really into esoterica, anyway. The walls were lined with bookshelves, but they hosted more than books. Crystal balls on silver pedestals sat nestled among live plants, candles of varying heights and colors, and mortars overflowing with herbs. An array of wands ranging from ornate pewter and amethyst to roughly hewn wooden sticks poked out from between book spines bearing titles such as *A Mage's Guide to Astronomy* and *Victorian Floriography for the Discerning Spiritualist.* The shelves were immaculate—not a speck of dust or even a wayward hair besmirched their appearance.

I looked up, marveling. The ceiling was painted to resemble the night sky, with shades from indigo to violet creating a backdrop for constellations illustrated with glittering metallic gold paint. In the center of the room were two long, dark wood tables covered in lamps and open books like you might find in an old Gothic library. In fact, the whole place very much gave off library vibes. Except for one thing.

The room was absolutely packed with ghosts.

Spirits faded in and out of translucence as they floated from one corner of the room to another. Some ghosts looked fully corporeal—I had to really examine them to see they were no longer living. Others were diaphanous shades of creamy blues and aquas. They seemed to come from different periods. Some looked freshly dead as they sported more modern looks. Others looked like they died some time ago—one ghost was wearing go-go boots and a beehive hairstyle. She had apparently died in a car accident. She was mangled, her body parts twisted in ways they weren't supposed to bend. Still, she was smiling ear to ear as she floated between clusters of spirits, moving from conversation to conversation with grace and ease.

I stood in mesmerized silence as my eyes followed them around the room. I'd never seen so many ghosts in one place. Finding a collection of spirits in the basement of a beachside cafe was enough to astound me. But their behavior, too, gave me pause. They were engaging with each other in ways I hadn't seen before. Sometimes, I came across pairs of ghosts—usually a husband and wife or sometimes siblings who had died together. But rarely did I see *groups* of ghosts. And never had I seen them mingling.

I mean, these ghosts were *cavorting*—traipsing about as if they were at their own private cocktail party.

It was curious. No, it was downright *weird*.

"What is this place?" Wrath asked as I continued to stare at the surrounding specters. An older woman in a long dress with a broken neck was laughing prettily with a pair of young men in fireproof racing suits. The two men were blackened, obviously burned to death.

I guess the suits were merely fire *retardant*.

"This is our headquarters," Victoria said. "We call it the Crypt because it's underground and because, well." She looked at me, head cocked to the side. "You tell me, Pride."

I looked at Wrath, eyebrows waggling. "This place is absolutely crawling with dead people."

Wrath froze, only his eyes darting around in the dark. "When you say dead people…You mean ghosts?"

I nodded. "Yeah. Dozens of them." I looked to Victoria. "This is some kind of ghost speakeasy."

Victoria's hand floated to the base of her throat as she laughed, a full sound that rattled my bones. "No one's ever called it that before, but I guess you're right. What an excellent description! Wait till I tell the others. Of course, *we* can't see them. But some of us are learning to sense them. Dozens, you say?" Victoria looked around with new interest, like this information might allow her to see what I saw. "They come from all around, I hear. Many of them are from Odyssey, of course, but I guess once word got around about our little haven, the other ghosts naturally found their way here. And we have no objections. I mean, really, a haunted sanctuary? You couldn't ask for a better setup."

Finding his voice again, Wrath cleared his throat and shook himself, no doubt shaking off a chill that shuddered through his body. "Exactly what kind of sanctuary is this? Headquarters for what?"

Victoria blinked in surprise. "The Society, of course. My apologies. I thought you knew. The Odyssey Paranormal Research Society. You met some of us gathered at the séance. We gather here regularly to compare notes and study. Among other things." She smiled, her eyes like sapphires in the shadows. "Anyway, this was the best place I could think of for some privacy to make a phone call." Victoria glanced between Wrath and me. "No objections?"

I pulled up Cecil's contact information on my phone and handed it to Victoria. "Do you know what you're going to say? This is our only chance, you know. If you screw this up…"

Victoria grabbed the phone and made a dismissive sound in her throat. "I know what I'm doing," she said.

Victoria dialed with the phone on speaker. My breath caught in my throat as it rang. But it just went on ringing. Cecil never answered.

"Let's call Jace," Wrath suggested. "Calling him on his *real* phone number, which he never gave to Tamora, should let him know we mean business."

"We don't have Jace's phone number," I reminded him.

Wrath chuckled and pulled out his phone, holding it up to his mouth. "Do a deep web search for Jace Harris Thornburgh's phone number in San Francisco, California."

A second later, the browser displayed a profile, complete with phone number, Jace's picture, address, birth date, and the same information for his closest relatives.

And that's why you can't just put all your information out on the internet.

Wrath dialed and handed the phone to Victoria.

It rang for a long time, and I was sure it would go to voice-mail. But then a voice answered.

"Hello?"

Victoria hesitated, licking her lips and swallowing. Then, she said, "Jeff? Oh my God, Jeff. Is it really you?"

Silence met us on the other line. Then, "Sorry, you have the wrong number."

Victoria tittered, turning her back to us. "No, wait, don't hang up." I couldn't see her face, but I heard the crack in her voice when she spoke. "It's me, Jeff. It's Victoria. We need to talk." She paused. *"They're back."*

The man on the other end sucked in a sharp breath. "Listen, lady, you have the wrong—"

"Oh, sorry. I might've mixed this all up in my silly head. Cecil, then? Is this Cecil?"

The man on the phone was silent, but he didn't hang up. Then he said, "Where did you get this number? Did Cecil give it to you?"

"No. I tried calling Cecil first, but he didn't answer. I wonder why that would be, Jace. Do you have any idea why he wouldn't answer his phone?"

Jace(?)/Cecil(?)/Jeff(?) sighed on the other end. "If you're trying to reach Cecil, he's…not here right now. But I can take a message."

Victoria snorted. "Oh, I just bet you can. I'm not actually looking for Cecil, though. I'm looking for Jeff Bishop. I understand Cecil knows where he is. I hear they've grown *close.*"

A long stretch of silence filled the air. Then he said, "Listen, Victoria? Is that what you said your name was? I think you have the wrong idea."

"Is this Jeff Bishop or not?" Victoria demanded.

The man on the other end sighed. "I—it's complicated. Can you please tell me who you are?"

Now, Victoria threw her shoulders back and lifted her chin, her eyes narrowed to slits. Her voice was smooth as ice when she said, "My name is Victoria Webster, and I'm close friends with Tamora Preston. I'm about to go to the police with everything I know about you. You're Jace Thornburgh, you're not Cecil Bradshaw, you're not a psychic medium, and you're trying to fleece my friend out of her fortune. You're a charlatan, and I can prove it. *You're not Jeff Bishop.*"

I froze, eyes darting to Wrath. He looked like I felt—cords in his neck stood out, his eyes wide and round. This was not what we had agreed to. Victoria was just supposed to pry into the poltergeists. But instead she was stealing our thunder.

The man sighed heavily. "No, I'm not. Not exactly."

"Are you the person my friend Tamora has been talking to or not? You owe me an explanation!"

"And I'm happy to give you one," the man said. He sounded weary. "But not over the phone. You wouldn't believe me if I did."

"You're probably right about that," Victoria spat. "So what do you propose? I don't think a video call will cut it."

"Cecil can come to Odyssey," the man said. "That's where you are, right?"

Victoria blinked in surprise. That was an answer none of us expected. "Really?"

"I knew—we both knew—it was only a matter of time before someone interfered in all this. I wasn't expecting anyone to call this number, but…Anyway, I need a few days to get my affairs in order. And I need to…scrape together the money for a plane ticket."

"Your expenses are on me," Victoria said importantly. "But this better not be another trick. I expect you here in Odyssey in a reasonable amount of time or I will call the police."

"I understand, and I appreciate the offer," the man said. "You have my number."

Then he hung up.

Victoria handed Wrath his phone and crossed her arms over her chest. "Well, that's done," she said. "Looks like we've caught ourselves a catfish."

"You were supposed to ask him about the poltergeists," Wrath grumbled. "But instead, you showed all our cards!"

"It doesn't matter," Victoria said with a shrug. "That guy is lying through his teeth, and if the two of you have any talent at all, you'll get him to confess everything on camera just like the network wants. You'll be heroes. Isn't that what you want?"

Wrath glowered but said nothing. I still didn't know what Wrath's ultimate desire was, so I had no idea why he'd come to Sinful House. He didn't strike me as hero-inclined.

But then, nobody at Sinful House was really who they

seemed. If I'd learned anything on this show, it was that you can't take anyone at face value.

Victoria turned to leave, and with a sigh, Wrath followed her up the stairs, leaving me alone in a swirl of gossiping ghosts. I didn't want to admit it, but at that moment, the idea of being a hero lit something inside of me, and my heart skipped a beat.

Just don't tell anyone I said that.

eleven

. . .

The next morning, Gluttony made breakfast tacos. He didn't put any magic in them, either, so I felt comfortable eating them. The "complimentary" muffins hadn't been the worst experience on earth, but you don't know how stupid it feels to walk around telling everybody how great they look and smell until it's actually happened to you. Seriously, try it if you don't believe me. People look at you like you've lost your mind.

Which says a lot about us as a society, I guess.

Anyway, I was waddling to my room after having stuffed my face with way too much sausage and eggs when I heard Sloth's voice call out my name.

I poked my head through her doorway and found her sitting cross-legged on her bed with Walt's computer in her lap. She was waving me over with a big smile on her face. "Pride, hey! You got a second? They reset the password for Walt's Chenoweth International account."

With everything else going on, I'd forgotten all about Mrs. Romanowsky and the case Sloth and I were supposed to be investigating on the side. I glanced down at my smartwatch. It was getting late, and I was tired, but for once, Sloth looked so upbeat that I couldn't turn away. So even though I wanted to lie down and wallow in my indigestion, I went into her room and plopped beside her on the bed.

"I just got the confirmation a few minutes ago," she explained. "I haven't even clicked on it yet."

I watched as she opened the email and clicked the shop link. The browser opened and the shopping page loaded up.

And, just as we expected, it was full of products for motorcycle enthusiasts. Helmets, jackets, other gear. Things like that. There were even parts for customizations.

In other words, completely worthless.

Sloth slumped beside me, the air going out of her like a deflated balloon. "This just doesn't make sense," she said. "I really thought we were going to find something more sinister."

"Sinister?" I asked. "Like how?"

Sloth laughed, her cheeks rosy. "I don't know, something like the Dark Web. You know what I mean?"

I drew my brows together, questioning. "You thought the motorcycle website was going to be a portal into the Dark Web?"

"What do you two dweebs know about the Dark Web?"

Sloth and I looked up to see Wrath coming into the room, a towel thrown over his shoulder. He was wearing board shorts with no shirt. Maybe he was going down to the beach later. Or it could be a fashion statement. You never could tell with Wrath. He ambled over to the bed and turned the laptop so he could see the screen. "What are you guys doing? Since when are you into motorcycles?" He shot me a dubious look when he caught me looking at his bare torso. "You're not going to tell me I have a beautiful chest, are you?"

"Shut up," I growled. "The spell wore off a long time ago."

"Well, thank goodness for that," he said, wiping a hand across his forehead in feigned relief. "Okay, but seriously, since when are you two into motorcycles?"

"We're *not* into motorcycles," Sloth said. "We're doing some sleuthing on the side." She quickly explained everything we knew so far about Walt Romanowsky, the organization, and Ping—the supe Walt had been hunting in Odyssey. She'd turned out to be a nine-tailed fox. "So we're trying to find out more about the organization Walt was involved with. We think he's hunting these creatures, but the email and website and everything are all about motorcycles. Here. Why don't you just look at the email yourself?"

Wrath pushed me aside, and Sloth and I made room for him on the bed. He took the computer into his lap and scrolled through the emails. He made quick work of them and then looked up at us, his eyes wide and round. "Are you two stupid or something?"

I jabbed Wrath in the side with my elbow and mouthed, "*Watch it!*" while jerking my head in Sloth's direction.

But Sloth rolled her eyes and dropped her chin into her hand. "Don't worry, I've been called worse. So…why are you asking if we're stupid?"

Wrath gestured toward the computer screen. "This is the worst code I've ever seen."

Sloth and I exchanged looks. "Code? Like computer code? What are you talking about?"

Wrath buried his hands in his hair, shaking his head in disbelief. "I swear, the two of you are so gullible. Did you really read these emails and think they were literally talking about motorcycles? They're *obviously* talking about something else. The motorcycles are code. Geez, didn't you ever watch spy movies?"

Spy movies aside (I was much more of a science fiction fan myself), Wrath's words tickled something in the back of my brain. I clicked the shop link one more time, bringing up the motorcycle parts page. I thrust the computer back at Wrath. "Can you do some of that technopathy of yours and see if there's more to this website than meets the eye?"

Wrath clucked his tongue against his teeth. "With my eyes closed," he said. "Browser, show me all gated content."

A new browser window appeared. For a moment, the page flashed to the motorcycle homepage. Then a second page flashed with a pop-up window. The motorcycle parts and gear page displayed again.

Then, a new page rendered.

It was still a shopping page, but this time, there were no motorcycle parts or gear.

It was equipment for…animals.

Cages, collars, leashes, you name it—this page had it all. As the three of us read over the descriptions, my heart tried to escape my chest. I pointed to a familiar product. "This is the cat carrier the cops found at the restaurant," I said. "Look at this description."

Wrath read it aloud. "Chenoweth Top Load Supe Carrier for Large and Medium Cats, Small Foxes, Small Tanuki, Small Dogs. Easy to get the supernatural in, and comfortable to carry, store, and clean. Chenoweth MagicBloc™ technology ensures supes can't escape or shift into another form while inside. The Top Load Supe Carrier comes with an adjustable shoulder strap for easy, hands-free carrying. It's also a cinch to store—just unzip and fold it down."

"You've got to be kidding me," Sloth breathed, her hand going to her mouth. "This whole motorcycle thing was a front. This is where Walter was getting his accessories. He was ordering them from this hidden website."

"Haha, check out this review," Wrath said, leaning forward as he continued to read. "3 stars. The Top Load Supe Carrier would be great except that, thanks to the MagicBloc™ technology, the carrier emits a slight glow when seen from the correct angle. If you're trying to fly under the radar, this isn't the carrier for you. Try the Front Load Supe Carrier with MagicThwart™ instead. It's not as convenient, but it doesn't glow."

I muttered something like, "Heh, that's funny," just to be polite, but I wasn't really listening. I was scanning the page, taking in as much information as possible. "What do you make of this?" I pointed to where the price should be for the cat carrier. "Says 5,000 points. Does that mean they don't accept cash?"

"You see that sometimes on these specialist commerce sites," Wrath said. "They use their own currency. It's points based. I'm guessing you earn points for completing certain tasks. When I worked in tech, our company gave us points for stuff like exercising regularly and completing our performance reviews on time. You could trade those points in for discounts on cell phone services, monitors, stuff like that. Or sometimes you could buy company swag with them."

I hrmmed, tapping my fingers thoughtfully against my chin. "Interesting. So, like, the more supernaturals you catch, the more points you get?"

"Or the rarer the catch," Wrath supplied. "Quality over quantity."

"I wonder what the motorcycles are code for," Sloth mused. "Maybe they're unicorns or—"

"Unicorns?" I snorted. "Come on."

"I don't see why *that's* so far-fetched," she said. "Not after everything else."

She had a point, but I wasn't willing to concede it. My worldview was still too small to include unicorns. "I wonder if the type of motorcycle is significant. He said they were SuperHawks. You think that matters?"

Wrath shrugged. "Don't know, but whatever the motorcycles

really are, sounds like Walt never unloaded them. At least, not to this guy. Do you know where his 'garage' is?"

Sloth shook her head. "No. But maybe his mom knows?"

"We should definitely ask her," I agreed. "Let's make time to go chat with her, okay?" While Sloth scribbled something down on a wayward receipt she was apparently using for a to-do list, I leaned over to Wrath. "Hey, is this the only gated page you found?"

My housemate shook his head. "No, look. There's a bunch. They're just in different tabs." He clicked over to the next tab and barked out a sharp laugh. "Well, there you go."

The page was titled, "Chenoweth Point Awards". It was broken down into a grid. In each cell was a photo of a creature, a name, a description, and the number of points each creature was worth.

"Look at this," I said, scrolling to the middle of the page. "The nine-tailed fox is worth 25,000 points."

"That's less than I would have thought," Sloth said. "That equals only five cat carriers."

"That's how they screw you," Wrath sneered. "They're stingy with the points they give out, and overcharge for the products you buy. That's why private currency is a slippery slope toward exploitation, man. It's not fair when the company owns both the product *and* the currency."

"Well, I'm not going to lose any sleep over people hunting supernatural creatures getting shafted," I admitted. "Is there any contact information anywhere on the site? An address, a phone number? Something like that?"

Wrath touched the screen. "Browser, show me physical addresses, phone numbers, and email addresses associated with this URL."

The browser returned nothing but the "Request Account/Reset Password" page we'd already visited.

"Doesn't look like it," Wrath said. "Whoever these people are, they're not interested in random jerks reaching out to them. But." He grinned, a mischievous look in his eye. "I bet if you make enough noise, they'll find you."

"Make noise how?" Sloth asked.

"I don't know, and I'm too busy to think about it right now," he said. "I've got a lot to do today." He stood, stretched, and walked to the door.

I looked up. "You do?"

"I've got, like, two raids to do with my guild, and I have to earn back the honor points I lost when you kicked me out of that PvP match."

"Gaming," I said. "You're busy with *gaming*."

"You got a problem with that?"

I shrugged. "It's your life. Waste it how you want."

Wrath paused in the doorway. "Leisure time is not time wasted. There you go again, Pride, equating value with production. Life is meant to be enjoyed, man. You can't gauge the value of your life based on capitalist—"

I shoved Wrath into the hallway and closed the door.

With Wrath gone, Sloth returned her attention to me. "I want to go talk to Mrs. Romanowsky today. Do you want to come with me?"

I gave a noncommittal shrug. "I've got time. When were you thinking of heading over?"

Her face brightened. "Right now!"

I glanced down at her outfit. She was wearing a t-shirt three sizes too big that looked like she'd slept in it. Her shorts used to be sweatpants, but she'd cut them off at the knee. They were covered in various stains and tattering along the edge. "Is that what you're wearing?" I asked.

Sloth's mouth twisted into a tight moue and her brows drew together sharply. "Not you, too," she scolded. "Do I exist just as an object of beauty for other people to admire? I don't think so," she said. "I'm allowed to look slovenly and sloppy if I want to. I don't owe you my attractiveness. Besides—beauty is only skin deep."

I blushed, chagrined. I'd heard Wrath giving Sloth this lecture a few days ago. She'd been crying in the bathroom—a sight I was getting used to, unfortunately—and when Wrath asked her what was wrong, she said some local women were making fun of her appearance. Wrath had gone into a full-blown tantrum, ranting that people rarely made such comments to men but felt free to hurl them at women. "Don't take that garbage from anyone, man," he admonished, his index finger pointing in Sloth's face. "Antagonizing women for their looks is patriarchal nonsense, Sloth. Self-confidence is punk rock, man. Loving yourself is a rebellion. Dress how you like. Do what you want. It's your life, after all."

"You're right," I said. "You don't owe anyone anything. And good for you for sticking up for yourself."

Her smile grew so bright, I could have used her face as a flashlight.

Almost skipping with joy, Sloth led the way out the front door, and a few minutes later, we were on our way to visit Eleanor Romanowsky.

twelve

· · ·

When we arrived at the Romanowsky place, Sloth rang the doorbell.

As we waited on the porch, I studied the street. The last time I was here, I'd run into a pair of ghosts, the spirits of a couple who had drowned. I didn't see them today, which meant nothing, of course. Ghosts didn't usually hang out in the same place unless they were haunting it. But that got me thinking about the headquarters for the Society. Why were those ghosts hanging out there? How did they find out about the place? Were they haunting it? It sure didn't seem like a standard haunting to me. Not that I'm an expert, but still.

Just as I was slipping deeper into these thoughts, Sloth grunted at my side. "Why isn't she answering?" She jabbed the doorbell several times with her thumb. But again, nothing happened.

With the laptop tucked against her side, Sloth began knocking on the door. "Mrs. Romanowsky?" she called out. "Are you in there?"

"Did you tell her we were coming?" I asked. "It doesn't look like she's home."

Sloth stood up straight and blew out a noisy breath through her nose. "She hardly leaves the house," she said. "That's why she gets so lonely, remember? But I guess it's possible. Let's go check the garage."

We walked around the side of the house to the attached garage. The windows were caked in dust and about a thousand years' worth of dirt. I shielded my eyes to peer inside. I could barely make out Eleanor Romanowsky's Cadillac—or, at least, someone's Cadillac. It could have been Walt's for all we knew. But it was a Cadillac, after all, which mostly only old people drive.

Listen, when you're investigating mysteries, sometimes stereotypes are helpful.

"Her car's here," I said. "But maybe someone picked her up. Does she use rideshares?"

Sloth gave me a look. "How should I know?" She shifted her weight, chewing on her lips thoughtfully. "No, Pride, something's not right."

We marched back around to the front of the house. Once more, Sloth banged on the door, calling out for Mrs. Romanowsky. When no one answered, I tried the doorknob.

The door swung open.

I started to enter, but Sloth put her free hand on my shoulder, tugging me back. "Hang on. Doesn't seem right to just barge in." She leaned her head through the door. "Mrs. Romanowsky? Are you—"

She didn't have time to complete the question, however. With the door open, we had an unobstructed view of the main hall leading into the living room.

The interior was destroyed. It looked like a giant had picked up the house and shaken it like a snow globe. Paintings that used to hang on the wall lay in a shattered heap on the floor. Furniture was overturned. I reached for my housemate. "Sloth—"

But before I could grab her, Sloth darted into the house. I followed on her heels, taking in the wreckage. The further we drew into the house, the colder my blood ran. Something terrible had happened here. And I had a feeling things were only going to get worse.

When we entered the living room, Sloth screamed.

I was right.

Mrs. Romanowsky lay in the middle of the living room floor, her body a crumpled heap. Like the hallway, the living room was ruined. Books, knickknacks, and dishes lay scattered over the floor amid trashed furniture. Someone had taken a blade to the upholstery and ripped out the insides. Cotton stuffing and shredded foam were everywhere. As I stood there surveying the damage, Sloth dropped to her knees at Eleanor's side. She pressed her fingers against the woman's throat, looking for a pulse. But when she looked up at me, her eyes were filled with tears.

"She's dead," Sloth said.

I nodded, pointing to the wound on her chest. "Yeah. She's been shot."

As if suddenly realizing we were in the middle of a crime scene, Sloth jumped to her feet, covering her mouth with her hand. "Oh, Pride. What if they're still in the house? What if they're still here and they know we're here and—"

Her voice was rising in a panic, so I grabbed her by the shoulders and shook her, forcing her to focus on me. "Nobody's here," I said. "We're alone, okay? We're alone."

"How do you know?" she said, her eyes still wild with fright. "How do you—"

"Because Eleanor's been dead a while. At least a day. Look at the corpse, Sloth. You can tell by the way—what?"

Sloth looked like she might throw up, the color draining from her face. "Don't explain," she said. "I shouldn't have asked. There's no…there aren't any other minds around, or I'd be able to hear their thoughts. It's just us."

I didn't think she would start screaming again, so I released her. She didn't move. "What do we do?" she asked. "Do we call the cops?"

I looked around and nodded. "Yes, obviously. We call the cops. I don't know what happened here, but it looks like someone was looking for something. This looks like a robbery, and poor Eleanor was just collateral damage."

Sloth swallowed and began to tremble, her teeth clattering. She was going into shock. "Collateral damage," she echoed, bemused. "She was a *person*, Pride. Not collateral damage. She was murdered in her own home just weeks after her son was killed."

A voice drifted into the room. "I'm pretty sure the two are related."

I looked up to find the ghost of Eleanor Romanowsky hovering at the far edge of the room. Her face was despondent, her eyes trained on her own corpse. "It's the only thing that makes sense," she said.

Gingerly, I stepped away from Sloth and toward the ghost, neatly avoiding the body in the middle of the floor. "I doubt that," I said flatly. "Walt's death was mostly an accident. You were…" I gestured vaguely toward the body. "You were obviously murdered."

Behind me, I heard movement, and a moment later, Sloth was pressed against my side. "Pride? Who are you talking to?"

I gestured at the ghost, but all Sloth could see was empty air. Her eyes searched the space but latched on to nothing. "It's Eleanor," I said. "Her ghost is here."

Sloth's eyes went wide as she pressed her hand to her mouth. "Mrs. Romanowsky? She's here?"

I nodded. "That's what I said."

Sloth stepped toward the ghost, and Eleanor backed away. For some reason, that struck me as funny. Even in death, people don't like having others inside their bubble. "Can you tell her something for me? Can you tell her I'm still trying to help?"

I smiled. "She can hear you," I said. "You can't hear her. But she can hear you."

Eleanor reached a hand toward Sloth in response, but her spectral form passed through Sloth's body. Eleanor paused, lifting her hand to her face, then tried again. Still her hand passed through Sloth. She shuddered, depressed, and let her hand fall limply to her side. "Please tell her I appreciate everything she has done for me so far."

I relayed the message to Sloth before returning my attention to Eleanor. "Did you see what happened here? Who did this? And why do you think it's related to Walt's death?"

In response, Eleanor lifted a hand and pointed toward the second floor. "They took my birds," she answered, her voice wavering.

I blinked in surprise. "Your birds? I don't get it. Why—"

But then I understood.

Suddenly, everything came crashing into my skull at once. The last time I'd been at this house, I'd noticed the birdcage glowing. Not all the time, and not if I looked directly at it. But if I looked at it from the corner of my eye, it glowed.

And then I remembered the cat carrier listing on the Chenoweth website. One commenter had mentioned that the MagicBloc™ technology had a visible glow.

"Your birds were shapeshifters," I said. "That cage was magic. It kept them from shifting. Did you know?"

Eleanor's hands were at her throat, her fingers winding around the delicate gold chain at her neck. "I didn't, not until the men came. But they were wearing outfits just like Walter used to wear. And I put two and two together. My son was a supernatural bounty hunter—and all this time, I had supernaturals in my house, and I didn't even know it." Again, she gestured toward her upstairs bedroom. "One of them went straight upstairs when they heard the birds twittering. I tried to stop him. That's when…" She looked down at her ruined chest. "That's when he shot me."

I looked at Sloth. "The SuperHawks," I breathed. "The birds were the SuperHawks."

Eleanor was speaking again, but I wasn't listening. I had to see for myself. I darted up the stairs and into Eleanor's bedroom. At the foot of her luxurious canopy bed was a giant birdcage. Someone had taken a pair of wire cutters and cut a hole into the cage. The two red and gold sun conures that had once chirped noisily from the cage were gone.

Back downstairs, Eleanor was floating around the living room, still wringing her hands in worry. When she saw me, she stilled. "You see? They're gone."

"Eleanor, I need you to think. What can you tell me about what happened here? Let's start with—how many people were here?"

Eleanor nodded. "Two. Two men, and they were looking for something. As I lay on the floor bleeding to death, they kept shouting at me, asking me where it was. But of course, I couldn't answer. And I had no incentive to, anyway. I knew I was dying."

I held out my hands, pleading. "What were they asking about, Eleanor? What were they looking for?"

Eleanor chewed her lips, glancing nervously between Sloth and me before she said, in a voice almost too quiet for me to hear, "Walter's laptop."

Stark dread washed over me, and I grabbed Sloth by the wrist. "We have to get out of here," I said.

Sloth stared, too scared to move. "Why? What did she say? Pride, tell me what's going on!"

"I'll explain later," I said. "We're in danger here."

I was heading for the door when Eleanor's voice stopped me in my tracks. "I know I'm dead," she called. "But please don't leave me here. I've been too afraid to leave on my own, and I don't know why I haven't gone to the other side. But I don't want to stay in this house with my own dead body a moment longer. Please. Please take me with you."

I paused only long enough to instruct Sloth to get into the car immediately. While Sloth hurried out of the house, I stalked over to Eleanor and gazed into her eyes. They were liquid and rheumy, but even in death, I saw the despair in them. "I don't know how to do this," I said. "I can't touch ghosts. And you can't touch me."

As if testing that theory, the old woman reached out to me. As had happened so many times before, I expected her hand to pass right through my body.

But it didn't.

Her fingers latched onto my wrist. An icy chill ran down my spine. The pressure on my skin where her fingertips met my flesh was unnerving. This wasn't right. I'd known my fair share of ghosts, and none of them, not one, could touch me.

But Eleanor was grasping me. I felt her trembling.

"Come on, then," I said, tugging the ghost toward the door. Unbelievably, she followed.

I darted from the house, dragging a petrified ghost behind me. As soon as we were inside the car, I started the engine while Sloth dialed the police. Then I stepped on the gas, and we flew out of there.

thirteen

. . .

"Where are we going, Pride? This isn't the way home."

I eased up a bit on the gas, my heart no longer throbbing in my ears. The more distance we got from Eleanor's house, the more confident I felt no one had seen us go in. No one knew we had the laptop.

I threw a sidelong glance at Sloth and sucked in a sharp breath. "We need to take Eleanor somewhere safe," I said. "I don't think Sinful House is the right place for her. She needs to be around others of her kind."

Sloth's eyes grew wide as she looked around the car. It's so funny when people do that. You tell them a ghost is around and they look for it, even though they know they can't see it. Human nature is wild sometimes.

"Take her—She's here? In the car?"

I jerked my head towards the backseat. "Sitting right next to the cameraman," I said.

The camera guy let out a little squeal as he squished himself into the corner, giving the ghost as wide a berth as possible. I chuckled under my breath.

"Why did you bring her? Not that I mind," Sloth said quickly, "it just seems like maybe she'd be better off at her house."

I shook my head. "Number one, she said she didn't want to stay there. But number two, if the people we're looking for—the same people who killed Eleanor—are supernatural bounty hunters, I figure they may have some knowledge about ghosts, too. The last thing I want is for them to get their hands on Eleanor. I don't know if you can torture a ghost. But I also don't want to find out."

I wasn't sure if my words made everyone feel better or worse, but it was the truth. I glanced at Eleanor in the rear-view mirror. "I won't let anything happen to you," I promised.

The ghost nodded mutely.

I parked outside Déjà Brew, and as the camera guy opened his door, I shook my head. "You're staying here," I said. "I can't let you in there."

The camera man gestured wildly toward the empty air in the backseat. "I'm not sitting in here alone with a ghost. The network doesn't pay me enough—"

"Calm down, compadre. The ghost is coming with me and Sloth. You're staying here alone."

Relief flooded his face, but he still gave me a petulant frown for show. "Network won't like it," he said.

I slammed the door, and Eleanor latched onto my wrist as I tugged her forward. "They'll live."

Inside the café, Felix was wiping down the counter, and the smell of espresso filled the air. Unlike the previous time I'd been at Déjà Brew, the place was filled with patrons. When he saw us, Felix straightened and dropped the rag to the counter. I'd like to say he was glad to see me, but that would be a lie. He looked perplexed.

"Hey, Felix," I said. "I hate to bother you. Do you remember me from the other day?"

The barista's eyes darted between Sloth and me as he fidgeted. "I remember you," he said cautiously. "You were here with Victoria."

I nodded. "Listen, can we talk in private? I need a favor."

Felix smirked and ran a hand through his hair. "I'm not usually keen on granting favors to people I barely know. However…" He glanced at our group again. "Why don't you come with me into the back." He pointed to Sloth. "The rest of you stay here."

I followed Felix into the back, and he closed the door that separated the kitchen area from the main house. Now that we were alone, he folded his arms across and pitched his voice low. "What happened to Mrs. Romanowsky?" he asked. "Why is she *dead?*"

My mouth fell open. "I – how did you—wait. Can you see ghosts?"

Again, Felix smirked. "You didn't think I'd operate a haunted guild hall from my basement without the ability to monitor what's going on, did you? Of course I can see them. Until you arrived, I was the only person in Odyssey who could. So, while I don't exactly think of you as a rival, I'm wary about you. To say the least."

Well, that tracked. I was wary of most people in Odyssey, too. "I see. Well, I need your help. Some dangerous people broke into Eleanor's house looking for something. When she didn't cooperate, they shot her. I don't know exactly what's going on," I admitted, "but I know Eleanor is better off here. I just get the feeling this place is safe. And I *know* her house isn't."

Felix dipped his chin toward his chest as he thought over what I'd said. He had no reason to trust me. After all, I was carting around the ghost of a murdered woman, the mother of a supernatural bounty hunter. But I'd come in with Victoria, and

Victoria and Felix were friends. I think. It was hard to tell. People in this town weren't always what they appeared.

Navigating the waters of Odyssey isn't for the faint of heart. I don't recommend it to anyone.

"Here's what we're gonna do," Felix said. His voice sounded like he'd rolled it in gravel. "Take her down to the basement, but don't tell anyone she's here. We don't need to attract any attention. Did anybody see you come here? Do you think anybody followed you from the house?"

I shrugged, digging my hands into my pockets. "I don't know. I don't think so. By the time we found Eleanor, she'd been dead for at least a day. I don't think the bad guys hung around that long. But I've been wrong before," I admitted.

Felix stroked his chin, still thoughtful. Finally, he said, "I guess that's a chance we'll just have to take. Take her downstairs. Like I said. Mum's the word."

I followed Felix back into the café, where he donned a cheerful grin for his patrons. I gestured for Sloth and Eleanor to follow me through the same doorway Victoria led me through. Quietly, we descended into darkness.

When we emerged into the Crypt, Sloth had the same reaction I did. Her eyes were wide as saucers as she wandered reverently through the room, taking in all the various accouterments of magic. She seemed especially enchanted by the astrology-painted ceiling.

But even more enthralled with this discovery was Eleanor. As soon as we were downstairs, she gasped audibly, freezing in her tracks as she took it all in. She was less interested in the wands and glass globes, though.

She was mesmerized by the ghosts.

"What is this place?" she whispered. "Are they all…like me? Are they all…?"

"They're all dead," I confirmed, nodding. "I don't know what they're doing here. But I thought if you can't stay home, you may as well have company."

Eventually, the other ghosts noticed they had a new member. Some kept their distance, surveying her from afar. But others were upon her like moths to flame, peppering her with questions.

"Eleanor? Is that you? Oh, come here, honey. Let me look at you!"

"Shot?! Who shot you? We need gun control in this country."

"Oh, my goodness, is everything okay? Of course it's not okay. You're dead."

"Mrs. Romanowsky, I'm so sorry to see you here. I thought you'd never die. I always said you would outlive us all! Which, I guess you did. Technically."

While Sloth examined her surroundings and Eleanor mingled with her new roommates, I scanned the room for ghosts who were more standoffish. A younger woman approximately my age stood watchful in the corner, her expression guarded. When I approached her, she stepped back, pressing herself against the wall. I stopped and held up my hands. "I don't want to hurt you," I said. Not that I could if I *did* want to. "My name's Pride. I thought I could ask you some questions."

The woman scoffed and raised an eyebrow. "Your name's Pride? What's the matter? Your mom not like you or something?"

I balked. "I never met my mother. She disappeared when I was an infant. But not because she didn't like me. At least, I have no proof of that."

The ghost looked like she was biting back a laugh. Then she said, "I'm Angelica Muñoz."

"Nice to meet you, Angelica." I didn't offer my hand, for obvious reasons. But no matter how many times I introduce myself to ghosts, it never stops feeling strange. "Can I ask you about this place? For starters, how long have you been down here?"

Angelica looked thoughtful, her image shimmering before my eyes. She must have been pretty in life. Her complexion was clear, her hair long and dark.

"It's hard to say," she breathed. "Once you're dead, time renders differently. I choked to death at a dinner party," she explained. "I kept waiting for that bright light everyone says you see when you die. But I never saw that. All I saw was my dead body lying on the ground while everyone around me cried and whatnot. Can you even imagine how disconcerting that is?" She huffed, turning up her nose. "Of course you can't. Why am I even asking? Anyway, I followed the ambulance toward the hospital before I realized—I'm dead. So I should make the most of it. You know. See the world."

She laughed then—at least I think it was a laugh. Her expression was very hard to read. "Turns out, though, traveling as a ghost is difficult, scary, and slow. At least for me. But as I was wandering the streets of Odyssey, I felt something call out to me."

I shivered, transfixed. "What was it?"

"It's hard to explain. It was like a voice in my head telling me where to go. So I walked—do ghosts walk? I guess I floated— until I found the place. It was a coffee shop, of all things, and I didn't even drink coffee in life. But Felix was there. He could see me. He welcomed me to the café and instructed me to go downstairs to where the others were. So here I am. I'm happy here, so I've never left. Although, I do much prefer it when the Society isn't in session. It gets so crowded. And it's already crowded enough. Even more so now that you've brought us another one."

"She had nowhere else to go," I pointed out.

Angelica sighed. "None of us do," she agreed.

I suddenly felt overwhelmed. Now that my adrenaline was wearing off, I felt my situation acutely. Mrs. Romanowsky had been murdered over a laptop now in Sloth's possession. My stomach felt sick, and my head was buzzing. I needed to go home and think. I thanked Angelica and went to find Sloth. She was hunched over a book titled *Fairies, Cats, and Other Annoying Creatures*. I tapped her on the shoulder. "Sloth. We need to go."

She glanced up from the book and blinked. She looked like she'd forgotten where she was. "Is everything okay?"

"Yes, but I need to get out of here and lie down for a while."

Sloth closed the book and slid it back into place on the book-shelf. She turned around and shouted in the shadows. "I'll come visit you, Eleanor," Sloth promised. "You're in good hands here."

Eleanor nodded, waving goodbye. "Thank you for all your help, dears. Please be safe."

We said nothing more as we went upstairs. Sloth thanked Felix, and then we headed home to Sinful House.

———

That night, I went to bed early, but I couldn't sleep. Sometime after midnight, I rolled over onto my back, my arm draped across my forehead. I was staring at the ceiling and contemplating going downstairs for a glass of warm milk when the air cooled, and a familiar shape shimmered into view.

"You did good today, you know."

The ghost was sitting cross-legged on top of my comforter, her chin propped atop her knuckles. I grinned in the darkness. "I did, didn't I?"

She nodded. "Eleanor would've been stuck in that house for a long time if you hadn't rescued her. You did the right thing taking her to Déjà Brew. She'll be happy there."

I rolled over onto my side, my cheek propped against my fist. I peered at the ghost, giving her a quizzical look. "How did you know about that? I mean, seriously, do you just follow me around in invisible mode all day? How do you know so much about my activities?"

The ghost giggled, covering her mouth with her free hand. "I'm psychic, silly."

"Psychic. Right." I knew that was a lie, but if she didn't want to let me in on her secrets, I wouldn't press the issue. "So I guess you saw me dragging her to the car. What I don't understand is how I could do that at all. You've tried to touch me a thousand times, but your hand always passes right through me."

The ghost reached out to pat me on the head, but as usual, her hand passed right through. "That is weird," she agreed. "I wonder how she was able to grab you."

"She tried to touch Sloth, but she couldn't," I said. "Is that normal?"

The ghost shrugged her slim little shoulders. "I don't know. I'm not an expert on ghosts."

"But you're a ghost," I chided. "So…?"

"You're a human," she retorted. "Are you an expert on humans?"

I chuckled. I guess she had a point there.

"Anyway," she said, switching her chin to her other hand, "Whatcha gonna do next? How are you gonna find those birds?"

I flopped onto my back and squeezed my eyes shut. "I'm not going to look for the birds," I said. I heard a sharp intake of breath, but I remained still. "It's too dangerous. Believe me, I've done nothing but think about this all day. But they killed Eleanor. Shot her in cold blood over a laptop. Listen, I have no idea what's on the computer, but I can tell you one thing. I'm not willing to die over it."

The ghost inched closer to me, and I could feel her disapproval radiating off her tiny spectral body. "You can't just quit," she said. "Eleanor was counting on you. Are you just going to tell her that her death wasn't important enough for you to look into?"

I grunted, sucking my teeth in annoyance. "Of course not. The cops will handle it. I know they're not the most talented police force in America, but they'll look into it. They'll do more than I can do, anyway."

The ghost threw up her hands in exasperation. "You don't know that! You know about the missing parrots and the laptop. The cops don't. They can't talk to ghosts like you can. They can't interview Eleanor. They'll probably treat it just like a typical robbery, and justice will never get served. And more importantly, nobody will ever find those poor birds."

I swallowed hard, squeezing my eyes even tighter. "I've thought about all of that," I repeated. "But it's just getting to be too much. It's too dangerous."

"Did you know sun conures can mimic human speech? They can also mimic telephones ringing and car horns, too."

"I didn't know that," I answered, relieved we were changing the subject. If she wanted to talk all night about babbling birds, I'd let her. If it meant we were done talking about the Chenoweth investigation, I'd stay up until the sun.

"You're scared. That's your problem."

So much for that.

I laughed, a bitter, dry sound that felt out of place. "Of course I'm scared! Someone was murdered! I'm way outside my league here."

"You handled cases like this all the time when you worked with the San Diego police force. So what's different now?"

I turned my head to face her. "The difference is, I was just a consultant. I didn't chase bad guys. Detective Hidalgo did that. And he had a gun."

The ghost shrugged as if this were the sorriest excuse she'd ever heard. "So get a gun."

I returned my gaze to the ceiling. "It's not that simple."

"You're scared, so you're giving up. I thought you were better than that."

I slapped my hands against the mattress. "And what would you have me do, O Bodiless One With No Skin In The Game? I have nothing to go on. I don't know who those men were, I don't know where to find Chenoweth, and even if I did—I'm not cut out for this. I'm just not."

"I don't believe you."

"Feel free to leave," I said, gesturing toward the door. "I'm trying to sleep, anyway."

But instead of leaving, the ghost inched closer. "What are you going to tell Sloth?"

"We already discussed it. And she agrees it's too dangerous. She's going to hand the laptop over to the police, and then we'll both be done with this. It's better and safer for everyone this way." I hissed out a long sigh. I didn't know why I bothered to justify myself to a ghost who wasn't even old enough to drive.

Silence filled the air between us. I rolled onto my other side, away from the ghost. After a while, I probed the air with my ghost whisperer senses, and I found nothing.

I was once again alone.

With a huff, I punched my pillow. I didn't owe Eleanor my safety. I didn't.

So why did I feel so guilty?

"I made the smart decision," I said into the night, hoping hearing my words aloud would convince me they were true. "Just because a ghost thinks I'm a coward doesn't mean I am."

Only silence answered me. I tugged the blanket up under my chin and squeezed my eyes shut. But the ghost's words echoed in my ears for a long time. It wasn't until pale sunlight struggled through my bedroom curtains in the early morning that I found sleep too much to resist and finally faded away.

fourteen

. . .

My phone rang early the next morning. Groggily, I answered, my eyes barely open. "Hello?"

"Good news," a woman's voice chirped. I didn't recognize it. "Cecil Bradshaw—or whoever he really is—will be in Odyssey in two days."

I rolled onto my back and shut my eyes. "Good morning, Victoria. That's great news. He has a ticket and everything?"

"Yes, everything's confirmed. I just got off the phone with him. Here's the kicker, though. He called from Cecil's phone number, but the man I spoke to was definitely *not* Jace Thornburgh."

I frowned. "What do you mean?"

"His voice was different. Similar, but different. It wasn't the same man we spoke to in the Crypt. At this point, I have no idea what that means. So what's the plan?"

I opened my eyes, brow wrinkled. "Plan?"

She sighed. "Yes, Pride. You need a *plan*. A little *showmanship*. How do you plan to confront him and get everything on camera in the most TV-pleasing way possible?"

I yawned and stretched. It was too early for this. "I don't know, Victoria. I hadn't really thought about it."

"Well, I have," she said. "You need to host a dinner party."

I sighed. There are three things I hate more than anything:

1. Shopping
2. Being woken up at the crack of dawn by people I barely know trying to get me to do things I don't want to do, and
3. Dinner parties.

"I don't know if that's such a great idea," I mused.

"Why not?" She sounded indignant.

"Because I don't want to," I admitted.

Victoria's response was something between a laugh and a sigh. "I'll make this very easy on you. I've already thought it out. Just listen."

While Victoria rattled off the details of her cockamamie dinner party plan, I hauled myself out of bed and got dressed. I definitely needed a shower and to brush my teeth, but I'd slept badly, and I wanted coffee more than anything. So while Victoria talked, I walked downstairs.

I found Envy in the kitchen. She had a shopping bag slung over her shoulder. "Morning," she said, her voice all sing-song and awake and slightly annoying. "How'd you sleep?"

I gestured to the phone and mouthed, "Busy."

But Envy kept talking. "I'm making a run to the grocery store," she said. "I could use your company. There's something I want to talk to you about."

Since the phone gesture didn't work, I held up a finger to quiet her. Into the phone, I said, "Yeah, that's fine, Victoria. No, I appreciate it. Seriously. It's just early and you caught me sleeping. Yeah, sure, I'll tell him. No, thanks a lot. Yeah, I'll see you."

I clicked the phone to disconnect and jammed it in my pocket. "What were you saying?"

Envy shoved a bag into my hand. "Grocery store. I'd like to get some alone time with America's Favorite Sin."

I groaned. "I wish you'd stop saying that."

Envy poked out her tongue. "The fact that it bugs you is exactly why I still say it. Didn't you go to grammar school?

I ignored her the entire way to the grocery store.

Inside, I volunteered to push the cart. Envy tapped a finger against her lips, eyes scanning the items on her list. "We can probably cut this in half if we let one of my elementals help."

I spun around on my heel and pointed a finger in Envy's face. "Absolutely not," I said. "First of all, do you think the citizens of Odyssey are ready for one of your elementals? It's one thing to have them around the house. It's another thing for them to be tearing around town on their own."

My housemate made an exasperated sound as she rolled her eyes. "Ugh, you're so dramatic. Don't worry. I'm not using the water or air elementals—they couldn't help, anyway. They're worthless at shopping. We'll use my earth elemental. And before you object," she said, holding up a hand, "he's not conspicuous. Unless you look *really* closely, he just looks like a short man. A very short man with round hips and a pointed hat," she amended under her breath, eyes darting sideways at me as she blushed. "But the earth elemental isn't even worthy of a second glance," she said in her usual speaking voice. "Usually."

"Number two," I said, continuing my objection, "the last time you summoned elementals to our house, the fire department ended up on our street. Don't you think you've caused enough trouble with them?"

Envy huffed, popping a hand on her hip as she narrowed her eyes at me. "If I don't keep summoning them, how am I supposed to get better at it? Besides. Back home, I *never* had any problems with the elementals. It's only since I've been in Odyssey that things have gone cockeyed. I'm not exactly sure why that is," she admitted, "but it's nothing a little practice can't fix. Trust me, Pride." She pressed her hand to her chest as she said this, offering me her best innocent smile. "It'll be fine."

When Envy had her mind made up, there was little I could say to dissuade her. So I dropped the subject and started pushing the cart. "What's the first item on the list?" I asked.

"Chicken," she said, her nose wrinkling, eyes scanning the rest of the list. "Why did I put chicken first?"

I shot her a confused glance. "Should chicken not be first?"

"Not on this list," she explained. "An unordered list just makes shopping tedious. Some people like to organize alphabetically, but even that's kind of a waste. I usually organize my list by shopping aisle. It's so much more efficient that way."

We were walking past an end cap filled with snack cakes. Envy grabbed one and threw it in the basket.

I shot her a look. "I thought the point of having a shopping list was so you didn't make impulse purchases," I chided.

Envy glanced sidelong at me, her lips pursed in displeasure. "I make lists so I don't forget things I need. That doesn't prevent me from buying things I *want*. Not that it matters. Every time I buy snack cakes, they disappear before I have a chance to eat them."

I recalled Gluttony eating my Chinese food out of the fridge without even an ounce of shame. "If you want something to yourself, you have to hide it. Gluttony has no boundaries."

Envy hrmmed as she selected a second package. "I'll keep that in mind. Anyway, listen. There's something I wanted to talk to you about."

We were headed towards the butcher for the chicken, which was on the other side of the grocery store. We walked past several displays—each containing nothing on our list—and Envy absently selected items from the shelves, tossing them into the basket. After throwing her third box of Velveeta into the cart, I stopped and looked her in the eye. "Envy. What's on your mind?"

Envy curled her lip beneath her teeth and sucked in a breath before answering. "Lust showed me that tiara you bought for her," she began slowly. "It's really nice. You chose well. I mean, I think wearing a tiara at our age is kind of weird, but that's not the point. She wanted it, and you bought it. Which was really nice. But which also raises some questions."

At the mention of my exchange with Lust, my stomach clenched. My personal business was my personal business, and I didn't really want to discuss it with Envy. This was stupid for several reasons, mainly because my personal business was being aired on TV, anyway. In fact, all over America, bloggers, vloggers, and influencers of all stripes were commenting on my personal life with wild abandon. As part of our contract, the network sent us updates on how we were being perceived in media—the "media" being everyone with a social media account. It's crazy to read strangers' opinions about yourself. They speculate and jump to wild conclusions. For example, there was an entire subReddit dedicated to analyzing our show, and several Redditors had posited that Shayda and I were never really together. That our entire relationship was a sham invented by the network to make me more sympathetic and normal.

It wasn't a bad theory. When it came to sympathy, I needed all the help I could get.

But that didn't make the theories true.

"So, what's your question?" I asked cautiously.

"You came on the show because you wanted to get your girl-friend back, yeah? But you and Lust seem to be developing something. Which is fine," she hurried to add. "But Lust is my friend. So I just wonder if your intentions about her are pure."

We were passing by aisle 7, which contained bread and

bread-related items. Envy had dinner rolls on her list, so I started to turn down the aisle. But Envy grabbed me by the elbow. "We're shopping the list in order," she said. "That's exactly why it should be organized when you…"

Her voice trailed off as she stared. Halfway down aisle 7, a short man wearing blue knickerbockers, a red hat, and a white shirt with red suspenders was throwing items into a cart half-filled with loaves of bread. His back was to us, so I couldn't see his face, but he looked suspiciously like a gnome. He was pushing the cart with one hand and grabbing items off the shelves with the other. I froze, gesturing to the man with a lift of my chin. "That's not your elemental, is it?" When she said nothing, I pressed on. "What's he doing?"

"It looks to me like he's having trouble making up his mind," she said. "Let's just give him a minute and see if it works itself out."

"I don't know, Envy. That doesn't look like indecision. That looks like mindless shopping. Like your elemental has an impulse problem."

Envy snapped her fingers and smiled brightly as she guided me away from the bread in aisle 7. "Impulse problem. That's a perfect segue, Pride. Did you give Lust that tiara as a token of your feelings, or do you just have an impulse problem?"

"Neither," I growled. "I bought Lust that tiara because I wanted her to have it. It's really as simple as that."

Envy huffed, peering at me quizzically. "There has to be more to it than that, Pride. You wanted her to have it, sure. But I want a Lamborghini. When should I expect that in the driveway?"

"That's a ridiculous question," I said matter-of-factly. "I can't afford a Lamborghini." *And I don't care about you getting what you want*, I thought, but I didn't say that. It would have been rude.

"Of course it's ridiculous. But it makes my point. You didn't just buy it because she wanted it. Heck, you didn't buy it because she wanted it *and* you could afford it. But I'm not sure why you *did* buy it. Was it for ratings? Or do you have feelings for her, despite your protestations about the girlfriend you claim you want back?"

I was working myself into a temper (*How dare she! Who does she think she is?*) when a voice over the loudspeaker announced in rising panic, "Cleanup on aisle 7. Cleanup and a manager to aisle 7!"

Envy and I turned to face each other, both of our eyes wide. We had just passed aisle 7. Without even needing to look, I had a sinking feeling I knew exactly what was happening.

We left the cart where it was and darted back to aisle 7, where, sure enough, the small man was throwing things into an overflowing cart. The pile of bread and bread-related items was towering out of the cart. Each loaf he tried to throw onto the pile bounced off onto the floor. And worse, the elemental was no longer choosing items one by one. He was grabbing armloads of bread, hurling them at the cart without looking.

The floor was covered with bread. And the mess was growing.

"Oh no, not again," Envy breathed. She raced toward the elemental, grabbing him by the suspenders from behind. "Elemental!" she hissed, trying to sound menacing while keeping her voice low to prevent a scene. "Elemental, you stop that *right now!*"

The elemental ignored her completely, reaching with its stubby fingers for a package of tortillas. Up ahead, someone gasped, shouting, "Young lady, you get your hands off that child this *instant!*" She was holding her phone up at arm's length. I couldn't tell if she was preparing to call the cops or making a video she hoped might go viral.

Envy looked up and snarled, "He's not a child. He's a gnome! And he's utterly out of control!"

The woman with the phone closed the distance between them, shaking her phone in Envy's face. "I don't know where you grew up, young lady. But in *Odyssey*, we don't make fun of people's disabilities! I'm sorry I called him a child, but he's certainly no gnome! That's a little person, and you need to get your hands *off!*"

"For somebody so worried about his rights, you sure are talking *about* him rather than *to* him!" Envy shot back.

The woman with the phone blanched, dropping the phone to her side. Her gaze shifted from Envy's face to the elemental she clutched by the suspenders. It was still trying to reach the loaves of bread. "I'm sorry," the woman said. "I didn't mean to—"

The elemental grabbed the woman's phone right out of her hand and threw it to the ground, where it shattered. Envy was so surprised that she let go of his suspenders, and the elemental went back to his madcap frenzy. But now, instead of carrying items off the shelves, he began sweeping them to the ground. Within seconds, he'd laid an entire shelf bare.

The shopping woman looked up at Envy with a steely gaze. "You need to get your friend under control," she snapped. Then, throwing her head back, she shouted, *"Can we please get security on aisle 7?"*

fifteen

. . .

We arrived home much later, exhausted, embarrassed, and bedraggled. The woman with the phone turned out to be a loud-mouth pet salon owner with a community newsletter and a penchant for armchair psychology. While Envy tried to get her elemental under control, the woman kept yammering about the importance of personal responsibility. "You have to own your mistakes," she said haughtily, nose tipped toward the ceiling as Envy tried desperately to constrain the gnome. "When you bring mentally handicapped people to the grocery store, you must be prepared for them to act out. I've written about this *extensively* in my newsletter."

The manager on duty called the cops. By the time they arrived, however, the gnome had despawned, leaving a tortured Envy to explain what had happened without actually explaining what happened. (You try telling the cops you summoned an earth elemental to help with the grocery shopping and see how well it goes over.)

After we put away the groceries, I trudged upstairs to my

room. I had fantasies of a long nap and maybe a bubble bath later. But as I was passing by Wrath's room, his door open, something nabbed my attention.

Whispering.

I know that's not enough reason to invade a person's privacy, but—call it intuition. I knew something was up. So I pushed the door open and stepped inside to find Wrath and Sloth huddled together on Wrath's bed, hunched over an open laptop.

A laptop I recognized.

"What are you guys doing?" I asked.

Sloth slammed the laptop closed, her mouth working, looking for words but not finding any. Wrath glared up at me, ready to excoriate me for coming into his room without an invitation. But then his face sagged, and he deflated. "Look, you said you didn't want to be involved anymore. So we didn't involve you anymore."

"That's Walt's laptop, isn't it?" I asked.

Sloth's face was pink, and she wouldn't meet my eyes when she whispered, "Yeah."

"You said you were taking the computer to the cops," I said. "You *know* it's not safe with us. What if whoever killed Eleanor figures out where it is? Do you really want them coming to Sinful House? You're putting everyone at risk!"

"No one knows we have it, Pride," Sloth said, finally meeting my gaze. "The cameras weren't with me when I picked it up."

"Maybe not, but it won't take a genius to track down Eleanor's associates. Geez, Sloth, you were on TV helping her find her missing son!"

"That doesn't mean she'd give me his laptop," Sloth objected. "For all anyone knows, the police already have it."

"Sloth—"

"We haven't found anything so far," Wrath interrupted, his scowl etched deep into his face. "But there has to be something here or else those goons wouldn't have wanted it so bad. But we can't find it. You know what that means, Pride? If *I* can't find it, even with my technopathy?"

I shrugged. "What?"

"It means maybe there's more to this laptop than meets the eye. What if I can't find it because this piece of junk's enchanted?"

I stared down at the computer, brow furrowed. "Enchanted? Is that even possible?"

"How should I know?" Wrath spat, leaning his head back in frustration. "But if it is, we gotta find someone who can detect things like that. See if they can find something we can't."

I threw my housemates a dubious look. "Guys, that just seems…unlikely. If there was an enchantment on the laptop, wouldn't it hide the emails and the website and everything? Maybe there's nothing more to find. Or maybe whatever's on it is so obvious, you've overlooked it."

"That's just it, though," Sloth said with a sigh. "There's like…*nothing* on here. No photographs, no porn, no half-written novels, no nothing. It's *suspiciously* empty."

I shrugged, thrusting my hands into my pockets. "Maybe Walt was a Luddite," I said. "He didn't have any tech in his room. No game systems. No Alexa. No 3D printer. So maybe there's nothing to find because there's *nothing to find*."

Sloth and Wrath shared a look I couldn't read. When Sloth looked back at me, she was frowning. "I want to send the laptop to this woman I know back home. She has psychometry—she can touch objects and sense things about them. She'll be able to tell us if anybody…you know. Messed with it."

"And what if they did?" I challenged. "Then what? Can this woman also erase hypothetical computer enchantments? Can she illuminate secret information we're too inept to locate?"

Sloth's face fell. "Well, no. But—"

"So you want to involve even more people in this when we still don't really know what we're dealing with? And even then, it won't really get us anywhere?"

Gingerly, Wrath slid the laptop off Sloth's lap and, to my surprise, handed it to me. When she saw what he was doing, Sloth shot up straight, eyes wide with objection. "Hang on, what are you—?"

"Pride's right," Wrath said, raising his voice just enough to drown out Sloth's protest. "We tried, Sloth. But whatever is on that laptop isn't for us to find. We've done the best we can. We need to turn this over to the cops and hope they can do a better job." At Sloth's crumpled face, he added. "It's too dangerous."

She nodded mutely and wiped at her nose. I tucked the laptop under my arm. "I'll take it to the station," I promised. "And I'll let Eleanor know. She wouldn't want to put us in harm's way, Sloth. I know she wouldn't."

Sloth slid off Wrath's bed and slipped past me into the hallway. When she was gone, I lifted a hand in a limp wave. "I'm gonna go have a nap or something," I said. "Thanks for siding with me on the laptop thing."

Wrath nodded. "When you're right, you're right. And you were right. We tried, we failed. Time to let the cops do their jobs. Even if I do think all cops are—"

"See you later, Wrath," I interrupted before going off to my own room, dreams of a nap and a bubble bath dancing in my mind.

———

Two days passed quickly, and the night of Cecil's dinner party arrived. Victoria came to the house early to help set up. The rest of us ran around like chickens with our heads cut off, making sure everything was in place. Even the cameramen were helpful for a change. I got the feeling they'd gotten an earful from the network about making this confrontation as successful and dramatic as possible. So instead of being surly and annoying, they pitched in, rearranging furniture and setting up the scene.

Sinful House was teeming with cameras, but most of them weren't hidden. The camera guys and Envy worked together to hide or remove cameras that were out in the open—all the better to catch Cecil off-guard. Victoria came up with the brilliant idea of assigned seats at dinner, so we'd know how to light the room to best capture Cecil's charade on camera.

The tricky part would be getting Cecil—Jace Thornburgh—to sign a release so the network could air the episode with him in it. But although it might cost the network a pretty penny, our producer, Tricia, assured us they'd worked with guys like him before. There was little Jace Thornburgh wouldn't do for money.

That's why we were in this predicament in the first place.

While the rest of us worked to set the stage, Gluttony prepared a meal fit for a king. He baked two different lasagnas—one with a mouthwatering combination of veal, pork sausage, and beef, the other with eggplant and mushrooms. In addition, he prepared three salads, several loaves of bread, rosemary butter, and home-churned lemon sorbet for dessert. The spread was beautiful. You had to hand it to Gluttony. The guy really knew how to create a five-star experience.

Greed sauntered into the dining room, his hands tucked casually in his pockets. After all my time at Sinful House, I still didn't know Greed well. He kept to himself, and even during our network-mandated house meals, he said little. Tonight wasn't much different. As he took in the spread, all he said was, "You went to a lot of trouble."

"I didn't," I corrected. "Gluttony did. He made all this himself. He saved our hides, really. None of this would be possible without him."

Greed offered a slight nod, still surveying the table. "I hope it goes well."

I paused. "Are you coming to dinner?"

Now, the barest shadow of a smile crept over his lips. "Wouldn't miss it. Though I'll be sure to keep strictly to the wine. It's store-bought, yes?"

I chuckled. "The wine is safe. But wine on an empty stomach?"

Greed smiled for real now. "Can't be worse than what you've got planned. And I like my secrets."

He said nothing more as he sauntered out the way he'd come in.

Curtain was in half an hour, and one by one, the housemates started trickling into the common rooms. Everyone was dolled up in their Sunday best. But of course, Lust put everyone else to shame. She was wearing the tiara we bought at the citywide garage sale. I couldn't decide if she looked majestic or insane and eventually settled on a combination of the two. Either way, I couldn't keep my eyes off her. Besides the crown, she wore a black dress that looked like she'd been poured into it. When she saw me staring, she blushed a bright crimson. I returned that blush and tore my eyes away, my pulse pounding in my ears.

As the housemates poured wine and Gluttony passed around hors d'oeuvres, Bailey Preston arrived. I gave her a quick tour of the house and offered her a glass of wine, which she accepted but didn't drink. She kept fidgeting with her jewelry and smoothing her hair into place even though she already looked perfect. She was worrying the rings on her fingers and biting her lip when she placed a hand on my elbow and gave a little squeeze.

"You really went above and beyond for this," she said. "I can't tell you how grateful I am."

I shrugged. "It was the least I could do. Anyway, this was all Victoria's idea. I know Tamora and I will probably never see eye to eye, but I can't stand the idea of someone being preyed upon like that. Everyone deserves to be with someone who loves them for who they are and not what they bring to the table."

Bailey nodded, her chin wobbling. "Is Tamora coming tonight?"

I shook my head. "We didn't invite her. I have no idea how this is going to go down, and we don't want to embarrass her. We'll show her the footage, though."

Bailey hrmmed, her lips pinched. "If this is successful and we get Cecil to admit who he really is, I want to arrange a *real* meeting between Tamora and Jeff."

Of all the things she could have said, I wasn't expecting that. "A real meeting?"

Bailey swallowed and fidgeted once again with her hair. "I know I said I didn't believe in the afterlife. And I still don't. Not really. But my sister does. So if we get Cecil on camera admitting how he duped my sister—and believe me, I can't wait to hear the details on that—it's going to destroy her. The only thing that'll help her heal is speaking with Jeff. The *real* Jeff. I think she needs to hear from him one more time."

Her request made a bitter sense. One day in the (probably far) future, Tamora would not only forgive us but be grateful we saved her from the nightmare of a fraudulent marriage. But in the short term, Bailey was right. Tamora would hate all of us when the truth came out. I didn't care about that, but of course, her sister did. Tamora might even slip into a depression like she had before. I cared somewhat more about that. I'd been depressed before. It's not fun. I wouldn't wish it on anyone.

However, I wasn't sure what I was supposed to do about any of this.

"I see ghosts," I admitted. "But I see them here on earth. Among the living. I can't cross over to the other side and find people. I'm not a medium."

"You're not," Bailey agreed, "but we both know someone who is."

I opened my mouth to ask for more details when Victoria bustled into the room. "Come on, you two. We have a show to put on. It's time to go catch a predator."

sixteen

. . .

At 7 p.m., the doorbell rang.

Everyone took their places, and I went to the door, my heart thumping in my throat. I didn't know why I was nervous. But I don't generally like surprises, and there was no telling how this would all pan out.

I tried to be prepared for anything. I braced myself for the man on the porch to be a stranger. I prepared for it to be a woman. I'd seen the MTV show *Catfish*. When it came to deception, human ingenuity knew no bounds. The person outside could be *anyone*.

With a breath to steady my nerves, I pulled the door open.

I blinked. Standing on the porch was Jace Thornburgh—the same man I'd seen in the Facebook photos and the startup articles online.

Kind of.

The pictures we'd found of Jace Thornburgh were of a good-looking middle-aged guy who drank dry martinis in polos and khakis and Docksider slip-ons. But this guy looked nothing like that. He was wearing a long white linen tunic over a loose pair of maroon linen trousers. He wore suede Birkenstocks revealing recently manicured toes. Around his left wrist, he wore a bracelet of milky jade mala beads. His wavy brown hair was growing out, almost touching his shoulders. Small gold hoops adorned both earlobes.

In short, he looked like a cross between Mahatma Gandhi and Jesus. Not a bad look if you're pretending to be a medium.

Finally, I found my voice. "Jeff?" I asked.

The man blinked and then smiled warmly. "Cecil," he corrected. "Understandable mistake."

I didn't know what to say. His voice sounded nothing like the man Victoria had spoken to on the phone. We stared at each other a moment before he cleared his throat and asked, "May I come in?"

I stepped aside and led him to the living room where everyone was seated. "I can't thank you enough for showing up," I said. "I hope you don't mind, but I've invited a few friends over to join us for dinner. Victoria you already know." At her name, Victoria nodded, smiling prettily. "And this is Bailey Preston, Tamora's sister. But maybe you already know that."

Cecil shook his head. "I'm afraid I don't. It's nice to meet you," he said, directing this comment at both Bailey and Victoria.

"The others are some of Tamora's more recent acquaintances. I figure if we're going to make this work—"

"Let me interrupt you," he said. He drew his hands to his chest, holding them in a prayerful position. "I know when you and Jace spoke on the phone, you had a lot of questions. It seems you may believe I'm here for…dubious purposes." He smiled awkwardly, fingers worrying the mala beads at his wrist. "But whatever you may think of me, I assure you I am who I say I am. My name is Cecil Bradshaw, and I'm a psychic medium. I channeled the spirit of Jeff Bishop into my body, where he continues to reside. Usually, I'm myself. But with just a little nudge in the right direction, Jeff comes to the front and takes over this body."

"Neat trick," Greed said, one leg thrown casually over the other. "So you can make this switch on command?"

Cecil hesitated. "I don't know if I'd say it's on command," he admitted. "I'd say more…when the time is right."

Victoria shot Greed a withering look as I escorted our guest to a loveseat where we both sat. Gluttony had set out trays of hors d'oeuvres, including watercress sandwiches and an impressive charcuterie board replete with a half dozen meats, cheeses, and fruits. "Dinner will be ready in just a minute," Victoria said, "But we thought we could begin the evening on a more casual note." Victoria tilted her head to the side. "I'd love to hear more about how—and why—you channeled Jeff into your body."

Cecil reached for a sandwich and popped it into his mouth. He brushed his hands together and crossed his legs as he leaned back into the sofa cushions. "Of course. Well, where do I begin? As a spiritual counselor, I do a lot of this kind of work: séances, automatic writing, past-life regression, things like that. But I'm also a medium. Most of that work is less about the spirit and more about helping grieving people heal. I channel spirits of the dead so their loved ones can move on. I work with families fighting over wills, wives who want to hear that their husbands still love them, things like that. So I was surprised when the person who came to me for medium services was not a friend or family member. It was a business associate of Jeff Bishop's. A man named Jace Thornburgh."

I gawped, my eyes going wide. *Wait, what? He* was Jace Thornburgh. I'd seen proof with my own eyes. I saw his Facebook profile. I saw his photo on the startup news site. The man sitting before us was a milquetoast guru, sure, but *he was Jace Thornburgh!*

Wasn't he?

I opened my mouth to state the obvious when Gluttony burst into the room, hands on his hips. "Dinner's on the table," he said. "Y'all best get in there before the food gets cold. I didn't spend all that time in the kitchen to let my hard work go to waste."

We knew better than to defy Gluttony, so we all climbed to our feet. As we headed into the dining room, I sidled up next to Sloth and whispered in her ear. "Well? What do you make of this? Is he telling the truth?"

Sloth's expression was serene. "It's super weird," she said, reaching for a pigtail to chew on. "I can't tell you if he's telling the truth. I tried to read his mind, but there was so much noise in there. Not normal noise, either. He wasn't just jumping from thought to thought like people do. It was like multiple conversations were happening at once, everyone talking on top of each other. I couldn't hear his thoughts over the conversations."

I quirked an eyebrow in surprise. "Have you heard anything like that before?"

Sloth shook her head. "No, not like that. Some people play noise in their heads to keep out intrusive thoughts. Like, a guy I know back home repeats lines from movies and song lyrics over and over again, so he doesn't have to hear himself think. But this was…different. I don't know what to make of it."

I sighed. "Well, don't worry about it too much. Between your mind reading and Gluttony's special dinner, I have a feeling we'll have our answers soon enough."

We took our seats around the table with Cecil at the head. As usual, Gluttony's feast was outstanding. Victoria acted as the hostess, preparing plates and passing them down the table. No one touched their food until everyone was served. Finally, when the last person had their dish in front of them, I turned to face Cecil.

"We asked Gluttony to prepare a special meal tonight," I said. "He's the best cook in the house. I hope you're hungry."

At the other end of the table, Victoria began pouring wine. As I pretended to cut into my lasagna, I watched Cecil from the corner of my eye. He took a huge bite, and ecstasy washed over his face as he chewed, his eyes rolling to the back of his head. "Oh my word," he exclaimed through a full mouth. "This is fantastic. Why aren't the rest of you as big as a house? If I lived here and I got to eat like this every day, you'd have to roll me out the front door."

We chuckled politely, but tensions were high. Cecil had already eaten several mouthfuls before the rest of us tentatively took small bites of the dinner. After all, we knew what was in the food.

After a few minutes of quiet chewing, Wrath said, "Since nobody else has the chops to say anything, I guess I'll do it. We've all seen Jace Thornburgh's photos, man. Unless he has a secret twin, you're him. I mean, you're obviously Jace Thornburgh, not Cecil Bradshaw or whatever. So why are you pretending…"

But Wrath didn't have a chance to complete the question. In the middle of his sentence, Wrath's words stuttered to a stop as he balked, eyes blinking rapidly as he stared at the other end of the table.

Confused, I turned to Cecil. It took a moment, but suddenly, I realized why Wrath had been shocked into silence.

Cecil changed right before my eyes.

One minute, he was a jovial, charming man with a casual command of the room. But now, he was scowling, brow wrinkled in confusion as he dropped his fork, which clattered to the floor. He pulled his hands away from the table and pushed up his sleeves until they revealed the mala beads at his wrists. Then, his head fell backward, and he sighed heavily. "Cecil again," he breathed, his voice low. "Why am I at Cecil's dinner party?"

The room went silent. The man speaking was not Cecil, but I

recognized this voice. I'd heard this voice on the phone in the Crypt.

The voice belonged to Jace Thornburgh.

The change was not dramatic, but it was noticeable. Cecil's voice was flowy and warm like he was trying to put you to sleep. This voice was sharper and louder, like he wanted you to sit up and pay attention.

But it wasn't just the voice that was different. His body language changed, his vibes palpably less relaxed. His shoulders were tighter; his jaw was clenched. Where Cecil had been open and welcoming, this man was guarded, like one of us might attack him at any moment.

He dropped his head into his hands, fingers buried deep in the roots of his hair. When he looked up, his expression was stern. "I agreed to let Cecil bring me here," he said. "But we agreed he'd stay until we got home. So...I'm not sure why I'm here and Cecil's not."

I stared, unable to reply. Did he think *we* had any answers? I was grasping for a way to respond when at the other end of the table, Greed inexplicably asked, "Who are we speaking to now?"

My head swiveled to face Greed. His eyes were trained on Cecil, and his expression was tender but professional, like a professor addressing a nervous first-year student.

I swiveled my head again to look at Cecil. I was beginning to feel like I was at a tennis match.

The man snorted out a heavy sigh. "Jace," he said. "My name is Jace Thornburgh."

I glanced over at Greed. He was leaning forward onto his elbows, his chin resting atop laced fingers. He was still wearing that eerie professor look. Frankly, it was the most of Greed's personality I'd ever seen, and it was creeping me out. He cleared his throat and asked, "Jace, are you the host?"

The man nodded. "Yes. You'd think I'd be used to this by now. But I guess you never really get used to it."

I was staring so intently at Cecil and trying to make sense of what I'd just seen that I almost jumped out of my skin when Wrath demanded, "What the heck is going on? Cecil?"

Greed smiled at Cecil(?) Jace(?) and dropped him a wink. "I can explain it," Greed said. It wasn't an offer to us, however. It felt like an olive branch to Jace. "But it is *you* we are speaking of, so perhaps you'd like to speak for yourself?" He softened his voice even further and said, "It's entirely up to you. *Jace.*" He put a subtle but unmistakable emphasis on the man's name.

Jace—look, even I could take the hint—looked like he'd rather be anywhere else on earth than sitting at this table with us. His skin had gone ashen, and his jowls sagged. "I, uh." He cleared his throat and looked down into his lap. "I have a psychological condition called dissociative identity disorder."

I chanced a look around the table. I had absolutely no idea what he was talking about, but no way would I admit as much. Thankfully, my housemates—all except Greed—looked just as perplexed as I felt. Greed made an encouraging motion at Jace, who sucked in a breath and tried again.

"It used to be called multiple personality disorder?"

I sank back into my chair, my hand covering my mouth in surprise. Oh. I'd heard of this condition, but only on TV shows and that one Sally Field movie. The man sitting at the head of the table had come to us as Cecil, an easygoing spiritual guru. But he wasn't Cecil now. Cecil had left the building.

This man was Jace Thornburgh.

Again, Jace shifted in his seat and continued. "I was diagnosed as a teenager," he said. "I don't know any of you, so sorry if I don't feel like giving you my entire medical history. But you invited *Cecil* to dinner, not me, so I guess I owe you an explanation of why I'm here, and Cecil isn't. But unfortunately, I don't have a great answer to that."

"Actually," Greed interrupted, "it is *we* who owe *you* an explanation." He gestured at the feast in front of us. "We tricked Cecil. Gluttony is a kitchen witch. He enchanted tonight's dinner with magic that makes people tell the truth. It's why we were hesitant to begin eating and why I'm confessing this now." He grinned and winked again. "I can't say for sure, but I suspect that's why you emerged when Cecil ate our food. You are the original personality, after all. Your body's true north. The magic forced the switch."

"I see," Jace said, voice low. "Well, under the circumstances, I'm gonna choose not to be ticked off. I assume you want to know how and why Jeff got stuck in Cecil's—and my—body."

"Or *if*," Victoria clarified, her voice icy.

"*If* isn't the question," Jace said, shaking his head. "That really did happen. And it's all my fault. Good grief, I hardly even know where to begin."

Envy was watching all this with rapt attention. "Begin at the beginning," she advised. "And when you come to the end, stop."

Jace grinned nervously. "Well, I can tell you what I know. I met Jeff on an Everest expedition. He sort of became my climbing buddy, I guess you'd say. When you go through something like that, even with a complete stranger, you form a bond with them. There were lots of other people on the expedition, of course. But I was attracted to Jeff not just because he was famous, but also because he was more like me than the others."

"More like you how?" Bailey asked.

"Uh, well…lots of the other guys were survivalists. They had Everest on their bucket lists, you know, so they were there to, like, prove something. Adrenaline junkies. But Jeff and I were different. We weren't there because we got off on the rush of danger. We were there trying to find ourselves. I know how that sounds," he scoffed. "But it's true. I like to think we would have become friends if we'd both survived."

I chanced another look around the table. All my housemates were as transfixed as I was. I guess it's not every day you meet someone with multiple personalities living inside one body.

"Jeff got sick in what they call the *death zone*. There's not much oxygen up there, and you're supposed to pass through that zone quickly. But the problem is, our expedition was overbooked. Imagine that. You finally get out of the hectic rush of day-to-day life only to stand in a queue to reach the top of Everest because the expedition was *overbooked*." He laughed again, a dry, mirthless sound. "Anyway, it's not uncommon for people to get sick in the death zone. That's why they call it the death zone. Jeff started hallucinating. He was talking to people who weren't there. Mostly, he spoke to Tamora, who I guess was his wife."

I shot a look at Bailey, but her expression was unreadable. She was watching Jace with as steely a gaze as I'd ever seen.

"He talked about private things that happened between them. Dinners they'd shared, jokes, TV shows. Stupid stuff like that. I tried to be there for him. But he was deteriorating fast, and—"

He sat up straight, his mouth drawn into a hard line. "I don't want to talk about Jeff's death," he said. "All I'll say is this. In my final moments with him, he was delirious. The last person he mentioned was someone called Tori."

It took everything I had not to look at Victoria to gauge her reaction. After all, Tori was her secret, and I wouldn't be the one to expose her. Instead, I asked, "Who's Tori?"

"I don't know," Jace admitted with a shrug. "He just kept saying he was sorry. He passed away before revealing the last of his secrets."

A collective sigh went around the table, and the energy shifted. It's always hard to talk intimately about death, even the death of a stranger. Humans have a tremendous capacity for empathy when we allow ourselves to feel it.

"Anyway, that's the backstory. When I got back stateside, it took me a while to acclimate to daily life, you know? Everest kicked my butt, and I watched someone die. It changed me. But after a while, I realized I needed to talk to Jeff. Not just about business, but about our experience. So I did something out of character. I asked Cecil for help."

"How?" Sloth asked. "I mean, I hope this isn't an ignorant question. But, if you and Cecil are the same person, then…?"

"I'm sorry, Sloth, but I must interrupt." Greed was leaning forward and craning his neck to address Sloth directly, who sat on the same side of the table as he did. "Cecil and Jace are *not* the same person. Or at least, not the same personality. They merely reside in the same body."

Jace was silent a moment. Finally, he looked to Greed and said, "You seem to know a bit about this. Are you a doctor or something?"

Greed's lips tightened into something like a smile. "I'm a psychiatrist," he said.

If you'd told me Greed was some kind of rock band dropout or a vampire cosplayer, I would have believed you. That's the kind of energy Greed gives off.

Never in a million years would I have guessed that guy to be a *psychiatrist.* I immediately felt terrible for his patients.

Greed shifted in his seat and said, "Dissociative identity disorder means there are several personalities—we call these *alters* —living inside the host. They can converse among themselves. Of course, psychiatry doesn't *really* understand how that happens. For as much as we like to think otherwise, the brain is still the great unknown. We know far less about how it works than we pretend."

"I guess that explains it," Sloth said almost to herself. She glanced over to Jace. "I'm a mind reader. My job tonight was to listen to your thoughts—sorry, *Cecil's* thoughts—to see if he was telling the truth. But when I tried, I heard so many other voices. I couldn't make out one from another. It was just so much chatter and noise."

Greed nodded. "You heard the alters having conversations. That's interesting. I'd like to talk to you more about that at another time." He adjusted his gaze to settle once again on Jace. "How many alters do you have?"

"Five that we know of," he mumbled.

No one knew what to say to that. It seemed intrusive and rude to ask more about the alters (even though I, for one, was dying to know more.) After a protracted silence, Wrath finally said, "So I guess I have to be the one to ask. *Again.*" He gave me a dirty look as he said this. "Can we talk to Jeff? I mean, can he come out to play?"

I threw Wrath a disgusted look, but he just shrugged and made bug eyes at me like he had done nothing wrong. I looked back at Jace, who was smiling. If he was offended by Wrath's question or tone, he didn't show it. "I wish I could help you there," he said. "But I don't have anything to do with Jeff. Not in his current state, anyway. That's all Cecil. And I can't *make* Cecil come out. That's not how this works. At least, not for me."

Without meaning to, I looked to Greed for confirmation. My housemate nodded sagely. "Some people claim they can switch alters at will," he explained. "But in my limited experience, most people can't. The alters come out when they are needed." Greed looked at Jace, his eyes narrowing as he tilted his head to the side questioningly. "What makes Cecil come out?"

Jace cleared his throat and adjusted in his seat. "According to my doctor, Cecil is an internal soother. He comes out when I feel stressed or I'm in a new, uncomfortable situation. His presence is very calming. Or so I'm told. When I deal with him behind the scenes, I don't find him calming. Mostly I just find him annoying." He grinned as he said this, color rising in his cheeks. "But he's useful."

"If he comes out when you're stressed, how come he didn't show up on Mount Everest?" Sloth asked, leaning forward eagerly in her seat. "Or did he?"

"That's a good question," Jace conceded. "The best I can guess is that Cecil couldn't have survived Everest. I was the one who trained, not him. My alters don't share their skill sets. Cecil can channel spirits and meditate and all that jazz—I can't. But similarly, I have what it takes to climb and survive Everest. I don't think Cecil would have made it out of basecamp."

The group was quiet for a long time, our dinner forgotten. Suddenly, Jace was on his feet, rubbing his palms on Cecil's white tunic. "I'm feeling a little on display," he admitted. "Especially sitting here wearing Cecil's clothes. Anyone mind if we pause this whole thing? I need a minute."

Jace didn't need our permission, of course, and he didn't wait for it. He bolted out of the dining room and disappeared around the corner. In the distance, a door opened and then slammed shut.

All eyes turned to Greed. He was leaning back in his chair now, and without Jace present, his relaxed, professional demeanor vanished. Now he looked like the Greed I was used to —wolfish and predatory. "I've never seen that happen in the wild like that," he said. "I've only treated a handful of patients with DID. Definitely never met anyone who channeled a spirit into their body. Can you imagine the papers I could publish about this? I've got to get Jace to sign a release form."

Lust growled, throwing Greed a disgusted look. "That poor man is suffering, and you're thinking about your career?"

"Not at all," Greed shot back. "I'm thinking about the *money*."

"You're disgusting."

"I'm honest," he quipped. "This could lead to book deals, movie rights, the whole shebang."

"That's so wrong, man," Wrath put in, sneering and shaking his head. "The poor dude's got an emotionally vapid millionaire stuck inside him, and all you care about is dollar signs. That's the trouble with our whole society! Capitalism is the death of humanity, man, I'm telling you!" He banged a hand on the table. "Greed is the perfect example of why this country is deteriorating! Our crumbling morals, our disregard for fellow man! Capitalism will destroy us from the inside out!"

I sighed and gave Wrath a weary look. "Now's not the time, Wrath."

"It's never the time!" he shouted. "But in actuality, it's *always* the time! When better to illuminate our system's flaws than when we're staring in the face of someone broken by it?"

"Stop it," I said, my voice taking on a threatening edge. "We just met this guy. You can't call him broken. It's not right."

"He's a mental case, man," Wrath said, shaking his head in despair. "But it's not his fault. He's a reflection of each of us, torn to pieces by an evil society."

"I have a question." We turned our heads to Sloth, who was chewing on a pigtail and dipping a finger into her red sauce. "If Cecil and Jeff conspired to marry Tamora together, what was the plan for when Cecil wasn't in charge of the body? Do Jace or any of the alters have girlfriends or boyfriends of their own?"

"Good question," I said. "But we won't get any answers unless we get Cecil to come out. But I don't know how to do that, and I don't want to pester Jace. Cecil agreed to this interrogation. Jace didn't."

"Technically, Jace agreed *for* Cecil," Victoria reminded me.

I ignored her.

Gluttony stood up and began cleaning the table. "All this

work for nothing," he muttered. "That's okay, though. I love lasagna. Even if it does make you tell the truth against your will. I'm gonna eat me some and hide out in my room where nobody can bother me. The rest of y'all are invited to do the same."

One by one, my housemates and I got up and cleared our places. Eating the lasagna in private was a good idea, so I wrapped up my food and placed it on the counter for later. First, I needed to go talk to Jace.

It took a while, but eventually, I found him down on the beach. He was sitting on the shore, his bare toes buried in the sand. He didn't tear his gaze away from the ocean as I settled down beside him. We shared a long, quiet moment with only the crash of the waves for company. The sun had already dipped below the horizon, and a cool breeze made my skin pimple over.

Without looking at me, Jace said, "I'm sorry about all this."

I shrugged, following Jace's gaze out over the ocean. I didn't have dissociative identity disorder, but my brain wasn't exactly normal, either. I struggled with anxiety, the inability to read social cues, reckless pride, and myriad other things. So I guess you could say I knew a thing or two about imbalanced mental health. "It's not your fault," I said. "I want to say we were trying to help a friend, but that's a lie. We were trying to win a contest for a TV show. But obviously, we had no idea what was really going on. If we'd known it would lead to this…"

I let my voice trail off. I wanted to believe I would have respected Jace's privacy, trading in my win for his wellbeing. But at that moment, I didn't know if it was true, so Gluttony's lasagna prevented me from saying it.

Let me tell you, that made me feel like trash.

"At least you're handling it well," he said. "Lots of people write me off as a lunatic."

"I see ghosts," I said. "So I know what that's like."

"Ghosts, huh?" He chuckled. "That's cool. Or maybe it's not. That's not normal, so. Maybe you should see a shrink."

"I do. Well, I used to. Not for the ghosts, though. For other stuff. I should probably make an appointment," I added, knowing I wouldn't.

Jace smiled. "I was just kidding."

"Oh."

Jace was quiet for a moment. Then he said, "What will you do if Cecil doesn't come out?"

"Nothing, I guess. It'll be up to Tamora at that point." I paused. "Well, hang on. How long are you staying?"

"I don't even remember getting here," he reminded me. "So I have no idea what the itinerary is." He dug a hand into a pocket and retrieved a phone. "This is Cecil's phone. We each have our own. I don't even know the passwords to some of them. But I know Cecil's." After flipping to the correct app, he said, "Looks like I'm leaving tomorrow evening."

I leaned back into my palms, the sand under my hands shifting with my weight. I grinned. "Well, in that case, we might be in luck. I think I know someone who can help."

seventeen

. . .

"I had begun to think I wouldn't hear from you again," Andromeda said. "And here you are, gracing me with the glory of your voice before I've even had my coffee."

I smiled into the phone, abashed. It was early in the morning—too early for a phone call. But after the previous night's shenanigans, it couldn't wait. "I didn't plan to call you," I admitted, "but we could use your help. Are you still in town?"

"I am," she confirmed.

"Great. Well, listen. If you're still in the mood to do a favor for Tamora, I've got an idea."

I told her my plan and was not at all surprised when Andromeda readily agreed. She'd grown up with Tamora, after all. She was a good friend and wanted to help.

"I don't know much about dissociative identity disorder," Andromeda said, "but this seems like a good plan to me. And Tamora agreed to this?"

I sighed, digging my free hand into my pocket. "I haven't talked to her yet, but Bailey is confident we can convince her."

"I hope you can," she said. "This will go better for all of us if she doesn't fight it. Good luck. You'll need it."

I disconnected and then called Bailey.

"Andromeda says she'll do it," I said. "Now we've just got to convince your sister."

"I'll convince her," she said. "Leave that to me. I'll meet you at Tamora's in thirty minutes. Have faith, Pride! We've got this!"

I disconnected without saying goodbye. Faith was something I lacked in spades.

When Bailey and I arrived at Tamora's house half an hour later, I was nervous. I didn't know why. I stood behind as Bailey rang the doorbell.

The door creaked open, and an exasperated Tamora deflated when she saw us. "What are you doing here?"

"Good morning to you, too," Bailey said, a forced cheerfulness in her voice. "I'm here to update you on what's going on. Can we come in?"

Tamora shook her head. "No."

"Fine." Bailey sighed and popped her hands on her hips. "We want you to host another séance."

Now, Tamora's eyes narrowed. "Another séance? What for?"

Bailey hesitated. "Tammy, there's something you should know. He's here in Odyssey. Cecil. And Jeff's with him. With your help, we can bring Jeff out and maybe release him from Cecil's body."

Tamora glanced from her sister to me and back again. "He's here in Odyssey? Why didn't you tell me? Why am I just hearing about this *now?*"

"We had to make sure it was really him," Bailey explained. "We had to protect you. But now you need to know. If this goes right, it'll be your last chance to talk to Jeff. With any luck, after today, Jeff won't be trapped anymore."

Tamora glared at her sister long and hard before directing

her ire at me. "How do I know you're not just trying to get me back for setting you up?"

I shrugged. "Holding grudges is a waste of energy. But if you don't believe that, look at it this way: I want to be likable on TV. Doing something mean to a widow seems like a fast-track to becoming Public Enemy Number One."

She pursed her lips, considering. Then, she rolled her eyes and threw up her hands. "Whatever. Do what you need to do, Bailey."

"I'm doing this for you, Tammy."

"If you were really doing this for me, you'd let me marry Jeff and get out of my business."

"Fine," Bailey said. "Then I'm doing it for you *and* Jeff. You can't just let him stay locked up in someone else's body, Tammy. Even you have to see how messed up that is."

Tamora didn't reply to this. Instead, she opened the door wider and stepped aside, bidding us entry. She gestured upstairs toward the library. "Guess you better get to work," she said. "I have other things to do."

Tamora disappeared around a corner as Bailey and I climbed the steps. "The séance begins in an hour!" Bailey shouted.

She turned to me, eyes wide. "That went better than I hoped." She gestured toward the library. "We haven't got a lot of time. Let's get moving."

An hour later, we were standing in Tamora's library with the rest of the guests we'd assembled. There were more people here today than at the last séance: Bailey, Tamora, and Victoria were present, along with Andromeda at the head of the table and all the housemates except Sloth. For my plan to work, we needed to keep Jace in the dark. Sloth was the designated babysitter, entertaining Jace downstairs while the rest of us set up for the big show.

The room felt stuffy and claustrophobic as we found our places around the table. It was a warm day, and the heat from the candles only added to the discomfort. It was also weird having a séance in the middle of the morning. Although Bailey had drawn the curtains, scant sunlight filtered through the windows. Birds chirped outside. The smells of Tamora's breakfast, fried bacon and coffee, drifted in from downstairs. The smells of breakfast muddled with Tamora's overpowering perfume and the scent of burning candles made me queasy.

There was a knock at the door. "Come in," Bailey said.

The door opened, and Sloth poked in her head. "You ready for us?"

Bailey nodded. "Perfect timing. Come on in."

Sloth pushed the door open wide and guided in a blindfolded Jace. He was dressed in Cecil's clothes: a navy-blue tunic and matching pants. I guess Cecil hadn't packed anything normal. He had pulled his hair into a ponytail and removed the gold earrings and mala bracelets from yesterday. He shuffled into the room with baby steps as Sloth guided him with her hand at the small of his back.

I watched Tamora's face as Jace stumbled toward his seat across from her. She'd never seen the man before her now, the man she'd agreed to marry. Jace was a good-looking guy, but he was no Israeli model. Her eyes followed him through the room, her face carefully blank. I wondered what was going through her head. Was she angry? Did she mind his looks? Was she worried? Confused?

I searched her face and body language for clues but didn't find any. No big surprise there, though. My catalog of Tamora's expressions contained only three entries: "Undeserved hatred for

Pride," "Moderately deserved annoyance at Bailey," and "Smug knowledge that she's right about everything."

Once Jace slid into place, Sloth sat next to him, maneuvering herself to within arm's reach of her charge. Jace's face was down-turned, and though I couldn't see his eyes, the shadows cast by the candles made his face look somber. Envy, seated to my left, leaned toward me, her voice low and soft in my ear. "Are we sure this is a good idea?" she asked, her gaze flitting to Jace's face. "It seems, I don't know… cruel."

"He agreed to it," I assured her. "Remember, we blindfolded him so he'll be shocked when he sees where he is. Jace said Cecil comes out when he feels out of his element. I'm hoping this is as out of Jace's element as you can get."

From unseen speakers overhead, a soft but morbid melody drifted into the room. Then Andromeda's voice cut through the darkness. "I've invited you all here today to commune with the dead," she said, her voice heavy and singsong. "It is a most gracious gift the dead offer when they deign to return to the phys-ical realm and share their wisdom with us, and for this, we are grateful. Now, as we attune ourselves to the vibrations of the after-world, I invite you, Sloth, to remove the blinds that prevent our good man Jace Thornburgh from seeing what he is meant to see."

Gently, Sloth reached over to untie Jace's blindfold. When the cloth dropped away, Jace blinked into the darkness. He took in the candles and the dozens of various crystals adorning the table. His eyes swept over the collection of animal bones, Tarot cards, astrological dice, and assorted daggers. He lifted his eyes slowly to the end of the table where Andromeda sat with her arms on their rests, a coy smile twisted on her lips. Her hair was piled high in a fluffy cloud of pink, held in place with Lust's tiara and dotted with plastic spiders tucked inside her many curls. She wore a black lace dress with long bell sleeves and a deep V neckline. Her lips were painted black, and she wore a velvet choker with a vintage cameo at her throat.

To summarize, she looked ridiculous. She looked nothing like the ethereal goddess her brand made her out to be. She looked like some kind of dollar-store Halloween matriarch, and not in a good way. I'm not even sure there *is* a good way to achieve that look.

(For the record, I had nothing to do with her costume. Andromeda and Lust concocted this cockamamie monstrosity on their own. I argued it would be enough for her to wear her usual attire, but I was outvoted.)

I held my breath, eyes trained on Jace to see if our work here made him uncomfortable enough to nudge him right out of his body.

And what do you know? It worked.

In an instant, Jace's body language changed. Confidence shimmied up his spine, and he sat up straight, his shoulders squaring. Even so, he looked relaxed. A smile broke over his face, and his eyes twinkled in the dim light. He looked around the table and tapped his fingertips together, nodding in silent greeting as he met each person's gaze. "It's good to see you all again," he said finally. "I trust I'm not interrupting anything?"

Tentatively, I asked, "Cecil?"

"In the flesh," he said, flashing us a wide smile. "Well, not exactly *my* flesh, but I assume you take my meaning."

With Cecil's arrival, the mood of the room changed. It no longer felt like we were leading a prisoner to his execution. Now, it felt like a gathering of friends performing crucial spiritual work. Which, if you believe in that sort of thing, was exactly what we were doing.

(I mean, I'm using the words *friends* loosely here, but cut me some slack.)

"I invite you all to link hands," Andromeda instructed. I took

Envy's hand in my left, Lust's hand in my right. At the touch of Lust's skin, a thrill ran down my spine. Seriously, one of these days, I just needed to ask her out on a proper date. The tension between us was getting ridiculous.

Focus, I reminded myself. Maybe sitting beside Lust hadn't been such a good idea.

"Do you know why we brought you here today, Cecil?" Andromeda asked.

Cecil nodded. "I have my suspicions. I assume you want to manifest Jeff."

Andromeda nodded. "Yes. The end goal today is to draw him out of your body and into my own. And hopefully, by releasing him from your flesh, we will untangle him from the multiples that already thrive within you. And then, when we are done, I will release him to his home on the other side."

Tamora's voice, sharp and icy, cut through the room. "And what if that's not what *I* want?"

All eyes shifted to Tamora. She was clutching Wrath's hand on her left and Bailey's hand on her right as she stared daggers at Andromeda. "Remember what I said? I *specifically* said I didn't want anyone else to channel him. You all promised. You *promised!*"

Andromeda huffed, lifting her chin in small defiance. "We *did* make that promise, Tamora. That was before we understood the extent of this situation. It's not just Jeff trapped within Cecil's vehicle. It's Jace and Cecil and the other alters burdened with a personality that isn't part of their system. We owe it to them to release Jeff. And we owe it to you."

I watched as Tamora's eyes grew soft, damp with tears. "It's not what I want," she whimpered. "Even if most of the time he's not present in that body, I still want to be with him for the few moments I can. Is that so terrible?"

Andromeda was silent for a long stretch. Then she said,

"Why don't we ask Jeff what *he* wants, Tamora? Wouldn't that be the right thing to do?"

Our host opened her mouth to speak, and for a moment, I thought she would refuse. But then, reluctantly, Tamora dropped her chin in a tacit nod. "All right," she whispered.

Andromeda cleared her throat and sat up a little straighter. "I invite you all to still your minds and open your hearts to welcome in the dead. As for you, Cecil, I ask that you release hold of your body and allow the universe to work through you in all its miraculous and wondrous ways. You are not merely a son of Adam. You are part and particle of the larger universe. Everything flows through you. You are stardust. You are ephemeral. And so I ask you to vanish and make room for the man we know as Jeff Bishop."

The room was silent and still. I felt Lust's breathing, the warmth rising in her hands. I waited with bated breath for the shenanigans to start. But unlike the first séance, there was no shaking of tables. No books fell from their shelves. Nothing levitated, no one screamed, and windows did not shatter. The only sign that something supernatural was happening was the slight drop in temperature.

I stared at the other end of the table, watching Cecil intently. He closed his eyes and breathed in deeply through his nose. After a while, he opened his eyes. He looked directly at Tamora and began to cry.

"Oh," he whispered, astonishment washing over him as he scrubbed his face with both hands. "Oh, Tam-Tam. It's really you." His voice was hoarse and heavy with the thickness in his throat. "I can't believe it. After all this time. I never thought I'd see that beautiful face again."

Tamora's face crumpled, and she, too, burst into tears. She chewed her lips and nodded as she sobbed, releasing Wrath's and Bailey's hands to press her fingers to her mouth. "It's me, baby.

I'm here. I've never stopped waiting for you. I knew I would see you again, I just knew it. I didn't know it would be like this," she said with a tearful chuckle. "But it's so good to hear your voice."

No matter how many times I'd seen it, hearing a voice that did not belong to the person using it was wild. I'd heard Jace Thornburgh use three different voices now. It was unsettling, but I couldn't deny the basic truth: the voice coming from him was not his own. Judging from Tamora's reaction, the speaker really was her husband, Jeff Bishop.

I'm telling you. Wonders never cease.

"There's so much I want to say to you," Jeff began. "I hardly know where to start." Then he looked around the table, noticing for the first time that he and his wife were not alone. "Bailey? Vic? Heh." He smiled, meeting each woman's gaze with a chuckle. But then the smile slid from his face, and he asked, "Who are these other people?"

"Just friends," Tamora breathed, shaking off the question. "Just people here to help the two of us find each other."

Jeff balked. Everyone I'd spoken to mentioned how private Jeff was, and apparently, they were right. When he realized he had an audience, he clammed up. He shrank back into his chair, chin trembling. "I don't know about this, Tam-Tam. It doesn't feel right to talk to you with these strangers here. Can't we go anywhere private? Can't we—"

"The spell will break," Andromeda said, her voice tender but decisive. "I'm afraid none of us can leave the table, or we may lose you again."

He looked around, taking in the faces of the attendants. His gaze fell first to Bailey. "Hey, sis," he said, a crooked smile forming over his mouth. "How's tricks?"

Bailey grinned, a single tear falling down her cheek. "Hey, Jeff. It's good to talk to you again. Are you…are you well?"

I knew from experience how weird it was to talk to dead

people. It's surprisingly awkward. You can't make small talk about the local sports team or what everyone's bingeing on Netflix. The weather is usually a safe topic unless the ghost is trapped indoors. But the point is, we're used to talking with people who are, you know, *living,* so we ask about *life.* Asking a dead guy how he's doing just seems like kicking a fellow when he's down.

"I'm hanging in there, all things considered," he said. He turned his gaze to Victoria, who looked like she'd swallowed a bug. "It's great to see you, Vic. I mean, really great. I have so much to say to you, too. But given our circumstances, I'll just say…I hope I made it up to you."

Victoria didn't move, but her mouth dropped open, and a tiny phrase emerged from her lips. "Thank you," was all she said.

A quick glance around the table told me that no one but Wrath and I understood the significance of the exchange. Even in death, Jeff still carried the guilt about his childhood with Victoria. Did he feel bad about the torture she endured at the hands of the poltergeists? Or was he sorry that his family dumped her when he went off to college, leaving her once again with nothing? It was impossible to say, and we might never know. But judging by the look on Victoria's face, none of that mattered.

She looked at peace.

At the other end of the table, Andromeda cleared her throat. "Jeff, I'm afraid our time might be running out. If there's something you'd like to say to Tamora, now is your chance."

Jeff shifted, rubbing his hands together as he peered at his wife. Her face was shining with tears, her chin wobbling. "I know we talked about getting married," Jeff said. "At the time, I thought it was a good idea. But that's because I accepted I might never cross back over. If I'm going to be stuck here, I'd rather be stuck here with you. But truly, Tam-Tam, I'd rather not be stuck here. Being an intruder in another man's body…it's awful. Most of the time, I have no control. It's like being asleep, but it's not restful. I only wake up when Cecil is in charge of the body. And even then, I can only wake up when Cecil's guard is down, which isn't often. Every time I wake up, I try to escape and return to the other side. But it's like the other personalities I'm with hold me back. It feels like I'm tied down. Restrained. I'm a captive. That's the only way to say it."

Jeff was quiet a minute, his nostrils flaring, lips trembling. "Remember our first trip to Puerta Vallarta? You lost your purse and the key to our Airbnb. You waited for me on the porch, but I'd left a note on the bed saying I had a surprise for you. I was waiting for you at that Mediterranean restaurant. You never showed up because you never got the note. Remember?"

Tamora sniffled at the memory. "Yes, of course I remember. I waited for you for hours. I had no way to contact you because I'd lost my phone. After that, I memorized your phone number." She smiled softly, her eyes shining in the candlelight.

"That's right. That's how I feel now, Tam-Tam, except worse. Like I'm anxiously waiting for you. Seeing you lights me up inside, but the waiting—the times I'm asleep or trying to claw my way to the front—it's the worst. It hurts."

Tamora lowered her head, her voice tremulous. "Please, Jeff. Don't do this. If you leave Cecil's body, you'll really be dead. Again."

"Being dead's not so bad, really. It's a lot less stressful." He cracked a smile at his joke, but it slid quickly from his face. "If I have the choice, I don't want to spend the next however-many years trapped in someone else's body. Can you understand that?"

Tamora was openly crying again, her shoulders quaking with each sob. I saw Bailey squeeze her sister's fingers, offering what small comfort she could. When Tamora gathered herself enough to speak, she said, "I don't know if I can go on without you, Jeff. I already lost you once. It's not fair to ask me to lose you again."

Jeff sighed, nodding thoughtfully as he mulled over Tamora's words. "We're going to lose each other again, one way or another," Jeff said. "Either I will watch you die while trapped in someone else's body, or you lose me today or some unknown time in the future. And think about it this way, my love. What if I'm not even in control of this body when one of us passes? What happens then? At least doing it this way means we can say goodbye."

Tamora was really crying now. My heart ached for her. Death was supposed to be the period at the end of the sentence. It was supposed to close old doors while opening new ones. But this coming back and forth? Not only was it unnatural, it was unhealthy. Humans need closure. It's how we know it's time to breathe again.

"I just love you so much," Tamora was saying. "And I just can't imagine the rest of my life without you."

"I want you to find happiness," Jeff said. "I want you to find love again. Enjoy your sister's company. Enjoy the friendships you formed on your own." He said this last bit while gesturing around the table. "You have so much life left, and so much light to give, Tam-Tam. I won't take that from you. I want you to move on."

Tamora devolved into tears again and couldn't respond. While Tamora sobbed silently, Jeff nodded to Andromeda and settled back into his chair. "I'm ready," he said.

The medium lifted her hands to the ceiling. "I call upon the harmonies of the universe, the vibrations that move through all things. I call to the Great Beyond, to the Eternal Hereafter, to the Far Shore. Open your gates to our friend Jeff Bishop. Shine a beacon that can call him home. Show us the way, O Darkness! Show us the way, O Light! If you, Jeff Bishop, wish to be free of your current prison, come unite with me. I invite you into my body. I make room for you in my body. I will celebrate and release you in this body."

A rush of wind whistled through the room, and the candles stuttered out. The table shook, the legs screeching across the floor just as they had during the first séance. The tarot cards rose from the table, spinning and flipping this way and that as they floated in the air. Next, the collection of daggers clattered to the floor as the table shook more violently. With a lurch, the table jolted into the air, levitating ever higher. An earth-rumbling sound like an oncoming train thundered through the room. And then, seemingly from everywhere at once, came Jeff Bishop's voice. "I accept your invitation, Andromeda. Bring me into your body so you can release me."

Jeff's voice was so loud, it rattled my bones. I felt like he was inside my head, hollering his brains out. Everyone else must have been experiencing something similar because they were all looking around the room with hands pressed to their ears.

Jace/Cecil/Jeff was slack in his seat. He'd fallen sideways, eyes closed, chin dipped against his chest. At the other end of the table, Andromeda's hair had come loose and was floating about her shoulders. Her mouth dropped open and her head fell back, and in the darkness, I heard a voice booming from her body, "I'll never stop loving you, Tam-Tam."

And then it was over.

The table crashed to the floor. Candles fell and rolled, toppling to the ground. Someone screamed. Someone else was crying. At my side, Lust was hugging herself and whimpering. As for me, I'd seen all this before. Amazing how, if you've seen one séance, you've seen them all. I didn't care about the room's wishy-washy relationship with gravity.

I only cared whether Jeff was gone.

As the room stilled, Andromeda slowly woke up. She blinked and shook herself, dusting stray plastic spiders from her shoulders as she looked down the table. "Cecil?"

I turned my head to find our guest of honor struggling into

wakefulness himself. He dug his knuckles into his eye sockets and rubbed. When he opened his eyes again, he said, "Is everyone okay?"

"We're fine," Andromeda breathed with a smile. "You're back. How do you feel?"

Cecil was quiet for a moment. Then he looked up and nodded. "Like myself. Like a burden has been released." He smiled, but there was a note of sadness in it. I think that was for Tamora's benefit. He looked right at her when he said, "I think Jeff is in a good place. I feel joy where I used to feel his sorrow."

Andromeda leaned forward. "So, he's gone?"

Cecil smiled. "He's gone. You did it. He's…free."

For a minute, no one moved. But then Tamora drew slowly to her feet. She walked over to where Cecil sat, her face as expressionless as a mannequin's. And then, surprising everyone, she leaned down and enveloped him in a hug. "Thank you for keeping him safe as long as you did," she said. "And thank you for coming here and letting me say goodbye."

Cecil stood and hugged her back, and the two stayed that way for a long time.

eighteen

. . .

There's nothing quite like being at Sinful House after you've completed one task but haven't yet started another. I got to spend my days however I wanted. Cameras didn't follow me around as I walked along the beach, digging my toes in the sand and enjoying the ocean spray in my hair. Nobody peppered me with ridiculous questions when I walked down to the bakery and ordered a box full of scones and croissants. And importantly, I could waste time doing nothing without feeling guilty. No nagging worries over the poor schmuck whose crime I was supposed to be solving. The days after completing a task were truly awesome. When you weren't mired in local politics or weird paranormal activity, Odyssey was actually a nice place to be.

So I was thinking about how I wanted to spend the day when I found Lust sitting outside on the porch doing a puzzle on the ground. She looked up when she saw me, a grin breaking out over her face. Man, she looked so good when she smiled. Not that she didn't look good when she wasn't smiling. And believe me, I'm not the jerk that tells people they should smile more. But when she looks at me like that? It just makes me feel like I'm the only person on earth. And who doesn't love to feel that way?

But even though I felt that way, I wasn't gonna own up to it. I donned my best air of casual disinterest and asked, "What's this supposed to be?" I toed the edge of the puzzle with my shoe.

Lust leaned back into her hands. "Baby raccoons," she said. "I picked it up at Target yesterday. We solved our case, too, you know."

I nodded. "Yeah, I heard. Congratulations. You, Greed, and Envy tracked down some old guy's stolen antique guns, right?"

Lust nodded. "Yes. Well, mostly it was Greed. He figured it out after helping with your case. He realized old Mr. Sampson had something called 'intermittent dementia' and hid the guns from himself. Or something. Anyway, we found the guns in a safe deposit box at the bank." She sighed and blew a stray lock of hair from her eyes. "It sure wasn't as exciting as your case. But I'm glad we're both through with the grueling stuff. It's nice to just poke around and work on jigsaw puzzles. Or do..." She smiled at me. "...Whatever."

You know how sometimes an opportunity presents itself, and you feel like you have to grab it with both hands, or else you'll end up the world's biggest loser? But at the same time, your monkey brain is telling you that risk = possible failure. And if you fail:

1. You'll end up miserable and alone
2. No one will ever love you
3. Rambunctious neighborhood kids will throw rotten eggs at your house every morning,
4. And you'll never smile again.

You know that feeling?

That's how I felt at that moment.

Ask her out, my brain screamed at me. And I knew I should. I knew she liked me. She'd told me so a million times. Well, maybe not a million, but at least five, anyway. And if she said no, the *worst* that would happen is I'd feel embarrassed for a while, and then I'd get over it. I didn't even own a house, so I didn't need to worry about rambunctious neighborhood kids.

But…I didn't want to be embarrassed. We lived together. I'd have to see her every day. And what if she told someone I'd asked her out, and they giggled about it like it was the funniest thing in the world? Because yeah, she was out of my league. Totally. But still…?

I must've stood there debating what to say for too long because Lust laughed and cut her eyes at me, her head cocked to the side. "Cat got your tongue, Freak Show? Come on, Pride. I know you. What's eating you?"

I quirked an eyebrow. "Eating me? Oh." I dug my hands in my pockets. "That's a metaphor."

She nodded. "Yes. What's *bothering* you?"

I sucked in a breath and closed my eyes. *Here goes nothing*, I thought. "The other day at the citywide garage sale, I wasn't the shopping partner you deserved. I want to make up for that."

Lust sucked her teeth. "You bought me a tiara. Consider that score settled."

"No, that's not what I mean." I opened my eyes and stared down at my feet. Why was I such a moron with words? I didn't want to be her shopping buddy! This wasn't about making things up to her! Why was it so hard to say what I really meant?

"It's just that I was wondering, if you're not busy, did you want to… I don't know. Spend the day with me?"

A sly smile spread over Lust's face. "My goodness, Pride. Are you asking me on a date?"

My face flushed so hot, I thought I might spontaneously combust. "Yes," I said.

Lust sat forward and brushed her hands together. "I accept," she said, climbing to her feet. She linked her arm in mine and led me back into the house. "What did you have in mind?"

I didn't have anything in mind. Literally nothing. As soon as Lust accepted my invitation, all other thoughts evaporated from my brain. I was a walking ball of goo with an IQ of -500 and the only thing running through my brain was *she said yes she said yes* repeatedly.

But finally, thankfully, I pulled myself together enough to ask, "What sounds good to you?"

"There's an art gallery I'd like to check out," she said. "You don't really strike me as an artsy person, but—"

"I love art," I blurted. That was a lie. I didn't know a thing about art except that a child could do it, and some art looked like a child *did* do it. But if it made me look better in Lust's eyes, I could love anything. Almost anything. I would never love shopping. "I'm a huge art fan. Did you want to go now?"

Lust chuckled. "Can I have, say, 20 minutes? I need to put my face on." She paused, then added, "I mean, I have to put on some makeup."

"Got it," I said. "I'll meet you back here in 20."

While Lust piled her face with products she didn't need, I scuttled back to my room to change into something more date-worthy. I shuffled through my closet, immediately rejecting every piece of clothing I owned. Grateful Dead t-shirt? Too casual. Pressed white button-down? Too formal. Cozy cashmere sweater? Way too warm. I rejected my favorite plaid pullover, my vintage Care Bear t-shirts, and my trusty knit jacket. Nothing was good enough, but so help me, I was *not* going to ask Envy for help, not after the last time she'd dressed me like a color-blind clown.

I was looking under my bed, hoping that's where the miraculous perfect outfit might be hiding, when a voice behind me said,

"She's not gonna care what you wear, you know. Since when do you care about appearances?"

"Since always," I answered. "Everyone cares about appearances. Anyone who says otherwise is selling something."

"That's not true," the ghost girl retorted. "And anyway, haven't you been through everything you own? Why isn't what you've got on okay?"

"It's gonna have to be," I grumbled, resigned to the reality that a trip to a shopping mall was in my future. I needed to invest in something better than a t-shirt but not as lame as a button-down.

"Where are you guys going? The museum? Ice skating? The dog park?"

"Neither one of us has a dog," I pointed out. "Why would we go to the dog park?"

The ghost ignored this. "Did you know dogs can have a sense of smell that's like one hundred times better than ours?"

"That sounds high to me," I grumbled. I was rifling through my sock drawer, looking for the twin to the Yoda trouser sock I held in one hand. "Maybe it's only like 10 times as good."

I could see the sock now. It was wedged in the back of the drawer. I wriggled the drawer in its tracks, trying to get the sock loose, but it was really jammed in there.

"No, it's like one hundred. Maybe even *two* hundred," the ghost girl insisted.

I didn't feel like arguing with her. It's fine if ghosts get their facts wrong. It's not like they're going to spread misinformation on social media and stir up trouble. And even if she did, what harm could it do to let people think dogs had supernatural powers of smell?

I tried to yank the drawer free, but it wasn't coming out. I jiggled and tugged, cursing the manufacturer. "You gotta be kidding me," I whined. Then I yanked the stupid drawer as hard as I could.

The drawer finally jerked free, but the force of my pulling shook the dresser so hard that the things I'd tossed up there fell and slid off. The lamp fell onto its side and rolled to the floor. But before it fell, it crashed into Walt's laptop. Both lamp and laptop smashed to the floor.

"Oh no," I moaned, dropping the drawer.

"I thought you were taking that to the police," the ghost said.

"I was supposed to," I agreed. "I just didn't make the time."

The laptop screen was cracked, and the plastic casing that attached the screen to the lid had come loose. I bent down to pick up the now-busted machine and noticed something strange.

I crouched over the laptop. The corner of a piece of paper was sticking out from behind the screen. Gingerly, I pulled the paper free and spread it across my knees.

"What the…? Is this what I think it is?"

The ghost girl was hovering over my shoulder, peering down at the recovered paper. "Looks like some kind of map," she whispered.

Intersecting horizontal and vertical lines were obviously streets, but none were marked. Squares with triangles on top were buildings—maybe houses or perhaps businesses, but again, none were labeled. Some squares were bigger than others, but I couldn't tell if that was because the map had been sketched quickly or if the difference in scale was intentional. There was no key. A collection of half ovals looked like they might be graves, but I couldn't be sure. The ovals were marked with a star, and scribbled across the bottom were the words, "Historic Odyssey Nexus of Power, 1902."

I sucked in a breath as realization struck me. *This* was the hidden information the laptop concealed. It wasn't a digital file at all, which was why Wrath couldn't find it. It was this piece of paper—this shoddily drawn, indecipherable, sorry excuse for a map.

"Somebody went to a lot of trouble to hide that," the ghost said, still whispering. "You should probably keep that safe. Put it somewhere good."

I left the broken laptop where it was and scanned my room. "Yeah, you're right. Whoever killed Mrs. Romanowsky likely killed her for this map," I said, more to myself than the ghost. "But I don't know where to put it. I wonder if I—"

My door opened, and Lust poked her head inside. As a house, we really needed to get better at respecting other people's privacy. "You ready?"

"Just one second," I said, hiding the paper behind my back. "Meet you downstairs in two?"

Lust pulled the door closed, and I carefully lodged the map between my mattress and box spring. It was a terrible hiding place and probably the first place a killer would look. But I'd have to find a more suitable place later when I wasn't in such a rush.

"Do me a favor," I said to the ghost. "Don't let anyone in my room until I come home."

The ghost rolled her eyes, her hands splayed out before her. "And how am I supposed to do that? I can't even touch anybody!"

I tossed her a wink and pulled my Yoda socks onto my feet. "You'll think of something," I said.

Then I rushed down the stairs, heart skipping into my throat as I headed to my first date with Lust.

———

The Odyssey Museum of Modern Art was a beautiful glass building by the sea. As Lust and I entered, her arm linked in mine and my hands dug into my pockets, I marveled that such a building could exist shoulder to shoulder with the strange things I'd seen in this town. How could something as mundane as a modern art museum exist in a city where ghosts had their own secret society and old ladies got murdered by supernatural bounty hunters?

Still, as we walked into the building, feeling the crisp, conditioned air riffle our hair, tension dripped from my shoulders. Even the cameramen tagging along weren't stressing me out for once. (I'd tried to escape without them, but they were insistent. "It's a great human-interest angle!" my camera guy asserted, jamming a peanut butter sandwich into his mouth. "Network would kill me if I let you lovebirds on a date alone.") I was content to be in an ordinary place doing everyday things.

Not that being on a date with a beautiful woman was normal for me. In fact, my hands were in my pockets to stop myself from pinching my arms to make sure I wasn't dreaming.

Ahead, a group of schoolchildren on a field trip ran from exhibit to exhibit, loudly and excitedly admiring the paintings and sculptures on display. Lust pressed her body against mine, smiling in excitement. "Where should we start?" She was craning her neck, her head swiveling from side to side as she scanned our options. "Do you want to browse on your own, or should we ask someone for a guided tour?"

Both options sounded terrifying. Being alone with Lust was what I wanted in theory, but then the burden of entertaining her would fall to me alone. On the other hand, a guided tour might be helpful, except I didn't want some rando tagging along.

However, the decision was wrenched from my hands when a young docent approached us, smiling with an enthusiasm usually reserved for toddlers and Golden Retrievers. He was college-age with rosy cheeks and a tan that indicated he might be a local. He was dressed in a crisp navy-blue blazer and tan chinos. "Welcome to OMMA," he said. "Have the two of you been here before?"

Lust shook her head. "First time!" she exclaimed. "Do you have any pointers?"

The docent clapped his hands together and faced Lust squarely, ignoring me. "Of course! We have several tracks to help our patrons enjoy all we offer. The exhibit starts on the bottom floor and winds its way up to the second, third, and fourth floors. If you want to see everything in the museum, expect to spend five hours on the premises. There's a lovely cafeteria on the second floor if you need to take a break. However, if your time is limited, we have story tracks that guide you on a more curated tour. You can choose from our tracks dedicated to local artists, female artists, artists with disabilities, or artists of color. Or, if a thematic tour is preferred, we have tours for mind-bending experiences, Americana, slice of life, and abstract appreciation. Or, if none of these options appeals to you, I can take you on a personalized tour highlighting some of my favorite pieces."

Lust turned to me, her face expectant. "It all sounds fantastic," she gushed. "What would you like to do?"

What I wanted to do was not make this decision. But it looked like I had to choose something, so I said, "A guided tour sounds great."

The young man took a step forward and pressed his palm against his chest. "Well, in that case, my name is Greg, and I will gladly be your docent for the day. And you are?"

"Pride," I said.

"And I'm Lust."

He was definitely a local (or maybe he'd just seen the show) because he wasn't at all surprised by our introductions. He extended a hand, which we both shook. "Well, it's a pleasure to have you at the museum. If neither of you has questions, why don't we get started?"

As it turned out, exploring the museum wasn't as arduous an experience as I feared. I usually associated modern art with splatter paintings or giant squares of a single color—neither of which I understood. But these paintings had soul. There were paintings of women screaming as they watched their children play at recess. A huge portrait showed a man crying in his corner office. Other images depicted animals, ocean landscapes, and, of course, they had obligatory abstract art. Interspersed with the paintings were sculptures. I liked the fiber art best. Some enterprising artist named Annabella Schwartz created a life-size pride of lions out of felt and yarn. It was an impressive display.

"I wanted to be an artist when I was young," Lust told the docent as we meandered up the stairs. "My parents couldn't be bothered with it, though. Sometimes I wonder about the artists who get to show at galleries. Did their parents support them from the beginning, or did they learn to fly on their own?"

"It's an interesting question," the docent said with a nod. "Everyone's story is different. We have a painting by a man named Pedro Fernandez who didn't start painting until he was 75."

The docent led us to the far corner of the second floor. "Over here is a personal favorite. This simple painting of a fisher catching a bass truly captures the zeitgeist and the profound loneliness and disappointment that most of us experience in our everyday lives."

I examined the painting. An angler adrift in an empty lake was reeling a large bass from the water. The line had snapped, and the bass was falling to the lake as the fisherman watched in bewilderment. Whether it captured the zeitgeist of loneliness or whatever was up for debate, but it was a nice painting.

Lust read the title of the piece from a placard on the wall. "*A Quiet Fisherman Drops the Bass*," she said.

The docent's eyebrows shot up. "*A Quiet Fisherman Drops the*

Bass," he said, correcting her pronunciation. She'd read "bass" like in music, rhyming with "base." He read it with a short a, rhyming with "pass."

Lust chuckled. "Well, it's sort of a double entendre, isn't it?" she asked.

The docent frowned, puzzled. "How do you mean?"

Lust shrugged and gestured at the title with a flick of her wrist. "Well, because of the word *bass*. It's obviously a picture of a fisherman, so you might read it as bass like the fish. But it's also a dubstep thing. When the bassline thumps hard, you know? They dropped the bass. So you could call this painting *A Quiet Fisherman Drops the Bass"* (She said it with short a, like the fish), "or you could read it *A Quiet Fisherman Drops the Bass"* (This time, she used a long a, like the instrument). "They're spelled the same way on paper but pronounced differently aloud."

The docent peered at her as though she had a second head growing out of her neck. "I assure you, the painting is titled *A Quiet Fisherman Drops the Bass*," he said, pronouncing bass like the fish.

She held up her hands defensively. "I'm not arguing. That could be how it's pronounced. But it could go the other way, too. I'm just saying it's a pretty clever joke."

"But it's not music," the docent insisted, his face pinched. His eyes flit briefly to me and then back to Lust. "It's a *painting*. It's *art*. It's not a record album."

Both Lust and Greg-the-docent had a point, and I wasn't sure who won the argument. But just as I was preparing to interrupt (their argument was going nowhere and I was getting annoyed), I noticed the complete title of the piece on the wall. The placard said, "*A Quiet Fisherman Drops the Bass* on canvas."

The words "on canvas" caught my attention, and I paused, my hand going to my mouth as my mind reeled.

Instantly, I was transported back to the séance where

Andromeda spoke in that strange voice and said to me, "Some of all profits on vinyl."

Andromeda thought it was the name of an album. But now, I wondered. Maybe it wasn't the name of an album at all. What if "on vinyl" just meant vinyl was the surface medium?

What if the voice coming from Andromeda's body was referring not to an album but a piece of art?

"Greg," I said suddenly, "are you familiar with the story of the Sam Lovelace commune that disappeared all those years ago?"

"Oh, yes!" Now that he was back on solid ground, the docent's thousand-watt smile returned. "I wrote my master's thesis on the commune's aims. Art that heals," he intoned, making a rainbow gesture with his hands. "Really a noble idea. Too bad they all vanished. Why do you ask?"

"Have you heard of an art piece that might have come from there called *Some of All Profits?*"

The docent twisted his mouth in thought. "I'm not sure," he said. "It sounds familiar, but..." He dug a phone from his pocket and clicked around. Then he snapped his fingers in the air with a nod. "Aha! Yes, here it is. It's owned by a private collector in Santa Barbara. Is this the piece you mean?"

He showed me the phone. A dozen records were glued together as a canvas onto which the artist had painted a troubling scene. A group of people with no faces were being attacked by a mob of unruly spirits while a robed wise man in the corner counted out his money without helping the others.

The piece was titled, *Sum of All Prophets* on vinyl.

I stared, my mouth agape. Another play on words, just like *Drop the Bass*. Not *Some of All Profits*, but *Sum of All Prophets*. That's why I never found a reference to it the night I'd googled the phrase with the ghost girl. I'd been using the wrong words.

"Lust," I whispered, "that's it. *That's* the clue I'm meant to find."

"Clue?" The docent tucked the phone back into his pocket. "Can I be a complete buttinsky and ask—a clue about what?"

"About my past," I said, my head still spinning. "I was the baby rescued from the compound. And I think that artwork was created by…"

Lust blinked, her eyes wide. "By *who*, Pride?"

I swallowed hard, remembering the eerily familiar voice that drifted from Andromeda's body that night. I knew now why some primitive part of me had recognized it. Some things are so sacred, they become imprinted on your brain. Or your soul. Or something.

I swallowed in a dry throat. "I think that artwork was created by my mother."

I glanced back at the camera crew. Man, the network was gonna have a field day with this.

nineteen

. . .

A few nights later, it was time for the mortifying task of watching ourselves on TV while we awaited the arrival of producer Tricia. Gluttony had set out trays full of hors d'oeuvres, and Lust was passing around a bottle of champagne. We were all watching the last episode of our first task. I have to say, it's weird to watch your life unfold weeks after you've already lived it. I mean, I get it. The network had to delay our episodes—it would be impossible to air the show in real time. Still, we were about to start our third task, and America had just seen the conclusion of our first.

I was sitting next to Sloth, both of us stuffing our faces with popcorn, when Tricia breezed through the front door. "Hi everyone! How's it going? Did everyone watch tonight's episode?"

I looked over my shoulder and waved. "Hi, Tricia," I said. "Yes, we watched. It was awful."

Tricia looked around the room. "Any problems with *editing* this time?" She directed this question at Wrath.

The surly technopath was still watching the TV, a scowl on

his face and arms crossed over his chest. "I still think they didn't give me a fair shot, man," he grumbled. "But at least I looked good in most of the episodes. Americans are shallow. They like anything that looks good. Which is a problem because unrealistic beauty standards established by Big Media reward—"

"Thanks, Wrath, I'll take your feedback to the rest of the team," Tricia interrupted. "I have the updates on your scores, everyone! Before I read these, please keep in mind that this is just the beginning of the season. You still have plenty of time to win over the viewers. So, if you didn't perform well this week, just remember, it's still early."

Tricia whipped out her phone and began reading. "In seventh place with 8% of the vote is Sloth. Greed, you came in sixth place with 10% of the vote. Gluttony, you're in fifth place with 11%. Envy, you got 12% and are in fourth place this week. In third place is Pride, with 14% of the vote. Lust, you're in second with a whopping 20%. And this week's winner, with a very improbable 25% of the vote, is—inexplicably—Wrath."

Cheers and jeers went up from my housemates. Everyone was laughing and pointing at Wrath, whose eyes were wide and round, his mouth open. Even he couldn't believe that he'd actually won this week.

"Well, bad editing aside, looks like you're doing pretty well for yourself, Wrath," Tricia joked, eyebrow cocked. "Got anything to say? Any vitriol to spew about your fellow Americans?"

Wrath shook his head and jammed his hands into the kangaroo pocket of his hoodie. "Well, you know what they say. People often make up in wrath what they lack in reason," he said with a sly grin.

"That's…not a positive for you," Envy pointed out.

"Maybe not, but I got the votes, and you can take that to the bank."

"But banks are the foundation of capitalism, Wrath! I thought you—"

"All right," Tricia interrupted again, smiling. "Are you all ready for your next assignments?" She didn't wait for an answer. With her face tipped toward her phone, she began reading. "For this week's task, the teams will be as follows. Wrath, since you are this week's winner, you'll be paired with Sloth. Pride, you will work with Envy. The last group will comprise Lust, Gluttony, and Greed."

"Together again," Greed said, making eyes at Lust. "Maybe this time, we'll bring home the win."

"I sure hope so," she purred, sidling up beside him and linking her arm in his. "I'm tired of playing second fiddle to these jokers."

I pretended not to watch them, but seeing Lust snuggling up next to Greed made me faint with nausea. What was she doing? And why right here in front of everyone? Okay, true, we weren't a couple or anything. But I thought we had something going.

But now, watching her make goo-goo eyes at Greed, I wasn't so sure.

Envy drew up beside me, nodding her head toward Lust and Greed. "I bet that makes you want to jam your thumb in your eye, huh?" she said, her mouth twisted in a frown. "I'm jealous on your behalf just watching them. I mean, seriously, get a room, you know? Have some shame, for goodness' sake."

I swallowed and turned my back to the confusing scene, trying to keep my expression light. "Don't worry about me," I said. "Lust can do what she likes. I don't own her, you know?"

"No, of course not. But it just doesn't seem fair. You bought her that tiara, you took her to the art gallery, you—"

"Envy, stop. It's fine." It wasn't. "I'm okay." I wasn't. "She's… I mean, that's who she is, right? She's Lust. A tiger can't change its stripes."

Envy scowled. "I guess. But—"

"No, I should have known better," I said, my throat dry. "You fall for a girl like that, and you're bound to get your heart stomped on. Listen, I'll be right back. I need to talk to Tricia before she leaves."

Tricia was already gathering her things and headed to the front door. I put a hand on her shoulder, and she turned. "Pride," she said. "What is it? Everything okay?"

Everything is not *okay*, I thought desperately. *I thought I met someone, I thought maybe someone was falling for me, and now I realize I'm just a name in her little black book. Why, WHY am I such a moron?!*

But instead of saying any of that, I swallowed down my panic. "I want to talk to you about my upcoming assignment with Envy."

Tricia's eyebrows shot up. "Oh? Did you have a question about it? I thought it was straightforward."

I shook my head. "No, we haven't even read it yet. Uh, I was wondering. I've been doing what the network wanted me to do. Looking into the Sam Lovelace thing."

Tricia nodded. "I've seen some of the footage from the séance," she said. "It's good stuff."

"Yeah, well, I have a request. Some new information came to light recently. It looks like I might have to take a trip up to Santa Barbara."

Tricia smiled. "Santa Barbara is gorgeous this time of year. Every time of year, really. Are you going up to the site? The place where the commune was before it vanished?"

"No," I said, though that was actually not a bad idea. "There's something I need to see. A piece of art. When Andromeda channeled that spirit that first night at Tamora's, it spoke to me, remember? It said, *"Find Sum of All Prophets*. Well, turns out that's an art piece owned by a private collector up in Santa Barbara. I've arranged to meet with him already."

Tricia stepped closer to me, her eyes twinkling. I could almost hear the *cha-ching!* of a cash register dinging in her mind. "That's *excellent* news, Pride! The network will be so happy to hear that!"

"Yeah, well, there's a snag, though. Santa Barbara's a good five hours from here. That's not a quick back-and-forth trip."

"It could be," Tricia said with a shrug. "I've done worse."

"Okay, but the point is, I'll need time while I'm up there. You know, to do some proper investigative work. Which means I might not have a lot of time left to work on whatever the network assigned me. So I'm just wondering…Maybe Envy and I can work on the missing commune case and skip whatever cocka-mamie mystery you put us on for this task?"

Tricia chuckled with a rueful shake of her head. "You know that isn't how this works," she said. "Everybody has to do their fair share. But don't worry so much. I think you'll like the task you and Envy got. Still, I encourage you to go to Santa Barbara. Take all the time you need. You might not win your challenge, that's true. But the viewer votes you'll get for following a lead in the missing commune case? It'll be well worth it. Our audience will eat that *up.*"

"That's not all," I continued. I checked over my shoulder to make sure no one was listening and that the cameras weren't trained on me. "I found something about Mrs. Romanowsky's murder."

Tricia narrowed her eyes. "I thought you decided to leave well enough alone. You said it was dangerous—and for the record, I agree. We never intentionally signed you up for harm," she said.

"I know. But I changed my mind. Now that I have a real lead, I can't let it go. I have to follow up on it."

Tricia weighed these words for a minute. Then she smoothed her hair behind her ears and cleared her throat. "That's up to you and Sloth, of course. You're both grown adults, and I can't stop you, not even if you're being foolish. But your task is your task."

"Tricia, I just think—"

"Well, don't," she said, patting me on the cheek. "You don't need to think. The network did all the thinking for all seven of you. See you soon."

She left me standing there with my mouth hanging open as she breezed out the door.

Frustrated, I wandered back into the living room to find Envy curled up on the couch, gazing into her phone. When she saw me, she waved me over and patted the seat next to her. "You ready to see what our case is?"

I shrugged. At this point, I couldn't care less. I was already investigating a missing commune and a woman's murder related to supernatural bounty hunters. Whatever dumb assignment the network had dug up for us couldn't possibly hold a candle to *that*.

But I didn't say any of that, of course. "Do us the honors."

Envy clicked on an email titled, "Envy and Pride: Challenge #3."

The email read,

"The temporary residents of Remembrance Home have been experiencing strange moments of clarity. The proprietors of the establishment would like help discovering the cause of this strange awakening."

Envy looked up at me and shrugged. "That doesn't seem so bad."

At the end of the email was a link that just said, "The details." Envy clicked it.

A screen loaded up. It said,

"Remembrance Home is a mortuary, and the embalmed corpses awaiting their final viewing have begun to talk. It's your job to find out how and why."

I looked at Envy and snorted, halfway because her expression was so funny and halfway because—well. That thing I just said about how my next task couldn't possibly be that interesting?

I guess I was wrong.

SIN & BONES

AMBER FISHER

LIGHTS, CAMERA, MYSTERY

3

intro reel (recap)

Welcome to *Sinful House*, a reality TV show where the 7 Deadly Sins live together in the sunny beach town of Odyssey, California, and compete to become America's Favorite Sin!

Previously on *Sinful House:*

1. Pride learned supernatural bounty hunter Walt Romanowsky believed local actress Charmaine Young might be a selkie—a shapeshifting seal.
2. While investigating Chenoweth International, Sloth and Pride recruited Wrath to hack Walt Romanowsky's laptop. They uncovered the organization's website, which included a shopping page for MagicBloc products and a marketplace for the buying and selling of supernaturals.
3. Sloth and Pride went to visit Eleanor Romanowsky to tell her what they'd found on her son's laptop. When they arrived, they found Eleanor murdered and her pet birds stolen…

4. …but Eleanor's ghost was still lingering around. Pride and Sloth took Eleanor to the Crypt, a secret underground location that serves as the headquarters for the Odyssey Paranormal Research Society.
5. Pride discovered an old map of Odyssey hidden inside Walt's laptop.

You're all caught up! Stay tuned for more rollicking adventures. And don't forget to vote for your favorite sin at the end of each challenge.

Happy watching!

one

. . .

"Sweet mother of pearl, what on earth is going on here?"

I had just returned from my morning jog on the beach to find Sloth, Wrath, and Greed milling around in the front yard. It was early, and Sloth should have been asleep. Instead, she was standing barefoot in the grass wearing her ratty bathrobe, a steaming mug of coffee in her hand. When she saw me, she waved me over, tittering.

"Isn't it amazing, Pride?" she asked, her voice thick with awe. "I mean, can you believe it? We haven't even been here a whole season, and already the Star of the Sea has paid us a visit."

My eyes traveled to the enormous mermaid statue that had appeared in our yard. It had to be at least 20 feet tall. It hadn't been there yesterday. Heck, it hadn't been there when I'd left for my jog earlier that morning. "What's it doing here?" I asked.

"Bringing bad luck," Sloth answered matter-of-factly. "At least, that's Greed's theory. That's why he and Wrath are trying to dig her up. If you ask me, it won't work."

I clucked my teeth. "Why not?"

Sloth leaned her head to the side and said sleepily, "All of us are right where we belong. Even the Star of the Sea. Our task is not to find fertile ground upon which to grow, but to learn to bloom where we are planted."

I scoffed. It was way too early to argue over cliched aphorisms (even if that particular saying was one of the most cockamamie things I'd ever heard) so instead I said, "I shouldn't be surprised by anything that happens in this town. And yet, I keep being surprised."

"That's a good thing," Sloth said. "When the world stops surprising you, it's probably because you're dead."

I wrinkled my nose and peeked inside Sloth's coffee mug. It didn't *look* like she'd spiked it with anything, but she sure was talking like she'd had one too many down at Sailor's Drink and Sink. Still, she wasn't entirely wrong.

Since coming to Odyssey, I'd seen a lot of weird stuff. I'd seen a woman turn into a nine-tailed fox, a dead man trapped in a psychic's body, and an army of wights working as servers in a Chinese restaurant. Mostly, I could explain these things. Well, not scientifically. But at least they jibed with my experiences. I could accept that shapeshifters existed. After all, I'm a psychic who talks to ghosts and has visions when I touch people. So I could accept that a dead man might get trapped inside another person's body. I could grasp how undead spirits consigned to an eternity of servitude might get roped into working food service. Death is unpredictable, is what I mean. So is life, for that matter.

But statues? Statues are usually predictable. And that's why, even after everything I'd seen, I was surprised to find the city's mascot looming over our yard.

"Last week, she was standing on the roof at JB's Groceries," Sloth said. She was watching Greed and Wrath alternate between pulling and pushing the statue to no avail. "Apparently, she was holding a bag of cash in one hand and an AK-47 in the other."

I chuckled. "Are those rifles even legal in California?"

"They are if you're a statue," Sloth answered, not missing a beat. "She's *supposed* to carry a lantern and a mirror. Her right hand lights the path ahead while the left reflects on the past. She's supposed to stand in front of City Hall to remind visitors of what is possible and how far the city has come."

I nodded. "Portia Cameron told me the statue disappeared from in front of City Hall a while ago. She's been traveling all over town. Nobody knows what to make of it."

"I tried asking her," Sloth said.

"Asking who? Portia?"

"No." Sloth sighed. "The Star of the Sea. I tried asking her what she hopes to accomplish by roaming the city."

I did a double take, but Sloth's expression was serene. She looked serious. "Are you for real?"

Sloth shrugged. "You never know if you don't try, right? She wasn't sharing her secrets with me, but maybe Wrath and Greed will have better luck." She giggled as she took a sip of her coffee.

Across the yard, Greed and Wrath were doing…something… to the statue. Wrath was wielding a shovel, trying with little success to dig up the earth around the mermaid. He looked hilarious—he was wearing skate shoes and black parachute pants with a white nylon pullover. The guy had obviously never done an honest day's work in his life, and it showed.

Digging my hands into my pockets, I ambled over to where Wrath had dug the shovel into the ground. He was bouncing on the step of the blade, trying to use his body weight for leverage. It wasn't working very well. "Morning," I said. "What's going on?"

Wrath didn't look up but gestured with a tilt of his head toward the statue. "What's it look like? The stupid statue's in the front yard! We have to get it out. This is a sign, man! She's not supposed to be here."

I rubbed the nape of my neck warily. "No, she's not supposed to be here. But why is it a sign?"

Greed used his hand as a visor as he peered up at the statue, an angry scowl scribbled over his face. "I had a premonition," he said.

Now, that piqued my interest. In the time I'd known Greed, I hadn't seen him do anything particularly psychic. To be fair, I mostly avoided him. He creeped me out. He gave off distinct vampire vibes with his aloofness and pale skin and long, dark hair. Not that I believed in vampires. But I still didn't want to spend time with people who looked like they might take a bite out of my neck, given the right opportunity.

Still, I *was* curious why the two least athletic people in the house were digging up the mermaid. "You had a premonition? About what?"

Greed's gaze drifted toward me, his expression icy. "An unexpected visitor will bring disaster and bad luck," he recited. He jammed his thumb in the direction of the wandering statue. "She's an unexpected visitor. Unexpected and *unwanted*. So I've recruited Wrath to help get rid of her."

I frowned. "Your premonition sounds like a bad fortune cookie," I mused. "Do they always sound like that?"

Greed returned his gaze to the statue. "Do you always *smell* like that?"

I took a step back, an embarrassed flush climbing up my neck. I'd just returned from a run on the beach. I wasn't supposed to smell like roses, but I guess I was a little ripe. "Well, that was rude," I muttered. "Anyway, Wrath seems to be the only one working. Are you going to help him dig?"

Greed folded his arms across his chest. "We're taking turns," he informed me. He said this like it was the most obvious thing in the world. "I sent Gluttony to the hardware store to get another shovel. Although our house is well-appointed, I guess no one expected us to do any actual yardwork. The garage and toolshed are both wanting. Since we only have the one shovel, only one person can dig at a time."

Well, that made sense. "Okay. I have another question. How do you know the unexpected guest is the statue? That seems like a stretch to me."

"Does it?" Greed's eyes narrowed, his lip curling in a flash of anger. "On the same morning I had the premonition, the statue appeared in our front yard. Doesn't feel like a stretch to me. In fact, I'm annoyed my premonition is lagging. Usually, I get at least a few days' notice before something happens."

I hrmmed noncommittally. "Right, okay. But how is getting rid of the statue supposed to change our future? The unexpected guest has already appeared, right? Does digging her out prevent the disaster or whatever?"

Greed stepped toward me, his expression changed. He no longer looked angry. Now, he was looking at me like I was stupid. I think I preferred it when he was angry. "You don't read tarot cards or anything like that perchance, do you, Pride?"

I scoffed. "Of course not. I may be a psychic, but I don't buy into that cockamamie nonsense."

Greed stretched his lips in a vampiric facsimile of a smile. "Cockamamie nonsense. I see. You do have a way of stating your position on things, don't you? No matter. If you did read tarot cards or perform similar work, you would know that no one's fortune is ever set in stone. All we can do is predict the most likely outcome based on a person's current situation and trajectory. For example, if a student continues not to study, he's likely to fail the test. If an employee continues to do mediocre work, he is not likely to get promoted, and may even lose his job. And if you continue to let an unwanted guest stand guard over your house, something terrible is likely to happen."

I frowned, scratching my chin. "The first two examples I get, even though the second is not necessarily true."

Greed snorted. "Isn't it? Mediocrity is seldom rewarded."

I shrugged. "Well, you've clearly never worked in corporate America. Anyway, even if your first two examples are sound, I'm not sure about the last. No, don't bother explaining it to me," I said, holding up a hand to stave off his interruption. "My interest in this topic is very low."

I turned my attention to the offending statue, really taking her in for the first time. She was beautiful. Cast in bronze with a white marble base, she was a wonder. I could see how she must have been a welcoming fixture in front of City Hall with her lantern and mirror. But now, both her hands were empty. Her palms were pressed to the sides of her face, the fingers curled inward. Her eyes were wide and round, and her mouth was open wide, her jaw stretched. She was screaming. The statue looked terrified.

My stomach flipped over. I didn't believe in omens as a rule, but when I got a load of her face, the strength of my belief system took a nosedive. There was something deeply unsettling about her, and the more I looked at her, the more I felt something twisted and dark settling into my bones.

I looked away.

"Have you reported this?" I asked. "To the mayor or whoever?"

Greed grunted. "What good would it do? Do you think the city will send someone to dig the statue out? Because if you do, please say so. I would gladly hand the manual labor over to someone else."

"You already did," Wrath grunted, still trying to overturn the soil. He chucked the shovel to the ground and propped his hands on his hips, leaning his head back in exhaustion. "I hate to admit it, but Pride might be right. We've been digging all morning, and the statue hasn't budged. Maybe we should call someone."

Just then, a car pulled into the driveway. Gluttony emerged from the driver's side and hauled a shovel from the backseat. He slammed the car door shut and stalked over to Greed, thrusting the shovel into his hand. "You owe me $20," he grumbled. "You can pay me later." Gluttony turned to me, his eyes flitting to the statue. "What do you think of her?"

A breeze blew, ruffling my hair, but it wasn't the warm, salt-scented breeze from the Pacific Ocean. It felt more like an electrical disturbance, an invisible current that passed right through me. I shuddered against the sudden cold, and my skin pimpled over.

Gluttony must have noticed because he looked me up and down and frowned. "Are you all right?"

I nodded, stammering. "Fine. It's just…there's something about that statue. Seeing her up close like this…she gives me the willies. I don't like her."

Gluttony grunted. "I guess nobody does. Me, I don't believe in bad luck, but y'all can think what you want. Greed and Wrath are out here busting their rumps because they think this here statue is bringing some bad juju. But me? I think she just wanted to be on TV." He lifted his chin toward the house.

I turned, following Gluttony's gaze. Sure enough, the camera crew had gotten wind of our new guest and was assembling on the porch, filming the whole thing. Wrath made a rude gesture at them. That would get cut in editing.

Greed tossed the new shovel to Wrath before retrieving the other from the grass. He attacked the topsoil with a vengeance. "I won't take this affront lying down," Greed said tersely. "If I have to dig all day, I will. But I'm not one to merely sidestep challenges fate has left in my path. I like to obliterate them. That's how I operate. That's how I've gotten this far in life."

"Well, good luck with that," I said, turning toward the house. "I guess I'll see you all at dinner?"

Wrath looked up, his brow creased. "Hold up, you're not gonna help dig? I've been at this all morning."

"Can't," I said with fake regret. "Envy and I are going over to the mortuary. We have a case of talking corpses to solve." I rubbed my hands together in mock anticipation and let the statue-inspired gloom roll off me. "Anyway, I hope the two of you get the statue out of here sooner rather than later. She doesn't look like she wants to be here any more than you want her here."

While Wrath grumbled something else that would get cut in editing, I disappeared into the house.

———

"If I were a dead person, I would absolutely want to be buried here. This is the kind of place I'm destined to sleep the eternal sleep in." Envy peered through the passenger's side window, her face pressed to the glass. "I didn't even think they had places like this in California. It looks like something you'd find in a Southern Gothic movie."

As I drove slowly down the driveway, I had to agree with her. If we hadn't just turned off Ocean View Drive, I'd never have believed we were still near the beach. I mean, the place had magnolias and weeping willows, for crying out loud.

Though, to be fair, we were pushing the boundaries of Odyssey. Remembrance Home was on the other side of town from Sinful House, tucked away in this idyllic glade.

"Place looks haunted if you ask me," the camera guy said.

My old camera guy had left the set for unknown reasons, and I had a new guy. This one was built like a refrigerator, with shoulders like boulders and biceps the size of a baby's head. He was wedged uncomfortably into the back seat, his knees practically pulled to his chest. I wondered why the network gave us such small cars if they were going to hire such big camera guys.

"Thankfully, no one asked you," I said absently. "Now zip it. You know the saying. It's better to be silent and be thought a fool, yadda yadda."

Beefy Camera Guy blinked in surprise but said nothing more as he turned to look out the window.

As we pulled through the long driveway, I slowed my pace to get a look at the building. Unlike most of the architecture in Odyssey, which was a cross between Spanish and beachy chic, Remembrance Home was one of those traditional colonial-style buildings. A broad porch wrapped around the weathered brick building. It even had plantation-style columns. In iron letters across the front were the words, REMEMBRANCE HOME. It looked exactly the way you would expect a funeral home to look. Polished, but not overstated. Elegant without being standoffish. And only mildly haunted.

We weren't going directly to the mortuary, however. The family who ran the place, the Thorntons, had an attached home on the east side of the building. As we walked up to the front porch, Envy placed a hand on my arm, giving it a gentle squeeze.

I paused to look at her. "Something wrong?"

Envy's eyes widened, and she shook her head, her face cracking into a smile. "No! Nothing's wrong. I just wanted to say I'm really excited to be working with you on this case."

"Oh." I hesitated, waiting for her to say something more. When she didn't, I gestured toward the door. "Okay if I ring the bell?"

She nodded enthusiastically. "Go ahead. I'm ready to get this party started."

I rang the doorbell.

A middle-aged woman opened the door. Her hair was a mousy brown and hung straight just past her shoulders. She wore a floral dress, nude stockings, and a polished pair of white flats. She looked nothing like the other women I'd met in Odyssey. She looked more like a preacher's wife in middle America. Not that I'm an expert. "You must be Pride and Envy," she said.

"That's us," Envy chirped. "I'm Envy. That's Pride. And that's the camera guy, but we don't know his name. So!" Her smiled widened. "We're here to see someone about corpses waking up in the middle of the night."

The woman smiled and extended a hand, which Envy and I both shook. "I'm Danielle Martin," she said. "Please, come in. Let's get acquainted in the living room."

We followed Danielle into the house. She led us into the kitchen where a breakfast table was set with lemonade and cookies. The three of us sat down, and Envy grabbed a snickerdoodle.

"I really appreciate your coming," Danielle said. "Before we get down to it, I thought I might explain what's been happening and why we asked RealTV to help. The whole thing has me a little flustered."

Envy chuckled. "I would get flustered, too, if I were embalming a corpse and it suddenly started talking," she said. "But don't let me get ahead of things."

"Well," Danielle said, "I wasn't the one embalming. My father, Edgar, is the mortician. He doesn't know I've asked you here to investigate this. Oh, I guess I should begin at the beginning."

Envy jabbed a finger into the air. "And when you come to the end, stop."

Danielle nodded. "It all started a few weeks ago. My family has been caring for Odyssey's dead for generations. My grandfather started the business. When my father passes on, my brother and I will inherit it. Anyway, Daddy was embalming Fiona Arquette when this whole thing started. Daddy was already in a bad place because he and Fiona were best friends, and he took her passing hard. In high school, everybody assumed they'd get married. That's how close they were."

"Were they sweethearts?" Envy asked. "I'm a sucker for a high school sweetheart story."

Danielle laughed. "No, never. From what I hear, Fiona was always sweet on Julian Gillespie. The three of them were like Gene Kelly, Donald O'Connor, and Debbie Reynolds in *Singing in the Rain*. Though between us girls, Julian has nothing on Daddy. Daddy is a genius, and Julian is a blockhead." She paused, shaking her head. "Oh, I shouldn't say that. He's the mayor now. Don't put that on the show," she rushed to add, blushing furiously. To Envy, she said, "He won't put that on the show, right?"

"Who, the camera guy?" Envy smirked. "He doesn't edit the content. He just shoots it. So, go on with your story. The mayor's an idiot, and your dad is the Smarty McSmartyPants of their friend group."

Danielle squirmed, shooting nervous glances at the camera. "Well, I don't know if I'd say the mayor's an *idiot*," she hedged, twining the pearl necklace at her throat around a slender finger. "He's just not the brightest bulb. I remember when he first ran for office, he was worried he wasn't electable because he didn't grow up rich. Odyssey is like that, you know. Very big on appearances."

"So we've noticed," I said.

"Right. Well, Julian badly wanted to win. So he asked Fiona if she would join his opposition's campaign and spy for them. Fiona, bless her heart, was willing to do it. But Daddy had to gently explain to both of them that no one would fall for that. Their friendship wasn't exactly a secret."

Envy laughed politely. "Sounds like your father has a good head on his shoulders."

"Oh, he does," Danielle gushed. "He does. But I do think losing his best friend has skewed his judgment. Not that I can blame him for that. Everybody loved Fiona, and I mean everyone. She was a performer and the life of any gathering. All the moms wanted her for their kids' birthday parties. She had these puppets, and she'd read these terrific kids' books, and she'd do all the voices and everything." A cloud passed over Danielle's face. "I hadn't seen her in years, though. Not since she developed the Alzheimer's."

As much as I didn't want to be rude, none of this was relevant to our case, and my interest in this woman's life story was very low. "Maybe we should get back to the talking corpses."

Danielle collected herself and nodded. "Yes, of course, sorry. I do go on sometimes, don't I? My husband always says if talking were an Olympic sport, I'd be sure to come home with the medal." She tittered and waved her hand airily. "Okay, sorry! Anyway, Daddy was working later than usual that night. I didn't think much of it because he's always been a night owl. I figured he was working slow because Fiona was a friend. The next day, he told us what happened. Just after 3 a.m., Fiona Arquette started talking."

Envy leaned forward. "What did she say?"

Danielle grimaced, wringing her fingers in her lap. "Well, I wasn't there, but Daddy said it was gobbledygook. It was all stuff like, 'Infrastructure costs are rising. Natalie agreed to lead next month's bake sale."

"That is strange," Envy said. "Who's Natalie?"

Danielle shrugged. "Who knows? Probably no one."

"Interesting," I said. "And was that the only time this happened?"

Danielle shook her head. "Not at all. Cougar Whitecastle and Jody Helmuth were the following night. And just like Fiona, they spoke gibberish. After that, Daddy got smart and recorded the incidents on his phone. I'll get you those recordings, though I have to tell you, they're confusing."

"Did the deceased have anything in common?" I asked.

"Nothing I can think of," Danielle said. "Just that they lived in town."

"How many talking corpses were there in total?" Envy asked.

Danielle thought for a moment. "Well, let's see," she said. "Fiona, Cougar, and Jody were first. Then there was Freddie McIntyre, Inez Montoya, Jack Wilcox—that was crazy because Jack shouted his message—and…oh, yes. Monica Stewart. I think that was everyone. So that's seven."

Envy glanced over at me. "Do you think that's significant? Seven corpses? Seven Deadly Sins?"

I grinned and shook my head. "Not everything is about us, Envy." To Danielle, I said, "So why did you ask the network for our help? Aren't there locals who dabble in this kind of thing?"

I was thinking specifically about the Paranormal Research Society operating underneath the coffee shop Déjà Brew, but I was pretty sure they were a secret, so I didn't ask directly. Danielle twisted her hands in her lap. "Well, that's the sticky wicket. See, Daddy doesn't want me or my brother involved in this at all."

"He doesn't? Why not?" Envy asked.

Danielle sighed. "He says he has it all under control. He says I don't need to worry about it—he's already handled it. A very Daddy thing to say, honestly," she added with a soft smile. "But it's not helpful. This is a family business. And like I said, one day, it will be half mine. If I'm inheriting a haunted mortuary, I think I deserve to know about it. And if it's *not* haunted and something else is going on here, I think I deserve to know that, too."

Envy nodded sagely. "Yes, you certainly do." She glanced at me and raised an eyebrow. "Pride, do you have more questions?"

"No," I answered.

"Well, in that case, unless there's more you want to tell us, do you think we can meet your dad? I've never met an actual mortician before."

Danielle brightened and got to her feet. Envy and I followed suit. "Well, sure! I'll take you back. Honestly, I thought he'd be in by now. Even for him, it's getting pretty late." She glanced at the clock. It was just after 9 a.m. I guessed he preferred to work at night. "Just do me a favor and don't mention anything we talked about, okay?"

Envy made a motion like she was zipping her lips and throwing away the key. We followed Danielle outside and down a little pathway that led to a side entrance. We padded down a wood-paneled hallway that led to a set of stairs going down.

At the bottom of the stairwell, we passed through a door marked *EMPLOYEES ONLY*, and the ambiance changed. Instead of rich carpet, the floors were tiled. Wood-paneled walls were traded for unadorned white drywall. Danielle pushed open a door marked *PREPARATION ROOM* and stepped inside. "Daddy, are you still working? It's already morning! I've brought someone who wants to meet…"

Her words fell away as she screamed. I hurried into the room, pushing Danielle aside. When I saw what caused her reaction, I stopped short, my throat tightening. Images of the screaming statue filled my mind, and my heart sank into my shoes. The bad luck Greed promised was apparently already starting.

Lying in the middle of the floor was a man's body.

He'd been shot in the chest.

He was dead.

two

. . .

"Daddy!"

Danielle rushed toward the corpse, falling to her knees at his side. Tenderly, she rolled him over and pressed her fingertips to his cardioid artery. It was obvious her father was dead, even to me, and I'm not exactly what you would call a professional. His skin had taken on an ashy pallor, and his limbs were stiff. He looked like he'd been dead for at least a few hours. Danielle pulled her hand away, choking with sobs. Then she grabbed him by the front of his protective garments, pressing her forehead to his chest. "Daddy, please wake up! Please wake up, Daddy!"

I pulled Envy aside and said, "I think you should probably call the cops."

While Envy dialed, I moved to Danielle's side, placing my hand gingerly on her shoulder. "There's nothing you can do for him now," I said, pulling her away from the body. "Come on. You shouldn't be looking at this. Let's get you somewhere else until the police arrive."

But Danielle didn't budge. "Who could do such a thing? My

father was the kindest, gentlest man anyone ever knew. Why would anyone murder him in cold blood like this? It just doesn't make sense. It doesn't make sense!"

I knew these questions were rhetorical, so I didn't answer them. Instead, I helped her to her feet and led her out of the room and back up the stairs. I didn't know the layout of the funeral home, so I had no particular destination in mind. I ended up dragging her along with me until I found a quiet corner for us to sit in. She collapsed into an armchair, her palm pressed to her forehead as tears streamed down her face. "What am I gonna tell Mama? I can't believe this is happening."

A moment later, I heard footsteps coming down the hallway. I looked up to see a man hurrying toward us, his expression troubled. He was very good looking, with a head of thick, dark hair and a strong jaw. He ignored me completely as he made a beeline for Danielle. When she saw him, she jumped to her feet and threw her arms around his neck, her sobs redoubling.

The man pulled Danielle close. "Dani? What's wrong? What happened? I heard screaming! Are you hurt?"

As Danielle continued to sob, the man's gaze slowly drifted to me, his eyes full of questions and accusations. I held my hands up, palms out, shirking off responsibility. "It's not my place to say," I began, "but we found something disturbing downstairs."

"It's Daddy," Danielle said, her words thick with grief. "Daddy's dead, Tony. We found him dead in the preparation room."

"What?" The man's body stiffened, and he drew Danielle away from him by her shoulders to look her in the face. "Daddy's dead? Are you sure? What happened?"

Danielle shook her head as her wailing continued. "He was shot! Somebody shot Daddy!"

"Envy's calling the police," I said. "They're on their way."

Tony glared at me again. "And who are you? What are you doing here?"

"I'm Pride," I answered. "Who are you?"

"Tony Thornton, Danielle's brother." He glanced down at his sister. "Have I lost my mind, or did this person just refer to themselves as *Pride?*"

I opened my mouth to respond, but Danielle beat me to it. "Tony, this is one of the psychics the TV show sent over."

Tony stiffened, his skin blanching. "Oh, Danielle. You didn't."

"He wouldn't let me help!" Danielle sobbed. "I needed to understand what's happening to our *business!*"

"Dani, you invited reality show parasites to Remembrance Home? These people aren't professionals; they're *actors!*"

"Common misconception," I said, "but not true. In my previous life, I was a paranormal investigator." Tony was still staring daggers in my direction, so I plundered on. "We might be able to help. Ideally, I'd like to interview the man who..."

As soon as I said the words, an idea struck me. The last time I'd encountered a dead body was at Mrs. Romanowsky's house. Amid the chaos, I had almost failed to notice that her ghost lingered behind.

I wouldn't make that same mistake twice.

"Excuse me," I said.

Before Tony could ask where I thought I was going, I made my way back to the preparation room. The room wasn't very large and had no good place for a ghost to hide. Still, some spirits were more obvious than others. Some looked like fully fleshed-out humans, while others were merely a glimmer of light. I didn't see any fully fleshed-out humans, so I waited patiently for something to catch my peripheral vision.

But I didn't see anything. For better or worse, Edgar Thornton's ghost wasn't in the room.

I heard motion behind me and turned to see Envy coming into the room. She walked over to me, but her eyes were on

Edgar lying stiff on the floor. "Who could do something like this?" she whispered.

I scoffed. "In *this* town? I'm starting to think treachery and murder are just casual pastimes. Ever since we've been here, terrible things keep happening."

Envy shuddered. "You're right. Which makes you wonder. Did the network choose this location because terrible things often happen here, or are terrible things happening because we are here?"

It was a good question, but one that had no answer, so I let it go. Plus, I didn't like to get philosophical this early in the morning. It set a rotten mood for the rest of my day. Not that my day was off to a great start.

"Let's go upstairs," I said. "This is a crime scene now. The longer we stay, the more likely we are to mess something up."

Envy cast a sidelong glance at the door. "I don't know, Pride. Don't you think we should investigate?"

I frowned. "Why would we investigate? You called the cops, didn't you?"

"Sure, but our task was to find out about the talking corpses. Once the police get here, everything will be out of our hands. If we're going to find any answers here, we need to look now. For starters, we need this phone." Envy strode over to where Edgar's phone lay on an embalming table and quickly stuck it in her pocket.

I gave Envy a dubious look. "You know you're tampering with evidence right now, don't you?"

But Envy waved this away. "Forget that. We need the phone more than the police do. And we need to do one more thing, Pride."

I already didn't like the sound of that, but I asked anyway. "What thing?"

Envy gulped. "I think you should touch him," she whispered.

"Isn't that a thing you can do? Touch corpses and have visions or whatever? We should know as much as we can about his death. Touch him, Pride. Let's see what he saw in his final moments."

I didn't think it was a good idea for lots of reasons, but Envy was right. If we wanted to win our challenge, data would give us a leg up. Cautiously, I maneuvered myself next to the corpse. I shot Envy one last hesitant glance before I closed my eyes and placed the flat of my palms against Mr. Thornton's cheeks.

I waited, my breath held in my throat. But after several seconds, I shook my hands and stood up.

"Nothing," I said. "I didn't see anything."

"How is that possible?" Envy asked, incredulous. "Don't you always see something when you touch a corpse?"

I looked back down at the man lying dead on the floor. There was nothing unusual about him other than the hole in his chest. But she was right. It *was* unusual for me to touch a dead body and not see anything at all.

"Try one more time," Envy said. "Come on, Pride. Not guts, no glory."

With a sigh, I pushed up my sleeves and grit my teeth, ready to lay my hands once more on the corpse when a gruff voice called out, "Stop right there. Hands where I can see 'em, pal."

I froze, my hands lifted in midair as I turned around. The cops had arrived and were now filing into the room, each of them throwing Envy and me dirty looks. I'd seen these particular cops before. They'd been on the scene when Walt Romanowsky was found dead in the walk-in freezer at Wights and Wongs.

One of them came over to me, notebook in hand. "You the two that found the body?" he asked. His nametag read "Farley."

"Can I put my arms down?" I asked.

Officer Farley glared at me. "If you promise not to touch any *evidence*," he said, glancing down at the man on the floor. "That's what you were about to do, wasn't it?"

"Yes, but it's not what it looks like," I mumbled, lowering my arms to my sides.

The cop scoffed. "I bet." He lifted his chin to the embalming table across the room. "Who's on the table?"

Without waiting for answer, Officer Farley sauntered over to the embalming table and took a quick peek. Then he stepped back, giving a low whistle. "Well, what do you know? Looks like Karen McMurtry finally bit it."

"You know her?" I asked.

"Of course I know her," he sneered. "You can't live in Odyssey without having at least one story about Karen McMurtry ruining your life." He gave the corpse another contemptuous look. I swear, if we hadn't been standing right there, he might have spit on her. "Not so high and mighty are you now, huh, Karen? Your life-wrecking days are over!"

"Can I just mention really fast that you're being extremely rude to a dead woman?" Envy interjected. "I mean, what the heck?"

Another officer, a woman, sauntered over to us, thumbs hooked in her belt loops. "Karen McMurtry had a reputation as a gossip," she explained. "And she was…I don't know, what's the adult version of a tattletale? Karen liked to tell people's business —especially business she wasn't supposed to know about, if you know what I mean."

I didn't know what she meant, but I wasn't about to admit that. "Was she a psychic?"

The second cop, whose nametag read "Underwood," snorted. "No, she was a busybody. She liked to say she was protecting the town from wickedness, but really, she was just raking the mud. Couple months back, she found out two members of the city council were having an affair. She told Stephanie Jones about it, of course. Those two were thick as thieves. Stephanie posted about the affair in her community newsletter. It was a huge scandal."

That piqued my curiosity, but also turned my stomach. I'd had my own run-in with Stephanie Jones, and it wasn't pretty. She'd spotted Envy and me at the grocery store wrangling an earth elemental that had gone haywire. Trouble was, she thought the elemental was a little person and published a furious write-up about the incident in her "newsletter"—which was little more than a thinly veiled gossip rag. She'd painted us as "ableist tyrants," an epitaph Envy took particularly hard. The network received dozens of complaints, and Envy lost some Instagram followers over it. It was an ongoing problem.

"So how did Karen die?" I asked. "Was it suspicious?"

Officer Underwood shrugged. "Don't know. Didn't work the case if it was. But if you ask me, if somebody did her in, they did this town a favor."

"Well, I didn't ask you *that*," I said, frowning.

Envy elbowed me in the side and turned an apologetic smile to the officer. "Did Karen ever do anything to ruin *your* life?"

The officer paused, her lips pressed into a line. Finally, she said, "Not unless you count stealing my boyfriend in high school. But maybe that was actually a favor. Sterling Longfellow was Mr. Popular back when we were kids—quarterback, prom king, you know the type. But I guess you could say he peaked in high school. These days, he's just a sorry slob, getting hammered over at Sailor's Drink and Sink with the other losers before noon. He doesn't even have a job. What a worthless—"

"Got it, thanks," I interrupted. The last thing I had time for was some pathetic story about the high school stud washing out as an adult. Why some people stay stuck in high school nostalgia is beyond me. "Are we still needed, or can we get out of here?"

Officer Underwood shrugged. "Do what you like. Just make

sure you don't leave Odyssey. Farley and I might have more questions later."

As we headed upstairs, Envy asked, "Can you imagine Karen McMurtry stealing Officer Underwood's boyfriend?"

I stammered, blinking back my confusion. "What are you talking about?"

"Well, I know she's dead, so she doesn't look her best," Envy said, "but did you *see* that woman? She wasn't exactly Hottie McHottiePants if you know what I mean. And Officer Underwood? All that long, red hair? What a looker! If I looked like her?" Envy sighed wistfully. "Well, I wouldn't be wasting my time interviewing psychics in a mortuary, that's for sure. I'd be staking out all the gyms in town looking for a hot guy to buy me drinks and wife me up, you know? I'd put even the likes of Lust to shame."

I filed that away as information to forget later. "Anyway, let's see if Danielle knows the passcode to her dad's phone. Otherwise, your evidence tampering will have been for nothing."

Envy nodded, completely oblivious to the reproach in my voice. "I was thinking the same thing. She's pretty emotional right now, though. Should we try the brother?"

I sighed. "We can try. I don't think he likes me much."

Envy patted me on the arm. "You're an acquired taste. Let's let him have another lick."

I filed that visual as something to forget immediately.

———

Back upstairs, we found Danielle and Tony in a large sitting room. A cluster of cops was off to one side, speaking in low voices. No one bothered the grieving family. But as soon as we entered the room, Tony Thornton's expression darkened, and he climbed to his feet, striding over to us.

"You're still here?" Grabbing us by our arms, he hauled us aside, out of his sister's earshot. "I assure you, your services are no longer needed. Talking corpses are the last thing my sister needs to worry about."

I folded my arms across my chest and lowered my voice. "I don't mean to be a jerk," I said, "but we're investigating this one way or the other. If something strange is happening in Odyssey, we have an obligation as a community to look into it. Don't you think so?"

Tony faltered, for a moment looking unsure of himself. But the expression was fleeting. He straightened his spine and adjusted the tie at his throat. "You're not even really part of this community," he hissed. "You're actors on a reality TV show. Show some respect. Let my family grieve in peace."

I was preparing another statement about grieving through action—some cockamamie nonsense I must have picked up from Dr. Xena— when Danielle joined her brother at his side. She placed a hand on his arm, giving it a little squeeze. "It's okay, Tony. I'm stronger than you think. And I want to know what's happening here."

"Dani, Dad said he was handling it! He didn't seem that upset. Maybe you should let it go."

Danielle sniffed and shook her head. "I want answers. I *deserve* them."

Tony grunted and threw me and Envy a dark look. "I need some fresh air." He didn't look back as he stormed out of the room.

Danielle watched her brother leave and then turned on an apologetic smile. "Please forgive my brother," she said. "He means well, but all of this makes him very uncomfortable."

"Psychics? Talking corpses?" I asked. "Or reality TV?"

Danielle hesitated. "It's not that he doesn't believe in psychics and fringe science and things like that. He does. Maybe too

much. He's one of those people who thinks these things are…
well, I don't want to say sacred, but not fit for public consump-
tion, anyway. He finds your show distasteful. He thinks people
with gifts like yours should be searching for a higher truth, not
flaunting their abilities for a quick buck."

"How about flaunting our abilities for a roof over our
heads?" I muttered. "Even psychics need to eat."

"I know, and I don't share my brother's position. However,
Odyssey is a unique town," she continued. "Many strange things
happen here. And when you grow up in a place like this, it can
make you hungry for answers."

Sheepishly, Envy pulled Edgar's phone from her pocket. "I
took this from the preparation room," she said, delicately
changing the subject. "This is the phone he recorded on, right?"

Danielle nodded. "Yes, that's right. I suppose you need me to
unlock it." She took the phone and tapped in the code. Then she
opened the settings and removed the security precaution. "There
you are," she said, handing the device back to Envy. "I hope
that's helpful. And please, if you find anything, let me know.
Don't let my brother dissuade you. Things have been…difficult
for him lately."

"And now his father's dead," Envy mused. "I imagine things
will only get worse."

Danielle nodded, stroking the back of her neck with her
fingertips. "It might be uncouth of me to share this, but financially, things have been strained for Tony. He joined a…well, I
don't want to say cult. That's such a loaded word. But these
people took him for everything he had. He was different before.
Now, he's so angry. Anyway, it damaged his pride, I think. He's
always looking for a way to get back on top. Have you ever heard
of cryptocurrency?"

I nodded. "Sure. It's like fake money."

Danielle frowned, her shoulders sagging. "I don't know if

that's accurate, but I see where you're coming from. He calls it investing. He says it's the way of the future. But to me? It just looks like gambling. He has no reason to believe these 'investments' will pay out over time. I wish he'd just invest in corn futures like everyone else."

"Not a lot of money in corn futures," I pointed out.

"Not a lot of money in crypto either, if the market crashes all the time," Danielle shot back. "He's lost so much already. He and his husband fight all the time. But anyway. Listen to me babbling on when you have more pressing matters to attend to." She shook off the previous conversation and let her breath out in a whoosh. "Now, my brother is right about one thing. I should be with my family. So, if there isn't anything else you need, may I walk you all to your car?"

It was perhaps the politest version of "Please get the heck out of my house" I'd ever heard in my life. I was impressed. Envy, the camera guy, and I followed Danielle out of the house and back out to the street. As we got into the car, Danielle leaned down to speak to us through the window one last time. "You can call me any time," she said. "My number's in Daddy's phone."

Once we were on the road back to Sinful House, Envy turned in her seat, angling her body to face me. "Okay. So what do you think so far? Did any of your psychic senses go off or anything?"

I shook my head, keeping my eyes on the road. "No, nothing. The place isn't haunted, that's for sure," I said, directing this comment to the cameraman in the back, who only grunted in response.

Envy sighed thoughtfully, running her fingers through her hair. "It's strange that you didn't see anything when you touched Mr. Thornton's body. Something about that funeral home just isn't right."

"Speaking of things not being quite right," I said, "what was that back there? Danielle just started telling us her brother's financial problems. I mean, I know she's talkative, but that was weird, right? Seemed like a very private thing to tell strangers."

Now, Envy made an irritated sound in her throat and rolled her eyes dramatically. "Oh, *that*. That was nothing. I have that effect on people. They don't call me a muse for nothing, you know."

I stole a quick glance at her. "A muse? What are you talking about?"

"That's my gift," Envy explained. "Or, one of them, anyway. I get people to talk. They muse aloud about all kinds of things—everybody becomes an oversharer. Or sometimes I just inspire them. Maybe they know just the right thing to say at just the right time. That's the most common. But sometimes, I give them a perfect idea, and the next thing you know, they're furiously drafting up business plans for an exciting new venture."

"I didn't know that about you," I said. "I thought you just conjured elementals."

Envy sighed. "Well, it's not something I like to talk about. I mean, it's depressing. Do you know how annoying it is that everyone around me is writing the Great American Novel or submitting fabulous new inventions to the trademark office while I'm stuck teaching second graders how to memorize 50 state capitals to the tune of *The Blue Danube?* As gifts go, mine is Stupid McStupidPants."

"So you don't have any great ideas of your own?"

Envy turned to stare mournfully out the window. "Not a single one."

three

. . .

When I got back to Sinful House, I made my way to my favorite location—the kitchen. With any luck, I'd find something tasty in the fridge. And if I was doubly lucky, it would be something tasty with no pesky magic baked in.

Living with a kitchen witch had its pros and cons. On the one hand, the kitchen was usually stocked with delicious meals and scrumptious treats. On the other hand, you never knew what magic might be lurking inside. I still wasn't over the time Gluttony put complimentary magic in the blueberry muffins, and I went around telling everyone how gorgeous their smile was for hours. It was humiliating.

Unfortunately, the kitchen was empty. So I made a sandwich, poured myself a glass of milk, and headed up the stairs. I was halfway to my room when Sloth peeked her head out her door.

"I thought that was you," she said. "Can I talk to you for a second?"

I shrugged. "You're talking to me now."

Sloth giggled like I'd said something funny. "Sure. Well, I just wanted to follow up about Walt's laptop. You did give it to the cops, didn't you?"

My stomach dropped into my shoes. Sloth was talking about the laptop Mrs. Romanowsky gave us before she was murdered. It was now a major clue in the case. I was supposed to turn it over to the police.

Which I hadn't done. But I had a good reason for it.

I wavered. "Yeah, so, about that. We should discuss this in my room."

I led Sloth into my bedroom and closed the door behind us. I gestured for her to take a seat on the bed, even though I wasn't sure I wanted her to do that. I couldn't see any visible signs of spilled food or coffee or juice on her clothing, but that didn't mean there wasn't something hiding. Sloth seemed to have a gift for grime.

"So here's the thing," I said. "See, the laptop…"

Sloth squinted at me. "What about it?"

I huffed out a sigh and strode over to the dresser, where the laptop was hidden under a mound of folded laundry. I swept the clothes aside and handed the computer to Sloth.

She looked down at the jumble of cracked plastic and gasped. "It's completely ruined," she said. When she looked up at me again, her eyes were wide and her mouth gaping. "How did this happen? What did you do?"

"It was an honest accident, I promise," I explained. "There was a sock stuck in the back of my drawer, and I was shaking the dresser trying to get it loose. The computer was on top, and it fell to the floor and shattered."

Sloth stared at the broken heap for a while before setting it aside with a melancholic sigh. "Poor Mrs. Romanowsky. She'll never get any justice now."

"Well, about that." I knelt at the side of my bed and slid my hand underneath the mattress. I found what I was looking for and handed it to Sloth. "When the laptop shattered, I found that inside."

Sloth peered down at the paper she was holding as she began chewing on the end of a pigtail. "What is this?" she asked.

"Obviously, it's a map of Odyssey, but I have no idea what part of town or anything like that."

Sloth flipped the paper over, saw that the back was blank, and then flipped it again. "This looks like a child drew it."

"Yeah. I don't know why it was hidden in the laptop. But I do know somebody really wanted that map. I think that's what they killed Mrs. Romanowsky to find."

Sloth traced her finger along the lines of the drawing, taking it all in. Not that there was much to take in. The whole map looked hastily sketched, and almost nothing was labeled. When her finger found its way to the lower right-hand corner, she paused and read aloud, "Historic Odyssey Nexus of Power, 1902." She looked up at me, her expression thoughtful. "What do you make of it?"

I sat down beside Sloth and examined the map over her shoulder. "Nothing yet. I mean, I don't know. But look at this right here." I tapped the corner of the map with my finger. The map depicted a collection of narrow mounds like skinny hills. Underneath the mounds was a star. "Don't these look like head-stones to you? Graves?"

Sloth cocked her head sideways. "I guess so."

I frowned. "If this was a cemetery back in 1902, it must still be here, right? You wouldn't just bulldoze a cemetery and develop it, would you?"

Sloth shrugged. "I mean, it happens. Didn't you ever see that movie *Poltergeist*?"

I hadn't seen it, but I wasn't going to admit that. "What does that have to do with anything?" I asked.

Sloth made bug eyes, looking at me like this was the stupidest question I'd ever asked. "Well, the whole point of the movie was that they built a housing development on top of a sacred Indian burial ground! That's why the houses in the neighborhood were all messed up. Geez, Pride, you really need to get out more."

I didn't say anything to that. I plucked the map from Sloth's fingers and set it aside before she could ruin it. While she was spoiling the plot of *Poltergeist*, I noticed a smear of peanut butter or maybe honey on her hands. "So, what you're saying is, in movies at least, nothing is sacred."

"I'm just saying, I wouldn't rule anything out," Sloth said. "You know, if you want to know more about how Odyssey *used* to be, we should talk to their historical society."

My eyebrows shot up. "There's an Odyssey historical society?"

Sloth shrugged. "Beats me. You didn't even check? Geez, Pride. That's like the first thing you should have done. Here."

Sloth pulled out her phone and started a Google search. The only relevant entry wasn't for a historical society at all, but for the City Hall. Sloth clicked the link, anyway.

"It says here the official historical society disbanded a few years ago. But it also says that visitors who want to know more about Odyssey's historic roots should direct their inquiries to Mrs. Pamela Arquette."

"Hold on," I said. "Arquette? Really?"

"Yeah." Sloth handed me the phone. "Why, does that mean something to you?"

"Sort of. The task Envy and I are working on involves a woman named Fiona Arquette."

Sloth clapped her hands together in excitement. "Ooh, that's fun! Maybe they're sisters!"

"Maybe, but Fiona's dead now," I said.

Sloth sighed. "Well, that's less fun for sure. We should email Pamela."

I clicked the link for Pamela Arquette. Sloth's email program opened in response.

"What should we say?" I asked.

"Well, we could tell her we found a crappy map of historic Odyssey hidden in a laptop and we'd like her to take a look at it."

I shook my head. "I don't want anybody to know about the laptop," I said. "After all, people are already dead over it."

Sloth nodded her agreement. "Okay, then let's just tell her we're on this show, and the network asked us to investigate Odyssey's roots. You know, as a human-interest story or whatever."

I shrugged. "It's as good a reason to ask for a meeting as any." I quickly tapped out a message asking for an appointment and hit send.

"So, where were you and Envy off to so early this morning?"

I handed Sloth her phone back. "Remembrance Home. We were supposed to investigate talking corpses. But when we got there, the proprietor had been murdered."

Sloth squinted at me, tilting her head sideways. "Hmm. Now that you mention it, you do look a little shaken."

"Well, that tracks," I said. "It was unexpected, to say the least. It's not like people get murdered every day."

Sloth smiled. "You're so naïve sometimes," she said. "People do get murdered every day. Though in Odyssey, it only seems to happen about once a week."

———

Later that evening, there was a knock at my door. Before I could answer, Envy stepped into my room, closing the door softly behind her. Her hands on her hips, Envy tipped her chin upward, turning her face from side to side. "Okay, so let me have it. What do you think? Is it embarrassingly obvious and desperate or do I just look refreshed?"

I frowned. "What do I think about what?"

Envy gestured to her face. "About my new look! I know it's a bit dramatic. But the dermatologist encouraged me to experiment and I don't know, I think I kind of like it. But maybe I don't. I can't tell! What do you think?"

I didn't think anything. Envy looked the way she always did, except her face wasn't moving around as much. She was usually more expressive. But you can't tell someone you don't notice anything when they're asking how they look, so instead I said, "Yeah, it looks great."

Envy took a step toward me, her eyes narrowing in suspicion. "You have no idea what I got done today, do you?"

Caught red-handed, I heaved a sigh of relief. "Nope. You look the same. Mostly."

"No, I don't. Though I'm not surprised you didn't notice. You're not the most observant person on the planet, I guess." She sighed and plopped down next to me on the bed. "I got my lips injected. I wanted a fuller, poutier look. It's not full-on Angelina Jolie, but it's pretty good. And then I let the doctor talk me into a round of Botox. Do you think it makes me look younger?"

I squinted. "You looked plenty young before," I said. "Besides, I don't know why people are so obsessed with youth. What's so bad about looking your age?"

Envy huffed and tossed her hair from her face. "Well, of course *you* can say something like that. You're gorgeous! You don't even try to look good, and you still have everyone around here swooning over you. I mean, you practically have Lust wrapped around your little finger."

I blushed furiously and looked away. Every instinct was to argue with Envy since nothing she just said was true, especially the gorgeous part. No, especially the everyone swooning over me part. Okay, both were equally ridiculous. But at the mention of Lust, my throat went dry. Something *was* developing between me and Lust. Or at least, I'd thought so. But then I saw her cozying up to Greed, and I was no longer sure I was even on her radar. I still felt something for her, though *what* I felt exactly, I was unsure of. Romantic relationships were not my forte. In all my life, I'd had exactly one girlfriend, and she dumped me because I was an inattentive moron. I didn't want to get too involved with anyone until I had my feet under me again.

Of course, I was also familiar with the adage, the best way to get over someone is to get under someone new. But I wasn't ready for that, either.

Nevertheless, none of this was something I wanted to discuss with Envy. "So did you want to talk more about your dermatological adventures, or should we get down to work?" I asked.

Envy shrugged and dug out Edgar's phone, tossing it into my lap. "All right, Business McBusinessPants. All work and no play. You can have the honors."

I opened Edgar Thornton's phone and located his audio memos. They were listed in chronological order, so I started with the most recent memo, titled "Monica Stewart." I pressed play.

It was a woman's voice speaking. The recording wasn't great, and the corpse wasn't speaking loudly, but if I closed my eyes, I could just make out what she was saying.

"Discussion, Madison Summerland. Having difficulty getting ahold of M at Summerland Memorial. Natalie will continue to try to contact. Might be a good idea to send cookies as a soft intro. Ginger to call Bake Some Waves for prices. Discussion, City Hall. Still no word on blueprints. Wilson to acquire papers from JG office. Action items, cookies, blueprints."

I looked over at Envy. "What does this sound like to you?"

Envy scrunched up her nose. "Like every work meeting I've ever been to. Maybe that's the wrong audio file."

"It's labeled Monica Stewart. According to Danielle, she was one of the talking corpses."

"Well, maybe he accidentally recorded over it. Try the next one."

I nodded and tried the next file. This one was labeled "Jack Wilcox." I pressed play and immediately cringed. The man was shouting instead of using his inside voice. But other than that, the content was much the same:

"Discussion, Portia for mayor. Cameron Realty, conflict of interest? PC to file papers. Discussion, community support for JG office. Do we want to start collecting pro-PC talking points? Discussion, Karen McMurtry. New gossip, anything to worry about? Anything to use against JG? Action items, PC to file papers, PC to meet with KM."

I stopped the playback and cocked an eyebrow at Envy. "This really does sound like meeting minutes. Maybe it's notes from the city council? I know Portia Cameron sits on the council."

Envy hrmmed and bit her lip. "Could be. Let's keep going."

The next file was labeled "Inez Montoya." I played it.

"Discussion, historical landmark. Anthony to add item to city council agenda to make Old Downtown a historical landmark. Discussion, member outings. We need to be more welcoming to new initiates. Might want to look into holding a meet and greet to set expectations. Perhaps cemetery tour? Discussion, initiation ceremony. Do we want to partner with Felix for coffee discounts? Status check, green. Action items, AT to protect our meeting space, protect Odyssey."

"Do city councils host initiation ceremonies?" Envy asked.

"Do they have meet and greets at cemeteries?" The more we listened, the less I understood. I navigated to the last file labeled "Freddie McIntyre" and hit play.

"The underground of the city is like what's underground in people. Beneath the surface, it's boiling with monsters. Discussion, new location. Wilson proposes City Hall for new location if we can get a friend or colleague into office. WB will ask Pam to order blueprints of emergency shelter. Outstanding questions, what are the dimensions for the room? Discussion, birthday party ideas for WB. Notes, WB is allergic to chocolate. The underground of the city is like what's underground in people. Beneath the surface, it's boiling with monsters."

Envy reached across my lap and tapped the Stop button. "Whoa, that one was different. What's that about the monsters?"

It was unsettling, but I didn't have any answers. I could see why Danielle was disturbed. Aloud, I said, "Why would a corpse wake up to relay this information to a mortician?"

Envy was chewing her lips, not quite meeting my gaze. "If you ask me, that's the wrong question."

"I didn't—okay. If that's the wrong question, what's the *right* question?"

Envy grinned wickedly. "Why would someone want to kill Edgar Thornton? And then, of course the real question—who?"

It was a moment before I saw where Envy was going with this. As she sat twisting her hands in her lap with her newly-plumped lips pressed together, I realized she was expecting me to say something, so I said the first thing that came to mind. "No."

Envy's face crumpled as much as the Botox would allow, and she folded her hands beneath her chin. "But *why?*"

"Well, to start, investigating Edgar's murder is not our task! We signed up to help Danielle unravel that talking corpses mystery. That's it."

"That was all *before,*" Envy said, rolling her eyes. "Things have changed. Everyone knows the local cops are idiots. They'll look in all the wrong places for the killer. Starting with investigating the most obvious suspect."

Despite myself, I said, "And who's the most obvious suspect in your opinion?"

Envy took a breath. "Danielle's brother, Tony. Think about it, Pride. We know he's having financial problems. And we also know Tony is poised to inherit half the business upon Mr. Thornton's death. He had motive *and* opportunity. The police will be all over it like bees on honey."

"But Edgar was his *father*," I objected.

"That doesn't mean anything," Envy snorted. "Haven't you heard of the Menendez brothers? Or Lizzie Borden? People kill their parents for money all the time."

I sat back, leaning my head against the wall. I wasn't so sure it happened all the time, but I took her point. "I see what you're saying. But let me guess—with all your profound experience, you don't think Tony Thornton did it."

Envy nodded excitedly, ignoring my sarcasm. "Exactly. While the police are busy investigating the totally wrong guy, you and I can find the real killer."

"But Envy, what about our *task*? Don't you want to win? We're only two people. We can only do so much."

Envy threw up her hands and let them fall into her lap. "Well…maybe our task and the murder are related."

"And maybe they're not." I sighed and rubbed my eyes. "Envy, let's just focus on the corpses, okay? Let's be smart and let the police do their job."

"That's just it, Pride," she said, sliding off my bed and heading for the door. "I'm not like you. I'm not a thinker. I'm a feeler. And I *feel* like I don't care about talking corpses when a man is dead."

And before I could think of anything encouraging to say, she was gone.

I sighed, closing my eyes. I knew I was doing the right thing.

So why did I feel like a chump?

four

. . .

Long after the rest of the house was snoring away peacefully, I lay awake in bed, staring at the ceiling. I couldn't sleep. I glanced over at the clock; 3 a.m. I heaved out a sigh and sat up, throwing my legs over the side of the bed. I stood, stuck my feet into a pair of porcupine slippers I'd inherited from Envy, and trudged downstairs for a glass of warm milk.

As I waited for my milk to warm in the microwave, I listened to the deep silence of the house. I thought I could hear the surf lapping against the shore, but it was probably just the ambient buzz of electricity. Sinful House was really a sound stage at its heart, and there were hidden cameras and mics everywhere. Even when you were alone, you weren't really alone. Which isn't as comforting a thought as you might think.

When the milk was ready, I took my refreshment outside to the front lawn. I settled into a plastic yard chair and stretched my legs. From my vantage point, I could only see the Star of the Sea's back. But although I couldn't see her face, I saw her hands were still pressed to her cheeks, so it was a good bet that she was still screaming.

As I sipped my warm milk, I wondered what it meant. Maybe nothing. Maybe something.

Now, I really could hear the surf. I closed my eyes and settled in, enjoying the cool air on my face. Peaceful moments at Sinful House were few, and I tried to enjoy them when I could.

"You know, they cast you as Pride, but they probably should've cast you as Scaredy McScaredyPants," a voice said.

Remember what I said about never really being alone? This was doubly true for me. Ghosts have absolutely no boundaries.

I turned to see the ghost girl who had been haunting me most of my life sauntering over, her hands on her hips. She sat down in the empty chair next to mine, pulling her knees to her chest. She wrapped her arms around her legs and pulled them close. "You are the biggest scaredy pants I've ever met."

"Scaredy McScaredyPants?" I said. "Did you get that from Envy?"

The ghost girl smiled. "She says stuff like that a lot, doesn't she? I like her."

I nodded. "Well, you would. She's a schoolteacher. She probably has a lot of experience with kids. I guess you could sense that about her."

But the ghost girl shook her head. "No, that's not why I like her. I like her because she's brave. She sees a job that needs to get done, and she won't let anything stand in her way. She's unstoppable."

I chuckled. "Unstoppable? I don't know if I'd go that far."

The ghost girl lifted her chin defiantly. "Well, I would. Since she's lived here, she's tried her best to make everyone else around her happy. That's why she summoned that water elemental. Because you guys are all slobs." She said this while gesturing to the shovels Wrath and Greed left lying in the front yard. "It wasn't her fault that the water elemental went crazy and started destroying

Sloth's bedroom. The smoke elemental wasn't her fault, either. Gluttony was upsetting her because he didn't believe in feng shui. Envy just wanted to create good energy in the house. Not just for herself, but for everyone. And even the earth elemental was her way of helping you with the shopping for your task."

I grunted, but the ghost girl was right. Envy's heart was always in the right place, even if her tactics didn't always work out so great. "I have a feeling you're going somewhere with this," I said.

"The whole reason you're in Odyssey is because a bunch of weird stuff happens here that only you and the other Sins can help with. Envy takes that seriously. And don't you think Danielle and her mother deserve to know why poor Mr. Thornton was killed?"

I took a long, slow drink of my milk. "Of course they deserve closure," I said. "But it's not my job to mete out justice for the whole world. Everyone has to pick their battles. And I'm choosing not to pick battles that will pit me against the local police. I just want to walk the straight and narrow."

"Why? You broke into a *morgue* to see what happened to Walt. And *he's* a bad guy!"

"Well, I didn't know that at the time," I muttered.

The ghost stared at me a while. Then she said, "That statue got into your head, didn't it? You're worried about disaster and bad luck, aren't you?"

Now that the ghost had said it aloud, I realized two things: One, it was ridiculous, and two, it was true. I was just starting to get comfortable in my new life. I had a nice place to live, people who tolerated me, and a purpose I felt good about. Things were looking up…and then a wandering statue showed up on my lawn and threatened to turn everything upside down. The last thing I needed was to go off-script with a bad luck omen staring me in the face. I just wanted to play the game, win my task, and move on.

But even as I thought this, I knew I was kidding myself. Envy was right: the police were known to be incompetent. And Edgar Thornton's story *did* deserve to be told.

"Envy and I are already in trouble with the network," I explained. "That stupid incident with the earth elemental at the grocery store has us on thin ice. I can't risk getting in trouble with the police after that. And like it or not, I don't have permission to get involved with an ongoing murder investigation."

The ghost girl spread her hands before her. "Well…why don't you just ask for permission?"

I opened my mouth to respond but quickly closed it again. Then I sat there blinking like a moron. Because, actually, I hadn't thought of that. "Do you think they'd have me?" I asked.

The ghost girl tucked a lock of hair behind an ear. "I don't know. I'm just a kid. You're the grown-up. What do you think?"

"I don't know, either," I admitted. "They say it's better to ask for forgiveness than permission. But I'm not really an ask for forgiveness kind of person."

"You're really not," the ghost agreed. "Did you know that a newborn Chinese water deer is so tiny, you can basically hold it in one hand?"

I cocked an eyebrow at the change in subject. "A Chinese water deer? I've never heard of that. I think you made it up."

The ghost shook her head. "I didn't. And when they grow up, instead of growing antlers, they grow long front teeth. That's why they call it the vampire deer."

"Now I know you're making that up," I laughed.

"I'm not! Cross my heart. And did you know rats can't vomit, and that's why it's so easy to poison them?"

I snorted and finished my milk. "I didn't know that," I said.

"I'm surprised that after all this time, you haven't run out of animal facts."

The ghost girl smiled brightly. "I'll never run out," she said. "No matter how long you're here on earth, you learn something new every day. Even scientists are finding out new things about animals all the time."

I smiled and leaned back in my seat, crossing my legs. "Is that right?"

The ghost girl shrugged. "I don't know. It's probably true."

We were quiet for a long stretch, the ghost girl humming to herself as I watched the statute, looking for some sign to indicate what she wanted from us. But the statue didn't move. I must have fallen asleep at some point because I woke up when my chin dropped to my chest. Taking that as the only sign I would get tonight, I got to my feet and stretched. "I guess I'll turn in," I said to the ghost girl. "You gave good advice tonight."

"I know," she said, her spectral form already fading into the night. "I always give good advice. Sometimes, you're even smart enough to take it."

And then she was gone.

five

. . .

The next day, I headed down to the precinct.

On the way over, I rehearsed what I would say. It wasn't like I could just walk in and ask to be put on the Edgar Thornton murder case. If I knew one thing about cops, they didn't like to ask for help. I understood that better than anyone. So I needed to make it look like they were doing *me* a favor. That's why I allowed my sidekick, Beefy Camera Guy, to come with me. If I gave the cops a story about how the network wanted to do a fluff segment on my past as a paranormal investigator, they might be more willing to give me an inch.

It was the best I could come up with, anyway.

When I arrived, the station was mostly empty. A woman in uniform sat behind the desk drinking a cup of coffee. She gave me a disinterested look from behind her mug. "How can I help you?" she asked.

I tried on my best smile, the one I'm told is sometimes pretty charming. I stuffed my hands into my pockets and said, "Do you know who the lead investigator on the Edgar Thornton case is?"

The desk officer shuffled through some papers scattered on

her desk. Then, finding what she was looking for, she tapped the form with a finger and said, "That's Detective Kelly Doyle."

I stretched my smile. "Great. Is she in? May I speak with her?"

The desk officer grunted. "*He* isn't available right now, but if you call and…"

The officer stopped speaking mid-sentence as the front door opened and someone swept into the station, bringing with her the strong scent of perfume. I turned to see who the officer was frowning at.

The woman striding through the front door was Portia Cameron.

Portia walked right up to the desk, edging me out of the way without actually acknowledging my presence. She folded her hands on the counter and leaned forward, her smile made of ice. "April, you were supposed to have security at my house 20 minutes ago. Where is my security detail?"

April blinked, looking from Portia to me and then back again. "I'll be with you in just a minute, Portia," she said. "I was just helping, uh…" She gestured toward me vaguely, her mouth twisted into a little moue.

"Pride," I said. Every time I used that cockamamie name, it got a bit easier. "You were saying? About Detective Doyle?"

April leaned forward onto her elbows, her expression skeptical. "And what do you want to talk to Detective Doyle about?"

"Isn't it obvious?" I asked. "I want to talk to him about the Edgar Thornton case."

"Well, if you think you know something, we have a tip line. However—"

"I don't need the tip line," I interrupted. "I want to lend my services."

April laughed, her eyes widening. "You want to help the detective on the case? Who even are you?"

I could have kicked myself. This was the opposite of what I had rehearsed. Not even five minutes into this ordeal and I'd already screwed it up.

But before I could drag myself out of the hole I'd just dug for myself, Portia cleared her throat and elbowed me aside. "April, this really can't wait. I'm supposed to have an escort to my meeting in San Leonardo. Remember? We talked about this. You said you would send two uniformed officers to my house. But nobody showed up, and no one has called."

April held up a finger. "You'll have to wait a minute, Portia. Pride and I aren't quite finished talking yet, are we, Pride?" She fluttered her lashes at me in a most un-officer-like way. "I assure you, we have the city's best detectives working the Thornton case. If you want the number for the tip line—"

"There's a paranormal aspect to the case," I said, the words rushing out before I could rein them in. As soon as I heard them aloud, I wanted to slap myself in the face. But there was no going back now, so what the heck? I went all in. "I'm not at liberty to discuss the details, but unless Detective Doyle can talk to ghosts, he might miss some important information only I can provide."

Portia turned on her heel to face me, her lips pursed. "Something about the Thornton murder is supernatural?" she asked, her eyebrow arched. "Are you sure?"

"No, I'm not sure," I admitted. "But I have reason to believe—"

"Is it possible the murderer has supernatural abilities? Or is somehow—to use your word—paranormal?"

I thought about Envy's suggestion that the talking corpses and the murder were related. Then I mentally played through the voices I'd heard on Mr. Thornton's phone. That weird line about underground monsters echoed through my brain, and a chill ran down my spine. "Yes, it's possible," I said.

Portia looked me up and down with a new expression—not

quite interest, but a step or two above disdain, anyway. "Do you have experience working with the police?"

"Yes," I said again. "I worked with the San Diego police for several years. Detective Hidalgo and I—"

Now April's hand flew to her mouth, and her eyes went wide as she gasped. "Hold on a sec! You're Sid Sheridan, aren't you?"

I cast a sideways glance at the camera guy. They would have to edit the segment later. We weren't supposed to use our real names on the show, even though everyone knew who I was, thanks to being the only survivor of the Sam Lovelace fiasco. "Yes. I'm Sid Sheridan, paranormal investigator. And I'm here to offer my services to Detective Doyle to help solve the Edgar Thornton case."

April was still staring at me like she'd just seen a movie star when Portia grabbed me by my arm and tugged me around the officer's desk and deeper into the station. Over her shoulder, she called, "I'll take care of this, April. You get on the phone and send those officers to my home immediately, or I will call Chief Ramsey myself. Don't make me badmouth you to your boss." Under her breath, she muttered, "Police efficiency at its finest. I'm so glad to see my tax dollars at work."

I tried to object, but Portia wasn't listening as she tugged me down the hall. She led me to a door marked "Detective Kelly Doyle" and stopped, turning to face me. "I'm the most influential person in Odyssey," she said. "Not even the mayor has the connections I do. This is *my* town. And if there's one thing I can't stand, it's watching my career go down the toilet because some superstitious simpletons think my town is full of ghosts and shapeshifters. Do you have *any* idea what that could do to real estate prices?"

"This town *is* full of ghosts," I said, crossing my arms in defiance. "I'm not sure yet about the shapeshifters." I gestured toward the cameraman with a lift of my chin. "Portia, the town's supernatural tendencies are already well-known. It's all over television, for crying out loud." I sighed, blowing out my cheeks. "So, is this the part where you tell me to take my cameras and go home or else?"

Portia hesitated, the muscles in her jaw going taut. Her blue eyes went dark as a cloud passed over her features. I could almost see the gears in her brain whirring. Then she lifted her chin and sniffed. "No," she said finally. "Believe me, I would rather threaten you than ask for your help. I have a duty to protect Odyssey's reputation as safe for commerce, development, and investment. But instead…" She lowered her voice and stepped closer to me. "If Edgar Thornton's murder does have supernatural connections, I want you to prove it. Find the people responsible. Promise me. Promise me you'll find them."

I didn't want to promise Portia Cameron anything, not even when our interests aligned. She was a snake in the grass waiting to strike, and I didn't trust her further than I could throw her. But I suspected I needed her influence to get on this case.

Plus, there was a note of something in her voice that gave me pause. Something that sounded eerily close to sorrow.

I sighed, blowing out my cheeks. "I promise I'll do my best to expose the truth," I said. "But I'm not on your team, Portia. I'm on Edgar's team. Danielle's team. So if you tell me you're on *their* side, then you've got a deal."

Portia's eyes narrowed, but her lips cracked a smile. "You're not as dumb as you look," she said. "Okay. You do your job. Find the truth. And if that truth happens to look strange from the corner of your eyes, dig deeper." She pushed open the door to the detective's office. "Let's make you a paranormal investigator again."

———

Walking into Detective Doyle's office, a wave of nostalgia washed over me. How many times had I walked into Detective Hidalgo's office to discuss a case or go over evidence? It was a comforting feeling, walking into a room and knowing you would be helpful. But now, things were different. Detective Kelly Doyle was not Detective Aaron Hidalgo.

Not by a long shot.

Detective Hidalgo was barrel chested and broad shouldered, with dark, weathered skin, a salt-and-pepper beard, and a ready smile. He laughed big and smiled hard. In contrast, Detective Kelly Doyle looked like a private investigator from a black-and-white 1940s noir film. He was elegant and thin, with oiled blue-black hair combed away from his face. He had a sharp nose and a square jaw with a 5 o'clock shadow, even though it was still morning. He wore a plain white button-down shirt with the top button undone. He sat away from his desk, legs crossed, manicured fingers laced casually in his lap as he squinted at us. He was as different from Detective Hidalgo as night from day.

Portia put her hand on the small of my back and pushed me forward, gesturing toward a chair before the detective's desk. "Have a seat," she said with a smile. She took the chair next to mine, crossing her legs and folding her hands in her lap. She offered a frosty smile to the detective who had still not greeted us. "I brought you a visitor," she said.

Detective Doyle studied me, his expression utterly blank. Then his eyes flicked to Portia, and he adjusted in his seat, re-crossing his legs and clearing his throat. "What are you doing here, Portia?"

Portia leaned back, her foot bouncing lazily. "I understand you're the lead investigator on the Edgar Thornton case."

The detective dipped his chin in small acknowledgment. "I am," he said.

"Terrible what happened to Edgar. I can't imagine what his

wife must be feeling. Tell me, have you spoken to Mrs. Thornton? How is she holding up?"

The detective studied Portia with the same empty stare he'd given me. "She's doing as well as one can expect. She lost her husband of 50 years. I imagine it's been a shock."

Portia nodded. "Indeed. Do you have any suspects?"

The detective chuckled, leaning his head to the side. "You know I can't discuss the details of an ongoing investigation with you, Portia. So why don't you cut the bull and tell me what you want?"

Portia reached over and laid a gentle hand on my forearm. "I want to introduce you to someone. Pride here is one of the housemates on that reality show filming in town—*Sinful House*." She turned to me, her brows peaked. "You were America's Favorite Sin after the first airing, right?"

I lowered my eyes as my cheeks flamed red. "That doesn't count," I grumbled. "That was basically a fluke."

"In any case," Portia continued as though I'd said nothing, "Pride also used to work for the San Diego Police Department as a paranormal investigator."

"It's nice to meet you," I said, trying on my charming smile.

Detective Doyle scoffed, his gaze flickering toward me. I said nothing, bracing myself for the worst. In my experience, when you tell someone you're a paranormal investigator, you get one of three responses:

1. Politeness. These guys mutter something banal and gracious like, "Oh, isn't that fun" or "I once played Bloody Mary in the girls' bathroom in high school." This is a blow off. What they really mean is, "You're a complete nutjob to believe in that cockamamie nonsense, and I'm low-key embarrassed for you right now."

2. Fascination. These people get really excited and start firing off questions. "How did you get involved with that? How many ghosts have you seen? What do they look like? Have you ever been so scared you wet yourself?" These people hear "ghosts" and they think of stuff like *Amityville Horror* or *The Legend of Hell House*. They don't realize ghosts are mostly ordinary people who happen to lack a heartbeat.

3. Inexplicable hatred. These people treat you like you just kicked their dog. They hate you and everything you stand for, and there's no good reason for it. Maybe you inspire fear, or doubt, or maybe they think you worship the devil. Or maybe they're angry because they think you're taking advantage of poor schlubs who naively believe in the occult. Who knows? But these people will do everything within their power to reduce you to the nothing they already believe you to be.

I'll let you guess which bucket Detective Doyle fell into.

"I don't have anything to say to you," the detective said, his eyes narrowing as he summed me up. "And, frankly, I find people like you—people who prey on grieving families—sickening. If it were up to me, I'd haul you out of Odyssey by your ear and lock you up if you ever tried to return."

At my side, Portia chuckled, winding the string of pearls at her throat around a finger. "That's no way to talk to our guest, Kelly. Furthermore, it's no way to talk to your new partner."

The detective barked out his astonishment as he reclined further and clasped his hands behind his head. "You never cease to amaze me, you know that? Your audacity is absolutely *boundless,* isn't it? I know you've got half the city tucked in your pocket and the other half wound around your little finger. Good for you.

Everybody needs a hobby. But you don't get to just walk in here and tell me I have a new partner. This isn't politics; it's police work. I have a job to do."

"Of course it's politics," Portia shot back. "Everything is politics. You want to catch bad guys. I want to preserve property values. We want the same thing, Kelly."

The detective leaned forward and slapped his hand on his desk. "No, *you* want what's good for Portia. I want what's good for Odyssey."

"Adding Pride to your team is what's good for Odyssey," Portia said. "You need someone with these talents."

"What for?" The detective's eyes were wide and filled with incredulity. "Ed Thornton wasn't killed by a demon or a monster or a wight. He was murdered by a human with a gun. There's no such thing as magic or psychics or life after death, okay? All this hocus pocus you're so worked up about *doesn't exist.*"

It seemed particularly obtuse to claim the paranormal didn't exist in a town with a wandering statue and a Chinese restaurant staffed with incorporeal entities, but I figured it best not to say so.

Portia glared at the detective. "Then explain Peyton," she said quietly.

Something passed between the two of them, but I didn't have the context to know what. Finally, the detective sucked his teeth and turned to face me. "What's *your* angle? What are you hoping to get out of this? Money? Information on the family? I know you're not here out of the goodness of your heart."

This was the very moment I'd been preparing for. Clearing my throat nervously, I gestured toward the camera guy and said, "It's for the show."

The detective blinked. "You want to help investigate a murder for your *show?*"

I nodded. "Yes. Like Portia said, I used to work for the San Diego Police Department. The network wants to do a segment on my life before I came to Sinful House. They thought showing me back on the streets would, you know, make me more relatable to the viewers."

The detective scoffed and shook his head. "Right. Well, humor me a second, will you? Why do you think the Ed Thornton case needs paranormal investigation in the first place? From where I sit, the shooting looks pretty cut-and-dried."

"You think it was Tony Thornton, don't you?" Portia asked, a devilish twinkle in her eye. "You are so predictable. I swear, if I—"

"Shut up, Portia," the detective cut in. "Really. Just shut up." Detective Doyle looked at me again. "Well?"

Now I had a choice to make. I wasn't really at liberty to talk about the talking corpses, but if I didn't let the detective in on this information, my involvement in the case wouldn't make any sense at all. I took a breath and said, "Mr. Thornton's daughter, Danielle, suspects Remembrance Home might be haunted. She contacted the show to ask us to look into it."

The detective nodded. "So you think the haunting—your word, not mine—and the murder are related?"

I shrugged. "I don't know, to be honest. But it seems an angle worth looking at."

Detective Doyle's brow furrowed as he considered this. "What *exactly* do you propose, Pride?"

"Let me work the haunting angle alongside your murder," I said. "If my investigation turns up any evidence relevant to your case, I promise to hand it over to you. And if you find anything that might help me…" I shrugged. "You'll do me the same courtesy. It's a grieving daughter's wish," I added, hoping I wasn't overplaying my hand.

The detective sighed heavily as he leaned back into his chair. He looked from me to Portia, who was grinning like she knew she'd just won whatever game we were playing. Finally, the detective said, "One way or another, I'll have to agree to this, won't I? If I say no, I'll just get a call from the chief telling me to reexamine my priorities. Isn't that right?"

Portia leaned her head to the side. "It's almost like you're a psychic yourself, Kelly. You have an uncanny ability to predict the future."

The detective glared at Portia and then turned that same anger to me. "I'll let you know when it's safe to visit the crime scene," he said. "Anything else?"

I hesitated. "I may need to talk to some people. But like I said, if I find out anything, you'll be the first to know."

Detective Doyle snarled at me. "Sure, no problem! Contaminate my witnesses all you want. Portia here doesn't mind, and everyone knows she runs this city. Right?"

Portia just sat demurely, saying nothing.

I cleared my throat again. "I don't want to be an inconvenience. I just want to get to the bottom of this. So, I know it doesn't mean much to you, but I really appreciate it."

Detective Doyle scoffed. "You're right. Your appreciation means absolutely nothing to me."

Both Portia and I stood and moved toward the door. With one hand on the knob, Portia looked over her shoulder. "It was nice seeing you again, Kelly. Please give your wife my love."

I heard the detective curse as we closed the door behind us.

In the hallway, I jerked my thumb over my shoulder. "What was all that about? Did the guy cut up your paper dolls when you were kids? You two act like you're mortal enemies or something."

Portia laughed as we headed to the front of the station. She gave April a parting glare as we walked out the front door and headed into the parking lot. "Well, of course Kelly and I are enemies," she said, opening the door to her silver BMW. "He's my ex-husband."

six

. . .

When I arrived back at Sinful House, I went immediately to Envy's room to tell her the good news.

I found her sitting at her desk, hunched over Edgar's phone, listening to an audio memo. When she saw me, she stopped the recording and pushed the phone away with a sigh. "I was looking for you," she said. "I've been listening to these recordings all morning. I still can't make heads or tails of them."

I sat at the foot of Envy's bed and nodded. "Yeah, they're confusing. That's okay, though. The messages might not be our only chance to find the truth."

Envy sat up straighter, her eyes going wide. "Really? Did you learn something? Where *were* you, anyway? I figured we'd get a jump start on the day, but when I went to your room, you weren't there."

I waved my hand, dismissing this concern. "Yeah, I had things to do this morning. But you'll be glad to hear what I was up to. I had a change of heart. Well, not a change of heart exactly. A change of perspective."

Envy rolled her hand in a "get on with it" motion, and I took a breath and pressed on. "Last night, I started thinking about everything you said. And you were right. We are uniquely qualified to help find Edgar Thornton's killer, assuming his murder had anything to do with the talking corpses. So I figured, why not just ask the police if we could help?"

Envy blinked, her expression dour. "Just ask them. You thought you could just *ask* the police to join an active investigation?"

The way she said it made it sound like the dumbest idea in the world. How come when the ghost suggested it, it sounded plausible? "Well, I just thought it couldn't hurt."

Envy leaned her chin into her hand, the fingers of her other hand drumming the desktop rhythmically. "So that's where you were? You went down to the police station behind my back?"

A tiny twinge of guilt slithered up my spine. "I wouldn't say that," I said. "I mean, I didn't go behind your back. That makes it sound like I purposefully left you out of it. In actuality, I just never thought to invite you along."

Envy snorted. "You know that's actually worse, right? I mean, that's totally way worse."

When I'd walked into this room, I was so excited to tell Envy the good news. Now, I felt like I was drowning in quicksand. This kind of stuff is why I prefer not to deal with people. "Well, think of it this way. What if they'd said no, and then you'd gotten your hopes up for nothing? This way, I could spare you the emotional rollercoaster."

Envy sighed, shaking her head as she leaned back and folded her arms over her chest. "Quit digging. You screwed up, but that's okay. It happens. Next time, don't forget about me. I'm your partner."

I made an X over my heart. "I won't," I solemnly swore.

Momentarily appeased, Envy's scowl evaporated and was replaced with a lovely smile. "Okay. So. What happened?"

I was so relieved she didn't ask for an apology that I nearly passed out. "Well, I met with the lead detective on the case. This guy Kelly Doyle. He's reluctantly agreed to let us look into the Thornton case. We have to promise to stay out of his way, and if we find anything promising, we have to turn it over to him immediately. But otherwise, we're good. We have free rein."

Without warning, Envy jumped from her seat and threw her arms around my neck, squealing in my ear as she hugged my head with all her might. "I can't believe this! That's so amazing! I mean, it was awful of you not to invite me along, but whatever, I forgive you. This is such great news, Pride!" She sat back down, her hands pressed to her mouth. "But now I don't know what to do. Like, where do we start?"

I leaned back into my hands, my brow furrowed. "One thing Detective Hidalgo taught me is sometimes you have to start with a story. A 'what if' situation. So let's try this. What if Edgar Thornton heard something from the corpses he wasn't supposed to hear? Or maybe someone *thought* he heard something he wasn't supposed to hear?"

"*Boring* information," Envy drawled, rolling her eyes. "I mean, those recordings are not exactly *Dear Diary* level stuff, you know? We heard everything Edgar heard, and…"

Envy gasped, her words stuttering to a stop. She covered her mouth again, her eyes growing round. "Wait a minute," she breathed. "When I played those memos, I was listening for something out of the ordinary. Something suspicious. But maybe the clue we need is in what's *not* recorded."

I frowned. "What are you talking about?"

Envy pointed to the phone. "When we found Mr. Thornton's body, there was another corpse in the preparation room, right? That woman Karen McMurtry. But there's no recording of her on the phone."

I blinked. I hadn't thought of that. "Go on."

"According to the cops, Karen was a busybody blabbermouth. If anyone in this town knew secrets and scandals, it was her. So what if the killer purposely struck before Karen woke up? It wouldn't keep Karen from talking—but it would keep anyone from listening."

"But like you said, all the corpses just recited meeting minutes." I objected. "So even if Karen did wake up, chances are she'd just be babbling about bake sales or something."

Envy shrugged. "If you were a killer with a secret, would you take that risk?"

I stared at Envy a moment, mulling over what she'd said. It was a good starter scenario. I got to my feet and started pacing around Envy's room, my hands clasped behind my back. I always did my best hypothesizing on my feet. "That's not bad thinking, Envy. Good job. Okay. If you're right, we need to know who else knew about the corpses. Do you still have Danielle's phone number?"

Envy reached for Mr. Thornton's phone. "Danielle said her number is in here. Should I call her?"

I nodded. "Let's do it."

We put the phone on speaker and dialed. It rang for a while but eventually went to voicemail. "Hi, Danielle," my housemate cooed. "It's Envy. Call me back when you can. Pride and I have some questions for you. Please take care of yourself."

She disconnected and placed the phone back on the desk. "Well, what should we do while we wait for her to call us back?"

I hesitated, chewing my lips. "I have an idea," I drawled, "but you probably won't like it."

Envy donned a delighted expression and rubbed her hands together. "That sounds juicy. What is it?"

I took a breath. "We should have a chat with Karen McMurtry's partner in crime."

A heartbeat passed, then two. Finally, understanding dawned

on Envy's face, and she groaned, folding over the desk in mock pain. "Oh, no. You think we should go talk to that awful woman with the newsletter? Stephanie Jones?"

I nodded. "She and Karen were thick as thieves, right? If Karen knew something murder-worthy, I'd bet dollars to donuts she told her blabbermouth friend about it."

Envy sat up, still frowning. "If you want, you can leave me behind just this once." A hopeful smile lit up her face.

I shook my head. "Nope. We're in this together. Come on, Envy. Let's go talk to your biggest fan. As long as you don't summon any little people, we should be fine."

She glowered at me as she climbed to her feet. "That's not funny, Pride."

I didn't respond to that. But I thought it was a little funny.

———

Stephanie Jones owned a pet grooming boutique in the heart of downtown Odyssey. The shop was named All Dogs Go to Odyssey. I think the name was supposed to be a cute pun or something, but it didn't make any sense. And I say that as someone who spent far too long trying to make sense of it because I hated it when other people got jokes and I was the only one who didn't. (That happened a lot.) The best I could come up with was maybe she was trying to compare Odyssey to heaven, but boy, was that ever a stretch. In any case, the name of the salon wasn't the only unfortunate thing about it.

The boutique catered especially to toy poodles. As soon as we walked in the door, we were greeted by the yipping and yapping of tiny purse dogs dyed every color of the rainbow. I'm not kidding. The whole place was set up like a beauty salon, with chairs, sinks, mirrors, stylists and everything. But instead of human clients, each stylist was working on a pooch. Puff balls ranging from pink to lavender to sky blue and sunshine yellow set barking and yapping in every corner of the salon. I wasn't a fan of tiny purse dogs. I was especially not a fan of tiny purse dogs that looked like cotton candy but acted like they wanted to chew my face off.

(I know how that *sounds*, but I'm not afraid of poodles. Not exactly. Whatever, I don't have to explain myself. Everybody has inexplicable fears.)

Stephanie Jones saw us as soon as we walked in. She scowled at us from behind the counter, dressed head to toe in black. She wore one of those old-fashioned pillbox hats with a little net veil that covered half her face. In addition, she wore a long-sleeved black silk blouse, a knee-length black skirt, and sensible black shoes. A mourning outfit. Amid the rainbow of pastel puff balls, she stood out.

We approached the desk, and Stephanie pursed her lips in disdain. "Well, do my eyes deceive me, or is it the local hoodlums come to pay me a house call? I don't suppose you have an appointment," she asked wryly.

I tried to look nonchalant, which is pretty rough when you're terrified of getting jumped at any moment by five-and-a-half pounds of pure fluffy fury. But I did my best. "Hi there, Stephanie. We don't have an appointment. We don't have any poodles, either," I added.

At my side, Envy squirmed uncomfortably. "Hi, Stephanie," she croaked.

Stephanie scoffed and pulled a face. "If you don't have any dogs that need grooming, why are you here?"

"We want to talk about Karen McMurtry."

Stephanie froze, real tears pooling in her eyes. She blinked quickly, trying not to let the tears fall, but I saw how the name affected her. She swiped her face with her fingertips and sniffed. "You're here to offer your condolences?" she asked, glancing toward the cameraman. "The network sent you, right? To ease the tension between us? I'm sure they're worried about ratings."

"Our condolences. Yes," I lied, recognizing an in when I saw one. "But the network didn't send us. We're neighbors, after all. All part of the Odyssey community. When one of us suffers, we all suffer." I must have picked up that schmaltzy malarkey from Dr. Xena. It wasn't something I would normally say.

Or maybe Envy was psychically inspiring me. I wasn't sure which I preferred.

My fake sympathy seemed to do the trick, however. Stephanie's expression softened as she nodded, her shoulders slumping in her grief. "Karen and I were peas and carrots," she breathed. "We've been friends since we were girls. We grew up next door to each other. We even dated each other's brothers at one point. No one was closer to Karen than me. No one."

I nodded. "If you don't mind my asking, how did she die?"

Stephanie reached into a pocket and retrieved a handkerchief to dab around her damp nostrils. "She had a heart condition and passed peacefully. And she will be missed every day by those who loved her." Stephanie covered her face with her hands and cried quietly into her palms.

I didn't say what I was thinking, which was that from what I could tell, no one loved Karen McMurtry. Even the cops at Remembrance Home practically high-fived her death. Instead, I said, "Stephanie, did Karen have secrets she didn't share with you?"

Stephanie looked up, blinking. She wore an expression I couldn't read when she said, "Karen's secrets? I'm sure she did, yes. Everyone does."

"No, that's not what I mean." I paused to rephrase the question. "I mean, did Karen have dirt on other people that she didn't share with you? Maybe something, I don't know…like blackmail?"

Envy kicked me and shot me a glance, but I ignored her. I was working on pure instinct, throwing darts in the dark. I just hoped Envy's ability would land me a bullseye.

Stephanie sniffled and shook the hair from her face. "Blackmail? That's such a dirty word. It sounds so salacious. Well, I don't know about blackmail, but Karen knew compromising things about everyone, of course."

"Even you?"

Stephanie pressed her lips into a hard line. "Well, I…Excuse me, but why are you asking? I thought you were here to offer condolences!"

"We are," Envy cut in, her voice as soft as butter. "I know what it's like to lose a friend. Girlfriends mean so much to each other, don't they? You've lost your closest confidante. We thought you might want to talk about her." Envy fluttered her lashes and put on her most angelic smile. Really, she was pretty good at this whole dealing-with-grieving-blabbermouths thing. Especially considering how much she didn't like Stephanie.

Stephanie swallowed, new tears forming in her eyes. "Everyone in this town is treating me like a leper," she admitted. "They're avoiding me so they *don't* have to offer condolences. They hated her, you know? Because she called things like she saw them. But she was my dear friend. Do you know how hard it is to grieve alone?"

"I do," Envy said. "No one should have to grieve a friend by themselves. So do you? Want to talk about it?"

Stephanie chewed her lips, considering. She glanced around the salon to ensure no one could overhear our conversation. Then she stepped out from behind the desk and took Envy by the arm. "Let's talk outside," she said.

Envy and I followed Stephanie out into the sunshine. The day was clear and bright without a cloud in the sky. A gentle breeze blew, and I heard the scream of seagulls overhead.

"Karen liked to gossip, it's true," Stephanie said as soon as the door to the salon closed behind us. "But she was more than just a gossip. She had a big heart. That's why she helped me with the newsletter. I don't have the nose for news that Karen did," she admitted. "Karen had a gift. And she willingly and *lovingly* shared important news with the community. Although," she added, "she didn't always share *everything*. Even Karen knew some information shouldn't be disclosed."

Envy and I exchanged a glance, and my heart rate picked up. This sounded exactly like the kind of clue we were looking for. All we had to do was keep Stephanie talking. And Envy was apparently great at that.

"You and Karen were both doing good work, you know," Envy said. "Protecting the community and everything."

Stephanie linked her arm in Envy's, and the two fell into a rhythm, their steps aligning. "Protecting the community! Yes! See, you get it. When we ran that story about you, for example, the purpose wasn't to hurt you. It was to protect Odyssey from bigotry and bullying."

Envy hrmmed in tacit agreement, though I knew she had to be thinking the same thing I was, which was, "What a crock." But if Envy wasn't gonna call her on it, neither was I.

"I imagine she took a lot of secrets to the grave," Envy pressed on.

"I'm sure she did," Stephanie agreed. "And as sad as I am about her passing, it does give me some small relief, if I'm being honest."

Envy tipped her head. "Why?"

Stephanie looked pensive as the ocean breeze ruffled her hair. Her little black veil fluttered in the wind, casting web-like shadows across her tear-stained face. "Sometimes, I worried for her physical safety," she said finally, the words sounding like they came straight from a confessional. "She knew things she shouldn't, and there were people in this town who weren't beyond threats. If you know what I mean."

My heart did a cartwheel. "Threats? Someone threatened her?"

"Oh, all the time," Stephanie guffawed, nodding enthusiastically. "Like I said, she knew things she shouldn't. I worried sometimes that she'd share the wrong secret and someone would hurt her. One person in particular."

Envy stopped short, her face imploring. "Who? Stephanie, who wanted to hurt your friend?"

Stephanie looked around nervously, her fingers worrying the delicate studs on her ears. She chewed her lip, eyes flickering here and there. "This is really…I could get in trouble," she whispered.

"We won't tell a soul," Envy whispered. To the camera guy, she called out, "Please put that away. In fact, can you give us some space?"

I expected an objection, but Beefy Camera Guy merely lowered the camera to his side and backed away a respectful distance. I eyed Envy with a new level of respect. My housemate took Stephanie's hand in her own and said, "Tell me."

Stephanie was silent a long time. Then she nudged Envy forward, and we were walking again. "This happened years ago, so forgive me if I don't remember all the details. Karen and I were making a birthday cake in my kitchen when my phone rang. It was Charmaine Young. Do you know Charmaine?"

I nodded. "Sure. She's an actress, right? Played Titania in the most recent ORCA production."

Stephanie nodded. "That's the one. Anyway, she was calling because it had finally happened. Charmaine got her first big audition. She'd been trying to land a Hollywood gig for as long as I can remember. But between you, me, and the fence post, she's only a mediocre actress, so her career wasn't going anywhere. So landing an honest-to-goodness audition was a huge deal. She wanted me to put it in my newsletter. I told her I'd love to interview her for my article, but I was up to my elbows in frosting and couldn't do her justice at the time. But I was being sneaky, see. I really was excited for Charmaine. So I sent Karen to her house to do a surprise interview. You know, like a paparazzi thing. I thought it would be fun to surprise her. But after what happened next, maybe that wasn't the best idea I ever had."

I slowed my pace. "And why is that?"

"Karen sneaked into the backyard through the side gate. She heard splashing in the pool, so she figured Charmaine was celebrating by doing a few laps. Charmaine loves to swim. She was a champion in high school. Anyway, Karen sneaked around to the pool with her camera in hand. But when she got to the pool, she saw…something."

I stopped dead in my tracks as my heart seized and my blood ran cold. I held up a hand, and both Stephanie and Envy halted. "What did she see?" I asked.

"I don't know," Stephanie said, her voice hard as nails. "I don't know, and Karen wouldn't tell me. What I do know is Charmaine grabbed Karen and knocked the camera from her hands and kicked it into the pool. Then she told Karen if she told anybody what she saw, she'd kill her."

"That's pretty dramatic," Envy said. "But people say things like that all the time, right? I mean, as a kid, I told my brother if he told anybody I had to wear headgear at night, I'd kill him."

Stephanie swallowed hard, wringing her hands as we began walking again. "No, you don't understand. Charmaine has a temper. She's an actress, so she's good at hiding it. But I've known Charmaine for years. She could get hot, you know. Violent. Karen said when she looked in Charmaine's eyes, she knew she meant it. If she ever told anyone what she had seen, Charmaine really would kill her." She shook herself, her bottom lip folded under her teeth. "I've never told anyone that story," she said. "Not a soul. I never ran the piece in the newsletter about Charmaine's audition, either. It just didn't seem right. Especially since she didn't get the part."

We'd made our way around the block and were now headed back toward the salon. With the building in view, Stephanie unlinked her arm from Envy's, her spine straightening. "Well, thank you for your visit," she said, "but I need to get back to work. Please, don't tell anyone any of this, okay?"

I thought it was pretty rich for the gossip queen to beg us for discretion, but I didn't say so. "Your secret is safe with me," I said.

"And me," said Envy.

"And me," said Beefy Camera Guy.

Stephanie pinched her lips and strode purposefully into the salon, the door swinging silently closed behind her.

seven

. . .

Once we were in the car, Envy turned to me and rubbed her hands together excitedly. "I'd say that was successful! We have our very first suspect! If Charmaine threatened to kill Karen to keep a secret, she might kill Edgar to keep that same secret, right? Should we go question Charmaine?"

I nodded and put the car into gear. "She's definitely on our list. But first, I'd like to speak to Danielle and find out if Charmaine knew about the talking corpses. Because if she didn't know, she has no motive."

Envy made a thinking sound in her throat. "That's not a bad idea, but I think you're being a little shortsighted."

I quirked an eyebrow in her direction. "How do you mean?"

"Well, if Danielle says *no one* else knew about the corpses, that's one thing. But if she says even one person knew, then we have no idea how many people actually knew."

"We don't?"

"Didn't you even go to high school?" Envy asked, incredulous. "Okay, look. It's like this: the likelihood of a secret getting out is equal to the square of the number of people who know the secret. So, let's say Danielle only told one person. That's three people that know: Danielle herself, Edgar Thornton, and the mystery person. Right? The square of three is nine. So if she only told one person, we're actually looking at a total of nine people who might know it."

I hrmmed, unconvinced. "Well, why stop there? If nine people know the secret, couldn't they tell someone, and then *they'd* tell someone, until the whole world knows the secret?"

"Mathematically, sure," Envy agreed. "But at some point, you run out of people close enough to the secret to care. No one cares about the friend of a friend of a friend of a friend who had an affair. It's got to be intimate to mean something."

I grunted noncommittally. Although Envy's logic added up, I wasn't sure where she got the equation from in the first place. (I did go to high school, but my friends weren't the gossiping sort. Or maybe I just wasn't the person others gossiped to. On further speculation, that's rather likely. I was probably the one they were gossiping *about*.) Still, it did make a very human kind of sense. People—even leaving aside the Stephanies and Karens of the world—liked to talk. So even if Danielle only told one person, there was no guarantee that person didn't tell someone else and so on and so on.

Honestly, now that I was thinking about it, it made me never want to tell anyone anything ever again.

"Fine, I see where you're going with this. But in the meantime—"

I was interrupted by the buzzing of my phone.

I answered, holding the phone to my ear with my shoulder. "Hello?"

The voice on the other end was breathy. "Pride! Great, so glad I caught you. It's Sloth. Are you busy right now?"

"Not really. Why?"

"Pamela Arquette just emailed me back. The woman from

the historical society. She's at City Hall right now. I thought you might want to meet me there."

I glanced over at Envy in the passenger seat and let the phone drop away from my mouth. "Hey Envy, do you have anywhere you need to be? I need to meet Sloth at City Hall. Is that okay?"

Envy's phone rang then, and she held up a finger. "Hang on, it's Greed." Into the phone, she said, "Yeah? Uh huh. *Really?* Yes, awesome! Okay, thank you so much. You're the best." She disconnected and slipped her phone away. "I've got no plans."

I spoke into the receiver again. "Okay, I'll meet you in 10 minutes."

I thumbed the phone off and put it aside. "What did Greed want?"

"To talk to me," Envy answered with an evasive smile.

"About what?"

She giggled. "Nunya."

I knew this joke, so I let it drop and rolled my eyes. "You are such a child sometimes," I said.

"And you're nosy. So what's going on at City Hall?"

She had some nerve calling me nosy and then asking about my business. But I was bringing her along for the ride, so I guess she had a right to ask. I sucked in a breath, my eyes drifting to the rear-view mirror. "Sloth and I are looking into the history of Odyssey," I said to the camera guy. "But it's strictly off-camera. No footage. I'm dropping you off on the corner. You can take a rideshare back to the house."

Beefy Camera Guy shrugged his huge shoulders. "That's fine. It's a nice day out. Just let me out here; I'll walk."

I was already preparing my mouth to counter his argument when I realized he wasn't arguing. Maybe this new camera guy would actually work out. I pulled over, and the camera guy climbed out of the back seat, leaving his equipment behind. He flashed me a peace sign and said, "Catch you later."

Envy pressed her forehead to the window, watching him as he walked the opposite direction. "He's kind of cute, isn't he?" she said. "He's got a cute butt."

If there was one thing I wasn't going to talk about, it was Beefy Camera Guy's butt. "Listen, Envy. I need to tell you something."

I quickly explained the details of the Eleanor Romanowsky case as I drove the rest of the way to City Hall. Not everything, but enough to get her up to speed on the murder, Chenoweth, the laptop, and the map I'd found inside. "So that's why we're meeting with Pam Arquette," I concluded. "We're hoping she can tell us something about the local cemeteries. Assuming the star on the map marks graves, which is what Sloth and I both think, it could be a big clue."

Envy was quiet a moment before saying, "Eleanor was killed over a map?"

I nodded. "That's right," I said. "And that's why I had to tell you before I dragged you into this. It could be dangerous. So if you don't want to get involved, say the word. You can get a ride back to the house. Nobody would blame you."

Envy rolled her eyes and tossed her hair over her shoulder. "It's like you've never met me or something. All I want in life is adventure and excitement. I get so tired of all the Boring McBoringPants things I do every day. I'm not afraid of a couple faceless bad guys."

"They're bad guys with guns," I reminded her.

Envy looked out the window. "Everything worth doing costs something," she said. "No pain, no gain."

That was good enough for me. I parked the car and we got out.

———

Ten minutes later, we walked into Pamela Arquette's office at Odyssey City Hall.

Sloth was already there when we arrived. She was sitting on a loveseat across from an impressive-looking elderly woman with silver-white hair styled in a chignon with mother-of-pearl combs. She wore a perfectly tailored aubergine skirt suit and an eggshell blouse ornamented with a simple string of pearls. Her fingernails were elegantly manicured and painted a conservative nude color. When she saw Envy and me, she stood and donned what I could only call a politician's smile. She held out her hand and, though I'm usually hesitant to touch other people, I shook it happily.

"You must be Pride," the woman said with a smile. "I'm Pamela Arquette. It's so nice to meet you. I'm glad you were able to meet here at my office. I've been underwater lately."

I glanced around the ornately furnished room. "Are you…the mayor?"

Pamela laughed, a sound like bells chiming. "Goodness, no. Our mayor is Julian Gillespie. If you're going to live in Odyssey, you should know that," she said with a wink. "No, I'm the city manager." She turned to Envy. "I'm sorry, I don't believe I've had the pleasure. You are?"

Envy flushed a deep crimson and held out her own hand. "Envy," she said as they shook. "Nice to meet you, ma'am."

The older woman laughed and shook her head. "Please. This is California. Just call me Pam."

I sat down next to Sloth, and Envy took a chair beside Pam. When everyone was settled, Pam scooted to the edge of her seat, her hands folded neatly on her knees, and said to Sloth, "So what is the nature of your inquiry, dear?"

Sloth shot me a nervous look and cleared her throat. "Well, we wanted to know the history of Odyssey."

Pam smiled brightly, like a nine year-old-boy who was just asked to explain the premise of his favorite video game. "All right. Well, that's a very broad topic. Where would you like to start?"

Sloth fingered the end of her pigtail, her mouth scrunched to one side as she thought. "Well, for starters, how old is this town? When was Odyssey founded?"

"1785. We are the second oldest city in California after San Diego." Pam's voice was rich with pride as she spoke. "Odyssey was one of the first Catholic missions located along El Camino Real. The city's original name was Santa Angela de la Cruz. The mission was run by two padres—Father Lucien Alvarez and Father Dante Figueroa. They are credited as the founders of Odyssey."

Sloth nodded and glanced over to me. "Are the padres… buried around here?"

I had to admire Sloth's segue into the topic we actually cared about. I wouldn't have thought her so capable. But maybe she was being affected by Envy's magic, too.

Pam nodded. "They are, in fact. They're both buried at Haven of Repose, our oldest cemetery. It's where our most notable citizens and founders are laid to rest. It's south of here, near the outskirts of town."

"Does Odyssey have many cemeteries?" I asked.

Pam's eyebrows lifted. "Not many, but a few. Are you looking for your progenitors? Do you have family that might be buried here?"

"No," I said. "All my family vanished."

Pam blinked in surprise, and Sloth tittered, her cheeks coloring pink. "Have you heard of the Sam Lovelace commune?" she asked.

"Of course. That artist colony up in Santa Barbara." Understanding swept over Pam's face, and she turned her wide, unblinking eyes on me. "You're the baby they found," she breathed. "The lone survivor. My heavens. A celebrity in our own midst!"

I felt my face flush hot. "It's really not that big a deal," I mumbled.

"Pride's also a ghost whisperer," Sloth said, warming up to the conversation. "So all this cemetery stuff is like, professional curiosity."

Pam stared at me a moment longer, her gaze penetrating. I held her eyes for as long as I could, but then I had to look away. It's mortifying to have someone stare at you like that. It's like they can see all your secrets. As though realizing what she was doing, Pam suddenly turned away, looking back to Sloth. "Well, I wouldn't say we have *many* cemeteries, but we have a number. My parents are buried at The Longest Night just up the road. We recently added a new cemetery only a few blocks from here—it's called Playa View Memorial Park." She turned her gaze to me once again. "As our very own ghost whisperer, would you be interested in hosting a haunted cemetery tour? I hear we have a number of citizens who would be interested in such a thing."

I had to school my face to keep from scowling. See, this is why I usually keep this stuff to myself. "Anything's possible," I hedged. Anything wasn't. I'd rather die than host a haunted cemetery tour.

"You should consider it," she said. "Odyssey is a very haunted city if you know where to look." Again, I had to bite my tongue to keep from laughing. I was well aware of Odyssey's ghost infestation. "In fact," Pam continued, "while we're dishing about ghosts, I'll share this with you. Every mission in California is said to be haunted, but our mission, the old Mission Santa Angela de la Cruz, was perhaps the most infamous. The story is that an indigenous medicine woman known only as Magdalena was accidentally killed and buried on mission property. At night, her soul wandered the city, looking for sick and injured to tend. Whenever her soul came upon someone close to death, she stayed with them and comforted them until they passed. Then she guided their soul back to the mission where she ministered to them until their soul was healed and could cross over into heaven. To this very day, the mission and the property it stood on is considered the very *heart* of Odyssey." She chuckled and offered a thin shrug. "If you go for that sort of thing."

Sloth opened her backpack and retrieved a piece of paper, handing it to Pam. "I think this is a rough map of Odyssey from 1902," she said. "None of the streets or buildings are marked, so I'm not sure what I'm looking at. Does this look at all familiar to you?"

I peered over Sloth's shoulder and noticed that the map Sloth handed Pam was not the same paper we'd found in the laptop. Sloth had reproduced it, leaving off the tell-tale star underneath the mounds. She also hadn't reproduced the weird phrase "Nexus of Power" or the title.

Pam studied the hastily drawn document, turning the paper this way and that. "Well, it's not exactly a work of art, is it?" she asked, giggling good-naturedly. "Oh, I hope that wasn't offensive. It wasn't your child that drew this, was it?"

"Our producer gave it to us," I said. The lie slid easily from my lips, and I threw a sideways glance at Envy, who smiled. This glibness had to be her doing. You know, if being in Envy's presence meant I always knew the right thing to say, maybe our partnership would work out great. "The history of Odyssey is for a segment the network wants to do. So do you recognize it?"

Pam tapped a finger against her chin and nodded. "Well, it's hard to tell, given the lack of…precision," she said, diplomatically. "But it looks like it could be a sketch of our original downtown."

That piqued my interest. "Downtown? Really?" I leaned forward and pointed to the map. "So those half oval shapes—

could they refer to a nearby cemetery? Maybe the one you said was only blocks away?"

Pam shook her head. "Playa View wasn't around in 1902," she said. "But anyhow, those aren't graves. Those are mission archways. Here, let me show you."

Pam rose to her feet and strode across the office to her bookshelf where she retrieved a large, hardbound coffee table book titled, *A Photographic History of Spanish Southern California*. She returned to her seat, flipping the book open on her lap. "Here. See this?" She pointed to a black and white photograph of an adobe-tiled building where a series of curved archways formed a long outdoor corridor. "This is what the California missions looked like. Spanish architecture featured these curved doorways and windows frequently. Many early maps used those arches to indicate a mission."

I stood to get a better look at the book. Peering over Pam's shoulder, I said, "Interesting. I never noticed any mission downtown, though. What happened to it?"

"I'm not sure exactly," Pam admitted. "It disappeared ages ago. But for a long time, we had a museum here honoring the mission and Odyssey's early history. It was small, but it housed some sacred relics from the old mission, including Magdalena's grave marker. And if I'm reading this map right, these arches align to where the museum would have been."

My heart was thundering away in my ears, and I had to swallow down my excitement. "And what's there now?"

Pam shrugged. "Well, now we call it Old Downtown. It's a very quaint, very trendy area. There's a nail salon, a day spa, and a lovely little café called Déjà Brew. There's been some talk about designating the area a historical landmark so it can't be further developed. I'm in favor, of course, but not everyone is. It's a heated issue around town."

A disembodied voice drifting through the room interrupted

my oncoming epiphany. "Yes, I'll take two of those. Just put it on my card."

I looked around quickly, scanning for the ghost that must have appeared. I didn't recognize the voice—it belonged to a man, booming and clear. But it didn't take long to realize the others heard the voice, too, so it couldn't be a ghost. I opened my mouth to ask what was happening when Pam sighed, stood, walked over to the wall, and pounded on it three times.

"The acoustics in these old buildings are notoriously mysterious," Pam explained, a chagrined smile on her lips. "The mayor's office is next door, and if he stands in just the wrong place, I can hear every word of his conversation. It's annoying."

"I know exactly what you mean," Sloth said, her mouth scrunching up in a sad little twist. "It happens to me *all* the time."

Pam cocked her head to the side, eyeing Sloth quizzically. I think she was about to ask what Sloth was talking about when the office door opened. An older, broad-shouldered man dressed impeccably in a charcoal suit strode into the office. He was swarthy, with white hair that glowed like a halo around a handsome, creased face. He was clearly elderly, maybe in his 70s, but he radiated vitality. I could tell just from looking at him he was a politician. And I could tell from the way Pam looked at him that this was the mayor.

"I was standing in the danger zone again, I know," he said, holding his hands up like he was under arrest. "I was ordering my wife's birthday present."

"You ordered *two* of whatever you purchased," Pam said, her brow arched. "How many wives do you have?"

"I bought her Baccarat candleholders," he said, laughing. "I couldn't get her just the one."

Pam raised a hand to her mouth, smothering a smile. "Julian, you do realize candlesticks are sold as a pair, right? You might want to check your credit card statement. Baccarat? I have a feeling you just spent a small fortune."

Julian blanched, his whole body freezing as he mentally tallied the amount of money he'd just accidentally spent. But then he laughed as he recovered, dusting his hands together and shaking his head playfully. "Well, that's why we pay you the big bucks, Pam. We can't all be beauty *and* brains." He flashed her a bright smile and looked around the room as though suddenly realizing he and Pam weren't alone. "My apologies, I didn't realize you had guests. I hope I'm not interrupting anything."

I had been enjoying their banter until that point, but with those words, I deflated. I hated it when people said things like that. Obviously, he was interrupting something. When people say things like that, the implication is that whatever they interrupted wasn't important. But whatever. He was a politician. It was his job to say meaningless words.

"I've just been giving the newest members of our community a history lesson," Pam said with a smile. "Mayor, these young people are from that reality TV show *Sinful House*. You remember the one. Finding the right location was all Portia talked about for months." She spoke Portia's name like the syllables might be poison. "This is Envy, this is Sloth, and this here is Pride. And this," she said, gesturing toward the mayor, "is Mayor Julian Gillespie."

The mayor went around the circle, shaking everyone's hand in turn. When my fingers closed around his hand, a lightning bolt shot down my spine. Images flashed before my eyes—a camping trip, a fishing expedition on a small boat, drinks by a fireplace. And in each of these visions, I saw the same face.

Edgar Thornton's face.

"My condolences for your loss," I said, not realizing I would say the words until they were already out of my mouth. The mayor's expression darkened, and I hurried to explain. "Sometimes, when I touch people, I see things. I saw you and Edgar fishing. You must have been close."

The mayor stared at me, his face blank. But his befuddlement lasted only a moment. He composed himself quickly, squaring his shoulders and dropping his chin to his chest as his politician's instincts kicked in. "Thank you. Edgar and I were close indeed. He was a good friend all the way from childhood, and I am devastated to have lost him." He looked to Pam. "In fact, if I believed in such a thing, I might say we should be on the lookout for more ill fortune. Within a short amount of time, I lost my best friend, and Pam here lost her sister. That's two tragedies. These things always come in threes."

The mention of ill fortune brought the Star of the Sea to mind, and my mouth went dry as I recalled the statue's posture, the way she held her face as she screamed. It was just a coincidence, though, wasn't it? Two deaths that touched the mayor's office had nothing to do with the statue's appearance on our lawn.

Still, I couldn't shake Greed's words: "An unexpected visitor will bring disaster and bad luck."

I shuddered and looked away.

Envy adjusted in her seat, leaning forward and touching Pam lightly on the arm. "I'm so sorry about your sister, as well."

"Oh, they weren't close," Sloth interjected. As soon as she said it, she covered her mouth and blushed bright red as she turned to Pam. "I mean…you were estranged, weren't you?"

Pam gawped, lips twitching as her mouth fell open. Her gaze fluttered to the mayor, who offered only a bewildered lift of his shoulders in response. "I'm sorry," the woman stammered, blinking quickly, "but why would you say that? Did you know Fiona?"

Sloth waved both hands in front of her face, her cheeks growing impossibly redder. "No, I…oh, geez, I'm sorry. It was an accident. I didn't mean to see it. It was just right *there*," she explained, making a plucking motion by her forehead. She looked over to me, her expression harried and desperate.

It took me a second to realize she meant she'd accidentally read Pam's thoughts.

I made a patting motion at Sloth, and she settled down, though she reached for a pigtail and began chewing on it with a vengeance. I gave Pam what I hoped was a reassuring smile. "Sloth is a mind-reader. Don't worry; she's very ethical. She really tries not to look at other people's thoughts. But I guess she couldn't help but see that you and your sister weren't close."

Still visibly flustered, Pam re-crossed her legs and settled back into her seat, eyeing Sloth warily. "I see. Well, you're right, my sister and I were estranged. It was a stupid disagreement over *property* of all things. She owned a bit of land downtown that I rented from her. I wanted to buy it, but she wasn't interested in a sale."

"Was that before she got sick?" Envy asked. "I mean, she had Alzheimer's, right? That's what Danielle Martin told us."

Pam sat motionless a long moment before answering. "No," she said finally. "It wasn't dementia. She developed a condition called *atypical alogia*." She spoke the words with clinical detachment like a doctor delivering a poor prognosis to a bereft family. "She was incapable of speaking much at a time; no more than a few sentences, and that was considered a lot. And when she did speak, she could only recite things she'd read. Her mind grabbed onto written words like a vice, and she could parrot them back. But she couldn't produce her own thoughts."

"That's so sad," Envy said. "I'm sorry."

Pam tried on a smile, but it didn't quite reach her eyes. "It's all right. As I've said, we weren't close."

"I'm not close to my sister, either," Sloth said, her eyes downcast. "I'm sort of the black sheep of the family, I guess. Hadley—

that's my sister—she's everyone's favorite. When we were kids, I worshiped her. She's the oldest. I wanted to be just like her."

Pam nodded. "Fiona was a year older than me," she said, a hint of sadness underlying her words. "So I understand."

"It's strange how sibling rivalries work," Sloth continued. "All I ever did was idolize Hadley. So it never made any sense why she hated me so much."

The room fell quiet, and we all averted our eyes. I didn't have any siblings, so I couldn't relate to this. But based on my admittedly thin knowledge of human nature, it rang true. People hated each other for no reason all the time. You just had to read social media for five minutes to see that.

"Well, I don't want to keep you," the mayor said suddenly, clapping his hands together to break the uncomfortable silence. "When you finish your visit, Pam, would you mind coming to my office? I'd like to go over the proposed Bozeman budget for next week's meeting."

Pam nodded distractedly, and the mayor bid the rest of us a polite farewell before disappearing out the door. When he was gone, Pam cleared her throat and ran a hand gently over her hair, smoothing it back. "I apologize for that disruption," she said. "But it seems the mayor needs me, so I really need to get back to work. Was there anything else you wanted to know?"

"I think that's everything," Sloth said, climbing to her feet. Pamela returned the map, and Sloth tucked it carefully away. "You've been so helpful. We would never have figured out the arches on our own. Who knew there used to be a mission here in Odyssey?"

"Few people, I assure you," Pam said with a chuckle. "Odyssey has grown so rapidly that most of our citizens are transplants. Few of us have been here for generations, and even the older families probably forgot about the museum." Pam guided us to the door, her hands folded neatly before her. "Well, if you think of anything else, don't hesitate to get in touch. I am always happy to speak to our constituents."

As we filed out the door, I could just make out the mayor's voice drifting from his office. "Yes, I heard about Portia Cameron running against me. Her candidacy is a *joke*. That woman must have mounds of skeletons that will tumble from her closet the minute my people start to poke around. At least one of her associates has already been to jail!" He paused. "No, come on, Harlan, I wouldn't stoop so low as to ask Karen McMurtry anything—I don't care how good her information is. Besides, unless you've got a Ouija Board, that's a no-go. Didn't you hear? She passed away."

The door behind us clicked closed, and Pam Arquette breezed into the hall, leaving behind the smell of lilac perfume. "I just thought of something," she said. "You should come to the Coldwater silent art auction. We're trying to fund a much-needed performing arts center out on the outskirts of town. Lower property taxes," she added with a wink. "It's coming up soon—I'll put your names on the invite list. Bring your camera man. It'll be great fun." She gave a little finger wave and then hurried into the mayor's office.

Envy looked at me, her nose scrunched. "I think I'll be busy washing my hair that night," she said.

I chuckled. "I think we'll *all* be busy washing our hair that night."

"Not me," Sloth said. "Sounds like fun. Besides, my hair hardly ever needs that much washing."

To her credit, Envy physically bit her lip instead of responding to this as we headed back to the car.

eight

. . .

When we arrived home, I made a beeline for the kitchen, visions of fried chicken and tacos with mango salsa dancing in my head. It was almost time for 'family dinner,' and if there was one thing I loved about Sinful House, it was Gluttony's cooking. Nothing got me out of bed faster than the smell of his homemade biscuits and gravy or peach-pecan buttermilk waffles. Even thinking about his food made my mouth water.

But to my utter heartbreak, I found the kitchen empty. Nothing was on the stove, and the countertops were bare. My stomach growled in response, and I patted my belly absently. It wasn't like Gluttony to forget dinner, so I went to go find him.

I didn't have to look long. I found him upstairs, huffing and puffing as he dragged a mattress down the hallway. Beads of sweat popped out along his brow, and his t-shirt was damp.

"Uh, Gluttony? What are you doing?" I asked. "Not to be an ungrateful jerk, but there's no dinner in the kitchen. Are we not eating together tonight?"

Gluttony frowned and shooed me aside as he tugged the mattress over the carpet. Not wanting to look like a complete twit, I grabbed the front of the mattress and pulled. "Where are we taking this?"

"Here," he grunted, turning into Envy's bedroom. Inside, he leaned the mattress against a wall. "Can't you see I'm busy? If you're hungry, there are leftovers from yesterday. I ain't your mama, and you ain't helpless. Go heat something up and leave me be."

I glanced around the room, my face twisted in a frown. "What's going on here? These aren't even Envy's things. Where's all Envy's stuff?"

Gluttony tilted his head toward the hallway. "Ask Greed about it. I'm just doing what I'm told."

I left Envy's room and found Greed down the hallway in his own room. He was standing in a corner, arms folded over his chest, wearing an expression I couldn't read. The room was a wreck, and that wasn't like Greed, who was meticulous. But then I realized that wasn't the only thing different. The room was a tangle of furniture, books, trinkets, and clothes—Envy's clothes.

"Greed?" I gestured around at the mess. "What the heck is going on here?"

Before Greed could answer, Envy popped out of the closet, a huge smile on her face. "Have you seen this closet?" she asked. "It's like twice the size of my old one. Look at this." She bounced over to the large set of windows that made up most of the western wall and spread her arms wide, indicating the view of the beach. "Remember when we first moved in, and I was *so* sad because my room faced east? Well, Greed's room faces west, and he's agreed to switch with me. That's why he called me earlier." She squealed, hopping up and down with excitement. "This is like, the best day of my life."

Greed was still standing quietly in the corner. He wasn't smiling. His gaze was soft and distant, and his lips twitched just a little. If I had to guess, I'd say he looked pensive, but my knowledge of Greed's expressions was minuscule. "Greed? You're switching rooms with Envy? Why?"

Lust sauntered into the room then, her hair falling in long, loose waves over her shoulders. As soon as I saw her, my heart skipped a beat. Man, she looked great. She was wearing a bright red midriff with white capri pants that showed off her curves. Her feet were bare, and her toes were painted bright red to match her shirt. I was halfway in love with her all over again before I scolded myself to get it together. Whatever I thought was happening between me and Lust was a figment of my imagination. I'd seen the way she'd snuggled up to Greed when our new assignments were handed out. She wasn't into me, she was just flirty. I couldn't forget that.

But it sure was rough.

"Greed had another premonition," Lust said, her voice all sultry and velvety. "It happened today while we were driving around town." She paused, glancing over at Greed. It was only now that I realized their expressions matched. They looked somber.

My stomach did a little flip. Something was wrong.

"What did you see?" I asked.

Greed was quiet for a long stretch, and with each word he didn't speak, my anxiety grew, inching up my spine. "Greed? Hello? What's going on? What was your premonition about?"

"You," he said simply, not looking in my direction. "And Envy. I saw you and Envy in a room full of fire."

The room fell silent. Envy stepped away from the window, coming nearer to Greed, but stopped at a heap of clothing on the floor. "What? You didn't say anything. Why didn't you tell me?"

"I'm telling you now," he said. "I don't mean to be glib. I was waiting for the right time, but the feeling is starting to fade, so it's now or never. I saw you and Pride in a dark room with flames licking up the walls. I smelled smoke. I heard screaming." He let his gaze fall on Envy. "I saw flames reflected in your eyes. And though I can't be sure," he drawled, "I think I saw one of your elementals. A being made entirely of fire."

Envy blanched, covering her mouth with both her hands. Ever since she'd arrived at Sinful House, Envy had been accidentally—well, sometimes on purpose—summoning elementals to help around the house. First, she summoned a water elemental to keep the house clean. That ended in disaster for Sloth, who found all her things drowning in the undine's continual deluge. Next, Envy tried to rid our house of negative energy by letting her air elemental cleanse the place with smoke. Of course, the elemental went crazy and the entire house was so smoke-filled, one of our neighbors called the fire department. Our furniture would smell like patchouli for weeks. And then, most recently, she summoned an earth elemental to help with the grocery shopping. She lost control of him too, and the gnome threw a tantrum, throwing bread everywhere until local blabbermouth Stephanie Jones called security and got us in trouble with the network.

Envy's track record with elementals was not great, to say the least.

I turned to Greed, hands held out before me. "I'm not following," I said. "What does this have to do with switching rooms with Envy?"

Greed chuckled darkly, his chin falling to his chest as he smiled. "Envy has wanted this room since the beginning. A quick Google search shows that having a bedroom in the western part of the home imparts a healing spirit to the room's inhabitants. I suspect that if her temperament is more balanced and her thinking clearer, she might be less apt to accidentally summon elementals she can't control. A fire elemental is dangerous enough. Coupled with the bad luck the Star of the Sea brings?" He sighed morosely. "I may be your competitor, but that doesn't mean I want you to *die*."

My thoughts drifted to something the mayor said earlier, and I muttered, "Tragedy always comes in threes."

As soon as I said this, Gluttony stormed into the room, his nostrils flared. "All right," he growled. "I've had enough of this talk about bad luck. I don't know what that statue in our yard is supposed to mean, if it means anything at all. All this doomsday talk about bad luck ends now. I want all of you to meet me downstairs in ten minutes."

Envy looked over her shoulder at the mess that was her new room. "Uh, but we're not fini—"

"*Ten minutes*," Gluttony growled again before stomping out of the room.

I listened for the sound of footsteps retreating downstairs. Then I shrugged. "You heard the man. Ten minutes."

Leaving Greed and Envy to finish their swap, I went back to my room and shut the door. Just as I was taking off my shoes and eyeing my favorite pair of Star Wars pajamas, my phone buzzed atop my desk.

Except it wasn't my phone. It was Edgar Thornton's phone. Envy must have put it in my room so it didn't get lost in the move.

I hesitated, unsure of the protocol for answering a dead man's phone. But when I saw who the call was from, I picked up. "Edgar Thornton's phone," I said.

The line was silent for a beat. Then, Danielle said, "Is that you, Pride?"

"It is. Danielle, why are you calling me on this phone?"

Danielle sighed heavily into the receiver. "I could ask the same question. I said you could reach me anytime, and that my number was in my father's phone. But I didn't expect you would actually call me from my father's number. Do you know how disconcerting it is to see a missed call from your late father? You almost gave my poor mother a heart attack."

I groaned as a flush crawled into my cheeks. She was right. That was idiotic of us. "I can only imagine," I agreed. It was as close to an apology as I could get. "It won't happen again. Listen, we called to ask you a question."

"All right. Whatever you need," Danielle said.

"We need to know who else knew about the talking corpses. Besides you, your brother, and your father."

For a moment, Danielle said nothing. "Well, it was a secret," she said at last. "We didn't want anyone to know."

"That doesn't answer my question. Look, this is important. It might be a clue in your father's murder."

Danielle was quiet a moment. When she spoke again, her voice was breathy. "Why are you asking questions about my father's murder? Are you working with the police?"

"Yes," I answered. "Sort of. Can you just answer me? Who else knew?"

I heard Danielle take a sharp breath on the other end. "Well…I don't know what use it could possibly be to you, but the only person I told was my realtor. I needed to know if a haunting would affect our property value," she explained.

My mouth went dry and my palms filmed over with sweat. "Danielle, your realtor wouldn't be Portia Cameron, would it?"

Danielle hesitated. "Yes, that's right. Why?"

"No reason," I said, my thoughts racing. "Hey, did you happen to tell her what the corpses said?"

"No, I didn't. Why do you ask?"

My thoughts were going a thousand miles a minute, and I wasn't ready to verbalize anything yet, so I said, "I'm just trying to piece together who knows what. Listen, I gotta go, Danielle. I'll talk to you later."

I hung up the phone, my thoughts drifting back to my visit at City Hall. What had Mayor Gillespie said about Portia's campaign? Something about a host of skeletons falling out of her closet once anyone started to look? He was probably right about that. As a mayoral candidate, Portia might have motive to silence the likes of Karen McMurtry, especially if she didn't know all the corpses just spewed indecipherable nonsense.

But I didn't have time to think about that in any detail. I needed to meet Gluttony and the rest of the house downstairs.

———

The kitchen table set with seven bowls of caramel popcorn—one for each housemate. The camera crew was already waiting for us, lined up against the wall, cameras rolling, their red lights blinking annoyingly. I sat at my usual place and waited for the rest of the house to appear. When we were all present, Gluttony folded his hands over his ample stomach and leaned back, his eyes narrowing as he studied each of us. "Ever since that statue appeared, y'all have been acting like we're doomed," he said, his voice grave. "Wrath and Greed made a huge mess in our front yard—and I'd like to point out that you haven't filled in that hole you made. I suggest you get to that. We don't need the HOA harassing us about it."

"Oh, they've already been harassing the network," Sloth chimed in helpfully. "The president of the HOA called Tricia directly. Tricia promised to send a landscape crew to fix anything we messed up."

"That's what we should have done in the first place," Wrath scowled. "Called a crew to remove the statue. I mean, look at these hands, man." He held them up, twisting them this way and that. "Do these hands look like they know how to do manual labor?"

"I didn't ask you all here to talk about the HOA," Gluttony cut in, his voice booming over the others. "I want to talk about your attitudes. Listen. I don't know much, but I know one thing.

Life is what you make of it. If you go looking for bad things, you will find them. Bad things are everywhere, statue or no statue. But I also know if you go looking for good things, you'll find that, too. So, I want y'all to eat this popcorn because it's delicious, and I made it myself. And then I want us to go around the table one by one and talk about something good that has happened since you've been at Sinful House."

If there was one thing I hated—well, it was shopping. But if there were two things I hated, the first was shopping, and the second was being forced into group activities. I wasn't in kindergarten. I didn't have to let Gluttony boss me around. But even though I wanted to object, Gluttony's heart was in the right place. And talking about good things that happened since we'd been at the house couldn't hurt.

I mean, I wasn't sure it would *help*, but whatever. The cameras were rolling, and cooperation would probably win me some votes. Plus, we had popcorn. I shoveled a handful into my mouth. It was sweet, buttery, sticky, and chewy, and I instantly felt refreshed when the sugar and salt hit my tongue.

"I'll go first," Envy said. "Since we've been at Sinful House together, I've gotten a brand-new bedroom that overlooks the ocean. Now I get to fall asleep listening to the waves crashing on the shore like I was destined to. I bet with all the amazing beauty rest, I'll get *so* many new Instagram followers."

"I'll go," Sloth said. "Since I've been at Sinful House, Gluttony has baked two dozen complimentary muffins just so I'd have a good day. That was really thoughtful of you," she said to Gluttony. "But that's not the only good thing that's happened. I also met a nice old woman who became my friend, and I cared for her quite a lot. Unfortunately, she ended up getting murdered."

Gluttony pounded the table, making our popcorn bowls quake. "Don't do that," he said. "I mean it. Good things only."

Sloth sucked in a breath. "You didn't let me finish. She got murdered, but we took her ghost to a really nice clubhouse for ghosts, and I think she's going to enjoy the rest of her afterlife there. The end."

When no one else immediately volunteered to go, I lowered my eyes and kept very still. I thought maybe if I didn't look at anyone, I'd become invisible, and I wouldn't have to play this absolutely mortifying game.

"I won last week's vote," Wrath said. "That's mine."

"And I signed a contract to publish a new article on personality disorders," Greed added.

"That's great, Greed. Congratulations," Gluttony said with a nod. "My sister had a baby. I'm an uncle."

Murmurs of congratulations went around the table before everyone went quiet. I felt my face burn hot. Had everyone gone? Was I the only one left? I held my breath and squeezed my eyes shut like a child who pretended if they couldn't see, they couldn't be seen.

Maybe I was still a kindergartener after all.

"Since I've been at Sinful House, I met someone who has become important to me. I've discovered that sometimes, your heart can take you for a wild ride."

I looked up to find Lust across the table, staring right at me. "I met Pride at Sinful House," she continued, "and that's made all the difference."

I was about one millisecond away from bursting into flames, so I dropped my gaze back into my lap, my palms practically dripping sweat. This was a plot twist I was not prepared for. What did she want from me? Was this an olive branch? Was this just Lust being Lust? Was she doing this for the viewers? I looked to Envy, hoping her expression might clue me in to how I should feel. But she was shoveling popcorn into her face, paying no attention to my absolute mortification.

"Pride," Greed said, "would you like to respond to Lust?"

Respond? To Lust? Right here in front of everyone? I would have sooner cut my finger off with a rusty pocket knife. But instead of saying that, I squeaked out, "I've enjoyed meeting you as well, Lust." Which was true, even though it left out the finer points of what meeting her made me feel.

"This is good," Gluttony said, his mouth also full of half-chewed kernels. "See, this is what I'm talking about. This is how a family is supposed to behave. It's your turn, Pride. What good things have happened since you've been here?"

"I don't want to do this," I admitted. "Not because nothing good has happened here, but what if…I don't know, what if talking about the good things jinxes it?" That wasn't the real reason I didn't want to talk about this, but I wasn't going to admit that in front of actual living humans. "It seems to me like shining a light on your blessings is asking the universe to snatch them away."

Gluttony scoffed, shaking his head. "That's not how the universe works. You don't jinx good things by talking about them. You make more good things happen. If you want something positive in your life, speak it into existence, Pride. If I learned nothing else from my mama, I learned that. The universe is always listening. Speak what you want into existence."

I scooped a handful of popcorn into my mouth just to buy some time. Finally, I said, "You know what I really want? I want things to be simple. I want things to make sense. I want people to say what they mean and mean what they say." I turned my gaze to Lust and stared at her until she pressed a napkin to her lips and looked away.

"I'll drink to that," Wrath said, tossing a kernel into the air and catching it in his mouth. "Anybody want to join me for an after-popcorn cocktail?"

As we all pushed away from the table and the others followed Wrath to the recreation room, I followed Gluttony to the kitchen.

Looking over my shoulder to ensure no one was listening, I asked, "So, what did you put in the popcorn this time?"

Gluttony raised an eyebrow. "The popcorn? What do you mean?"

"You know," I said. "So? What's in it?"

"Well, all right, I guess I can share my secrets with you. Didn't take you for a candy-maker, though. That caramel is made with butter, cream, sugar—"

"Hilarious," I interrupted. "That's not what I'm talking about. I'm onto you, Gluttony. You always put magic in our food when you think there's a problem. So what did you add this time?"

My housemate grunted, picking up a rag to wipe down the counters. "Don't worry about it, Pride."

"But I *am* worried about it," I pressed, "because I don't like surprises. I don't want to be forced to tell the truth, I don't want to get chatty with strangers, and I don't want to walk around telling people how beautiful they are! So what did you spike the popcorn with?"

Gluttony heaved a sigh and shook his head. "Well, if you have to know, I put good luck in it. Y'all are so worried about that statue outside, and since we can't seem to move it, I thought I'd counterbalance it with some good juju."

I frowned. "So does that mean you believe the statue is a bad omen, too?"

Gluttony shook his head. "No. But y'all do. Beliefs matter, Pride. Your brain creates your reality. If you believe a thing, you manifest a thing. So go on, get out of my kitchen. Go enjoy your good luck." He winked and gestured toward the recreation room. "I'd start with Lust. She obviously has a thing for you."

"There's nothing obvious about Lust," I grumbled under my breath. "At least, not to me. But anyway, thank you. For the honesty and the good luck magic, I mean. Just…thanks."

I ambled out of the kitchen and trekked up the stairs to my room. I was feeling better already. With each step, I could literally feel my luck changing. Maybe Greed's weird feng shui would stop Envy from lighting us on fire, maybe it wouldn't. But with Gluttony's good luck magic coursing through my veins, I no longer had to worry about it.

For the first night in a while, I slept like a baby.

nine

. . .

"You're crazy if you think I'm not coming with you."

Sloth and I were slipping on our shoes and heading out to Déjà Brew when Envy cornered us, hands on her hips and determination in her eyes. "We're partners, Pride. Remember?"

I pushed around her, reaching for the door. "It's not a good idea, Envy," I said. "Sloth and I just need to take care of something really fast, and then you and I can go back to working the talking corpses case later today."

But Envy was not dissuaded. She elbowed me aside and planted herself in front of me, one hand on each side of the doorjamb, blocking my path. "You're not leaving this house without me," she said. "I need excitement, Pride. I'm so tired of watching everyone else's life on social media. My baby cousin got married last weekend, and you know how my love life is? I haven't had a date in six months! My other friends are climbing the corporate ladder and progressing their careers, and I'm still stuck in the same teaching position I've had for the past 10 years. And I love teaching. But I want something exciting to show for my life, too. It's not fair for everyone else to have all the fun. So if you think you're getting out of this house without me, you've got another think coming." She paused. "Do you want to take it right now?"

I growled. "Take *what* right now?"

"Your other *think*," she said with a grin. "You have one coming, after all."

I sighed and turned to Sloth, looking for help. But Sloth just shrugged and gestured with her chin toward the car. "If she wants to come, I say we let her. Three heads are better than two and everything."

I didn't think that was true, but it looked like I was outnumbered. With a dejected sigh, I nodded wearily. "Fine. Just let me and Sloth do all the talking, okay? And when we get there, don't touch anything. And whatever you do, don't *summon* anything."

Hands still planted in the doorway, Envy glowered at me and rolled her eyes. "*Obviously* I wouldn't summon anything. *Obviously* I'll be on my best behavior." Then she clapped her hands in excitement, bouncing on her toes as she squealed. "Oh my gosh, I've never been to a haunted café before! This is going to be the best day of my life."

As we headed for the car, I heard the soft whir of a spinning motor followed by a quick slurp. I turned around to see Beefy Camera Guy with his bag slung over a shoulder, drinking what looked like green sludge from a personal blender.

"Oh no, not you," I said, holding up a hand. "This is personal business. You're not invited."

"I'm real sorry, but the network says I've been too lenient with you," he said, licking a smear of green smoothie from the corner of his mouth. "They'll give me my walking papers if I don't tag along everywhere you go today. I've got a wife at home and a new baby on the way. I can't lose this job."

I did feel a twang of guilt at that, but there was no way I was letting the camera guy tag along. I didn't even want to get Envy involved. "Listen, this is my call, and I'm not taking 'The network said so' for an answer. I may have signed a contract, but I still have a personal life. Don't make this weird."

The camera guy laughed and gave me a genial clap on the arm. "Can it *get* any weirder?" he asked. "This is the weirdest job I've ever taken, and I worked on the set of *Dating Bigfoot*."

"And if you want to live to shoot *Marrying Bigfoot*, you'll go back inside and pretend you never saw us."

He huffed, huge shoulders sagging. "Fine. Have it your way, boss. But don't be surprised if your numbers go down this week. Again."

I said nothing to that, but I brooded over my tanking popularity all the way to Old Downtown. When we arrived at Déjà Brew, we had to stand in line for nearly 10 minutes as only one barista was working. Thankfully, that barista was Felix. As soon as he saw me, however, his expression darkened. "Can I get you something?" he asked, eyes darting nervously around the room.

"You definitely seem capable," I said, trying on my best movie-star smile, which, let's be honest, was C-list level at best. "We were just headed downstairs. I assume that's okay?"

Felix folded his arms across his chest and shook his head. "Afraid not. New rules. The Crypt is off-limits until further notice."

I blinked. That was a predicament I didn't see coming. "Off-limits? Why?"

"I've been having trouble with one of the ghosts," Felix explained. "Somebody has been sneaking up the stairs and scaring the bejeezus out of my customers."

I quirked an eyebrow. "How? What's the ghost doing?"

"Shouting," Felix said with a sigh. "First it was pieces of poetry. Then it was corny jokes like you'd find on popsicle sticks. Most recently, it was recipes. The upside is, now I know how to make potatoes au gratin." Felix chuckled, shaking his head. "Anyway, I figured if we keep the door closed, the ghost can't sneak up here. So for now, no one goes into the Crypt."

I furrowed my brow in frustration. "Well…why don't you just ask the ghost to quit?"

"I tried that," Felix said. "But it didn't work. And it doesn't help that I can't see the culprit."

I frowned, tilting my head to the side in thought. "Wait a second. You can't see this ghost? It's invisible?"

"Appears so."

Sloth elbowed me playfully in the side. "Appears so. Get it? But it's invisible?"

"But you can hear it?" I asked, ignoring her. "And the *customers* can hear it?" That was the strangest news of all. Most people could neither see nor hear ghosts unless they were whisperers like me and Felix.

"That's right. Anyway, you can appreciate that I didn't want a ghost running around shouting recipes at my customers. So until I have time to figure that all out, nobody goes downstairs."

I ran my fingers through my hair. "Okay, but Felix…ghosts can go through walls."

"I know that," he grumbled. "But I'm hoping if I don't disturb them, they won't disturb me. The woman who owns this property was in here about a month or two ago. She's thinking of selling to a developer—condos, you know? She was real nice about it—said she'd give me a cash for the trouble of moving the store. So the last thing I need is for ghosts to mess that up for me."

"They're gonna turn Déjà Brew into condos?" I wrinkled my nose in distaste. "But this place is historic! Didn't there used to be a mission here or something?"

Felix shrugged. "I don't know. Maybe."

"Well, what about the ghosts?" I asked, my mind still turning. "Where will they go?"

"Yeah, that's a concern," Felix agreed. "Also, the Society will have to find somewhere else to operate. There's a lot of moving parts. Now, can I get you anything?"

Sloth sauntered up to the counter, chewing idly on the end of one of her pigtails. "Actually, can I get a double espresso?" As if underscoring her needs, she stretched her arms overhead, yawning noisily. "These early mornings are for the birds."

Felix quirked an eyebrow. "It's 10 a.m.," he said.

Sloth dug her knuckles into an eye socket and rubbed sleepily. "Yeah, that's what I mean. Better make that a triple. It's for Sloth."

The three of us found an empty table and slid into our chairs. When we were sure Felix wasn't paying us any attention, Envy leaned forward and whispered, "So, you know what we have to do, right?"

I raised an eyebrow. "What's that?"

A slow smile curled over her lips. "We'll have to come back here tonight when the place is closed and sneak in."

Sloth raised an eyebrow. "Sneak in? You mean *break* in."

I held my hands out in front of me, palms out as I shook my head. "Hold your horses there, Catwoman. We're not breaking into anywhere. No chance. Going to jail isn't part of my contract."

"There's a new moon tonight," Envy continued as though I hadn't spoken. "That means it'll be dark. We'll come down here late—maybe around two, three in the morning. We'll sneak into the café and go downstairs and investigate. It shouldn't take long, right? An hour, tops? We'll be out of here long before the commuter crowd even wakes up."

"Envy," I said, my voice sounding strained even to my ears, "this isn't a game. This is real life. You can't just break into someone's business. It's wrong on so many levels!"

"Well, we have to investigate that map," she pressed on.

"What's down there? Why is there a star in the spot where Déjà Brew is today? People are *dead*, Pride. And this map is our best clue why."

"Yes!" I threw my hands up in exasperation. "Exactly! People are dead! That should be a starred reason in the Why We're Not Doing This Column, Envy!"

"Well, it's not," she retorted. "People have gotten killed over this, and the three of us are the only ones looking into it. But hey. If you don't want to go?" She gave a carefree shrug and turned her attention to Sloth. "You'll do this with me, won't you?"

Sloth traced a finger lazily over the table, making designs in the sugar someone had spilled. "Me? Yeah, I guess so. Sure, I'm in."

Envy gave a crisp nod and sat back in her seat, a smug smile playing over her lips. "So then it's settled. Sloth and I are on the case. Pride, you can stay home and watch TV or paint your nails with all the other girls."

I knew she was trying to goad me. This was, like, Reverse Psychology 101. I wasn't going to fall for it. I wasn't. I *wasn't.*

I turned to Sloth and gave her my best look of reproach. "You know this isn't a good idea," I said. "Come on, Sloth. This is nuts."

"Yeah, it kind of is," Sloth agreed, "but Envy's right. We haven't come this far to give up now. At least, I haven't. So if you want to sit this one out, that's fine. But I'm with Envy. Besides." She offered me a reproachful look of her own. "You didn't think you could peer pressure me into being a weenie, did you?"

Busted. I absolutely thought I could do that. I should have known better—Sloth looked harmless, but she was actually pretty hardcore underneath her jelly-stained pajamas. "Fine." I blew out my cheeks in defeat and leaned back in my seat. "Let's say I go along with this. Do you even know how to break into a building?"

"Not exactly," Envy admitted. "But look at the front door. It uses one of those electric keypads. And I just bet we know someone who'd make quick work of locks like that."

"Absolutely not," I objected, banging my hand on the table. The silverware rattled in response, and the table next to ours shot me a dirty look. I lowered my voice and jabbed a finger at Envy's chest. "Seriously, Envy. *No.* We're not dragging Wrath into this."

"To be fair," Sloth drawled, sticking a sugar-laden finger into her mouth, "Wrath is already involved. He knows about Chenoweth and the laptop. He's as involved as anyone."

"Then let me be honest," I said. "I don't want to work with the guy. *Again.* I just got rid of him! I don't know if you've noticed, but he's kind of a lot to handle, you know?"

Envy smirked. "I don't know if *you've* noticed, but so are you."

If you want to bruise a person's ego, let it slip that they're just as annoying as the person they're complaining about. It works every time. My pride wanted to object to Envy's well-placed but entirely unnecessary barb, but what could I say? I knew I was difficult. I had trouble with social situations. I rarely understood nuance or figurative language, and dealing with people sometimes made me want to stab myself with a fork. (That's not figurative language. I do sometimes *want* to stab myself in the thigh when people try to make small talk with me. But I don't because I have what Dr. Xena calls *impulse control.* And that's the difference between *wanting* to text your ex in the middle of the night but not actually *doing* it. Not that I have any experience with that kind of thing.)

But even with my flaws, I wasn't the one running around preaching the evils of capitalism and telling anybody who would listen that patriarchy and white supremacy were ruining Western society! I was the lesser of two evils! Surely my housemates could see that.

Right?

"Whatever," I said, soothing my battered ego by sniffing importantly and refusing to make eye contact. "I'm sure there will be nothing obvious about four people trying to break into a building after dark. This plan gets better and better by the second."

"I agree," Envy said, turning my sarcasm against me. "Just think about it, Pride. When it's all said and done, this will make for such an awesome story on TikTok."

"Triple espresso for Sloth?"

Sloth got up as her name was called and walked over to the counter to retrieve her coffee. When we were alone, Envy started picking at her nails and said casually, "You know what your problem is?"

"Yes," I sighed. "I suffer from a mix of social anxiety disorder and—"

"Your problem is you've played it safe your whole life," she interrupted. "Your parents vanished off the face of the earth when you were a baby. Your whole background is a mystery. I get that. Maybe if my whole life was overshadowed by some freak incident, I'd be more like you. But life is risk versus reward. If you never risk anything, you never get anything, either."

"I'll keep that in mind," I muttered, knowing I wouldn't. "Anyway, to change the subject, I finally got in touch with Danielle."

"So what did she say? Did she tell anybody about the talking corpses?"

I nodded. "You were right. She couldn't keep that secret to herself. She claims she only told one person. But guess who that one person was?"

Envy's eyes were bright with excitement as she shook her head. "I have no idea! Tell me."

I smiled. "Portia Cameron."

Envy blinked. "Who?"

Sloth returned just then, sliding into her seat as she slurped her espresso. "The woman who just announced she's running for mayor," Sloth put in. "Remember? Mayor Gillespie was shouting about it."

Envy snapped her fingers, eyes going wide. "Right! Now I see why you look so smug. Suppose Karen McMurtry had something on Portia, and Portia knew about the chatty corpses. In that case, she might worry that her secret wasn't, you know—taken to the grave, as they say."

I nodded, my brow furrowed in thought. "I know. But it's still kind of a weak motive. We all have secrets we don't want getting out."

"But we're not all running for office," Sloth said.

"And as much as I dislike Portia," I continued, "and I really dislike her, like, a lot—I'm having a hard time seeing her as a murderer. I mean, shooting an old guy in cold blood?"

"Well, how well do you really know her?" Envy asked. "People have murdered for less. You can't assume what people are capable of just by having a passing acquaintance with them, right?"

I grunted. "I guess that's true."

"So have you shared this with Detective Doyle yet?"

I shook my head, drumming my fingers on the table. "No. I don't know how to relay the information in a way that makes sense. I mean, you and I know Portia has motive. But the detective doesn't know about the talking corpses and almost certainly wouldn't believe us even if we told him. So how can we make this make sense?"

Envy pressed her lips together and scooted to the edge of her seat, giving me a pointed look. "You're overthinking this. Just tell the detective you got some evidence suggesting Edgar Thornton may have known a secret Portia didn't want to get out. You don't have to tell him Edgar heard the secret from a dead body."

I hated to admit it, but Envy was making sense. "Yeah, you're right. Let me give him a call."

I pulled out my phone and dialed.

"Doyle."

I cleared my throat and took a deep breath. "Hi, Detective. This is Pride. I have some information on the Edgar Thornton case to share with you." I glanced at Envy, who made encouraging motions with her hands. "Well, we've been talking to some people around town, and it seems Edgar might have stumbled upon a secret about Portia Cameron she didn't want getting out."

The detective grunted. "We all have secrets we don't want getting out," he said.

I turned to my housemates and made a *See? That's what I said!* face, but they couldn't hear the other side of the conversation, so it had little effect. Into the phone, I said, "Right, but Portia just announced she's running for mayor next term. And if there's one thing I know about Portia Cameron, she's cutthroat. She's not much interested in losing."

The detective barked out a laugh. "You know I was married to her, right? I think I have a pretty good bead on her myself. So. You called to tell me I need to look into my ex-wife as a suspect. Well, isn't that rich? She digs her nose into my business and gives you the green light to investigate my case, and here you are telling me she's got motive. Well, sometimes life just hands you good news on a platter, doesn't it? Any idea what the secret was?"

"If I knew that," I drawled, "it wouldn't be a secret."

"Don't get smart," the detective growled. "I was just beginning to like you."

That was a lie, but I let it slide. "Quid pro quo, detective. Did your people find anything interesting at the crime scene?"

"Honestly, not much," the detective admitted with a weary sigh. "The scene was pretty clean. The only unusual thing we found was a used fogger. You know, the stuff you use to bomb the house when you have a bug infestation. Seems the mortuary must've been crawling with cockroaches."

That imagery was something straight out of a horror movie, and I shuddered violently. "You found that in the preparation room?"

"Yep. Well, we assume it's a bug bomb. Not familiar with the brand. The label just said 'CI'. Is there anything else?"

"No, that's everything," I said absently. I was still mulling over the can of bug poison left behind. Sure, a mortuary could have a bug problem just like anywhere else. But the preparation room? The immaculate room where morticians prepared the dead for viewing? It wasn't like you munched on chips and sandwiches in that room. So why would it have a bug problem?

"Well, I appreciate the tip on Portia," the detective said. He didn't really sound appreciative. "I'm sure nothing will come of it. As much as I'd like to hang this on my ex-wife, I'm not sure she's really the murdering type."

"It's not your job to guess," I said. "It's your job to uncover facts."

The detective scoffed into the receiver. "Right. Well, I can't say it's been a pleasure."

The line went dead.

I turned to Envy and Sloth and shrugged lamely. "They didn't find anything at the crime scene. Just a used canister of CI bug poison."

Sloth tapped her chin thoughtfully with a forefinger. "A canister of bug poison? Brand-name CI?"

I nodded. "That's what he said."

Sloth dug out her phone and tapped out a quick text message. "Hang on just a sec," she said, her face all squinched up as she typed. "I have a hunch, but I need Wrath's help."

A moment later, Sloth's phone pinged. She looked down to

read the message, and her face lit up as she smiled with excitement. "Yep. That's what I thought. Here, Pride. Look at this."

Sloth handed me the phone, and I looked down to see a return text message from Wrath. He had attached a screenshot from a website I was now familiar with. It was the Chenoweth International website—specifically, their secret shopping page. The screenshot was of a product called MagicBloc™ Bomb. The canister looked just like a standard fogger, except the label was nondescript, bearing only the letters CI.

Of course. CI for Chenoweth International.

"It's a fogger, but it's not bug poison," I said, stating the obvious. "It's that MagicBloc stuff. Okay, wow. Now it all makes sense." I banged my forehead with the butt of my hand, aghast at my stupidity. "When I touched Edgar's corpse, nothing happened, remember? I should have felt something, especially after such a violent crime. I didn't, but now I know why. Somebody set off this fogger, dousing the whole room in MagicBloc, preventing my ability from firing." I looked at Sloth. "Chenoweth is the link. Edgar Thornton's murder and Eleanor Romanowsky's murder are related."

Envy grinned. "Still have cold feet about coming back here tonight?"

I shook my head. "Not anymore," I admitted. "There's too much at stake. Chenoweth has to be taken down."

ten

. . .

The four of us sneaked out of the house just after 2 a.m. Wrath took no convincing at all—in fact, he was excited to do his part to "flip the tables on a fascist organization." How he decided Chenoweth International was fascist, I had no idea. But then again, nothing about Wrath really made sense to me.

We parked the car two blocks from our destination and walked the rest of the way. Just as Envy predicted, the night was dark. The sliver of new moon gave off little light as it played peekaboo with the clouds. Still, we all wore dark colors to blend in with the night. I'd donned a black hoodie and jeans with the hood pulled tight around my face. We crept along Odyssey's streets without speaking, keeping our hands in our pockets and our heads ducked low.

As we neared Déjà Brew, we slowed our pace. Envy nudged Wrath to the front of our line, where he moved with quiet caution toward the door. He glanced over his shoulder and then tried the door handle. "Locked," he said.

"Of course it's locked," Envy hissed impatiently. "It's 2 o'clock in the morning! That's why we brought you in the first place. Now hurry up and do your magic or whatever it is you do. We need to get off the street."

Wrath scowled and made a rude gesture at Envy but leaned forward toward the lock just the same. When he was eye level with it, he whispered, "Okay, open up you piece of—"

An electric whir and the metallic sound of something clicking was all we heard. When Wrath tried the doorknob again, the door slid soundlessly open.

"We're in," he grinned. Then he disappeared through the door, and the rest of us followed.

We paused inside Déjà Brew, getting our bearings and letting our eyes adjust to the dark. At night, everything looks sinister. My mind played tricks on me, convincing me I saw the shadowy profiles of the bad guys we were hunting waiting around every corner. Taking a deep inhale to steady my nerves, I motioned for my housemates to follow me as I led them to the back room and down the secret staircase that led into the Crypt.

At the bottom of the stairs, I flipped a switch, and dim, honey-colored light infiltrated the darkness. The ghosts were still milling around, looking unperturbed by our late-night arrival. Most of the ghosts sat around in little clusters, chatting with their friends or reading books. It was the reading part I found interesting. In all the years I'd been dealing with ghosts, I'd rarely seen them interact with physical objects. But several of these ghosts were doing just that, flipping through the pages of various tomes on topics such as cryptozoology, telekinesis, and UFOs. I wondered idly if ghosts could *learn* to touch things. I'd have to look into it later.

"So," Sloth said, interrupting my thoughts. "What exactly are we looking for?"

I surveyed the room, taking in the possibilities. The Crypt was filled with arcane books and paraphernalia, containing everything from Ouija boards to prints of sacred geometry. "I'm not sure, to be honest. All I know is this place is important to Chenoweth for some reason. Just look for weird stuff, I guess."

Sloth gestured around sleepily. "Yeah, okay, but this whole place is weird stuff, Pride."

I grunted. "I don't know what else to tell you. Just start searching."

The four of us split up, each taking a separate section of the room. Nobody spoke, but I felt the heaviness of our task hanging in the air. All we had to go on was a star on an old, crappy map. We could be looking for anything, and that thought was too depressing for words.

But then I remembered Gluttony and the magic he put in the popcorn. Good luck magic. So I took a breath and got to work.

As I was opening drawers and rooting through the contents, I heard a familiar voice behind me. "Hello again."

I turned around to found to find Angelica Muñoz floating behind me. She looked chipper, and I was glad to see her. "Hi yourself," I said, smiling. "How's death treating you?"

"I can't complain. There's no one around to listen." She glanced around the room at the rest of my housemates. "What are you all doing here?"

I ran a hand through my hair and heaved a noisy sigh. "Well, we're looking for something, but we're not sure what. Something out of place or unusual. You live down here, so maybe you've seen something out of the ordinary?" I asked hopefully.

The ghost tapped a finger to her lips thoughtfully. "Well, it's just a basement. A very fancy basement, but still. Mostly it's just a place for ghosts to mingle and the Society to do…whatever it is they do. Which isn't much."

My rising optimism sank. "No? What *do* they do here?"

"They gossip," the ghost said with a roll of her eyes. "*So* much gossip. You would think these people had better things to do with their lives. But I guess they don't have to work for a living, so how else are they supposed to fill their time? You know what they say: Great minds discuss ideas. Average minds discuss events. Small minds discuss other people. And I assure you, the Society is filled with the smallest-minded people I've ever met."

I chuckled wryly. "What do they gossip about?"

Angelica sighed. "All kinds of things. Who's dating who, who's cheating on who, who lost money in the stock market, stuff like that. Honestly, it's like an endless episode of *Real Housewives of Odyssey, California*." The ghost smiled and leaned her head to the side, thinking. "Sometimes, they talk about city business. At least a handful of them are on the city council."

That piqued my interest. "Really? Who?"

"Well, let's see. There's this blonde woman. I think she's named after a car? Mercedes or Lexus or—"

"Portia?"

Angelica nodded. "That's it. Portia. You know her?"

"Yes," I stammered. "But…wait, she's a member of the *Society?* Are you sure? She hates the supernatural!"

Angelica shrugged. "Yeah, well, she acts like the leader of the crew. The *actual* leader is this woman Victoria, but Portia wears the pants in that relationship, if you know what I mean."

I was positive I'd seen both Portia and Victoria wear pants, so I wasn't sure why that was relevant. The ghost continued, "There's also this guy, Anthony. He's not so bad—easy on the eyes, anyway, if you know what I mean. And then there's his friend, Wilson. He's a giant nerd, and he *clearly* doesn't care about politics. Beats me why he sits on the council at all—he looks *so* bored any time they stop talking about hauntings or astral travel and start yammering about propositions and elections. And then there's this other woman, Natalie—she seems okay. Kind of a wallflower. But they all sit on the council together."

I whistled. "Four Society members are also on the council?

That seems like a lot. How many council members does a city like Odyssey have, anyway?"

Angelica shrugged. "You're asking the wrong chick. Politics is not my bag. Anyway, I don't pay too much attention to what they do or what they talk about. I wouldn't have spent time around people like that in life, and I certainly try to avoid them in death."

I was opening my mouth to respond when I heard a sharp intake of breath and Envy saying, "Pride, come check this out."

I excused myself and drifted over to where Envy was peering into the pages of a spiral-bound notebook. Her brow was creased as she read. "What did you find?"

"You tell me." She pressed the notebook into my hands. "It looks like meeting minutes. Does any of this sound familiar to you?"

I looked down into the handwritten notes and began skimming the pages. It wasn't exactly riveting, just a bunch of mumbo-jumbo about dues, initiation ceremonies, fundraisers, and—

And then it hit me. These words *were* familiar.

I read aloud from the page. "Discussion, new location. Wilson proposes City Hall for new location if we can get a friend or colleague into office. WB will ask Pam to order blueprints of emergency shelter. Outstanding questions, what are the dimensions for the room? Discussion, birthday party ideas for WB. Notes, WB is allergic to chocolate."

I looked up and shut the book. "This is what we heard on Edgar Thornton's phone." I scrunched up my face in bewilderment. "The stupid corpses were relaying Paranormal Society meeting minutes? What for?"

Envy chewed on her bottom lip, shaking her head in equal dismay. "I don't know. There's got to be a connection between the Society and the deceased. Or maybe a connection between the Society and Edgar? Maybe he was a member?"

"Maybe," I agreed, handing the journal back to Envy. "Great find on the minutes, even if I don't know what it means yet. Hang onto those, okay? They might come in useful later."

Envy stuffed the notebook into her purse and I drifted away to continue looking around. The Paranormal Society had a lot of curious memorabilia. The walls were lined with paintings, strange photos, and even old lithographs. I was turning away from an aged gravestone rubbing when something about it caught my eye, and I doubled back.

I blinked, re-reading the words I had glossed over a moment before. I didn't speak Spanish, so I didn't know what they meant. But as I read the words aloud, a shiver ran down my spine.

"Magdalena. Ahora con los angeles, protegiéndonos desde arriba."

A voice at my side startled me. "Magdalena. That must be the medicine woman Pam told you about."

I looked over to find the ghost girl fidgeting beside me. Her face was upturned, and she stood on tiptoes to better see the rubbing. She pointed at the framed paper and scrunched up her face. "Can you get that down for me? It's too high to see."

"Since when are you interested in headstone inscriptions?" I asked, gently lifting the rubbing from its nail. "I thought you were only interested in random animal facts. Can you even read Spanish?"

"No," the ghost said, pressing herself close to peer at the artwork. I kneeled low so she could get a better look. "But it's pretty, don't you think? How are these made?"

"You cover a headstone with a lightweight paper like vellum and then you gently rub over it with charcoal or a pencil until you've captured the engraving on the paper," I explained. "It's very tedious and time-consuming to do it well because you don't want to damage the headstone."

The ghost nodded. "It was worth it. Her headstone must have been beautiful. This flower looks like the California poppy," she said, pointing. "It's kind of hard to tell, though. But this is definitely a quail, the California state bird. Did you know the common quail can run almost 40 miles per hour?"

I was about to say that seemed impossible given their short legs when a voice behind me said, "It says, 'Now with the angels, protecting us from above.'"

Angelica moved next to me, too, until the three of us were huddled together over the grave rubbing. "Magdalena is one of the folk saints of Odyssey. Unofficially, of course. But it's said she looks over us. She guides us."

"Who's us?" I asked. "The people who live in Odyssey?"

"No," the ghost girl whispered somberly, her eyes wide and round. "The people who die in Odyssey." She looked around, a slow smile spreading on her cupid bow mouth. "There's power here," she said. "Don't you feel it?"

I opened my mouth to say I didn't feel anything when an image popped into my mind—handwritten words on a carefully hidden piece of paper that read "Nexus of Power," accompanied by a star that marked the very location I was standing in now.

Goosebumps broke out along my skin, and the hairs at the back of my neck stood up. I rose to put the artwork back where I'd found it, but as I moved to place the frame on the nail, I stopped short.

An inch beneath the nail was a small, circular indentation in the wall. It almost blended in perfectly with the texture of the drywall, but it was faintly outlined.

It wasn't merely an indentation. It was a button.

"What the...?"

The ghost girl pressed herself against my legs. "What is it?"

"I don't know," I said, my words barely a whisper. I placed a forefinger against the button and, my lip folded beneath my teeth, pressed it.

A deep grumbling filled the Crypt, followed by shouts and squeals of surprise. Quickly, I placed Magdalena's grave rubbing back on the wall and backed away, my eyes searching the room for the source of the disruption.

"This can't be happening," Wrath breathed.

I followed Wrath's gaze, and my mouth fell open. On the other side of the room, a giant bookshelf had slid aside to reveal a corroded metal door bearing the same keypad lock as the front door to Déjà Brew.

"I think we found what we're looking for," Sloth said.

"Wrath?" I whispered. "Can you open that?"

Envy slipped her arm through mine, trembling at my side as we approached the door. Wrath pushed up his sleeves and took a deep breath. He leaned forward, whispered something to the lock, and the door beeped.

With my heart in my throat, I reached out, fingers closing around the doorknob. I turned, and the door creaked open.

eleven

. . .

"A secret passage?" Envy breathed, digging her fingers into my bicep. "Are you *kidding* me? Oh wow, this is the best day of my life. I had no idea when I woke up this morning I would be living in a Sherlock Holmes novel. Eat your heart out, Becca Daniels!"

"Who's Becca Daniels?" Sloth asked.

"Third-grade teacher," Envy answered. "She thinks she's hot stuff because she has 10,000 followers on Instagram. It's just because she likes to show off her—"

"Quiet." I brought a finger to my lips and disentangled from Envy as I stepped into the darkness. The hallway was cool and damp and smelled of algae, decay, and saltwater. Up ahead, the hallway met another hallway, forming an intersection. We appeared to be in some kind of tunnel network, connecting unfinished passages beneath Old Downtown. Everything around us was stone or concrete, and as soon as the door behind us closed, we were plunged into total darkness. Wrath pulled out his cellphone and activated its flashlight.

That's when we noticed this side of the door had no lock. And no handle for that matter.

"This has to be some kind of joke," Wrath said, cursing under his breath. "Are we trapped down here? Can we get back inside?"

Sloth placed a hand on Wrath's shoulder and squeezed. "We'll cross that bridge when we come to it," she said. "Come on. Let's find whatever we came down here to find."

She pushed Wrath forward with a comforting smile. But I saw the way her lips trembled when his back was turned.

Quietly, we padded down the corridor, hardly daring to breathe. At the first intersection, I looked both ways and then placed my right hand on the wall. "Right-hand turns only," I instructed. "As long as I keep contact with the wall, we should find a way out. I think," I amended under my breath.

"Where do you think we are?" Sloth whispered. Her voice echoed through the underground. "We're not underneath Déjà Brew anymore."

"Definitely not," Wrath said. "We seem to have stumbled into some kind of underground railroad. I had no idea something like this would exist in California."

"There are tunnels just like these underneath Los Angeles," I said, keeping my voice low and my hand on the wall as we walked. "They were originally used for streetcars, safer ways to transport money between banks, and finally for bootleggers. The tunnels are mostly unmapped, so they're not really safe to use. But they still exist today."

"I wonder if this tunnel system was part of the original mission," Envy mused. "Do you think anyone even knows they're here?"

"Someone knows," I said. "That's why the door we just went through was both hidden and locked. You wouldn't want anyone to sneak into your business via these tunnels. I assume Felix knows. And if he does, others do." I thought about Envy's equation about secrets. Old Downtown consisted of three different streets. If half the proprietors in the area knew about the tunnels…well, you do the math.

"Look," Sloth said, pointing. "A door."

We paused before an old door painted with chipped, faded green paint. It was coated with grime, rust, and spiderwebs. It evidently hadn't been used in a while, though it at least had a handle. Wrath stepped toward it, hands deep in the kangaroo pocket of his hoodie. "Should we try it?" he asked.

"No guts, no glory," Envy said, nodding.

Wrath reached for the handle and pulled. Unsurprisingly, the door didn't budge. It was locked from the other side. Wrath bent down and whispered the same way he'd done for the locks at Déjà Brew.

Nothing happened.

Frowning, Wrath stood up. "This one must be mechanical instead of electrical," he said. "I can't get us inside that one, man. Maybe we'll have better luck with the others."

A little further on, we came to another door. Just like the green door, this one was old and rusted. Wrath tried his technopathy again to no avail. We moved along, continuing to make right-hand turns and trying any doors we came across. So far, Gluttony's good luck wasn't exactly panning out.

"Here's another one," Wrath said, coming upon another ill-used door. He reached for the handle and pulled. Like the others, nothing happened. "This is getting old, man. I'm starting to get claustrophobic."

"You're the one who wanted to come," Envy reminded him.

"You're the one who asked me!" he hissed. "You think I was just jonesing to go spelunking in the middle of the night?"

"Just try to open the door," Sloth reprimanded, "and quit whining."

Wrath huffed out a sigh, ran his hands through his hair, and put his palms on the door. His voice trembled only slightly when he said, "Time to open up, old buddy, old pal."

To my surprise, a familiar whirring sound was followed by an electric click. We gasped collectively as Wrath's hand found the door handle and pulled.

The door swung open.

No one spoke as we entered the room. Like the tunnel, it was pitch black, illuminated only by the thin glow of Wrath's phone. A sound like the buzzing of an air conditioner or maybe the hum of electronics filled the air. It lent an eerie quality to our already creepy surroundings. Gradually, my eyes adjusted to the darkness, and when I realized what I was seeing, my heart fell into my stomach.

"What the hell is this place?" Envy asked aloud.

"It looks like some kind of laboratory," Sloth answered.

Wrath found a light switch and flipped it. Fluorescent lights buzzed on, casting the room in a cool, white light. The room was large and square, maybe 60 x 60 feet. In the middle stood long metal tables laden with scientific equipment: Beakers, Bunsen burners, microscopes, flasks, and test tubes. The floor was clean linoleum tile. There was no dust anywhere—it seemed the place had been recently used. It appeared, like Sloth said, to be a chemist's laboratory.

That is, until I saw the cages.

Locked, metal enclosures of varying sizes were stacked against the walls. Some were small, maybe rabbit-sized, while others were large enough to contain a pair of full-grow people. These larger cages were additionally outfitted with chains and handcuffs that hung from the tops of the cell. Dark stains marred the floor around some of the larger corrals. I looked away, swallowing around the huge lump in my throat. If that was blood, I didn't want to know about it.

On the far side of the room, another empty cage sat apart from the rest. It was large, big enough for a person. It was outfitted with a neatly made cot, a water pitcher, and, strangely, an icebox containing fresh, raw ocean fish. Unlike the other cages, this one looked like it hadn't been used.

"Tell me this isn't what I think it is," Wrath said.

"This is Chenoweth property," I said. "This is where they bring the supernaturals."

As soon as I spoke the words aloud, I knew them to be true. I thought back to when I'd found Ping in the alleyway, her eyes wild with fear. "You don't know what they do to my kind," she said, terrified. "Experiments. Torture."

Experiments. Torture.

Her words rang through me as I took in the totality of my surroundings. This was the place Ping was so afraid of. This was the place we'd been looking for. The star on the map didn't note Déjà Brew at all.

It marked this place. *This* was the Nexus of Power.

I was about to suggest that we split up to search the hidden laboratory when a scream ripped through the room. My head shot up, eyes flying wide as I whipped my head around, trying to locate the source of the sound.

"Over here!" Sloth ran to a corner of the room where something was covered with a quilted moving pad. She grabbed a corner and tugged until the blanket slipped to the ground, revealing a plain, metal birdcage. She gasped, hands flying to her mouth as she stared.

Inside the cage were two brightly colored sun conures.

"Pride! It's Mrs. Romanowsky's parrots," she exclaimed. "This proves it. This is Chenoweth. We've found their hideout. These are the birds they stole."

The birds were flapping wildly in their cage, screaming and banging their wings against their metal confines. Feathers flew everywhere. The enclosure was much smaller than the one Eleanor kept for them—this one was not much larger than a cat carrier.

Sloth grabbed the cage and hugged it to her chest, her jaw set. "Tear this place apart if you have to. If there are any other supernaturals in here, we have to rescue them. Don't just stand there, guys. Get moving."

Sloth didn't need to ask twice. The four of us split up as we began our frantic search for more kidnapped supernaturals. We searched under tables, overturned boxes, threw open cabinets and closet doors, searching every nook and cranny. We couldn't leave a single creature behind. But after several minutes of frenzied hunting, we found nothing besides the parrots.

"What should we do now?" I asked once the laboratory was secured.

"We have to tell someone about this place," Sloth said. "Where exactly are we? What business connects to this place? We have to know—"

But Sloth's speech was interrupted when Wrath threw his hood away from his face, sniffing the air. "Do you guys smell that? It smells like—"

I sniffed the air. Hot metal. Melted plastic. Smoke.

The laboratory was filling with curls of black smoke. I spun around to see Envy at the back of the room with her hand buried in the roots of her hair, jaw clenched, her whole body shaking. And then I saw what loomed behind her—a towering pillar of fire with long, thin, humanoid limbs and a furious expression on its uncannily human face.

"Envy," I breathed, stark terror rising in my chest. "Tell me you didn't summon that. Tell me that's not one of your fire elementals."

"This place is evil," she said, her voice thick with rage. As she spoke, her skin lit up with the bright yellows and oranges of the flames burning behind her. "I don't have to let this stand. This place shouldn't be here. So I'm destroying it. This ends now."

No sooner were the words out of her mouth than the fire elemental exploded, raining a torrent of flame and burning ash down on the room, lighting the equipment, the walls, the furniture on fire.

"Envy!" I screamed. "What did you do? *What did you do?*"

The birds, too, were screaming, their fevered screeches matching my own. Sloth clutched the cage tighter to her chest and turned her back, protecting the birds from the inferno with her body. Wrath grabbed me by the wrist, hauling me across the room as we dodged the flames burning hot and furious around us. "No time for lectures, man," he cried. "We gotta get outta here! Like, *pronto!*"

We ran. The laboratory had to be connected to a street-level room the same way the Crypt was connected to Déjà Brew. But though we searched every corner, we couldn't find any door leading up and out of the underground. The heat in the laboratory was terrifying. The fire was spreading so much faster than I would have thought possible. I pressed my nose into the crook of my arm, eyes watering as I searched for an escape.

"We have to go back into the tunnels." Sloth was shouting over the roar of the fire growing around us. "There's no other way out."

"If we go back into the tunnels, we'll die for sure," Wrath shot back. "All the doors we found were locked!"

"We didn't search everywhere," I said, trying to keep my cool. That was becoming more and more difficult as the conflagration closed in. "There might be another exit. Sloth's right; we can't stay here. Let's go!"

We practically tripped over each other as we pushed our way out of the laboratory and back into the tunnels. Wrath had the good sense to close the door behind us. Maybe that would contain the blaze for a little while. Maybe not. We ran down the twisting corridors in stark darkness, made all the more blind by our fire-seared retinas. I fumbled my phone from my pocket, trying to thumb on the flashlight. But I was shaking so badly, the device slipped from my fingers and crashed to the ground. The glass interface shattered.

"Up here!" Wrath shouted ahead. I snatched up my phone, sticking it in my pocket as I dashed to catch up with my housemate.

"What did you find?" Sloth was breathless, her fingers gone bloodless as she squeezed the wire of the cage in her grasp.

Wrath was standing before a metal grating about half the height of a normal door. He kneeled down and pried his fingers into the gaps and tugged. The grating came loose, revealing a narrow crawlspace just large enough to traverse if we hunched down. We scrambled into the cramped space with Wrath leading the way and Sloth and the parrots bringing up the rear. At last, the corridor emptied out into another hallway, at the end of which stood a stairwell leading up. We rushed up the stairs to find a rusted metal door locked from the other side. Wrath shouted at the lock and pulled the handle.

The door groaned open.

Quaking with adrenaline and relief, we poured through, panting and sweating, to find ourselves on the street on the other side of the building from where we'd started.

"Is everybody okay?"

Sloth's teeth were chattering. She was still clutching the bird cage tight against her chest. Her face was smudged, maybe with dirt, maybe soot. I couldn't tell in the pale starlight. The night air smelled of smoke and chemicals. I guess closing the door didn't do as much good as I hoped.

"We're fine," Envy answered for the group, looking us all over. She scrubbed her face with her palms. "We're all okay."

"No thanks to you," I spat. "How do you keep *doing* that? We could have died back there! Why can't you—"

"Maybe later for this," Sloth interrupted. "We have to get back to the house. We're all on the edge of shock, and it's gonna hit real soon. No one should be behind the wheel when that happens."

No one argued further. We headed swiftly for the car, heads bent low against the night. I reached into my pocket for my phone, yanking it free. As I peered down into the shattered screen, I saw how badly I was shaking. Sloth was right. We were all in for a bad night.

But it could be worse. After all, we were lucky. We were alive.

Thank you for the good luck, Gluttony, I thought as I climbed into the car and slammed the door, listening to the distant wail of sirens growing nearer.

———

The next morning came way too quickly. I'd watched each hour tick by on the alarm clock on my nightstand as I trembled beneath my sheets. I'd still been awake at 6 a.m., but I didn't remember seeing 7, so maybe that was around the time I finally fell asleep.

Either way, it was still too early when a knock came at my door.

Wonderful, I thought. *My housemates finally learned to knock and it's at the most inopportune time.* I pulled myself to seated and rubbed the sleep from my eyes.

"Come in," I croaked.

The door opened slowly, and when I saw who stood at the entrance, I knew I was about to have a very bad day.

Detective Doyle stepped into my room and closed the door

behind him. He looked me up and down. "Rough night?" he asked.

I faked nonchalance with a shallow lift of my shoulders. "Oh, you know how it goes. We Hollywood types are always looking to have a good time. I guess we had too much fun last night."

The lie came effortlessly, but I felt like a schmuck saying it aloud, especially because I could see all over the detective's face that he didn't believe a word. However, he didn't call my bluff. He remained standing in the corner, arms folded over his chest. "I'm here about your tip," he said.

Tip? What tip? I was so groggy and hungover from the previous night's adrenaline that I could barely think straight. "What are you talking about?"

"Portia's alibi is airtight," he said. "The night Ed Thornton was shot, Portia was having dinner with the mayor. At least half a dozen people saw her."

I rubbed my face with my palms, trying to wake up. I didn't dare stand— I couldn't even remember what I was wearing. If I somehow had on my favorite unicorn pajamas, I would die of mortification. "Okay," I said. "So it wasn't Portia. Good, I guess. You came all the way here to tell me that?"

Now, the detective stepped closer to me, his expression darkening. "Not exactly," he said. "Let's be frank with each other, Pride. One investigator to another. I might not be a psychic, but I've been doing this job for a long time. And when you've been on the streets for as long as I have, you develop intuition about people. There's something you're not telling me, and I want to know what it is."

I shook my head, refusing to meet the detective's eyes. "I have no idea what you're talking about. Everything I know about this case, I've told you." That was a lie. I was sure Edgar's murder and Eleanor's murder were linked, and I hadn't shared anything with the detective about that. But it was too early and

I was too messed up to get into it now. "That was the deal, right?"

Detective Doyle nodded. "It was the deal, all right. I'm just not sure you're holding up your end of it."

I sighed. "Look, detective. Can we do this later? I could use a shower and some coffee. And some, you know. Clothes."

"Would you prefer to do this at the station?" A snide smile quirked over his lips.

"That wouldn't be my first choice," I admitted, "but right now, I'd rather be anywhere than half naked in my bed being interrogated by the cops." Especially the night after my comrades and I had accidentally-on-purpose set downtown on fire.

The detective heaved a sigh and stuffed his hands into his pockets, rocking back onto his heels. "All right. If that's how you want to play this, I get it. You're holding your cards close to your chest. I have no evidence to suggest that you're withholding information about Ed's murder, but if that should change, please know I will not hesitate to arrest you. Big Hollywood star or no, I take my job seriously."

I felt even more like a schmo now that he used my own Hollywood line against me.

The detective turned to go. But just as he reached my door, he snapped his fingers and turned around. "I almost forgot." He walked over to the bed and withdrew something from his hip pocket, tossing it into my lap.

It was a wallet. *My* wallet.

I stared at it, frosty dread climbing from my stomach into my throat. When I looked up again to meet the detective's eyes, he wasn't smiling.

"Found that on the street in Old Downtown," he said. "I guess you heard about the fire."

I closed my eyes and let my chin fall to my chest. My heart was pounding so loud, I was sure the detective could hear. The stupid wallet must have fallen from my pocket when I'd been fumbling around with my phone. "I don't know what you're talking about," I managed. "What fire?"

"Old Downtown burned last night," he said. "Whole town's talking about it. Weird that you didn't hear."

I scoffed. "I just woke up, detective."

The detective grunted noncommittally. "I see. So then, I guess this is the part where you tell me you don't know where or when you dropped that."

I didn't trust myself to speak. I could've dropped that wallet at any time—it didn't mean anything. The detective had to know that.

And I had a feeling he *did* know that—and more he wasn't sharing.

I gave a slow shake of my head. "No idea," I squeaked out.

The detective clucked his tongue against his cheek and turned to go. "That's too bad, Pride," he said. "If you think of anything, you have my number."

And in the next moment, he was gone.

twelve

. . .

"Envy, what the star-spangled devil were you thinking?"

Of course, I didn't say 'star-spangled devil.' I said something more explicit that isn't polite to repeat in mixed company. The four of us were huddled together in Sloth's room, me pacing back and forth while Envy perched on the foot of Sloth's bed, arms crossed over her chest, a deep frown scribbled over her features. Sloth was at her desk, her bathrobe half-tied at her waist, cheek propped against her fist. Wrath was standing in the corner, his hoodie pulled low over his face and his hands dug into his pockets. All of us were on edge. Well, maybe not Sloth. I wasn't sure she had any edges.

"I don't see what the big deal is," Envy said for the third time that morning. "You saw that place. Those people were doing unthinkable things down there. To animals or people or shapeshifters—it doesn't matter. I saw cages, handcuffs, and blood with my own eyes, Pride. And so did you. I did what had to be done."

"You burned down an entire historical district!" I shouted,

throwing my hands in the air. "Don't you have the slightest remorse about that?"

Envy shot me a dark look. "No! And keep your voice down! We don't need the whole house knowing what we did."

"What *you* did!" I fired back.

"You know what I *do* feel bad about?" she continued. "Evil organizations getting away with murder because people like you and me are too chicken to do anything about them. So last night, I did something about it."

Incredulity made my voice shake. "But you burned up all of our evidence, too! If we had gone to the police, they could have done a proper investigation. We could've looked for fingerprints. Some telltale sign of the people behind the evil we found down in the tunnels. But your fire obliterated all of that. My goodness, Envy, depending on how you look at it, you actually did the criminals a favor!"

Sloth yawned and fluttered her eyes sleepily. "Guys?"

"I hate to say it," Wrath said, "but I agree with Envy, man. We didn't find anything illegal down there. It's not like we found a meth lab. We found some birds. If we'd turned the case over to the authorities, what could they have done? They'd probably need a search warrant or whatever, man. And by the time all that went down, the bad guys woulda cleared outta there anyway. And let's say the cops did go down there," Wrath pressed on. "What would they have done? Probably just fined those guys or something. And that's the problem, man. Fines disproportionately hurt the poor more than the rich. Until we start enacting fines as a percentage of income, then—"

I dug my hands into my hair, my frustration mounting. "But we're not talking about poor versus rich, Wrath! Listen to yourself! How do you manage to turn every conversation into some anti-capitalism rant? Envy burned down the Chenoweth laboratory and any potential evidence along with it! How are we supposed to catch the guys behind this now?"

"You're blowing this out of proportion," Envy said. "I destroyed their secret base. So we didn't catch them this time. But we hit them where it hurts, and that counts for something."

"I don't want to hear another word from you," I snapped, pointing a finger in Envy's face. "You've got an answer for everything. How about accepting some personal responsibility, huh?"

My housemate gaped. "Are you seriously lecturing me about personal responsibility? You're the one who can't apologize even when you're *clearly* in the wrong! If you had just apologized to your stupid girlfriend, you wouldn't even be in this mess in the first place!"

My face flushed hot with fury and embarrassment. "So you admit it's a mess!" I thundered. "Now admit it's *your* mess, Envy! You and your stupid elemental—"

Sloth cleared her throat. "Guys?"

"I don't have to sit here and listen to this," Envy said, climbing to her feet. "I did what I did and I'm not sorry. If you've got a problem with me, Pride, take it up with the network. Maybe Tricia will give you a new partner."

"Oh, I'm already thinking about it," I fumed. "I'd rather forfeit this round than spend another minute—"

"*Guys!*"

We were so unused to the sound of Sloth raising her voice that the room fell silent as all heads turned toward her. Her cheek was still propped against her fist, but her face was red now, her mouth pulled into a frown. "Can we talk about this later? We have more pressing issues to deal with."

We all followed Sloth's gaze to the cage sitting in the corner of her room. She'd covered the birdcage with a blanket, and the parrots were blessedly quiet—so quiet, we'd forgotten about them. "So. What are we going to do about the birds?" she asked.

"Well, I guess we should get them out of that MagicBloc cage," Wrath said. "Then…well, I guess we'll see. I'll go see if we have any wire cutters."

While Wrath disappeared from the room, Envy sat back down on the bed, and I took in a deep breath to calm my nerves. "I didn't mean to shout at you," I said. It was the closest thing to an apology she was going to get, and I hoped she appreciated that. "It's just you put us in a really bad position. You know the detective was here this morning?"

Now Envy's eyes widened in surprise. "Detective Doyle? He was here? Why?"

I scoffed. "Ostensibly, to tell me Portia's alibi checked out. She wasn't the one who shot Edgar. But he also wanted to drop this off." I tossed my wallet onto the bed. When Envy saw it, her hand drew to her mouth, and the color seeped from her face.

"Oh no," she breathed. "That's not your wallet, is it?"

"He knows we were there," I answered. "Or at least, he knows I was. And if he's on to me, there's a good chance he's onto the rest of us."

"You could've lost that wallet last week for all he knows," Envy said. "That's not enough evidence to put us in trouble, is it?"

I shrugged. "I don't know. On its own, probably not. But I'm guessing the detective knows more than he's letting on. So what I'm saying is, this wouldn't have happened if you hadn't loosed that ridiculous elemental on the town."

Envy opened her mouth to object, but Sloth held up her hand and snapped her fingers. "Not again," she said. "If you guys want to argue about this, take it to another room. What's done is done. We're a team. If one of us goes down, we all go down. So we need to have each other's backs."

The bedroom door opened, and Wrath slipped inside, a pair of wire cutters in his hand. He strode over to the birdcage and lifted the blanket, tossing it to the ground. The parrots chirped enthusiastically as Wrath took to the cage, grunting and swearing as he worked at the wires. A moment later, I heard it: the snap of metal as Wrath pulled the side panel free and dropped it to the floor.

The birds huddled in the corner of the cage, not moving. "Come on now, you stupid birds," Wrath said. "Cage is open. Just come out, will you?"

Sloth giggled from her chair. "Just take them out, Wrath. You're not afraid of them, are you? They're just parrots. They can't hurt you."

Pushing up the sleeves on his hoodie, Wrath reached into the cage. The birds danced away from him, but they couldn't move far. The cage was only so big. Finally, Wrath lifted one in his hand and withdrew it, placing it on the carpet. He reached in for the second bird and placed it beside the first. The parrots were stunned motionless and silent. But then one parrot lifted its foot, and I noticed the silver rings on their feet.

"Sloth, do you have anything we can cut these little coils with? The wire cutters are too big."

Sloth went to her bedside table and retrieved a pair of nail clippers. "Will these work?"

I took the clippers and carefully pinched at the metal until the birds' feet were free. At first, nothing happened. But slowly, the parrots began to shimmer as a faint light bloomed around them. There was a sound like a lightbulb popping, and the birds snapped together like magnets, melding to each other at the sides. Gradually, the parrots began to transform, blending into each other as the prismatic light pulsed and grew brighter until I had to turn away to save my eyes. When I looked back, I shrieked.

Sitting on the floor stark naked was…

… *Portia Cameron?!*

I stared at Portia with my mouth agape, unable to process

what I was seeing. When she realized she was naked, Portia drew her arms over her chest and turned away from us, a pink blush crawling up her neck and into her cheeks. Sloth jumped to her feet, retrieved the blanket that had been on the parrot cage, and draped it over the woman's shoulders. Portia gathered the blanket around her and looked up into Sloth's face, gratitude blooming all over her features. Her eyes were wide and glassy, and she looked enchanted. Or hungover. Or something.

But this didn't make sense. How could the parrots be Portia? I'd just seen her!

Tentatively, I stepped toward her. "Portia?"

Portia looked up at me and blinked. She opened her mouth as though trying to speak, but no words came out. She bit down on her lip and drew a deep breath, trying again. "What day is it?" she managed finally.

"Tuesday, I think," I said.

Portia's brow furrowed, and a shadow passed over her features. Then she said, "Sorry. The date? Can you please tell me the date?"

My housemates and I exchanged nervous glances. Envy walked over to the woman and kneeled beside her, placing a hand on her forehead. She whispered something in Portia's ear, and the woman froze. "That can't be right," she breathed, shaking her head in denial. "That would mean…that would mean I was in that cage for over a year."

I stared at her, my mind reeling. Finally, I blurted, "Portia, what are you talking about? What's going on?"

The woman tightened the blanket around her shoulders. "I'm not Portia," she said. "I'm Peyton. Portia and I are twins."

I stared mutely until the words made sense. Peyton. I recognized that name—I'd heard Portia say it in Detective Doyle's office. They'd been arguing about the existence of the supernatural, and the detective had maintained it was nothing but fancy. And Portia had shot back, "Then explain Peyton."

I gave a long blink. This was Peyton. Portia's twin sister.

Portia's twin sister was a supernatural.

I was only beginning to register the implications of this revelation when Envy walked across the room to Sloth's closet and pulled out a stained but otherwise clean sweatshirt and a pair of dark leggings. She handed these to Peyton. "Why don't you get dressed," she said, keeping her voice soft. "We need to get you somewhere safe."

Peyton accepted the clothing with a bashful twist of her lips. "Can you take me to my sister? Please?"

I pulled out my phone. "I'm on it. What's her number?"

Peyton gave me her sister's number, and I dialed as we filed out of the room to give her some privacy. In the hallway, I leaned against a wall, phone pressed to my ear.

"Portia Cameron's phone," an assistant answered.

"Put Portia on," I said. "It's an emergency."

"I'm sorry, but Portia—"

"Put her on immediately or so help me I will hunt your whole family down."

That did the trick. A moment later, a disgruntled Portia was on the other end, breathing loudly into the phone. "Who is this? I'm in the middle of—"

"Portia, this is Pride. Please don't interrupt. Meet me at your house in fifteen minutes." I sighed, closing my eyes. "I can't explain over the phone. You wouldn't believe me if I did. Just be there. I have something you want. Don't be late." I disconnected without waiting for a reply. To my housemates, I said, "This day's gonna need coffee. Lots of it."

I was heading toward the kitchen when Envy sidled up to me and tugged on my sleeve. "Can we talk?" When I didn't stop walking, she caught up with me, matching my pace. "I know you're angry with me right now," she began, "but let me come with you to Portia's. I know this isn't part of our case, but I'd really like to see the two sisters reunited."

I narrowed my eyes at her. "This isn't one of your 'get-famous-on-TikTok' schemes, is it? I'm not letting you use their tragedy for personal gain, Envy."

My housemate's face darkened, her mouth drawing into a hard line. "Whatever else you may think about me, Pride, I would hope you know I have common decency. Yeah, I want to be social media famous, but I'm not a monster."

I hesitated, examining her face. I don't know what I was looking for—under the best circumstances, I couldn't tell what people were thinking or feeling. But Envy looked sincere. And while I *was* angry with her, I knew she wasn't a monster.

"All right," I said, softening only a little. "You can come. I'll see if Sloth wants to come, too."

While Envy disappeared into her room to get dressed, I found Sloth downstairs. She was in the kitchen making breakfast—coffee with jam on toast. She left a trail of crumbs everywhere, and she'd dribbled heavy creamer all over the counter. She didn't even seem to notice. But after the night and morning we'd just had, I figured extending a little grace was the least I could do.

"Envy and I are taking Peyton over to Portia's," I said. "Do you want to come? After all, this is all part of the Romanowsky case. And that case was yours from the beginning."

But Sloth moaned, shaking her head. "No, thank you. I've had more than enough excitement for a while. You guys go. I'm feeling overwhelmed, and I need to recharge my social batteries." She offered me a smile, but I noticed for the first time the half-moons beneath her eyes. She really did look wrung out.

"All right," I said. I reached for the coffee, pouring myself a mug. "So, can I ask you something?"

"Sure," she said. "What's up?"

"I was wondering." I took a sip of the coffee. It was too hot to drink, but I was stalling. "The other day at City Hall, you mentioned you saw Pam's thoughts because they were, you know. Right there." I cleared my throat. "Have you ever…I don't know, accidentally picked up on Lust's thoughts? You know, because they're *right there?*"

Sloth took a bite of toast, leaving a smear of jam on the tip of her nose. "I pick up stuff from everyone," she said. "You guys are all very loud thinkers."

That got me blushing, but I tried not to focus on it. If I went down the rabbit hole of which of my thoughts Sloth had picked up, I'd surely wind up buried alive. "Well, I was wondering if you ever heard Lust thinking about me. And if she does think about me, well…"

"You want to know how she feels about you," Sloth finished.

"Yes," I breathed, relieved I didn't have to spell it out. I felt like I was in 6th grade again, sliding notes to my crush's best friend. "Does Lust like me? Check Yes or No."

Honestly, having feelings is so undignified.

Sloth sighed and licked her lips. "I can't tell you that, Pride. It wouldn't be ethical. But here's the thing. You don't need a mind-reader to find out if Lust likes you. All you have to do is *talk* to her."

"I can't," I said, shrugging lamely as I stepped away. "I wouldn't be able to get the words out. Emotions, relationships… they're not really my strong suit," I said.

"Avoiding rejection is a lonely way to live," Sloth said from around another mouthful of jam and toast. "Sometimes, you have to be vulnerable. You know, I can help you with that."

I quirked an eyebrow. "Really? How?"

Sloth grinned. "In my day job, I'm a professional cuddler. I hold people and make them feel safe and secure. I could do that for you if you want."

My mouth dropped open. "You're a…*what?* You hug people for a living?"

Sloth nodded. "It's low energy, and I'm good at it. Do you want—"

"No," I said, a little louder than I meant to. "Thanks, but that sounds like a nightmare. No offense."

Sloth shrugged lightheartedly. "None taken. Well, if you change your mind, you know where to find me. It's not as weird as you might think. It can be very therapeutic."

I heard a sound and turned to find Peyton coming into the kitchen. She was dressed in Sloth's oversized sweatshirt that hung limply from one shoulder and baggy leggings that bunched around her ankles. It was only after seeing her fully clothed that I realized how thin she was. As parrots, she'd looked healthy. As a human, she was little more than skin and bones. A sharp collarbone peeked out from her shirt. Her cheeks were gaunt, her undereyes gray and sunken. Maybe she'd always been thin, but there was *thin,* and there was *emaciated.*

When she saw me looking, Peyton blushed, glancing down at her outfit. "I've never stayed in animal form for so long," she said, trying to smile. She looked like a scared child. "I guess it took a toll on my body. But I'm sure I'll fill out again eventually."

I said nothing and looked away. Whoever had done this to her would pay.

"Thank you for the clothes," she said to Sloth. "I promise to return them."

Sloth shook her head and sipped her coffee. "Keep them. I'm just glad you're safe."

"Okay," Envy said, jogging into the kitchen. "I'm ready." For a delinquent who had just summoned an elemental to torch all of Old Downtown, she looked remarkably like a retiree on a cruise. She wore a pair of linen culottes and a blue and white striped boatneck shirt. Her freshly Botoxed face completed the look. "Let's get this show on the road."

When we pulled into Portia's driveway ten minutes later, Peyton pressed her hands to her mouth, her eyes wide. "It looks just how I remember," she breathed. "She's redone her landscaping, it looks like. But otherwise, it's the same. How can so little have changed?"

I didn't have an answer for that, so I said nothing. We got out of the car and marched up to the house. As we approached, Peyton lagged behind, cowering after me. I paused to look at her, noticing the way her lips trembled and her eyes darted around. "Are you all right? Is this what you want to do?"

Peyton hesitated a moment before biting down on her lip and giving a crisp nod. "Yes. I'm just scared, is all."

I offered what I hoped was a reassuring smile. "There's nothing to be afraid of," I said. "Come on. Let's get you home."

I pressed the doorbell.

A few moments later, the front door flew open. Portia's expression was stony, her cheeks flaming red. By the way she bared her teeth, I could tell she was ready to issue me an epic tongue lashing. *Nobody tells Portia Cameron what to do!* and *Who do you think you are?* and all that jazz. But the moment she saw her sister, Portia froze in the doorway. All her ferocity melted away, and she stared in blank shock. A protracted silence followed, and then finally, Portia whispered, "Peyton?"

No one said another word. Portia rushed forward, pulling her sister into a fierce embrace. Peyton pressed her face into the crook of her twin sister's neck, and the two women huddled together in the doorway and sobbed.

thirteen

. . .

Once the shock of seeing her sister wore off, Portia ushered us inside and took us into the living room. She instructed the house staff to prepare food while she situated her sister on the couch. She surrounded Peyton with comfortable pillows and fluffy blankets, even though it wasn't cool in the house. Peyton welcomed them, however, burrowing down in them like a small animal.

Portia nestled into the couch beside her sister, taking her twin's hands in her own. The stark difference in their weight was made evident when Portia's fingers, nearly chubby by comparison, caressed her sister's skeletal phalanges. "I never thought I would see you again," Portia said. Her voice was raw with emotion. "You were gone for a whole year, Peyton. *An entire year.*"

Peyton nodded and sniffled, wiping away a stray tear that had leaked onto her cheek. "I know. They told me. I can't believe it's been that long. But you know, time passes differently for me when I'm…" She glanced over at Envy and me as stricken panic flashed over her face.

"We know about shapeshifters," I said softly. "It's a long story, but we know. And don't worry. Your secret is safe with us."

At my words, Peyton relaxed slightly and nodded, returning her attention to Portia. "Anyway, I don't remember much. I suppose that's probably a blessing, given the way I look." She glanced down at her body, and I assumed she was referring to her weight. "Nothing hurts, though. I don't see any scars or anything. So they couldn't have hurt me too badly."

"They stole a year of your life," Portia cut in, her words punctuated by palpable anger. "They took you away from your family. That's time we can never get back. So maybe they didn't leave any visible marks, Peyton, but they hurt you terribly. You and me both."

Peyton shuddered and pulled the blanket tighter around her body. "I guess you're right," she said.

Softening her voice, Portia asked, "Do you remember anything? Do you remember who took you—who is responsible?"

Peyton squeezed her eyes shut, doing her best to conjure up a helpful memory. "I remember a little. Charmaine Young and I had gone shopping at the city-wide garage sale. She wanted to find some vintage curtains, and I'd never been to city-wide before. It sounded like fun. We took Charmaine's car. I guess we'd been shopping for a little over an hour when I got hungry. I went over to concessions while Charmaine kept shopping. After I ate, I had to pee, so I went to the ladies' room. And before I even made it to a stall, a man grabbed me from behind. He slapped handcuffs on my wrists and I..." She sniffled and pressed her knuckles into her eye. "I shifted."

"Do you know who it was, Peyton?" Portia was rubbing her sister's back, her voice as soft as feathers. "Was it someone you knew?"

"It was Walt Romanowsky," I said. "When she was parrots, I

saw her at his house. I didn't know it was her, of course. I didn't know they were supernatural parrots for that matter." I turned to Peyton. "But then someone kidnapped you from Walt's house, right? And they took you underground. Do you know who?"

Peyton shook her head. "No. They wore masks. But I'm pretty sure one of them was a woman. Two men and a woman," she repeated, as though confirming this with herself.

I nodded, deep in thought as I considered everything Peyton shared. "So, Charmaine was the last person to see you before you disappeared," I mused aloud. "Portia, did the police ever interview her? Did Doyle?"

"This is the first I'm hearing that my sister was even with Charmaine," Portia admitted.

Now, Peyton frowned, her chin wobbling as she looked up into her sister's face. "No, that can't be right. She must have reported me missing. When she couldn't find me that day? We went to the event together," she insisted. "She must have looked for me. And then when she didn't find me, surely she came to you. Right? I mean, you'd be the first person she'd call."

Raw anger crept up Portia's spine, changing her body language and blooming crimson in her face. "She never called me," Portia whispered through a clenched jaw. "I had no idea she was with you. I had no idea you'd been taken from city-wide garage sale. All I knew was you were gone. I didn't know *what* happened to you. I suspected your disappearance had to do with your ability. Mom and Dad always said if anyone found out about you, it could be dangerous. But it was only unfounded suspicion."

"Portia," I drawled, "is that why you wanted me to be on the lookout for supernatural involvement on the Edgar Thornton case?" I asked. "Did you think maybe I'd find something that would lead to your sister?"

Portia sniffled, new tears seeping from her eyes. "I never

thought I'd see Peyton again," she admitted. "But yes. Tell me you don't see a connection. Wights? Talking corpses? A traveling statue? A sister who can shift into an animal? Don't you think all of this is somehow related?"

"Yes." I answered before I even realized I would, and I didn't know until I said it that I believed it. "I don't know how. But yes. It's Odyssey."

"I hate it," Portia spat. "I hate it all. I lost a year of my sister's life because of…what? The paranormal? The supernatural? I want it all gone. Whatever it takes to root it out of my home, I'll do it. I will burn Odyssey's supernatural proclivities to the ground."

"Don't say that," Peyton said, snuggling into her sister's arms. "This is our home. And it's weird but it's wonderful. So don't say that. Don't even think it. We don't know why I am the way I am, but I'm still me."

"Well, I know one thing," Portia said, hugging her twin tight. "We know Charmaine knew something. I never considered her a friend, but I never would have thought she'd be complicit in your disappearance."

"She wasn't complicit," Peyton objected. "At least, I have no reason to believe—"

"She didn't *say* anything, Peyton! She should have gone directly to the police! To Kelly! To me! But she never said a *word.*"

"We should go talk to her," I said to Envy.

But as I got to my feet, Portia peeled away from her sister and stood, shaking her head sternly. "No. I know I told Kelly to let you help, but you've done enough. This is kidnapping and conspiracy and heaven knows what else. Now isn't the time for an amateur investigation. It was reckless of me to let you get involved in the first place."

"You might be right about that," I agreed. "But please,

Portia. Charmaine's also a suspect in Edgar Thornton's murder. With everything else that's been happening, we haven't had a chance to dig into it. But we want answers, too."

Portia's face darkened. "If she's involved in a kidnapping *and* a murder, that's more reason to stay far away from her. Let the professionals handle it."

"Pride *is* a professional," Envy said. "If you want to get to the bottom of this—and I know you do—there's no one better to have on your team than Pride. I ought to know."

For a moment, I was speechless. Even after the way I'd treated her that morning, Envy still had my back. I was so moved by her small praise that I just stood there gaping. But I finally came to my senses and touched Portia lightly on the arm. "Just give me a head start on the cops. Envy and I will head over to Charmaine's right now. Envy's good with people. It's a gift—she gets them to talk."

The steely determination in Portia's face remained a second longer but then melted away as her shoulders sagged and she nodded. "Fine. I guess I owe you that much. But I'm only giving you a few minutes head start before I call Kelly. So whatever you want to ask her, you better ask her soon as you see her. Because I intend to put that cow away for the rest of her life for what she did to my family. Do you understand?"

Envy and I were already heading for the front door. "Understood. Ten minutes, Portia. Ten minutes."

And with that, Envy and I bolted out the door.

———

Charmaine lived in a quaint area of Odyssey, one of the older parts of town that hadn't been revamped to be some sort of Hollywood beach town fantasy. It looked like a place where normal people lived. Well, normal people and a possible shapeshifting seal, but still.

"What's the address again?" I asked.

Envy looked down into her phone. "1821 Seabreeze Way."

I pointed to a pink-and-white stucco house with a patchy grass yard and a classic Cadillac parked in the driveway. "It's this one," I said. "I would have thought Charmaine would live in something…I don't know, grander."

Envy unbuckled her seatbelt and opened the door. "Let's not sit here lollygagging. We only have a 10-minute head start, remember? The cops will be here any minute. Hop to it."

We strode up to Charmaine's door. I had no idea what I wanted to say—I just knew I had to get the truth out of Charmaine before the cops arrived. If she knew anything about Chenoweth, I had to get that information from her. Who knew how many others might be in danger? I thought of the bounty page on the Chenoweth website and shuddered. There were so many creatures listed.

No, not creatures. People.

I pounded on the door. "Charmaine! It's me, Pride! We have to talk."

There was no answer.

"We don't have time for this," Envy said. She tried the doorknob, and the door swung open. We barged into the house but didn't get very far before we both drew up short. My heart sank through the floor.

The house had been ransacked. There was no furniture overturned like at Mrs. Romanowsky's, but knickknacks and tchotchkes that had been placed on the mantel and wall shelves were knocked to the ground. A glass table in the middle of the living room lay shattered.

I didn't need to be a detective to know that a struggle had taken place here.

"Search the house," I instructed.

Without arguing, Envy began shouting for Charmaine, going in and out of rooms before finally running up the stairs. While Envy searched, I examined the carnage looking for clues. It didn't take long to find what I was looking for.

Standing conspicuously upright in a room filled with things lying broken on their sides was a used canister of MagicBloc fogger.

Envy came running down the steps. "She's not here," she said. "She's gone."

"Chenoweth was here," I said. "They kidnapped her."

"Kidnapped?" The word hung heavy in the air between us. "Why? Why would they kidnap Charmaine?"

I paused. "I heard a rumor she might be a shapeshifter. Looks like the others might have heard the same thing."

Dizzy with this revelation, Envy was about to sink down onto the couch, but I caught her and shook her. "This is a crime scene," I said. "You can't sit on or touch anything. In fact, we should get out of here." I didn't wait for an argument as I hauled her out the front door.

Outside, I heard car doors slamming and I cursed, glancing down at my watch. That was the fastest ten minutes on earth. Detective Doyle met us on the sidewalk, his face a mask of fury. I jammed my thumb over my shoulder. "Something's happened to Charmaine," I said. "She's not there. It looks like someone took her."

"Someone?" The detective's eyes were wide and round, and a fire burned behind his irises. I half-expected smoke to shoot from his ears. "What are you *doing* here? How is it that everywhere I look, you turn up?"

I faltered. "Detective—"

"No, I don't have time for this. I'll deal with you later." The detective elbowed past me and strode into Charmaine's house.

Alone again, Envy turned to me, her hands twisting at her chest. "What do we do now?"

"We have to find the people behind Chenoweth," I said. Then I cursed and shot Envy a dirty look.

Envy's eyes narrowed. "Why are you looking at me like that?"

"I hate to remind you of this after so short a time, but we would know exactly where they would have taken her if you hadn't *burned it to the ground*."

Without warning, Envy punched me in the shoulder before shoving me aside and stalking to the car. "I guess everything's my fault!" she shouted, her back to me. "Go ahead and blame me for it all!"

I sighed and dropped my chin to my chest. While Envy threw a tantrum, the detective came out of the house, his cell phone pressed against his ear. "I need a crime scene unit here immediately," he said. "Charmaine Young is missing. A cursory perusal of her home suggests possible abduction."

The detective disconnected and slipped his phone away, never tearing his eyes away from mine. "Let me be very clear," he said. "I don't want to see you at any more of my crime scenes. I don't want to find your name attached to any more of my victims. I want you out of my way or there's going to be trouble. Do you understand what I'm saying to you?"

I held up my hands in virtual surrender. "I had nothing to do with this," I said. "You talked to Portia. You know what's going on. I was merely following up on what Peyton said happened to her."

Anger flashed behind the detective's eyes, and he stepped forward, his large frame looming over mine, a finger pointed threateningly at my chest. "It wasn't your place to come investigate," he hissed. "You should have let Portia call me immediately. Is this a game to you? No, wait. Don't answer that." His face transformed into a snarl, nostrils flaring as he stepped even closer to me. I fumbled backward in response. "I know the real reason you're here. You're just a no-account D-lister hoping for your 15 minutes of fame and some *ridiculous* wish you think a TV network can grant you. But if you muck up one more of my cases, I'll make your life a living hell, and nothing anyone can offer you will be worth it. I promise you that."

I swallowed around the lump in my throat. I'd been talked down to by police officers before. It was never a walk in the park —I mean, they're cops. Half their job is to be intimidating. But this time was different because I felt something more than low-grade fear.

I felt *sad*.

For one thing, the detective had completely misjudged me. Yes, I was on this cockamamie TV show to win a prize. But that wasn't why I was *here*, standing in front of Charmaine's house. I was here because I cared. I was here because I wanted to see justice served. I wanted to be a force of good in a sea of human evil.

But it wasn't my job. Detective Doyle was not Detective Hidalgo, and Odyssey wasn't San Diego. Here, I was no one.

I mean, I was no one everywhere. I guess here, it was just more obvious.

"I understand, Detective Doyle. You won't see me again," I said. "I'll stay out of your way."

The detective gave a crisp nod. "Good. Now get out of here before I arrest you for—"

"Interfering with an ongoing investigation, yeah, I got it." I turned away from the detective, hands thrust into my pockets. I felt like a dog with its tail between its legs as I retreated to the car. When I got inside, I rested both hands on the steering wheel, leaning my head backward as I closed my eyes and let out a long, slow exhale.

"Everything okay?" Envy asked.

"I think we've worn out our welcome with the detective," I said. "Anything else we do regarding the Edgar Thornton case? We need to be stealthy about it. I don't want to give up," I said before Envy could object. "But we have to be careful. The detective threatened to arrest me if I get in his way one more time, and I believe him. So. The question is, what do we do now?"

"I think we should talk to the ghosts at Déjà Brew," Envy said. "Maybe one of them saw something. Someone going in or out of the secret passageway or something. It's worth a shot."

With my eyes still closed, I shook my head. "The Crypt might not have burned down, but it's got to be badly damaged. Plus, the detective practically accused me of arson. We won't be allowed back over there."

I heard Envy shift in her seat as her seatbelt clicked. "Sounds like we'll just have to sneak in. Again."

I opened my eyes and looked over at her, expecting her to be smiling or giving some other indication that she was joking. But Envy looked dead serious. "Sneak into Déjà Brew *again?* Are you out of your mind? Didn't you just hear what I said about the detective?"

Envy shrugged. "I heard you. But do you have a better idea?"

"Yes. My better idea is to *not get arrested.*" I pinched the bridge of my nose. "Forget about Chenoweth for a minute," I said. "Let's focus on Edgar Thornton. What do you want to do about that?"

Envy smiled. "Same thing. When we were down in the Crypt, I found those meeting notes, remember? If there's a relationship between the Crypt and what was happening at Remembrance Home, the ghosts might know something about it."

I gripped the steering wheel until my knuckles turned white and hung my head to my chest. "You're just not gonna stop until I'm behind bars," I said, shaking my head in defeat. "And although I hate to say it, I think you may be right. No matter which case we investigate, all paths lead to Déjà Brew."

Envy turned her face away from mine and pressed her forehead to the window. "Well, good news is, the cops will be busy at Charmaine's for a while. So this is our chance. Breaking and entering, part two. This time with hopefully less fire damage."

I listened for a telltale sign that Envy was joking. But I got nothing.

"Too soon, Envy." I said. "Too soon."

Then I did the only thing I could do. I drove us back to Déjà Brew.

fourteen

. . .

Getting into Déjà Brew was easier the second time. We just walked in through the back door. Or rather, the lack of a back door. Inside, the walls were covered in soot, and I saw signs of water and smoke damage on the ceilings and floor. Counter tops were covered in soot and ash, and as we walked, we left a trail of footprints through the debris.

Great, I thought. *More evidence for the detective. Why don't I just leave my wallet here again?* But I kept my sarcasm to myself as Envy and I found our way down the steps and into the eerie darkness of the Crypt.

As expected, the room was badly damaged. The ceiling was crumbling, with tufts of pink insulation falling through. The walls were blackened, the paint bubbling on the surface. Much of the furniture had been surprisingly spared, but most of the books were destroyed, charred to nothingness.

Yet even among the wreckage, the ghosts still milled about almost as though nothing were wrong. As I surveyed the crowd looking for a familiar face, Eleanor floated over to me, her eyes liquid. Her fingers absently worried the string of pearls at her throat, and her lips trembled. "I'm so glad you're here," she said. She sounded breathless and rattled, like she'd been crying, though I wasn't sure ghosts could cry. "Damn not having a body! I'd like to give you a big hug. Well, no matter. I don't suppose you can spare an old woman some news? What happened here? How did the fire start? The reports I'm hearing are conflicting."

I took a sharp breath and avoided looking at Envy. It wasn't nearly as satisfying to poke her when she could only hear half the conversation. "Well, the details are a little murky. But I guess the fire started in another building and spread more quickly because of the underground tunnel system. Did you know about that? That Old Downtown is connected by a series of tunnels?"

Eleanor waved a hand. "Well, of course I knew that. All of us old-timers remember. We used to go on field trips through those tunnels when we were children."

"Is that right? Strange field trip, taking kids to see tunnels where criminals ferried illegal hooch."

Eleanor laughed and clucked her tongue playfully. "Now, see, that isn't what they told us children! They told us the tunnels were for electricity. Or maybe I remember that wrong. Well, my word. I guess you learn something new every day. And here I thought death itself imparted great wisdom! But I'm afraid I don't know much more today than when I kicked the bucket, pardon my language. Oh, ignore me, Pride," she said, her voice still full of apology. "I'm just a silly old woman."

"You're not old anymore," I reminded her. "You're dead. It's a very different thing."

Eleanor chuckled and waved a hand dismissively. "Oh, you."

"What's she saying?" Envy demanded.

"She doesn't know anything about the fire," I said. To Eleanor, I said, "Have you ever seen anyone using the tunnels? Going in or out of the secret passageway there?" I nodded toward the door we'd uncovered.

But Eleanor shook her head. "No, never."

I turned to Envy. "It's a negative on the secret passageway, too."

"Well, ask her what she knows about the talking corpses."

Eleanor's eyes widened. "Talking corpses?"

I explained briefly about the connection between the Society's meeting notes and the disturbances at Remembrance Home, but Eleanor just shook her head. "I'm sorry, I don't know anything about that. I haven't been down here that long, but maybe some of the others might know something."

"You're right," I said. "Thanks, Eleanor. Sloth sends her regards."

With Envy on my heels, I picked my way through the crowd, looking for someone who might want to talk, but most of the ghosts either ignored me or actively avoided me. Dead people were much like living people—they stuck to what they knew. And so I wasn't surprised when the only other ghost that seemed interested in my presence was Angelica.

When she saw me, she beckoned me over with a coy grin. "I thought I might see you here soon," she said. "Though I wasn't sure whether you'd be alive or dead when you returned."

I quirked my eyebrows. "Why?"

"Well, you went through that door and then the fire started. I never saw you come out. So I figured, you know." She sliced a finger across her throat and made a gross sound with her mouth.

"We found another way out," I explained. "Speaking of the passage, though, have you or any of the other ghosts ever seen anyone use that door in the Crypt? Ever seen anyone go in or come out?"

Angelica whistled. "No way. We were just as surprised as all of you when that bookcase slid away. Nobody's ever been in or out that door—not that any of us have noticed, anyway."

That wasn't the answer I hoped for, and my shoulders slumped in defeat. "Well, there goes that lead," I said.

"Things around here have been crazy," Angelica continued, unfazed by my downward turn. "Ghosts running around like chickens with their heads cut off. I mean, not literally. But you know what I mean."

"I'm surprised you're all still here," I said.

Angelica frowned. "Why?"

"Well, that's how you clear out unwanted ghosts and spirits and things. With smoke," I said.

"That's right," Envy chimed in. "Or air elementals."

I gave her a withering look. "Don't start."

"Well, I'm sure some of us would have moved on if we could have," Angelica said. "The thing about the Crypt though, is it seems to be where ghosts go when they don't have another choice. It's kind of like jail in that way. The accommodations are mediocre and the food isn't that great, but one is able to secure lodging instantly and without a reservation." She laughed and tossed her hair over a ghostly shoulder. "Seriously, though, where else are we supposed to go? Most of us are tethered here. There are only a few of us who have no trouble coming and going, and most of them have moved on. I took Fiona's departure especially hard. She was a gas."

I blinked. "Fiona Arquette? She was here?"

"Oh, sure. Crazy old bat. She used to amuse herself by scaring the pants off some of the others. She'd go invisible, sneak up on someone, and scream in their ear. You haven't lived until you've heard a ghost shout in fright." She chuckled at a memory. "Sometimes, she floated around here reciting Shakespeare in an English accent. You know, she was a ventriloquist, so I guess that's why she was so good with voices. Or maybe it's the other way around."

While Angelica had been talking, my brain was running a

mile a minute, putting everything together. "Angelica, could Fiona leave the Déjà Brew?"

Again, Angelica nodded. "Yeah, she was one of the few that could. She liked to sneak out in the middle of the night like a teenager sneaking out to a party. At least, that's how I liked to think of it. It's fun to think that old Fiona was getting away with something."

A new realization struck me. "So…*she* was the one sneaking upstairs and shouting at the customers?"

Angelica laughed out loud, her shoulders shaking. "Oh man, that was *great!* You have to hand it to her—the old bat had a twisted sense of humor. By the time Felix started keeping the door to upstairs shut, it didn't matter anymore anyway. Fiona had already crossed over, and we never saw her again. God rest her soul."

"When?" I asked, my heart rate picking up. "When did Fiona cross over? Was it the same night Edgar Thornton was murdered?"

Angelica snapped her ghostly fingers and nodded. "You know what? Now that you mention it, yeah. I think it was."

I turned to Envy, a slow smile spreading on my face. "Envy, I think we finally got a break in this case. Let's go back to the house—I'll tell you everything, I promise. But first, I want to read those meeting minutes. That's the key to solving this whole mystery."

Envy squealed, bouncing on her toes and clapping her hands in glee. "So you know who killed Edgar?"

"No," I said, waving this away. "No idea. But I know why the corpses appeared to be talking."

Envy's excitement immediately drained away, and her shoulders sagged. "What? I thought we were supposed to be solving Edgar's murder?"

I reached out and pinched Envy on the cheek. "We just

solved our assignment, Envy. You can thank me later, but you're one giant step closer to becoming America's Favorite Sin."

Envy squealed again and threw her arms around my neck. "I knew you were the best partner! I just knew it. Hang on." Envy pulled out her phone and drew herself close to me, her cheek pressed against mine. "Say cheese!"

She snapped a photo before I could object. She was typing furiously when she said, "I'm making the announcement on Instagram. There you go. It's official. We completed our assignment! And since I'm pretty sure we're the first, those Good Samaritan points are in the bag, baby!"

I was still standing there like a slack-jawed moron when Envy flew up the stairs. "You coming?" she called down.

I turned to Angelica. "Thanks for your help," I said. "If you want, I'll see what I can do about helping you cross over. I can't promise anything at all, but you've helped me, so I'd like to help you."

The ghost smiled and shook her head. "Thanks, but it's not a tit for tat thing, you know? You help people because it's the right thing to do. That's all." She blew me a kiss and a wink. "Just promise to keep visiting me. And whatever you do—keep kicking butt until *you* become America's Favorite Sin."

———

When we arrived back at Sinful House, I immediately retrieved the Society's meeting minutes and took the book back to my room. I hunkered down until I had read every page multiple times. With each read, a weight lifted from my shoulders. I liked when things made sense. And now, everything was adding up. Here's what I learned:

1. Whispers of real estate development meant the Society needed to find a new headquarters. This jibed with what I'd already heard from Felix.
2. The Society figured that if they could get a friend or colleague into office, they could move to the emergency shelter beneath City Hall which was private, secure, and unused.
3. Some Society members thought it would be better to make Old Downtown a historical landmark, which would protect Déjà Brew and the Crypt from development.
4. Someone objected (spoiler alert: it was Portia Cameron) that Old Downtown was prime real estate and had no historical value whatsoever.
5. Portia decided to formally run for mayor against Julian Gillespie. That caused a big fuss: half the Society members thought it was a great idea, while the other half worried Portia would sabotage their plans to protect Old Downtown. Portia wanted it noted for the record that she neither wanted nor valued anyone's opinion on the matter.
6. Natalie Buchanan moved to eliminate further Council talk from Society meetings. She was outvoted.

I found Envy in her room painting her nails. She barely glanced up but motioned with her chin for me to have a seat on the edge of her bed. "I can't stop now or my nails won't dry right," she said. "But go ahead and tell me everything. I'm listening."

I told Envy what I'd figured out—how Fiona left the Crypt in the middle of the night to speak to Edgar. "According to Angelica, Fiona had a twisted sense of humor. She probably thought it was hilarious to scare Edgar's socks off while he was working. The corpses were never talking—it was Fiona the whole time."

Envy hrmmed thoughtfully. "Well, why was she reading meeting minutes? Seems a weird choice to me."

"Do you remember what Danielle said about how Fiona was willing to spy for Julian Gillespie's first mayoral campaign? I think she was doing the same thing in death—helping his campaign."

"Helping how?"

"I read over those minutes you found, and the Society talked a lot about city business behind the mayor's back," I explained. "They were even planning to run someone against him just so they could get access to City Hall's emergency shelter. I think Fiona was trying to warn him. She was a spy."

Envy scoffed. "So why not just *warn* him? Why read meeting —ohhhhh." Envy's face brightened as understanding hit her. "She had that brain thing. She could only repeat things she'd read. She couldn't form her own sentences."

I grinned, glad my partner and I were finally on the same page. "Bingo. My guess is Fiona would have told the mayor directly if she could have, but according to Danielle, Julian's kind of a numskull. He might not have put two and two together like Edgar did."

"Do you think Edgar knew it was Fiona all along?"

"Probably not at first, but by the end, yeah," I said, smiling. "When people are that close for that long, they learn to recognize each other's quirks."

Envy tucked a lock of hair behind her ear. "So do you think Edgar warned the mayor in time? I mean, before he died?"

I leaned back, sinking my weight into my hands. Envy's mattress was soft—way too soft. I couldn't imagine sleeping on a bed like this. My back would be wrecked for weeks. "I don't know. According to Danielle, Edgar said he'd handled it. So I'd say he did. However…

maybe we should tell the mayor what we know, just in case. Nothing we learned is earth-shattering, but politics should be done in public, not in underground, ghost-laden sanctuaries. If people from the city council are stabbing the mayor in the back, he deserves to know."

Envy blew on her nails while nodding. "I agree with you in theory, but man, haven't you ever heard of the Freemasons? Or the Illuminati? The whole world is governed from the shadows by rich people with an agenda."

"Now you sound like Wrath," I scolded, the slightest laugh rounding out my words. "When did you become a conspiracy theorist?"

"I'm not," she objected. "I just pay attention."

I chuckled. "Right. Anyway, Pam invited us to that Coldwater event, right? I guess the mayor will be there. We can try to talk to him then."

Envy glanced up and rolled her eyes. "Ugh, that fundraiser? Pride, I'd rather stab my eyes out with a fork than go to that. Why don't we just make an appointment to see Pam?"

"Well, Sloth already said she wanted to go, and we can't let her go alone. Plus, you're thinking about this all wrong," I pressed. "Imagine: you in a slinky dress, me in a debonair pantsuit." I didn't own a pantsuit, let alone a debonair one, but Envy didn't need to know that. "Us mingling with important people, Beefy Camera Guy there to film the whole thing? You have to think about your public image. It will look great on camera. Plus, who knows? Maybe there'll be celebrities there."

Envy only looked half-convinced, but I knew I was in. She would do anything for the 'Gram, plus, she really wanted to win this competition. Finally, she blew out a breath, her hair fluttering away from her face. "Fine. But as soon as I get bored, I'm leaving. And if there are no celebrities there? Then you owe me one. A nice dinner out or something."

I stood up and ran a hand through my hair. "So, how do you feel? It's fun to win an assignment, isn't it?"

Envy half-smiled and gave a shallow shrug. "I guess. But can I be honest? I really wanted to solve the Edgar Thornton case. Or the Chenoweth thing. Or find Charmaine. You know? I mean, I get it. We're just TV personalities. But I thought… I don't know. We were onto something big. Something *real*. And now I guess I feel kind of shallow."

I didn't want to say anything, but I knew exactly how Envy felt. She had just articulated how I'd been feeling ever since I had promised the detective I would stay out of his way. Figuring out how and why corpses were talking to Edgar Thornton was one thing. Figuring out who murdered the poor man was quite another.

"Keep the faith, Envy," I said. "Everything will happen exactly as it's supposed to."

I didn't know why I said that cockamamie nonsense. I didn't even believe that. As I turned to leave, I heard Envy mutter under her breath, "That's basically what I'm afraid of."

fifteen

. . .

We arrived at the Coldwater Mansion a little before 8 p.m. The gala was exactly what I promised Envy—rich people clad head to toe in glamorous outfits, carrying flutes of champagne and smiling prettily into flashing cameras. The event was a veritable Who's Who of Odyssey's cultural elite, and I couldn't help but feel a small swell of pride that my housemates and I had been invited. For her part, Envy looked to be on cloud nine. Her phone was glued to her hand, and she snapped pictures of everything that moved, making sure to use her front-facing camera as she posed for her audience.

Even Sloth looked genuinely happy for once. Envy had loaned her a dress, and her blonde hair was done up in a chic chignon. She actually cleaned up pretty well for a woman who spent her life cuddling people in stained pajamas. Even Beefy Camera Guy had dressed for the occasion, wearing a pair of tuxedo pants and a slim-fitting white t-shirt under a velvet smoking jacket.

We milled around the hors d'oeuvre tables piling our plates high with miniature quiches and tiny sausages until a voice drifted in from a nearby speaker. "Mayor Gillespie will begin his speech in exactly five minutes," the voice said. "We invite you into the main courtyard for the address."

I snatched up a second helping of tiny quiches as Envy groaned and downed the rest of her champagne. "You know, if we arrived fashionably late like I suggested, we wouldn't have to sit through the stupid speech." Envy caught the attention of a passing server and traded her empty flute for a fresh one. "Honestly, Pride. Your whole 'play-it-by-the-book' attitude is seriously cramping my style."

"Look at it this way, Envy," I said from around a mouthful of eggs and pastry. "If we arrived late, you wouldn't have so many photographs to post to your Instagram account."

That seemed to cheer her up, and the four of us piled into the main courtyard. I headed for the back row, but Sloth tugged me by the elbow to the front and shoved me down into the first empty seat. "You wanted to speak to the mayor," she reminded me as she slipped into the seat beside me. "What better way to snag his attention than to be right up front where he can't overlook you?"

Slowly, the folding chairs filled in as Odyssey's royalty and even a handful of ordinary citizens took their places. After a little while, the mayor strode onto the dais where he beamed his 1,000-watt smile at us. Pam was seated to his right, dressed smartly as ever in an elegant, crisp wool suit and pillbox hat. Small applause broke out around us, and the mayor placed his hands on either side of the podium and began to speak.

"First of all, I'd like to thank everyone for coming," the mayor said. "It's not every day I get a chance to address my city like this, and I cherish every moment we have together. I'd also like to thank the organizers—the volunteers and paid staff who put in so many hours to make the night possible. Can we give them a round of applause?"

Hoots and whistles broke out through the crowd, and even Envy clapped excitedly as she looked around. Sloth leaned toward me, whispering in my ear. "I love it when they thank the volunteers," Sloth said. "Putting on events like this actually takes so much effort. People don't realize it."

The mayor continued. "As most of you know, the purpose of tonight's fundraiser is to support a new expansion—the annexation of 200 square acres of land just outside city limits onto which we'd like to architect an important piece of Odyssey's future. Throughout our city's history, we've seen a lot of change. Odyssey used to be a small, undisturbed beach town, home to no more than 50,000 people. And long before that, it was a Catholic mission. Today, Odyssey is one of the fastest-growing cities in America."

Again, an enthusiastic group of applause met the mayor's words. I had a feeling he was stretching the truth more than a little. There was no way Odyssey was growing as fast as, say, Austin, Texas, or Boise, Idaho. It couldn't even if it wanted to—it was bordered by the Pacific Ocean, so only so much development was even possible. Plus, while the likes of Portia Cameron and her cronies would love to see Odyssey become the next Beverly Hills, there were still families like the ghost Angelica that wanted to keep Odyssey's growth to a minimum and were working to make that happen.

So, he was pandering. Of course he was. None of people at the gala cared about Odyssey's gentrification problem. And the people who were most likely to be affected probably hadn't been invited to this shindig.

I squirmed in my seat. This kind of thing is why it's better not to have friends like Wrath whispering in your ear. Once you notice the man behind the curtain, the shine is totally off the penny.

Not that Wrath was my friend. But you know what I mean.

"As our city grows, we will experience growing pains. I have already asked the council for a plan to address our issue with the elementary schools, which don't have enough desks per classroom. I've also asked the council to put out an RFP for a developer—the high school football stadium is in dire need of an update. Go, Sirens!" He paused, presumably expecting applause, but the crowd was silent. No football fans among the social elite, apparently. The mayor collected himself quickly and plowed on. "For tonight, however, our focus is expanding the cultural arts in our beloved city. We will never compete with the likes of San Francisco, Los Angeles, or New York without a proper venue for opera, theater, or symphonies. So if you would, please reach deep into your pockets as you peruse the art on offer tonight. The auction will last until midnight, but there is a buy-out option on every piece."

I glanced over to see Envy fidgeting in her seat, tapping something I couldn't read on her phone. This was another reason we should have sat in the back. It was one thing to not pay attention when no one could see you. It was another thing entirely to not pay attention right in someone's face. I felt a hot flush of embarrassment crawl up my neck. I put a hand on Envy's knee and squeezed, but she made a disgusted sound and kicked my hand away.

"Before I let you all go tonight, there is one other thing I would like to address. As many of you know, we lost a good man recently. My good friend Edgar Thornton was taken from us much too soon. And though the police are doing their best to find the brute responsible, I fear Edgar's murder harkens to a deeper, uglier truth about Odyssey. And as mayor, I feel it is my job to bring light to the shadows and reveal the truth as I see it."

Now, I sat up a little straighter. Even Envy stopped typing, slipping her phone out of sight as she peered up at the mayor through the long false lashes she'd donned for the occasion.

"Edgar and I spent many hours together alone in a fishing boat, sometimes speaking only a few words here and there for long stretches at a time. But the thing about friendship is, it weathers all things, including silence. Sometimes, no words are needed between friends. Yet at other times, it's your friends who illuminate a truth you've been too busy, too naive, or too unwilling to see."

On stage, Pam shifted in her seat, fingers skimming the necklace at her throat. Her eyes darted over the crowd. This obviously wasn't what the mayor was supposed to say, which of course made the spectacle that much more interesting. Usually, when politicians went off-script, it was a train wreck.

I leaned forward in anticipation. What can I say? I'm human; schadenfreude is my favorite pastime.

"Through Edgar, I learned of some disturbing goings-on here in Odyssey. It seems that a certain group of individuals—and they know who they are—have taken it upon themselves to form a secret society operating right beneath our fair city. These individuals masquerade as our friends and yet they stab us in the back. They pretend to have Odyssey's best interest at heart, and yet they plot the destruction of our friends and neighbors. But I'll have you know that as your trusted public servant, I will not take this affront lying down. Although the fire downtown has made it necessary for these grifters to temporarily relocate, I assure you that when they resurface, I will be there, ready and waiting, to grip their organization by the throat and squeeze until they are snuffed out. The underground of the city is like what's underground in people. Beneath the surface, it's boiling with monsters. But we will not allow *nefarious wickedness* to flourish here in Odyssey."

For a moment, the crowd was silent, unsure how to react. But little by little, people began politely clapping—more of a nervous trickle than actual applause. But something the mayor said grabbed me by the throat. "Boiling with monsters," I repeated. "I've heard that before."

"It's something that horror movie director Guillermo del Toro said," Sloth replied. "I read it in an interview."

I blinked. "Huh. Well, I guess we wasted our time. He obviously already knows about the Paranormal Society and their plot to move their headquarters to City Hall. But maybe—"

"Shh!" Sloth hissed, her body going rigid. She gripped my thigh, fingers clamped down hard on the muscle. Her skin had gone stark white, her jaw clenched and her eyes open wide. I faltered, blinking in confusion. "Sloth? Are you—"

"The killer's here."

She said the words without emotion, and for a second, I thought I misheard. But then I saw the way her eyes darted around and she bit down on her lip. I sat ramrod straight. "What? Here? Are you sure?"

She nodded. "I head their thoughts when they mayor was speaking. I don't know who it was, but I heard it clear as day."

My heart began hammering against my ribs. "What did you hear?"

Sloth pressed her hands to her face. *"I guess I didn't have Edgar killed soon enough,"* Sloth said.

I opened my mouth in shock, but no words came out. Quickly, I pulled myself together and began scanning the crowd. I don't know what I hoped to see. It's not like I was gonna see the word *MURDERER* stamped across someone's forehead. But maybe someone looked nervous? Guilty? Ashamed?

But most everyone just looked confused and/or bored at the mayor's off-script ramble.

On stage, the mayor was finishing up his speech, gathering his papers and stepping down from the dais. Around us, the assembled crowd also began to disperse. I realized then that the clock was ticking. If we were going to find the killer, we needed to act fast, before people started leaving. I held my hands out before me. "What do we do?" I asked Sloth.

"There's only one thing we *can* do," she said. "And you're not gonna like it."

I braced myself. "What is it?"

My housemate took a deep breath. "You need to touch them, Pride. You need to touch everyone here and see if you have one of your visions."

I felt myself blanch. She was right—I didn't like that at all. If I'd learned anything about Odyssey, it was that almost everyone here had a secret, and I had no interest in seeing their dark thoughts.

But on the other hand, Sloth was right. I didn't see an alternative.

Envy grabbed me by the wrist and tugged me out into the center of the courtyard. "Just act natural," she said. "But move quickly, while everybody is still kinda bunched up. Like this."

Envy began winding through the crowd, placing a hand on the guests as she passed them—a touch on the shoulder here, a gentle brush against an elbow there. She smiled and purred as she weaved a path through the guests. She made it look effortless. But then again, she didn't have to worry about seeing anything awful or jarring.

Who knew what I might see?

But every moment I stood there deliberating was time wasted. So I took a deep breath, squared my shoulders, and followed Envy's lead.

I moved like a snake through the crowd, mumbling, "Excuse me," and "Beg pardon" as I slithered through the guests, touching them discreetly. The first person I touched showed me nothing. Nor did the second or third. The fourth person gave me a small jolt—an image of ashes falling from the sky and distant shouting. I shook it off as I moved past, making sure to casually bump into as many people as I could. But although I got flashes of memories here and there, I didn't see anyone thinking of Edgar's murder.

"This is hopeless," I said to my housemates under my breath as we moved into a cluster gathered near the art auction entrance. "I'm not seeing much. Nothing relevant, for sure. Sloth, do you hear anything else? Can you give me any clues?"

"I think it was a woman," she said, "but I'm not sure. The voice was hushed—angry. And the thought was quick—they immediately pushed it aside, like they knew better than to think about it. You know?"

I heaved a sigh and looked around. There were so many people; it would take all night to touch everyone, and I was already growing mentally exhausted. I was about to head toward another cluster of people when behind me, a familiar voice stopped me in my tracks. "Pride! I'm so glad to see that you all made it."

I turned around to see Pam standing behind me, hands clasped before her as she smiled brightly, head tilted slightly to the side. She was radiant as usual—whatever nervousness she'd experienced during the mayor's impromptu speech had clearly evaporated. She once again looked like the Head Woman in Charge. "Are you having a good time? Shall I fetch you a glass of champagne?"

I shook my head, stammering. Do you know how weird it is to go from looking for a murderer to being schmoozed by the city manager? It's enough to make your head spin.

"I've had my fill tonight, but thanks. It's a great party," I said, feigning a smile. "Though I have to admit, I do feel a little under-dressed."

Pam chuckled prettily and clucked her tongue against her teeth. "Clothes do not make the Sin," she admonished jokingly. "And anyway, your presence is more than enough. I don't know if you noticed, but some of our more celebrated guests have been eyeing you all night. Envy and Sloth, you too. The three of you don't seem to realize how popular you are. Have you mingled? Gotten to know anyone? Oh, speaking of that." Pam lifted a hand as her gaze shifted to someone standing behind me. She beckoned them over, and a moment later, a man was standing at Pam's side. He was dressed impeccably in a dark suit with a silver bowtie. He looked like he just stepped out from the pages of GQ magazine.

"This is my good friend, Travis Thornton. His husband Anthony is on the city council—Anthony's my right-hand man. I have to keep on his good side, since he knows where all the bodies are buried." She laughed and patted Travis's arm. "Travis, I'd like to introduce you to our town's newest citizens. Meet Pride, Envy, and Sloth."

I extended my hand, which Travis accepted graciously, his teeth flashing behind a handsome smile. "Wow, this is a real treat," he said. "I watch your show religiously. I can't believe I'm getting to meet you in person. Oh, *where* is Tony? I want him to meet you, too." He craned his neck, observing the crowd. "Oh, there he is." He wrapped his hands around his mouth and shouted. "Tony! Come here, babe, there's someone I want you to meet." Turning back to us, he scrunched his nose and said, "If he doesn't get excited, don't take it personal. He doesn't watch the show. I know. There's no accounting for taste."

A moment later, a man appeared from the crowd, sidling up next to Travis. When we saw each other, we both blinked in surprise, drawing up short.

"Tony Thornton," I said, offering my hand. "We meet again."

Tony smiled politely, accepting the handshake. "Nice to see you again, Pride. You clean up nice. I trust everyone is enjoying the evening? Pam, you look gorgeous as ever."

But even as he spoke, spewing compliments like a seasoned politician, I hardly heard a word of it. Because as soon as his fingers closed over mine, a scene flashed behind my eyes.

I was standing in a dark room, unfurnished but for a wall of metal shelves stuffed with cardboard boxes. Behind the boxes was a pegboard holding an assortment of tools—screwdrivers, hammers, a drill. Above, a bare light bulb hung from the rafters, doing little to illuminate the darkness.

And before me, gagged, blindfolded, bound with rope, and seated on a folding chair, was a woman.

I didn't recognize her at first. The blindfold covered most of her face, and her hair was tied back. She wasn't wearing any makeup, and her cheeks were wet and tear-stained. But then I noticed the way her nose twitched, and I thought I saw a glimmer of something that looked like whiskers.

It was Charmaine.

In my mind's eye, I was turning away, leaving Charmaine to whimper behind me. I was moving up the stairs, slamming the door behind me. And then I was in the living room. My eyes glanced over the walls, and I saw family portraits—a husband, another husband, and a young child.

I recognized the men in the portraits. One of them was pumping my hand even as this vision flashed through my mind.

Fleetingly, I saw a degree in mortuary science on the wall. I saw a pink backpack on the couch with the name *Rebecca* embroidered across the front.

I dropped Tony's hand and blinked, wiping my palm on my slacks to erase the memory from my mind. The vision hadn't lasted more than a few seconds, but it rattled me to my core. I was dizzy and light-headed, but I couldn't let on that anything was the matter. So I summoned my best reality TV smile and dredged up every ounce of charm at my disposal.

Turning to Travis, I said, "Say, I don't usually do this, but you wouldn't happen to have kids, would you? A little one at home who might like an autographed picture of an up-and-coming celebrity?"

As the words tumbled out of my mouth, I wanted to stuff them back in. Even Envy was looking at me like I'd lost my mind, and I couldn't blame her. It was easily the most cockamamie, asinine thing that had ever come out of my mouth, but I was operating on pure adrenaline and instinct. And the champagne I'd consumed wasn't helping, either.

But Travis's smile only brightened. "Our daughter Rebecca is eleven. She's asked to watch the show—apparently, all her friends are tuning in. I don't know if it's appropriate for children, though, what with Lust and everything. So I haven't let her watch with me. But she would be thrilled to have an autographed photo to show off for her classmates."

I stretched my lips in what I hoped was an approximation of a smile. "Why don't I have one sent to your house?" I said. "Here." I unlocked my phone and handed it to him. "Put your address in here, and I'll get that out to you. For Rebecca, you said?"

Travis typed and nodded. "Rebecca, that's right." He handed the phone back to me. "That's really generous of you. Thanks."

I glanced down, confirming the address. Then I slipped the phone into my pocket and gestured at Envy and Sloth. "Well, we don't want to keep you. I'll be sure to get that photograph in the mail. And I'll see if any of the other Sins want to include theirs, too. Anything for a fan, right?" I added with a wink. I glanced back to Tony. "Great seeing you again, really. Tell Danielle I said hi."

As we separated from the trio, Envy sidled up to me, clenching me by the elbow. "What was that all about? It's like you were channeling Greed or something. Where did you get that weird charisma from?"

I draped my arms around Sloth's and Envy's shoulders as I guided them hurriedly toward the exit. "I know where Charmaine is," I said. "I know who kidnapped her."

"Who?"

I gestured vaguely with a toss of my head. "Tony Thornton."

Envy gasped. "*No!* Danielle's brother? Edgar Thornton's son?"

"Charmaine is at his house," I said. "I saw it when I shook his hand. That's why I cooked up that signed photograph malarky. It got me his address."

Envy looked up at me, eyes blinking in what I think was admiration. "That was some pretty quick thinking," she breathed. Then she gestured to the camera guy. "We've got to get him back to Sinful House. We can't—"

"I'm not taking an Uber," the camera guy said. "Sorry. The Uber drivers in this town are—"

"No time to argue," I said, practically shoving my housemates through the entrance and out onto the street. Beefy Camera Guy was right on our heels—he really would not be left behind. "We need to get over there now while Tony is distracted by the party. Let's just pray their kid went to the babysitter's house and not the other way around."

The four of us crowded into the car, and I pulled up Tony's address on the GPS. A moment later, we peeled out, hearts racing, praying we weren't too late.

sixteen

. . .

We parked a few blocks down from Tony and Travis's house. Thankfully, the street was dark, with few lights to give away our presence. By now, I was getting pretty good at breaking into places. It wasn't exactly the sort of thing I could put on a resume, but I'd be lying if I said it wasn't coming in handy.

The four of us sneaked around to the back of the house, looking for our way in. The back door was locked up tight. I could break a window if I had to, but that would make noise and possibly rouse the neighbors, inviting attention we didn't need.

"Let me see if I can find a key out front," Sloth whispered. "You guys wait here."

"You're not just gonna find a key lying on the patio," Envy whispered back. "Maybe we can use a hairpin to pick the lock."

"Oh, you never know," Sloth countered. "People find house keys on porches all the time on TV shows and movies. It must have a basis in reality."

Envy looked as dubious about that as I felt, but it was worth a shot. Beefy Camera Guy, Envy, and I waited while Sloth ran around the front of the house. From behind the house, we could just make out the sounds of pottery shifting around. A few moments later, Sloth appeared, a triumphant smile on her face as she brandished a key before her.

"It was hiding under a flowerpot, just like I predicted," she said, pressing the key into my palm. "See? All those shows I watch are really paying off."

I stared at the key in my hand, stunned someone was actually trusting enough to leave a key to their house on the porch where anybody could grab it. But I didn't have time to ponder the galactic stupidity of my fellow humans. I slipped the key into the lock and turned.

The door swung quietly open, and we all stepped inside, finding ourselves in the kitchen. Except for the illuminated clock on the microwave, the house was pitch black.

"Leave the lights out," I instructed. "We don't want to alert the neighbors that anybody's home. Let's use the flashlights on our phones and search for Charmaine. We have to be fast. There's no telling when they'll be back."

The four of us split up and began searching the house. I moved quickly from room to room, checking every corner for Charmaine's whereabouts. I wanted to shout her name to see if I could hear any scuffling or scraping or maybe some muffled sounds of her trying to alert me of her presence. But I was also worried about being overheard by the neighbors, so I kept my mouth shut.

Searching a house for a potential kidnap victim is more tedious than you might think.

I knew from my vision that Charmaine was in a basement somewhere. The trouble was, I didn't see any entrance to a basement. I checked every door I could find, but all I found were more rooms. I looked underneath rugs, checked baseboards for some telltale sign of a trap door beneath our feet. But I found nothing.

"I hate to say this," Sloth said, wiping her hands on her jeans as she joined me in the living room, "but I'm wondering if maybe you saw something else? Maybe the vision you saw wasn't in Tony's house?"

I pointed to a portrait on the wall. "I saw that in my vision," I said. "Tony definitely came up the stairs and landed in this room. There has to be a door to the basement in here somewhere. What am I missing?" I asked, mostly to myself.

"I don't know," Sloth said, peering around. "Maybe if we had a blueprint of the house, but…"

"That's it," I said, snapping my fingers. "Sloth, you're a genius." I said nothing more as I whipped out my phone from my pocket and dialed the only person I knew who might be able to help.

"Portia Cameron," the voice on the other end said.

"Portia, it's me, Pride. Listen. I need a huge favor. Do you deal with residential real estate at all?"

"Yes, of course. Though it isn't as lucrative as commercial."

"Do any of the residential homes in Odyssey have trapdoors? Hidden passageways? Stuff like that?"

Portia chuckled lightly. "Why? Are you thinking about making Odyssey your home permanently?"

"Portia, please. This is serious," I said.

"I'm being serious. And actually, yes, some do."

"How do you open them?"

Again, my question met with a pregnant pause. "Well, the mechanism differs from neighborhood to neighborhood. Different builders, you see. Bradley and Sons was the most sought-after builder during Prohibition, and they're infamous for—"

"Not now, Portia," I interrupted. "I don't have time to

explain, but believe me when I say, this is a life or death situation. Are you familiar with the homes in this neighborhood? Uh, around 5508 Sundial Parkway?"

Portia was quiet for so long that for a moment, I wondered if I'd lost the connection. I looked down at my phone, but we were still connected. "Portia? Please. This is important."

Portia drew in a breath. "That's the Wateredge neighborhood," she said. "What are you doing there, Pride? Can you even afford real estate in that area?"

"Portia! For crying out loud!" I hadn't meant to shout, but this conversation was dragging on much too long. "I said this was life or death! Please!"

"All right!" She huffed loudly into the receiver. "Go into the living room. You should see a fireplace. Reach up behind the lintel until you find a button."

"What the heck is a lintel?" I screeched.

"It's the horizontal bar above the firebox. Just go feel around inside the fireplace along the top."

"That's it?" I asked. "Just press the button?"

"I can't guarantee what will happen when you press the button," Portia said. "Most people who have secret passageways and secret rooms in their houses go to great lengths to make sure the areas are secure so pets or kids don't get trapped inside. I can't tell you if they have installed a custom trigger or modified the solution another way." She was quiet only a moment before saying, "Pride, is everything okay? This conversation is troubling me."

I didn't have time to engage Portia in this line of conversation, so I disconnected and stuffed the phone into my pocket. I pointed toward the fireplace. "Portia says there's a secret button inside here."

I got down on my knees and reached up into the fireplace, feeling around in the dark. It was hard to discern what I was feeling. The bricks were very bumpy, and I couldn't really distinguish one brick from another. As far as I could tell, there was nothing in there except soot and dirt.

But just as my anxiety shot to astronomical levels, I found it. Something smooth, round, slightly protruding, and plastic-like. I almost missed it; it was smaller than I expected. With my breath held in my throat, I pressed the button.

For a moment, nothing happened. But then I heard a click, and the slightest movement caught my attention from the corner of my eye.

Sloth noticed it at the same time I did. "The bookcase," she breathed. "I think it just…"

She hurried over to the large wooden bookcase on the other side of the room. Placing both her hands on its side, she gave a shove.

The bookshelf moved aside, revealing a staircase leading into darkness.

"This is just like an episode of *Scooby-Doo*," Beefy Camera Guy said. "Are you sure we should go down there? Maybe we should call the cops or something."

"Do what you want," I said, hands balled into fists at my sides. "I'm going in." I nudged Sloth aside, held my breath, and began my descent down the stairs.

At the bottom of the staircase was a light switch. I flipped it on, and a single, bare bulb hanging from the ceiling flickered to life.

The room was not so much a basement as a small cellar. It smelled of dirt and stone and something else I couldn't quite place. Musk? Body odor?

But then, of course it did. Because in the corner of the room, bound and gagged and perched awkwardly on the edge of a folding chair, was Charmaine Young.

Her eyes flew open in disbelief as she took in our ragtag

group. As I strode over to her, she was trembling so hard, I thought I heard her bones rattling. But maybe that was the chair thudding against the floorboards.

Nope. On second thought, those were my teeth. I, too, was shaking like an unbalanced washing machine.

"It's okay, Charmaine," I said, going the extra mile to make my voice sound much calmer than I felt. My heart was thundering away in my ears, my monkey brain shouting out each second that went by like a sadistic countdown timer. "We're gonna get you outta here. It's okay." I said it as much for her benefit as mine.

I eased the gag from her mouth, and Charmaine heaved a haggard breath, licking and chewing on her lips. "How on earth did you find me? How did you even get down here? No, it doesn't matter, you can tell me later. Just please, get me out of here!"

Her hands were bound behind her back. The skin was raw and bruised where the bastard had tied her down. The knot was tight; I couldn't get it loose with my fingers. "Anybody got a knife?" I asked. "We're gonna need to cut her free."

"I'll get one from the kitchen," Envy said, darting up the stairs.

"How long have you been down here?" I asked, still working the knot with my fingers.

"I don't really know," Charmaine said. "Not long. I was at home reading lines for an audition when I heard someone in my house, and Anthony Thornton ambushed me."

A moment later, Envy placed a knife in my hands, and I cut through Charmaine's binds. She drew her hands to her chest, fingers rubbing the raw spots on her wrists. She would have some nasty bruises for a while—maybe even a scar. The rope had bitten into her skin pretty severely.

"Come on," I said, drawing Charmaine to her feet. "We need to get out of here."

"Oh, you're not going anywhere."

Charmaine froze mid-gasp as the rest of us spun around. My heart leaped into my chest as my eyes focused on the man coming down the steps, a gun in his hand.

A shadow fell across Tony's face as he glared at us from across the room. "Get your hands up," he barked. I threw my hands into the air—the others did the same. I felt Envy stumble next to me, her hands raised so high, she looked like she was about to do the wave at the local college football game.

"I see you found my selkie."

"Selkie?" Envy whispered. "What's a—"

"Shapeshifting seal," I answered. "He means Charmaine."

Tony snarled, his eyes darting from me to my companions and back again. "And here I paid good money for a home with a secret room. Seems I didn't exactly get my money's worth." He smacked his lips and offered a carefree shrug. "But it doesn't matter. I may not know how you got down here, but I know how you'll be leaving." The self-confident smile on his face widened, and he cocked his head to the side. "What is that they always say in the movies? The only way you're leaving here is in a body bag."

Under different circumstances, I might have thought it a very cheesy thing to say, and I would have made a smart quip about his lack of imagination or the quality of the movies he'd been consuming. (I mean, really, any time I hear mention of a body bag, I can't help but think about that scene from *Karate Kid*, and once someone makes you think of that flick, you just can't take them seriously anymore.)

But the truth was, in all the years of working for the San Diego Police Department, not once had anyone pulled a gun on me. It's one thing to have a clever remark at the tip of your tongue when the sun is shining, the wind is blowing through your hair, and the sand is shifting underneath your feet. It's quite another thing when you're staring down the barrel of a literal gun.

"You don't have to do this," Sloth said, her hands shaking in the air. "We don't want any trouble. We don't know anything about what's going on here. We just came for Charmaine. Just let us walk out of here, and nobody has to get hurt."

Tony sucked his teeth and dropped Sloth a sardonic wink. "We're long past that, though, aren't we? I mean, I just had to leave my husband alone at a party, and now you've invaded my house. I'd say this has gotten personal."

"You're a member of Chenoweth," I said, trying to keep the fear from my voice. "You're a bounty hunter."

Tony grimaced, something like disgust rolling over his features. "That's one way to look at it, I suppose. But I didn't join Chenoweth for the material rewards, though the prizes are pretty sweet. No, it was philosophical. Existential. Hunting supernaturals is just a means to an end."

"What's the end?" Envy asked. "What do you hope to gain?"

Tony gave a limp lift of his shoulders. "Status. Wisdom. Power. Why do people join the Freemasons or Skull and Bones or the Odyssey Paranormal Research Society? So we can grasp the numinous. So we can learn the secrets of the universe. There's great power in the world if you learn to harness it. Some of us understand that."

"Some of us?" Envy pressed on. "Who else? Walter Romanowsky?"

I threw a glance to Envy, ready to make my best "Now isn't the time for a Come-to-Jesus pow-wow with the crazy guy with a gun!" face at her. But when I saw the set of her jaw, I knew what she was doing. She was trying to force her muse ability to coerce Tony into talking. If we were lucky, he'd tell us something useful. But if we weren't…

"Walt? That moron?" Tony scoffed, disgust etched all over his face. "He never bought into our philosophy. He was just a greedy twit who wanted to watch Odyssey burn."

"Is that why he kidnapped Peyton?" Envy asked.

Tony gawped, taking a step forward. Instinctively, we all moved a step back. "*Walt?* Are you kidding? Walt didn't capture Peyton Cameron! That was me!"

The room fell silent, and Tony cursed, his arm shaking. "When I went to city-wide garage sale that day, I just expected to capture another supe," Tony continued. "I'd been tracking Peyton for a while. When you've been doing this as long as I have, you learn how to sniff out a shifter. The problem with Peyton was her high profile. She was Portia's twin. Capturing her at home or work was out of the question. But city-wide was my shot, and I took it." He grinned like a wolf. "I was 10,000 credits shy of a brand new Viking stove, and Peyton would put me over the top. But I wasn't ready for what happened when I snapped those bracelets on her wrists. I expected her to shift into a cuddly rabbit or a cute little kitten, but no! Peyton Cameron shifted into not one bird but *two!* My future changed in an instant. To hell with a Viking stove—a shifter that could split was worth actual *money* to the right buyer. Good money."

Envy scoffed. "I thought you didn't join Chenoweth for the money."

"I didn't join for the money," he agreed. "But that doesn't mean I don't *need* money. It's expensive trying to keep up with the Joneses in Odyssey. I thought cryptocurrency was my ticket, but." He tsked and shrugged. "I was wrong. I lost a lot of cash, and that didn't go over great with Travis. Those birds were gonna save my marriage. So how do you think I felt when someone stole them right out from under me?"

No one said anything, of course. Envy's ability was working. All we had to do was let it run its course. The longer Tony talked, the more time I had to figure out a plan.

Except as far as plans went, my brain was coming up with zilch. Instead of hatching an escape, I just started praying for Gluttony's good luck mojo to kick in.

"It was my own fault," Tony continued. "I should have left the moment I captured her. But I set the cage down to browse a pile of vintage men's coats, and the next thing I knew…" He made a poofing motion with his free hand. "The birds were gone."

Now, I know I should have been wracking my brain for an escape route, but I was utterly transfixed by the notion of someone eschewing a profitable escape so they could explore the crummy wares at the city-wide garage sale. I'd been there before with Lust. And for the life of me, I didn't understand the appeal. The place was full of dusty old junk that should have gone into the trash heap. And yet this guy just confessed that he made the biggest score of his career and instead of running home to cash in, he was browsing old coats!

I'm telling you, some people just don't have the good sense God gave a woodpecker.

"I looked for those birds for months, but it was like they vanished into thin air. So you can imagine my surprise when I stumbled upon them at Walt's house a year after I'd lost them. His mother had them all along—and he was probably the one who stole them, that sleazy bastard. He must not have known what he had or else he would have sold them a long time ago."

"Walt's family is rich," Sloth said. "He didn't need the money."

"You know what people with money want more than anything?" Tony asked. "More money. No, my bet is he had no idea what he'd stolen from me. He was probably shopping for deals at city-wide like the rest of us when he saw the glow from the corner of his eyes. Stupid MagicBloc! I should have invested in a MagicThwart cage. Not as easy to get the supes into, but at least they don't glow."

I was too stunned to say anything. Were we really having a conversation about the pros and cons of different supernatural bounty hunting supplies?

"But birds are hard to offload if you don't know what you're doing," he went on. "The average supe collector doesn't want them. They're loud, and they don't cuddle. So I'm not surprised that doofus had trouble unloading them. But at least he took care of them. He'd acquired a bigger cage, and the birds looked healthy. So I confiscated them—after all, they were rightfully mine—and took them back to our lab at Chenoweth. After a few necessary experiments, I was *finally* going to capitalize on my find. But then you all burned the lab down and stole my birds. *Again.*" Noting the alarm on my face, he smirked. "Yes, everyone knows it was the idiots from *Sinful House* that caused the fire. Don't worry, though. I'm sure your network will take care of any impending charges."

For a moment, no one spoke. But then Charmaine's voice squeaked out, "Wait. Is Peyton alive?"

"You killed Eleanor Romanowsky," Sloth said, ignoring Charmaine. "You murdered an innocent old woman."

"Yeah, Wilson wasn't too happy about that either, actually," Tony admitted. "Fit of passion. It was never my intention to kill her. I just needed to make some money. And after losing the birds again, I still do. Do you know how infuriating it is to lose a windfall *twice?*" He turned his gaze to Charmaine. "A selkie isn't worth nearly what those birds were, but I never did get my Viking stove, so."

"Please, Anthony." Charmaine's voice was ragged, her words coming out a cross between a plea and a sob. "I swear, if you let me go, you will never see my face again. I'll leave Odyssey. I won't tell anyone anything. Just please, *please* let me go."

"I'm sorry, Charmaine. You're worth something alive, but your friends?" Our captor returned his gaze to me. "Not so much."

Tony raised the gun until the barrel was level with my chest. Then he fired.

…Or tried to. He pulled the trigger, but nothing happened. The world stood still for about a second before Tony realized he'd neglected to release the safety. He growled, thumbed the safety off, and aimed again.

But as his finger moved back to the trigger, someone hollered, an animal-like roar that filled my ears. I saw a blur of movement as Beefy Camera Guy plowed past me, throwing 260 pounds of pure protein shake-fueled muscle directly at Tony.

The momentum knocked the gunman to the ground. His hand crashed against the floor, and the weapon skittered from his fingers. Tony cried out with both surprise and pain as he tried to fight the cameraman off him. I was too stunned to do anything but stare. Thankfully, Sloth had the good sense to pick up the gun, her hands shaking so badly, she nearly dropped it.

"I don't know what to do with this!" she shrieked, unsure how to hold it or where to point it. The two men were still wrestling on the floor, and Envy and I were paralyzed with fear, neither of us able to utter a word. "Tell me what to do with this!"

"Drop it."

The sound of a new voice startled me out of my stupor. I turned, blinking with shock and confusion as another shadow descended down the steps. I knew that stance—the outstretched arms, the gun properly clasped in steady hands, finger off the trigger.

It wasn't another bad guy coming to escort us to our graves.

It was Detective Doyle.

"Nobody move," he said, coming fully into the room, his gun

trained on no one in particular. "Drop the weapon, Sloth. Hands where I can see them. *Everyone! Now!*"

Sloth practically threw the gun down, her hands flying into the air. My shoulders were beginning to ache from holding my hands up, but I was so relieved to see the detective, I could have wept. My arms shook, but I raised them higher.

"Is everyone okay?" the detective asked as he turned toward the two men on the ground.

"I think so," I stammered. "You got here just in time. How did you—?"

"Portia called me," he said. "After she spoke to you, she called me, worried you were getting yourselves into trouble. Looks like she was right." He looked over to Charmaine and blinked. "Charmaine Young? Is that you? Are you all right?"

Charmaine pointed a shaking finger at Tony. "It was Anthony Thornton, officer," she croaked. "He's the one who kidnapped me."

Detective Doyle turned his gun on Tony. "Anthony Thornton, you're under arrest for the abduction and unlawful imprisonment of Charmaine Young. You have the right to remain silent. Anything you say…"

The detective moved in, angling the now-huffing and puffing camera guy out of the way and wrenching Tony's hands behind his back as he cuffed and Mirandized him. The rest of us watched in stark, disbelieving awe as the detective forced Tony to his feet.

"You'll save yourself a lot of grief if you tell me who else was in this with you," Detective Doyle said, guiding Tony toward the stairwell. "I know you're not the brains behind this. So who are you working for?"

"He murdered Eleanor," I called out. "He mentioned having an accomplice that day. He called him Wilson."

Doyle clapped Tony on the shoulder, barking out a dry laugh.

"Let me guess, your city council buddy Wilson Brenner? Wow, the next issue of Stephanie Jones's newsletter is going to be a doozy!"

As the detective led Tony Thornton up the stairs, the sounds of sirens welled in my ears. The five of us stood in the basement in a near-circle, gazing at each other stupidly. Nobody knew what to say.

I turned to Beefy Camera Guy and licked my lips. "You saved my life," I said, my voice cracking with emotion. "You—I can't even—you really saved me." I bowed my head a little. "Thank you."

"Craig," he said. His eyes were steely, and his voice didn't tremble. "My name is Craig. So you can stop calling me Beefy Camera Guy behind my back." He looked down and gestured vaguely toward his midsection. "Anyway, this isn't all muscle. Some of it's fat. What? I like pizza as much as the next guy."

Moments later, the basement filled with uniformed officers. Someone wrapped a blubbering Charmaine in a fuzzy blanket and led her somewhere private to talk. The others took our statements.

I didn't know how long we were down there. But much later, when I was finally back at Sinful House and alone in my bedroom, I took off my shoes and lay down on my bed, eyes wide open. I was afraid to shut them. I was afraid I'd see that gun behind my eyelids.

I hadn't been lying there long when there was a knock at my door. I didn't answer, but the door creaked open, nonetheless. Sloth came in, padding quietly across the room until she reached my bed. She sat down and placed her hand on my shoulder.

"Pride," she said, "are you all right?"

I nodded mutely, unable to actually speak the lie aloud.

Sloth said nothing as she climbed over me, placing herself between my back and the wall. She slipped underneath the blanket and stretched her body along mine, and then draped an arm over my chest. At my back, she whispered, "It's okay if you need to cry, Pride. I'm a professional cuddler, remember? If you need to let loose, I'll take care of you."

Nothing happened for a few minutes. But slowly, a tear slid down my cheek. Sloth's fingers ruffled through my hair. I shuddered with the memories that came flooding back and squeezed my eyes shut. Sloth said nothing, didn't even move, as I quietly cried in her arms.

I must have cried myself to sleep, and when the ringing of my phone woke me the next morning, Sloth had already gone.

seventeen

· · ·

I rubbed my eyes groggily and swung my legs over the side of the bed. I had half a mind to ignore the call, but when I saw the name on the screen, I blew out a hot breath and put the device against my ear.

"Charmaine, hey." My voice came out thick with morning phlegm, and I cleared my throat noisily. "Is everything okay?"

Charmaine was silent for a while. Then a small voice came over the receiver. "Pride? You weren't asleep, were you? I'm sorry to wake you. I…I just needed someone to talk to. I didn't sleep very well last night."

"No, I guess not," I said. "You've had a very traumatic experience. Are you okay?"

Charmaine chuckled darkly. "I'm not sure if I'll ever be okay again, if you want to know the truth. As long as I can avoid emotions for a while…" She snorted. "*That'll* really put a damper on my acting career."

I had to smile at that. If Charmaine was worried about her acting career after everything she'd been through, she wasn't as bad off as I'd feared. "I can recommend a therapist if you're interested," I said.

"Oh, I don't think that'll be necessary. Like I said, I just need someone to talk to." I was about to inform Charmaine that that was exactly what a therapist did when she pressed on. "I could really use some company. Would you mind coming over? I can make breakfast."

I couldn't imagine that Charmaine was worth much in the kitchen, but my stomach rumbled at the thought of breakfast anyway. I glanced down at the time. It was barely 9 o'clock, and I was usually not functional this early in the morning. But now that I was up, I *did* feel certain questions bubbling to the surface that only Charmaine could answer. "All right," I said, "breakfast sounds great. However… Can I ask you something?"

"I suppose so," she drawled.

I took in a breath. "What are you still doing in Odyssey?"

Charmaine was quiet for a long while. Then she said, "I'm not sure what you mean."

"Well, the police have Tony in custody, and I assume they'll nab Wilson for the break-in at Mrs. Romanowsky's soon enough. But…you and I both know someone else was behind all of this, Charmaine. And that someone is still at large. If they came after you once, they'll come after you again. Maybe not now—they're probably smart enough to wait until the dust settles. Still, staying in town seems dangerous. So, don't you think it's best to get out of Dodge? At least for a while?"

Charmaine sighed heavily. "Right. Well, that's very practical advice, and I appreciate your concern. But I'm not going anywhere. This is my home."

I nodded. "All right. I'll be there over there in about 15 minutes."

"Wonderful. Oh, and Pride?" She paused. "Please come

alone. The things I want to talk to you about don't need to be aired on television."

And then she hung up.

Fifteen minutes later, I was sitting on Charmaine's sofa, a plastic tray of croissants on the table before us and a fresh mug of coffee in my hands. For someone who had just been kidnapped, Charmaine looked remarkably calm and collected. Her hair hung in a loose ponytail at the back of her head, and she was draped in a fuzzy gray housecoat with matching slippers. She sat with her legs nestled underneath her as she leaned against the sofa's arm. "So." She took a long drink of her coffee before setting it on the table and clasping her hands in her lap. "How did you find me?" she asked.

"I got your address from Portia," I said.

Charmaine stared at me a second before barking out a laugh. "No, I mean, how did you find me at Tony's?"

I ran my hands through my hair and blew out a long sigh. "It's kind of a long story."

Charmaine tilted her head. "Tell me anyway."

I told her the whole thing, from finding Peyton to touching Tony at the party. When I was through, Charmaine bit down on her lower lip and nodded, her eyes welling with tears. "It's terrifying to be taken from your own home," she said. "At first, I thought he wanted to kill me. But then he was tugging me out the door, and I realized he was kidnapping me. That's when I tried to shift into my true form. Into a seal." Her cheeks blushing red at the confession. "I figured if I shifted, he'd never be able to haul me from the house. I'd be too heavy. But I couldn't shift, and I panicked. It wasn't until I was halfway out the door that I saw the can of MagicBloc fogger and understood. He was preventing me from shifting. I guess kidnapping a woman is easier than kidnapping a seal."

She wiped her face with the back of her hand and squared

her shoulders. "Once he had me, though, he was so erratic. He kept going on about the trouble he'd be in if his husband or daughter found me. Of course, they didn't know about the secret room. He made sure to tell me that, too. To dash my hopes of discovery and rescue, I guess." She shook her head then, pressing her knuckles to a leaky nostril. "Honestly, I don't know how you live in a house for *years* and never know that you have an entire basement beneath you."

"According to Portia, some people pay good money for those homes. Presumably, those people have a lot to hide."

"Yes, I see that now," Charmaine agreed. "I did everything I could to get rescued. I screamed and banged on the walls, but then Tony tied me up and gagged me. He kept complaining that I wasn't supposed to be there in the first place. He wanted to move me somewhere else, but I guess that place burned down in the fire." She looked away, a far-off look in her eye. "That might be what saved my life."

I frowned. "What do you mean?"

"He didn't have a big enough cage for me," she said with a self-deprecating laugh. "If his headquarters or whatever hadn't burned down, he'd have a cage. And I'd be…" She shrugged. "God only knows where."

Halfway across the world was my bet, but it wouldn't do any good to say it aloud, so kept that to myself. "Charmaine, how did he even know about you? I mean, he was a bounty hunter, but he came for you very quickly after we rescued Peyton from the lab. Like he already *knew* about you."

Charmaine snorted and took a sip of coffee. "I was the worst kept secret in Odyssey," she explained, "thanks to that idiot Karen McMurtry. She just *couldn't* keep her mouth shut after she caught me in my natural form in my pool. I threatened to kill her if she told anyone, but I guess I'm not very convincing. Which more than one Hollywood casting agent has told me," she pointed out wryly. She sighed, shoulders sagging. "If it weren't for Walt, one of those Chenoweth idiots probably would have nabbed me long ago. But Walt used his family's money to keep me safe. To make sure no one laid a hand on me. But then he died, and his protection went up in smoke. I never even considered that until it was too late."

I fidgeted in my seat and took a sip of coffee to calm my nerves before settling back into the couch. "Charmaine…I have to ask. Why didn't you ever come forward with what you knew about Peyton's disappearance? Why didn't you tell anyone you'd been with her at the city-wide garage sale when she vanished?"

Charmaine squeezed her eyes shut and pinched the bridge of her nose. "I've asked myself that many times," she began. "Why didn't I look for her harder? Why didn't I call Portia? Why didn't I come forward after I knew for sure she was missing?" The actress opened her eyes and blinked back tears. "And the truth is, I don't know. The Camerons are wealthy. I figured if Peyton was really missing, Portia would find her. Her money would find a way. Just like Walt's money kept me safe."

"What do you mean if Peyton was really missing?" I asked.

"Peyton and I were friends, but we weren't besties," she said. "When I couldn't find her at city-wide, I called her cell and left a message. I texted her. But when I didn't hear back from her… look, I know this sound suspicious in hindsight. But at the time, I figured she just went home. And when she *never* returned my call or my text, I assumed she'd hightailed it outta here, you know? Took a last-minute trip to Ibiza or wherever. Like I said, we weren't inner-circle friends. And by the time I realized she was actually *missing* missing…it was too late to come forward. I was scared I'd get in trouble. And plus, I didn't know anything anyway. So, what good could it have done?"

"It would have given the cops a lead," I said, incredulous. "That's how investigations work. You have to start somewhere!

They could have found security footage. They could have interviewed vendors. They could have asked around if anyone saw her go in or come out. But you denied them that chance by withholding information. And as a result, you cost her a year of her life."

Charmaine slammed a hand to her thigh, her eyes wild. "I know that! When I realized she was still alive, it was like a knife in my heart. I can't imagine being a caged bird for that much time. But I can't go back and undo what I did. And now, Portia will destroy me. I'm ruined in this town." She folded over, dropping her head into her lap, her shoulders shaking as she cried.

I let Charmaine cry for a while without offering her any comfort. For one, I wasn't sure whether she deserved sympathy. And for two, I don't like comforting people. It always made me feel like a phony.

After a few minutes, Charmaine finally calmed down. She took our plates and mugs into the kitchen, and when she returned, she looked almost normal. Her face was still red and splotchy, but at least she didn't have tears and snot running down her face anymore. She walked to the living room window and folded her arms over her chest as she looked out over the clear day. "May I ask one more question?" she asked. "Did you guys burn down their headquarters on purpose? Because the police are saying it was an accident."

I hadn't heard that, and the news made me smile. At least I wouldn't have to add *arsonist* to my resume. "Not exactly. Sort of."

Charmaine smirked. "Right. How did you find it?"

I considered lying, but I decided it wouldn't hurt anyone if I told her the truth. "I found a map inside Walt's laptop."

Charmaine turned to me, her face twisted in a confused frown. "A map?"

"A drawing of Old Downtown, with the old mission marked with a star and a comment that just said 'Nexus of Power.'"

Charmaine was silent a moment, her lips opening into a small *o*. Then she coughed out a guffaw of disbelief. "He kept that after all these years? The map he got from that crazy psychic woman?"

Now, it was my turn to stare blankly. "What crazy psychic woman?"

Charmaine chuckled again, shaking her head as she tucked a stray hair behind her ears. "When we were teenagers, there was a woman who made a living pretending to see into the future. She'd dole out advice, and sometimes, she'd draw a picture of what she saw. And, of course, if she saw *darkness* around you, it only cost $100 for her to perform a ritual to cleanse your future." She rolled her eyes and huffed through her nose. "Anyway, Walt was enamored with her. He was really into stuff like that. One day, she drew a map of old Odyssey with that stupid phrase at the bottom. I'll never forget what she said when she gave him the drawing. She said, '*This place will be your beginning and your end.*'" Charmaine shrugged and continued looking out the window. "I can't believe he kept that piece of trash."

"It obviously wasn't trash," I said, frowning. "That paper led us to Chenoweth." I licked my lips, my pulse quickening as an idea blossomed in my brain. "Charmaine, tell me more about the psychic woman. What was her name? Does she still live in town?"

Charmaine leaned her head to the side as she thought. "Her name? Hmm, I'm not sure I recall. Daphne? Deborah? Something like that. Angelica Muñoz was her daughter; she was in my graduating class. But they both passed away some time ago."

At the mention of the daughter's name, I sat up straight, my eyes shooting wide. "Angelica Muñoz? You're sure?"

Charmaine turned away from the window to meet my gaze. "Yeah, that was her daughter. Why? Does that name mean something to you?"

I bit down on the inside of my cheek, my excitement growing.

"Yeah, it does. And you said her mother drew that map for Walt?"

Charmaine nodded, her brow knit in confusion. "Yes. Why? What are you thinking?"

I got to my feet, wiping my palms on my jeans as I stood. "I've got to go," I said. "I need to go talk to Angelica."

Charmaine held her hands out before her, beseeching. "I told you, she's dead."

I smiled. "Yeah, she is. See you later."

I left Charmaine bewildered by her window while I got in my car and drove once again for Déjà Brew.

eighteen

. . .

"Oh, sure. My mom was a psychic. Everyone who grew up in Odyssey knows that."

I was sitting at a half-burned table with Angelica Muñoz in the Crypt. The other ghosts were giving us a wide berth, or at least appearing to do so. From the corner of my eye, I saw a few nosy specters lingering, their ears cocked in our direction. I surveyed the assemblage, looking for Eleanor. But I didn't see her anywhere.

"Was she the real deal?" I asked, returning my attention to Angelica with my arms folded across my chest. "I mean, I hope that doesn't come off as insensitive. But you know how it is. Some people will do anything for a buck."

Angelica sniffed, looking mildly affronted. "My mother didn't charge for services." Her face colored a bit, and she tittered, wobbling her head from side to side. "Well, at least not my class-mates. She did that psychic stuff because she couldn't really help herself, you know?"

I huffed out a grunt of agreement. I knew. Being a psychic certainly had its ups and downs, but one of the downs is you can't always control who your gift is meant for. Sometimes, when I touch someone and I see something, I know deep down that I'm supposed to ask them about what I saw. Maybe offer comforting words or advice. I don't always want to. But if there's one thing I've learned about life, it doesn't really care one way or another what we want.

"Did she ever talk about the things she saw? Or was she more private about her gift?"

Angelica leaned her head to the side, murmuring to herself. "We talked about it sometimes. You have to understand, though, that my mother's psychic visions were personal. She didn't think it was right—you know, ethical—to share everything she saw. But sure, we talked about some things." Angelica leaned forward and tossed a stray lock of hair over a ghostly shoulder. "I have a feeling you're going somewhere with all of these questions, Pride. Call it paranormal intuition. Maybe you should stop being so cryptic and just get to the point."

I shifted, leaning my elbows onto the table between us. I wasn't sure why I was nervous about mentioning this to Angelica. It wasn't like what I had to say could put her in danger. She was already dead. Still, a chill ran down my spine. I had a feeling ears were listening that didn't need to hear what I had to say. But it wasn't like I could take Angelica somewhere else to have a more private conversation. Déjà Brew would have to do.

I gave a stiff nod. "Yeah, you're right. There is something specific I need to know. Do you remember that guy Walt Romanowsky?"

Angelica nodded. "Of course I do. Why?"

"Your mother had a vision about him. Apparently, he came to see her a lot. Does that ring a bell?"

Angelica shrugged. "I don't know how many times he came around, but I'm sure he did. He was kind of a weirdo. And my mother was kind of a weirdo, too. So I guess they sort of had an affinity for each other." She grew thoughtful then, her eyes narrowing as she peered into the surrounding darkness. "You know, he never came around here. I mean, as a ghost after he died. I never saw him here."

"Well, not everyone who dies ends up here," I said.

"No," she agreed. "But it seems like he should have."

I got that chilled feeling again, and I rubbed my arms absently. "Why?"

"I don't know," she admitted. "It's just a feeling."

The question of who became a ghost and went to Déjà Brew *was* a matter I wanted to investigate further, but now was not the time. "That doesn't matter," I said, waving this information away. "Your mother gave Walt a map one time. This is important. Do you remember anything about that?"

Angelica chewed her lips and shook her head slowly. "No," she drawled, "I don't think so."

"Think harder," I said. "It was a map of old Odyssey. And scribbled along the bottom were the words 'Nexus of Power.' Does that help?"

Now Angelica's eyes flew wide, and she snapped her fingers as memory struck her. "Oh! The Nexus of Power maps. Yes, I remember those. Well, I don't remember the maps themselves exactly. My mom was a psychic, but a great artist she was not."

Something Angelica just said snagged my attention. "Wait, *maps?* Plural? There was more than one?"

The ghost nodded excitedly. "Yes! See, sometimes—rarely, but sometimes—my mother had visions that were shared between people. Like, she might have a vision about a cheating spouse or something. And of course, she would have the same vision for both the husband and the wife. Once in a while, she had a vision shared between people with no connection to each other. But with the map—she had the vision twice. The first time was for Walt. But the second time, she had the vision for someone else."

My heart stilled as my blood ran cold. "Do you remember who?"

Angelica's brow furrowed in thought as she made thinking noises in her throat. "I think so. Some woman? Walt was my age —that's why I remember his more clearly. I don't really remember all the old people that came in. I mean, you know, they weren't *old*, but I was a teenager, so."

Under ordinary circumstances, Angelica's rambling would have been annoying. But now, I found it absolutely insufferable. Still, she was doing me a favor, and I was the one who needed this information. So I took a breath to steady my growing anxiety and clenched my fists. "Angelica, please. Did she make a second map? Who for?"

Angelica tapped a finger against her chin thoughtfully. "Yeah, it was definitely a woman. Patricia? Penelope? Paula? Any of those names sound familiar?"

They didn't, but it wasn't like I knew every woman in Odyssey. We were getting nowhere, and with each passing second, I grew more anxious. "You don't remember the last name? This is really important," I repeated. I knew that reminding her of the importance wouldn't help jog her memory, but it was all I could do. I had to get her thinking and talking. I knew in my bones this information was crucial.

"Polly? Pepper?"

I froze. These were all P names. I breathed in deep and prepared myself for the worst. "Peyton?"

But the ghost shook her head. "No. Priscilla?"

My mouth went dry, making it difficult to swallow. My voice came out a squeak when I said, "Portia?"

As soon as I said this, though, Angelica snapped her fingers, and a wide smile spread over her face. "Pamela! That's it. Some lady named Pamela. She told both Walt and Pamela that this place of power would be their beginning and their end."

I breathed a sigh of relief. The last thing I needed was to find out Portia was behind everything I'd been through. "Okay, good. We're getting somewhere. What does it mean?"

Angelica sighed and shook her head. "I don't know. I'm sorry, but I guess that's a secret my mother took to the grave. I do remember one thing, though."

My emotions were already all over the place, so despite my better judgment, I went ahead and got my hopes up. "What?"

"Soon after Mom had that vision, someone bought Old Downtown. Almost exactly the property she'd drawn on that map, too. It was big news even back then—Odyssey has always gossiped about real estate. Mom was *so* annoyed about it. She said something like, if she'd known her vision would lead to such a large real estate transaction, she would have asked for a finder's fee." She winked at me, laughing at the memory. "So I guess you were right about my mom trying to make a buck. Just not in the way you thought."

I closed my eyes as I let these facts coalesce in my brain. Angelica's mother had a vision, and soon after, the property she'd envisioned got purchased. That couldn't be a coincidence. "Do you remember who bought the property?"

Angelica smirked. "Of course I do. Like I said, it was all anyone talked about. *What does a ventriloquist want with downtown real estate?* They said 'ventriloquist' like it was a dirty word, but that's how people get when they're jealous. Mean and petty. You should have heard the rumors. Some people even said—"

"Wait. Stop." I blinked hard, puzzle pieces slowly falling together in my brain. "Ventriloquist? Angelica, did *Fiona Arquette* buy this property?"

"You got it," Angelica said with a smile. "Though I'm not sure she was happy to end up down here. She kept muttering about monsters underground—she meant the Society, of course. She didn't like them much. I can't say I blame her. They are kind of an odious bunch."

An odious bunch indeed. Some might even say—*nefarious*. I thought back to the mayor's speech about friendship, monsters underground, and nefarious wickedness. I thought of the Paranormal Society's meeting minutes, their discussions of city business, Fiona's alogia, and her friendship with both the mayor and Edgar. I thought of Pamela, the supernaturals, the Nexus of Power, and Chenoweth. I thought about underground tunnels and Spanish missions and the heart of Odyssey.

Two secret organizations had operated in the tunnels beneath Odyssey. Edgar had been talking about one. But it was the other that got him killed.

Suddenly, I understood everything.

A sick feeling welled in my stomach and suddenly, I was shaking like a leaf as I pushed back from the table. "Thanks, Angelica. I think I understand now. Oh man, I gotta get back to the house. I need to call the detective. I think I just figured out—"

The words were hardly out of my mouth when a voice behind me said, "Well, fancy meeting you here."

I cursed under my breath and turned slowly to see Pamela Arquette standing at the bottom of the stairs, a gun pointed at my chest.

You might think if you've already been through a scenario like this, it wouldn't scare you to pieces the second time. I'm here to tell you, you'd be wrong. "Hello, Pam," I managed.

"Hello, yourself. I've heard that criminals like to return to the scene of their crimes. Still, it's quite a thing to see it with your own eyes." She offered me a tight-lipped smile, her head lilting genially to one side. "You burned down my laboratory, didn't you? No, don't lie, we both already know. Do an old woman a kindness. Tell me, how did you find it?"

I licked my lips. "Walt's map," I said. "The one I showed you when we first met."

Pam paused, bewildered, before bursting into laughter. "Are you serious? That terrible drawing was the map Devra made for Walter Romanowsky? *That's* what I sent Anthony and Wilson to retrieve? Oh, I wish I had known! I had no idea! My own map was carefully rendered. Not exactly a work of art, but not scribble, either. Oh, the irony!" She dabbed at her eyes and gave a rueful shake of her head. "That damn map. At least I had the good sense to destroy mine. I'd have destroyed his, too, if I'd managed to acquire it. But I guess you beat me to it. And now, here we are."

There we were, indeed. Surrounded by nothing but ghosts and the charred remains of the Crypt, I was keenly aware of how alone I was. Tonight, I didn't have Beefy Camera Guy to tackle my assailant. Detective Doyle was unlikely to come to my rescue. I'd managed to evade death once. Twice was asking for too much. But if I was going to die today, I would at least die with answers. "It was you all along, wasn't it?" I said, eyes trained on Pam's gun. *"You* killed Edgar. You killed him because you thought he knew about Chenoweth."

Pam blinked, surprised, but kept her gun aimed at my chest. She was doing that weird thing people sometimes do in movies, where she held the gun in her pocket and pointed her pocket at me. In the movies, the point is to prevent some random onlooker from seeing someone with a gun. Of course, that always struck me as odd for several reasons. The foremost is that if you see someone holding another person hostage with their pocket, you have to know there's a gun inside. But more importantly, we were alone in the Crypt. There was no one but us and the ghosts.

Pam heaved a sigh, her shoulders drooping in resignation.

"Well, not *me*, but my men. It had to be done, you understand. I didn't want to kill him. Not at all."

"So why did you?"

"Sharing an office wall with Julian was usually only mildly annoying," she said. "Most of the time, I might hear him tapping noisily on his keyboard or laughing hysterically about something stupid he saw on social media. But occasionally, he'd stand in the danger zone, and I'd have to listen to every word of his conversation. The day before Edgar died—"

"You mean the day before you had him murdered," I cut in.

"—he rushed into Julian's office," she continued. "I couldn't hear everything—he wasn't standing in the danger zone for the entire conversation. But I heard him say something evil was lurking below the city. Monsters underground or something ridiculous. He said he'd uncovered something that could destroy Odyssey. That was the word he used. *Destroy*. He was so dramatic."

"You assumed Edgar meant to tell the mayor about Chenoweth," I said. "So you killed him."

"The mayor and I were headed to a meeting, and Julian told Edgar they would discuss the matter later. Edgar was adamant, but Julian sent him away." She tsked and rolled her free hand. "I knew at that point it was only a matter of time. You know what they say about the likelihood of a secret getting out. The probability equals the square of the number of people who know the secret."

I stared. While I was busy memorizing the quadratic formula to the tune of "Pop Goes the Weasel," apparently everyone else was learning this arcane but radically more useful piece of knowledge. My high school teachers had some explaining to do.

"I thought I got to Edgar before he told anyone what he knew. But you heard that little speech Julian gave at Coldwater. It seems Edgar got to Julian before I got to Edgar."

I sucked in a sharp breath and shook my head. "Edgar didn't tell the mayor about Chenoweth," I said. "He didn't know anything about it. Edgar was warning the mayor about the Paranormal Research Society!"

Hearing these words, Pam faltered, her eyes narrowing in the darkness. "That's ridiculous. The Society isn't dangerous," she spat. "They're just a bunch of layabout pretenders! Surely Edgar didn't think—"

"When Fiona died, your sister's ghost was pulled here to the Crypt, where the Society holds their meetings. She overheard them discussing city council business. So she went to Edgar and warned him that the Society was planning to run Portia against Julian next term. The Society operated here. *Underground*. Those were the monsters Edgar was talking about. It had nothing to do with you. You killed him for nothing."

Pam was silent for a long stretch. Then she said, "No, it wasn't for nothing. It was for Chenoweth and the important work we were doing here. I couldn't risk anyone finding the laboratory. Our work was groundbreaking. It was going to change everything."

I gaped at her, eyes wide in disbelief. "You were trafficking supernatural people for profit! How was that important work?"

Pam sucked her teeth and rolled her eyes but kept the gun trained right at my chest. "You think I joined Chenoweth for the money?"

"I think you—wait." Something she just said stopped me cold. "You *joined* Chenoweth? You didn't start it?"

Pam stared at me a moment before devolving into giggles, covering her mouth with her free hand. "Me? The founder of Chenoweth International? Goodness, no! You're giving me far too much credit. I started the Odyssey chapter, yes, but the whole organization? Of course not. We're worldwide. What, did you think I was manufacturing MagicBloc technology on my own?

That I had warehouses of magical cat carriers and bird cages just down by the beach? That I was orchestrating the buying and selling of creatures during my lunch break? Really, Pride. I thought you were smarter than that."

To be honest, I thought I was smarter than that, too. Now that she'd said it all aloud, it was obvious she wasn't singlehandedly responsible for all Chenoweth was doing. The realization rendered me both disillusioned and petrified. Even if I got out of here alive and managed to turn Pam over to the cops, somewhere out there was an entire global organization hunting, capturing, and torturing supernaturals.

It was almost enough to push me over the edge.

But Pam was still talking, so I forced myself back into the moment. "Anyway, no, selling the creatures wasn't the point, but I did have to be rid of them once they served their purpose. The real work was in *studying* the creatures that Walt, Tony, and Wilson captured. How do they transform? What do they have that we don't? Can their essence be distilled, replicated, and absorbed by simple humans? That's what I want to know. *That* is my destiny!"

I cringed. People who tossed around words like *destiny* couldn't be taken seriously. When I was six, I thought it was my destiny to become the youngest member of the Harlem Globetrotters. But Pam still had a gun pointed at me, and I wasn't ready to join the ranks of the recently disembodied. So I gritted my teeth and asked, "Your destiny how?"

"It started with a map," she said, "and Devra Muñoz's vision. She told me this place was my beginning and my end. When I heard those words, I knew this property had to be mine. A 'nexus of power' right here in Odyssey? Tangled up in a psychic vision about *me?* I had to have it! But I made a mistake." A flash of sorrow crossed her face, and her nostrils flared. "I made the mistake of sharing that information with my sister."

Pam sighed, her eyes going soft and unfocused. "Like everyone, I adored Fiona. And I was so excited to tell her about Devra's vision. Even if she didn't believe in it, I thought she'd be happy that I found something special to pursue." She shrugged, and her expression edged toward anger. "How could I know Fiona was a double-crossing Judas who wanted me to fail? How could I know she secretly hated me for reasons I never really understood? How could I know my own sister would betray me?"

Understanding dawned on me like a baptism, and I heaved a slow sigh. "Fiona bought the property before you had the chance," I said. "Just to spite you."

"Not just," Pam said with an empty grin. "Also to *rent* me a place. To make me pay her each month for a basement room when the whole city block should have been mine. But she didn't even stop there. She recently decided to sell this place to a developer! Historic downtown! I told her I would buy it, but she refused me. Out of pure spite."

Growing up an only child, I'd always wished for a sibling, someone who got my sense of humor and shared my crooked nose. Someone I could blame for eating the cookies that mysteriously vanished from the jar. But after hearing Sloth and now Pam bemoan sisters who hated them for no reason, maybe fate had done me a solid.

But then I thought of Peyton and Portia snuggled together on the couch and thought, maybe not.

"At first," Pam went on, "I was devastated, then furious—at least until Anthony proposed we petition the city council to have this area preserved. Portia threw a wrench in that plan when she decided to run for office with her pro-development platform. But perhaps now that Peyton is home safe, she'll change her mind."

Pam's arm wobbled then, a subtle motion that quickened my heart. People don't realize how difficult holding a gun for long is. The body starts to ache. And Pam was already elderly; I wasn't sure how much longer she could hold out. As my hopes rose that maybe I'd get out of this intact, Angelica sidled up beside me, clearing her throat to gain my attention. "Pride? You realize—"

"Everything you've done is beyond unforgivable," I said to Pam, ignoring Angelica. "You kidnapped people. Experimented on them. *Sold* them. And then you murdered Edgar. And what did you learn, Pam? Did you even learn anything at all?"

The city manager scoffed, waving the gun in a circle. "We were close. I just needed more time. The answers are here, Pride! In this place of power! Everything that makes Odyssey unique, the reason wights and ghosts and shapeshifters are drawn here— it's all right here, under our feet, flowing through the earth. Don't you feel it? Don't any of you feel it?"

I opened my mouth to answer but then shut it again. I looked around—we were still alone. So, who was she talking to? I blinked, my brow wrinkling. "Any of *who*, Pam? Who are you talking to?"

"She's talking to *us*," Angelica said, her voice thick with exasperation. "Wow, are you ever dense. Haven't you figured out yet that she—"

"She can see ghosts?" I asked, incredulous. I hadn't forgotten about the gun, but my professional curiosity was eclipsing my human need for self-preservation. Never let anyone tell you the human brain is logical. "Pam, can you see ghosts?"

Angelia threw up her hands in disgust. "She *is* a ghost, idiot! That's what I've been trying to—"

"I am *not* a ghost!" Pamela spat, swinging the gun toward Angelica. "Don't be foolish! I was attacked, but I got away! I was smarter, I was faster…I was…*better*…"

"You're *dead*," Angelica replied, her voice low and even. "I hate to break it to you. But you're dead. Finito. Dearly departed. El kick-o el bucket-o." She made a slicing motion across her neck with a finger, accompanied by a grotesque slurping with her mouth. "That's why you can see me. That's why you can see all of us." She gestured around at the ghosts lingering in the shadows. "Could you see ghosts yesterday? This morning, even?"

Pam swallowed, her hands quivering as she lowered the gun to her side. "No," she admitted. "But that doesn't mean…it can't mean…"

"Lots of these folks didn't realize they were dead at first, either," Angelica said, gesturing at the surrounding ghosts. "I don't know how. When I died, I saw my body. I knew what was up. But anyway, it's not unusual."

My phone rang then, and I dug it from my pocket, pressing the shattered screen to my ear. "Look, now's not a great time," I said.

"Pride, where are you?" The voice on the other end belonged to Envy, but she sounded strained. "You need to come home. There's been a development."

"Development?" I glanced over to Pam, who was no longer paying attention to me. She walked to an empty armchair and sank down into it. "What development, Envy?"

"It's the mayor," she said. "He's been arrested."

I blinked in surprise. "Arrested? Wait, why? What for?"

Envy was silent for a moment. Then she said, "For the murder of Pamela Arquette."

I let that sink in as I looked over at Pam. She was watching me intently with an expression I couldn't read. Now that I knew, I couldn't believe I'd missed it before. She shimmered slightly, and she had a dark bruise at the base of her throat. Maybe a crushed windpipe? I tried not to think about it. "Okay," I answered. "I'm on my way." I ended the call and slipped the phone back into my pocket. "You don't have a gun at all," I said to Pam. "You tricked me. You're a ghost—you can't hold a gun."

Pamela smiled sadly and removed her hand from her pocket. She was making a finger gun with her thumb and forefinger. "I've never owned a gun," she admitted, "but I've seen enough movies to know you don't need a gun to hold someone at gunpoint. You just need a pocket and conviction. Oh, I wasn't sure you'd fall for it," she admitted. "But it was worth a shot. And look at us! It worked! I guess fear does funny things to people."

"What were you going to do with a fake gun?" I asked, bewildered. "What was your plan?"

She patted her hair and leaned her head to the side. "Old Downtown may have burned up, but these tunnels are hardy. Surely there's a cage or two left at the lab. I was just going to lock you up and throw away the key if you want to know the truth."

She smiled then, and a shiver ran down my spine. She was so calm and cool, like locking another person in a cage meant nothing to her. But I guess if you'd done it once, you could do it again. Except, I didn't think she *could* do it again because she was a ghost. But apparently, she didn't know that. "How did you even know you'd find me here? And how did you know I was onto you?"

"Oh, I didn't," she said. "I didn't plan to come here at all. I was just…pulled. Same as Fiona, I guess."

I glanced over at Angelica, who was nodding with understanding. She, too, had been pulled to the Crypt after death.

"But when I saw you," Pam continued, "I hatched a plan. My supernaturals may be gone, but a ghost-whispering psychic wasn't a bad alternative for study. Especially one who was also the sole survivor of the Sam Lovelace commune." She laughed then, a dry, mirthless sound. "So no, I didn't know you were onto me. Not until you accused me."

"You're a sick, evil woman. But I guess now you're a sick, evil corpse. Murdered by your own colleague. The mayor."

The smug expression slipped from her face, and her eyes glazed over. "The mayor," she repeated, nodding softly to herself. "That's right. He attacked me in my own home. Yes, I remember now. He came to my home to tell me the police connected Charmaine's kidnapping and Edgar's murder thanks to the foggers Anthony left behind. Idiot. He named me, of course. After everything I did for him. Getting him on the council, getting him into Chenoweth…Well, I should have known better. If you want something done right…"

She shrugged, a wan smile playing over her lips. "Julian may have been a dolt, but he did one thing right. At least he had the guts to avenge his best friend's murder himself."

"Pamela," I said, my throat going dry, "did you say *Tony* left the fogger behind at Remembrance Home? Does that mean Tony killed his own father? Just because you asked him to?"

Pam smirked and looked away. "I told you," she said. "Family isn't all it's cracked up to be."

I turned to Angelica. "I have to go," I said. "Is it okay to leave her here with you? She's a murderer," I reminded her. "You don't deserve to be burdened with her, but I don't know what else to do."

"Don't worry about me," Angelica said. "Go home and get some rest. You've earned it."

———

When I arrived back at Sinful House, Envy was waiting for me on the stoop. Without a word, she ran up to me and threw her arms around me, pulling me close.

And the crazy part was, I let her.

When we disentangled, I said, "I saw Pam. It's a long story, and I'll tell you everything later, after I've processed it. But the short version is, Pam was behind the Chenoweth chapter in Odyssey. With her and Walt gone and Tony and Wilson behind bars, the supernaturals in this town are safe."

Envy looked up into my face, her eyes shining. "That's great,

Pride. That's…wow." She smiled, shaking her head. "This day is really coming around."

I lifted an eyebrow. "What do you mean?"

"Well, I have some good news of my own." Envy smiled and ran a hand through her hair. "I think all this is over. Whatever we were supposed to do or learn…I think we did it."

I frowned. "What are you talking about?"

Envy gestured to the surrounding yard. "See for yourself. Notice anything?"

I stepped away from Envy and looked around. "Not really," I began. "What—"

But then I saw what Envy meant. Or rather, I *didn't* see.

The Star of the Sea, that mysterious harbinger of tragedy and misfortune, was gone.

nineteen

· · ·

"So Fiona was behind the talking corpses the whole time?"

Envy and I were sitting with Danielle Martin and her husband Hank at Remembrance Home. My housemate and I had taken the two armchairs, and the Martins were ensconced on the couch. Beefy Camera Guy—no, *Craig*—was on his feet, filming from the wings.

"That's right," I said. "Thanks to her alogia, she couldn't relay the information she discovered in her own words. The best she could do was recite the meeting notes to your father. But to his credit, he was smart enough to figure out the significance of what she said. And then he told what he knew to Julian."

Danielle's lips pinched, and her face blanched a little. "That information got my father killed," she said, her voice breaking. "And my own brother pulled the trigger."

My face burned hot at that, and I dropped my gaze. When we'd first begun this investigation, Envy and I both knew the police would target Tony Thornton as their number one suspect. We were sure that was wrong, and that's why we'd gotten involved in the first place. Of course, that was right, just for all the wrong reasons. He hadn't killed his father to quickly inherit the business and get out of debt. He'd killed his father because he was fanatically committed to an organization that had no respect for the value of human life.

I couldn't imagine how difficult it must have been for Detective Doyle to tell Danielle that her brother murdered her father. Looking at her now, I saw the despair all over her face. In a matter of days, she'd lost her father and her brother. It was heart wrenching.

"He used the MagicBloc fogger to douse the preparation room. He wanted to make sure your father never told anyone what happened. Talking corpses, after all," Envy explained. She folded her hands in her lap. "I'm so sorry to tell you all this."

Hank reached for his wife's hand and gave it a little squeeze. "Hopefully, Tony will get the rehabilitation he needs in prison. And now your father is in a better place."

I leaned forward, my fingers steepled beneath my chin. "Well, actually—"

Envy cleared her throat, and when I glanced at her, she tucked a lock of hair behind an ear and gave her head a little shake. It was a subtle enough gesture, but I deciphered it well enough. *Shut it, Pride*, she was saying.

I shut it.

"I'm really thankful for everything you discovered," Danielle said, oblivious to my little exchange with Envy. "I knew I could count on you." A soft but sad smile spread over Danielle's face. "I hope I never *need* your services again, but if I ever do, can I call you directly?"

I drew my eyebrows together in confusion. "Call us directly? You mean…like your own personal investigation team or something?"

Danielle tittered, her cheeks blooming pink. "Well, when you say it like that, it sounds ridiculous. I guess that's not what I meant, anyway. I just meant…I don't know, as a friend?"

In all the years I'd been helping people find the culprits behind their loved one's deaths, no one had ever asked if I would be their friend. I was so choked up for a moment that I hardly knew what to say. I looked at Envy, hoping she knew how to fill the silence. It seemed the situation was so strange that even her muse magic wasn't working on me.

Thankfully, my housemate clapped her hands together and giggled happily. "Of course! We should all get together and have lunch sometime. I hear Jorge's on the Coast has great seafood and beautiful dinnerware—we could take *great* photos for Instagram!"

Danielle laughed as she nodded, the last of her grief melting away. "Wonderful. I'd really like that."

The four of us stood, and the Martins led us outside. Hank walked us to our car while Danielle stayed behind on the porch, waving on her tiptoes.

"Drive safe," he said, shutting the driver's door as I buckled in.

As Envy fiddled with her seatbelt, I turned on the radio, cranking up the volume louder than usual. I felt a weird sensation forming in my chest, just behind my rib cage. It felt warm, like I was developing a fever. It also tickled, like I was about to develop a cough or a sore throat. But I didn't feel fatigued or run down.

And then I found myself smiling like an idiot and even jamming to the music a little. Because I realized I wasn't getting sick. I was just really happy.

———

Days later, it was time for our inevitable house gathering with Tricia Woodward to hear our weekly results. Usually, Gluttony whipped up something delectable for the event, but today, he'd sent me out for treats. I carried a pink box filled with pastries from Bake Some Waves into the kitchen and plopped them down next to a stack of paper plates.

"Honey, I'm home!" I shouted. I selected a pastry for myself and headed into the rec room where the rest of the cast and our producer was already waiting. Tricia was dressed in a heather gray t-shirt dress and a pair of white canvas tennis shoes. Her hair was pulled into a messy bun atop her head, and a simple pair of pearl earrings studded her earlobes. She looked picture-perfect as usual.

As I entered, she looked down at her watch and tsked. "You're late," she admonished. "We've been waiting for fifteen minutes. Where are the snacks?"

"Kitchen," I said, jamming a thumb over my shoulder. "Do you want me to bring you a plate?"

Tricia scrunched up her nose and gave a disdainful shake of her head. "I haven't eaten carbs since the 90s," she said. "Well! Now that we have everyone, let's get started."

I wedged myself on the couch between Sloth and Gluttony. "I didn't know we were on a schedule," I muttered, taking a bite of lemon bar. The ooey gooey sweetness melted on my tongue. The tartness made my toes curl. "Did you know we were on a schedule?"

"I bet you're all dying to know how you did this week," Tricia was saying. She was standing at the front of the room, shining her 1000-watt smile around the room. "But before I read the results, I want to remind you that the viewers haven't seen any of your footage from your most recent challenge. These are the results from the episode which just aired tonight."

"We know that, Tricia," Gluttony said. "You tell us the same damn thing every week. We ain't dumb. Just get on with the numbers." To me, he said, "Yes, of course I knew. That's why I sent you to get the snacks. I didn't have time to cook nothing."

"You could've given me a heads up," I whispered. "Should I bring the pastries in here?" I turned to Sloth. "You won't make a mess, will you?"

"I also want to remind you," Tricia continued, unruffled by the interruption, "that these numbers are not cumulative. These are only today's results. So! Drumroll, please!" She brought out her phone and peered down into the screen. "Without further ado, tonight's results are as follows!

"In seventh place with 7% of the vote is Greed." Tricia pulled a face of mock sorrow and sucked her teeth. "Ooh, better luck next time, buddy. Pride, you came in sixth place with 10%." She clucked her tongue against the roof of her mouth. "I guess you should have gone to Santa Barbara to check out that art piece like we talked about."

My jaw dropped. Tricia was still talking about Santa Barbara and finding clues about that stupid missing commune? Did she not realize I'd just been involved in a case where two people were murdered, one was kidnapped, and an elemental on a rampage burned an entire city block to the ground?

And she was coming at me about *artwork?*

"I guess I was busy," I muttered, not wanting to appear too flustered. The truth was that 10% was a blow to my ego. Nobody likes to lose, but that was just *harsh*.

"In the future, when I give you advice, you should take it," Tricia said with a breezy shrug.

"Wait, hold on." Wrath was on his feet now, hands planted on his hips. "You've been giving audience-winning tips to Pride? What about the rest of us?" He gestured wildly at the other housemates. "What are we to you, chopped liver? Or are we just not as valuable for your precious capitalist ratings?"

"Pipe down, Wrath," Lust said from her seat. "Tricia gave me some tips, too. Why do you think I've started wearing more red? Red pops on camera."

"I don't notice what you do or don't wear," Wrath said, rolling his eyes.

Lust blinked in mock surprise. "You don't?" As she said this, she tugged down the front of her blouse just a little.

Wrath blushed and sat down, arms folded over his chest. "All I'm saying is, I want a fair shot. That's all."

"You won last week," Tricia reminded him. "So I think you're doing just fine."

Sloth must have noticed my despondency because she leaned into me, throwing her arm around my neck. "Don't listen to Tricia," she said. "She's the producer. She gets paid to bring drama to the house. For what it's worth, I think you made the right decision to put off going to Santa Barbara. Your task was a whopper." She grinned, showing charmingly crooked teeth. "Anyway, just my two cents. But I know my opinion doesn't really count."

"It counts," I said, offering her a genuine smile. The more time I spent with Sloth, the more I liked her. Even if she did leave crumbs and smears of jelly everywhere she went. "Thanks."

"No problem. So, do you think your old girlfriend watches the show? And if so, do you think she votes for you?"

My hands turned to ice, and I stammered, rubbing the nape of my neck as a hot flush crawled into my face. "I have no idea," I said. "Probably not? She doesn't watch much television."

Sloth twisted her mouth in thought. "Well, my family doesn't watch that much TV, either. But they watch *Sinful House* because I'm on it. So maybe your girlfriend is watching, too."

"She's not my girlfriend anymore," I answered automatically. As soon as the words were out of my mouth, I lifted my gaze to find Lust watching me from across the room, a coy smile on her lips.

I blushed even harder and looked away.

"What's going on there?" Sloth asked, her eyes flitting toward Lust. "I noticed you've been avoiding her."

I huffed and chewed my lips. "Nothing's going on there," I said. "I just…I don't know, maybe dating someone at the house isn't the right move. This is work, you know? Better to keep business and personal separate."

Sloth hrmmed and twirled a pigtail around a finger. "Maybe," she drawled. "But maybe not. Whatever you decide, you should make it clear to her. For both your sakes." She ruffled my hair with her fingers and winked.

I chanced another glance at Lust and saw she was going out of her way not to look at me. I wasn't sure what that meant, but Sloth was probably right. The tension between us needed to be addressed one way or another.

Just maybe not tonight.

"…everything for next week," Tricia was saying, apparently wrapping up her announcements. "For now, please congratulate Sloth and Envy on this week's tie! Well done!"

Tricia was already heading over to offer Sloth a congratulatory hug before I had processed what I'd just heard. I turned to my housemate and smiled. "You won?"

"First time for everything!" she beamed. "Mom and Dad will be thrilled! Take that, Hadley!" she said, making a rude gesture in her sister's honor.

She sank back into the sofa and pulled out her phone. "So, should we check our next assignment?" she asked.

I blinked and ran a hand over my hair. "Our assignment? We're on the same team?"

Sloth laughed and nudged me in the side with her elbow. "Wow, you really weren't listening to Tricia at all, were you?"

"No," I admitted. "I was talking to you."

Sloth chuckled and wriggled back into the cushions. "I guess that's fair. Most people can only really pay attention to one conversation at a time. I have an advantage." She tapped her temple with a forefinger. "Tricia's a loud thinker. I plucked my teammate right out of her skull."

On my other side, Gluttony cleared his voice. "It's us three this week," he said. "And with our combined talents, I think we have a really good shot."

"We do," I agreed. "You know, I've been meaning to thank you and just haven't had the chance."

Gluttony grunted. "You're welcome. What for?"

"For the good luck popcorn," I said. "You were right. The whole house was acting like we were doomed, and we really needed that little pick me up. And for what it's worth, it really came in handy. I think it saved my life. Twice."

A slow, embarrassed grin spread over Gluttony's face. "Ayo, if something saved your life, it wasn't my good luck magic."

I blinked. "What do you mean?"

"I mean I ain't never put no good luck magic in that popcorn. I just said I did because y'all was acting like you'd been condemned. Look, far as I know? Ain't no such thing as good luck or bad luck. It's all in your mind," he said, tapping his temple for emphasis. "Things happen. There's nothing either good or bad. It's *thinking* that makes it so."

"*Hamlet*," Sloth said with a smile. "My favorite Shakespearean play. And you're right," she added thoughtfully. "There's no fate but what we make."

"*Terminator!* Nice one." Gluttony and Sloth high-fived each other right over my head. "Should we read our assignment?"

"Hold on," I said. "No fate but what we make? Then how do you explain Greed's premonition? He predicted Envy would summon a fire elemental that put us in danger, and she did!"

"Or," Gluttony drawled, "she did *because* Greed put the idea in her head. If he had never said anything, would she still have summoned it?"

"What's really going to bake your noodle later on," Sloth intoned, "is would you still have broken it if I hadn't said anything?"

"*The Matrix!* Dang, girl. That's good." Gluttony pointed at Sloth with admiration.

"Reality is shaped by your beliefs," Sloth said with a definitive nod. "That's why I try to keep my thoughts clean and positive. And also why I watch a lot of sci fi."

I was still grappling with the realization that Gluttony had lied to me and that magic hadn't saved me at all. The fact that I wasn't dead was just pure, dumb…

…well, luck.

But I didn't have the chance to dwell on any of that because Sloth opened up her email and leaned over me so all three of us could get a good look at the screen. "Ready?" she asked.

"Let's get it," Gluttony said.

Sloth navigated to the email with the subject line, "Sloth, Pride, Gluttony Task #4," and clicked it.

It read:

"Local fashion designer Julio Villarreal has opened a new boutique attracting huge crowds from all over southern California—but for the wrong reason. The Star of the Sea appeared at his doorstep, and gobs of tourists are camped out at the site of the miracle. Julio says it's ruining his small business. Your task is to discover the Star of the Sea's mysterious secret and put her back in her rightful place once and for all."

"More statue nonsense," Gluttony grumbled. "I thought we was *done* with homegirl."

I looked up to see Tricia ambling toward us, arms folded nonchalantly over her chest. "Everybody good here?"

"Just looking over our assignment," I said. "This one hits close to home."

"Portia Cameron specially requested you for this task," Tricia beamed. "She said putting the statue to rest would help with her campaign. She's running on an anti-supernatural, pro-business platform."

I blinked. "Really? She's still running? I assumed after finding her sister, she'd change her mind about running for mayor."

"Well, someone has to," Tricia pointed out. "According to Odyssey's laws, in the event the mayor becomes unable to perform his duties, an emergency election must be held. And since Pam Arquette was the city manager, well, it means Odyssey is hurting for leadership right about now."

I snorted. "Well, she can't be serious. How can she run on an anti-supe platform when her own sister is a supernatural?"

"People act against their own best interest all the time," Sloth said with a knowing nod. "We're complex creatures, Pride. You, me. Even Portia."

I gave an unconvinced grunt. Sure, maybe that was true. But if I knew Portia, there was more going on with her than met the eye. Her interest in the statue wasn't just about winning an election. She wanted to uncover the mystery of what made Odyssey…well, Odyssey.

And though I hated to admit it, so did I.

"I guess that's true," I conceded, sticking the last of the pastry in my mouth. "Well, with any luck, no one will turn up dead this time."

The producer shrugged and offered a mysterious smile. "Well, don't speak too soon. Stranger things have happened in this town. And just think of the ratings!"

I didn't like the sound of that, but I didn't have a chance to dwell on Tricia's ominous message for long. As the producer walked away, Sloth slipped her phone into her pocket and looped her arm over my shoulders. "One thing about Sinful House," she said, "this place is never boring. I guess that's why we're still on the air. Right, Gluttony?"

"That's right," he agreed. "And we about to keep it that way. I hope that mermaid is full up on sightseeing because her traveling days are numbered."

I blew out a hot breath and swallowed down the last of my lemon bar. I had no idea how to catch a wandering mermaid, but if there was one thing I'd learned in my time at the house, it was that Odyssey, California was full of surprises.

thanks for reading!

Lights, Camera, Mystery was so much fun to write, and I'm thrilled to share these adventures with you.

I'd love it if we kept in touch.

If you'd like that too, please sign up for my newsletter on my website.

If a newsletter isn't your jam but you'd still like to support me, please consider leaving a review. This is the easiest and best way to help other readers connect with the weird and wonderful cast at *Sinful House*.

See you soon!

about the author

Amber Fisher is the author of urban fantasy and paranormal mysteries ranging from sweet and delightful to dark and morbid. She lives in Austin, Texas, where she enjoys watching sci-fi shows, making things, baking, and playing tabletop games with her husband.

Connect with me at: amberfishermedia.com

Facebook at: facebook.com/amberfisherauthor

Sign up for the newsletter: bit.ly/332eurl